Raves For The Quarters Novels:

"I love the way Huff writes. She creates rich, complex fantasy worlds, populates them with likeable characters, includes lots of humor and action, bright, lively dialogue, and in this case, an 'all's well that ends well' ending that is perfect. Unputdonable." —*Voya* for **No Quarter**

"It's great fun, but Huff plays some interesting variations on love, family, and the balance between love and dependence." —*Locus* for **No Quarter**

"Only a storyteller of Ms. Huff's considerable merit could create the extraordinary characterization to bring this unusual storyline to full and vivid life." —*Romantic Times* for **No Quarter**

"Mercedes Lackey fans take note—this latest fantasy in the 'Quarters' series is good reading in the same vein as Lackey's 'The Last Herald-Mage' series." —*Locus* for **The Quartered Sea**

"A richly complex story set in a magical world that could almost be a part of our own history." —*Science Fiction Chronicle* for **Sing the Four Quarters**

"Tanya Huff moves the story along briskly but without skimping on details. There are some good scenes showing tenderness, humor and anger between the two pig-headed leads, and all the secondary characters could support their own stories. Recommended." —*Starlog* for **Sing the Four Quarters**

"This isn't fluff, and it isn't light—but it has so much heart to leaven its dark moments that is a someplace-that-isn't here in which to find belief in redemption." —*The Magazine of Fantasy and Science Fiction* for **Fifth Quarter**

THE QUARTERS NOVELS

VOL II

NO QUARTERS

THE QUARTERED SEA

Tanya Huff

DAW BOOKS, INC.

DONALD A. WOLLHEIM, FOUNDER

375 Hudson Street, New York, NY 10014

ELIZABETH R. WOLLHEIM
SHEILA E. GILBERT
PUBLISHERS

www.dawbooks.com

NO QUARTER

For Cap'n Dave Nelson, who taught me the most important lesson I learned in seventeen years of formal schooling by giving me my first C in English. When I protested, saying another student had written a much worse paper and had gotten an A, he replied, "If that student had written you paper, they'd have gotten an A. But from *you*, it's worth a C."

One

Motes of dust spun in the sunlight slanting into the upper hold through an open hatch. At the edge of the shadows, a slight, dark figure held a round shield, turning it this way and that so its polished surface caught the light.

"And I thought Bannon was vain," Vree muttered.

It's not vanity, Gyhard protested.

As the quiet voice in her head spoke with unusual seriousness, the ex-assassin, late of His Imperial Majesty's Sixth Army, snorted but continued tilting the shield.

There. Hold it there.

Vree stared into the makeshift mirror, feeling as though she were seeing her features for the first time. Her dark brown eyes looked too big for her face. Her chin was ridiculously pointed. Six days at sea under an unrelenting late summer sun had darkened the deep olive of her skin. She looked thin and much younger than her almost twenty-two years.

*You *are* young.*

Her lips pressed into a thin line. *You told me you couldn't hear my thoughts.* When Bannon had shared her body and it had been her brother's voice she heard, their thoughts had merged and, with their thoughts, their identities. It had very nearly destroyed them both. With Gyhard, however, it had been easy to draw the line between them. Until now.

I can feel strong emotions, Vree. Gyhard's reassurance was almost gentle. *So can you. There's no need to panic.*

You don't know . . .

I have a good idea. He'd been there from the beginning. As Governor Aralt, the leader of a rebellion whom Vree and Bannon had been sent to assassinate, he'd stolen Bannon's body. When Vree had appeared, carrying her brother's life, her brother's kigh, tucked in with her own, he'd blackmailed her into helping him get close enough to a young Imperial prince for him to make yet another trade. But a broken piece of his past had taken the prince and they'd ending up chasing him across half the Empire. Together. He'd seen how close she'd come to losing herself in sharing herself with her brother. *I'm not Bannon, Vree. His weaknesses aren't mine.*

Neither are his strengths. Until Gyhard had driven them apart, Bannon had been the center of her life. No. Her teeth ground together. Gyhard had not driven them apart. For reasons she could not yet admit, she'd chosen to save his life by making it a part of her own and now had to face the consequences of that decision. Forcing the tension out of her shoulders, she stared down at her reflection. *Are you done?*

In a minute.

What do you think you're going to see?

Who I am.

*Who *I* am. . . . Did you hear that?* Brows drawn in, she set the shield aside and started for the ladder leading up to the deck.

Hear what?

Lookout's spotted a sail. Callused fingers and toes barely touched the polished wooden rungs and a heartbeat later, Vree crossed the deck to a knot of sailors gathered at the rail. "What is it?" It was the one sentence she could say in Shkoden and be certain she'd got it right.

"Pirates."

The word was close enough to Imperial that she understood the meaning before Gyhard finished his translation. Shading her eyes with her hands, she peered back along the side of the ship. Just moving into the current behind them was a sleek, two-masted, narrow-hulled vessel.

"The *Raven*." It sounded like a curse. Two sailors spat over the side, giving water to the sea for luck, and a third traced the sign of the Circle on her breast, muttering, "Probably bin followin' us since the outer islands." When the lookout confirmed the identification a moment later, the crew of the *Gilded Fancy* raced to defensive positions.

Vree put herself in the path of a running sailor and he

skidded to a stop. The third night out, she'd barely managed to keep from killing their best knife fighter when he'd challenged her right to the long dagger she wore. After her easy victory, the crew treated her with the same wary respect she'd received from those around her most of her life. While they might not know what she was—had been—they'd been made very aware of what she could do. "Can we . . ." She hated having to search for words but her Shkoden was up to little more than the most basic of conversations. *Gyhard, how do you say, outrun her?*

When he told her and she repeated it, the sailor shook his head, scalp locks whipping his ears. "No stinking way. They're in the same stinking current, ahead of the same stinking wind, and they're built for speed which we sure as fish shit aren't."

"What will . . ."

He didn't wait for her to finish. "Happen? They'll board us. Anyone who survives the fight'll go over the side. Less, of course, they've got some stinking skill Edite i'Oceania . . ."

i'Oceania?

She's claiming the sea as her mother, Gyhard explained. *It's probably not true.*

Probably?

". . . thinks she needs—healers, or sail makers, or stinking carpenters. You, don't know what she'll do about you, but the hucksters, his stinking Lordship, and his stinking Lordship's servant, she'll hold for ransom."

The hucksters were a pair of Imperial merchants and His Lordship was a Shkoden noble, who was involved in some way with the ambassador at the Imperial court. Vree knew nothing more about any of them, nor did she really care. As the sailor ran off to join others performing complicated and inexplicable maneuvers with a rope—the decks looked like an anthill stirred with a stick—she took another look at the *Raven*.

Even in that short time, it had pulled closer—close enough to see that all exposed timber had been painted a deep matte black.

That's conceit, Gyhard growled. *All that black paint must've cost her a fortune. No wonder she turned pirate.*

Conceit. Vree frowned.

She felt Gyhard stir uneasily within the boundaries of her mind. *What are you thinking?* he demanded. *Vree . . .*

I'm thinking that there may be an alternative to going over the side with a pirate's ax splitting my skull.

What alternative?

She turned from the rail. *The usual one.* Ignoring the chaos growing around her, she made her way past frantic men and women fighting to get the last bit of speed out of the *Fancy* to the arms locker where the armsmaster was methodically setting out bundles of barbed arrows. As he'd spent some years in the Empire and spoke fluent Imperial, they'd not have to waste any of their rapidly decreasing time on translations. "Tell me," she demanded without preamble, "about Edite i'Oceania."

"Good at what she does," he grunted, not bothering to look up. "Almost as good as she thinks she is. Shkoden navy controls most of the sea-lanes through the Broken Islands, but they can't catch her. And the Circle knows they've tried. From what I've heard, her crew adores her. They should. She's made them rich. They'd die for her." He pulled oilskin-wrapped packets of bowstrings out of the locker. "And some of them are going to."

"What about her? Would she die for them?"

The armsmaster laughed, but the sound held little humor. "Her type thinks they're immortal."

"How would she respond to a knife at her throat?" The tone of Vree's voice lifted the armsmaster out of his crouch and turned him toward her. "Would this pirate call off an attack in exchange for her life? Would her crew listen if she did?"

"Aye, the crew would likely listen," he said slowly, studying her face, a slow realization dawning. "But i'Oceania wouldn't give that order. If she's taken alive, she'll die ashore and she knows it. You kill her, though, and her crew becomes the stinking rabble it was before she forced order on it. Captain Edite's the only thing holding that murdering bunch of cutthroats together. If she dies, they'd fall apart. If they fall apart . . ." His eyes still on her face, he closed his fist around the hilt of his short sword. "I can beat them."

Vree nodded and spun about on one bare heel.

"Assassin."

She paused.

"Do it quickly or there'll be no point in doing it at all."

Down in the forecastle, ignoring the fire crew readying its station, Vree unrolled her pack and began buckling on the wrist sheaths that held her throwing daggers. Up above, she could hear the armsmaster shouting orders. As she understood it, the captain—a thin and hairy man she'd barely seen—commanded all nautical situations and the armsmaster commanded defense. It would never have worked in the Imperial Army, but it seemed to work at sea.

If the armsmaster commanded, then the *Raven* was close.

You're very quiet, she said a moment later as she regained the main deck.

I thought we'd agreed that it would be best if you told no one what you were.

*I didn't *tell* him.*

You gave him enough for him to figure it out. He must've been suspicious ever since you won that knife fight . . .

Teeth clenched, Vree cut him off. *Look, you can jump into the nearest slaughtering pirate if this body dies. I can't. So shut up and stay out of my way.*

I can't talk you out of this?

No.

She had a mental image of Gyhard spreading his hands— Bannon's hands, because those were the only ones she'd ever seen him wear. *Then I guess I'm along for the ride. Wait a minute! Where are you going?*

Surefooted despite the constant movement of the ship, Vree started up the rigging by the stern mast. *You know that long thing sticking out from the front of the *Raven*?*

The bowsprit.

Whatever. Swinging up onto the bottom spar, she moved out to the end. The armsmaster had obviously said something to his bowmen, for the three she passed stared at her wide-eyed and twisted out of her way as much as their position some fifteen feet above the deck allowed. *I'm going to jump from the end of this crosspiece thing down onto it.*

You're going to what? Each word was carefully and separately enunciated. He sounded impossibly calm.

There's enough rope coming off it that it shouldn't matter if I miss a little.

Are you out of your mind! The calm had disappeared so completely it might never have existed. *That is *not* possible!*

Rolling her shoulders, Vree squinted back at the *Raven*, now close enough to make out the individual pirates crowding the rail. She could almost see the single line that held them together. The line she was about to cut. *It's not impossible, just very difficult. In fact, I'll aim for that rope between the whatever-you-called-it and the front mast and not worry about my footing. I can swing straight from there to the deck.*

*No you can't. *No one* could do that.*

Vree merely shrugged and watched with interest as a flaming ball of pitch landed with an angry hiss and a gout of steam just short of the *Raven*. Familiar with the huge siege engines the Imperial Army used, she'd been fascinated to discover, upon exploring the ship, a much smaller catapult on the carved stern of the *Gilded Fancy*.

The *Raven's* answer was a canister of metal fragments. The *Raven's* armsmaster was a better shot. Vree heard the impact; heard wood splinter; heard someone scream; could smell smoke.

What happened on the *Fancy* was no longer her concern. All her attention shifted to the enemy.

*Vree! Listen to me! You *can't* do this! I don't care how much training Imperial assassins go through; you can't jump from a moving ship to a moving ship!*

Concentration broken, she snapped, *How do the pirates intend to board us?*

That's different!

Only in degree.

They'll wait until they've dropped sail and grappled!

I haven't time to wait, and I know what I'm capable of. You don't. So shut up. And if you try to take over even an eyebrow, I'll push you right out of my head! Do you understand me, Gyhard?

I don't want to die, he said softly, ignoring the threat neither of them wanted to explore.

Good. That makes two of us. But as his concern was

in her head, she had to feel it. And the feeling was a distraction. Because assassins couldn't feel. Not while they were working. *Gyhard . . .*

At least they won't be expecting it, he sighed, surrendered, and drew back until he was barely a whisper in the depths of her mind. Vree suspected the whisper would remain even if Gyhard's kigh should find another body.

She forced her attention back to the *Raven.* Looked through the arrow fire. Ignored the howls of both pain and fury. Found a wild-haired woman in a scarlet shirt and boiled leather armor conducting the attack, a sword in one hand, and a basket-hilted dagger in the other. She marked the defenses and defenders she'd have to pass and found two of the pirate ship's other officers.

Compressing her focus, she shifted her gaze to the bowsprit.

The world became a rope, two sets of movement, and the distance between them.

The distance narrowed.

A grappling iron clanged against the side of the *Fancy,* only a hand's span short.

Vree jumped.

She was holding the rope but still falling when the *Raven*'s reinforced bow rammed into the *Fancy*'s side. The rope took up most of the shock, her arms the rest. Her right hand lost its grip, gained it again as the rough hemp burned a line across her palm, but the dagger in her wrist sheath twisted out and into the sea.

Shit!

She let her weight on the rope swing her in over the deck. As the ship rose, cresting a wave, she dropped, rolled, and sprinted for the stern.

Survive to reach the target. She'd been seven when she'd started training. Bannon had been six. They'd survived the training—two out of three didn't. She couldn't remember how many targets they'd survived to reach.

The world became a scarlet shirt and the pale column of throat above it.

In the confusion of boarding, few of the pirates noticed her. Those that did, she avoided although one took a wild swing and slashed a shallow cut diagonally across her back.

When Vree reached the sterncastle, a narrow three steps above the main deck, she leaped, without pausing, up and over the railing, landing directly in front of her target.

The captain broke off bellowing orders and began to laugh. A large woman, carrying very little of her weight as fat, she towered over the short, slender Southerner. "Have you come to challenge me, little sprat?" her voice cut through the bedlam and heads began to turn on both ships. "I think not."

Her heavy sword slammed down into the deck, splintering the wood, but Vree had begun to move before she'd finished speaking. Virtually too fast to follow, the point of her long dagger slipped in under Edite's left ear, drew a graceful line across the captain's throat, and slid out from under the right ear. She finished the motion by flicking her remaining wrist dagger down into her hand and sending it hilt deep into one of the brilliant blue eyes of the sailor on the tiller.

Edite scowled and began to choke, covering the immediate area with a crimson spray. Sword and dagger fell from fingers that curved to clutch futilely at life. With her windpipe and all major blood vessels severed, she didn't live long. As she slammed into the deck, still twitching, a roar went up from her crew. As one, their prize forgotten, they turned on Vree and, screaming with rage, they rushed for the stern. A few, already on board the *Fancy*, returned to join the enraged mass. A high-pitched voice, shouting for them to continue the attack, was ignored.

An ax splintered the deck at Vree's feet and a javelin cut through the place she'd been an instant before. Fortunately, most of the howling pack forgot the missile weapons they held in the desire to personally rip their captain's killer limb from limb. Backing rapidly into a corner of the stern, Vree's hips hit the rail. The first half-dozen crew members charged toward her past their captain's body, faces twisted in identical masks of hate.

Vree!

She hit the water in a clean dive some distance from the *Raven*'s ebony hull and stayed deep as long as she could.

I didn't know you could swim.

The relief in Gyhard's mental voice was so great that Vree very nearly laughed aloud. *The Sixth Army's garrison was at Harack, on the coast. When I was eleven, we had to swim about five miles back to shore in the middle of the night.*

*When you were *eleven*?*

Bannon was ten. The swim wasn't so bad, but the sharks were annoying.

Sharks!

This time she did laugh as her head broke the surface, the water pulling her dripping hair back off her face. *I'm kidding about the sharks.* Bobbing up and down the swells, salt burning in the cut across her back, she turned until she could see the battle raging on the two ships. Although she thought she could hear the *Fancy*'s armsmaster yelling orders, she had no way of knowing who was winning.

If the garrison was by the ocean, why didn't you know what a bowsprit was called?

Because it wasn't important; we had too many other things to learn, and a ship has no throat to slit. I guess we should go back and . . .

Large hands closed around Vree's waist and dragged her under. Released her, grabbed her shoulders, and pushed her deeper. As the water closed over her head, she fought a heartbeat's panic, then pointed her toes and pushed up against the water, trying to go deeper still. It almost worked. Her attacker lost his grip on her shoulders but caught a painful handful of her hair.

Taken by surprise, her lungs were nearly empty. She needed to breathe.

Most assassins died after taking out their targets, success having made them careless.

Her chest burned. A primal panic clawed at the inside of her mouth and throat.

The sea closed around her ribs and squeezed, trying to force her to inhale.

Through slitted eyes, she could see a huge, dark shape in the water above her.

Facing her.

Throwing the strength of arms and shoulders into a backstroke, she drew her legs up and, knees touching her own forehead, drove both feet past his arm and slammed them up under his jaw. Pulling herself over and around, she sucked in great lungfuls of air as her face broke the surface and finished the circle, coughing, gasping, with an unnecessary dagger in her hand.

I think you crushed his throat.

Forcing her breathing to slow, Vree sheathed the dagger and started swimming for the ships, ignoring the choking, thrashing pirate just over an arm's length away.

Aren't you going to finish him?

He's finished. And I'd rather not put more blood into the water. Arms and legs growing heavier with every heartbeat, all she wanted to do was get back on board the *Fancy* before the last of her energy gave out.

I don't understand why they're carrying on like this.

Through Vree's eyes, Gyhard watched as the crew of the *Gilded Fancy* celebrated by lantern light. The captain'd had two casks of sweet Imperial wine brought up on deck and most of the toasts drunk had been to Vireyda Magaly, the savior of the ship. Gyhard could feel her confusion and recognized its source. While any of the Seven Armies might rejoice at the removal of an enemy commander—for the lack of a battle no lives were lost—they'd been trained to make no fuss over the assassin who, after all, had only been doing her job. But Vree was no longer in the Imperial Army and she'd just done the impossible. *You've never worked with an audience before. Usually, the people who see you don't survive the experience.*

She shifted uneasily. *So?*

So, you do impressive work. He remembered the first time he'd seen her kill; by the time he'd thought she should start moving, it was all over. Her concentration, he'd just discovered, was as complete as it appeared—nothing got in her way. Fueled by that concentration, her speed was terrifying. If he ever took control of her body, the difference would be night and day, her deadly grace lost. *If he ever took control of her body . . .* He buried the thought as deeply as possible, lest she feel it.

He'd wanted to remind her, back when she'd been worrying over how assassins couldn't feel, that she wasn't an assassin any more. Except that only an Imperial assassin with years of brutal training both mental and physical behind her could hope to make that jump, and as she obviously intended to make it and he had no choice but to go along . . .

In the corner of her vision, he caught sight of the two Imperial merchants and felt the memory of hair rising off the back of his neck. Although both merchants held heavy metal goblets, their expressions were anything but celebratory and when one of them, believing herself unobserved, glanced at Vree, she was scowling.

In the Havakeen Empire, assassins were named the blades of Jiir, the goddess of battles, and their terrifying, deadly skills were controlled by the army. The citizens of the Empire were constantly assured that assassins were not only rare but safely sheathed, killing only on order of their commanders. Trained from early childhood that the army was their only family, assassins never left . . . home.

As an added reassurance to a nervous population, it was well known that if, in spite of incredible odds, they should desert, they would be targeted and quickly killed.

But Vree had been trained with her brother and that attachment had been strong enough to break all the rest. She'd killed the man sent to kill her and had bought her freedom from His Imperial Majesty with the life of his youngest son.

Gyhard, though born in Shkoder, had lived most of his hundred and thirty-six years—most of his lives—in the Empire and could understand the fear on the merchant's face. *This* assassin was not sheathed by the army and she'd just made her own decision to kill—without orders. If that were possible, how could anyone be safe?

How indeed, Gyhard wondered. When the celebration was over, it would only take a couple of voices to turn the admiration to fear. *"Listen to me, I come from the Empire, I know . . ."* She was too fast. Too deadly. Too impossible to stop. And they had all seen what she was capable of. Assassinating both merchants before the warnings could start seemed a bit extreme even if he could convince Vree to do it. Besides, after the afternoon's exhibition of her abilities, the authorities wouldn't need a bard to discover who'd wielded the knife—Vree was deadly but hardly subtle.

As Vree turned slightly to watch a sailor juggling three

torches, an ax, and a dead chicken, Gyhard took a better look at the merchants. There was nothing obviously wrong with the male of the pair: young enough, reasonably good-looking. Suppose he could convince Vree to push him into the male merchant? Once there he could easily silence the rumors by arranging an accident . . . except that even should Vree prove willing—which she wouldn't—Gabris and Karlene had made it clear what the bards would do if he acquired a body by taking a life.

"As we can neither remove you nor bring you to justice for the lives you've so callously ended as long as you remain in Vree's body, you have, for the moment, found sanctuary. You'd best not forget what you owe her for that." Karlene's voice had made it a warning, not a reminder. *"But this is where we draw the line. If anyone else dies because of you, anyone, the bards will see to it that your kigh goes back into the Circle so fast you won't know what hit you."*

That Karlene and Gabris were a very long distance away in the Empire meant little when they both Sang air and distance meant nothing at all to the kigh.

He felt Vree's foot tapping in time to the music as a battered squeeze-box, a fiddle, and a pair of pipes began to play. The army had gone to a great deal of trouble to present the assassins as weapons; perhaps it would help if Vree were seen as flesh and blood. *Why don't you dance?*

To his surprise she shifted uncomfortably. *Don't you start.*

Start what?

The whole time Bannon shared my body, he kept trying to push me into having sex with someone, anyone. You. Karlene. He didn't care just as long as he got to experience it from the other side.

It's just a dance, Vree.

He could feel her tension as she chopped a hand at the leaping, stomping, sweating bodies that filled the deck. *If you think this won't end in a sacrifice to the horizontal gods, you never spent much time expecting to die.* She snorted. *How stupid of me; of course you didn't. If you expected to die, you just . . . jumped ship.* Wiping damp palms on her cotton trousers, she added, her voice flat, all sarcasm gone, *Not for Bannon. Not for you.*

It didn't take much to recognize where the tension originated. First Bannon. Then him. *It's been a while, hasn't it?*

Shut the slaughter up!

Vree, I'm not your brother. I don't want to be with you—in you—while you're with someone else. The thought of her wrapped in the arms of a man or woman, taking what he couldn't give her, drove daggers into his heart and twisted. She might not know how she felt about him, but he knew exactly how he felt about her.

Don't say it.

They could feel each other's strong emotions.

Vree . . .

No.

When the *Gilded Fancy* made her way into Pitesti Harbor—the only harbor in the Broken Islands deep enough for a merchant ship of her draw—followed closely by the *Raven,* the hysterical reaction on shore could be both seen and heard from the foredeck. Bells rang out, fishing boats ran themselves aground, and the broad pebble beach curving between the town and the sea began to empty.

"Fools think they're being invaded," the armsmaster snorted, jerking his head at the masts where the flags of Shkoder hung limp and unreadable. "Think i'Oceania's crew has both ships."

Vree glanced toward the *Raven* where the late captain's body had been lashed to the bowsprit. The surviving pirates were secured belowdecks and the sailors now guiding her in past the breakwater were a skeleton crew off the *Fancy.*

On shore, the beach began to fill again as archers took up their positions behind the curved shields of overturned dories and siege engines were uncovered at both ends of the crescent.

"Pitesti was the last place to fall when Shkoder took the Broken Islands," the armsmaster told her, leaning unconcernedly on the rail. "They're proud of that. Obviously, they don't intend to fall again."

Vree squinted at the town silhouetted against the setting sun. "I'd feint at the harbor, land troops on the other side of the island and take the place from behind."

The armsmaster nodded. "You and King Mikus."

Should we be worried? As far as Gyhard could tell, the catapults were being loaded with what looked to be bales of hemp soaked in pitch.

Under the circumstances, it seemed a reasonable question, so Vree repeated it.

"No, we're just at the edge of their range." As the armsmaster spoke, the anchors were dropped. "Captain'll send a boat in. With any luck they won't sink it."

From the expressions on the faces of the boat crew, they were aware of their danger; postures visibly relaxed when the keel scraped gravel and the mate stepped safely ashore. Her hands out from her sides, she moved a body length from the boat, and stopped. There seemed to be a lot of shouting going on although no one on either ship could make out the words. After a moment, she half-turned and waved an angry hand toward the harbor.

As though the mate had commanded it, a sudden evening breeze unfurled the crowned ship of Shkoder flying from both the *Fancy* and the *Raven* and a last, long ray from the setting sun bathed both ships in a golden light.

The cheering carried clearly over the water and the bells of Pitesti began to ring again.

"Always said Kirston had a touch of bard. Couldn't have done that with more style if she'd Sung the kigh." The armsmaster pushed off the rail. "You'd best get ready. They'll likely want you ashore."

"Why?"

He chuckled, the sound almost fatherly. "You killed Edite i'Oceania. That makes you a hero in these parts, Assassin."

I wish he'd stop calling you that.

Vree nodded slowly. She didn't know why but the armsmaster's reinforcement of her past made her uneasy as well.

Bonfires were lit on the beach that night, but most of the sailors, exhausted by the effort of bringing two ships safely to harbor with what remained of a single ship's crew, crawled into their hammocks and stayed there.

The next morning, the town council and the captain of the *Gilded Fancy* hung Edite i'Oceania's body in an iron cage on the harbor headland.

"And she'll soon have company enough," growled an old woman. Dry fingers wrapped around Vree's forearm and drew her away from the crowd clustered under the dead woman's dangling feet. "I'm Ilka i'Gitka, the eldest on the council. You're the Southern girl who cut that second smile 'neath her chin, aren't you?" Before Gyhard could finish translating or Vree could answer, she went on, "Slip of a girl like you doing what the entire Shkoden Navy couldn't; that's going to make them feel like a bunch of unenclosed fools, isn't it? Looks good on them. We'll have the trial this afternoon, you'll tell your story—that's you, the *Fancy*'s armsmaster and anyone else who feels like they've got an anchor to drop—the pirate scum'll tell their story, then we'll likely hang the lot of them. Until then, you let folk make a fuss of you, you hear? Few enough heroes in the world as it is."

A muffled exclamation drew them both around. The man who'd made the noise was staring wide-eyed at Vree.

"Looks like you've made an impression on young Tomas," Ilka cackled.

Did she say *young* Tomas? Vree frowned. The man was at least forty; possibly older, the broad faces of the Northerners made judging age confusing.

Look at the robe, Vree.

Tomas' robe hung off his narrow shoulders in full folds of green and blue. Other than a white splash of seagull shit, Vree couldn't see anything special about it.

He's a bard!

Oh. Bards knew. In ways she couldn't understand, they could sense both of the lives she carried. Even injured and in the dark, Karlene had known.

Make friends with him, Vree. He keeps these people connected with the world and his opinion carries a lot of weight.

She set her jaw. *Why should I care what he thinks?*

Gyhard watched through her eyes as the pair of Imperial merchants came ashore and, keeping as far from the assassin as possible, joined the crowd. He hadn't wanted to tell Vree his suspicions, but now he had no choice. Quickly, he outlined the damage he thought the merchants could do.

Vree's hands curled into fists. *The next time you see danger at my back,* she said, her mental voice an edged weapon, *tell me or this slaughtering . . . *thing* we have won't last very long.*

I just thought . . .

No. You didn't think. I can't protect myself against enemies I don't slaughtering well know I have. She turned to the councillor, who'd been talking about bards and heroes and how the former could create the latter while she and Gyhard had been holding their silent conversation. A quick bow cut off the flow of meaningless words. "If I may be . . ."

Excused, Gyhard broke in. *Not dismissed. Let's not remind people of the army right now.*

". . . excused, the bard and I have . . . something to talk on."

Discuss.

That's what I said. Her tone made it clear he was far from forgiven.

As Vree approached, Tomas stopped nervously cracking his knuckles and tried, not very successfully, to smile.

The Bardic Hall in Pitesti occupied the seaward corner of the top floor of the four-story Healers' Hall. It was the tallest building in the town and Tomas' balcony—a ten by twenty cedar-covered section of the third-floor roof—had an unobstructed view out over the harbor. As he Sang, Vree watched the leaves of potted herbs flutter against the wind and wondered what Karlene would tell him.

His voice quavering just a little, the bard Sang a gratitude and sent the air kigh on its way. Although the salt breeze was cool, he wiped a dribble of sweat from his brow before he turned to face his guest. Guests. "We won't get an answer for a while," he explained. "Would you like some, well, lunch?"

Well, would I?

She could feel Gyhard's approval. *Lunch is good.*

Lunch is all. I don't care how friendly we need him.

*Having touched Bannon's mind, I can see how you might have gotten this impression, but not *all* men think about sex *all* the time.*

"And if it's all right, I'd like my partner to look at you," Tomas continued, taking her silence for assent. "He hasn't a full healer's talent, but he's a good diagnostic and I'd like to show him proof that the fifth kigh exists. That is, if you and, uh . . ."

"Gyhard," Vree prompted.

He has the worst memory of any bard I've ever met.

I don't think he wants to remember.

"Yes. Gyhard. If the two of you don't, well, mind?"

"No." When his face fell, Vree frowned. "Yes?" When he only looked confused, she sighed. "The words in your language get . . . mixed." Hands spread, she said very slowly, "You may bring your healer."

"Good." The bard finally managed a smile. "I hope you like fish."

What do you man, he doesn't want to remember?

Isn't it obvious? This whole slaughtering fifth kigh thing, you being here in my body, has screwed up everything he thought he could be sure about in his entire life. Vree perched on the edge of a huge fan-backed wicker chair and, out of habit, adjusted her daggers. *You're good at that.*

Vree, are you about to begin your flows? You seem unreasonably angry.

Jiir forbid I should be angry at you for destroying my life? For nearly killing my brother? For deciding what I do and do not need to know about potential danger?

For loving you?

Yes. No. She sagged into the chair. *I wish you'd quit bringing that up. It doesn't have anything to do with . . .*

You?

Oh, shut up.

Gyhard tried to remember how close they were to the next dark of the moon. There were aspects of occupying a woman's body that had never occurred to him during the previous six lives he'd lived. He thanked all the gods the Circle contained that he wasn't facing those complications alone. If Vree had made it to his/Aralt's chamber before her brother and he'd taken over her body . . . He shuddered.

Brow furrowed, Tomas listened to the message the kigh brought out of the Empire and tried to keep from glancing over his shoulder to where Vree—*"No, Vree and Gyhard,"* he corrected himself silently—sat talking quietly with Adamec. His partner had been first skeptical and then, after laying on his hands, ecstatic. He'd had a thousand questions. Tomas only had one.

"You can trust Vree completely," Karlene told him through the kigh. *"She'll kill to survive, but I believe that's it. Ignoring for the moment the implication I would've even considered sending a maniacal murderer to Shkoder—Imperial assassins don't work that way. If anything, they're too controlled. All she wants is to talk to our healers and see if there's anything they can do to find Gyhard a separate life."* The kigh paused and their ethereal noncolor seemed to darken. *"Gyhard, on the other hand, you can't trust. He's spent over a hundred years jumping from body to body—I don't know how he does it; I wish I did—and this is the first time he's been in a willing host. It's also only the second time he hasn't killed the host and the first time with Vree's brother Bannon was, as I understand it, a fluke. He says he loves her, but I personally am not sure I believe him."*

Tomas grinned a little at that as the emotional nuance the kigh gave to the words indicated that Karlene herself had an intimate interest in the tiny, Southern woman.

"Even if he does love her, I doubt it would be enough to change his basically amoral nature. This is, after all, a man who has removed himself from the Circle. We can't do anything about justice as long as he's sharing Vree's body but he seemed to believe Gabris and me when we explained that if yet another host died because of him, that would be it. I explained the whole thing to Captain Liene, and if I'd known Vree'd be stopping at Pitesti, I'd have let you know as well. Final chorus—as long as it's Vree in control of her body, I wouldn't worry about it."

"You wouldn't worry about it," Tomas muttered after Singing a gratitude and dismissing the kigh. How was he supposed to tell who was in control of the assassin's body? With two kigh in a place where there should be only one, all nets came up empty. Why did he have to be the first bard to deal with this situation? *"All right, third bard,"* he amended, granting first and second place to Gabris and Karlene. Not for the first time, he felt completely inadequate. Although most bards who anchored the country at a Bardic Hall Sang all four quarters, he'd been given Pitesti because he Sang the two most common, air and water, very strongly and because King Theron and the Bardic Captain

had agreed that a returning native might be more acceptable to the Broken Islanders than a perceived foreigner.

As he turned, he heard Adamec say, "I wish you could stay! There's so much we could learn from you! So much we could learn to do deliberately instead of instinctively."

"Trained instincts," the young woman replied, "can be a powerful . . . tool."

Crossing toward them, Tomas wondered what she'd intended to say. What had been discarded in that pause? Weapon, perhaps? *She doesn't look dangerous,* he mused. *With that pointy little face she looks almost fragile.* Then she stood and the way she moved suddenly made him think of several deadly predators. It took him a moment to find his voice. "If we're going to be on time for the trial," he managed at last. "We'll have to leave now."

Vree nodded but remained where she was. "What did the air spirits, the kigh, tell you?"

"Well . . ." He weighed the information and separated what he thought he should pass on. "Karlene says I should trust you."

"Are you going to?"

Meeting her steady gaze, Tomas saw strength and vulnerability about equally mixed and found himself in sudden sympathy with this strange young foreigner. "Yes," he said, a little surprised by his reaction. "I am."

I wonder what Karlene told him about me, Gyhard muttered.

Vree snorted. *I think you already know.*

"Bertic a'Karlis step forward."

Vree watched in horror as the armsmaster obeyed the bard's command.

"Bertic a'Karlis, you will speak only the truth."

Are they going to do that to me? She remembered the terrifying feeling of being held by an invisible fist the night they'd broken into Karlene's chamber at the Healers' Hall in the Capital. She'd broken the spell by having Bannon take over her body, but she didn't have Bannon with her now.

Calm down, Vree. They just want to make sure they're getting at the whole truth. People's lives are at stake here. Don't worry, it doesn't hurt.

I wasn't worried about it hurting, she snapped. *I don't want anyone controlling my body ever again.*

He won't be controlling your body. In a minor way he'll be controlling your mind.

*That makes me feel *so* much better.*

They don't need your testimony as such, but if you refuse, you'll be playing right into whatever rumors those merchants started.

They'd definitely started something. Vree could feel the hostility rising from whispering clusters scattered through the crowd and wrapping around her like a dark fog. She'd seen mobs work before and couldn't ignore the danger.

"Vireyda Magaly, step forward."

It wasn't as bad as she'd thought it would be, but without Gyhard's constant murmur of comfort, she doubted she'd have been able to stand it. When it finally ended, she was covered in a clammy film of cold sweat.

As Gyhard predicted, her cooperation, combined with the apparent approval of Tomas and his partner, returned the hero status the Imperial merchants had nearly managed to destroy.

The *Raven*'s carpenter and sail maker, impressed from captured ships and tortured to maintain their compliance, were set free. Unfortunately, the sail maker was no longer exactly sane. Three women in the early stages of pregnancy were taken aside—their sentences commuted until their babies were born. The rest, condemned out of their own mouths, stood bound on the beach before the council. Most of them looked numb, a few cursed softly, a couple wept. They all wore the marks of rotten eggs and fruit. The crowd had stopped throwing things only after the council had threatened to move to the privacy of the council chamber.

From her central seat in the semicircle of driftwood chairs, it was clear that Ilka's position as eldest not only allowed her to run the council but also everyone on it. "You're lucky we're not on the mainland," she declared, looking as though she considered them lucky indeed. "On the mainland you'd have to go through all this again before the king at a Death Judgment. Fortunately for us, our distance from His Majesty ensures a certain autonomy in dealing with the sort of people who have, over a period of some years, slaughtered, individually and collectively, upward of two hundred men, women, and children. In short, in dealing with scum like you." She stood, accepted a staff carved with an entwined pattern of kelp and crowned with a leaping dolphin, and slammed its metal-bound butt three times into the smooth stones of the beach, "By the power invested in this council by Theron, King of Shkoder, High Captain of the Broken Islands, lord of a whole bunch of places that don't mean fish shit out here, I pronounce sentence—hang them."

The crowd released a collective, satisfied sigh and Vree thought she saw Tomas wince as he said, "Witnessed."

"Of course she's dangerous. She just put an end to the most vicious crew of mass murderers we've had in these waters since my grandfather's time." Ilka nodded in satisfaction as the seventh pirate was hoisted kicking and writhing into the air at the other end of the beach, then turned her attention again to the pair of Imperial merchants. "Tell me something I *don't* know."

"Honored Councillor, you don't understand." Although he spoke Shkoden fluently, the merchant's accent put strange inflections on the words. "Assassins are trained only to kill or be killed, for them there is no middle ground and they are never away from the army. For this one to be as she is, deciding to kill as she has, is wrong."

"Very wrong," affirmed his companion. "It is as though a sword moved through the world, striking and killing with no hand wielding it."

The elderly councillor studied them, weighing their fear. "How do you know there's no hand wielding her?" she asked at last. "Perhaps she's been sent to kill someone in Shkoder, no one saw fit to tell the two of you, and you've just blown her cover to the other side. That's treason, isn't it?"

The young man paled. Frowning, the woman shook her head. "Assassins travel only as part of an army. They are targeted and released by the army. The Empire is not at war with Shkoder, nor do we wish them to be. War is very bad for trade."

"It is that." Hand disappearing into her robe, Ilka

scratched at the white line of an old scar, received the day Pitesti fell. "So what do you want me to do about this wild sword of yours? If she's too dangerous for Shkoder, she's an unenclosed sight too dangerous to hold here. Even if we had a reason to hold her. Which we don't. And besides, she spent the morning with the bard and if she was any kind of a threat, he'd have told me."

"We know nothing of bards, Honored Councillor, we merely thought that someone should be told what we know of assassins."

"Well, someone's been told. In fact . . ." The sudden shrieking of a pirate brought face-to-face with his own imminent death cut her off. She waited until the noise stopped before continuing. "In fact, from the whispering I've been hearing, hasn't just about everyone been told? Didn't it occur to you that she could get *annoyed* about that and, if she's as dangerous as you say, maybe you'd be better off not attracting her attention? You think on that, and I'll think on what you've told me. Ass-kissing bottom feeders," she added after the two recognized a dismissal, bowed, and scurried away.

"Still," she sighed, a pair of pirates later, "personal admiration probably shouldn't stand in the way of national security. Kaspar!"

A balding fisherman hurried over to her chair. "Yes, Grandmother?"

"Wasn't there a Shkoden diplomat of some kind on the *Fancy*?"

"I think so, Grandmother."

"Go find him, and tell him I want to talk to him."

Imrich i'Iduska a'Krisus, diplomatic courier between the Shkoden ambassador to the Empire and King Theron, stroked the point of his beard and frowned. "We've been on the same ship for nine days; I wonder why they didn't bring this information directly to me."

"Because you're an officer of the Shkoden court, and I'm a sweet, approachable old lady." She threw up her hands. "How in the Circle should I know? The point is, you have the information now. Forget it or pass it on, it's all the same to me."

*   *   *

Vree stood out on the bard's deck and watched the dark silhouettes of the hanged pirate crew swinging in the night. Although the air was warm, she shuddered.

Tomas, who'd been about to ask if she wanted something to eat before Adamec started in on her again, saw the movement and asked instead, "It bothers you?"

She shrugged without turning. "It is a slow, painful, messy way to kill."

"You're saying you could've done it better?" He couldn't stop the incredulous question, recognized how insulting it sounded, and hoped Karlene's assessment of the assassin's temperament was correct.

"I am not . . . an executioner. I say, it is a slow, painful, messy way to die. And, yes, it bothers me."

The bard swallowed and risked touching her gently on one shoulder. "It bothers me, too."

When Vree turned to face him, her face was carefully expressionless and her tone matter-of-fact. "But they expect it to bother you. Please tell Adamec I will be in . . . soon."

He could possibly have Sung his way past the barriers, but he suspected he wouldn't have known what to do with what he found, so he merely nodded and went back inside.

Vree? What's wrong?

I'm in a strange country, speaking a language I barely understand, and I want to go home.

We can.

No. She stared at the harbor without really seeing it. *I miss the army.* Her fingers dug into the soft wood of the railing. *I miss Bannon. I have no one around me I can trust.*

He didn't so much understand her pain, as share in it. *You can trust me.*

The sound of the rope rubbing against wooden cross beams drifted up clearly from the beach.

Vree?

TWO

"Vireyda Magaly."

Vree turned and, even in the midst of the chaos on the docks, easily identified the woman who'd spoken her name. It almost seemed as though she could see a line drawn in the air between them.

Bard, Gyhard murmured.

That would explain the robe. But his single word had sounded nervous and Vree regretted the sarcasm. All at once, she found herself wondering how Gyhard felt about returning to Shkoder. He hadn't asked for her interference back when he'd left Bannon's body. She'd just grabbed him out of nothingness and since then she hadn't once considered that he might have feelings that didn't involve her—for all that she refused to acknowledge his feelings that did. The sudden realization froze her in place.

Go on. She's waiting.

Gyhard, I . . .

Not now. Something in his tone suggested he could read the direction of her thoughts and found himself mildly amused by them.

If he didn't want to come here, he should've said something before *we left the Empire.* Less easily defined emotions lost in irritation, Vree gritted her teeth and made her way toward the bard. The quartered robe covered a stocky body, condensed by age but far from frail. Above the robe, deep lines bracketed eyes and mouth in a well-weathered face and her hair hugged the angles of her head like a steel cap. She leaned on a heavy, no-nonsense cane that to Vree's practiced eye had enough heft to make an effective club. Amidst the seemingly formless pandemonium that surged back and forth against the harborfront of Elbasan, the elderly bard stood surrounded by a nearly visible circle of competence and calm.

This is someone, Vree thought with relief as she ducked under a swinging net of cargo being unloaded from the *Fancy*'s hold, *who can tell me what to do.*

Weight on her cane, fingers drumming against the quartered pattern carved into the handle, the Bardic Captain dragged her attention from the pair of kigh the young woman carried—despite the urge to begin investigating them immediately—to the young woman herself. She was younger than Liene had expected. *But then again, these days,* the captain grunted silently, *everyone is.* She was also smaller than expected and her lack of height, combined with her youth and the pointed features, resulted in an almost fragile appearance.

But there was nothing fragile in how she moved through the confusion on the docks. She used exactly the space available, sliding from opening to opening, never in anyone's way, never allowing anyone to be in hers.

Assassin. Liene turned the word over in her mind. She'd never met a person who'd taken a life who hadn't been, at least for that instant, insane. Karlene had insisted that the Empire had turned this young woman into a weapon without destroying her. Perhaps. Karlene had also insisted that her personal feelings had nothing to do with that analysis. Not likely.

Now this assassin was in Shkoder, asking for help; offering in return a chance for bards and healers to study the suddenly impossible to ignore fifth kigh. And it had to be done in Shkoder not the Empire where an assassin would be no more than a part of the military infrastructure for, in spite of the evidence, the citizens of the Empire barely believed in the original four kigh.

Original four kigh. Liene shook her head. That seemed to imply a possibility of further discoveries. A sixth and a seventh kigh perhaps? Perhaps. All things were enclosed in the Circle. *But for now,* she told herself emphatically, *we have enough to concentrate on without adding further complications.*

Upon dismissing the kigh who'd brought Karlene's message,

Liene had gone over every recall in the Bardic Library that mentioned Imperial assassins. It hadn't taken long. Although bards had gained access to the Havakeen Empire twenty-two years before when Princess Irenka had joined with the Empire's crown prince—now Emperor—not one of them had met an assassin until they'd encountered Vree and her brother. Apparently, as few people had the necessary combination of skills it took to kill on command as had the perfect pitch and desire to Sing the kigh. Uncomfortable with the analogy, Liene hastily put it aside.

A small amount of the available information had been gleaned from the military. The rest, unfortunately, was nothing more than rumor and hearsay. When she'd had the kigh contact Aurel, the bard Karlene had replaced at the Imperial court, he'd expressed doubts that assassins actually existed.

No doubt of that now. The young woman who turned to acknowledge a shouted farewell from the *Fancy*'s stern with a truncated wave, had danger wrapped around her like a crimson cloak. Danger to what, though; that was the question.

Was Vireyda Magaly a danger to crown or country? Karlene believed not and, more importantly, Gabris had agreed with her. But they had both warned her to watch Gyhard i'Stevana.

"According to Gyhard, unless Vree pushes him, he can't jump to another body without killing the body he's in. He says he has no wish to do that, but then he's not likely to tell Vree otherwise, is he? Vree has agreed not to help him if it means the taking of a life, but we have little doubt that while he is in her head, he'll attempt to convince her otherwise. He has been outside the Circle for so long, we cannot trust him." The kigh had grown very agitated at that point, making the rest of the message difficult to understand.

"We suggest, Captain, that the bards and healers both watch him closely."

Liene snorted, remembering. Neither bard had been able to suggest how they were supposed to watch a man reduced to kigh and sharing a body with another.

As the young woman drew nearer, it became more and more difficult to be aware of anything but the two kigh she carried.

A good thing I came myself, the captain mused. *A younger bard might lose the larger picture in the smaller. Might find a pair of kigh completely overwhelming.* Bardic Captain for twenty-nine of her sixty-eight years, Liene considered herself long past the possibility of being overwhelmed by anything. She held out her fist as the ex-assassin stopped an arm's length away. "Liene. Bardic Captain."

Touch the bottom of your fist to the top of hers and tell her your name.

She knows my name, Vree protested, shifting her weight forward onto the balls of her feet.

It's the way they introduce themselves in Shkoder. Just do it.

He was definitely nervous. Under the circumstances, Vree decided to do as he suggested and ignore the tone he suggested it in. "Vireyda Magaly. But I am always Vree."

"Vree." Liene nodded. She'd noted the signs of a silent conversation and, abruptly, decided to acknowledge the situation. Ignoring it wouldn't make it go away. *More's the pity.* "And your companion?"

Vree started and glanced around. No one in the surrounding crowd of buyers, sellers, sailors, and city folk seemed to paying them any attention. "Uh, Gyhard i'Stevana."

Maybe I didn't want them to know.

You think Karlene or Gabris hasn't already told her? She's their captain.

It isn't a military organization, Vree.

Then why are they using military rank?

She's like the captain of a ship.

Then she's still the person in charge and they'd still have told her.

"Is Gyhard not able to speak for himself?"

"No." When Liene's eyebrows rose, Vree found herself elaborating. "Not without I give him control of my body."

The captain half smiled. "Unless. Not *unless* you give him control of your body. Which, as I understand it, is probably not a good idea."

As she didn't seem to expect a response, Vree waited.

"Is that all you brought with you?" Liene used her cane to point at Vree's pack.

"Yes."

"Good." She half-turned and, still using the cane, pointed to a cluster of stone buildings just visible above the slate roofs of the city. "That's the Citadel, there on the top of that hill. That's where we'll be walking to." The last phrase emerged like a challenge and when the expected protest wasn't voiced, the Bardic Captain shook her head in disgust at her own defensiveness. "Most of the bards and some of the healers seem to think I can't walk across a room anymore, let alone halfway across the city," she snorted as Vree fell into step beside her. "My joints stiffen up in the damp, especially my hips and knees, but I've walked across this whole country in my time and I *won't* be coddled."

Am I supposed to say something? Vree asked, a little confused.

I don't think so.

"Kovar thought he should be the one to come to the harbor to meet you." Her cane hit the damp cobblestones of Upper Dock Street with unnecessary force and a young man pulling a wheeled dolly loaded with bales of raw cotton moved hastily out of her way. "I had to remind him that I remain Bardic Captain until Third Quarter Festival and he can just live with it."

What is it about you and old ladies? Gyhard wondered as they followed the captain around the edge of the Dock Market, the roar of buying and selling making audible conversation impossible. *All of a sudden, you seem to be attracting them. First in Pitesti and now here.*

Maybe it's something Bannon left behind. He was always the one getting pinched and patted.

Probably enjoyed it, too. He watched through Vree's eyes as Liene exchanged noisy greetings with half a dozen people, questioned the price of a pound of jasmine tea, and arranged for it to be delivered to the Bardic Hall at the lower price all without breaking stride. *I'm curious about why the Bardic Captain herself came down to meet us.*

Vree glanced up at the stone towers of the Citadel rising from the center of Elbasan like a crown. Although the steepness of the hill made an estimate difficult, it looked like they had some distance to cover and, with the captain's age slowing them down, they were going to take a while to cover it. *Seems like we'll have plenty of time to find out.*

Remember you've got to . . .

. . . make a good impression with the bards. She sighed.
I know. But I can't be something I'm not.

Be yourself.

Yeah. Right.

The bitterness took him by surprise.

The noise of the market became a background growl as
the two women turned onto a narrow avenue and started
the long climb up the hill.

"Cotton Street," Liene explained, following Vree's gaze
to where thick skeins of thread dyed all the colors of the
rainbow hung twisting in the breeze between the open shutters of a shopfront. "Use to be West Wharf Street, but
about fifteen years ago everyone started calling it Cotton
Street and about five years ago the city council finally
changed it. They buy bales of the stuff raw off the ships
from the South, spin it, dye it, weave it, and sell it all
around here. Don't sell a lot of it, mind, as the price is one
unenclosed amount higher than the linen coming locally
out of Vidor. The cloth doesn't last as long either." Then
her voice changed, and it suddenly became impossible not
to pay attention to what she had to say. "Lower Dock
Street, then Hill Street to the Citadel would've been more
direct, but at this time of day there'd be people all around
and we need to talk without being interrupted. What do
you want from us, Vree?"

"Karlene . . ." Vree began defensively.

The Bardic Captain shook her head. "No. I've heard her
version, now I want yours."

"Gyhard . . ."

"Forget Gyhard," the older woman commanded. "Or if
you can't forget him, disregard him for the moment. What
do *you* want from us?"

I want everything to be like it was before. Except she
didn't. Not really. Or she'd have let Gyhard disappear
into oblivion.

"I want Gyhard to have a body for his own." Ignoring
Gyhard's soft, *Of his own,* Vree clutched the hilt of her
dagger with her left hand, fingers opening and closing convulsively, and added, "But no one can die for it."

"Why not?"

She saw the face of Edite i'Oceania, a crimson line of

death across her throat; Commander Neegan's face, her
father's face, finding his only possible peace as her blade
found his heart; Avor's face, a friend's face, as he realized
he was going to die; too many faces to remember the names
or the reasons. Her own face, reflected in a polished shield.

What do you think you're going to see?

Who I am.

Who I am . . .

"Vree?"

She blinked and realized that she'd stopped walking. The
captain had moved a few paces ahead, had turned, and was
watching her. She couldn't read the expression on the older
woman's face and had no better idea of the expression on
her own. Her arms were folded tightly over her stomach,
as though she'd been slashed in the belly and had to hold
in her guts. Slowly, she released the white-knuckled embrace she had on each elbow and held out her hands.
"There has been enough death. I don't want to see death
when I look at him."

To her surprise, the Bardic Captain took a step forward
and enclosed her fingers in a gentle grip. Vree found herself
looking into a dark gaze that reached past all the years of
blood and all the training that had come before to find a
seven-year-old who was suddenly no longer a child. It hurt
more than any wound she'd ever taken. Somehow, she
found the strength to drag her eyes away.

Liene released the girl's icy fingers and began walking
toward the Citadel once again, her only outward reaction
to the pain she'd seen a spasming of the hand that held
her cane. Never good with emotions unconfined by chord
and chorus, this was far more than she was capable of dealing with. More, she suspected, than the Healers' Hall could
deal with. *Karlene has a greater perception than I gave her
credit for. This child is so tied in knots she's no danger to
anyone but herself.*

She'd intended to ask a lot of other whys, but they were
no longer necessary.

"I don't want to see death when I look at him."

It was a love song with enough tragic potential to rip
out hearts and tear them into tiny, bleeding pieces. Teeth
clenched, Liene wished she'd sent Kovar to the docks so

that she could've received these first impressions filtered through his recall.

Gyhard felt Vree tremble and silently cursed his inability to hold her, to comfort her. He hated the Bardic Captain for what she'd done and his anger sizzled around the parameters of his existence. If only he had hands. . . .

Don't.

He forced himself to withdraw although he knew at that moment she couldn't have stopped him from taking control.

The moment passed.

Are you all right? he demanded, fighting to suppress the anger for both their sakes.

Don't leave me.

If he'd still had a body, that quiet plea would've left him struggling to breathe. This was the first time, since the initial impulse that had gathered up his kigh, that Vree had shown him her heart. If confronted, she probably wouldn't admit to the thought but he'd heard it—felt it—and nothing, not hatred, not anger, was worth hanging onto in the face of it. *Don't leave me.* Catching hold of them before they could fade, Gyhard gathered the words up and locked them away in his memory. Then he waited.

He felt her chin rise. *I'm fine,* she told him, lengthening her stride to draw even with the Bardic Captain again. Her tone implied she didn't care if he believed her or not.

"I half expected that you'd be carried off the *Fancy* on the shoulders of her crew," Liene observed, stepping aside to allow a tailor's apprentice, arms loaded with a bolt of sea-green fabric, to pass. It suddenly seemed important she find a subject with a little distance.

Vree shrugged. "They were happy to come home. They made me a hero in the Broken Islands. That was enough."

"From what Tomas told me, I imagine it must've been." The image of a row of hastily-constructed gallows, filled as quickly as they were built, rose in Liene's mind. The crowd of dead behind the young assassin grew. "You speak Shkoden very well," she said, searching for yet a safer topic.

"Gyhard taught me."

The older woman stifled a sigh. It appeared there were no safer topics. "Well, he did a good job. I assume he translates for you, too?"

"Less now."

Liene grinned at Vree's tone. "Don't like depending on other people, do you? I can appreciate that." Then she frowned. "Gyhard hears through your ears? Sees through your eyes?"

"Yes."

"Then we shouldn't talk about him as though he isn't here." She turned that over, examined it from all sides. When she spoke again, they'd moved some distance up the hill. "From what Karlene has told me, I think you and he and your brother have proved that the body is merely meat worn by the kigh and that what we all consider the person, *is* the kigh. So." She took a tighter grip on her cane, forcing herself to give credit where credit was due. "Gyhard, thank you. Although a number of the bards speak Imperial, none of the healers do. You've made all our lives less complicated." Sweeping a piece of trash into the gutter, she snorted. "Well, less complicated as regards language, at least."

I'm not sure that granting me any kind of individuality is such a good idea. Gyhard lightly touched the place where he ended and Vree began, felt her recoil, and drew back. *If I'm given a little, I may be tempted to take the rest.*

You can try.

Vree, I'm serious.

Then we'll deal with it ourselves because I'm not going to tell her. It's obvious she thinks I'm, we're, unstable. We don't need to prove her right. Conscious of Liene's gaze, Vree added aloud, "He says, you're welcome."

The Bardic Captain shook her head. "No, he doesn't. Didn't Karlene tell you that you can't lie to a bard?" With everything filtered through Vree, they'd have no way of telling if Gyhard was lying—a realization that left the captain feeling distinctly less than happy—but they could certainly tell when she was. "Now then, what did he actually say?"

Okay. That's it. Ever since Ghoti, Vree'd had to continually draw lines between herself and the world. Time to draw another one. *How do I tell her that's none of her slaughtering business?*

Vree!

Never mind. This woman was the head of all the bards; Vree'd dice with the gods on the odds the Bardic Captain understood Imperial. "That's none of your slaughtering business," she repeated aloud, glad to be speaking her own language again and discovering an unexpectedly pleasant freedom in no longer being bound by the rules of rank. A similar response to an Imperial Army Captain would've resulted in six lashes and time in the box.

The Bardic Captain understood Imperial. She stopped in the middle of the street. Her cheeks flushed an alarming purple as she spun around and glared into Vree's face. "If you want our help—" she began.

Vree cut her off. "If you want to study the fifth kigh, we're going to have to trust you enough to let you poke around in our lives. If you want that kind of trust, you're going to have to give it in return."

"Gyhard i'Stevana has removed himself from the Circle!" Liene snapped.

"And we're asking you to put him back in. Doesn't that count for anything? All we want is a chance to start over, and if you're not willing to give us that chance, then we're on the first boat out of here and you can whistle up information on the fifth kigh without us."

It wasn't a bluff. Liene suspected assassins were unable to bluff. And, it was the truth. All they wanted was a chance to start over. At least, it was all Vree wanted and if it wasn't what Gyhard wanted, she believed he did. Still standing in the middle of the street, disregarding the audience they'd attracted, the Bardic captain drew in a deep breath and released it slowly, releasing her anger and her suspicion and her fear at the same time.

Then she held out her fist. "Liene. Bardic captain."

Vree stared at it for a long moment. "Vireyda Magaly. Vree," she said at last, touching it lightly with her own. "Gyhard i'Stevana."

"Welcome to Shkoder."

"Thank you."

"That Southerner giving you trouble, Bard?" a heavyset woman called from a second-floor window. "You want I should come down there?"

"No need," Liene replied, her tone suggesting the curious return to what they'd been doing before the shouting started. "But thank you for the offer." She waited until her champion waved cheerily and withdrew, before turning her attention back to Vree. "Are we all right, you and I and Gyhard?"

"I think so."

"And what does Gyhard think?"

Muscles still tensed, Vree's gesture took in the end of the argument. "That starting over's a good idea."

We'll have to play a careful melody here, Liene thought as they continued up the hill, squinting in the late afternoon sun: *This child has been tuned so tightly she's going to start breaking strings. I guess it's a good thing I didn't let Kovar meet her at the dock,* she decided silently to herself. *If I don't stay on top of this, it's never going to work. Someone's going to have to remember there's more involved here than the fifth kigh.*

"She threatened you?"

Liene drummed her fingers on the edge of her desk. "She threatened to leave. Which is her right, she's not a prisoner."

The waxed ends of his mustache twitching, Kovar slapped his palms down on the polished wood. "But she lied to you!"

"If someone called me an unmitigated horse's ass— which, upon reflection, is how I was acting—would you tell me?"

"Of course not."

"You'd lie to me."

He didn't pretend to misunderstand. "It's not the same thing."

"Ah." Liene nodded. "One rule for you. A different rule for her."

Kovar sputtered for a moment and finally grabbed onto the one affront he was certain of. "She is voluntarily carrying the kigh of a man who removed himself from the Circle!"

"True. Which means there's a great deal we can learn from them concerning the fifth kigh." She leaned back in her chair, considered putting her feet up on the desk, and reluctantly decided her hips weren't up to it. "They help us, we help them—which, if you'll recall, was the whole point of them coming here—and we all act like civilized people while we do it."

"How civilized is assassination?" the younger bard demanded.

"How civilized is prejudice!" Liene snapped. Painfully conscious of how her own preconceptions had caused her to react, she was determined Kovar would be less inflexible. The bards had not come across in the best of lights this afternoon.

"Are you trying to tell me that you met this woman completely unconcerned about her past?"

"I'm trying to tell you that after I met this woman, her past became unimportant. She followed orders, exactly as she was trained to. Frankly, I'm a lot more concerned about the people who trained her."

"You have a point," Kovar murmured after a moment's reflection. Liene was pleased to note that he'd stopped reacting and started thinking. "But what about the past of the kigh she's carrying?"

"That," Liene admitted, "I am concerned about. But if Vree can't control Gyhard, we can. If only for her sake, he deserves a chance."

"For her sake?" Kovar shook his head and dropped into the wood and leather chair facing the desk. He directed a searching gaze at his captain's face. "You sound like Karlene."

Liene spread her hands, the gesture clearly allowing the comparison. "The girl's beautiful, intense, and tragic. I can understand what Karlene saw in her."

"Beautiful, intense, and tragic," Kovar repeated, rubbing the creases out of his forehead, unable to maintain suspicion in the face of his captain's certainty. He sighed deeply. "Then she's just what we need around the Bardic Hall."

"Afraid you'll have the youngsters falling in love?"

He looked up from under his hand and his mustache lifted as his mouth curled into a weary smile. "No. I'm afraid I'll have to spend the next dozen years listening to overheated, overwritten ballads. If there's one thing a bard can't resist, it's a tragedy. You'll be well out of it."

"I'll be retired, not dead," Liene pointed out curtly.

The ends of the mustache lifted higher as the smile grew. "I beg your pardon." Then he sobered and stood. "I suppose I'd better meet her—meet them—before they're surrounded by healers."

"Kovar."

He paused by the door, turned, and lifted an inquiring brow.

"Remember what Vree said about trust. They *have* to trust us in order for us to learn anything, so we're going to have to offer trust in return. Keep in mind who they were but deal gently with who they are."

Shadow screening her from the courtyard, Vree studied the wall below her second-floor window. *I could get down that,* she said with satisfaction as she straightened.

Why do you want to?

I don't. But I might need to. Bannon wouldn't have had to ask. Bannon would've understood. *Let it go, Vree,* she told herself sternly. *Even if you'd let Gyhard die, you and Bannon couldn't have gone back to what you had. You'd come to know each other too well.*

You know, talking to yourself seems a bit redundant under the circumstances, Gyhard told her dryly, wishing he'd been able to pick the content out of the buzz of thought. *Are you expecting trouble?*

Expecting trouble keeps you alive. A squint into the small fireplace showed the chimney too narrow to climb although it appeared to open up into the larger stack just past her fingertips.

Vree, what are you doing?

Checking.

For what?

Escape routes.

But we aren't in any danger.

Now.

Unable to get past the surface agitation to the cause, Gyhard muttered, *You weren't this paranoid on board ship.*

I understood the rules on board ship. I stay out of the way, I let them do their jobs, they take me where I've paid to go. The heavy plank door opened in and would be easy to secure from the room. Not so easy from the corridor. *And they don't want us here. Their captain made that plain.*

They want us, but they're afraid of us. Of you, because you're an assassin. Of me, because I'm outside the Circle.

Outside the Circle? What the slaughter does that mean?

It's a religious thing. I'm sure they'll explain it, he added caustically.

I want you . . . She froze, head cocked to one side. *Someone's coming.*

I hear them, but, Vree, you aren't the only person in the Bardic Hall. Other people will be using the . . .

A brisk rapping cut him off.

Vree checked that her knives were accessible, swore softly when she remembered that one of her wrist daggers lay on the seabed in the Broken Islands, and positioned herself where she'd have the greatest freedom of movement should there be a fight.

Are you going to tell them to come in? Gyhard asked when the rapping grew louder. *Or wait for them to break the door down?*

Wait.

Vree!

I'm kidding. A quick glance over her shoulder defined the distance to the window, just in case. "Come in."

By all the gods in the Circle, it's true! The girl is carrying two kigh! Kovar stood in the doorway, fingers clutching the latch, trying to sort out what his eyes told him and what he knew. One slender young woman stood facing him in the center of the small sitting room, but two separate people occupied that space. Until this meeting, he'd dealt with Karlene's incredible tale purely intellectually. Having taken over most of the day-to-day administration of the Bardic Hall, he'd made arrangements for the girl's stay, he'd set up schedules with the healers, he'd worried about bringing both an assassin and a man who'd dared to remove himself from the Circle into Shkoder. Upon coming face-to-face with the unarguable evidence, however, he found himself far more overwhelmed than he'd believed possible. *Two separate and distinct kigh! What we could learn from this!*

Would it be rude to tell him to close his mouth? Vree asked, not sure whether she should be amused or annoyed.

Almost as though he'd heard her, Kovar's mouth

snapped shut and he released his white-knuckled grip on the latch, jerking his fist forward. "Kovar."

"Vree." She moved toward him just enough to touch her fist to his, carefully avoiding his gaze. "And Gyhard."

And Gyhard. Two kigh. "Did Liene mention me?"

"Yes."

He couldn't remember her stepping back, but she stood, once again, in the center of the room. "Were you told about the necessities?" How would a male kigh react to a female body? Or was gender a result of physical form?

Privies, Gyhard explained.

"Yes."

"And the dining hall?" Would she have to eat enough to sustain two lives?

"Yes." Vree's pulse began to slow as the inane dialogue convinced her this tall, balding man with the impressive mustache was not a threat.

"The bards who have rooms in this part of the hall are all out Walking, so you should have plenty of privacy. If you need anything, just ask." He paused, then added. "Either of you."

"Thank you."

"I have a thousand questions to ask."

Vree waited, the bard's last statement so obvious she didn't think it needed a reply.

About to begin on the first of the thousand, Kovar stopped himself. Something about the young woman's stance, so clearly defensive, reminded him of his daughter the day she'd arrived at the Hall to begin her training, her talent an inheritance from a father she barely knew. Superficial differences between the two disappeared beneath a shared, desperate bravado. It would be distressingly easy, he realized, to lose sight of the needs of one kigh in the wonder over two. "You've nothing to be afraid of, Vree," he said gently.

Startled, Vree looked him full in the face, her need to keep a distance between herself and these strange new people lost in her need to find out just what he meant. He didn't seem to be mocking her. "I'm *not* afraid."

"I beg your pardon." Four years learning to be a father to Olexa as much as many more years of bardic training made the apology believable. If the captain, by her own admittance, had not been welcoming, it was time to remedy that. "The bards and the healers are both very glad that you're here, Vree. You and Gyhard. By allowing us to study your unique kigh, you're doing us a tremendous favor and we'll do everything we can to take care of your problem in return."

"Uh . . ." To her horror, she started to shake and could feel tears burning behind her lids. *Gyhard, why is he being so nice to me? I haven't done anything for him.*

You're doing him a favor—he said so himself—besides, he's a bard. They're supposed to be nice. Gyhard struggled to keep his own emotions under control lest his anger push Vree over the edge. The mere fact that she couldn't deal with someone being unexpectedly nice to her told him more than he wanted to know about her life before he became a part of it. He wanted to grab Kovar by the shirt and shake him until he was sure the bard understood. *Do you see what they've done to her?*

Behind his gentle smile, Kovar gritted his teeth, certain he saw another intelligence flash for a heartbeat in Vree's eyes; pure animal rage one moment, gone the next. Gyhard. All at once, he thought he understood what Vree was afraid of. *She's carrying a kigh that's been over a hundred years outside the Circle.* Before he could say anything—before he had any idea of what to say that wouldn't make her situation even worse—the sound of a gong struck twice filled the building.

"Dinner gong," he explained, amazed at how still Vree had gone. "I'd be pleased to have your company this evening."

Heart pounding, Vree struggled through her confusion and finally nodded. Anything would be better than facing a roomful of strangers alone.

Not quite alone.

No, she allowed. *Not quite.*

"So what will it be? Do we arrive late to get the reactions over all at once, or do we arrive early so that you only have to go through it one bard at a time?"

"Reactions?"

"To the pair of kigh." Kovar spread his hands and smiled encouragingly. "I'm afraid there's no way around it, you're going to be the center of attention for a while. Unless you'd rather I had something sent up? You could eat in your room."

"No." Her chin rose. "I don't hide from confrontation."

"Well, with any luck, it won't go any further than acknowledgment."

Considering that Vree's reaction to confrontation usually involved knives, Gyhard sincerely hoped the bard was right.

Three or four heads turned when Vree and Kovar entered the dining hall, reactions turned three or four more and, in a moment, every one of the dozen bards in the room stared openmouthed in their direction.

During the heartbeat of absolute silence, before the babble could begin, Kovar took a step forward. Using enough Voice to hold their attention, he said, "This is Vree, a citizen of the Havakeen Empire who has graciously consented to assist us in our studies of the fifth kigh. Yes, she *is* carrying two kigh and if you must know the whole story, Karlene has sent us a copy of her recall which will be in the library by tomorrow morning. If you have any questions, bring them to either the captain or myself. **Do not pester Vree with them. Is that clear?**"

Heads nodded.

"That said, I expect you to make her feel welcome. She speaks Shkoden fluently . . ."

He has a loose definition of fluently, Gyhard observed.

". . . but it wouldn't hurt for some of you to use this opportunity to practice Imperial." His voice lost its overtone of command and picked up a distinct note of amusement as he added, "That's all; enjoy your meal."

Her expression carefully neutral, Vree followed Kovar across the dining hall, skin crawling under the heated focus of a dozen intensely curious pairs of eyes. Assassins worked unseen and not even the greenest of recruits was fool enough to satisfy curiosity by staring at the blades of Jiir. Vree could hear Kovar's footsteps against the plank floor and her own blood roaring in her ears; nothing else.

The silence stretched and grew brittle.

Then a very, very old woman in a wheeled chair leaned toward her neighbor and said, in what she imagined was a whisper, "She's a pretty little thing, isn't she?"

The silence disappeared in the mutual embarrassment that followed. By the time Vree set her plate of cold beef and vegetables on the table across from Kovar, she was the topic of every conversation but no longer the center of attention.

That's your third old lady.

So? Vree watched Kovar carry a piece of meat to his mouth on the tines of an implement she'd never seen before and carefully imitated his action. *What is this thing?*

How would I know?

You're from Shkoder.

A hundred years ago. And I was never in Elbasan and I never actually met a bard before Kars.

That's why you're so, she settled on, *tense. You keep being reminded of Kars.*

I'm so tense because everyone around us would as soon Sing me back into the Circle as look at me.

I think you're overreacting.

I'm not the one planning to climb up the chimney, he snapped. He didn't want to be reminded of Kars—not by Vree, not by the bards. Unfortunately, what he wanted didn't seem to matter because every bard he saw reminded him not only of Kars but of how he'd failed him twice; the first time by pushing him into insanity, the second by leaving him there. Gyhard didn't know whether Vree had felt his reaction through their close contact or had come to it on her own; either way he didn't like it much.

But it's okay if you know what I'm feeling?

Stay out of my thoughts, Vree.

Strong emotions, remember?

You going to answer Kovar's question or sit there like an idiot?

Vree jerked and found Kovar staring at her from across the table. "I'm sorry. Could you repeat, please?"

He waved a hand at her plate. "I just wondered how you liked the food."

"The food?" She looked down and realized she'd eaten most of it. "It's, uh, fine. Better than army cooking." She couldn't actually remember how anything tasted, but it seemed a safe comparison.

"And Gyhard?"

"He tastes what I taste."

Kovar leaned forward, trying not to appear too anxious. "And do you like the same things?"

Conversations died as every bard still in the dining hall waited for her answer.

Vree's ears grew hot. She had no idea what Gyhard liked.

You never asked.

You could've told me!

She felt the memory of a shrug. *It wasn't important. Besides, I was busy learning about you.*

What? And I'm not supposed to learn about you?

Kovar sat back. "I'm sorry; have I started something?"

Before Vree could find the words, the double doors to the dinning hall slammed open and a short, dark-haired figure charged in.

"Is she here? I heard she was here!" Without waiting for a reply, the young woman—girl—swept her gaze across the remaining occupants of the room. Quarry spotted, she flung herself forward, racing to Vree's side, her eyes gleaming. "You *are* here! And you *do* have two kigh! This is so amazingly amazing. When they told me you were coming, I just couldn't believe it. I'd have been here sooner, but I had garden duty this afternoon."

"This is Magda i'Annice a'Pjerin," Kovar interrupted. If he had anything more to say, not even bardic training gave him the chance to say it.

"Maggi. Almost everyone calls me Maggi. You're Vree, right? And Gyhard? Captain Liene told me all about you." She grinned as she took in Vree's expression. "You have no idea who I am, do you? I'm the healer, well, all right, apprentice healer who Heals the fifth kigh—it has something to do with my mother saving my brother's life before I was born, but they're still trying to figure out the particulars. Karlene *must* have told you about me. I'm the one who's going to find Gyhard a body." She shoved a thick fall of curls back from her face with weed stained fingers. "I think that what you did was the most romantic thing I've *ever* heard of."

Vree blinked, as stunned by the delivery as by the actual flow of information. *I feel old.*

She felt Gyhard twitch. *You feel old?*

Three

Vree's eyes snapped open and she stared at a crack in the rough plaster ceiling over her head, momentarily uncertain of where she was. Then she remembered. Senses extended, she swept the tiny bedroom. There was no danger. She was alone.

Not quite alone.

Vree–ee . . .

Wha–aht? she mocked, throwing back the thin blanket and sliding out of bed. The braided straw mat gave way to painted boards underfoot as she made her way silently into the sitting room. In the liquid light of early morning, she could see that none of the carefully arranged furniture had been moved during the night.

Gyhard gathered his scattered thoughts, flung out of sleep by Vree's sudden, complete, and irritating return to consciousness. *Do you *have* to wake up so unenclosed quickly?*

Yes. The single hair she'd laid across the latch remained in place. *Wake slow. Die fast.*

So you've said, he muttered, wishing he had teeth to grind. *But you might take under consideration, nothing's trying to kill you.*

You don't know that until you're awake.

You do this wakey-wakey thing to me on purpose, don't you?

No, she replied as she pulled a long-sleeved shirt over her head. Without the weight of wrist sheaths and throwing daggers, her arms felt unnaturally light. *It's training.*

Yeah. Right. Training. Why can't you train yourself to wake up a little slower?

Vree grinned and headed for the privy at the end of the hall. *Because I don't want to.*

Similar conversations had become part of their morning ritual, comforting in a situation where they were making up the rules as they went along.

When her reluctant knock brought a brusque reply, the page pushed open the morning room door and blushed a brilliant scarlet to find both king and consort staring at her, their expressions neutral at best. "Begging your pardon, Majesties, but the chancellor asks if *His* Majesty could find a moment to speak with her. She says it's urgent."

Theron, King of Shkoder, pushed his chair away from the table with something very like relief. "Nadia, isn't it?"

The blush darkened. "Yes, Majesty."

"And it's urgent, you say?"

"Yes, Majesty. The chancellor awaits your pleasure in the small audience chamber."

"Tell her I'll be with her in a moment."

"Yes, Majesty."

As the paneled door closed behind the girl, Lilyana shook her head. "What can be so urgent it can't wait until after you finish your breakfast?" she asked with a sigh.

Theron glanced down at his food. Melon slices, bread with only a thin scraping of butter, a small amount of cold beef, and mint tea; not a sausage, not an egg, not a mug of ale in sight. He'd rather have the chest pains. It was difficult not to regard the chancellor's request as a kind of reprieve although, for Lilyana's sake, he tried not to let that show. "I'm sure Rozele has a good reason to call me away from my meal," he said as he stood, burying his plate under the snowy folds of his discarded linen napkin. "She's never abused her privilege."

"True." While the chancellor had the right to claim the ear of the king at any time, usually the times she claimed were more convenient. Lilyana frowned. "Perhaps I should . . ."

"Stay right here and eat." Coming around the corner of the table, Theron bent and kissed her lightly. "There's no point in both of us having our morning disrupted." He smiled down at her and, suddenly struck by how worried she looked, added, only half jokingly, "If it's trouble, you'll need to keep up your strength."

Rozele i'Natalia, chancellor to the King of Shkoder,

turned as Theron entered the small audience chamber and bowed deeply, one hand clutching the dark purple skirt of her robe, the other sketching an apology in the air. "Please forgive me for disturbing you at your meal, Majesty, but I have just been given news I thought you should know immediately."

"I trust your judgment, Chancellor." Theron settled onto the tapestry cushion his younger daughter had worked to soften the uncompromising seat of the carved rosewood throne and indicated that the page following him should set her tray on the round table by his elbow.

Under other circumstances, fully aware that neither sausage rolls nor ale were on the diet the healers had drawn up for the king, Rozele would have faced royal disapproval and pointed it out. This morning, she was far too distracted. She fidgeted until the heavily paneled door closed behind the page, then stepped forward and began.

"Majesty, this morning I met for breakfast with Imrich i'Iduska a'Krisus, a diplomatic courier from your ambassador in the Havakeen Empire."

The king wiped grease off his fingertips. "You met him for breakfast?" he asked, brows lifting slightly.

"Yes, Sire. I thought as we both had to eat we might as well combine the meeting with food and save time."

"The day isn't long enough?"

The chancellor looked confused. It was midway through Second Quarter; of course the days were long. "Majesty?"

"Never mind." Years of practice hid his sigh. While Shkoder appreciated the zeal with which Rozele fulfilled the duties of her position, Shkoder's king occasionally thought she ought to get a life. "Please, continue."

"Yes, Majesty. The report out of the Empire will be on your desk this afternoon, but Lord Imrich gained additional information during the journey home." She paused, gathering her thoughts.

Theron put down his mug and straightened. In the seven years they'd worked together, the chancellor had never needed to gather her thoughts. In seven years, she'd always known exactly what she'd intended to say. This didn't look good. . . .

"Majesty, the Empire has sent an assassin into Shkoder."

*   *   *

"Majesty, the Empire has *not* sent an assassin into Shkoder."

Eyes narrowed, Theron tapped an index finger against the arm of the throne. "Then perhaps you would be good enough to tell me just *what* is going on."

The Bardic Captain shifted position slightly, the hem of her robe whispering caution against the polished parquet floor. In her younger days, she'd walked through blizzards warmer than the king's tone. "Chancellor Rozele has upset you unnecessarily, Majesty. Vireyda Magaly is an ex-assassin . . ."

"As I understand their training," the chancellor interrupted indignantly from her position to the right of the throne, "there is no such thing as an ex-assassin. Or did your bard in Pitesti not inform you of the pirate she killed?"

"She killed the pirate, Majesty," Liene made it very clear to whom she spoke, "to protect the ship she traveled on."

"She killed the pirate, Captain, by leaping between two moving vessels, making her way through an armed and bloodthirsty crew, and slitting the woman's throat." Theron leaned forward. "This does not indicate ex-anything to me."

Liene spread her hands. "Should she not use her skills to protect herself, Majesty? If we had thought she was a danger to the realm, we would not have allowed her to enter the country."

"*You* would not have allowed her to enter the country?" the king repeated incredulously, half rising. "Since when do the bards make those decisions? You gather the information," he snarled as he sat down again. "I decide what to do with it."

"Yes, Sire. However, if you received every detail the bards gather without some sort of filtering process, you'd have no time to deal with anything else, and as this was a bardic matter . . ."

"A bardic matter? An Imperial assassin entering Shkoder is a bardic matter?" Theron leaned back and smiled tightly. "I think I'd like to hear your reasoning."

I think I should have retired a year ago. Liene considered and discarded the option of telling the king only that Vree had acquired a second kigh and leaving it at that. Unfortu-

nately, filtering out trivial information and deliberately mis-
leading a sovereign lord were two entirely different pieces
of music. Shooting the chancellor a withering glance, Liene
began with Karlene's recall, a sizable document she'd spent
half the night reading, and finished with both her and Kovar's personal impressions.

The tight smile remained. "Why didn't the younger
bard—what's her name?"

"Karlene, Majesty."

"Yes, Karlene. Why didn't Karlene inform His Imperial
Majesty, the Havakeen Emperor, that this Gyhard continued to exist in the assassin's body?"

That was the first easy answer of the morning. "As Gyhard was in some manner responsible for a number of
crimes against the Empire, formulating rebellion as Governor Aralt, not to mention intending to murder an Imperial
Prince and take over his body . . ."

"Not to mention," Rozele repeated dryly.

Liene ignored the interruption. ". . . Karlene assumed
that if the Emperor knew of his continued existence, he
would order Gyhard's death. This would be impossible
without destroying Vree, and His Majesty must admit she
personally has done nothing to merit destruction."

"Except perhaps saving the abomination," Theron
growled, but his gesture conceded her point. "So," he
leaned back and steepled his fingers, "you are suggesting
that for the sake of one ex-assassin, I harbor a traitor to the
Imperial Throne. I had thought that his Imperial Majesty
required those bards who served in the Empire to swear
on their music that they would not act contrary to the needs
of the Empire while living there."

"That is true, Majesty. However, those oaths specifically
state that earlier oaths take precedence; oaths to Shkoder,
oaths to the Bardic Hall."

"And this was bardic business?"

"Precisely, Majesty." Liene's voice deliberately left no
room for doubt. "And it continues to be bardic business.
It is an excellent opportunity for us to study the fifth
kigh, Majesty."

"Oh, yes, the fifth kigh." The king's words took on a
distinct edge. "I'm glad you reminded me of that." He
jabbed at the air with an emphatic finger. "This assassin is

not, do you hear me, *not* to come in contact with my niece!"

Magda sighed and wished that both the Bardic Captain and the chancellor—who bracketed the throne like a pair of scowling old buzzards—were somewhere else. Theron-her-uncle could be got around; not as easily as her father, perhaps, but the principle was the same. Theron-the-king was another matter entirely. "Majesty, I promise you I'm in no danger."

He shook his head. "Child, you have no idea what this assassin is capable of."

"But I *do,* Sire. I read every available reference in the Bardic Library and I'm probably safer with her than I am with anyone. Assassins kill for only two reasons." She held up a finger for each point. "Because they've been ordered to and because they're in mortal danger. That's why she killed the pirate, to save her life. You'd have done the same yourself."

Magda's tone implied that he *could* have done the same himself and Liene hid a smile at a mental picture of Theron leaping from ship to ship with a knife in his teeth. Sixteen years in constant company with bards had taught the girl a trick or two—or perhaps it was those same sixteen years spent wrapping her father around her little finger.

"They're very predictable," Magda continued, leaning forward, practically quivering with intensity. "And besides, she *needs* me. I'm the *only* person in the whole *world* who has any chance of finding Gyhard a body."

The name chased away any amusement Theron might have been feeling at her emphasis. "And what of the abomination?"

"Gyhard doesn't want to hurt me. He needs me, too. Without me, he'll never hold her or love her or . . ."

"Maggi." Theron lifted a hand and cut off the list. "You can't know what an abomination needs."

Yes, I can. But she didn't say it; even though the whole thing was really very simple, true love wasn't the argument that would convince her uncle, the king. She held out both hands and said instead, trying to make it sound as if there could be no question, "I can handle him."

Before the king could speak, Liene leaned forward.

"Majesty, she might very well be the *only* person in the *whole* world who can handle him."

"I'm . . ."

Surprised.

". . . surprised they let you be alone with us."

Magda grinned. "We aren't exactly alone."

"I know." Her tone low and matter-of-fact, Vree kept her eyes on the flagstone path beneath her feet lest she provoke a reaction. "Two people watch us from the middle window on the second floor, one from the roof of the building on the east side of this courtyard, and a guard with a crossbow who believes the ivy at the end of the . . ."

Cloister.

". . . cloister is hiding him." She lifted her head and glanced at the girl circling the courtyard with her. "But still, I expected . . ." A wave over the empty herb gardens indicated the hordes not present.

Her brows drawn into an indignant ebony vee above her nose, Magda glared at the places Vree'd listed. "I *told* them you weren't dangerous," she muttered.

"If I were targeted on you," Vree told her softly, "even the crossbow wouldn't be fast enough."

"Really?" Magda's eyes widened. "Wow." Then she smiled. "But you aren't targeted on me, and you won't be, so you're no danger to me. Right? And besides, you need me. Actually, they're more worried about Gyhard."

"Then the crossbow is less than useless."

"I've always thought so. You should see my father with a mountain bow. Or even my brother." She dropped onto a weathered plank bench with careless grace and patted the place beside her. "But that wasn't what I meant when I said we aren't exactly alone."

Vree turned her face into the breeze, and the breeze moved away to dance across the tops of the flowering mint. "Kigh."

"Uh-huh."

"Can you . . ."

"Sing them? Nope. I thought you *knew*; I'm not a bard, I'm a healer. Well, I will be a healer. Eventually. They keep saying that I Sing the fifth kigh, but I don't, not *really*. It's more like I *know* the fifth kigh." Her right fist thumped into her chest. "In *here* and when I reach out, I can touch it. I can't do much with it yet, but I'm learning. My mother says she can hear me Sing while I do it, but I'm not so sure that it's me she's hearing." Kicking off a sandal, she brushed the bottom of her bare foot over the thyme growing between stones of the path. "Why did you expect there'd be more people around?"

Wrinkling her nose against the smell of the crushed herb, Vree sank down onto the bench. If she sat facing Magda, she could keep an eye on the guard with the crossbow. "Everyone thinks you're special."

"Really?" Magda looked pleased, then shifted uneasily. "They weren't supposed to tell you."

"I already knew about the fifth kigh."

"Oh. That."

Vree waited patiently. She was good at waiting, most people weren't. Most people had to do something or say something to fill the time.

After a few moments, the tips of her ears bright red, Magda murmured, "My mother's the king's youngest sister, but you're not supposed to know, so please don't tell them I told you."

That explains a lot they didn't say, Gyhard murmured thoughtfully.

Doesn't it. "They said your mother is a bard."

"They didn't go on about her, did they? I mean, that's *so* embarrassing."

"No, mostly they *hummed* at me."

Her giggle held as much relief as amusement. "Was it Petrelis? He always hums when he's concentrating. He's leaving on a Long Walk this afternoon, and he wanted to get the shape of a kigh before he left." Pulling a damp curl out of the corner of her mouth, she tucked it behind her ear and grinned. "You don't understand, do you? That's okay. You see," her fingers sketched patterns in the air, "a fifth kigh is usually an intricate part of the body it wears, everything all mixed up together, and it's really hard to tell where the kigh ends and the body begins. But if you want to do anything with the kigh, it's *really* important to know where the boundaries are. *I* know, but it's hard to explain it to other people. With you—well, with you and Gyhard—

the boundaries are really clear. His kigh is almost completely distinct from you."

"Almost!"

Magda blinked, a little stunned by the near panic in that one word. Her voice gentled. "It's all right." Needing to heal, she reached out to touch Vree's kigh and found herself pushed back.

"No. It isn't all right." Vree turned and stared down at the stone between her feet. "My brother and I nearly lost ourselves in each other. Gyhard and I have to stay separate. I can't go through that again."

"Ah." Magda nodded slowly, understanding dawning. "So *that's* why you're afraid to love him. Nothing tangles two kigh as tightly as love."

"I'm not . . ." But there wasn't any point in saying it because the girl knew and she'd already made it clear that she thought it was the most romantic thing she'd ever heard of.

Vree, she's our only chance.

For what? Never mind. Getting angry wouldn't solve anything. Walking away would solve even less. Vree pleated a fold in her wide-legged trousers, her fingers leaving damp prints behind on the fabric. "Look, can we just leave it?"

"Sure, we can leave it. But I want you to know that I only want to help. Really."

"I know." And to her surprise, she did.

You trust her? Gyhard sounded as surprised as she felt. *I don't want to discourage this, Vree, but why?*

Because she isn't afraid of us. Of either of us.

The Imperial Ambassador to the Court of Shkoder stared at the Imperial sunburst on the packet delivered the night before by the mate of the *Gilded Fancy* and sighed deeply. He hated opening packets that bore the Imperial seal as they invariably contained something unpleasant, but he'd delayed opening this one as long as possible. Taking a last, slow swallow of the orange juice he imported from his sister's estates in the Seventh Province, he pushed the dishes from a late lunch aside and picked at the golden wax with one gleaming fingernail.

"I hate unpleasantness," he murmured. There had been trade difficulties of late between Shkoder and the Empire. Shkoder had been complaining for some time that the much larger country to their south had been flooding their market with cheap iron. The complaints had become more forceful, and something was going to have to be done—the Empire had no desire to cut exports. The very nature of the Empire insisted it had to keep expanding, one way or another.

"I hate trade." The ambassador sighed deeply as he broke the seal. "It's such a lousy reason to start a war. If I'm really lucky, this will be nothing more than another Imperial kidnapping."

The details of Prince Otavas' abduction had been under the last golden sunburst he'd received. He'd been informed only because a Shkoden bard had been involved.

He read the thick parchment packet twice.

The Empire had sent an assassin into Shkoder and not just any assassin, but one of the two who'd recently rescued His Imperial Highness and been released from her oaths as a result.

Technically, she was no longer an assassin.

Nor did she think she'd been sent.

She was staying with the bards.

"And just what exactly am I supposed to do with this information?" he asked himself, wondering why everything in Shkoder always seemed to come back to the bards.

When Bannon had shared her head, it had been difficult to find where her thoughts ended and her brother's thoughts began. Their shared lives had created a tangle of hers and his and theirs. Thinking about it afterward, she'd been surprised that Bannon had been able to pull free so easily when the chance came to return to his body. Thinking about *that* later still, during the long days she'd spent wandering the confines of the bardic suite in the Imperial Palace, she realized Bannon had always known which parts were him. Why shouldn't he? She'd defined him all their lives.

Gyhard was different. He was always there, but he never tried to be where she was. She could think around him and be reasonably certain he wouldn't become tangled in the thoughts.

Tucked into the thick window embrasure, Vree stared

out over the Citadel wall and down at the city, her hands busy with a dagger and whetstone, needing no guidance after so many edges. If she wanted to leave, they couldn't keep her. She was small enough to fit out of the window, and the jump to the top of the wall—her lip curled—would be less than challenging. The wall itself would be ridiculously easy to descend.

And then what?

Until Gyhard, Bannon had been the one person in her life. There was the army—a living, breathing, single creature—there were targets, and there was Bannon. Occasionally, bits of the army would become more separate than other bits—Emo had almost become a person—but it never lasted. Anyone outside the army was lumped under "other" and forgotten.

She'd had to notice Gyhard; he'd been wearing Bannon's body. Then there'd suddenly been Karlene, just when she needed a hand and Bannon's no longer reached for her. Now, there was Magda, who so desperately wanted to help she was next to impossible not to trust. Three people to take the place of Bannon and an army. . . .

From a room higher in the four-story building, Vree could hear a voice lifted in song. From the other end of her floor, two instruments clashed, sorted themselves out, and began to make music. A breeze lifted her hair off her forehead, and Vree slipped down off the windowsill and inside. If the bards were going to watch her with the kigh, she wasn't going to make it easy for them.

Slipping the dagger into its sheath, Vree caught sight of her reflection in the blade and suddenly wondered if the sifting of her past originated with her or with Gyhard. Was it the situation that drove her to self-discovery or was it him?

Hey.

Hey, what? he answered and her awareness of his presence grew.

Are you messing around in my head?

I wouldn't think of it. She saw the memory of his smile as he spoke. Bannon's smile. No. Bannon's face. Gyhard's smile. *I'm leaving everything exactly as I found it.*

Liar.

The bittersweet sense of inevitability accompanying that single word closed off further conversation.

There were a number of things Gyhard wanted to say, but he couldn't, not without letting Vree know that he had access to more of her thoughts than she realized. Perhaps her need to consolidate her identity did come from him, he had no way of being sure.

He'd seen a man once who'd fallen from a bridge and broken his neck. Against all odds he'd lived, even though the closest thing around to a healer was the village midwife. The man could see and hear and speak, but he couldn't move or do anything with the body he wore. Gyhard had wondered at the time how he'd kept from going mad.

He found himself wondering it again.

The bardic touching, the tracing of his boundaries, had left him restless. Strengthening his sense of self was quite probably the most dangerous thing they could do. He wanted . . .

He wanted Vree. To hold her. To love her. To be held by her. To be loved by her. He wanted them to be able to make a future together. Whether death would eventually have a part in that future, he wasn't sure.

It had been enough just to be with her.

Had been. Now, he wanted a body of his own.

And this is after only one day of poking about at us. Carefully, he reached out and touched Vree's memory of the moment she dragged him back from oblivion. She'd been willing at that instant to do anything rather than lose him. He was trying very hard to do the same.

"Well, can you do it?"

Magda carefully anchored the scroll she'd been studying, one hand resting lightly on a faded line drawing of a caraway plant. Talent made up only a very small part of being a healer and healer's apprentices spent a lot of their evenings in the library. She twisted lithely until she could look the Bardic Captain in the face. "I'm not even sure I know what it is I'm supposed to do."

"Find the abom . . . Gyhard a body with no one dying to provide it."

"Uh-huh. And how am I supposed to do that?"

Liene scowled, drummed her fingers against the head of her cane, and finally stomped away.

Magda shook her head and went back to her reading. It

was a good thing both her mother and Stasya had warned her that the old woman's bark was worse than her bite. Although Stasya *had* pointed out that Liene still had all her teeth.

They'd warned her about a number of other things as well, but she'd happily disregarded most of them.

Sighing, Magda brushed a curl away from her face. "A body without a kigh is a dead body and I can't just shove his kigh into a dead body." She made a disgusted moue at the thought. From the mice the cats used to leave on the steps of the keep to those the healers had not been able to save, dead bodies were *not* among her favorite things.

The pass between Shkoder and the Empire looked as though a giant had carved it out of the Smitts Mountains with a knife. Sheer rock walls rose up on either side of a broad passage years of use had made as easy to travel as any lowland road. Long before the current king's grandmother had convinced their duc to join the kingdom, the miners of the mountain principality of Somes had traded iron ore with the First Province of the Empire through that pass, picks and shovels amending what nature began.

As Jazep approached the guard tower on the Shkoder side, he could just barely make out through the early morning haze the Empire's sunburst flying next to the crowned ship at the midpoint of the pass.

Two of the three guards came hurrying out to meet him.

"Jazep? Is that you?"

A huge smile split the bard's grizzled beard. "Nastka! I was wondering why I hadn't seen you in town!"

"Now you know." Tossing her helm to her companion, she returned his hug with equal enthusiasm, leather armor creaking. "What brings you up here? Not crossing surely? We had two of those Imperial fledglings up here during my last shift. Who was with them? I know, Tesia. She took them to the halfway point and said she was letting them feel the difference you get in earth kigh when you're standing on your own soil. She wasn't kidding me, was she?"

"No. The kigh can always tell when you've come home." He shifted his feet and his smile faded. "I backtracked a disturbance in the kigh to the pass."

"Do tell." Nastka retrieved her helm. "Trouble?"

Jazep shrugged. "I don't know. Troubling. It's almost as if they're afraid."

"The kigh? Afraid? I don't like the sound of that."

"No, neither do I." He turned and looked toward the Empire. "Can you remember what and who came through five days ago?"

"I can do better than that. Mila—oh, this is Mila, by the way." The second guard nodded shyly. "It's her first shift at the pass. Jakub's up at the beacon. You remember him, skinny guy with too much red hair?"

"I remember."

"Of course you do. Mila, go get the lists." As the younger woman ran back to the tower, Nastka grinned proudly. "Duc's seeing to it that everyone in the guard can read and write."

Jazep had actually heard that from the Duc of Somes herself, but the disturbance in the kigh had driven it right out of his mind. "Her Grace has a lot of good ideas."

"Her Grace is going to put this place in a song."

"I saw Jelena when I went through town."

Nastka's grin softened and her dark eyes shone. "She's grown into a beautiful woman, hasn't she?"

"She has." Jazep reached out and gripped the guard's shoulder. "Just like her mother."

A few moments later, he frowned down at the rough sheet of paper and shook his head. "Two wagons and a single traveler. Not exactly a busy day. Do any of them stand out?"

"Well, the old man . . ." Mila began, then lapsed into an embarrassed silence when both Jazep and Nastka turned to look at her.

"Go on," Jazep urged, using just enough charm to put the girl at ease.

"It's just he was so old. I couldn't believe he was able to walk at all, let alone cross the mountains from the Empire into Somes. He said he was looking for his family."

"Is that all?" It was difficult to imagine how one old man could so upset the kigh.

"No." Mila shook her head, frowning as she remembered. "As he walked away, he said, 'Come, Kait.' But he was all alone."

Four

"His Imperial Majesty desires your presence in his private audience chamber."

On his way out of the palace to an assignation with a very obliging young wine merchant, Bannon stared in disbelief at the guard blocking his path. "The Emperor wants to see *me*? Why?"

"I did not presume to inquire." She managed to sound simultaneously sanctimonious and disapproving.

"But I bet you know." The ex-assassin grinned, his tone evoking the shared camaraderie of uniform.

For a moment, he thought she was going to tell him, then, after a barely perceivable shake of her head, she snapped, "I know only that His Imperial Majesty desires your presence in his private audience chamber."

It's trouble and she's keeping her distance. Imperial assassins were trained to recognize danger in all its unexpected forms and, while his mind raced, trying to work out what he'd done to merit the personal attention of the Emperor, Bannon fought to calm the pounding of his heart. Whatever the danger, he wasn't going to get out of it on the edge of a blade. He needed information. "Have I time to change into a clean tunic?"

"No." Her eyes remained focused on the wall just behind his left shoulder.

"Prince Otavas is with the Empress; I should let him know where I am in case he sends for me." Considering he was the prince's personal bodyguard, it was a reasonable request.

"If His Majesty decides His Highness should know your location, His Majesty will have His Highness informed."

Big trouble. She turned, beckoned with her pike, and Bannon fell into step beside her, still with no idea of what he'd done. His unease grew as they walked through a palace complex crawling with courtiers and servants and the less easily defined classes between and passed no one he knew. By the time they reached the narrow flight of stairs leading up to the section of the palace reserved exclusively for the Emperor, sweat stained his tunic. Not even the tight muscles of the guard's butt moving under her uniform kilt as she led the way up the stairs distracted him for more than a moment or two and, as he climbed, he became increasingly conscious of the empty space at his back. *Vree, where are you when I need you!*

The half-dozen soldiers of the First Army waiting in the antechamber ignored him until he reached the small, iron-bound door. Then the corporal stepped forward and demanded his weapons. Bannon had been at the palace long enough to know that no one approached the Emperor armed but something in the corporal's tone lifted the hair on the back of his neck.

Slowly and deliberately, he drew the long dagger off his belt, unbuckled the two wrist sheaths, slid the extra throwing dagger out of the sheath strapped to his left shoulder, and removed the slender blades from the ornate leather tongues of his high sandals. Under other circumstances, he would've found the corporal's expression hilarious as he reached under his kilt and drew the three throwing stars out of their strap on the front of his sling. As it was, he merely added them to the pile and waited for the door to be opened.

When it closed behind him, habit scanned the room for avenues of escape—there were none. Marshal Usef, commander of the First Army, stood rigid behind the throne, his face below his crested helm twisted with rage, both hands crushing his heavy belt as though that grip alone kept his hands from Bannon's throat. Seated on the throne, his calm a stark and frightening contrast to the marshal's agitation, the Emperor lifted a hand and beckoned him forward, rings flashing in the lamplight.

With his mind shrieking, "Danger!" loud enough to drown out the pounding of his heart, Bannon dropped to one knee at the edge of the dais, needing Vree beside him so badly he almost saw her there.

"Is the tale you told my son the truth?" the Emperor

asked. In spite of the gentle tone, each word emerged as a separate and distinct threat.

Startled, Bannon looked up. What could he have told the prince that would . . .? Then, all at once, he understood. Part of the story had slipped out when Otavas asked him why he was so angry with his sister and, once started, the rest just seemed to follow.

Silk whispered against silk as His Imperial Majesty leaned forward. "There are no secrets from me in this Empire," he said. "Did your sister save the spirit of the man who led a rebellion against me? A man who intended to take the life of an Imperial Prince? And did you lie to me about it, telling me that this man was dead?"

His mouth gone too dry for speech, the stink of his own fear in his nose, Bannon nodded.

"Treason," Usef hissed, and his hand moved from his belt to close around the jeweled hilt of his sword.

Even weaponless, Bannon knew he could defeat the marshal. But then what? His mind raced. There were guards outside the small door to the antechamber and undoubtedly guards outside the larger door leading to a less private audience hall. One word from the Emperor and a good part of the first army would be in the room. He couldn't fight them all. Not alone. But if he silenced the Emperor? A fist closed around his throat, and he couldn't breathe. Lay hands on the Emperor? He didn't think he could. He didn't want to die. "Majesty, I . . ."

"You lied to protect your sister," the Emperor cut him off. "I understand that."

Bannon's eyes widened as he suddenly realized that the treason Usef referred to was not the treason he'd committed in presenting Prince Otavas' body for Gyhard's use—a direct breaking of his vow to protect the Imperial Family. The Emperor only knew that Gyhard was alive, and he understood about the lesser treason of the lie. Bannon's relief was so great, he had to fight to keep himself from trembling and at that moment he'd have walked through fire had the Emperor commanded.

"Why the bards lied, I do not yet understand." For a moment, the Imperial voice evoked shadowed rooms and heated iron. "But I will. Unfortunately, as they are both away from the Capital training our native-born bards, answers will have to wait." Bannon found himself caught in a dark gaze that seemed to strip away skin and muscle and bones and stare straight into his heart. "For now, we will have no further lies between us." the Emperor leaned back. "Marshal, relax. This young man is not a danger to me. He wants to help. Don't you?"

"Yes, Majesty." His voice sounded hoarse, barely under his command. "Yes, Majesty," he repeated; clearer, firmer. "I want to help."

"Good." Imperial approval touched him like a benediction, filled for a moment the empty space where Vree had been, then disappeared. "I want this Gyhard back in the Empire. I want him to pay for his crimes. I want you to go to Shkoder and bring him back to me because, after the great wrong he did you, I believe *you* have the right to bring him to justice."

Bannon ground his teeth at the thought of Gyhard paying for what he'd done, paying for every instant he'd spent usurping Bannon's body. And then, through the hate, he remembered. "But, Majesty, my sister . . ."

"The sister he took from you? The sister he controls?"

"Controls?"

The Emperor spread his hands. "How else would you explain her denying her training? Her denying everything she lived for? Her denying you?"

How else?

Back at last in his own body, Bannon felt Gyhard turn his head to stare at Vree, felt the surge of the other man's emotion, and heard his voice say, "I love you."

Then he pushed, viciously throwing the intruder from his body, and was alone.

"NO!" Vree's denial held as much pain as rage.

Because he'd shared her mind for so long, he knew what she was going to do and why and he was powerless to stop her.

How else could he explain her choosing Gyhard over him? Bannon's hands opened and closed as though they held the other man's life and slowly crushed it.

"I give you your sister's life. I want only the one who was Aralt."

Not as much as Bannon did. "But, Majesty, the bards

said they couldn't remove Gyhard without hurting Vree."
It was, he told himself, the only reason he'd supported the
lie. He even half believed it.

"If you return your sister to the Empire, I will see to it
that the bards will be able to do exactly as I command
them. We are no longer dependent on *Shkoden* bards."

It might work. Vree would hesitate, unable to raise her
blade against him. He would capture her, blindfold her, and
contain Gyhard until they returned to the Empire. Rubbing
his palms together, Bannon frowned. "Majesty, if the bards
are protecting him, I won't be able to get close to Vree.
The moment those kigh things tell them I'm coming, they'll
hide her."

"Which is why I am sending the Prince Otavas to
Shkoder to visit his uncle, the king." The Emperor's voice
softened as he spoke of his son. "The boy has had a dis-
tressing experience and needs his mind turned to other
things. As Otavas' personal bodyguard, you will go to
Shkoder with my son's household. The palace is very close
to the hall of the bards. It will be natural for you to seek
out and spend time with your sister. I will speak with Otavas tonight and you will leave as soon as possible." He
pointed at the assassin kneeling before him, and Bannon
could feel the weight of his commission. "I am loosing you
at a target. A target only the very best could hope to strike.
Bring me justice for the Empire; justice for yourself."

"I will not fail you, Majesty."

"I know that you won't."

Recognizing a dismissal, Bannon stood, bowed, and
backed to the door. Soon, the empty space in his life would
be filled. Soon, the person responsible for emptying it
would pay.

As the door to the antechamber closed, the Emperor
nearly smiled. "He never looked; did you notice, Usef? He
backed straight to the door, absolutely positive he knew
where it was. Can you imagine having that certain a sense
of place?"

"He is dangerous, Majesty." Stepping forward into the
Emperor's line of sight, Usef was nearly purple under the
force of his emotion. "The blades of Jiir should not exist
outside the sheath of the army."

"But you forget. Neither he nor his sister are assassins any longer."

The marshal bit back a reply that would have stretched Imperial indulgence. His Majesty himself had said training did not permit an ex-assassin, but if His Majesty wished to be facetious, there was nothing he could do about it.

"It seems, Usef, that you were right; it was a mistake to send the woman to Shkoder. But it seems also that I was right; we have found a use for her brother."

"Begging Your Majesty's pardon, but why manipulate this, this fool into bringing her back? They are both guilty of treason, Majesty. Treason! They lied to *you*. You should have them killed!" Then he realized what he'd said. "Not *should*, Majesty, I would never so presume. It is merely my belief that they should not be permitted to live."

The Emperor lifted a forgiving hand. "Perhaps they won't be, but first I desire to speak with this Gyhard and I need Bannon to bring him to me. He's the only person in the Empire with the slightest chance of actually capturing the body Gyhard wears."

"But you can't trust Bannon, Majesty. He's proved that."

"Did you know that I've never lost a hawk, Marshal? Every single hawk I have ever flown has come back to me." He studied the scars on his left wrist, the marks of talons made in spite of gloves and padding. "That's something very few can say. Young Bannon has proved only that he's unwilling to see his sister hurt. *I'm* willing to allow him to believe in her safety in exchange."

"In exchange for what, Majesty?"

"Think about it, Marshal. What does this Gyhard have that any sane person would desire?"

Usef frowned as he attempted to follow his Emperor's line of thought. "Control of an Imperial assassin?"

"Immortality, Marshal. Immortality."

. . . first time was an accident. When the brigand speared me, I only knew that I didn't want to die. When oblivion began to close around me, I fought it—fought my way through it and out the other side. The next thing I knew, I was in the brigand's body and he was in mine. When I tried to go home, they only saw the body I wore.

Perched on the edge of the bench, forcing herself to remain still, Vree repeated Gyhard's story. Not until she finished did she turn and look at Magda.

The apprentice healer sat, bare feet up beside her, legs tucked into the circle of her arms, chin resting on her knees. Her dark eyes were locked on Vree's face. "What about the second time?" she said softly.

The second time? Vree felt Gyhard move restlessly within the limits he'd set on himself. *The second time,* he repeated, *was no accident. . . .*

He'd been Hinrich for seven years and that was seven years too long. In the beginning, hunted away from his home because of the body he wore, he'd thrown himself into his new identity. If his own family would treat him as a brigand, than a brigand he would be. He suspected that he hadn't been entirely sane those first few years although as he could remember every excess, every disgusting or violent act, insanity didn't seem like much of a defense.

Later, after thieving and whoring had lost its appeal, he'd made a living of sorts from an ability to brutalize those smaller and weaker than himself. Finally, he'd ended up as a caravan guard for traders too poor or too stupid to hire anyone better. He'd crossed the mountains into Cemandia with two ramshackle wagons full of junk and after drinking away his pay, such as it was, in a Cemandian tavern, he found himself heading back into the mountains again. He didn't know why. He only knew he didn't want to be Hinrich any longer.

Three nights later, sober, cold, and hungry, he followed a stream to a shadowed pool, drawn by the smell of woodsmoke and roasting fish.

"Lord and Lady!" The young man behind the fire snatched up a staff. "Where did you come from?"

He turned and pointed back along the stream. "From Artis Falls." He thought that was the name of the town, but he was so hungry he wasn't sure.

"Are you lost?"

Was he lost? Clamping his teeth around a bitter laugh, he nodded, then, drawn by the smell of the food, he staggered forward another two steps.

"Are you hungry? No, wait." A luminescent smile flashed in the dusk. "That's a stupid question. You're obviously starving. Well, the dogs caught their own dinner earlier on, so there's plenty for two." The crooked staff pointed across the fire. "Sit. It's almost done."

Sitting turned into a barely controlled fall and a few moments later he was stuffing fish into his mouth too fast to taste it. Some kind of roasted roots followed—their Cemandian name meant nothing to him—and by the time he finished all he was offered, his brain had started working again. "Shepherd?" he asked as the sounds drifting in from the night began to make sense.

"That's right." Again the smile. "Tomas."

"Hinrich." But not for much longer.

Tomas stirred the embers, a shock of dark hair falling forward over brilliant eyes. "You talk funny. You're not Cemandian, are you."

"From Shkoder."

The shepherd laughed. "If you're heading home, you've missed the pass."

"I have no home."

"Oh. I'm sorry." Tomas shifted about, then launched into a long story about his own home to cover his embarrassment.

He didn't want to know about the shepherd's home. Or his past. Or his life. Knowing he was a shepherd was almost too much. He stood.

Tomas paused and looked a question at him.

"I need to wash." That was undeniable. He stepped toward the pool.

"Be careful, it's deep."

That would make it easier. Heart pounding, he knelt and stared at the water. The surface was bright with reflected starlight, but when he slid his hand beneath the surface, it disappeared into darkness. *This has to work,* he thought as he let himself fall forward. *I can't be Hinrich anymore.*

He'd known all along what he had to do, but he'd never been able to find the courage. He still hadn't. Desperation would have to serve.

Terror nearly flung him back to the surface, but he added the weight of those seven years to the weight of his sodden clothes and he drew in a lungful of water.

Except for the panic trying to claw its way free, it was almost peaceful.

He felt a hand close around his arm. Felt himself dragged upward. He twisted. And released the panic.

He was dying!

No!

Drowning!

No!

There was a shape above him, a patch of darkness with no stars.

A face.

Time stopped as he launched himself toward a pair of brilliant eyes. He fought for room, shoving everything that got in his way—images of sheep, dogs, parents, friends— viciously back behind him.

Then he was staring down through an inch of water at a sandy-haired man with a bristling red beard and a face contorted in unbelieving horror. Shifting his grip, he held him under until the struggling stopped, then he let the body float away.

He wasn't Hinrich anymore.

He was Tomas.

Tomas, Gyhard repeated. He felt Magda touch Vree gently on the shoulder, felt Vree turn to face her, and lost himself in a wave of pity. In seven lives over a hundred and thirty years, no one had ever pitied him. He wanted to hide. He wanted to scream. In the end, with an image of Vree standing guard at his back, he did neither.

"It took a long time for Gyhard to heal," Magda murmured.

That's no excuse. But he was surprised by how much he wanted it to be. *I'll tell you what I told Vree, don't make me a tragic hero. I knew exactly what I was doing.*

"I know. But I don't think you can ignore why you were doing it."

"Wait a minute." Vree held up both hands and scowled at the girl. "You heard him?"

Magda nodded, eyes wide.

Can you hear me now? When it became obvious she didn't, he repeated the question, much louder.

Vree winced and Magda lightly laid a hand on her knee. "Are you okay?"

"I'm fine."

Sorry. He knew the apology sounded terse, but his isolation had been broken for an instant and now it seemed that instant was over.

"I heard him." Magda looked down at her hand, still resting on Vree's knee. "I heard you. You said sorry. Say something else."

You must need physical contact.

She lifted her hand. "There's only one way to find out."

A moment later Vree muttered, "He wants you to touch me again."

Why is this happening? Gyhard demanded, when Magda's fingers lay against Vree's palm.

All three of them considered it for a moment. Finally, Magda shrugged. "I think it's because I touched your kigh."

Vree fought down a completely irrational flash of jealousy. "And?"

"And I think it's sad that a man so terribly afraid of dying thought he had to keep dying to live."

When Jazep saw the cluster of villagers hurrying out of Bartek Springs to meet him, he knew it had to do with the disturbance he'd been following in the kigh. The path led right by the village; too close not to have affected the people who lived in the cluster of half-timbered houses.

"Jazep!"

He dipped lightly into recall for the name of the woman who hailed him. Memory had Celestin's braid more brown than gray, but there could be no mistaking either the strong beauty of her face or the focused determination in her movements. As the only priest for at least three days in any direction, she took responsibility for the spiritual well-being of an extended Circle. Drawing closer, he was surprised to see her expression held equal parts fear and relief and his worry about what he followed grew.

When she reached him, she gripped his arm as though she gripped a lifeline. "Thank all the gods enclosed by the Circle that you've come. Did Brencis meet you on the way?" She leaned a little to the right in order to see beyond his bulk. "Where is he?"

"I'm afraid I haven't seen Brencis." Jazep closed his hand lightly around the priest's as the clump of villagers murmured behind her. In spite of the Second Quarter heat, her fingers were freezing. "What's wrong?"

Celestin took a deep breath and let go of his arm. "We sent Brencis out to find us a bard. Something . . . something has disturbed our dead."

"Scavengers?"

"No." A younger woman Jazep didn't know made an emphatic denial. "Not scavengers. Scavengers don't . . ."

Celestin cut her off. "I think you'd better see for yourself."

As they hurried through the village, she refused to elaborate, saying only, "I want your opinion unclouded by our fear."

In the graveyard, a young man stood protectively over a blanket-covered mound that lay a short distance from a disturbed grave. Jazep frowned. There was something wrong about the way the earth had been piled. *Almost as if . . . No.* He shook his head. *Impossible.*

The young man watched warily as the bard approached. His eyes were red and swollen, and he looked as though a gentle breeze could push him over whatever edge it was he tottered on.

"Dymek," Celestin called. "This is Jazep. He's a bard. Let him see."

"Bard?" Dymek repeated hoarsely. Hope skirted around grief. "Can you tell me what happened? Can you help Filip rest?"

"I'll do what I can," Jazep assured him gently. He gestured at the blanket. "May I?"

Dymek nodded, his head jerking up and down as though he had little control over its movement.

The young man under the blanket had been dead for only six or seven days. Unfortunately, six or seven days in Second Quarter was five or six days too long to be out of the ground. Jazep waved a cloud of flies away, swallowed hard, and breathed shallowly through his mouth. Filip had obviously died of massive trauma to his lower body. His legs within the unbleached linen burial clothes seemed strangely flat and the single foot hung unnaturally from a crushed ankle. But the position of the body . . .

Jazep stood, thankfully took a deeper breath, and looked

back toward the open grave. He moved closer, squatted, and Sang.

No kigh responded.

They were there. He could feel them. Could feel the same disturbance he'd followed from the border. Still Singing, he slid out of his pack, unhooked his tambour, and added a compelling beat to the Song. A lone kigh rose partway out of the ground, squat body radiating distress. Jazep Sang it comfort for a moment, then changed the Song to ask it what had happened. It disappeared and refused to return.

The Song slid into silence. Gnawing at his lower lip, Jazep stood, drum dangling from one hand.

"Jazep?" Celestin prodded.

He looked at the grave, at the body, at the priest, at the villagers, and realized he'd come to the same conclusion they had. "It seems," he said slowly, "that something or someone partially unburied Filip and he dragged himself the rest of the way out. That he pulled himself over there on his hands and then he collapsed."

"He was dead when we buried him," Dymek whispered. "He was *dead*. I swear it."

"I believe you," Jazep told him, using enough Voice to be believed in turn and catching him barely in time when he fainted.

"Dymek found him two mornings ago." Together, bard and priest watched as those villagers able to overcome their fear took turns redigging Filip's grave. "His scream dragged me out of a sunrise service and up here at a run. He was kneeling, just over an arm's length away from the body, reaching out but too terrified to touch." Celestin turned enough to see Dymek sobbing within the circle of his parents' arms. "He'd only just begun to accept Filip was dead; now this."

"He loved Filip very much," Jazep murmured.

Celestin nodded. "He did. He does." She looked at Jazep, her cheeks ashen. "This thing you've been following, this thing that's frightening the kigh and hurting my people, what precisely is it doing? I mean, besides reanimating the dead."

"I don't know."

"What are you going to do when you catch up to it?"

Jazep shook his head, one hand lightly stroking the bellows of his pipes. "Stop it."

When all the loose dirt had been dug out, Filip, wrapped again in a linen winding cloth, was lowered back into the earth. Standing at the head of the grave, Celestin traced the Circle on her breast with a fistful of dirt. "We give back to the earth as we have taken from it," she said as she scattered the dirt on the body.

"The Circle encloses us all," Jazep answered with the villagers. In the prayers that followed, he could hear an undertone of uncertainty; hardly surprising as this was the second time the prayers had been said. When they were finished, he stepped into the priest's place, settled the drones on his shoulder, and began to play.

He played grief that a young man was dead, anger at the disinterment, comfort to Dymek, to the rest of Filip's family and friends, and then he called the kigh. They came this time with an enthusiasm that suggested they were as interested in making this right as he was. The pile of dirt slid down into the hole, spread itself, and enfolded Filip back into the earth's embrace.

That should've been enough, but when Jazep tried to leave the graveside, he found he couldn't move. The kigh held him in place.

Tucking the pipes back under his arm, he Sang. Reluctantly, the kigh moved away.

"What is it?" Celestin asked, hurrying to his side.

"I don't know."

Dymek jerked forward, eyes wide, his hand stretched out toward the bard. "Is it about Filip?"

"No, not about Filip," Jazep told him gently, catching hold of the younger man's fingers for a brief moment of reassurance. "They want me to help a lost kigh."

"I can feel him, you know. It's like I can reach out and he's there."

Celestin moved to put an arm around his shoulder. "He'll always be in your heart."

Dymek shook his head, tears spilling down his cheeks. "No. It's like he's still *here*!"

As Dymek's parents led their son from the graveyard, their own faces twisted with grieving, bard and priest exchanged a helpless glance. Time would have to heal what they could not.

"Will you stay for a while?" Celestin asked when they were alone beside the grave.

"No. I have to catch up to whatever's causing this before it can reach another village."

"And do the same thing."

Jazep nodded grimly. "Or worse." He stepped toward his pack and found the kigh had anchored his feet once again. When he asked them why, he got the same answer he had before. They wanted him to Sing home a lost kigh.

"How can a kigh be lost?" Celestin wondered when he told her.

"They can't. At least, I never knew they could." Brow furrowed, he Sang a different question. He changed the phrasing. He changed the pitch of the Song. Finally he gave up. "I don't know what they're talking about," he admitted, pulling at his beard in bewildered frustration. "They just keep repeating the same thing, over and over." It almost tore him in two, but he couldn't take the time to learn what they wanted—not when past experience said it could take days.

They made him Sing his feet free every step across the graveyard. When he had to Sing the kigh away from his pack, Celestin lightly touched his shoulder.

"Perhaps you should stay."

"I can't." The words ripped great holes in his heart.

"Have you told them why?" She gestured at the ground.

"They don't *understand*." The final word became a plea for understanding from the priest. When she nodded, he swung the pack up onto his shoulders. "Look, Brencis is still out there trying to contact a bard. Sooner or later, he'll come home with one. If they can Sing air, have them send your recall to the Bardic Hall—everyone should know about this. If they can Sing earth . . ." For a moment he was unable to go on. "If they can Sing earth, ask them to help the kigh."

The earth tugged at his shoes as Jazep hurried away from the village. Voice tight in his throat, he sang to the breezes as he walked, hoping one of them would carry the news to a bard who could hear it.

* * *

Head cocked, one hand lifted to stroke the air, Annice frowned. "Something's wrong."

"At the keep?"

"No." The bard squinted up the length of the valley to bring the distant stone bulk of the keep into better focus. "It's definitely not Stasya. In fact . . ." Her frown deepened as she slowly pivoted, trying to pinpoint the source. ". . . it's not really a Song, it's more a . . . feeling."

Pjerin, Duc of Ohrid, stepped back from the stooked corn, swept an approving gaze over the work continuing in the rest of the field, and finally turned to face Annice. While he'd come to appreciate bardic abilities over the last seventeen years, he'd spent a lifetime learning that good weather seldom lasted so close to Third Quarter Festival. He wanted the field stacked by dark, and that wasn't going to happen if *something* was wrong.

"A feeling?" he repeated irritably. "Annice . . ." An imperious wave of her hand cut him off and he folded his arms across his chest with a scowl. The scowl lightened as he realized the extent of her concern and, watching the play of emotions across her face while she called the kigh, he began, himself, to feel a faint sense of unease.

Although the kigh seemed skittish, they couldn't answer Annice's questions. "Too far," she muttered at last, having Sung an unhappy gratitude.

Ohrid stood on the border between Shkoder and Cemandia, the farthest of the five mountain principalities from Elbasan. The farthest from the Healers' Hall. Pjerin stepped forward, as though to close the distance. "Is it about Magda?"

"No, I don't think so."

He turned on her, violet eyes narrowed. "You don't think so? If you're not *certain,* check."

His tone left no room for disagreement. Under other circumstances, Annice would have disagreed anyway, on principle—growing older had only intensified Pjerin's fondness for having his own way—but not this time. Hearing the fear behind the arrogance, she called the kigh back and Sang the four notes of their daughter's name. She didn't believe the wrongness had anything to do with Magda but, now that the possibility had occurred to Pjerin, she knew he'd not let it rest until he was convinced their child was safe.

"Shall I have them check up on Gerek as well?" she wondered. Although Gerek was not her son by birth, she had long since come to consider him hers, much the same way she'd come to consider all of Ohrid hers.

"Gerek," Pjerin growled, "is a grown man and does not need you peering over his shoulder!"

"Magda is . . ."

"A child," her father declared.

And that was that.

Over half the crop had been stacked by the time the kigh returned with the unmistakable message that all was well at the Healers' Hall. Magda was in no danger the kigh could discover.

The wrongness remained, a shadow over the Circle; faint and undefined, impossible to ignore.

"If not Magda," Annice asked herself, growing increasingly concerned, "then who?"

"Tadeus!" Magda flung herself past Vree, across the courtyard, and into the arms of a slight man standing just at the edge of the cloister. He laughed as the force of her greeting rocked him back on his heels and Vree, who'd spun around into a defensive position at the sound of footsteps behind her, relaxed slightly.

I think she knows him, Gyhard observed dryly as Magda dragged him forward.

When Tadeus stepped out into the late afternoon sun, Vree realized that the shadow covering his eyes was a narrow black leather band cut to perch on his nose and loop back over his ears. *He's blind.*

So it seems.

He's also not alone. Tadeus' companion moved hesitantly out of the cloisters and Vree was astounded to see he was Southern. In fact, if she had to place him more precisely, she'd say Sixth or Seventh Province based on the cinnamon-brown of his skin.

"Vree, Gyhard, this is Tadeus.". Tucked in the semicircle of his right arm, Magda smiled proudly at the bard as though he were something she'd thought up on her own. "He's one of my name-fathers. Tadeus, this is . . ."

"The young Imperial citizen who carries the two kigh." His smile held a warmth Vree felt herself responding to. "It's actually you I've come to see."

"Tadeus!"

Ignoring Magda's exaggerated protest, he half-turned toward the Southerner and beckoned him forward. "Ullious here is one of the four remaining Imperial fledglings, and when he heard you were in the country, he expressed a very natural desire to meet you." A breeze ruffled silver-shot curls as he reached out an unerring hand and pulled the fledgling to his side. "Ullious, this is Vree and Gyhard who are sharing a body. Vree, Gyhard, this is Ullious who has an astonishing command of air and a truly amazing tenor."

"Better than yours?" Magda dug an elbow into his ribs.

"Don't be impudent, brat, or I'll tell your mother you've quit your studies, taken up hayla dancing, and are living with a drunk who beats you."

"She'd never believe that."

"You're right." Garnets glittered in his ears as he cocked his head to grin down at her. "But I could always tell her you were looking pale and I didn't think you were eating properly."

Magda winced. "She'd be here the next day."

"Or sooner," Tadeus agreed. He pinched her chin. "So why don't you tell me what you *have* been doing, I'll pass on what I think Annice should know, and the rest can be a secret between us."

"But Vree . . ."

"Can spend a few moments with Ullious who I'm sure would love to speak his own language with someone who doesn't confuse verb tenses." Tadeus turned and Vree had the strangest feeling he was smiling directly at her although he couldn't possibly see anything through the leather band. "You don't mind me stolen my name-daughter away for a little while, do you?" he asked in Imperial.

"Stealing," Ullious murmured. "Not stolen; stealing."

Tadeus winced. "Verb tenses," he muttered. "Hate 'em. Come along, Maggi, we'll sit over here and you can tell me all about the hearts you've broken while I was gone."

"I'd rather hear about the hearts *you've* broken," Magda declared as they walked toward a bench set into the far wall of the courtyard.

Vree thought she'd never heard anything quite so engaging as Tadeus' laugh. "When you're older, child," she heard him say. "When you're older."

"He's still friends with every lover he ever had," Ullious observed quietly. "And he has a lot of friends."

I'll bet. Gyhard sounded so appreciative, Vree couldn't help but smile. The expression seemed to reassure Ullious.

"You're not what I expected," he said, nervously brushing at his narrow mustache.

The smile faded. "Because I'm an assassin?"

"No, I've met assassins. I spent four years in the Seventh Army—Third Division, Second Company, Second Unit, First Squad." He looked a little startled at the involuntary completion of the list, then he went on. "It's just that you're you, and Gyhard's himself, and there's so obviously two of you in one body. When the kigh brought us the news about you, I guess I expected things would be mixed up a little more."

"Does *everyone* know about us?" Vree growled.

Ullious shook his head. "Oh, no. Only the bards who Sing air."

"And there're how many of those?"

"Actually," he shrugged a bit sheepishly, "most of the bards Sing air."

Vree couldn't keep from glancing up into the square of sky framed by the courtyard. A shadow flickered on the west roof of the Healers' Hall as an archer moved back out of sight. *I wonder how many of them are watching us now.*

You could ask.

Think he'd tell me?

"You were talking to him, weren't you?" Ullious leaned a little forward, eyes shining.

"Yes."

The blunt monosyllable stopped conversation cold. In the distance, Vree could hear Magda filling the older bard in on the details of her life. As usual, she didn't appear to be bothering to breathe.

"You're not what I expected either," Vree admitted at last. "I thought fledglings were supposed to be young."

Oh, that's tactful.

"Younger," she corrected hurriedly.

Ullious ran a self-conscious hand over his thinning hair. "The Emperor has only allowed citizens to be tested over the last four years," he explained. "When I heard, two years ago—news travels slowly to the South . . ."

Unless it comes with a tax collector, Gyhard added and Vree remembered he'd been, as Aralt, governor of a Southern region.

"I sold my carting business and went to the Capital. The bard Karlene met me at the South Gate saying the kigh told her I was coming." He flushed with pleasure at the memory. "She didn't have to test me. She spoke of you."

Vree blinked. "Two years ago?"

"No. Twelve days ago. Tadeus had me practice Singing the kigh over long distances and from up the coast to Karlene was the longest distance we had. She said I was to see that you weren't lonely." He spread his hands. "Can you be lonely? I mean under the circumstances?"

She could feel Gyhard waiting for her answer. "Homesick," she said at last, "but not lonely." All at once, as though they'd been waiting for her to admit it, the pale gray stone of the buildings, the scent of the surrounding herbs, even the clothes Ullious wore seemed strange and unsettling. Hurriedly, she focused on his face, which could have been any of a hundred faces from home. "And you?"

"I am learning to be a bard, with bards. Lines drawn on a map mean nothing to that. But still . . ." He reached out and, fleetingly, touched the back of her hand. "It's good to see someone from home." Then he grinned, lightening the moment. "If only because everyone in Shkoder is so slaughtering tall."

Vree laughed, as much at the army curse coming from the fledgling bard as at the observation. "*I'm* small even for a Southerner. Magda is the first person I've met since I arrived that I can look in the eye."

As though she'd heard her name, Magda's voice rose momentarily over the background drone of the bees. ". . . realized when I touched her kigh that she still blamed herself for the death of her baby. Once we knew that . . ."

"She's very special," Ullious murmured as they both

turned to look. "She'll be able to heal a lot of people who would otherwise have no hope at all."

Like us.

Like us, Vree agreed. Then she thought of Gyhard in a body of his own, and heard Ullious ask again, *"Can you be lonely?"* She'd already lost Bannon.

By nightfall it was obvious that the thing disturbing the kigh was moving east along the mountains. It crossed from Somes to Bicaz at a ford in the Spotted Fish River and Jazep would've given his left leg to have been able to Sing to the water kigh at the crossing. He still had no way of knowing if more than the earth was upset.

As he drew closer, the kigh became more and more agitated and harder to reach. If he hadn't known better, he'd have sworn they were afraid. Certain he was only a short distance behind, he walked until he nearly put out an eye on an overhanging branch, then reluctantly made a quick, cold supper and rolled up in his blanket for what remained of the night. Although cloud cover made the dark impenetrable, he didn't think it would rain.

He was wrong.

By dawn, he was wet and miserable and hoping he'd run into his quarry soon so he could make the most use of his mood. Grinding up a mouthful of dried fruit, he swung his pack up onto his back and turned toward the rising sun.

"With any luck," he muttered, "this thing'll keep going all the way to Ohrid and Annice can help deal with it."

Then he frowned and put down his pack.

There was something he was forgetting.

Something important.

Something to do with Annice.

No, Annice's daughter.

Magda. A year ago, Maggi had gone to the Healers' Hall in Elbasan for training. She not only had an incredible talent for healing, but she also Sang—or did something as near to Singing as made no difference—what they were calling a fifth kigh.

His legs folded under him, and he found himself suddenly on the ground, mud soaking through his trousers. It took him three tries to find the pitch, but when he finally regained control of his voice, the kigh appeared as a seemingly solid barrier between him and the way he'd been traveling. This time, he knew what questions to ask.

Dymek said he could feel Filip's presence.

The lost kigh was not an earth kigh.

You have to Sing it home.

Jazep felt physically sick. He knew why it had looked as though Filip's body had climbed out of the grave. It had.

But if he went back, he risked losing his chance to catch the thing he followed.

But if he didn't go back . . .

His hands were shaking so badly he could barely trace the sign of the Circle on his chest. If he didn't go back, Filip's kigh would remain lost between life and death, lost outside the Circle.

Brencis might have already returned with another bard.

But no, he couldn't have, for the kigh were still desperate that he return.

He had to choose. Had to weigh what could happen against what already had. He hoped he'd never have to make another choice like that again because he doubted that the scars from this choice would ever heal.

Sunset turned the lower margin of the clouds a sullen orange when Jazep reached Bartek Springs. He wasted no time entering the village but went directly to the graveyard. A trio of curious dogs followed him for a while but would not approach Filip's grave.

His heart lurched when he saw a body sprawled at the edge of the loose earth—he'd half-expected to see that the dead man had dug himself free once again—and began beating normally when he realized it was Dymek.

The young man lifted his head and peered at Jazep through a tangled curtain of dripping hair. "He's here," he said, his voice hoarse from crying. "I can feel him. He's here."

"Yes." Jazep slid out of his pack and untied the padded oilskin bag that held his drum. "He is."

Dymek pushed himself up onto muddy knees and stared at the bard. "You mean that."

It wasn't a question, but Jazep answered it anyway. "Yes," he said again. "Filip is the lost kigh they want me to Sing home."

"How?"

"I don't know." He only knew that it *had* to be done. "Will you help?"

Turning to look at the dirt piled over his lover's body, Dymek whispered, "I'd die for him if it would help."

Jazep took hold of his shoulder and shook him gently but said nothing because there was nothing to say that wouldn't sound like a meaningless platitude. He sank cross-legged to the ground and settled his drum on his lap. If a fifth kigh existed, which it did, then it could be Sung. The earth kigh believed he could Sing it, so he had to believe them. "Tell me about Filip."

"He had hazel eyes," Dymek told him, his own eyes locked on the past. "But he always said they were green. I used to tease him about it sometimes. He was a little shorter than me and . ."

As Dymek spoke, his voice growing stronger with every memory, Jazep stroked a heartbeat out of the drum and listened past the words. Gradually, he became aware of a presence matching the undertones of Dymek's detailing of Filip and he opened himself to contact.

Terror so intense it bordered on insanity slammed into him. His spine bowed backward, muscles spasmed, and he screamed.

"Filip, stop it! He's trying to help!"

Jazep felt the terror turn. Tried to warn Dymek. Couldn't find his voice. Found himself lying on his back, staring at a darkening sky, blinking rain out of his eyes.

"Bard?"

Either Filip could touch only those with bardic talents or love had kept him from hurting Dymek. Which, at this moment, Jazep neither knew nor cared. Shaking, as much with rage that someone would dare to so abuse a kigh as in reaction, he forced himself into a sitting position and picked up his drum.

"Bard? He didn't mean it."

Startled, Jazep peered at Dymek through the dusk. The younger man's face was a pale blur against the approaching night but his expression clearly matched the worry in his voice. The sudden realization he was grinding his teeth gave Jazep the clue he needed. "I'm not angry at Filip," he explained. "I'm angry that such a thing was done to him." Drawing in a deep breath, he forced himself to find a measure of calm before he continued, "But I know how to help him now."

There were very few bards who Sang only earth. And there were very few bards who knew the Circle as well as Jazep did. He followed the turning of the seasons from the inside—birth, life, death, out of death a rebirth and Circle comes around once again. Filip's kigh had been ripped out of the cycle. Jazep Sang it back onto the path.

He felt a surge of joy, as strong and all encompassing as the terror had been, then he and Dymek were alone by the grave. He could just barely see new tears cutting channels through the dirt on Dymek's cheeks.

"The Circle," Jazep said softly, laying aside his drum, "encloses us *all*."

"I think that was supposed to be my line."

The two men turned as Celestin materialized out of the darkness. With a strangled cry, Dymek leaped to his feet and threw himself into her arms. Jazep stood a little more slowly.

"I heard your Song," the priest told him. "I had to come. What . . . ?" She paused, reconsidered the question and settled for, "What happened?"

"Dymek can tell you." Jazep heaved his pack up onto his shoulders. The rain had stopped and if the kigh were willing to help him hold the path, he might make it back to the river by midnight.

"Surely, you're not . . ."

"When Brencis returns with the bard," he interrupted, "have Dymek put under recall. Whoever it is will know what to do."

"But Jazep, it's dark. It's wet. Can't you stay until morning?"

He moved close enough to see her face clearly. "There are other villages in its path." When understanding dawned, he stepped back and turned. There were other villages in its path, and he had lost a full day from the hunt. The ground smoothed beneath his feet as the kigh guided him out of the graveyard. Trusting their touch, he started to run.

Five

The closed lamp hanging by the head of the bunk swung back and forth with the motion of the ship. Leaning against the cabin wall just past the shifting edge of light and shadow, Bannon watched Prince Otavas sleep and wondered if he dreamed and, if he dreamed, what about.

Held captive for seven days by an insane old man, surrounded by the living dead, the seventeen-year-old prince had seen more horror in that short amount of time than many saw in their entire lives. In Bannon's opinion, this trip to Shkoder would be good for him. Too many things in the Imperial Palace—including Her Imperial Majesty, his mother—kept reminding him of his kidnapping. Although outwardly His Highness still appeared to be the carefree darling of the court, Bannon—who saw so much more of him—could see memory lying over the superficial gaiety like an oily scum, and not even the lamp that burned all night by the prince's bed could keep the darkness from haunting him.

"But could any of it have been as bad as looking up from a dying body and seeing your own face laughing down at you?" Bannon silently asked the sleeping prince. *"Or watching another live in your body and be helpless to stop it?*

"Or realizing that the one person you trusted completely had betrayed you?"

A sound up on deck shifted his weight forward onto the balls of his feet, a dagger appearing in his hand. When he became certain it was only one of the many creaks and groans of a ship at sea, he relaxed again.

Vree had no right to save Gyhard's life, not when justice owed it to him. Even the Emperor had seen it. If he couldn't convince her of that with Gyhard in her head, he'd carry her blindfolded back to the Empire and convince her after Gyhard had been destroyed by the Imperial bards. It shouldn't, wouldn't take much for her to realize she'd made a mistake—Bannon had seen how much their separation had hurt her—and they'd be together again, just like they used to be.

Otavas moaned.

A heartbeat later, Bannon stood at his prince's side, gently pushing him back against the thin mattress and pulling the heavily embroidered coverlet up over cold shoulders. "It's all right, Highness," he murmured. "I'm here."

Soon, someone would be there for him. Just like she always had been.

This is Ghoti.

The Gyhard outside the dream identified the rounded walls of orange stucco even while the Gyhard participating walked the empty streets toward the Governor's stronghold. It was quiet, as if the city had emptied, and the knowledge that death waited around every corner ate its way through his composure. He had lived his long life by repeatedly opening death's door and, at the last moment, pushing someone else over the threshold. Death could not love him for it.

He heard a footstep behind him and forced himself to turn. Three soldiers of the Sixth Army blocked his retreat. All three carried crossbows that tracked him unerringly despite the black leather bands that covered their eyes and prevented him from jumping to another body. His heart began to pound. As he couldn't go back, he went on.

The remainder of the army, similarly shielded, waited in the area he'd cleared around the tower wall. He couldn't count the number of crossbows aimed at his heart. He tried, then decided it didn't matter when one would be enough. A slight figure dressed in black beckoned to him from the top of the wall.

Suddenly, he stared down at where he'd been and, from that exact place, Vree stared up at him.

"Time to die," announced a familiar voice.

No. Before he finished turning, a noose settled around his neck.

Vree smiled and pulled it tighter. "Long past time to die."

He fought the hands that shoved him to the edge of the battlements but for every one he pried off his flesh, two returned. Some, he thought he recognized. His pleas, his curses, neither made any difference. Tottering over oblivion, he turned to ask why and saw it was Bannon not Vree who held the other end of the rope, his eyes shielded like all the rest.

Vree stood below, hands outstretched to him, eyes uncovered.

She was too far away.

He screamed her name as he fell.

And jerked awake in her head.

It was her heart he could feel pounding. Her blood roaring in her ears. His own terror . . .

His fear of dying slammed into the barriers so carefully maintained between them, and they fell. His kigh surged out into Vree's body, shoving hers aside in a panicked need for the control so long denied him. Arms. Hands. Fingers.

Then he remembered. Her eyes had been the only eyes uncovered. With a strength he thought he'd long since abandoned, he stopped, lightly touched his/her cheek with his/her hand, and forced himself back to the space she allowed him.

He felt her tremble—in reaction, not fear—and suddenly realized . . . *Why didn't you try to stop me?*

I'd just woke up.

You wake up instantly, he snapped, tipping the terror that continued to sizzle through him over into anger. She was hiding something. He didn't know what. The urge to shake her sent his kigh racing down into her hands and it took almost all he had left to yank it back. *Did you *want* me to kill you? I shove you out of your body and then the bards Sing me into oblivion? Have you had enough? Is that it? Is it?*

Her anger rose to meet his. *If I've had enough of you, I'll deal with you myself.* She threw herself out of the bed, bare feet slapping against the floor. *And what the slaughter makes you think that I would even consider killing myself over you? You think I can't live without you?*

What *had* he been thinking? He hadn't. Terrified by the dream, further terrified by what he'd nearly done, he'd reacted by striking out and that kind of a reaction, he realized now, could get one or both of them killed. *Vree, I . . .*

*You what? Maybe you wanted me to kill *you*.* She stomped into the sitting room, flung open the shutters on the single window and gulped in desperate lungfuls of the night air. *Maybe you think oblivion's a better idea than spending more slaughtering time with me.*

The emotions raging about inside her head had cut him off so completely, it took him a moment to realize what was wrong with her voice. *Vree, are you crying?*

No!

Gyhard didn't bother confronting her with the lie, not when they both knew it for what it was. *Vree . . .* Uncertain what he'd intended to say, he paused. In a very short time they'd gone through fear, anger, and into an emotional storm he couldn't understand. *Why didn't you stop me when you knew I could've killed you?*

At first, he thought she wasn't going to answer him. She stood silently staring out the window, searching the sky for familiar stars and not finding any. He could feel the cool air against her skin—cooler against lines of moisture on each cheek.

"I didn't believe you would," she whispered at last to the night and, for an instant, her fear slipped out from behind the confusion.

Fear not of him but of the feelings that had defied training and kept her from defending herself.

He wanted to accept the gift. He wanted to assure her that he'd never hurt her more than he'd ever wanted anything over the course of a very long life. But he couldn't. *Vree, I love you, but I can't guarantee that will always be enough to protect you. This time I stopped, the next time I might not be able to.*

So I have to be strong enough for both of us? Her mental voice had picked up a bitter flavor. Both the fear, and the emotion behind the fear, might never have existed.

Until he'd met her, Gyhard had thought he was dead to shame. It irritated him to discover he wasn't. *Vree, I . . .*

It's okay. Her eyes were dry and he had the feeling he'd just missed accepting something very important. Their kigh were more separate than they'd been in a long time. *I'm used to it.*

*   *   *

"You don't look so good." Magda folded her arms, cocked her head, and studied Vree clinically. "In fact, you look like you're *significantly* short of sleep. You're not coming down with something, are you? I mean, this *is* a different country with different sicknesses and stuff, so I suppose we *should've* expected you to catch things."

Vree shrugged. "Gyhard had a nightmare."

"If he wakes up, you wake up?"

"Something like that." She'd woken up with him because she'd·been dreaming with him, but if she hadn't told that to Gyhard, she certainly wasn't going to tell it to Magda.

What are you hiding, Vree?

None of your slaughtering business. Her dreams merging with Bannon's had led to a terrifying loss of self and she'd lost as much self to Gyhard as she intended to.

"I expect it's colder at night than you're used to," Magda observed, turning and walking backward down the corridor so she could see Vree's face. "It *is* almost Third Quarter but you're *probably* feeling the damp more than the cold. *I* did when I first got to Elbasan because the air's a lot damper here than it is in Ohrid. Of course we don't have an ocean right outside the keep. I know!" She stopped so suddenly that Vree nearly ran her down. "We'll go out and get you some warmer clothes. You haven't been outside the Citadel since you got here." Her eyes gleamed. "A little shopping'll be a great break for you."

Shopping. Vree couldn't think of anything she'd rather do less. Then she caught sight of a familiar shadow at the end of the corridor as a guard ducked back out of sight. Outside the Citadel. She smiled. "Why not. The security arrangements alone ought to be worth a laugh."

"Tadeus has a cousin who's a draper; we'll go there first. I got some *beautiful* wool cloth from him back in First Quarter that I had made into a *gorgeous* cloak. Uri was *so* jealous; he said it was the exact color he'd been looking for and now he couldn't use it."

"Did you buy all of it?" Vree asked as she mapped all visible exits from the street.

"Well, no, but he could hardly have a cloak made that looked exactly like mine. That would be *so* scrubby."

"Scrubby?"

"You know, less than fine." Magda laughed and tucked Vree's hand into the crook of her elbow. "I guess you don't know, do you? Do you mind if we walk like this?" As Vree twitched, she added, "That way Gyhard won't be excluded. I'd hold onto you, but you're wearing long sleeves."

If it upsets you . . .

A muscle jumped in Vree's jaw. "I don't mind."

"Good. So what's the problem?"

Vree made note of a cistern pipe that would probably hold her weight. "Problem?"

"Between you and Gyhard." Maintaining contact, she laced her fingers together. "Yesterday your kigh were like this. Today . . ." Her fingers folded into fists butting against each other.

Lovers' quarrel, Gyhard said shortly.

"If you're telling me it's none of my business—" Magda began.

Vree cut her off. "Gyhard thinks I shouldn't trust him. That I should always be on guard in case he can't control the urge to take over my body."

It's not that simple!

It was last night, she snarled.

I don't want to hurt you.

Then you take the responsibility for not hurting me! I'm tired of always holding the knife. "What's so funny?" she demanded as Magda smiled.

"Just that Gyhard was right; it is a lovers' quarrel because love can't exist without trust. You two really are so—"

Vree cut her off a second time. "Don't say we're so romantic."

"But . . ."

"No."

The draper, the tailor, and the cobbler took most of the afternoon. A life spent in the army had equipped Vree with neither the skills nor attention span Magda considered necessary for picking out clothes, so for the most part she merely endured the younger woman's opinions. When Gyhard suggested high boots instead of low, she ignored him.

"You'll need oilskins if you want to go outside in Third

Quarter," Magda reflected, piling packages into the arms of the cobbler's senior apprentice who seemed more than willing to quit the shop for the remainder of the afternoon. "But I think we've done enough for one day."

More than, Gyhard agreed.

"No. There's something else." Vree twisted her left wrist and her remaining throwing dagger dropped into her hand. "I lost the other one at sea. I want to replace it."

"I guess you'll need a blacksmith . . ."

Gyhard translated; Vree shook her head. "Blacksmiths shoe horses and beat swords into plows. I need a weapons crafter."

"Izak a'Edvard." Finding himself suddenly under close scrutiny, the bits of the boy's ears visible under an untidy shock of light brown hair turned bright red, "He's the best." His eyes widened while Vree balanced the dagger on the callused tip of one finger before she flipped it back up her sleeve.

"Who says he's the best?" she asked. "Besides you."

"Alise i'Dumin."

"Who is?"

"W–weapons master for the city guard. She's my Aunt Dasa's partner," he added when it seemed like more explanation might be demanded.

Vree, that's an assassin's weapon . . .

If I'm not an assassin, then I'm not dangerous, and that trio of palace guards who've been trying to keep up with us all afternoon have been wasting their time. If I'm not an assassin, what am I? Nothing.

Frowning slightly, Magda reached out to touch Vree's hand.

She jerked it back. "I still have some of the coins the Emperor gave me." Pulling a purse out of her belt-pouch, she passed it over. "Is it enough?"

"I have no idea what a dagger like that would cost," Magda admitted, peering into the calfskin purse at the two silver Imperial starbursts barely visible among the less valuable copper. "But you'd have to change this into Shkoden money before you could spend it anyway. If the dagger's that important to you . . ."

"It is."

". . . we'll just charge it to the Bardic Hall like the rest."

Handing back the purse, she grinned. "Captain Liene told me to be sure you had *everything* you needed." She pulled a gull out of her own purse, realized the apprentice had his hands full, and stuffed the coin into his pocket. His blush deepened. "They might make you leave our stuff at the gate but that's all right because someone will come out to carry it in from there." Leaning forward so his master, cutting leather on the other side of the open shop, couldn't hear, she added in a conspiratorial whisper, "We'll cover for you later if you want to tell him you were delayed at the Hall."

Muttering an inarticulate protest, the boy jerked into motion.

"Hold it," Vree snapped.

He stopped so quickly he almost lost his grip on a fleece hat.

"Where is the weapons crafter's shop?"

"Uh, Ironmonger's Street. Far end. He uses a wooden sword crossed with two wooden daggers as a signboard." When it appeared that Magda was about to move closer and say something, he insisted he knew no more and headed up the hill at a stiff-legged trot.

"What was *that* all about?" Magda muttered as they picked their way across the debris on the street and into Tether Alley.

"I think it had to do with warm breath against his ear."

"Mine?"

"Not mine," Vree told her, even as she checked the half-timbered buildings that flanked the narrow lane for routes to the roof.

"Really?" The apprentice healer paused and peered back around the corner. "I don't think so," she said after a moment. Tucking Vree's hand back into the crook of her elbow, she started them walking again. "He's too young."

"He can't be that much younger than you are, if he's younger at all," Vree pointed out.

"Yes, but women mature *earlier* than men. Healers have known that for years. I mean, when you were growing up, didn't you feel so much more adult than all the boys you knew?"

"Assassins are treated as assassins from the moment they start training."

"Well, yes, but if you were seven, you were still a child. They couldn't change that."

Vree didn't understand why Magda's innocence hurt so much. "I was an assassin," she said, and that ended the conversation.

"Lookie what we have here." One of the three young men lounging about the sunny front of Izak a'Edvard's shop pushed himself up onto his feet as Vree and Magda approached. "You two an item?" He flicked the beaded ends of his mustache with a forefinger and arched his back enough to stretch his sleeveless tunic tight against the undulating ridges of his chest. "Or does a charming, sophisticated, handsome fellow like myself stand a chance?"

"No," Vree replied before Magda could answer. Her posture clearly indicated she expected him to get out of her way.

"Vree . . ."

Magda sounded so worried, Gyhard tried to keep the amusement out of his mental voice—and failed. *People usually accept it when an assassin says no.*

"He doesn't know."

And you're not to tell him.

"We got us a grumpy one, boys." His friends grinned encouragement and shifted position on the bench to get a better view of the fun. "You the little healer's personal bodyguard, Southie?"

Vree started around him, but he grabbed her shoulder with a scarred hand and pushed her back.

Oh, oh.

"I asked you a question, Southie."

Doesn't smell like he's drunk; he must be stupid.

"Vree . . ."

"Is that your name, Southie?" He laughed. "It sounds like the noise a pig makes when you slit its throat. Vreeee!" Bowing slightly toward Magda, he purred, "Excuse me, *healer,*" his emphasis indicated he was fully aware of the apprentice circle on her badge, "but I'm going to have to teach your little friend here a lesson in manners."

Clutching Vree's hand tightly, Magda glared at him. "Look, you're making a mistake."

He held his hand out from his chest, just even with the top of Vree's head. "Somehow, I doubt it."

"She looks dangerous, Jak." While the warning held a certain amount of derision, it was a warning for all of that.

Jak spread his arms. Muscles rippled from shoulder to wrist, the pattern of scars a moving history of other fights. "She's half my size, Ziv. How *dangerous* can that be?"

One of Vree's instructors had told her that women made marginally better assassins than men because they didn't posture.

No blades!

Responding instinctively to the sound of a direct order, Vree changed the direction of her initial movement and launched herself into the air. Planting a hand on each of Jak's shoulders, she flipped over his head, smacking her knee into his chin as she passed. She slapped the cobblestones, rolled, and regained her feet an instant later.

Bellowing with pain and rage, Jak spat out a bloody tooth, whirled, and charged. A few moments later, loyalty dragged his friends into the fight. By the time the trio of palace guards arrived, short swords drawn and wondering what they were going to tell their captain if the Southern woman got killed, it was all over. They stared wide-eyed from the groaning men to Vree, who was wiping a trickle of blood from her nose on her sleeve.

I'm surprised they touched you.

It wasn't intentional. These idiots don't know how to fall.

Accidents happen?

Only once.

Feel better now?

She grinned at his tone. *Much. Thanks for reminding me not to kill them.* To Gyhard's surprise, the thanks were sincere. *I thought you never served?*

I didn't. But I spent sixty years as Governor Aralt and over the years he, I, gave a great many orders.

"You're hurt!" Magda rushed forward and patted the air in front of Vree's nose. "Let me Heal that!"

"It'll heal itself in a minute." All at once, she became aware of the dozen or so people who'd been drawn out of the surrounding buildings at the sound of battle. Most wore singed leather aprons, the rest wore the weapons they'd come to this street to buy. None of them looked happy.

"No one can move like that," muttered a smith, her hands wrapped around the shaft of a heavy hammer.

"She doesn't look Shkoden,"

"She doesn't move like she's human."

"Demon. I'm tellin' ya, she must be a demon."

Magda whirled on them, hands on her hips. "Don't be ridiculous. She's from the Havakeen Empire. And if these three braggarts couldn't finish what they started, it's *hardly* her fault."

It might've worked had the three members of the palace guard not suddenly decided to make up for arriving late. As they moved into a defensive position around the two women, the rumbles from the crowd grew ugly.

Her breathing back to normal, Vree studied patterns and planned her attack, just in case. *This is stupid.*

Granted. But it doesn't make it any less dangerous.

Granted.

Don't tell them what you are. Were. You'd stand a better chance with them believing you a demon.

"No one her size could take down three people their size," the smith declared. "It's impossible!"

Magda sighed. "You've always been the strongest, haven't you? You hate the thought of anyone so much smaller than you being able to defeat you."

"What're you talkin' about?" the smith snarled. She shifted her grip on the hammer. "This ain't about me. It's about her." Raising a beefy arm, she stepped forward. "Now git out of my . . ."

Whether she intended a blow or merely a shove became irrelevant as a pair of strong hands grabbed her from behind and threw her to the ground. The hammer bounced out of her reach, striking sparks off the cobblestones. When she tried to rise, the point of a sword at her throat changed her mind.

The tall young man holding the sword, tossed a straying strand of ebony hair back over his shoulder and slowly swept an arrogant violet gaze over the area. His looks and his bearing as much as the sword, silenced the crowd. "Maggi," he sighed at last, "what is going on here?"

Everyone started talking at once.

"I was speaking to my sister." The gentle admonishment had steel behind it. A bard couldn't have done it better.

"It wasn't my *fault*, Gerek," Magda told him. "Vree and I just wanted to go into this shop and these three buffoons wouldn't let us."

"And?"

"And so Vree fought them."

"And?"

"And she won."

"And?"

"And now these people think she's a demon!"

"Maggi, demons don't really exist. They're stories told to frighten children."

Magda glared at her older brother. She didn't know what he was doing in Elbasan and while she appreciated him dropping out of the Circle to save her, if indeed he had saved her, she didn't appreciate his tone. "Don't tell me," she snapped. "Tell *them*."

"These are adults," Gerek pointed out facetiously. "They know that."

So fascinated was everyone by this exchange that they forgot about the men who'd started it and had Jak not bellowed as he surged to his feet, he might've had a slim chance of success. As it was, Vree's dagger caught the loose fabric where the wide legs of his trousers joined and buried itself guard deep in the wall behind him. Jak stared down at the pommel, just visible at his crotch, and fainted.

"Hope he tucks left," someone murmured.

One of the palace guards snickered. The tension dissolved in shouts of raucous laughter.

About to demand an explanation, Magda caught the expression on Gerek's face and stopped cold. She'd seen that expression before. Frequently. It was the last thing she wanted to see in this time and this place.

Gerek was in love.

"All right. Let me see if I understand this." Gerek paced across one of the small rooms in the suite set aside for the Duc of Ohrid at the palace and stared over at the lights of the Bardic Hall. "Not only does Vree have two kigh, but they're in love with each other."

"That's right."

He sighed, turned, and propped one leg on the polished marble window sill. "That's not love, Maggot. That's masturbation."

"Gerek!"

His teeth were very white against the shadow of whiskers on his chin. "You've been studying here for almost two years. You must've run into the word."

"Of course I've run into the word and stop grinning at me in that stupid way!" Magda spat a curl out of the corner of her mouth and glared at her brother. "You haven't been listening to anything I've said! Vree and Gyhard are two separate people!"

"In one body."

"Yes!"

"In one beautiful, desirable, very sexy body."

"No!" She snatched a tapestry cushion up off a padded chair and threw it at him.

Stretching out a languid arm, he lazily plucked it out of the air before impact and tossed it back onto the chair. "Are you saying she's *not* beautiful?"

"Of *course* she's beautiful. I'm not *blind*."

A single ebony brow swept upward in an interrogative gesture Magda'd hated all her life. The only way she could get a single brow to rise was if she tied the other one down.

"Gerek! She's my patient!"

He spread his hands, the gesture as elegant as everything he did. "Not mine."

"Look, Gerek, Vree's *really* vulnerable right now and she hates feeling vulnerable and that makes things even worse." Gathering up her robe in one hand, Magda crossed to his side and stared earnestly up at him. "She truly loves Gyhard, but she's afraid of her feelings because assassins are taught only to love the army. And being assassins. If it hadn't been for Bannon, Vree'd *never* have been able to do what she did."

"I thought you said his name was Gyhard?"

"Bannon's her brother. For some reason I'm not *entirely* clear on, mostly because I haven't wanted to ask, they were trained together, against all tradition, and she loved him. That made it possible for her to love Gyhard even though she's having trouble handling the emotions. This entire experience has *completely* messed up her whole identity. Her kigh is so *confused* all the time . . ."

"All the time?" he prodded when she paused.

"Okay, it wasn't confused this afternoon. This afternoon she knew *exactly* who she was."

"And Gyhard loves her? Whoever she is?"

"Yes."

"What? No accompanying diagnosis?"

She bit her lip. "He's afraid that someday his love won't be strong enough to stop him from taking over her body."

"And what are you afraid of, little sister?" Gerek asked gently, cupping her chin with his palm.

"The same thing," Magda admitted with a sigh. "Gerek, you've got to promise me you'll stay away from her." Wrapping his hand in both of hers, she searched his face for any sign of capitulation. "The last thing Vree needs right now is you panting all over her, further confusing the issue."

He freed his hand. "I don't pant."

"You know what I mean."

"Have I ever hurt anyone?" Before she could answer, he added, "Intentionally?"

"Well, no, but . . ."

"Then trust me."

Gerek fought the urge to scratch as he accompanied the page through the section of the palace that held the royal family's private apartments. It might have been more politic to shave before this visit, but having discovered upon arriving in Elbasan that beards were now the fashion, he had no time to waste. He clasped his hands behind his back to keep them from his chin. *Because it's too late to do anything about it now.*

When the page pulled open a gleaming section of paneling carved with the crowned ship of Shkoder, he tugged at his tunic and followed her into the room.

"Gerek a'Pjerin, Majesties."

He bowed extravagantly, sweeping the thick carpet with an imaginary hat—the way Tadeus had taught him when he was seven—and straightened to see the Queen approaching him with outstretched hands and a fond smile.

"It's good to see you, Gerek, and a little surprising to see you so soon after your arrival. I'd have thought Elbasan had more interesting claims on your time."

"How can you say that when I have thought of nothing but Your Majesty's beauty . . ." He laid a gentle kiss on the back of each of her offered hands. ". . . and grace from the moment I left my father's keep."

"You've been spending too much time with the bards, Gerek," the king called from his chair by the empty hearth. "You're starting to sound like one."

"Nonsense, Theron." Llyana returned to her own chair, her cheeks lightly pink. "I've never had a bard say anything half so pretty to me."

"Then you ought to spend more time with Tadeus if you're feeling the lack. Give that one half a chance and he'd say pretty things to me."

"Yes, dear, but not to me."

Theron grunted and laced his hands over his stomach. "Sit, Gerek," he commanded, nodding at a third chair. "I can't stand the way you and your father insist on towering over people."

Gerek grinned as he sat. "I'll try to be shorter, Majesty, but I'm afraid I can't speak for my father."

"Who can," the king agreed dryly. "How is he?"

"He sent his respects, Sire, and his deepest regret that he would be unable to attend the Full Council. He only hopes that my humble attempt to take his place will meet with your approval."

"Well, you're more of a diplomat than he ever was, but you can stop forking it off the manure pile, boy; I've known you most of your life. How is he really?"

"When I left, he was furious about a ram that'd been pulled out of a breeding program without his approval."

"Of course he was. And how is my sister?"

"Equally furious, sir. Nees was the one who removed the ram."

The king shook his head and exchanged a speaking glance with his consort. "Of course she was," he said. "And how are you? Besides having unfortunately lost your shaving kit."

"Theron, he's obviously growing a beard," Llyana declared as Gerek's ears reddened. "Before you say any more," she reached over and tugged at the gray-brown curls adorning His Majesty's chin, "you should remember how you looked when your beard was growing in."

Family matters took a certain amount of time to cover as Annice had entrusted Gerek with a number of messages to her brother that she didn't think needed to be sent through the Bardic Hall. Servers were setting out wine as they discussed the lack of action on the Cemandian border and the slow but steady growth of trade.

When the servers had left and the three were alone again, Theron stared down into his goblet as if he might read answers in the wine. "So, Gerek, why *did* you come to see us so soon after your arrival?"

Half smiling at the emphasis, Gerek admitted he was concerned about his sister.

"Ah. She's told you about the assassin."

"Yes, Majesty."

"We have them under constant surveillance. Besides the kigh, there are always guards within crossbow range."

"Begging Your Majesty's pardon, but that didn't do much good this afternoon."

"How fortunate that you arrived when you did then."

Gerek's jaw dropped. "How did you know . . . ?"

"Don't be ridiculous," Theron advised gently, setting the goblet on the small marble table by his elbow. "I'm the king. When those close to me are involved in a street brawl, I'm informed. So, what's your suggestion?"

"Majesty?" The abrupt question had taken him completely by surprise.

The king smiled. "I know the two who raised you, Gerek. Given that, given them, I can't believe you don't have a better way of dealing with the situation in mind."

Not entirely certain he liked being read so easily, Gerek spread his hands. "I had thought that perhaps I could be used as an additional guard, one who could stay much closer than those now assigned."

"Magda was very insistent that there be no guard at all. What we have now is an attempt at a compromise. The guards are discreet and she pretends they aren't there."

"But she can hardly object to me, Majesty. I'm her brother."

Brow furrowed, Theron considered the offer from a

number of angles; unfortunately, with no idea of the only relevant one.

If she realizes she's a healer with a healer's privileges instead of just my little sister, she won't ask me to stay away from Vree, she'll order it. She's like that. Stubborn. Certain she knows what's right. Gerek couldn't let that happen. He had to get closer to the Southern beauty who'd stolen his heart.

"I have to admit I didn't like Maggi being so far from the guards," the king allowed at last. "If you think you can get closer, go ahead, and if she gives you any trouble with it, tell her you're there on my order."

"Yes, Sire." He stood. "Thank you, Majesty, I . . ."

"Father?" The Heir paused in the open door and looked slightly embarrassed. "My apologies, Majesty, I didn't realize you were . . . Gerek! How nice to see you back in Elbasan."

"Your Highness." His bow to the Princess Onele was significantly less flamboyant than to her parents. The odds were good that when he became duc, she'd be Queen—his direct liege.

"What brings you down from Ohrid?" she asked, her gaze frankly appreciative.

Having attracted that kind of response his entire adult life, Gerek had long since learned to ignore it. "I'm here to sit as my father's proxy on the Full Council, Highness."

"I'll be looking forward to your participation." She smiled and reached behind her, pulling her oldest daughter out from her shadow and into the room. While her relationship with her consort had grown to be distant at best, she doted on both her daughters. "Look who's here, Jelena."

Jelena took one panicked look at Gerek, turned bright red, dropped her gaze to the embroidered toes of her slippers, and murmured something unintelligible.

Gerek smiled kindly down at the girl. "But the princess Jelena was a child when I saw her last; this is a young woman."

"I was twelve then." Jelena glanced up, met his gaze for an instant, and returned her attention back to her slippers. "I'm over fourteen now."

"What was it you wanted, Onele?" Theron asked, taking pity on his granddaughter.

"It's not important, Father. It can wait until tomorrow." The Heir herded her daughter back out into the hall. "As I said, I didn't realize you had a guest. Good night, Gerek."

He bowed again. "Good night, Highness."

"I think we can take it as read that Jelena still has that crush on you," the king mused. "I had hoped she'd outgrown it in the interim."

"I would never take advantage, Majesty."

"Don't be an idiot. Of course you wouldn't."

When he was gone, Theron shook his head. "I'm getting old, my dear. I forgot to warn him about looking into the assassin's eyes. Suppose this Gyhard decides to leap into his body?"

"I'm sure Magda will warn him. And if not, Gerek's obviously made himself familiar with the situation. He's a smart young man. He'll be fine."

I don't like him.

Why not?

Isn't it obvious? He likes you too well.

Vree turned to look at Gerek, who stood smiling down at his sister as she told him for the eighth time that afternoon just how much she didn't want him around. *Obvious?*

He's continually staring longingly into your eyes. When you look like he does, you know how effective that can be. If he'd had teeth, he'd have ground them. As it was, Vree felt a muscle tighten in her jaw. *Remember, I can feel your response.*

Look at him; a corpse would respond. Which was as much reassurance as she was going to give. Bannon had needed to be told constantly he was the center of her world and she had no intention of setting that up again. Either Gyhard trusted her, or he didn't. *It seems like he's getting to you more than he's getting to me.*

Watching Gerek through Vree's eyes, Gyhard wished he could jump across one of those longing looks and throw the arrogant little shit right out of his body. *You just pray,* he thought, shielding it carefully, *that I never manage to convince Vree just how perfectly your body would fit me because all it would take is one little shove.*

Six

The Imperial Ambassador stared down at the golden sunburst sealing the parchment package that had, moments before, been placed on his desk. "Didn't I just receive one of these?" he asked the empty office. When no answer was forthcoming, he sighed and rubbed at throbbing temples with his fingertips. Two messages directly from His Imperial Majesty during the same quarter were unprecedented during his tenure as ambassador. That it had been sent up the coast on one of the sleek little ships kept for moments of extreme diplomacy did not reassure him in the least.

Muttering "Fear, fire, flood," under his breath, he reached for a horn letter opener and slid the blade beneath the seal.

His Royal Highness Prince Otavas will be arriving in Elbasan shortly on the Imperial Navy vessel, Deliverance.

The rest of the package primarily contained lists of the prince's preferences in food and drink and accommodation.

"Will be arriving *shortly?* Oh, that's useful." Shaking his head, he stood, scooped up the papers, and headed for the door. One of his attaches—a career civil servant as opposed to the distant Imperial cousins who made up most of the rest of his staff—fell into step beside him as he left the room.

"His Royal Highness Prince Otavas will be arriving in Elbasan shortly," he said as they moved together down the hall. The attaché turned enough to see the ambassador's face. "Shortly?" she asked.

"Funny, that was my response. I'm on my way to inform Their Majesties—if I change quickly, I can catch the end of the morning audience. You take care of things here and see about the status of our suite at the palace—I'll need to be accessible to him. And find a reasonably responsible translator close to his own age. I don't imagine he speaks much Shkoden. He's traveling by sea, but I'll let King Theron's people deal with the Harbor Master. The last time I tried, I very nearly disrupted trade all up and down the coast."

"Hardly that bad, sir."

"You weren't there, Tysia." He threw her a smile as he turned down the corridor leading to his private apartments. "You weren't there."

A few moments later, as his valet hurriedly dressed him in official robes, he pondered the implications of the sudden visit and began to work out how best to use it to the Empire's advantage. If he were very lucky, when the prince arrived, he might be informed exactly *why* His Imperial Majesty had decided to so abruptly send his youngest son to Shkoder.

And if not, he sighed silently, lifting his arms so that the folds of the saffron undertunic could be adjusted, *it might be best to keep King Theron's sentiments in mind and remember that nothing coming out of the Empire is ever exactly what it seems.*

On one knee, both hands pressed against the earth, Jazep stared through the trees at the cluster of buildings. The extended families who made up the settlement called it Fortune, after what they hoped to take out of the silver mine they jointly worked. He hadn't been here for about six years but, by risking a light trance, he could touch the recall and compare it with what he could see.

Although a few small cottages had been built, it appeared that most of the people continued to live communally—a sensible way to conserve heat during the long, hard mountain winters. The kitchens should have been busy with the preparation of the evening meal, but no smoke rose from any chimney. The only sound he could hear was the high, thin crying of an unhappy baby.

Jazep closed his eyes for a heartbeat and fought with the still, small voice in his head that told him to leave as quickly as he could, to not face this thing alone. He'd been walking without kigh since dawn; the earth had been as empty of their presence as the settlement was of visible life. Without their guidance, he'd spent the day feeling crippled and lost but kept continually moving in the direction all his senses told him to stay away from. Whatever it was he followed, it had to be stopped.

Now, it seemed he'd finally caught up to it. Until this moment, his greatest horror had been the thought of another emptied grave and a kigh brutalized as Filip's had been, but as he lifted his eyes to a flock of buzzards circling the buildings, he began to realize the terrifying possibilities.

Had there been kigh, they would have warned him he was no longer alone.

A strong arm wrapped around Jazep's chest and callused hand clamped tightly over his mouth. After the initial, involuntary jerk, he twisted enough to find himself staring into the frightened face of a pale young man.

Bard? The young man mouthed, hope beginning to dawn.

Jazep nodded.

Be quiet. When Jazep nodded again, he removed both hand and arm and stood. He stared, wide-eyed, as Jazep rose and shrugged back into his pack, then he motioned for the bard to follow.

The woman waiting at the makeshift shelter lowered her club and sagged against a tree as the two men came out of the underbrush. "I thought they had you," she whispered, relief not quite enough to banish the fear. "I thought they had you."

"Evicka, he's a bard." The young man crossed the clearing and took hold of her shoulders. "A bard!"

Evicka straightened and looked past him to Jazep. Her face began to lighten with a sudden incredulous joy; then, just as quickly, the shadows returned. "A bard," she repeated. "What is *one* bard going to do?"

"What does he have to do?" Jazep asked quietly.

"The old man wandered in yesterday morning. I never thought anything that old could be alive." She pushed her hair back off her face and laughed bitterly. "Maybe it can't. Anyway, he came and we fed him and sat him in the sun because, well, we're all enclosed in the Circle, aren't we?" Again the bitter laugh. The young man reached out and closed his hand around her arm. She covered it with her own and went on. "Johan had taken down one of the deer that's been stripping our gardens, a big buck, so tough they practically needed the picks to take it apart, but after long enough in the pot, well, anything tenders up and it was venison stew for last night's meal. Everyone ate in the big hall—stupid to let that kind of bounty go to waste and with a dozen cousins off to Bicaz with a load of ore there was lots to go around—but me and Krisus had just been joined a few days and well, we were in one of the cottages. We didn't eat any of the stew.

"About full dark, they woke us up. Everyone was sick. First the old and the young, then everyone else. By the turn of the night, six people were dead. A couple hours later . . ." She paused and swiped at her eyes. ". . . everyone."

"We thought at first the meat had been diseased." Krisus took up the tale when Evicka fell silent. "The only ones in the whole place who weren't sick were us and Amalia's baby—she's still on the tit. Even Great-grandfather had a bowl of the broth. There wasn't anything we could do. We don't have a healer."

Evicka spread her hands. "We just watched them die. Then . . ." She shook her head and tried again. "Then . . ."

Jazep thought he understood the terror that kept her from going on. "Then you watched them live again?"

Two pairs of shadowed eyes locked onto his face. "How did you know?"

He couldn't tell which of them had spoken. Maybe they both had. "I've been following the thing that did it, trying to stop it before . . ."

"Too late." Hysteria hovered around the edges of Evicka's interruption. "And it isn't a thing, it's the old man. And he Sings. We heard him."

"*Sings?*"

"Yeah, like a bard. He took hold of my brother's hand, my brother's dead hand, 'cause I'm telling you I watched Justyn die, and he Sang, and my brother came back. Or at least part of him did."

. . . and he Sang . . .

Jazep scrambled to his feet and made it to the edge of the clearing before expelling the contents of his knotted stomach all over a bush. He retched until there was nothing left and then he retched some more. When he finally straightened, they were both watching him blankly; their concern had been used up on greater things and nothing remained for a bard who'd just realized he'd been following not a thing, but an old man—an old bard.

Wiping his beard on the back of his hand, Jazep turned and murmured, "How many?"

"Don't know. We ran. You couldn't stay around them."

As far as we know," Evicka said, shoulders hunched against a chill only she could feel, "we're the only survivors. Us and Amalia's baby—and we're not going nowhere without her."

"Except we can't go back. We've tried, but we always end up going around, finding ourselves on the other side without knowing how we got there. It's like your head was pushing you aside from something, something it doesn't want you to see."

Jazep stared at them in amazement. At the moment, they were the bravest people he'd ever met. "You tried to go back?"

"We aren't going nowhere without Amalia's baby," Evicka repeated, then her lower lip started to tremble and her eyes filled with tears. "But she's been alone all night and all day and we can't get to her and she's just three months old and she's probably dead by now, too."

"She's alive." Jazep used just enough Voice to leave no room for doubt. Evicka, wrapped in Krisus' arms, looked up. "I heard her crying. She's not happy, but she's alive."

"But we can't get to her."

"I can." Trembling with anger and fear combined, he knelt and began unbuckling his instrument case.

"This is as close as you can get before your head starts pushing you away." Evicka's fingers dug into Jazep's arm. "What are you going to do?"

He settled the drones on his shoulder. "First I'm going to get their attention, then I'm going to Sing the dead to rest."

"All of them? All at once?"

"Yes." There were times when Jazep felt limited Singing only a single quarter, but this wasn't one of those times. All his life, he'd followed where the earth had led, and the earth kigh were tied to the turning of the Circle in unmistakable ways. When the old man had Sung the kigh back into the dead of Fortune, he'd ripped them out of the Circle. They were lost, like Filip's kigh had been, and like Filip's kigh they needed to be shown the way home.

And then; then he'd deal with the old man.

"Deal how?" asked a little voice in his head.

He didn't have an answer, so he ignored it. "I want you two to stay out here until I stop Singing. We know the old man is dangerous so let me take care of him before you move in."

Krisus shifted in place defensively, wanting to be the one who rode to the rescue and, in spite of himself, resenting the bard for being able to do what he couldn't. "What are you going to do? Sing to him?"

Sing to him . . . The old man was as much out of the Circle as the dead he abused. Perhaps . . . Jazep reached out, took hold of the idea, and gathered it close. Perhaps the old man, too, was lost.

"Yes," he said gently, as fear and anger fled to be replaced by sorrow so overwhelming his knees nearly buckled beneath its weight. "That's exactly what I'm going to do. I'm going to Sing to him."

The late afternoon sun threw long shadows through Fortune as Jazep walked out from under the cover of the trees and onto the rutted track. He felt as though he were pushing against an invisible wall; each step requiring more effort than the one before.

I know the path, he told the wall, fingers moving purposefully up and down the chanter, blowpipe clamped between his lips. *You cannot keep me from following it. The walking dead are to be pitied, not feared.*

The resistance ceased so suddenly, he stumbled and nearly fell. Both Krisus and Evicka had described their failure to approach the settlement as having had their heads push them aside. It was personal horror and disbelief that had to be overcome, Jazep realized, living kigh simply preferred not to deal with the dead returned.

He would have preferred not to deal with it himself, preferred that whatever it was that had driven the old man so far out of the Circle had never occurred but, as it had, he had no choice.

The call of the pipes rose up into the unnaturally quiet air and, as the bard followed the track between the first two outbuildings, the dead began to answer.

Filip had been crushed in a rock fall and buried three long days in the heat of Second Quarter. The people of Fortune had been poisoned and so it was harder to see the seven drawn, one by one, through the door of the largest building as dead. They moved with a careful deliberation, as though they'd had to relearn the use of arms and legs and they wore identical blank expressions that would, Jazep assumed, grow more identical as death began to wipe away physical differences.

Why these seven had been chosen out of all the poisoned dead, he had no idea.

He could feel their kigh, confused and frightened. Although they hadn't wanted to die, neither had they wanted to return, thrust back into shells of lifeless flesh. Jazep felt no terror, only the pity he'd earlier assumed. The thought of the desperate loneliness that would allow the old man to commit such an injustice, to drag other lives so brutally out of the Circle, nearly broke his heart.

Spitting out the blowpipe, he took a deep breath and began to Sing. His voice, deep and resonant, filled the spaces between the buildings and gently covered the dead. He Sang of their life the way it had been, drawing on the recall of his last visit, adding to it the story Krisus and Evicka had told. He redefined the individual paths of their lives and then he walked them to the one path all life followed around the Circle and he Sang them home. It was so very simple, it was the most powerful Song he'd ever Sung.

One by one the bodies began to fall as each kigh took up its journey, once again.

As the afternoon deepened into dusk, the last of the walking dead remained standing above the empty husks of her companions. Jazep could feel her kigh being torn, needing to go, needing to stay, and he paused in his Song to better listen to hers.

Had he not been a bard, he might have missed the baby's cry; it had grown so weak and faint it barely made it out of the building. The woman turned toward the cry, stretching out a graying hand. When she turned back to Jazep, her face as expressionless as before but her pain impossible

to mistake, he Sang of how Evicka and Krisus had overcome their fear for her baby's sake, that although she
couldn't stay, her baby would never lack for love or
protection.

The dead cannot cry, but her kigh wailed its sorrow as
it fled and her body faced her baby when it fell.

Tears streaming down his face and into his beard, Jazep
Sang the Circle's welcome. He could feel its comfort enclosing him and had to force himself to put that comfort aside.
Shaking himself vigorously, feeling as though he'd just
emerged from a trance state deeper than any he'd ever
reached before, he let the Song trail off to silence.

There were still no earth kigh about, but he could deal
with the implications of that later. Before he did anything
else, he had to get to that baby.

He'd taken only a single step when he saw the bent and
ancient figure emerge from the shadows. He'd thought,
when Evicka had said she hadn't believed anything so old
could live, it was merely youth defining the parameters of
old. He was wrong. Although the old man was alive, his
kigh was somehow as trapped as the kigh of those he'd
killed to hold.

Their eyes met over the distance. The old man's face was
wet and twisted with longing. Much as the young woman
had reached for her child, Jazep stretched out his hand
toward him and opened his mouth to Sing again.

NO! NO! NO!

It slammed into his awareness, a kigh too far gone in
insanity to reach.

Not the old man's kigh.

Then who?

Jazep screamed, felt muscles tear as his back arched impossibly far. He clawed at the air as the attacking kigh
clawed his spirit. Red and black waves of pain ripped
through his head. Worse than his pain was the pain of the
other kigh. He could feel every tortured nuance tearing
through him again and again and again.

He heard the old man call out a name and had barely
enough self remaining to realize that if he'd known Kait's
name sooner, he might have been able to find her Song.

Too late.

The pain became more than even he could bear.

Holding tightly to the only Song he could remember, his kigh fled and his body fell to lie beside the other seven.

"Annice!" Drawn by the long, low moan of pain, Stasya raced across the garden, dropped onto the wet dirt beside the kneeling woman and gathered her into the circle of her arms. "What is it, dearling? What's wrong?"

"I don't know." Her body rigid, her face wet with tears, Annice slowly opened the fingers of one hand. Nestled in her palm lay a clump of earth, compacted by the pressure of her fist. "I don't know," she repeated. "But it just got worse."

"So, Vree." Kovar smiled kindly across the desk at her, the waxed ends of his mustache rising. "How are you finding your stay with us?"

Finding? What does he mean, finding? I haven't lost anything.

Vree felt her lungs expand and contract as Gyhard sighed. *I'm going to assume you don't know enough Shkoden to make puns. Our Bardic-Captain-in-waiting here, wants to know how you are, relative to where you are.*

Oh, that makes just *as much sense.* She nodded at Kovar, her expression carefully unreadable, and said, "Fine." Since arriving in Shkoder, she'd discovered it was a good, all-purpose answer for those times she didn't quite understand the question. Unless, of course, she was talking to Magda, who'd be all over it, like fire ants in a bedroll.

"The food's all right? The room? The bards aren't pestering you too much?"

The bards didn't actually see her. Most often, they saw two kigh and reacted accordingly. Occasionally, they saw some sort of romantic nonsense she didn't understand. Of all the bards who'd Sung at, around, and to her since she'd arrived, only the Bardic Captain had actually responded to her, as herself, and Gyhard, as himself, instead of treating them like some strange new piece of music to be learned.

What about Tadeus? Gyhard asked. Since his return, Tadeus had used his age and position to co-opt more than his fair share of their time.

He does it, too, although he's so slaughtering charming about it, it's hard to mind.

And Kovar? He seems worried about you.

He's not worried about me. He's worried about some-one he thinks is me. Realizing that Kovar was waiting for an answer, Vree shrugged. "The food is good. The room is more than I've ever had. The bards have been very interested."

Kovar frowned and lightly drummed his fingers on the desktop in unconscious imitation of Captain Liene. He sus-pected there was more to Vree's response than an imper-fect command of Shkoden, but as he also suspected that the cause of her unhappiness was a perpetual eavesdropper on her life, he didn't dare ask for further explanation lest she suffer for it later.

"Interested," he repeated. "That's one word for it. You've been a great help to us, Vree. I don't know if she mentioned it to you, but Karlene believed that part of being a bard involved an ability to Sing the fifth kigh. That we've all always done it without realizing it. That every time we touch an audience, one listener or one hundred, we're Sing-ing the fifth kigh. Thanks to you . . ." His pause was so short that anyone but another bard would have missed it. Another bard or an assassin trained to notice the smallest detail connected to survival. ". . . and Gyhard, we're dis-covering that Karlene was right. We're beginning to find out why some Songs work, why some don't. If we can learn to consciously Sing the fifth kigh, we could reach so many more people."

Or they could fine-tune the way they manipulate emo-tions. All for the greater good, of course.

Karlene said bards aren't like that.

Karlene's a bard, Vree. She's not exactly unbiased.

Noticing Vree's blank stare, Kovar shook his head. "I'm sorry; I'm lecturing, aren't I? Bad habit of mine, I'm afraid. Have you heard the songs the fledglings are writing about you?"

"Songs? There's more than *one*?" Vree's cheeks grew hot at the memory of the lengthy and overly tragic ballad she was already aware of. Hearing it sung in front of Magda and her brother had been the most embarrassing moment of her entire life. When the young bard had left, Gerek had summed up her feelings pretty much exactly.

"Don't you wish you were still an assassin?" he'd caroled,

surrendering to the laughter he'd charitably suppressed while the fledgling was within earshot. *"I bet you wish you could use your daggers right about now."*

"On me or on him?" she'd asked miserably. Gyhard's amusement hadn't helped.

And now she'd been told there was more than one. "Are the rest as bad?"

Kovar hid an involuntary smile at her tone. "Very likely. Never mind, Vree, the pressure'll be off you in a little while. The bards will be too busy to drown you in their creative juices and there'll be more Southerners around, so the Citadel, at least, shouldn't look so strange." When he saw he had her full attention, he went on. "According to the Imperial Ambassador, your young Prince Otavas is coming to Shkoder for a visit. His ship will be arriving sometime tomorrow." The panic that flashed in her eyes disappeared so quickly he thought he might have imagined it. "Vree?"

She stared at him but saw another face—a younger face; Bannon's face.

Vree?

Why is he coming here?

You don't know that Bannon is still with the prince.

Rising, Kovar came around the desk and stood, outstretched hand not quite touching Vree's rigid shoulder. "Are you all right, child?"

Before she could answer, or not answer, the door to the office burst open and Captain Liene threw herself into the room. "Open the window, Kovar! Quickly!"

Propelled across the room by Liene's voice, Kovar flipped up the latch that held the multipaned window closed. It flew open with such force that he lost his grip and it slammed back against the wall. The howl of the wind drowned out the crash of breaking glass.

The two bards tried to calm the half-dozen agitated kigh that spun around them, drenching them both with the rain the window had been closed to keep out. It wasn't until they raised their voices in harmony that the kigh's message began to make any sense.

A young bard named Marija had been intercepted by a hysterical teenager and taken to the small town of Bartek Springs where she'd found that something had caused the dead to walk. Fortunately, Jazep had arrived before her and Sung the dead to rest—her relief at the older bard's intervention was the strongest part of the message. Unfortunately, before she'd arrived, he'd then gone hunting the abomination that had done such a horrible and hideous thing—here the kigh grew agitated again and had to be soothed. Marija had Sung the notes of Jazep's name to an air kigh and sent it to find him. When it returned, it told her that Jazep no longer was. She'd sent another, and another, and another. The answer didn't change.

The final part of the message was less a Song than a wail. *What should I do?*

Liene groped her way to a chair and sat heavily, fingers white around the head of her cane. Kovar stared out the window as though he could find an answer in the blowing sheets of rain. Neither noticed that Vree was no longer in the room.

"Jazep." The Bardic Captain fought for breath, feeling as though she'd just been hit in the chest. "Marija has no ability in earth and that's the only quarter Jazep Sings. I need to get out of the city and hear what the earth kigh have to say."

Kovar shook his head slowly, as though even that limited motion was almost beyond him. "She didn't say that the air kigh couldn't find him, Liene. They told her he no longer was."

"That's impossible!"

"No. It isn't." His shoulders sagged. "You *know* the only reason they would have told her that."

"But Jazep . . ."

"Is dead. And we'll mourn him later." He lost his voice in grief, swallowed, and found it again. "Right now, we have a living bard who needs our help. What is Marija to do?"

Liene closed her eyes, feeling her age tighten around her. She touched a recall of Jazep as a fledgling. The only one in his year unable to Sing air, he'd never resented the others' easy communication with bards in other parts of the country; he'd just smiled his slow smile and been their anchor. The breadth of his shoulders and the heavy muscles in his arms made his legs seem short and out of proportion to the rest of his body, but everyone who met him saw his kindness and *then* his great strength. He had a tendency to fuss. She'd taught him the tambour and he'd soaked up the knowledge as effortlessly as the earth soaked up rain.

She'd mourn him later.

Straightening, Liene opened her eyes to meet Kovar's concerned gaze. "It seems," she said, "that if the dead are walking, the abomination of Karlene's recall has crossed the border from the Empire. Who else is in that area?"

"It's almost to the border, Captain. There's no one close. Jeremias is near the south end of the Coast Road, but he's only got two quarters—air and water, I believe . . ."

"All right." An upraised hand that trembled only a little cut him off. "Marija needs the description of the old man from Karlene's recall. We need the recall she's carrying about what happened at Bartek Springs. The Duc of Somes needs to be warned what's walking her province. We can't do anything with bits of information scattered all over the country so we have to consolidate, and we have to get a bard who Sings earth into those mountains. Jazep must have left a Song."

"With Jazep walking that way, we've spread the others with earth over the rest of the kingdom and with this opportunity to study the fifth kigh, we've shortened a number of walks . . ." His face went blank as he worked out the rough locations of the bards they could use. Suddenly, animation returned. "I'll go. And we needn't send the courier. I can ride with the recall myself."

In spite of everything, the corners of Liene's mouth quirked up. "Kovar, when was the last time you were on a horse?"

He frowned. "Ten, twelve years ago, why?"

Bards walked. It kept them connected to the land and the people. The few times it became necessary for a bard to ride, younger bards, those closest to their lives before the Bardic Hall, were invariably chosen.

"I think," Liene told him kindly, "we'd best leave this to those who ride for a living." When it looked as though he were going to protest, she added, "You wouldn't ask a courier to Sing the Fourth Quarter service, would you?"

"No." He sighed. "No, I wouldn't." His chin rose. "All right, then what?"

"That depends on His Majesty's orders." Liene stood

and smoothed down her robe, her palm lingering over the brown quarter. "I'll request an immediate audience. But, no matter what His Majesty says, this much is definite: Marija is not to try and find Jazep's body until she knows what she may be facing. We have few enough bards to risk their lives so foolishly." She could see a pair of kigh just outside the window, waiting for an answer to Marija's final question, their presence a reminder of the message they'd brought, a reminder of Jazep's death. All at once, she wanted to smack their pointy little ethereal faces. "Could you send her my decision please, Kovar. I don't think . . ." She shook her head and blinked away tears. "I don't think I could Sing right now."

By the time the Bardic Captain had slammed the door all the way open, Vree had been out of her chair reaching for the daggers she didn't wear within the Bardic Hall. When the winds blew into the room, she'd kept her back to the wall and slid toward the door. While the two bards were trying to calm the air spirits, she'd slipped out of the room.

This was bardic business, not hers. If they wanted her to know later, they'd tell her. A quick glance showed she hadn't been missed.

Aren't you the least bit curious about what the kigh are telling them? Gyhard asked.

No. Whenever the air spirits . . .

The kigh.

She rolled her eyes. *Fine. The kigh. Whenever *the kigh* blew around Karlene that violently, it was always bad news.*

Gyhard tried to remember every time the kigh had come to Karlene and decided, after a moment, that Vree was right. *I'd still like to know what they had to say.*

You know what we used to call people who always had to know what was going on? Jiir's targets—and then we'd bury them.

But this message might have been about us, he argued. He let her feel his desire to turn her around, back toward Kovar's office.

That, she declared, ignoring the feeling with the ease of much practice, *is all the more reason to make ourselves scarce. If they want us, they can find us when they calm down.*

After a moment's consideration, Gyhard muttered, *That's not a bad idea.*

Yeah, well, a lifetime in the army teaches a number of useful survival skills.

Halfway up the stairs, a bard Vree'd forgotten the name of rushed past, eyes streaming tears. The ex-assassin froze in place, head cocked.

What is it? Gyhard demanded.

A breeze touched Vree's cheek and moved on. "There's a lot of air moving around in here," she murmured.

What?

Something's wrong. Can't you feel it? Silently, she sped down the stairs to the first floor and headed for an exit. Although she had no reason for believing it, she was convinced that the arrival of the air spirits and the weeping bard were connected. *This building suddenly seems too small for what it has to hold.*

Fully aware that Vree's instincts had been developed by years of brutal training, Gyhard examined that statement from every possible angle. *I think you've been spending too much time with the bards,* he concluded as they stepped out into the rain.

Maybe. But listen.

From one of the upper windows came the same four notes, repeated over and over and over. The raw emotion lifted the hair off the back of her neck and made it impossible to tell if the voice was male or female. Eddies of wind, given definition by the rain, spun around the building.

Unwilling to leave the Citadel, Vree made her way to the cloister where she and Magda most often spent their afternoons. With a minimum of effort—more for practice than anything—she slipped unseen into the Healers' Hall and then out into the cloister. Choosing a bench that gave her a clear line of sight on both doors leading back into the building, she sat and stared out at the herb garden, deserted because of the rain.

What are we doing here? Gyhard demanded, moving restlessly within the confines of Vree's mind. *If we're hiding, we're not doing a very good job.*

We're waiting for something to happen.

Like what?

If I knew, we wouldn't have to wait. We could go looking for it.

She reminded him of a cat, sitting by a hole gnawed in the wall, certain that, in time, a mouse would appear. It wasn't that she was focused—he could almost feel her concentration spreading out to cover all possibilities—it was that *all* she was doing was waiting. It made him very uncomfortable although he wasn't entirely certain why. *Did they train you to do this?* When she nodded, he wondered if maybe that was it; that perhaps she was, in a way, training him, and he didn't want to learn to be an assassin. He wanted to fidget, to pace, to twiddle his thumbs—except that he didn't have thumbs of his own to twiddle. *Shouldn't we be doing something?*

Like what? she demanded in turn.

When Gyhard couldn't find an answer, he decided it might be time to change the subject. *Vree, about Bannon; I'm sure if you don't think you can face him, it can be arranged so that you don't have to.*

First of all, she snapped, * what makes you think I don't want to see him? And second, what makes you think anyone here could stop him if he wanted to see me?*

Her mental voice suggested she'd be equally unaffected by either scenario, but she couldn't block the chaotic mix of emotions churning just below the surface of her thoughts. Though it was far from that simple, guilt, longing, and fear seemed to predominate.

What are you more afraid of, Vree? Gyhard asked quietly. *That he won't want to see you or that he will?*

Maybe I'm afraid that the moment you see him, you'll jump back to his body. It suited you well enough before.

He couldn't be angry, not when he could feel her frightened uncertainty and knew she lashed out at him only because he was there. He could, however, be irritated by her desire to pick a fight rather than face an emotion or two. *I can't jump unless your body is dying or you push me out. So if I end up back in Bannon's body, it won't have been *my* choice.*

Just for a moment, he caught the memory of her thigh brushing his with nothing between them but scented water. Before he figured out whether it was his memory or hers, it was so strongly suppressed it took other, less heated memories, with it.

There's just so slaughtering much between us. Gyhard recognized Bannon in the plural rather than himself. *Or maybe,* she continued as she remembered a strained good-bye on the docks of the Capital, *it's that there's nothing between us anymore at all. That we used it all up. Besides . . .* She flicked one finger at a dead leaf back of the bench, the closest Gyhard could ever remember her coming to fidgeting. *He probably still hates you and you're still with me.*

A lot of people don't get along with their sibling's partners.

Vree snorted. *You're not exactly a partner. You're more like a . . .*

A parasite.

The lengthy silence became agreement.

She stared out at the rain, watching it bead on the broad leaves of the boneset, listening to it run down the cistern pipes, tasting it with every breath. Finally, she sighed. *We have to find you a body. Soon.*

Gyhard fought the urge to nod her head. *No argument here.*

The main door into the cloister flew open and Gerek charged through, momentum taking him right out into the garden.

That boy is too good-looking, Gyhard grumbled as Vree straightened out of her defensive crouch.

Murmuring a distracted affirmation, Vree stepped forward enough to be seen.

For a heartbeat, Gerek's worried frown disappeared, returning when he saw she was alone. Ignoring both the rain and the herbs crushed under his feet, he jerked forward. "Have you seen Maggi? I can't find her anywhere!"

"What's wrong?"

"The kigh are saying that Jazep is dead—it's all over the Citadel. He was one of Maggi's name-fathers. She's going to need me."

"Name-fathers," Vree repeated.

Gyhard made the connection first. *Didn't Magda tell us that Tadeus was one of her name-fathers?*

"Tadeus!" The name cast a deeper shadow over Gerek's

face when Vree asked Gyhard's question aloud. "Of course! He's going to be in pieces. She'd have headed right for him!" Spinning on one heel, he ran back into the building with Vree close behind.

No one got in their way.

They raced into an ominously quiet Bardic Hall, took the stairs to the third floor two at a time, and pounded down the corridor. As they neared the end of the hall and began to slow, a door opened.

Magda staggered from the room, pushed out by the hoarse sound of crying. When she saw her brother, her face crumpled, as though, seeing refuge at last, she'd let go of an artificial strength. She threw herself at him and burst into tears.

"Jazep . . ."

"I know, Maggi. I've heard." Enclosing her in the circle of his arms, he rested his cheek on her curls.

"I felt it when Tadeus found out," she sobbed. "I was on my way to a lesson and his pain, it just *hit* me and *hit* me and *hit* me. When I got here, he was Singing Jazep's name, over and over. It was like there was a whirlwind in the room with him—the kigh wouldn't let me get close to him. Then that Imperial fledgling he has, Ullious, he showed up and he Sang the kigh enough away that I could touch him and Tadeus just *looked* at me like his heart was broken and he stopping Singing and he started to cry and, oh Ger, I couldn't. I just couldn't."

"Couldn't what, Maggi?" Although his own face was wet, Gerek's voice was gentle and calm.

She twisted the loose folds of his shirt up in both fists. "I couldn't handle his pain and mine. He was . . . I was . . . It just *hurts* so much."

"Is Ullious still with him?"

"He is, but I'm *not.* I should be in there, Gerek. I'm *supposed* to be a healer!"

Trembling a little at the sudden rush of emotion, wishing there was a target she could hit to make it all better, Vree reached out and gently gripped Magda's hand where it was tangled in her brother's shirt. "Wounded healers need bandages themselves. You can't save anyone if you bleed to death."

"I'm not *bleeding.*" Her protest emerged damp and muffled from Gerek's chest.

"Your heart is bleeding. You've done what you can for Tadeus. Now you need to heal yourself."

"But . . ."

"No buts," Vree interrupted. She gave the younger woman's hand a final squeeze, released it, and stepped back, holding tightly to her own control.

Gerek swung his little sister up into his arms where she clung to him, her face pressed into the angle of his shoulder, the curve of her neck below the tangle of dark curls looking vulnerable and lost. "I'll take her to her room and stay with her," he said. "Where will you be if she needs you?"

Startled, Vree stared at him. "Needs me?" she repeated.

Settling Magda more securely in his arms, Gerek rested an expression on Vree that held too many variables for her to understand. "Yes, needs you. Where will you be?"

"I guess my room, but . . ."

"No buts."

She watched him carry his sister down the hall and moved only when they disappeared into a stairwell.

Where to now? Gyhard asked, the tone of his voice reminding her of Gerek's expression.

I guess to my room. Wondering how much pain a blind man had to be in to *look* at someone as though his heart were broken, she turned on one heel and walked silently back to the room she'd been given.

Kovar arrived just as she did. His eyes were red and his lashes clung together in clumps. "Have you heard?" When she nodded, he swallowed and visibly squared his shoulders under the quartered robe. "How much?"

"Only that a bard named Jazep is dead."

There's more, Gyhard murmured.

No slaughtering shit. She opened the door and gestured for Kovar to enter. "You look like you need to sit down," she said abruptly. "I can make tea."

"No, no tea, thank you." But he accepted the offer of a place to sit, lowering himself into a chair as though he'd broken ribs and not taken the time to have them bound. Lacing long, ink-stained fingers in his lap, he looked up at her and said, "We need your help."

Vree cocked her head to one side and moved her weight forward onto the balls of her feet. Not quite a fighting stance but ready for the eventuality. "You want me to kill the person or persons who killed Jazep."

The Bardic Second was so surprised his mouth opened and closed, but no sound emerged. Finally, he managed a strangled, "Not that. No."

"Then what?" Vree relaxed slightly, refusing to acknowledge the relief his answer gave.

"We need your knowledge of the abomination who was Kars."

Kars?

She couldn't entirely prevent Gyhard's cry from leaving her mouth. It burst past her lips as a truncated, wordless wail. Regaining control, she wrapped herself around him, protecting him as she would have protected Bannon had he been hit from ambush.

Kovar misunderstood. "I know. You're shocked. You thought that part of your life was over. But something is in Shkoder causing the dead to walk, and we can't think of who or what else it could be." He drew a shaking hand across his forehead. "We have Karlene's recall, of course, but if we are to defeat this thing, we need to add your knowledge as well."

Vree waited. Silently.

"Yours and Gyhard's."

Gyhard stirred out of his shock. *They want to put *me* under recall?* When Vree repeated his questions and the bard nodded, he asked, his mental voice incredulous, *Do they know what that means?*

They should by now. "Sorry," she said, spreading her hands. "I can't risk that."

Looking as though he'd expected her response, Kovar nodded, somehow managing to sound both disappointed and relieved. "I understand, but I had to ask."

Vree, what are you doing? He could sense the lie but not what it was about, memories of Kars—as a young man, as an old man—kept getting in the way.

Before she could answer, Kovar continued, his tone so incredibly reassuring Vree suspected he was using some sort of bardic trick and she steeled herself against it. "We still need your memories, though, and I personally assure you there'll be no danger of Gyhard trying to take control while you're in recall."

Why that suspicious, son of a . . .

Shut up! Vree snapped and added aloud, "All right. When?"

"It'll have to be tomorrow morning. There isn't a bard in the hall who could do it tonight." His face folded along lines drawn by grief and he looked ten years older as he slowly pulled himself out of the chair and back onto his feet. He paused at the door. "Thank you for helping, Vree. We'll be Singing for Jazep at the Center tonight; you're welcome to attend."

As the sound of his footsteps faded down the hall, Vree closed the shutters, lit a lamp, and pulled her pack out from under the bed.

Vree, what are you doing?

Kars is our business, not theirs.

I can't . . .

Can't what? she interrupted. *Can't face him? You've said you failed him twice.* Gyhard jerked as her intentional blow hit home and, making no effort to block out the pain she'd caused him, she forced herself to go on. *I say that third time pays for all.*

We don't even know where he is!

Then we eavesdrop a little and find out where the message came from. I can track him from there. One of the bulky knit sweater things took up more room than she liked, but if it was about to get as cold as everyone said, she supposed she'd better take it.

Vree.

What? You started this, Gyhard, don't you want to finish it?

Not exactly. I want it to be finished. He could feel the memory of the ancient throat between his hands—Bannon's hands—could see behind the rheumy eyes the young man he'd pushed over the edge into insanity then abandoned an impossible number of years before. He could have—would have—killed him then, but one of the walking dead had intervened. He wasn't sure he could bring himself to that point again.

You were alone last time. This time, you've got me.

Stop reading my mind.

He felt her almost smile. *Strong emotions, remember?*

But if you're afraid I'll take control . . .

The almost smile disappeared. *Is that why you think I refused to let them recall you? You think I'm stupid enough to believe you'd try to take over with half a dozen slaughtering bards marching through our minds?*

No, but . . .

What happened between you and Kars is private. You shouldn't have to share it with everyone who can carry a tune. She bent over to fight with a stiff buckle and Gyhard suddenly realized she was embarrassed, that she was trying to distance herself from her words.

I'm sorry.

She shrugged. *It's all right.*

And thank you.

Look, I said it's all right!

He drew back before she could push him away, willing to give her what little space he could, maintaining too tenuous a hold on his own emotions to deal with hers.

Vree laid her daggers out on the bed and lightly touched the empty wrist sheath. Allowing for slight differences in weight, Bannon had an identical set—except, of course, that Bannon still had a *set*.

For the moment, memories of Kars had wrapped Gyhard in an emotional soup too thick to see through. It hadn't yet occurred to him that in going after his past, they'd be avoiding hers.

Seven

Twisted up in memories of Kars, Gyhard had been paying little attention to Vree's preparations. He'd roused briefly when she'd discovered that the dead were walking in Bartek Springs and then allowed himself to be sucked back down into a roiling mix of emotions. As he hadn't noticed her turn off the lamp or open the shutters, it came as a bit of a shock to realize they were perched on the window ledge outside her room and he hastily quelled an urge to propel her body back inside. *Vree, why are we going out the window?*

So no one sees us. We're going to need as large a lead as we can get.

But . . . He refused to look as she pushed off the narrow ledge, dropped, and caught herself on fingers and toes. The pack pulled at her shoulders and she compensated for its extra weight. *But we're heading down into an enclosed courtyard. We're going to have to go back into the Hall or over the . . .*

Wall? she finished for him, dropping onto the worn flagstones. They were still damp from the day's rain, but the sky was clear overhead, the bowl of night filled with stars. After an unhappy glance up at the unfamiliar constellations, she followed the shadow path along the foundations of the building.

Vree.

Look, since you're new at this, I'll explain. The windows overlooking the courtyard held no signs of life. Based on their evidence, the Bardic Hall might well have been empty. *We can't go out the gate—there's always a bard on it and we can't exactly pretend to be someone else. Nothing overlooks this piece of wall except the Bardic Hall.

The bards are at the center, Singing for Jazep. If we go over the wall here, no one will see us.*

It very nearly made sense. *The kigh can see us.*

So slaughtering what? By the time the bards ask them where we've gone, we'll be a good six or seven hours closer to Kars. Splaying both hands out against the huge, squared stones used to build the wall around the Citadel, she smiled. Although the outside rose perpendicular from the street, the inside, in the interests of strength and stability, angled gently in from the base to the crown. *We're not hiding, this is a race,* she continued as she started to climb. *We have to get to Kars first.*

And when they use the kigh to send messages ahead?

To stop us? Lying flat, she rolled across the top of the wall and started down the other side. *I don't think so.*

About to protest further, Gyhard remembered that Vree had been a military assassin for five years. Two years longer than assassins usually managed to outwit the odds. She'd never gone after a target that hadn't known she was coming, and they'd never been able to stop her. What chance would the bards of Shkoder, who really had no idea of her capabilities, have against her? He only hoped that would occur to the bards of Shkoder.

He briefly noted how fast Vree was moving and how tiny the edges of stone she gripped were, then quickly turned his attention elsewhere. It wouldn't take much of a twitch to send them plummeting to the ground. The trouble was, elsewhere almost immediately became thoughts of Kars.

Gyhard had wondered once if new love had called back the old, if the gods or the fates or the Circle or whatever anyone of a dozen different religions wanted to call it had set Kars in his path in order for him to close the door on the past and open it on the future. He didn't believe in coincidence, especially not when he'd had his nose rubbed in the past with a thoroughness that had made it impossible to ignore.

That he'd failed Kars a second time had been no fault of his. He'd done everything he could.

Apparently, it wasn't enough.

The knowledge that Kars continued to live, somewhere, could be ignored. He'd had lifetimes of practice ignoring

it. But something had propelled Kars across the border into
Shkoder. And something had seen to it that he got the
news.

He was being given another chance.

Vree was right. He had to take it.

Staying in Elbasan and letting the bards deal with the
situation would release Kars from the trap but leave him
in it. If he and Vree were to ever have a life together—
even as strange a life as they were living now—he had to
be the one who finally laid Kars to rest.

As Vree dropped to the street and checked to make sure
they'd been unobserved, Gyhard gave himself a mental
shake and decided it was probably a good thing they were
leaving the bards behind. Melodrama appeared to be
catching.

They taken maybe six steps on level ground when they
heard horses approaching from behind, shod hooves chiming against the cobblestones.

Vree?

The wide road encircling the Citadel wall provided no
cover and the night was too bright to hide them.

Vree refused to turn although she could feel how much
Gyhard wanted to. *Ignore it. It has nothing to do with us.
Even if someone saw us going over the wall, they wouldn't
have sent out the cavalry.*

The horses drew closer. Close enough to hear the creak
of harness, to catch a whiff of the stable, to feel the warm
bulk of the animals looming up behind them.

"We'll get there a lot faster if we ride."

"We?" Vree demanded before she finished turning.

Magda let the hooded cloak fall back. An afternoon of
crying had left her face blotchy, but her eyes were dry and
she carried her chin at a determined angle. "I knew you
were going as soon as I worked past Jazep being dead and
actually thought about how he . . . how he died. Gyhard
has responsibilities to Kars he *has* to honor or they'll eat
at him, at both of you, all the rest of your lives. I have
responsibilities to you. I *can't* let you go alone."

"You can't go with us."

The younger woman held out the extra set of reins. "You
can't stop me. I won't go back willingly and if you take me

back, you know you won't get out again. This is your only chance to get to Kars first, and I'm afraid I'm a part of it."

Vree's eyes narrowed. "I could knock you out and leave you here. Take both horses. It might be a couple of hours until you're found."

"You won't."

"You're very sure of yourself."

"No." Magda shook her head and half-smiled. "I'm very sure of you."

The generous curves of her mouth pressed into a thin, irritated line, Vree secured her pack behind the saddle and mounted. "The king, your uncle, is not going to allow this."

"The king, my uncle, will have to catch us." Magda flicked a wet curl out of the corner of her mouth. "These are the same horses our couriers ride—the same horses Imperial couriers have been riding since His Majesty got the idea and the stock from the Empire, so you *know* how fast they move. By tomorrow morning when they notice we're gone, we'll be three or four stations down the Coast Road and even if the bards get a message ahead of us, we'll have a huge lead."

"If the bards get a message ahead of us," Vree pointed out acerbically, "they'll try to stop us."

The pale oval of Magda's face tilted to one side. "Stop *you?*" she asked.

As Vree had said almost the same thing to Gyhard, she had little room left for argument. "This is going to get you into a lot of trouble."

"Why? I'm not a prisoner here." Her chin rose in a motion Gyhard recognized from days and nights of watching Vree. "I can leave if I like."

"What about studying to be a healer?" Vree leaned forward and stroked a silken neck. "What about stealing these horses?"

"I'm not *stealing* anything," Magda protested indignantly. "Healers are *allowed* to use the couriers' stables so they can get to emergencies as fast as possible. Now I may only be an apprentice healer, but I think that the dead walking in Shkoder qualifies as an *emergency*. As for the rest, you're my patient. I can't abandon you. That's covered under Healers' Oaths. Besides . . ." She sighed and her tone gentled. "I heal the fifth kigh, and healing Kars is part of healing you."

She has a slaughtering answer for everything.

Vree, she can't come. It's going to be hard enough dealing with Kars. If she's there . . . Gyhard's voice got lost in the painful prospect of once more seeing the ruin the years and his interference had made of Kars. *Dying has to be easier than having your heart ripped out over and over.* The ancient image grew younger; the chin pointed; the hair grew thick and brown and curly; the skin darkened; the brows lifted to a sardonic angle. Not Kars. Bannon. Which was when he realized that neither the pain nor the thought accompanying it was his alone

The second realization seeped around the edges of the first. Bannon would be arriving shortly with Prince Otavas. If they went after Kars, Vree wouldn't have to face him. His rush of anger at having his personal demons used as an excuse to avoid hers smashed apart the barriers between them, crashed into her fear, and ground to a halt, its momentum destroyed.

Vree stiffened. The horse, who'd been standing quietly while she'd been adjusting the stirrups, began to move forward. *Bannon can wait. Kars can't.* She yanked back on the reins. *If the bards get to him first, you'll have lost your chance.*

You were hoping I wouldn't notice. You didn't want me to know how afraid you were.

Her teeth were clenched so tightly together both temples throbbed. *Assassins are trained to face their fears. I . . .* The barriers were down. She had no self-image left to save. *I can't face him. Not yet.*

Then it's a good thing you're not an assassin anymore, isn't it?

I'm sorry. She didn't know what exactly she was sorry for, so she hoped he did.

"It would be a healthy thing, a distinct step forward if you two managed to resolve *something* in your lives. At least you both know what has to be done in order to deal with Kars."

Breathing heavily, Vree looked down at Magda's fingers lying across her wrist. Until the young healer had spoken, she hadn't even felt the touch. If she needed proof she was no longer an assassin, there it was.

This was a private conversation, child, Gyhard told her shortly.

Magda snatched her hand back as though the fingers had been burned. Her lower lip started to tremble. "I only wanted to help. Vree was looking so . . . I mean, I'm a healer, and I have to do *something!*"

Gyhard used Vree's lungs to sigh. *You know, her wanting to go along probably has as much to do with a response to Jazep's death as with us.*

No shit. As Magda sniffed, Vree reached between the horses and gently grabbed her shoulder. "He's . . ." *How do you say pissed off in Shkoden?*

I don't need you to explain me to her, Vree.

"He's upset because we have so little privacy and so every bit we lose seems too large." She tightened her grip for a moment then let go. "But it's a good thing you're going with us."

"Really?"

"Yeah."

Vree!

Maybe healing Kars is a part of healing you. Us. Besides, she's right. We don't have a choice. We have a saying in the army: don't waste your strength trying to push a dagger through armor. It only dulls the blade and irritates the enemy.

Very profound.

Thank you.

The moist sound of horseshit hitting cobblestones echoed against the Citadel wall. Magda giggled, just a little hysterically. "We'd better get moving before we're caught by a garden-wagon and escorted home at pitchfork point."

As Vree settled into the rhythm of her horse's gait, she revised travel plans. If they managed to avoid bardic entanglements, Magda's presence had cut their time on the road at least in half. Which had to be weighed against Magda's presence complicating things rather significantly.

Then let's look at the bright side, Gyhard put in wearily. *If the king's niece, the only healer they've got who can heal the fifth kigh, has to go tearing around the country, at least there's no one she's safer doing it with than you.*

Vree grinned, thinking of the omnipresent trio of guards,

and of Gerek who shadowed every moment she and Magda spent together. *You really think His Majesty and her brother are going to believe that?*

About as much as I think His Majesty and her brother are likely to sprout wings and fly.

"I assure you, Your Majesty, that Magda is completely safe."

"You also assured me," Theron growled, both hands pressed white-knuckled against his desk, "that the assassin would remain under bardic control. Now you tell me she's galloping down the South Coast Road with my niece." He held the Bardic Captain in a basilisk glare. "Which am I to believe?"

Projecting a calm she wasn't entirely feeling, Liene spread her hands. "The kigh are watching them, Majesty. They're not trying to hide."

"That's very helpful." The words squeezed out from between clenched teeth. "But I don't care about the kigh. What are *you* going to do?"

Liene blinked. "Do, Majesty?" They hadn't realized until they'd sent a fledgling to her room after breakfast that Vree was gone—they'd thought she'd merely missed the meal and had been concerned that she might be ill. When she wasn't in her room, they'd assumed she was with Magda and sent the fledgling to the Healers' Hall only to find Magda missing as well and an irritated Captain of Couriers demanding to know why an apprentice had signed for two horses.

Kovar had immediately Called a kigh—his summons so peremptory four of them appeared and nearly blew him over—and sent them searching for the missing assassin. The two senior bards then began to put the pieces together and by the time the kigh reappeared, their answer came as no surprise. Liene had headed immediately for the palace. She hadn't actually thought of much beyond getting to the king before he heard his niece was missing from a non-bardic source.

"Do," she repeated. "Majesty, as I said, Magda is in no danger. She was, according to Cecilie, the bard on the gate, under no compulsion when she left the Citadel. We believe that the three of them—Vree, Gyhard, and Magda—are heading into Somes in order to deal with Kars."

"Who is—if I remember Karlene's recall correctly, which

I assure you, Captain, I do—an insane Cemandian who Sings the dead to life and has recently killed a bard." Theron's face began to darken. "Not to mention, he was once Gyhard's lover and was not killed by this same assassin although she had every opportunity to do so and had apparently been trained never to miss. You'll have to explain to me, Captain, how you can possibly stand there and say that Magda is in no danger!"

Considerably more worried about the vein throbbing on Theron's temple than she was about Magda, Liene stepped toward the desk. "Majesty, please believe me when I say that both Vree and Gyhard view Magda as the only person who might possibly be able to help them. They would never, ever hurt her and will, in fact, do everything they can to protect her. There is no one in Shkoder, Majesty," she continued soothingly, "who would be able to get past Vree to Magda."

Unfortunately, the king was past being soothed. "No one except this bardic abomination!" His left hand curled into a fist. "The very thing she's rushing off to face! I want her stopped, do you hear me! Send a kigh to every bard between her and Somes!" He paused and his left shoulder flexed forward, but before the Bardic Captain could explain that they'd already begun to move the only bard in the area, he went on. "And *then,* you throw everything you've got at this thing that is killing my people!" His expression changed between one heartbeat and the next, pain wiping out anger.

"Majesty?"

Beads of sweat suddenly appeared on his forehead, combining and trickling down both temples. He opened his mouth, but no sound emerged. Right hand clutching at his tunic front, he slumped forward, his face smacking into the desk.

"Majesty!" Liene raced to his side just as a tentative knock sounded against the office door. "What!" she snapped, one hand pressed on a pulse point in the king's throat, relief that he still lived overwhelming fifty years of vocal training.

A section of paneling swung open and a page stepped into the room. "Majesty, the . . ." Her jaw dropped.

"Get the king's healer! Now!"

The page whirled around and raced away, leaving the door ajar behind her.

As Liene eased Theron back against the leather padding of his chair, the second page on duty poked his head into the room. Eyes impossibly wide under ginger brows and every freckle standing out against pale skin, he crept forward, shoes making no noise against the thick carpet. "Majesty?"

Liene jerked around. "Don't do that!" she snarled.

The page ignored the old woman, his gaze locked on the king. "What's wrong with him?"

"Do I look like a healer?" When the boy seemed about to cry, she clutched at control and managed to gentle her voice. "I don't know what's wrong, but he needs your help."

"My help?"

"That's right. Go get Her Majesty and bring her here as quickly as you can. Be careful not to frighten her."

He sniffed. "What about the Heir? Should I get Princess Onele?"

Her hand on Theron's shoulder, Liene nodded, grateful that the boy had thought of it. *He's ten years younger than I am. This shouldn't be happening.* "Yes. Get her, too."

"Where you headed, Healer?"

"Somes." Magda covered a yawn with the back of her hand then scrawled her name across the bottom of the form that would get them fresh horses. She began to make the apprentice symbol, realized what she was doing, and flushed.

The stablemaster only laughed. "Haven't been a healer too long, have you?"

"No, in fact, I . . ." Exhaustion wiped out the rest of the thought and she stared blankly up at him, unable to remember the lie she'd been about to tell.

"Never mind." He looked as though he were about to pat her on the head. "I'll just check this against the list the Healers' Hall sends me out from Elbasan." Yanking open the single drawer under the scarred table, he pulled out a folded sheet, swept aside some straw and spread it out. "Can't just have anyone riding off on the King's horses," he explained as he ran a thick finger down the first column of names.

Vree shifted her weigh forward and wished she had her second throwing dagger.

Gyhard quickly shifted her weight back. *You're not going to have to kill him.*

How do you know?

Magda would never put us in a situation where that was the only option.

She's tired. Tired people make mistakes.

Not one that so completely contravenes everything she believes in..

Big words. What the slaughter do they mean?

She wouldn't make a mistake that big.

"Ah, here you are. See that loopy bit there? Unmistakable." He turned frowning slightly. "I see you're still an apprentice on the Second Quarter list. Funny you should make full healer before Third Quarter Festival."

Magda shrugged, making no effort to hide how exhausted she was. "*I'd* have waited, but they need my specialty as soon as possible in Somes and they couldn't spare a healer to travel all that way with me. If I was going to go, and I had to, I had to go as a healer."

"Poor thing. Missed your ceremony, then tossed on a horse and pounded against a saddle for days on end." Clucking his tongue, he looked over at Vree. "If you're her helper, Southerner, you ought to be helping her up to bed. She's nearly dead on her feet."

Startled, Vree took a closer look at the younger woman. They'd been on the move since just after full dark and it was now well into morning. Stops had been infrequent and the two previous times they'd changed horses, Vree hadn't bothered going inside. There were purple-gray shadows under Magda's eyes, her mouth was slack, her shoulders slumped, and she carried her head as if it were too heavy for her neck.

You're used to your own rather remarkable endurance, Gyhard reminded her, feeling her guilt. *You're not used to traveling with someone who doesn't share it.* He well remembered how Bannon's body had effortlessly done everything he'd asked of it.

Vree shoved aside a memory of Gyhard/Bannon riding beside her, laughing, eating, bathing . . . and lightly touched Magda on the arm. "He's right. You need to rest."

"We need to keep moving." But it was almost a question.

"You'll do no one no good if you fall off the horse and break your neck, Healer," the stablemaster pointed out, kindly. "I got a nice quiet corner of the mow for just this kind of situation. You two head up there and lie down and I'll see that you're woke in three hours."

"Three hours," Magda repeated.

Vree met the stablemaster's eyes. There appeared to be nothing behind his smile but an honest desire to help. "Come on." She put her arm around the younger woman's shoulders. "We can spare three hours."

A horse blanket spread over the straw was a better bed than many Vree had slept in. Taking a deep breath, she allowed her muscles to relax and was nearly asleep when an unfamiliar sound snapped her fully alert. Unfamiliar to her; Gyhard obviously knew what it was.

Imperial Army service starts at fifteen, he murmured. *Don't soldiers ever get homesick?*

Not around assassins, she told him shortly, rolling up on one elbow. Rays of sunlight, glittering with dust, slanted through cracks and knotholes, providing more than enough light to see thin shoulders shaking. "Magda? what's wrong?"

"Jazep's dead." Nearly lost against the crook of her elbow, the childlike wail took years off Magda's age.

Vree reached out a hand, but left it hovering in midair, uncertain of what to do.

Hold her.

Are you sure?

Trust me.

I don't know how. She'd meant it as a bald statement of fact, but it came out more like a desperate apology.

Yes, you do. He didn't want to say it, didn't want to remind her, but he couldn't allow her to believe she was unable to give comfort, couldn't allow jealousy to cause her such pain. *Just pretend that Magda is Bannon.*

Bannon? Slowly, hesitantly, ready to pull back if it were the wrong thing to do, Vree reached out and drew Magda into the circle of her arms.

Magda pressed herself against Vree's side. Her sobs

turned to ragged breathing, evened out, and in a few moments she was asleep, too tired to grieve further.

Resting her cheek on the soft cap of dark curls, Vree shifted to settle herself more comfortably beneath the warm weight and tried to work out how long it had been since she'd held another person; if she'd *ever* been granted the kind of trust that allowed sleep in such a position. Breathing in the scent of sweat and hay and horses, she forced herself to relax and grant that trust in return.

Just before sleep claimed them both, Gyhard realized that Vree hadn't reacted to his instinctive control of her body down in the stable and he found himself suddenly unsure if that was a good thing or a bad.

Her Royal Highness, the Princess Onele, Heir to the crown of Shkoder, looked grim as she left her parents' bedchamber and entered the solar where the Bardic Captain and the Chancellor were waiting, their mutual animosity lost in shared worry. She nodded at Liene. "He wants to see you." Her lips twisted up in a humorless smile. "And he says you're not to start composing any eulogies."

"Highness, is he . . ."

"In a very bad mood," Onele interrupted. "Use as much Voice as you have to to keep him from losing his temper."

"Yes, Highness."

Neither of them meant it, but the exchange lightened the tensions in the room just a little.

"When His Majesty is finished with you, come and see me. We have things to discuss."

"Yes, Highness."

As the Bardic Captain left the solar, leaning heavily on her cane, Onele took a deep breath and squared her shoulders under the faded shirt she'd been wearing when summoned from the stables. Unlike most children, she'd been raised with the full knowledge that one day her father would die. *"When you are Queen, Highness . . ."* had begun every lesson, the implication clear, and she had to admit that increasingly over the last few years she'd been impatient to get on with the job she'd been trained to do. She was thirty-four years old. Long past time to finish her apprenticeship. Now that the job was almost hers, she found that she wouldn't mind putting it off for a little while yet.

"When you are Queen, Highness . . ."
When my father dies . . .

"Highness?"

The Heir gave herself a shake and focused on the Chancellor.

"Highness, Prince Otavas' ship has passed the outer harbor and will be mooring shortly. Everything is in readiness, but . . ." Chancellor Rozele spread her hands.

Onele nodded. "But obviously I can't go down to greet my Imperial cousin as planned. I don't suppose Aunt Milena's boy is still here?"

"No, Highness, he went home." And, good riddance, her expression added. "I had thought perhaps His Grace, Heir of Ohrid . . ."

"Perfect. It'll keep him from worrying about his sister and there's only what, five years between them?"

"Four, Highness. Unfortunately, we haven't been able to find His Grace." Her lips pursed. "He didn't spend the night in the Citadel and has not yet returned."

Onele briefly closed her eyes. It was just like Gerek not to be around when he was needed. "Who's left?"

The Chancellor glanced down at the floor, as though looking for inspiration in the polished wood. "Princess Jelena is barely three years younger than Prince Otavas, Highness and, as Heir Apparent, would bring a certain diplomatic sense of rank to the meeting."

Jelena's mother frowned. "But she's so shy."

"The pressure on her will be slight, Highness. Although an official duty, it is also a family duty." The shared knowledge that Princess Jelena would, given her position, have to overcome that shyness, lingered behind the Chancellor's words. "If one of the older bards took the duty, she'd feel like she had someone to depend on."

Olena sighed. It seemed her father's illness would also force her daughter forward into new responsibility. "Have her sent to my quarters. I'll tell her myself while I change." Her hand on the door, she paused. "I want to see His Grace when he returns to the palace."

"I'll have him informed, Highness."

Uncertain of what to expect when she entered the royal bedchamber, Liene swept her gaze over healer, consort, and king.

The Healer, Jokubas i'Brigita a'Jokubas, looked too young for the critical position he held—although honesty forced Liene to admit that, of late, everyone looked too young. Standing by the head of the bed, one thin hand resting lightly on Theron's shoulder so that he could constantly monitor the king's condition, his expression was far too serene to give anything away.

Light diagnostic trance, Liene noted as she approached.

Llyana, sitting close against the bed and holding one of Theron's hands in hers, could not maintain a mask over her emotions. Fear, grief, fear, love, fear—they chased each other around her face. Her grip suggested that if the turning of the Circle intended to take the king from her, it would have to pry him loose one finger at a time.

The king himself was a pleasant surprise. Propped up on a pile of pillows, his face had regained its normal color, and, although he looked very tired, his eyes were clear.

"You're to tell Annice she's to stay right where she is."

Not entirely finished bowing, Liene frowned. "Majesty?"

Theron snorted. "I know my sister, Captain. Her daughter is racing toward an insane bard in the company of an assassin and I've been confined to my bed. One such incident alone would have been enough to bring her here, the two together surely will." Theron sipped at the mug he held and grimaced. "Willow bark tea. Apparently, I've got to drink a cup of this swill every day for the rest of my life."

"It will help you live a good long time, Majesty," Jokubas murmured.

Theron swallowed and his upper lip curled. "I'm so thrilled."

Llyana leaned forward—fear, grief, fear, love, fear making another circuit. "The Bardic Captain will have to leave if you grow excited," she warned.

He pulled his fingers free and patted her hand. "You want to see excited? Dealing with Annice, that would excite me. Captain, see that she stays right where she is. King Rajmund's not quite as ambitious as his mother but I don't trust him not to try and take advantage of the situation when he hears I'm laid up. The last thing we need is a war with Cemandia, so Annice must stay on top of the situation at the pass. Tell her that and make sure she listens."

"Majesty," Liene sighed, thankful she was no longer

strong enough to Sing a kigh all the way to the border and that the Song would fall to Kovar, "if you have a way to make Annice listen, I'd love to hear it."

"Nees?" Sitting on a stump at the edge of the creek, Stasya watched Annice pace, more than a little worried by how quiet she'd grown. They'd spent the night Singing for Jazep at the small Center in the village, had shared memories of him with Pjerin and the others who'd been touched by his Song, and had been walking alone together with their grief when the kigh carrying Kovar's message had found them. "Nees, are you all right?"

Annice started, pulled out of her reverie. Her eyes were red and puffy and she moved back and forth along the path as though movement kept dark possibilities at bay. "I will be when we hear that Maggi's safe," she said, although she didn't sound convinced.

"We should tell Pjerin . . ."

That stopped the pacing. "We tell Pjerin nothing until we know Maggi's okay. We don't want him charging off after her like a hero out of a bad ballad."

Stasya, who considered Magda to be hers as much as Annice's or Pjerin's, and who'd Sung a kigh in pursuit immediately upon hearing Kovar's message while Annice still stared openmouthed and disbelieving into the air, dropped her gaze to the muddy toes of her boots and forced herself to ask, "And if Maggi isn't okay?"

"She is." Annice lifted her head and a muscle jumped in her jaw. "She has to be. Kovar wouldn't lie to us about something like that." Her tone made the words very nearly a warning.

"And His Majesty?"

"He seems to want me to stay here."

"Are you going to?"

"I don't know." Ignoring the damp, she sank cross-legged to the ground and picked up a double handful of earth. "First Jazep's killed, then Maggi runs off, then Theron's heart tries to quit—I feel as if someone's been smashing at my head with a . . . with a . . ."

"Nees?"

Eyes locked on the soil dribbling out from between her fingers, Annice murmured, "Stas, something's wrong."

"Center it, Annice! Stop saying that!" Exhausted by a night of grieving and the morning's news, Stasya had reached her limit. She leaped to her feet and, breathing heavily, glared down at Annice. "Either tell me exactly what's wrong, or shut up about it!"

"The dead are walking, Stas. I can feel the earth recoil from their tread. Life flees before them. Sorrow travels by their side."

"Annice, stop it!" Arms wrapped around her body, Stasya shivered as the sun disappeared behind the tattered edges of a gray cloudbank. "You're scaring me!"

Blinking in the dull light, feeling as though she'd just been granted a glimpse of the horror that existed in shadows beyond the safe enclosure of the Circle, Annice wiped her shaking hands against her thighs. "I'm not surprised; I'm scaring me." She drew in a long breath and let it out slowly, searching for strength. "There's more."

"More? More what? More dead?"

"Jazep . . ."

Stasya squatted down and brushed a strand of hair back off Annice's face. "Nees, we know Jazep is dead," she said gently. "Don't you remember? The kigh brought the news last night."

"An air kigh brought the news." Annice caught up the other woman's hand in hers and stared up into the dark eyes. "But Jazep Sang only earth. I have to *do* something, Stas. I can't just sit here and let this go on."

"But His Majesty said . . ."

"His Majesty said what?" Annice snapped sounding more like herself. "That I wasn't to go to Elbasan?" She stood, hauling Stasya up with her. "He doesn't want me by his sickbed, fine." Her tone suggested it wasn't fine at all. Stasya winced. "As it happens, I have no intention of going to *Elbasan.*"

Wakened by the clash and clatter of a procession going up Hill Street toward the Citadel, Gerek dragged himself out of bed and stumbled naked to the window, cracking the shutter just enough to peer outside. The flags and pennants flying above the crowd told him everything he needed to know.

Looks like Prince Otavas arrived safely. Realizing that

his mouth tasted like the inside of a boot, he turned and tried to remember what he was doing in what was obviously the best room in a less than quality inn.

He'd left Maggi at the Healers' Hall and gone to the service the bards were holding for Jazep at the Center—where it had finally hit him that the man who'd brought him an orphaned fox cub tucked down inside his vest, was dead. He'd gone out and gotten drunk. Very drunk. After that, things became a little less clear.

Crossing over to the washstand, he sniffed the water in the chipped pitcher and drank the lot, ignoring the handleless mug.

"Better," he husked, wincing as the cheering outside momentarily increased in volume. He didn't see why the prince couldn't travel through the city just a little more quietly.

His pants were under the bed and as he dragged them out, a brass button spun across the floor. Teeth gritted, he bent and picked it up. Stamped with the crowned ship of Shkoder, it seemed to have been torn from the uniform of His Majesty's navy.

Gerek sighed as the memories returned. He didn't feel any better about Jazep being dead but, all things being enclosed, he'd gained new respect for the navy. As the young woman he'd spent the latter part of the night with had long since left—he vaguely remembered her explaining she had to be back on board ship at dawn—he dressed and headed downstairs to pay the reckoning.

Not feeling up to either the crowd on the street or the chaos Prince Otavas would be causing at the Citadel, he spent an hour in the common room remembering Jazep over biscuits and sausage gravy. When he finally stepped outside, a wind blew up in the harbor and nearly knocked him over.

He recognized Annice's touch. For the last seventeen years, ever since Maggi's mother had come to live in Ohrid, breezes that blew where breezes had no business blowing had pushed him around.

Fear quickly took the place of his initial irritation. As far as he knew, Annice was still in Ohrid—as far from Elbasan as possible while remaining in Shkoder. In order for her to be sending the kigh after him instead of just sending a message through one of the bards at the Hall, something had to be wrong. Very wrong. More wrong than Jazep's death alone could account for.

Breathing Magda's name like a prayer, he raced up the hill, wishing he'd picked an inn a little farther from the harbor. When his heels hit the cobblestones, painful reverberations bounced about his skull. Breezes continued to swirl around him, completely oblivious to the direction of the actual wind. He wasn't surprised when the bard on the gate was waiting for him.

"What's she want?" he panted. "What's she trying to tell me?"

Ziven frowned and Sang the notes that made up Annice's name. Half a dozen kigh expanded their circle to include him then, message finally delivered, sped off in different directions—one of them twisting its ethereal body around so that it appeared to blow in one of Gerek's ears and out the other as it left. "She says that you're to go after your sister and then find Jazep."

"You mean, find Jazep's body?"

"That's what I mean, but that's not what Nees said." Ziven blinked back tears and half shrugged. "She probably doesn't believe it's true. She probably doesn't believe he's really dead."

"I find it hard to believe myself," Gerek admitted. "And what does she mean 'go after my sister'?" He wiped the sweat off his brow with the sleeve of his shirt and scowled. "What's she talking about? When I left last night, Maggi was safely tucked in her room. Where's she gone?"

Glancing pointedly at the pair of guards also on duty at the gate, Ziven said, "Princess Onele wants to see you."

No answer could only be a bad answer. Heart pounding, Gerek stepped forward, anxiety and frustration warring against a lifetime of training. He was younger, bigger, stronger—his fingers curled to grab the bard's tunic—he'd find out what happened to Maggi if he had to shake Ziven so hard his teeth shattered.

Ziven made no attempt to move away. "Princess Onele," he repeated calmly, his tone adding a quiet counterpoint of both sympathy and warning, "wants to see you."

*   *   *

"I asked you here to arrange for you to spend some time with His Highness."

Ullious, who'd met the Imperial Ambassador twice in the three years he'd been studying at the Bardic Hall—just after he'd arrived and at a court function he'd been Witnessing under supervision—stared at the man in astonishment. "Me, sir?"

The ambassador bit back a sigh. Having been informed at the last possible moment that the king was under a healer's care, he'd had an exhausting morning tiptoeing around the wide-eyed self-consciousness of the *child* they'd sent to welcome the prince. He'd been as diplomatic as he knew how, but Princess Jelena had not responded well to the formal phrasing. The highlight of his morning had involved Prince Otavas telling him to stop being such a bully and then moving to stand between him and the grateful young princess in a blatant breach of protocol.

"Yes, you," he said shortly. "His Highness likes bards. You're studying to be one. It is the duty of all Imperial citizens in Shkoder to make His Highness welcome. You're an Imperial citizen. I don't see where there's a problem."

Ullious flushed and tried to explain, using the most formal of the ambassador's titles in order to stress the seriousness of his objection. "Imperial Voice, I was only a carter before I began training to be a bard. I'd have no idea of how to behave around an Imperial Prince."

This time, the ambassador allowed the sigh to expand. The people of Shkoder were raised with very clear ideas of the liberties afforded to bards. The citizens of the Empire were not. He'd always believed that this would be the hardest adjustment that the Imperial bards would have to make. "Just behave like a bard. His Highness will accept that."

"I beg your pardon, Imperial Voice . . ." There was no trace of actual apology in Ullious' voice. ". . . but His Imperial Highness accepts such behavior from foreigners. Will he accept that kind of behavior from one of his own?"

"A very good point," the ambassador admitted, studying the ex-carter/almost-bard with increased respect. "I guess we'll have to find that out together."

A cursory knock brought Tysia in from the outer office.

"Begging your indulgence, Ambassador," she murmured. "But there's someone here I think you'd better see." Her hand signal indicated that the matter was extremely urgent and, if he hadn't known better, the ambassador would have sworn she was afraid.

He stood and motioned for Ullious to remain where he was. "Wait here," he said. "We still have a schedule to arrange." Sweeping Tysia out of the inner office before him, he closed the door between the crisis and the bard. "What is it?"

Silently, she handed him a square of leather stamped with a black sunburst.

The ambassador's gaze slid off the assassin's calling card, traveled across the room, and locked on the slight young man standing by the window. *How . . . interesting,* he thought. *Two Imperial assassins in Shkoder when assassins have never previously been allowed out of the Empire.* His hand began to rise toward his throat. He forced it back to his side.

Ullious would never have considered eavesdropping had the ambassador's assistant not sounded so frightened. *An Imperial citizen,* he told himself as he made his way to the window, *even one who's spent years in Shkoder, would never think of asking a bard for help.* Whistling softly, he sent one of the multitude of kigh that hung about the Citadel to peer into the next room and asked it to repeat everything it heard.

"Unfortunately, Bannon, your sister is no longer at the Bardic Hall."

Bannon's easy smile disappeared. "Where is she?"

Rubbing his thumb over yet another gold Imperial seal, the ambassador reflected on how this was all becoming absurdly complicated. First one of the assassins that helped to rescue the kidnapped Prince Otavas, then the prince himself, and now, apparently the second of the assassins. *Who's next?* "I have been informed that she disappeared some time last night."

"Informed by who?"

"A reliable and discreet source whose anonymity I would prefer to maintain." *None of your business* didn't seem like

the politic thing to say to an assassin looking for his sister.
The hem of the ambassador's official court robes whispered
against the floor as he walked over to a high-backed chair
and lowered himself into it.

"His Imperial Majesty," Bannon reiterated, a minor
change of posture making him look imminently dangerous,
"wants me to bring my sister back to the Empire."

"And I obey His Imperial Majesty in all things." Stee-
pling his fingers together, the ambassador refused to surrender to the subtle intimidation. "I will offer you every
assistance I can, but destroying a contact it has taken me
years to establish will not help you and will certainly not
advance the Emperor's interests in Shkoder. Your sister
has left Elbasan with the king's niece, a young healer of
some rare talent. I have no idea where they are heading,
but my source seems to think it has something to do with
the bard who died."

"What bard?"

"A man named Jazep." Anticipating the next question,
he added, "In Bartek Springs, a small town in the principality of Somes. Tysia, if you would be so kind as to find our
guest a map?"

Tysia jerked into motion. Her attempt to walk toward
a multidrawered cabinet while continuing to stare at the
assassin—the attractive, dangerous, deadly assassin—was
not notably successful. When, fully aware of her interest,
he flashed her a charming smile, she cracked her knee on
the cabinet's corner and grunted in pain.

Bannon made a graceful gesture of sympathy that only
flustered her further, then turned his attention back to the
ambassador. "If this Jazep is dead, what good's a healer
going to do?"

"An excellent question. The young woman apparently
heals the fifth kigh." To his surprise, the assassin nodded in
understanding. "There was something said about the dead
walking . . ." Under the full force of the young man's stare,
his voice trailed off. "What is it?"

"Is this Bartek Springs near the border? Near a pass?"

"It's the principal trading town by the Giant's Cleft, the
pass between Somes and the First Province. Why?"

Shaking his head, Bannon propped a thigh on the windowsill and ran a hand through thick curls. The gold rings

he wore in both ears gleamed in the sunlight, matching the gleam in gold-flecked eyes. "Do you know about what happened to the prince? To Vree and me?"

"Essentially. Something took over your body, your sister saved you, together the three of you and a bard saved the prince. Although, to be honest, I am unable to understand any motivation but yours and your sister's."

Bannon snorted. "You don't understand hers either. The thing that took over my body didn't die. It's still alive and it's in Vree. That's why the Emperor wants her back, to destroy it."

"In the report, everyone involved swore it was dead." Eyes narrowed, he studied the assassin. "Swore to the Emperor."

"Yeah, well I was *convinced* by the bards. They wanted to study it."

Of course they did. And the ambassador had never yet met a bard—Shkoden or Imperial—who didn't, deep down, believe that he or she knew best.

"From what the Emperor told me . . ." Bannon leaned forward as a breeze ruffled the hair on the back of his head. ". . . those bards, Gabris and Karlene, are going to be in for a nasty surprise when they get back to the Capital."

"I think you'll find that the Empress has Gabris sufficiently under her protection."

"Him maybe, but not Karlene," he said with satisfaction. He'd never liked the possessive way the Shkoden bard had looked at Vree.

The ambassador slowly shook his head. "I'm not sure you should be spreading that around."

"No one ever repeats what they're told by an assassin," Bannon told him with a feral smile.

"A very good point." As Tysia, having gotten a grip on her reactions, presented the deadly young man with the maps, the ambassador silently considered how, once again, everything had come around to the bards. "You realize that the Shkoden authorities are not going to be happy about having you careening about the country after your sister."

"How are they going to stop me?"

Wincing slightly, the ambassador raised a cautioning hand. "Please, allow me to attempt to arrange an approach less likely to pitch us all into an unpleasant situation."

*   *   *

Ullious whistled a quiet gratitude, dismissing the kigh. He'd heard enough.

He was an Imperial citizen and interfering with the Emperor's justice would be treason. Nervously, he ran his thumb over the narrow edge of his mustache and desperately searched for a solution that would keep not only Karlene and Gabris but himself alive.

"Her Royal Highness considers Kars to be a bardic problem, and we're to deal with it." Ignoring Kovar, who'd moved out from behind the desk, Liene lowered herself onto the pile of faded tapestry cushions heaped in her favorite chair. "I am far too old to deal with a third Sovereign Head of Shkoder. Far too old. You were right. I should have retired at Second Quarter Festival. If I had, I'd be sitting in my garden right now with nothing more to worry about than worms in the apples. Bardic problem. Hmmph."

"It is essentially what Karlene concluded in her recall. She did point out that we'd have to deal with him eventually."

Liene glared up at her second. "I know that." She pounded the tip of her cane against the floor. "But I should have been the one to tell Her Highness, not the other way around. *It's a bardic problem, Captain,* she said. *When you've worked out a plan for dealing with it, come back and see me.* Of course, it's a bardic problem. It's destroyed one of our own."

"So, what shall we do?" Kovar asked calmly, resting one leg over the corner of the desk and using as much Voice as he thought he could get away with.

"Stop trying to calm me," Liene snarled. "I'm not angry at Her Highness. I'm angry because Jazep was thirty-three years younger than I am, and he's dead and I'm not. And stop looking at me like that! I don't want to be dead, I want *him* to be alive. Her Highness would also like us to send a message to Marija at Bartek Springs and arrange to have Magda and Vree stopped."

"Stopped?"

"Apparently the how and why is a Bartek Springs problem. I suppose she'd best stay and not go on to the Duc of Somes. Once Jeremias is there, and the recall's there, they'll have to Sing each other the particulars." A tentative knock on the door jerked her head around. "What!"

A little startled by his reception, Ullious stepped into the office. "Captain, Kovar, I believe I have at least a partial solution to the problem in Somes."

"You mean a solution to Kars?" Kovar asked.

"Yes, sir."

Kovar shook his head. "I doubt you have all the information necessary to . . ."

"Oh, let him talk," Liene interrupted, leaning forward, gnarled hands clasped over the head of her cane. "It's not like the Circle's been spitting out great ideas at us. Besides, anyone who can run a successful business under the weight of the Emperor's taxes deserves to be listened to."

Ullious bowed in the Imperial fashion at the Bardic Captain—and then, to be politic, at Kovar. "Recently," he began, falling into a storytelling cadence, "in order to test my range, Tadeus had me Sing to Karlene in the Empire. Both she and Gabris were out Walking with the first group of Imperial fledglings to return home and were, at the time, quite close to the border. If they remained on their intended route, they're closer to the border now. Very near, in fact, to the pass into Somes." He paused. Singing Karlene into Shkoder would betray the Emperor's plans. As an Imperial citizen, suggesting it would be treason. However as a bard, if he were told to send a message across the border, he'd only be following orders.

"If she's that close to the border, she's the closest bard we've got," Kovar mused. "And having recently dealt with Kars, she's already familiar with at least part of the situation."

"Doesn't Sing earth though," Liene put in thoughtfully.

"Granted. But she Sings a strong three quarters and has proven ability in Singing the fifth kigh. She's also proved she can track this enclosed abomination." Kovar turned to face the Imperial fledgling, even the waxed curls of his mustache looking more hopeful than they had a moment before. "Can you find her again?"

"Yes, sir."

"Good. We'll work out a message to send her that can't be misinterpreted. Gabris can explain things to the Emperor."

Ullious prayed to Kattinni, god of cartage and the personal deity he'd brought with him into Shkoder, that Gabris was as protected as the ambassador believed. "There is one other thing. You are aware that Vireyda Magaly's brother Bannon is Prince Otavas' bodyguard?"

"Of course we're aware of it," Liene snapped, then her head jerked back and she stared, wide-eyed, up at Kovar. "Center it! Jazep's death pushed Bannon completely out of my head. All things being enclosed, I imagine *he'll* have an opinion to express about this as well."

"Your Grace, with the lead your sister and the . . ." Onele paused and frowned. ". . . and the other young woman have, you won't catch up to them before they reach Bartek Springs where they'll be stopped and then returned here. I neither want my cousin with her unique and irreplaceable talents endangering herself by confronting this bardic abomination, nor do I want an assassin with two not entirely stable kigh wandering around Shkoder."

"Then allow me to go to Bartek Springs," Gerek pleaded. "I can escort them back to Elbasan."

The Heir leaned forward and rested her chin on her fist, her father's signet on her index finger. There were shadows under her eyes that had not been there earlier. "Tell me why," she instructed. "Do you believe she's in danger from her companion?"

"No, Highness! Vree would never hurt her."

"What about Gyhard? He may not be able to jump to another body without Vree's help, but suppose he pushes her out and takes over the body he already has?"

Gerek shook his head. "It wouldn't happen, Highness."

"Why not? Because he allegedly loves her?"

"Your Highness is very well informed . . ."

Onele straightened. "There's an unstable Imperial assassin staying at the Bardic Hall. You're unenclosed right I'm very well informed and I haven't got time for your vague petitions. Why is it so important that you go after your sister?"

Gerek felt his cheeks grow hot. He glanced down at the carpet, noticed the toes of his boots were filthy with street grime and wished he'd taken the opportunity to clean up while he was waiting for Her Royal Highness to have time to see him. Finally, he murmured, "It isn't entirely my idea, Highness."

"Annice sent the kigh after you?" Onele smiled for the first time since she'd been summoned to the king's side. "I thought she took an oath not to use the kigh as weapons?"

"She doesn't exactly use them as weapons, Highness. If she feel the situation merits it, she sends messages it's difficult . . . no . . ." He reconsidered, scratching at his beard. ". . . impossible, to ignore."

"While I'm inclined to say that this is your problem, not mine, I'll speak with the Bardic Captain. You're twenty-two years old, it's time Annice stopped trying to run your life. The Circle knows your father and Stasya should be enough for anyone."

Under normal circumstances, Gerek would have jumped at the chance to have Annice's interference pared back. Under these specific circumstances, however, he'd just realized she was his strongest argument for going after Maggi. "Highness, please, for a moment, put yourself in her position. Your only child is galloping toward the insane thing that just killed one of your oldest friends. Duty prevents you from intervening personally. Wouldn't you do everything you could?" He spread his hands. "And I assure you it isn't just for Annice's sake that I want to go. Maggi is entirely too trusting. Vree is in a foreign land and I'm one of her only friends. And, if you think that once Maggi's set her mind on facing this thing you can get her back to Elbasan in anything short of chains, think again. I'm one of four people she actually listens to and the only one close enough to get to her in time."

Leaning back in her chair, Onele exhaled noisily. "I can't decide, Your Grace, whether you've become an excellent politician or you've just spent too many of your formative years among bards."

Gerek bowed, recognizing capitulation. "You won't regret it, Highness."

"At the risk of sounding clichéd, I already regret it." She rolled her eyes at yet another knock on the door; there hadn't been less than three things at a time claiming her attention all day. "Come."

"We have a solution, Highness," Liene declared as she came into the office. "Oh. Hello, Your Grace. I heard about your message from Ziven. Hiding inside?"

"Actually, Captain, I'm just about to leave. I'll be catching up to my sister and her companion in Bartek Springs and escorting them back to Elbasan."

"Will you? Well, I wish you luck, but I don't think you've thought the thing through."

"What do you mean?"

"Your sister's companion is an Imperial assassin. If she decides not to return to Elbasan with you, there's no way you can make her."

"Captain," Onele interrupted, "if I give orders that this person is returning to Elbasan, she *will* return."

"I don't doubt it, Highness, but before you go making an enemy of someone whose business it is to sneak past armed guards and slit throats, I have a suggestion. Perhaps Gerek could take his own companion along. Vireyda Magaly is not the only assassin in Elbasan."

Onele and Gerek both stared at the Bardic Captain.

"And that's supposed to be good news?" the Heir demanded.

Liene shrugged. "From what I hear, he's likely to go off on his own. I merely thought that it might be a good idea for us to maintain some control over his actions."

"Why would he want to travel with me?" Gerek wondered.

"Charm and good looks aside, Bannon's in a strange country where he speaks almost none of the language. Even an Imperial assassin will need a translator."

Both Onele's brows rose, her expression suddenly making her look very much like the king. "I wasn't aware you spoke Imperial, Your Grace," she said dryly.

"Tadeus had him learning under deep trance," Liene explained before Gerek decided on his best response. "The two of them had some stupid romantic notion it would make him more attractive to Vree. Normally, I'd suggest we send young Bannon off with a bard, but I doubt he'd go for that. I understand he doesn't care much for bards."

"Why not?"

The Bardic Captain glanced pointedly at Gerek. "One of them cared a bit too much for his sister."

Eight

"I'm not so sure you should go back to the Capital," Karlene muttered as she fastened the straps of her instrument case to her pack. "Ullious' message had undertones I didn't much like."

"I can't say as I cared much for the message itself," Gabris told her, morosely scraping his thumbnail along his jaw. "Jazep Sang the strongest earth I'd ever heard."

"A grave loss to Shkoder."

Gabris sighed. "I wasn't actually thinking of Shkoder. You probably didn't know him very well, but he was only six years younger than me. We were good friends."

Karlene straightened. "I'm sorry, I didn't know."

"We used to Sing the Fire and Earth duets together whenever we managed to be at the same Center at Festival. After I came south with the Princess, he'd send long letters with diplomatic couriers, traders, the new bards . . ." He raised an eyebrow at the younger bard. "You brought one with you. I came because Her Highness—Her Imperial Majesty—asked me to, but I think I was only able to stay because of Jazep's letters."

"There were always the kigh . . ."

"The kigh are not usually interested in carrying a wealth of personal detail. Nor," he added, scowling at the sky, "are they infallible. They should have told us when Jazep died. A bard does not die unremarked even if he only Sings earth."

"He does if Kars killed him. The kigh couldn't bring the news because there were no kigh around; they'd all fled." She tucked a strand of pale hair back into her braid and whistled a terse **Stop that!** as long, ethereal fingers tugged it forward again. "Frankly," she admitted, acknowledging the sick feeling in the pit of her stomach, "I'm more worried about what happened after he died."

"You think that Kars could have . . ." Gabris let his voice trail off, as if putting the fear into words made it more possible.

"I don't know." Shoving her arms through the straps, Karlene heaved her pack up onto her shoulders. "There's only one way to find out."

Gabris pulled her into a quick and awkward embrace—awkward both because of the pack and because neither was, by nature, overtly demonstrative. "Be careful."

"You, too." At his protest she added, "At least I know what I'm facing. You don't. I found what Ullious didn't say in that message to be very disconcerting."

"Her Imperial Majesty's protection will, I'm certain, be sufficient."

Karlene studied him for a moment, brows drawn in, then she shrugged, allowing him his belief that in any contest between Their Imperial Majesties involving him, the Emperor would lose. She'd asked him once, just after she'd first arrived from Shkoder, what exactly his relationship with the Empress was.

"I'm Her Majesty's lifeline to home," he'd told her.

"That's all?"

"Anything else is not your song to sing."

And that had been that.

"Do you think you can get this lot back to the Capital on your own?" she asked, turning enough to gesture at the four Imperial fledglings sprawled out in the shade of a giant cottonwood tree.

Gabris snorted. "I think I'm up to it."

As though she'd been waiting for Karlene's signal, Virine rose gracefully to her feet and stepped forward. In her late twenties, barely a full Quarter younger than Karlene, she'd been an acolyte in the temple of Eddam, the three-headed, androgynous god of music. When Gabris and Aurel had reminded the priests of her temples that technically speaking she would still be an acolyte—the sphere of her devotion having merely grown larger—they'd voted four to three in favor of allowing her to become a bard. Of the ten Imperial fledglings, she was the only one to Sing all four quarters.

"I think I should go with you," she said.

"Why?"

"Two reasons. The first, you don't Sing earth. I do. And the second, Jazep taught me recall. He was . . ." Virine frowned as she searched for the exact word then spread her hands expressively. "He was kind. I want to help."

Karlene shook her head. "First, Singing earth didn't help Jazep and he had a lot more years' experience than you do. Second . . ." Her second objection got lost in memories of Jazep teaching *her* recall. As his single quarter had kept him at the Bardic Hall in Elbasan almost every Fourth Quarter since he'd been fledged, there couldn't be a bard under thirty he hadn't taught. She remembered his gentle smile, his joy in life, his kindness. "Third," she went on, her voice rough-edged, "this is going to be dangerous and frankly, Virine, you are just too precious a resource to risk."

"But . . ."

"No buts. You're the only Imperial bard who Sings all four quarters and you may remain alone in this ability for some time."

"Gabris?" Virine's face fell as the older bard shook his head. Her sigh brought a kigh in to lightly brush her cheek. Although the gaze that met Karlene's was steady, her eyes were bright. "Then, when you find his body, will you Sing my good-byes?"

"And mine," said one of the three fledglings behind her. The other two murmured a quiet agreement.

Not trusting her voice, Karlene nodded. She scrubbed the back of her hand across her cheeks and started along the road toward the border.

"Karlene!"

When she turned, she saw that the four fledglings had moved up to stand by Gabris' side.

"You were right," he called, tears glistening silver in the gray of his beard. "Jazep's death *is* a grave loss to Shkoder."

"You will be traveling with His Grace, the Heir of Ohrid." The Imperial Ambassador's voice held a warning that narrowed Bannon's eyes to speculative slits. "His Grace's sister is traveling with your sister, and he is as anxious as you are to return them to Elbasan." As Gerek stepped forward, he added, "His Grace speaks some Imperial."

Bannon touched his heels together and nodded. His gaze flickered down the length of Gerek's body, noting and dismissing both sword and dagger. *Too big and too slow,* said the lift in his lip. *I don't need you.*

Gerek smiled and made an obvious point of looking down at the much shorter man. "Your sister told me so *little* about you," he said.

Layers upon layers and practically a bardic emphasis. Liene made a silent note to have a word with Tadeus about the tenor of his linguistic lessons when grief allowed.

"My sister is not for you to discuss."

"Your sister makes her own choices."

"My sister . . ."

"Is probably halfway to Bartek Springs by now," the ambassador broke in, stepping forward—although not quite *between* the two. "I think it would be best if you wasted very little time in beginning your pursuit."

A few moments later he dropped onto a bench and sighed deeply. "Frankly, Captain, you weren't much help."

Liene grinned. "You seemed to be doing fine on your own. I suspect they're going to have an interesting trip."

"Interesting?" The ambassador rolled his eyes. "You bards have such a way with words." He supposed he should be thankful that it would be interesting some distance away from him.

"Of course you have my permission to go after your sister." Prince Otavas clasped his hands together behind his back, hiding the way his fingers had begun to tremble. "She's in danger the closer she gets to that . . . that . . . to Kars. Stop her. Bring her and my cousin back to safety. And if this Gyhard has other ideas, well, do what you have to."

"Thank you, Highness." Bannon frowned slightly as he studied the prince. It was evident to the trained eye that the younger man was very afraid. "Highness, you'll be perfectly safe. There's no one here who wishes to harm you, and Kars is not only far away but they say the bards . . ." With an effort, he kept the distaste from his voice. ". . . are preparing to deal with him."

Otavas tossed his head. "Of course I'll be safe," he snapped, irritated that Bannon had recognized his fear. "Why wouldn't I be?"

"No reason, Highness." The Emperor had ordered him to return Vree and Gyhard to the Capital. Gyhard had to pay for what he'd done; for his treason, for Vree's betrayal. But the prince . . . Bannon shook his head, confused. He had a target and the target should be everything. But the prince's safety was his responsibility. If the prince was afraid, then he'd failed. *And who will guard his dreams while I'm gone?*

"Is there something else?"

"No, Highness." Bannon bowed. "I'll return as quickly as I can."

"Take the time you need," Otavas told him. He managed a shaky smile. "I'll try to stay out of trouble while you're gone."

"Thank you, Highness." If Bannon's answering smile was steadier, it was only because he was a much better liar.

"Don't trust him."

"Why not?" Gerek jerked the strap tight on the bulging saddlebag. "Because he's an arrogant, amoral, little shit?"

Kovar snorted. "Because he's an Imperial assassin."

"So's Vree."

"Exactly. And as Vree has proven herself capable of killing without orders, it's very likely that Bannon can, too. Vree, however, needs our good will; her brother does not and therefore has no external controls on his actions."

"So you want me to control him?"

"Don't be ridiculous." Kovar paced across the bedchamber and back, his agitation sounding through the slap of his soles against the polished wooden floor. Only the Duc of Ohrid had refused carpet in his palace suite. "You couldn't control him if you wanted to. If it comes to a fight, you'll lose—don't ever forget that."

Gerek's lip curled, the expression making him look remarkably like his father. "Anything else?" he snarled.

"Yes. Don't trust Gyhard either. And don't forget that according to Karlene, Bannon hates him."

"Vree seems to be the only one who doesn't." Throwing open the trunk at the foot of his bed, Gerek waved away the smell of cedar and began to rummage through his clothing. "Oh, and Maggi," he added, without looking up. "She feels sorry for him."

Kovar snorted again, the waxed curls of his mustache trembling. "Your sister is very young and I believe that Vree is afraid."

"Afraid?" Gerek straightened to stare indignantly across his bedchamber at the bard. "Vree isn't afraid of anything."

"I think I have been a slightly more impartial observer than you, Your Grace, and I have seen this fear."

"I didn't think anyone's impartial observing Vree, she's carrying too much history. However," Gerek held up a surrendering hand as Kovar opened his mouth to protest, "I suppose I may be more partial than most. So, what's she afraid of?"

Kovar drew in a deep breath and let it out slowly, wondering if the younger man was being deliberately obtuse. "Gyhard. She's afraid of Gyhard."

"I don't think so." He threw a sweater up onto the bed with unnecessary force. "As much as I wish she weren't, she's in love with Gyhard."

"Is she? Is it logical that she would be? This man, this abomination, destroyed her life, drove a wedge between herself and her brother, and now sits like a parasite in her mind. Why would she love him? Isn't it more logical to believe that she does what he wants because she is afraid of him but, unable because of her training to admit fear, she calls it love instead?"

Both Gerek's brows went up. "I think you've been listening to too many fledgling ballads, Kovar. Even by bardic standards that doesn't make any sense."

"Doesn't it?"

Unfortunately, it did. "Maggi says . . ."

"Magda is little more than a child." It was Kovar's turn to raise a cautioning hand. "This whole situation is much more complex than a simple love story. I'm not asking that you believe me, Gerek, just keep it in mind. Please."

"Yeah. Sure." He shook his head as if trying to settle unsettling information. "Anything else?"

"Yes. Be careful." Kovar used enough Voice to make his concern plain. Due to the circumstances of Gerek's upbringing, the bards considered the Heir of Ohrid to be one of theirs. "I'd hate to have to tell your father that he'd lost you."

"You're the entire country away from my father," Gerek reminded him with a not entirely successful laugh. "If I were you, I'd worry more about telling Annice."

"My mother's death was what made me an assassin." So strange to say *my mother* and *made me* when it had been *our mother* and *made us* for so long.

Magda paled under the color the sun had laid across her cheeks. "You didn't . . . I mean, you were only seven, you couldn't have . . ."

"No. I didn't." Unable to decide if she were amused or hurt by the assumption, Vree's voice held no expression at all.

"I'm sorry, Vree." The younger woman reached between the horses and laid her hand lightly on Vree's arm. "That was a stupid thing to say. I forgot the most important lesson the Healers' Hall tried to bang into my head." When Vree lifted a questioning brow, she lifted her hand and explained. "Brain first. Mouth second."

She was so contrite, it was impossible not to smile. "I always thought I hid my reactions better than that."

"Not from me. I've been learning your kigh, remember "

"And when you've learned it, you'll know me better than anyone?"

Magda grinned and tucked a curl of hair into the corner of her mouth. "Not quite anyone."

About to say, *Bannon,* Vree felt Gyhard's kigh stir and realized that her brother hadn't really known her at all. "And will I know you better than anyone," she asked.

"That depends on you."

If they hadn't been riding down a public road, she might have surrendered to the unexpected lack of barriers between them. Might have. As it was, she had no real desire to fall off the horse.

She felt Gyhard withdraw enough to keep them separate. *There'll be other times,* he promised.

The reins gripped between damp fingers, Vree suddenly needed to fill the silence. "*My* teachers always said, throat first, eye second."

"Eye?" Magda asked uncertainly.

"Through the socket and into the brain. Takes a more specialized dagger, though. Longer, narrower blade. You can slit someone's throat with your teeth if you have to."

"Vree, that's really gross."

"Only if you forget and swallow."

Magda swiveled in the saddle and stared at her, aghast. As far as Vree could remember, she'd never seen anyone look so disgusted. Although she tried to keep a straight face, she couldn't stop herself from laughing. "It's a joke, Maggi, a joke."

Is it? Gyhard wondered, and then wished he hadn't because it stopped the laughter.

Mostly.

Two days' travel into the mountains, a pair of ravens led Karlene to the scattered remains of a body by the side of the road. A shallow indentation scratched into the dry soil and an oblong pile of fist-sized rocks indicated an attempt at burial, but such pitiful protection had been no protection at all against the local scavengers.

Wrinkling her nose, Karlene squatted by a piece of bone and was astonished to see that desiccated tissue still clung to it. Although the body had been torn apart, none of the flesh appeared to have been eaten.

"That's very odd," she muttered as she stood.

Cocking an ebony head, one of the ravens fixed her with an amber eye, its cry sounding very much like loud and raucous laughter.

"Easy for you to say," Karlene told it derisively, then she stopped and took a closer look at its perch. Cracked and faded, the leather collar that had held Kait's head erect on her broken neck was unmistakable. Needing no further confirmation, she turned away before she chanced to spot Kait's head.

While her right hand sketched the sign of the Circle over her breast, Karlene Sang the kigh a question. Considering what had happened when Kars' other companions had fallen, the answer surprised her.

Kait's kigh was nowhere around.

It was very strange.

*   *   *

The timber-holding stood at one end of a narrow valley close by where the river broadened into a natural basin to hold the logs sent down from the cutting crew upstream. Although a high wooden stockade surrounded the buildings, the gate was open and a small herd of shaggy cattle were grazing around the stumps in a cleared pasture.

Had he come out onto the lip of the valley anywhere else, the trees would have blocked his view and he very likely would have missed the holding entirely. Sinking down onto his haunches so that the necklace of bone he wore tucked under his robe clattered against the ground, Kars stared at the cattle, at the buildings, at the stockade, and wondered where he'd seen them all before.

"In a dream," he murmured. "Or in the memory of a dream?"

Perhaps the shadow of familiarity that lay over the valley was an omen. He didn't think he believed in omens, but as he couldn't remember exactly what he believed in, he supposed it didn't matter.

"There are people there, Kait." She brushed the back of her hand against his cheek and he smiled, teeth still surprisingly whole and white between cracked and bleeding lips. "Our family. Yours and mine." There had been a family before the Song . . . before the Song . . . . the Song . . .

NO! NO! NO! NO! NO!

Trembling, tears spilling over into wrinkles so deep the moisture disappeared within the crease, Kars held up a placating hand.

"I won't leave you," he said softly. "I promise." How could he leave her? She'd given him reason to live when he'd lost his heart for the second time. She'd stayed with him even after her own Song had ended. She was all he had. "We'll be a family again. Like we were." When she nodded, he smiled again. "Your legs are younger than mine, child. Go down there and look around. See if they'll welcome us."

He watched her move down into the valley, skimming the ground, swirling around rocks and trees like pale smoke. She looked so much better without the brace. He remembered how pleased he'd been when she'd put it aside.

As she passed, the cattle rushed to the far side of their pasture and stood, shaggy orange rumps against the fence, heads turned toward the open gate of the stockade.

Trouble coming.
How can you tell?
Shoulders hunched against the driving rain, Vree tossed her head to clear the water from her eyes and said, *There's a horse galloping hard toward us. In this weather, you don't ride like that unless there's trouble.*
I can't see anything. He could see the rump end of Magda's horse and Magda slumped forward in the saddle. Past her, he could see another horse-length, maybe two, of the ribbon of mud that Shkodens referred to as a road— the Empire spent considerably more tax dollars on road building than on music and, at the moment, Gyhard whole-heartedly approved—but then the translucent curtain of rain became opaque.
Listen.
Rain. Creak of wet leather. Hooves lifting out of and falling back into wet earth. *I don't hear anything.*
Listen for what doesn't belong.
He heard it then, the low pounding like an angry drum roll, held against the ground by the weather. From the way Magda straightened, he suspected it had now come too close to ignore.
Head cocked, wet hair plastered tight to her skull, Magda tried to figure out not only what the sound was, but where it was coming from. The rhythmic pounding seemed to bounce off the individual drops of rain and surround her. "Which is ridiculous," she told herself, pulling her mount's reluctant head around.
Diagonal across the road and turned toward Vree, she didn't see the rider burst suddenly into view. Her horse slammed back onto its haunches, Magda fought to keep her seat. And lost.
A moment later, Vree knelt on the shoulders of a very wet young man. Gasping for breath, he stared up at her, unable to understand how he'd been on the back of a galloping horse one instant and on his back in the mud the next.

"You should watch where you're going," she said, her voice devoid of inflection.

Gyhard had a sudden memory—it had to be one of Vree's—of Avor lying in the same position. The only difference had been, the Sixth Army Messenger knew how he'd ended up flat out on the road and how long he had left to live.

"Vree?"

Rising lithely, Vree moved to where Magda sat pulling mud out of her hair. "Are you hurt?"

"I don't think so." Her confused expression was, in most ways, identical to that of the young man.

"Can you stand?"

"I don't know."

Grasping Magda's left wrist, Vree slowly pulled her up onto her feet, ready to stop if she gave any indication of pain. "Does anything hurt?"

"No. No," she repeated, her voice growing stronger as she looked down at the imprint of her body in the mud. 'I guess I was lucky I didn't land on a rock." She spotted her horse and Vree's, bulky shadows cropping grass by the side of the road, noticed a third horse a little way off, then noticed the rider carefully getting to his feet. "Who's he?"

"The idiot who ran into you."

"What happened to him?"

The corners of Vree's mouth curled up into what was only peripherally a smile. "He stopped to make sure you weren't hurt."

Magda glanced from Vree to the filthy young man and came to the correct conclusion. Rolling her eyes, she stepped toward him. "Are you all . . ."

He charged past her, fists raised.

". . . right?" she finished as he hit the ground again.

When he grabbed for his dagger, Vree stepped on his wrist. "I wouldn't," she said quietly.

He stiffened, then saw his own mortality in the dark eyes looking down into his. The fight went out of him so completely, its absence left him trembling.

Gyhard was pleased to see that the boy wasn't a total fool.

"Dusty?"

"Your horse?" Magda asked as she squatted beside him. "It's right over there. It didn't go far after you . . ." She paused.

"Fell off?" Vree offered.

". . . parted company. *Are* you all right?" Licking rain off her lips, she rested her palm lightly on his chest. "It's just that I'm a healer and . . ."

"A healer!" He jerked up out of the mud and clutched at her hand. "I was riding for a healer!"

The village had been built just above the high tide mark down on the flats where a broad creek spilled fresh water into the sea. Small boats were pulled up on the gravel beach and empty drying racks made skeletal outlines against the gray on gray of sea and sky.

"Why is it all fishing villages look the same?" Vree wondered. "Put this on the coast anywhere in the Sixth Province and it wouldn't look out of place."

Maybe it's because all fish look the same.

They didn't stop at the village but pounded right up to the crowd of people standing on the clifftop overlooking the bay. The young man was off his horse before it had actually stopped moving.

"I didn't have to bring Raulas, Mother! I found a younger healer just up coast!"

Magda dismounted almost as quickly.

Younger healer? Gyhard wondered as a thin woman with pale hair hurried toward them.

"Thank all the gods in the Circle and then some!" She grabbed Magda's hand and pulled her toward an oiled canvas tarp propped tentlike over two still forms and the bent figure of her son. "We've kept them as dry as we can, but we didn't want to move them any farther!"

"What happened?"

"Didn't Dumi tell you?" She broke off as Dumi moaned and ran out from under the tarp toward the edge of the cliff. "Dumi! Stop! It's gotten worse! Don't go past the ropes!"

Dumi ignored her. A few of the villagers began moving to intercept him, but they seemed to be carrying the weight of the world on their shoulders and were obviously not going to get to him in time.

Vree slammed her heels into her horse's ribs and when the astonished animal leaped forward, she slipped free of the stirrups and drew her feet up under her on the saddle. As they drew level with her quarry, she yanked back hard on the reins. The sudden stop catapulted her forward. She flipped in the air and landed with knees bent, palms against the ground, facing a still running Dumi. Straightening her legs, she drove her shoulder into his stomach and, a heart-beat later, knelt on his shoulders for the second time that afternoon.

The only sound on the clifftop was the angry pounding of waves against rock.

Impressive, Gyhard murmured, feeling as though he hadn't quite caught up.

Thank you.

You know, people would pay good coin to see some-thing like that.

Yeah? Well, maybe we'll let them; the bards aren't going to feed us forever.

"You don't understand!" Dumi wailed, tears running back into his hair. "Celja's still down there."

Vree twisted as she stood. The edge of the cliff had the raw look of a fresh wound. "Down there?"

"Stupid, stupid place to build a house. Stupid."

Nice view, though.

Maybe yesterday. Grabbing onto Dumi's wrist, Vree hauled him to his feet. "Celja's house fell off the cliff?"

"Her father's house." He rubbed the back of his hand under his nose, but before he could continue, another voice cut in.

"It'd be more accurate to say the cliff fell out from under the house." A heavyset woman, wet gray hair plastered against a round head, exhaustion turning her face a slightly paler shade of gray, closed her fingers around Dumi's arm and stared tiredly at Vree. "It's all sandstone around here. Stuff gets wet enough, it starts to slide. The boy's right though, it's a stupid place to build. You're with the healer, Southerner?"

"I am."

"When we sent him . . ." *To get him out of the way,* her tone added. ". . . we thought he'd have to go up coast to old Raulus i'Ilka at Eel Cove. He's been retired for years and he's older than spit, but he's the closest healer around."

Dumi twisted in her grip. "Gran, I have to get to Celja!"

"You can't get to her, boy. Things are worse than when you left. The rest of it's going to go any minute."

"NO!" Dumi jerked free, but before Vree could knock him down for the third time, one of the village men got him in a secure hold and dragged him back from the sagging rope barrier.

His grandmother sighed. "She passed up her little brother and got the ropes around her father before the house slipped right off. We dragged him out through a wall. Didn't mean to, but the wall ended up where he was. Now Celja's tangled in the wreckage, can't climb out and we can't get a rope to her, because every time someone steps over that line, the whole enclosed mess starts to slip."

Vree studied the area, well aware that the villagers were studying her. "Are you sure she's still alive?"

"She was a few minutes ago."

"If someone goes over to get her, the house will fall and both girl and rescuer will die?"

The heavyset woman shrugged. "That's about it."

"If no one goes over to get her, the house will fall and the girl will die?"

The silence was answer enough.

"There's no chance she'd survive the fall?"

Vree.

Calm down. I'm just asking.

"You don't know what's down there, Southerner." Vree allowed herself to be led about thirty feet along the cliff. "If you're careful, you can crawl out there and look over." The old woman pointed at a rain-slick patch of grass that extended out to where land met sky.

Taking the reference to crawling literally, Vree dropped to her belly and crept forward. When she got her first view of the wreckage, she sucked air through her teeth. The upper third of the cliff had collapsed. The house—the remains of the house—balanced between a steep slope of loose rock and a nearly perpendicular drop fifty feet into a churning sea. While she watched, a wave lifted a tabletop and smashed it into kindling against the cliff.

She crept a little farther forward and allowed the upper

half of her body to drop over the rim. "Someone could climb down here and work their way over level with the house."

Someone?

Behind her, Dumi's grandmother snorted. "Don't be ridiculous. There's no holds on that face big enough to support an adult, and I'll not send a child down."

"There's holds," Vree said, still scanning the rock.

"We haven't time to anchor a safety line way over here." But the protest held less force than it had.

"Don't need one. Just drop two lines down by the house."

"It can't be done." Colored by hope, it was almost a question.

Vree rolled over and looked up at her. The rain had stopped, but the sky was still a sullen gray. "Yes, it can."

Why, Vree? Gyhard's thoughts paced the confines of Vree's mind as though looking for a way to escape. *Why risk both our lives for a girl you don't know? Her own people have given up!*

I don't leave people to die.

He bit back a protest as he realized that emotionless statement made a warped sort of sense. Death and Imperial Assassins were active partners. Besides, from his position inside her head, he could see that it would be no use trying to talk her out of it. *Are you sure you can do this?*

I could do this in the dark under the noses of guards who would desperately like to kill me. As Dumi's grandmother shouted orders, Vree began stripping off her sodden clothes.

Yeah, but can you do it in daylight under the noses of people who desperately want you to succeed?

First time for everything. Naked, she began to limber up.

Uh, Vree . . .

What? Gyhard's unease drew her attention to the various reactions of the watching villagers. *They look like they've never seen skin before.*

Well aware that Vree had no nudity taboos—they were impossible to maintain in the army and, as most Imperial citizens spent at least two years in uniform, they'd disappeared almost entirely throughout the Empire—Gyhard could only assume the embarrassment he felt was his own. The problem was, they weren't in the Empire. *Is this really necessary?*

Before she could answer, Dumi's grandmother asked much the same thing.

Vree flexed the muscles across her shoulders. "Wet clothes are heavy. They also get in the way."

"But protection . . ."

"From what?"

"Scrapes. The rock."

Is she kidding?

You're a new experience for them, Vree.

Spitting on her palms for luck, she dropped over the edge of the cliff. She could hear Dumi calling and a faint answer rising up from the ruin of the house. *The tricky part's going to be remembering not to kill her when I get there.*

Another joke?

Mostly. Now shut up, I need to concentrate.

Drawn back into himself as much as possible, Gyhard felt her attention shift to the cliff face. Her thoughts cleared until they focused on nothing but moving down and across, fingers and toes. The world became rock.

The rock under her right foot crumbled. Her left foot, already in the air, could find no purchase.

She dangled, her entire weight on fingertips alone.

Then the toes of her left foot found a crack; the side of her right foot, a crevasse.

Breathing heavily, she rested her forehead against the wet stone, unable to tell if the roaring she heard was her blood in her ears or the sea, waiting hungrily below.

A few moments later, still some distance from the slide, she felt a shiver deep in the rock. *If it goes now, we'll go with it.* Her thought. Gyhard's. It wasn't important.

Knees and elbows were bleeding when she finally reached the house. The area was remarkably contained, loose debris having already fallen into the water. She was reaching for one of the two waiting ropes when the world shifted.

One chance. Everything risked on it. Lips pulled back in a vicious parody of a grin, Vree launched herself off crumbling holds at the wildly swaying rope. Rock careened off the cliff around her. Wood shrieked as timber framing twisted like taffy. She closed her fingers. The rough hemp cut into her palm. Something slammed into her shoulder. She snarled and hung on. The noise pounded at her.

Flung back and forth on the end of the rope like a rag doll, she fought to get her other arm up. To double her chance of survival.

Then it was over.

Her first thought was for Bannon. The sight of the second rope, hanging empty, nearly accomplished what the rock fall had been unable to do. Then she remembered and her heart started beating again.

Miraculously, the house had not yet gone all the way over.

Climbing back up to the lower edge of the slide as quickly as she could, Vree tied the ends of both ropes around her waist and then dropped back down even with the canted wall now the bottom of the building.

"I need more line," she yelled. "Play it out slowly. Keep the . ."

Tension, Gyhard offered.

". . . tension the same!"

Cries from the clifftop seemed to indicate they'd thought she'd fallen.

"Talk it over later!" she screamed. "Just give me some slaughtering rope!"

She'd yelled in Imperial, Gyhard noted. It didn't seem to matter. Her tone appeared to be enough for results.

Muttering under her breath, she moved sideways toward the smashed remains of a window that appeared to open out of a floor. When she reached it, she was astounded to see a young woman her own age peering out. "Celja?"

Celja smiled and brushed at the line of blood dribbling into her eyes. "Hello. Do I know you?"

Shock?

Good guess. "Celja, can you move toward me?"

"Sure. My legs are free now. They weren't before, you know." She crept forward on her elbows, looked down, and added. "I don't think I could swim right now. Maybe I'd better stay here."

"Come a little farther," Vree told her, ducking as a splintered chunk of wood dropped past her ear. "Just a little."

"I don't think so."

"Dumi's waiting for you up top," she said, untying the second rope.

Her face brightening, Celja pulled herself another few feet closer to rescue. "Do you know Dumi?"

"Not very well." Her toes gripping the rock, Vree leaned out, slid the free end of the rope under the young woman's arms and tied it off.

"You're not from around here, are you?"

"No." Easing back, she began to slide Celja out of the window.

The world shifted again.

One hand gripping the front of Celja's tunic, Vree flung them both away from the slide, hoping the arc of the rope would be long enough.

It was.

Just.

Celja was unconscious but alive when they pulled her up.

Half a dozen hands reached for Vree as she came over the rim, most of her weight on the rope. Someone untied the knots, someone else threw a rough wool blanket over her shoulders. The scene had taken on a clarity she recognized and her blood sizzled the way it did after a target had been taken out. All that was missing was Bannon. And a body.

The villagers were shouting things, but she didn't understand most of them. Everything seemed to be happening some distance away from herself.

Then she saw Magda kneel by Celja's side. The healer looked up, caught her gaze, and nodded.

It's funny, she murmured.

What is?

If I hadn't been so thoroughly trained to kill people, that girl would have died.

Her need overwhelming caution, Gyhard extended his awareness and pulled the blanket more tightly around her, leaving his/her arms wrapped around her/his body.

She shivered.

You're cold.

No . . .

"One double pallet or two singles, my lord?"

Scowling, Gerek pushed wet hair back off his face. "What?"

The innkeeper sighed. The Circle enclose her away from nobility determined to rough it. "One double pallet," she repeated, "or two singles? The double'll cost you half an anchor; the singles, a gull each. You two sleeping alone or together?"

"Alone," Gerek told her indignantly, reaching for his purse.

"Very well, my lord. There's stew in the pot if you and your .." She took a good look at Bannon, reassessed both her first and second opinion and decided she didn't want to know. ". . . companion want a late supper. Quarter-gull each, bowl of stew, bread, and beer. Bowl of fruit's another quarter-gull."

"Fine." Gerek laid a half-gull beside the two copper coins already on the scarred counter. Until he'd spent the last few days in the saddle pounding at a full gallop down the South Coast Road, he'd thought he was in good shape, but every time they'd changed horses he'd mounted a little more slowly. The short walk from the stable to the inn—an establishment chosen purely on the basis of proximity—had nearly crippled him. All he wanted was to sit for a few minutes on something that wasn't moving, shove some food into his abused body, then fall over. That Bannon appeared to be completely unaffected by the punishing ride irritated him more than he could say, and he strongly suspected that had it not been raining so hard, the southerner would have expected them to reach the next station before stopping for the night.

The public room was nearly empty. Although the three trestle tables could probably hold close to thirty people if they were willing to be friendly, this evening there were only six other customers. Two old men sat by the empty hearth pushing tricolored game pieces around a strategy board, and four young women sitting in the seats closest to the door giggled over mugs of beer.

Shoving his saddlebags under the table with the side of his foot, Gerek began to drop onto the end of the bench nearest the counter.

Bannon lightly touched his arm. "No," he said. "You sit on the other side of the table."

Gerek felt his lip curl—about the only protest he had the energy for. "Why?"

"Because this the only seat in the room where you can see all four entrances."

"Four?"

"Door to the outside; door to the kitchen; stairs to the second floor, chimney."

"Chimney? That's not an entrance!"

"It is when there's no fire lit."

Grinding his teeth, Gerek shuffled around the table. "Fine," he snarled. "Sit there. And I wouldn't be surprised if someone came down the chimney and tried to kill you."

Bannon bowed mockingly. "*Tried* to kill me, Your Grace. This way, I can protect *your* back."

The giggling grew louder. Although they didn't understand the language, they understood the tone.

As much as he resented both the implication that he would be unable to provide a similar protection and the reaction it had evoked, Gerek let it go. His father was fond of saying, *Never fight with a man trying to pick a fight with you. Even if you win, you'll lose.* When Annice demanded to know what he meant, he'd add, *The boy understands.* It drove her crazy. Sometimes, Gerek thought that was why his father said it, except that he *did* understand.

"Suit yourself," he said, slowly lowering his aching body down onto the bench.

Bannon bowed again, playing to his audience. When one of the girls called out something, he frowned—not because of what had been said, but because he suddenly remembered who'd have to translate it for him.

As the realization showed in Bannon's expression, Gerek smiled guilelessly. "Did you want something?" he asked.

The young woman added a longer statement along with a lecherous waggle of pale brows. Her friends continued to giggle and one of them shrieked, "Kasya!" in exaggerated horror.

The gist was unmistakable and Bannon couldn't stand not knowing the particulars any longer. "If you could tell me what she said, Your Grace?"

Gerek dropped his chin onto the heel of his left hand. "You know," he drawled, "that's the first time you've used my title and haven't made it sound like an insult."

"And it could easily be the last, *Your Grace.*"

All at once, he was tired of the posturing. Maintaining it

took more energy than he had to spare. "She said you had a nice *bow,* emphasis obvious, then she said it was too bad the table blocked so much of the view."

"Did she?" Gerek forgotten in the possibilities, Bannon took two running steps, leaped lightly onto the table, flipped in the air, and landed on the far side. He bowed a third time, then made his way back to his seat by the more conventional route.

The giggling stopped and after a moment's stunned silence, a low-voiced argument ensued.

"End of round one?" Gerek asked as Bannon sat down, impressed in spite of himself.

Bannon smiled, his expression for the first time since Gerek had met him, free of anything but the moment. "The advance, as we say in the army, is on her front."

The innkeeper put a heavily laden tray down between them. "You break anything," she growled, with a pointed look at Bannon's damp footprint on the tabletop, "and you pay for it."

The food was surprisingly good; the stew no more than two days on the fire and the bread soft enough to dip into the gravy without breaking.

Bannon took a cautious sip of the beer and set it aside.

"Too strong for you?" Gerek asked facetiously.

"A strong beer slows your reaction time." Bannon moved his gaze deliberately from Gerek to Gerek's half-empty mug.

Gerek ignored him. He wasn't in the mood.

They were almost finished when the door slammed open. The flames flickered in the half-dozen flax-oil lanterns and one of the old men muttered a curse without looking up from his game. The five men who stomped in, rain dripping from grimy clothes, wore an assortment of scars and identical scowls.

The innkeeper laid a metal-headed club on the counter. "Get out," she said. "I've told you before Jonakus a'Vasil, I don't want you and your boys in here."

The eldest, lamplight reflected in the beads of water on his greasy bald head, held up a purse in a three-fingered hand. "We got money."

Weighing the nearly empty room against her expenses, the innkeeper's eyes narrowed. "One drink each."

"Just one." Jonakus smiled. Under the mashed remains of his nose, most of his teeth were missing. "Sit, boys. I told you she'd do right by us."

Five heavily-muscled bodies dropped onto the benches at the far end of Gerek's and Bannon's table. The old men ignored them, all their attention on the game. The young women nervously shifted positions in order to keep them in sight.

"Hey, Pa!" A sausagelike finger pointed down the table at Bannon. "Look at the pretty little man."

Five heads swiveled on bull necks.

"I hear that in the South they cut off their balls to make 'em that pretty."

"What did he say?" Bannon asked.

Gerek shook his head. "You don't want to know."

"I heard," offered one of the others through scabbed lips, "that if you stroke a Southerner just right, they squeal like a pig."

"You squeal, Southerner?"

Teeth clenched, Gerek began to rise.

A viselike grip around his wrist stopped him. "It's me they insult," Bannon said quietly. "So it's my slaughtering fight. Tell me what they said."

Two of them squealed. Three of them laughed.

Gerek told him. Bannon's fingers tightened around his wrist. "I don't need your help," he growled.

"There're five of them."

"I *can* count, Your Grace."

Scowling, Gerek sat back down. *Fine,* he snarled silently. *He thinks he's such hot shit, he can prove it. I'll be here to pull his butt out of trouble when he gets in over his head.*

Over his head seemed an apt observation when the four younger men stood.

"Jonakus!"

He waved a placating hand at the innkeeper. "Don't worry. The boys won't bust nothin' but the pretty little Southerner."

"I'm warning you . . ."

Her warning came too late. Bannon somehow managed to spit in three out of four faces.

Over the next few moments bellows of rage turned to

shrieks of pain that didn't quite drown out the wet crack
of more than one joint separating.

Gyhard watched with his mouth open and barely managed to get it shut in time to yell, "Don't kill anyone!"
before it was all over.

Eyes glittering, Bannon stroked one of his daggers across
Jonakus' throat. "Squeal," he said in heavily accented
Shkoden.

Sweat beading the dome of his head, Jonakus stared in
horror at the broken, bleeding bodies of his sons and squealed.

Bannon moved the point of the blade to the stubbled
chin and lifted Jonakus' head until their eyes locked. "I see
again," he told the older man quietly, "I kill."

The sudden smell of urine and a spreading stain indicated
just how much Jonakus believed the threat.

Stepping back, Bannon gestured at the door. "Go."

Three of them carrying two of them, they went.

The innkeeper picked the abandoned purse up out of a
puddle of beer. "This oughta cover the damages."

Wondering why he was the one panting when Bannon
had been in the fight, Gerek stared at her. "That's a pretty
minor reaction! Does this sort of thing happen often?"

She snorted. "Not usually until they've had a bit more
to drink. Then they get ugly."

"What did she say?" Bannon asked, cleaning off his
daggers.

When Gerek translated, the ex-assassin laughed, his eyes
still gleaming. "I'd hate to see them any uglier."

"No one's ever beaten them before," the innkeeper
added. "I'm impressed."

"Only impressed?" Gerek shook his head. "As much as
it pains me to admit it, I'm amazed!"

Shrugging, she started to clean up. "Keep an inn long
enough and nothing amazes you, my lord. We had a two-
headed calf in here once. Still alive it was, too."

"What did she say?"

By the time Gerek finished translating the information
about the calf, both men were laughing so hard they had to
sit down. A soft touch on Bannon's arm drew him around.

Kasya stood looking down at him, eyes half-lidded,
cheeks flushed, moist lips slightly parted. "I think," she

sighed, drawing one finger lightly along Bannon's jaw, "that I'm in love."

Bannon didn't bother asking for a translation.

Far to the south, at the Sixth Army garrison, the corporal of the watch stood over the huge brass drums and pounded out the pattern that began the day. A soldier for fifteen of his twenty-one years, Bannon obeyed the command and woke. He lay testing his surroundings for threat then rose silently to his feet. In the pale gray, predawn light, he scanned the loft, not moving, barely breathing, until he was certain he and Gerek were alone.

He'd returned to the inn when Kasya had fallen asleep, slipping away from the warm comfort of her embrace and back to the security of a companion he knew was no threat. While he regretted leaving, and doubted the necessity, he couldn't break the caution of his training. Assassins had died of warm comfort before. For all Gerek a'Pjerin was an arrogant millstone hung around his neck, he was also an ally.

And an attractive ally, too, Bannon admitted, his gaze tracing the line of dark curls running over ridged muscle and disappearing behind a loosened waistband. Had circumstances been different . . . He put desire aside with little difficulty, Kasya having taken the edge off.

Wearing only breeches and wrist daggers, he slipped down to the inn yard. In the Empire, inns even smaller than this one would have a bathhouse. "Well, what can you expect from barbarians?" he sighed, glancing disdainfully at the hand-pump and trough by the door.

Back to the rising sun, he began his morning exercises. As he moved through the increasingly complicated pattern, he couldn't help but imagine he was no longer alone. Every now and then, out of the corner of his eye, he'd actually see Vree in her accustomed place and it hurt every time when he turned to face her and she wasn't there.

She should be there. Beside him.

This was the time of day when he missed her the most; missed the sound of her, the smell of her, the mirror image as they moved together in the assassin's deadly dance that promised an eternal partnership. He'd get her back. He had to get her back.

And what then? asked a little voice in his head. *Do you return to the army?*

No. Not the army.

What about the prince?

The prince needed him. He needed Vree. But somehow he couldn't seem to bring those two needs together.

The prince is mine. Not Vree's. Not the army's. Not our-slaughtering-father-the-dead-commander Neegan's. Mine. In his whole life, the only other thing he'd ever had of his own had been Vree. Until Gyhard had taken her.

Gyhard.

He twisted in the air, his heel slamming into an imaginary throat, a dagger suddenly in each hand. Once Gyhard was dead, everything would be like it used to be between him and Vree.

Rolling up off one shoulder, he saw Gerek cross the yard to the privy and his lip curled. *He's hobbling like a slaughtering old man.* When he emerged, a moment later, Bannon was as far from the privy as he could be without leaving the yard. He wanted to be alone with his memories of Vree. He didn't want to put up with the facetious comments of the slaughtering useless noble foisted on him by a ball-less ambassador.

Ignoring the hint, Gerek crossed the yard and stood just outside the danger zone. He had a good eye, Bannon reluctantly acknowledged. One of the more common scars in the Imperial Armies came as a result of standing too close to an assassin's morning exercises.

He went on a little longer and a little more strenuously than he would've without this particular audience, but finally, torso shining with sweat, he had to stop.

"What?" he demanded.

"Nothing." Gerek spread his hands, determined not to be provoked. Maybe the Southerner could be a pain in the ass all the way to Bartek Springs, but he had better things to do with his energy than reply in kind. "I watched Vree exercise one morning back in the Citadel and you two move exactly the same way." Uncomfortably the same way, actually. Although not usually attracted to men, he thanked the Circle for loose trousers.

Unbuckling his wrist sheaths, eyes locked on the sweaty

leather, Bannon scowled. "And why were you up that early, Your Grace. Because she was?"

His implication colored the question. "We didn't sleep together, if that's what you're asking." Making an obvious point of considering it, Gerek added, "I guess I'm not Gyhard's type."

Bannon's head jerked up. "My sister makes her own choices!"

That was more, much more than Gerek could resist. "Funny, that's what Gyhard said. You may have a greater amount in common than you think."

Even half-expecting the attack, it still came faster than he was able to react. He survived only because Bannon ignored a lifetime of training and tried to throttle him barehanded. Fighting for air, Gerek threw himself forward. The impact with the ground broke the smaller man's hold. He managed to get in two good blows before something that felt like a steel bar drove up under the center of his ribs and he found himself flat on his back, gasping for breath, staring up at a dagger point suspended terrifyingly close over his left eye.

Oh, shit. The moment he could speak, determined to hide the fear even if it killed him, he gasped, "Your nose . . . is bleeding."

Startled, Bannon touched his upper lip with the fingers of his free hand and gazed in astonishment at the crimson smear.

Gerek tried very hard to look past the dagger. "The four guys last night . . . didn't even touch you."

Rolling his weight back off Gerek's shoulders, Bannon stood, shaking his head as though to settle in unsettling information. He picked up his wrist sheaths, and walked, still shaking his head, toward the inn.

With his left arm clamped against his chest, Gerek got to his feet. "Well, I hope that shook up your worldview," he muttered at the closing door. "You arrogant little prick." Then, with the memory of that dagger poised to take out his eye sending him limping back to the privy, he added, "Remind me never to do that again."

Nine

On his hands and knees in a stand of larch, Kars gently picked another mushroom. He examined the pale yellow cap for blemishes, ran a finger lightly over the white warts, turned it over to check that the gills were open and free of insect damage, and, satisfied, placed it with the others in a fold of his robe.

"We're very lucky," he said softly. "In a few weeks, it will be too late. Do you see, Kait? This little veil here, it becomes a collar when they're old."

Kait whispered something, but he couldn't hear it over the gentle patter of dead larch needles falling from the trees. He didn't ask her to repeat herself; he knew how frustrated she was that she couldn't help. He wished she'd believe him when he said it didn't matter, that he loved her for what she did and loved her no less for what she could no longer do. But she was young and the young always felt they had to prove themselves. Being dead wouldn't change that.

The inner flesh of the mushrooms was firm and white. He tested each with the point of a ridged fingernail to be certain they hadn't lost their moisture to age. It was late afternoon before he found enough. When he'd finally filled the fold in his robe, he straightened, ancient joints protesting the damp, and carried the fungus carefully back to the hollow where he slept.

He had the rocks ready—one with a hollow and one with a curve—and his small, fire-blackened pot, and a green glass flask that had once held . . . once held . . . He couldn't remember. It had last held the same promise he would pour into it today.

Who had told him about the mushrooms? Who had

shown him how to crush them for their juices? It had to have been the dead, but there had been so many dead.

So many.

One hand rose to stroke the necklace of bone; a remembrance from each of them as they'd left him. He had lost them all. All but Kait.

"Now we've found a new family," he told the shadow of the girl hovering protectively around him. "A family the stockade will help us to protect."

Kait knew where they kept their beer. They took all their water from a single well.

He hummed as he poured the cloudy liquid from the pot to the flask. Kait moved closer to listen. He could only remember one Song.

Eyes narrowed, Karlene rocked back on her heels and watched a guard wearing the double sunburst of the Second Army efficiently search her packs. He'd obviously been on border duty long enough, or often enough that he didn't have to actually think about what he was doing. His bored expression never changed as he rummaged through her meager possessions.

"Please . . ." When he looked up from her instrument case, she added, "Be careful with that."

A few minutes later, she was back out in the drizzle and moving up the gentle slope to the pass. She'd been prepared to use Command to get across the border, but no one in the customs house seemed to think it strange she was going back to Shkoder—after all, the Empire now had bards of its own. Shoulders hunched against the wet, she walked quickly through the Giant's Cleft.

The moment she passed the midpoint, the world felt different. It shouldn't have, as she didn't Sing earth, but it did and in a multitude of ways she couldn't define, she knew she was home. Her step lightened as she hurried toward the guard tower at the Shkoden end of the pass. When a helmed figure stepped forward, she Sang her name.

"Bard?" Nastka pulled off her helm and peered across the border, as though she were checking to be sure that this unexpected bard was alone. "What are you doing here?"

"I've been called home." Remembering why destroyed

her pleasure in it. "I've been in the Empire for the last two years."

"Well, since you're not Gabris, you must be Karlene. I'm Nastka i'Milena." Holding out her fist, Nastka laughed at the other woman's expression. "This is the easiest pass through these mountains. We make it a point to know about any prominent Shkodens on the other side." Her other fist lightly pounded her leather armor. "If the Empire tries anything, we'll be ready."

She seemed so proud that Karlene didn't have the heart to tell her the Empire barely thought about Shkoder at all and that its most likely venue for "trying something" would be dumping surplus production and not an armed invasion. Shkoder's natural defenses were too good to attempt the latter and the trade imbalance too great to ignore the former.

"So, what do you Sing?"

"Air, fire, and water."

"You going to be in the area for Third Quarter Festival? Jazep's around somewhere and if the two of you could get together in the next couple of days, you'd have all four quarters. You might even get *me* into a Center to hear that."

"Jazep's a friend of yours?"

"Oh, yeah, we go way back. We thought my eldest girl, Jelena, was his. Turned out she wasn't, so he stood as her name-father." As Karlene's expression changed, she frowned. "What is it?"

There were a hundred ways to tell her, but they all came down to the same thing. "Jazep's been killed. That's why I've been called home."

Nastka stood perfectly still for a long moment, her complete and utter lack of reaction speaking of a greater loss than weeping and wailing would have. She blinked once, silent tears cutting a warm path through the rain on her face. "Was it the thing he was following? The thing that scared the kigh?"

"Yes."

"And you're going after it." Not a question; but then, it didn't need to be. "Do you know what it is?"

Karlene sighed and nodded. "It's a Cemandian bard."

"I thought the Cemandians hated bards."

"They do." Remembering the abomination Kars had become, she added, "They tortured him because he could Sing the kigh. They made him insane."

The information elicited no sympathy. "Him? It isn't an old man, is it? Looks too old to live?" When Karlene's eyes widened, she explained about Jazep's visit and about the old man who'd come into Shkoder at around the right time. She didn't mention that he'd called out a name as he crossed the border. He was crazy, after all. "If we'd known," she growled, grinding the knuckles of her right hand into her left palm, "we could've stopped him. Jazep might still be alive."

"Or you might be dead."

A jerky rise and fall of armored shoulders was her only response. "Two days and I'm finished this shift. I've got free time coming. I want to help."

"Thank you, but **no**." Karlene used just enough Voice to push the last word over into Command. "I've faced him before, and I think I know his Song. He doesn't seem to have any protection against bards."

"Tell that to Jazep," Nastka reminded her grimly.

Just down from the pass, Karlene sat under the umbrella of a huge old pine and listened in astonishment to the message the kigh brought from Marija at Bartek Springs. Her Royal Highness wanted Vree and the healer she was traveling with held? Captain Liene had told Marija to deal with it? It would've been laughable had the potential for disaster not been so great. She Sang back a single word.

"How?"

While she waited for an answer, she reflected that Vree's imminent arrival—or perhaps more accurately, Gyhard's—came as no surprise. Gyhard had unfinished business with Kars. His past seemed determined to interfere with whatever future he and Vree could cobble together.

"Her Highness leaves how up to us. We don't have to hold her long, her brother is close behind."

"Bannon?" Karlene whistled away a kigh unbraiding her hair, and frowned. "What's Bannon doing in Shkoder?" Then she remembered, the fledglings and Jazep had driven Prince Otavas' trip to Elbasan right out of her head. Given that Bannon was in the country, sending him after Vree made sense. He was probably the only living person with a chance of stopping her.

It wasn't going to be pleasant. Bannon hated Gyhard and the last she'd seen them, he wasn't getting along that well with his sister either.

Had she a way to do it, she might have warned Vree. "All things being enclosed, probably a good thing I can't." Neither Her Highness nor the Bardic Captain would be very happy about it. "On the other hand, I'd better warn Marija.

"Remember that Vree has two kigh. Neither Charm nor Command will hold her long."

When it came right down to it, Karlene would've welcomed Vree's company, but she wanted Gyhard stopped. He'd had his hands around Kars' throat once before and Kars had gotten away. Now, Jazep was dead. She didn't trust him. Didn't trust the bond between the two men. She'd deal with this herself.

There was no reason for her to go to Bartek Springs. It was far more important that she catch up with Kars; the sooner she got to him, the sooner people would stop dying.

The reaction of the kigh told her Kars was east, up in the mountains. She heaved her pack up onto her shoulders and started off cross-country, the kigh choosing her path.

"A woman trained to kill, who's immune to Command and Charm because she has two kigh." Marija sighed deeply and ate another butter cookie. "Why me?"

Celestin smiled. "Think of what a great song this will make."

"Yeah, wonderful." The priest had proved to be a valuable ally when the Bartek Springs town council had decided, much as Her Highness had, that this was a bardic problem. Imperial assassins were not for them to deal with. Marija brushed crumbs off her shirtfront. "I knew I should've walked north this quarter, but, oh, no, I wanted to be in the mountains when the high berries ripened. Are you sure that shed will hold her?"

"It held the bear."

"I get the distinct impression that this Vireyda Magaly is more dangerous than a bear."

*   *   *

"Are you all right?"

Slumped in the saddle, a breeze pushing her curls first over one eye and then the other, Magda forced a close approximation of a smile. "I'm fine. Why?"

Vree swept a critical gaze over the younger woman. "You look like you've been riding under the horse, not on it."

"So I'm a little tired." She tried to straighten, then sighed and sagged again. "They keep saying that healing energies have to come from somewhere."

"You told us that the sugar-water you drank would take care of it."

"I lied."

We should've left her in the village. Gyhard's tone had a distinct *I told you* flavor.

Granted. Vree guided her mount around a low branch—Magda merely sagged lower, the yellowing leaves that announced the coming Third Quarter brushing her head. *But since we didn't, what do we do now?*

Go on without her.

And just leave her like this?

*Vree, she's slowing us down. We already lost a day in the village while she dealt with the accident. Pursuit *can't* be far behind. If they catch us before we get to Kars . . .*

I won't let that happen.

How are you going to stop it? Suppose His Majesty sent a whole troop of guards? It's not unlikely, considering that Magda's not only his niece but a valuable healer and he doesn't trust us. Even you can't kill that many people! He felt her wince. *Vree, I'm sorry but . . .*

No. You're right. I can't. She twisted around and looked back the way they'd come. Unfortunately, although some of the leaves had turned brilliant shades of orange and yellow, very few had actually fallen. She couldn't see a thing even though their path had been rising all morning. Similar geography back in the Sixth Province would've left everything below them exposed. *This country has too many trees.*

Homesick?

Closing her eyes, she saw the village spread out around the garrison wall; pots of flowers bloomed on red slate roofs, olive groves lifted silver-green leaves to a brilliant blue sky and, in the distance, the heat shimmered over plateaus of orange stone. Behind her, she could hear the soldiers of the Sixth Army; the metal on metal of a practice bout, a corporal calling cadence, dice rattling in a cup, men and women laughing, lying, belonging. Breathing in, she could smell the omnipresent odor of cooking onions. And at her back . . .

Vree?

She opened her eyes and stared at the trees. *I have no home.*

"See anything?" Magda asked.

"No." Turning to face forward once again, she left the past lying where it had fallen. *I can't gallop off and leave her behind.*

*Why not? I guarantee that whoever is after us poses no danger to *her*.*

I've never left a wounded comrade behind, and I'm slaughtering well not going to start now.

She's not wounded.

She's not well! End of argument. "Magda, can you canter?"

"No, but I've been told I have an attractive trot." When Vree's eyes narrowed, Magda raised a hand and cut off the response. "Joke." She sighed deeply and, her voice wistful, added, "I thought we were sparing the horses?"

Although they were still riding courier horses, they were no longer galloping wildly down the Coast Road. They'd left the line of stables—extending from Elbasan to Somesford where the Duc of Somes had her principal residence—when they'd turned toward Bartek Springs.

"No, not now. We wouldn't ask except . . ."

"That you think we're going to be stopped. That whoever His Majesty, my uncle, has sent after us is breathing right down our necks because of me." Magda's chin rose. "Was I supposed to just let those people die?"

Vree stared at her in some confusion. "We never . . ."

"I told you right at the beginning I wouldn't slow you down. I can do *anything* I have to do!" She slammed her heels into her horse's ribs and, clutching the saddlehorn with both hands, pounded away up the track.

Where did that come from? Gyhard wondered.

Exhaustion. We'd better catch up before she bounces off and breaks her neck.

Which would certainly not be what we were hoping for when we wanted her to find us a body.

As they raced after the young healer, Vree realized it had been days since she'd thought of Gyhard in a body of his own.

"Yer less than a day behind. See, that's the problem. They come pounding in just after dawn this mornin'. My boy gets me up and I checked the healer's mark against the list—she's an apprentice on the list, but that don't mean squat—and I mount them, see?"

It took an effort, but Gerek managed to keep his expression pleasant. "So what you're saying is that the only horses you have are the two my sister and her companion rode in on this morning?"

The stablemaster beamed at him. "That's it Yer Grace. That's it exactly. And you see, the problem is, the horses, they don't go out again unless they got a full day's rest." She shrugged apologetically. "I ain't never had four riders in so close together before, being at the end of the line as it were 'cepting for the Duc's stable at Somesford."

"Is she refusing to mount us?" Bannon asked quietly from his place behind Gerek's left shoulder.

"Essentially. The horses require a day's rest and they haven't had it."

Bannon turned and stared into the corral where a bay and a black were standing nose to tail in a patch of late afternoon sun, lazily swatting at the last, hardy flies of the season. "They don't look tired."

"She says Vree and Maggie rode in just after dawn."

"Dawn? Then they rode all night? I don't think so, there was no slaughtering moon."

Gerek nodded. "You're right." They'd spent dark till dawn on opposite sides of a haymow for that very reason. "Do you know how far they'd come?" he asked the stablemaster, who'd been staring at Bannon in rapt fascination.

She shifted her slightly protruding gaze back onto Gerek. "Oh, yeah, they just come from Three Rock Cove, see?

Just up the coast a fish, skip, and a jump. Terrible accident there day 'fore yesterday. Healer saved three lives. Southern girl— This one's sister is she? Thought as much. Look right alike. —She rescued young Celja right off the side of the cliff. Plucked her out as handy as a kid stealing eggs from a gull. My Gerri, he was there doin' what he could, he says everyone was some impressed." She nodded sagely. "Did it with no clothes on, too."

"What's she babbling about now?" Bannon muttered.

The stablemaster sighed happily. "I do love to hear him talk Southern. Sounds so pretty."

Gerek just barely managed to stop himself from saying something very rude. He sighed and squared his shoulders, his voice dropping into an almost bardic cadence. "Stablemaster, these horses have been ridden a very short distance by two very light riders. At most, we have only a couple of hours until dark. The track to Bartek Springs is not one you can go galloping down even in full daylight without risking your neck. We have no desire to risk either our necks or the horses'. I give you my word that if you mount us now, we will treat these animals as if they were my own."

"Yer own?"

As assorted breezes lifted ebony curls, he spread his hands and turned the full force of his smile on her, teeth gleaming in the dark depths of his beard. "As if they were my father's."

She blinked and flushed. "Yeah, that's more like it. You gots a tongue like a bard, Yer Grace. And if I gots yer word, you gots the horses."

"What the slaughter was *that* all about?" Bannon demanded as she led the animals from the corral.

"We have a saying in Ohrid: you can get more flies with honey than you can with vinegar."

"We've got one like it," Bannon admitted suspiciously.

I just bet you do, Gerek thought, remembering how charming the southerner could become when he wanted something. He gestured at the stablemaster saddling the bay. "I got us a pair of flies."

"So we'll catch them tonight?"

"No. Probably not until tomorrow. But the less time they

have to be held in Bartek Springs before we arrive, the better the odds are they'll still be there. I don't imagine Vree's going to like being held."

"You *can't* imagine." Bannon's chin lifted. "You know nothing about my sister."

"I know enough not to refer to her like she was some kind of possession. You say 'my sister' like you say, 'my knives' or 'my boots'."

"I don't . . ."

"You do." Gerek turned away, took a single step, then turned back. "And I'll tell you something else," he added, catching the shorter man's gaze and holding it, "if anyone talked about *my* sister the way you talk about Vree, I'd beat the living shit out of him."

Bannon's right hand curled into a fist, but his left touched his nose, still slightly swollen.

Splintered finger ends clattered together as Kars lifted the necklace of bone over his head and hung it carefully on a broken spur of branch. While he hated to leave the mementos of his old family behind, they had, in the past, made it difficult for him to acquire a new family and this time he was taking no chances.

"I will return for you," he murmured, lightly stroking the memories of those who'd been his companions over the years, "when things are settled down below."

He checked that the green glass flask—now full of cloudy liquid—was safely tucked into a corner of his worn, leather pouch then settled the broad strap on his shoulder. As he looked down into the valley, he had the feeling that this was what he'd been searching for all along.

"Come, Kait. Let's go home."

Standing in the open gate of the stockade, Kiril a'Edko i'Amalia shielded his eyes against the late afternoon sun and squinted in the direction his youngest son was pointing. "You've got eyes like a hawk, boy, if you can tell that's an old man from this distance."

"A very old man, Papa." His stance identical to his father's, Edko narrowed his eyes a little more. "Older even than Granduncle was before he died."

"Older than Grandmother?"

The boy snorted. "No one's older than Grandmother."

"Can't argue with that," Kiril laughed. "Not when she says it herself." Folding his arms over a barrel chest, he leaned against the huge peeled log that anchored the gate. "Wonder what he's doing way out here."

"Wandering?"

"From where to where, that's the question. And why?"

Edko shrugged. "Why does he have to have a reason?"

"Everyone has a reason, lad, even if they don't know it themselves."

"There's something kind of funny around his head."

"Funny?"

"Yeah like, uh . . ." He cocked his own head, but it didn't help. "I dunno; funny."

Kiril straightened and stared searchingly at his son. Of late there'd been indications he'd be a bard once his voice changed. "Kigh?"

"No, Papa, not kigh." His voice held all the weary disdain of a twelve-year-old who was tired of hearing adults plan his future.

"Probably just the light being behind him, then."

"Yeah, I guess." But he didn't sound convinced. "Are we gonna take him in?"

"Well, we're not going to leave him standing at the gate. Frankly, I'm amazed he hasn't been eaten by something before now."

"Maybe he's too old and tough?"

"Show some respect for your elders, boy." He swung a three-fingered hand in the general direction of his son. Grinning broadly, the boy danced back. "Day after tomorrow being Third Quarter Festival and all, I'd just as soon we stayed on the good side of the gods. No point in moving farther from the Center of the Circle than you have to. I'd better go tell your Aunt Ales there'll be company for supper."

Edko wrinkled his nose. "Better tell someone to heat up the bathwater, too."

Kiril took another long look and nodded. "Good idea."

As his father turned and ambled inside, Edko trotted toward the fenced pasture and the waiting cattle. He sang as he ran, his pure soprano wrapped incongruously around a disgusting ditty involving cow patties in the spring.

Because he was moving, he didn't realize that, for the first time in his life, no breeze answered his song.

"Bartek Springs?"

"Uh-huh." Magda pulled a damp curl from the corner of her mouth. "Kind of pretty, isn't it? Pity we're not going in."

Vree turned her gaze from the town—they'd arrived at dusk, just as lamps were being lit in the windows of half-timbered houses—and looked at the healer. "We're not?"

"If they're going to stop us anywhere, they're going to stop us here. You know that as well as I do. If you planned on going in, you planned on getting caught and then leaving without me."

I thought she didn't read minds, Gyhard grumbled.

Magda smiled sweetly at them. "I have an older brother. I'm harder to ditch than that."

"And you're exhausted," Vree told her bluntly, not bothering to deny the accusation. "You need to rest."

"Have I slowed you down?"

Vree sighed. "No."

"Then I think it should be my choice, whether I go on or not. Don't you?" She rested her elbow on the saddle horn and her chin on her cupped hand. "Well?"

"Yes. It should be your choice . . ."

Vree.

". . . but I think you should stay here."

"No. Everything I said back at the Citadel still stands. You're my patient and I won't abandon you. Kars needs healing, and I won't abandon him either."

Vree!

You're the one who said she has an answer for every-thing. You want her to stay here so badly, you come up with a good reason. "So where do the good people of Bartek Springs put their dead?" she continued aloud when Gyhard remained silent.

Looking worried, Magda straightened. "Their dead?"

"Tombs or graves or something. If Kars is making the dead walk, he needs fresh bodies."

The younger woman winced at the matter-of-fact reference. "According to the bardic maps I studied back in El-basan, there's a cemetery on the far side of town."

"Then let's get going." Guiding her reluctant horse off the main track, that would very shortly become the town's main street, Vree nudged him with her heels until he lengthened his walk.

"But it'll be dark by the time we get there," Magda protested.

"So we'll get an early start tomorrow morning."

"We're spending the night in the cemetery?"

"It's okay. The bards said that Jazep took care of what Kars did here."

Magda urged her horse after Vree's. "Yeah, but . . ."

"Unless you'd rather go into town?" When Magda muttered something Vree couldn't quite catch, the ex-assassin almost smiled.

You're mean.

She's a healer, Gyhard. She's going to have to learn to deal with dead bodies.

Try to see it from her side. A dead body means she failed. For you, dead bodies meant success.

And for you?

She felt herself sigh; knew it was his reaction. *Only that I was still alive,* he said softly.

Wishing that there was a little more light, Vree dismounted and stretched. She could just barely make out the dark on dark slabs of gravestones on the other side of the low stone wall and she wondered just what it was the Shkodens did for their dead. In the Empire, army dead were most frequently buried in mass graves with the rites performed once for the lot and their only memorial in the memories of their surviving comrades. The rich stacked their dead in stone tombs along the Great Roads. She didn't know what the poor did.

"It's spooky," Magda whispered, pressed tightly against the comforting bulk of her horse.

"Without the kigh, there's nothing left but meat."

"I know."

"Meat can't hurt you."

"I *know*."

You have such a comforting way with a metaphor, Gyhard noted as Vree unbuckled the saddle girth.

Hobbling the horses—fortunately, they'd been able to

water them on the way around town—the two women ate
quickly and settled down for the night, wrapped together
in their blankets to conserve warmth.

"You know, this close to Third Quarter this far up in
the mountains, we could *easily* have a touch of light frost
before morning."

Vree tucked her chin closer to her chest. "I'm so
thrilled."

As sleep claimed them, the night seemed to take on the
rhythm of their breathing. Leaves danced with the breeze
to the same slow time; the thousand and one noises of the
creatures who made the darkness their own became a gentle harmony. At first, the music was only an extension of
the breathing, the breeze, the creatures, but then it took
on a definition all its own. Promising security, it lay over
the sleepers like another blanket.

When it finally trailed off, the other sounds went with it
and the night was, for a moment, perfectly still.

On the far side of the graveyard, Celestin pulled her
fingers from her ears and yawned. "Is that it, then?"

"That's it." Marija Sang a quick four notes and a kigh
danced on the wick of the lantern she held. "I can't guarantee it'll hold them until morning, but we'll have time
enough to lock them safely away."

The priest shook her head as she beckoned her nephew
and three other men forward into the light. "I don't much
like this."

Marija shrugged and rummaged a bit of hard candy out
of a pocket. "You won't have to not like it for long. According to the kigh, they'll only be our problem until
noon tomorrow."

Clean and fed, dressed in a borrowed robe better than
any he could remember wearing, Kars lay on a pallet by
the hearth and listened to the sounds of people sleeping.
Tomorrow, they'd told him—speaking slowly and loudly for
he understood very little of the language—the cutters
would be coming in and everyone would be home for the
festival.

Everyone would be home.

He would wait.

*   *   *

Eyes still closed. Breathing regular. If anyone was watching, they'd think she remained asleep. She was in a building. A small building. She was alone—or at least Magda was no longer with her—and her weapons had been removed.

Vree?

Quiet.

The urgency in the command and the surge of adrenaline accompanying it penetrated Gyhard's usual waking fog and he found himself completely attuned to Vree's senses.

It wasn't a stable, although it had held an animal. She could smell a faint hint of musk behind an overlay of soap. The pallet beneath her was clean. The blanket, the one she'd fallen asleep under.

She could hear dogs barking. A rooster crow. Farther away, a baby cried fretfully. She could hear only her own breathing.

She opened her eyes. Before her lids were all the way up, she stood, hands out from her sides, in the center of the shed.

Logs as big around as her thigh had been sunk into the ground to make a square, each wall a little longer than the pallet they'd laid her on. Light and air came through a multitude of tiny chinks. Something large and angry had gouged lines of parallel claw marks into the wood. The roof had been built of more logs with sod laid on top. The door dragged open outward on bullhide hinges and had been braced or barred. The dirt floor showed signs of having been recently repacked around the base of the walls. There was a jug of water by the bed and an empty, covered pot in the opposite corner.

A cautious look outside showed a field, a dirt yard and a fence, the back of a building, and the side of what smelled like a cow stable.

Moving back to the center of the floor, she drew in a deep breath and let it out slowly through her nose, teeth clenched too tightly to allow even the passage of air. "What happened?"

Offhand, I'd say there's a bard in Bartek Springs.

A bard did this?

Probably Sang us a lullaby.

Vree flexed her fingers around an invisible throat. "I'm beginning to understand the Cemandian attitude."

"So you stuck her in a shed that used to hold a bear? You locked her up like an *animal?*"

Marija was beginning to regret ever having mentioned the shed's previous occupant. "She's an Imperial assassin; I doubt very much Celestin's house would hold her."

Eyes blazing, Magda stomped across the room and jabbed her finger at the bard. "You have no business holding her at all! For that matter, you have no business holding me!"

"Her Highness commanded . . ."

"What? That you break your vows and use the kigh against an innocent pair of travelers!"

"I haven't broken anything!" Astonished to find herself shouting, Marija took a deep breath and regained a measure of control. "You know as well as I do that Singing a lullaby involves no kigh."

Magda smiled triumphantly. "Does, too. Fifth kigh. And you can't argue with that because *I* know."

"I was just following orders . . ."

"Oh, sure, convenient excuse. If they'd ordered you cover us in honey and stake us over an anthill, would you have done *that*, too?"

Marija sighed. "Maybe not yesterday."

"What's *that* supposed to mean!"

Raising both hands, palm out, the bard stood. "Look, Magda, as much as I personally find it difficult to understand, the powers that be want you back in Elbasan. They also want your companion, an Imperial assassin with two not entirely stable kigh, back where she's under some kind of supervision."

"And they don't consider *me* sufficient supervision?"

"Apparently not." With one hand on the door, she cautioned the young healer against approaching any closer. "I've done what I was told to do and in a very short while you won't be my problem. The kigh say your brother and her brother are a very short distance from town."

"Her brother?"

"His name is Bannon. He came into Shkoder with Prince

Otavas and was recruited to help out. That's all I know."
Nodding at the table she added, "Try a little jam on the
oatcakes, they're really good." Then she left.

"Oh, sure." Magda slapped a spoonful of jam on an oat-
cake with one hand and dashed away angry tears with the
other. "*I'm* not sufficient supervision for an Imperial assassin, but Gerek *is?* Like *that's* fair."

"Magda is locked in the priest's spare room, Your Grace.
We felt her companion . . ." Under the intensity of Bannon's stare, Marija cleared her throat and began again.
"That is, under the circumstances and considering everything we'd heard about her ability, we felt her companion
should be put someplace a little more secure.

As Gerek translated, Bannon shifted his weight forward
and flexed the muscles across his back. Although he looked
ready for a fight, all he said when Gerek finished was,
"Where?"

Someone's coming. Vree rolled up onto her feet and
held her breath as she sifted the quiet sound of approaching
footsteps from the sounds she'd been listening to all morning. Whoever it was, was walking softly. Not furtively, as
though expecting to reach the shed unnoticed but with a
sure and quiet tread that kept the weight balanced and the
noise to a minimum.

Whoever it was . . .

Vree! Are you all right?

No . . .

Vree, breathe!

She jerked and sucked in a frantic lungful of air just in
time to expel it as a name when the footsteps stopped.
"Bannon."

"He's made you weak, Vree. These people should never
have been able to catch you." His voice dripped disdain;
for Gyhard, for her, for the people who'd caught her.

"Their bards don't exactly fight fair."

"What was it Commander Neegan used to say? The survivors determine what's fair?"

"Things are more complicated now," she said, turning to
follow the sound of his movement as he circled the shed.
"Survival isn't everything."

"Does *he* think so, too, sister-mine?" He used to say it like an endearment. Now, it was more of a reminder. "Remember what he's done in the past to survive."

"We remember."

"We?" His voice picked up an edge, just as arrogant but a little less certain. "You'll never share his memories the way you shared mine, Vree, because you'll never share his life the way you shared mine."

"What makes you think I want to?" She watched his shadow flicker silently past the chinks between the logs.

Finally, it stopped, a hand's span to the right of the door. "So it's like that, is it? I might have known. Do you let him use your body? Does he touch you with your hands?"

Vree rolled her eyes. "Is that all you *ever* think about?" she demanded. "Bannon, what are you doing here?"

"I've come to take you back to Elbasan."

"By whose command?"

"As a favor to the crown of Shkoder."

"Then as a favor to me, let me go."

Bannon laughed. "That'd be a favor to *him,* not to you. It isn't you that's running after Kars, it's him. It isn't you that needs to be stopped, it's him." His voice grew slightly shrill. "It isn't you who left me, it's him!"

"I chose."

"NO!"

His pain ripping great holes in her heart, Vree took a step toward the wall. He was the younger brother she'd loved and protected her entire life, and she wanted to destroy the thing hurting him so.

Vree.

Not you; me.

I know. He gave her his strength and was surprised when she used it.

"Bannon, even if I'd let Gyhard die, things could never have been the same between us. We can't go back into the past."

"I know that. I'm not stupid, Vree. But why can't we go into the future together?"

She laid her hand against the logs. Saw bits of him mirror the movement on the other side. "Because we'd drag the past with us and it would drag us down. I'm not going back to Elbasan with you."

"Yes, you are." His hand fell away. "If I have to knock you out and tie you to the slaughtering horse."

Can he? Gyhard asked as they listened to the footsteps move away.

Trying to remember if her palms used to sweat, she dried them on her thighs. *No. If it came to a fight, I'd know every move he'd make before he made it.*

Wouldn't he know yours the same way?

My life revolved around him. So did his.

Vree, if it came to a fight . . .

As the sound of Bannon's footsteps blended with the sounds of Bartek Springs, she shook her head. *He can't kill me. He wants me for something.*

What? Besides the obvious.

Settling back cross-legged on the edge of the pallet, she snorted, the sound more sad than indignant. *Don't you start. I don't know what he wants but, trust me, I know when he's hiding something.*

Vree?

Don't . . .

Can you kill him?

She closed her eyes and touched the memories of her brother. *I hate you sometimes, you know.*

He let his control move down into her arms. Once again, she allowed his embrace. *I know.*

"Gerek, things are happening here that you don't understand!"

He dropped his head into his hands and sighed. It'd been a long hard ride and this accusation was not what he needed at the end of it. "What don't I understand, Maggi?"

"If you force us to go back to Elbasan with you, you'll have completely *ruined* Vree's life. Destroyed *any* chance that she and Gyhard might be able to create some kind of a future together."

"How?" Suddenly suspicious, he studied her through narrowed eyes. "You're not thinking of putting Gyhard into Kars' body are you?"

Magda made a disgusted face. "Yuk, no."

"Then explain how I'd be destroying anything."

"Sometimes the past is like, like a millstone around your neck and it keeps dragging you back whenever you try to go forward. Kars is that kind of a millstone for Gyhard. As long as Gyhard was just killing time . . ."

"Not to mention assorted young men."

Magda ignored him. ". . . then he didn't have to deal with all the feelings of betrayal and guilt, but the moment he fell in love with Vree, then it all came to the surface like, like a festering boil that has to be lanced."

"Lovely imagery, Maggot," Gerek muttered, curling his lip. "Don't tell me—you're the healer to lance the boil?"

"Yes!" Throwing herself to her knees at his feet, she gazed up at him, using an expression that had, in the past, softened his resistance. "Singing the kigh back into the dead for all these years, Kars has taken his *own* kigh out of the Circle. Gyhard and I *together* are the only hope of stopping him." Grabbing his wrists, she shook him as hard as she could—unfortunately, it made little impression. "If you can't help us for Vree's sake—who, I'd like to remind you, you were so *infatuated* with such a short while ago— then do help us for Shkoder. Who *knows* what terrible things will happen if Kars isn't stopped!"

Shaking free of her grip, Gerek captured her hands in his. "Listen, Maggi, I know you're used to being the only one who can do certain things, but Captain Liene has called Karlene from the Empire to deal with Kars. She's faced him before. She knows what to do."

Magda shook her head, her dark eyes suddenly bright with tears. "She'll die, Ger. She'll die like Jazep did."

"Jazep only Sang earth, Maggi." His voice gentled, he wiped tears from her cheeks with his thumbs.

She sniffed and pulled away. "Karlene's a bard. Kars needs to be *healed*. She won't be able to reach him and she'll die. Vree and Gyhard need to be healed, and I need *Kars* to do that." Rising, she walked to the window and stared in the direction of the shed. "This is *a lot* more important than keeping me safe or keeping Vree under some sort of supervision."

"Maggi, it wasn't only Her Highness. Annice sent me after you as well."

"*Mother* wants me back in Elbasan?"

"She sent me to find you."

"But did she tell you to take me back to the Capital?" Gerek frowned. "Well, no, but . . ."

"Then *maybe* she wanted you to help me." Hands on her hips, she turned and glared at him. "Did you even *consider* that?"

"Help you?" There were times . . . "Maggi, when she sent the kigh to me, she had no idea of what you were going to do. She still doesn't."

"Are you sure?"

"What?"

"If you think, under these circumstances . . ." Waving arms emphasized the circumstances. ". . . Mother hasn't had the kigh watching both of us, you're not half as smart as you think you are."

"Look, even if Annice does want me to help you," he sighed, his tone suggesting it was highly unlikely, "I've been given a direct order from Her Highness to bring you back."

Lips pressed into a thin line, Magda pivoted on one heel and stared out the window once again.

"Maggi . . ."

She shook her head.

Gerek sighed and left the room. It had seemed so simple when he'd left the capital. Stepping out the back door he saw Bannon approaching across the yard. Something in the Southerner's face, or his posture, or the way that he moved, made Gerek frown.

All at once, he suspected that his little sister was right.

Things were happening here that he didn't understand.

Ten

Singing softly, Karlene tried to work out what was wrong with the kigh. They weren't frightened, although the air trembled still with the faint reverberations of Kars' passing. They weren't trying to warn her of danger; if anything, they seemed sad. Even after she Sang a gratitude, three or four hovered about her head not, as they would usually, in order to make mischief but almost as though they thought she might need the support.

She began to get a very bad feeling about walking into Fortune.

From where she stood, the mining settlement seemed normal enough. A little quiet perhaps, but as it was barely noon, it seemed logical to assume that most of the activity should be going on out of sight at the mine. The breeze shifted and from one of the cottages she could hear the faint wail of an angry baby.

As one, the kigh around her head spun up and out of sight.

"Fickle," she muttered. Squaring her shoulders under the weight of her pack, she walked slowly along the track. At the point where it spread out and became the central square of the settlement, a trio of huge, rough-coated dogs bounded out to meet her. Their greeting seemed subdued. Two of them were strangely submissive, the third sniffed her outstretched hand, then turned and ran barking back the way it had come.

Karlene stayed where she was, waiting for someone to respond to the barking and taking a closer look around. In spite of a Third Quarter chill in the air, all the doors and windows were open in the two, large, communal buildings fronting the square. Except for the dogs, the place seemed deserted. Even the baby had stopped crying.

Then a young woman stepped out of one of the small

cottages, pulling the door closed behind her. The way she moved spoke of both fear and suspicion. Karlene thought she saw a shape stir at the window and the fine hairs lifted off the back of her neck as she felt herself watched.

"What do you want?" the young woman called, one hand resting lightly on the dog's broad head.

Karlene Sang her name.

To her surprise, the young woman started, raised both hands to her mouth, and burst into tears.

"Why didn't you send word to the duc? Or even down to Bartek Springs?"

"How?" Krisus demanded, bouncing a now smiling baby on his lap. "We had so many people to bury and Ilka to take care of—she's not even weaned yet—and . . ."

Karlene laid her hand lightly on his shoulder and cut off the flow of bitter words. "I wasn't criticizing," she explained gently. "It's just that you've been through so much, I'm amazed that you managed without sending for help."

"We couldn't leave them," Evicka declared defensively. She poured warm milk into a glass flask and deftly tied a cloth nipple to the top. "What if the others had come home while we were gone and found only bodies?"

"You're right." Astounded by the strength these two just barely out of their teens had shown, Karlene didn't bother being subtle with her voice. She let all her admiration and her sympathy and her sorrow show.

Krisus sniffed. "After what happened . . ." No need to actually say what had happened; the memory lay like an oily film over the settlement. ". . . it was almost a relief that they were dead." He jerked and stared at the bard, horrified by what he'd said. "Except for Jazep, I mean. I wasn't . . . I didn't .. when he Sang . . . If it wasn't for Jazep, they'd still be walking around and Ilka would have starved and I didn't mean we were relieved that he was dead."

"I know." And they had to believe her.

Only the baby, feeding with the single-minded intensity of the very young, remained unaffected. After a moment Evicka cleared her throat. "Could you Sing over the grave? We said what we thought we should, but the nearest priest is in Bartek Springs and it feels unfinished."

*   *   *

The mound of stone at the edge of the forest was larger than Karlene expected, larger and sadder.

"There's rock close to the surface up here," Krisus told her. "I had to dig near the trees to get down far enough that they wouldn't get dug up again by scavengers." He looked at the dirt ground into the creases of callused hands. "I—we, haven't been back to the mine since it happened. I grab onto a pick and all I can think of is . . ." Words failed him, and he waved toward the mound.

Evicka shifted the baby from right arm to left. "We put Jazep's body in with the others. We didn't know what else to do. If the bards want him . . ."

"No. Let him lie where he is." The body without the kigh was an empty shell. Karlene knew that, had seen the proof of it, but it was harder, far harder, to believe it when the body belonged to a friend. "He liked to have people around him."

"We didn't get to know him very well."

Blinking back tears, Karlene remembered what Virine had said. If Jazep had to have an epitaph, she couldn't find one better. "He was kind."

"And brave," Krisus added.

"And one of many." Karlene straightened and drew in a deep, cleansing breath. "Tell me about the others."

"Just the seven that walked?"

"No, all of them."

It was one of the longest Songs, she'd ever Sung, but when it was over, she felt curiously clear-headed as though more than just the dead had been Sung to rest.

Evicka smiled tentatively, then looked guilty when she'd realized what she'd done. Krisus pressed his lips against the top of the baby's head, who woke up and started to fuss.

"One thing I still don't understand," Karlene murmured as they walked back to the cottage. "In the Empire, when Kars did what he did, babies died. How did Ilka survive?"

"Her mother was one of the dead?"

"A possible reason, but I doubt that's it."

"Our babies are tougher?"

Karlene shook her head. "Nice to believe, but I don't think so." Turning and walking backward, she tickled Ilka's nose with the end of her braid. "What is it about you, baby? Why are you still here?"

Ilka shrieked with laughter and stretched out chubby fists. To Karlene's surprise, she wasn't reaching for the braid.

The kigh slid its elongated body through the infant's grasp and, twisting back on itself, stroked both her cheeks with ethereal fingers.

Too stunned to notice where she was putting her feet, Karlene tripped over a rock and sat down. Hard. To her companions' astonishment, she stayed where she was, and Sang a question to the kigh. When they answered, she bounced up, took Ilka, and swung her in the air.

"All four quarters! You little music box, you!"

"What are you talking about?" Krisus asked, his hands extended to retrieve the baby but unwilling to insult the bard as long as Ilka herself seemed to be happy with the situation.

Eyes gleaming, mouth stretched out in so large a smile her cheeks hurt, Karlene handed the laughing child back to her anxious guardian. "She's a bard. Or she will be in time. *And* all four quarters. This is incredible. This is absolutely incredible! I've got to tell the Captain!" Opening her mouth, she noticed the expressions on the two people facing her and closed it again. "What's the matter?"

Evicka stroked a rounded cheek, much as the kigh had. "Will she have to go away?"

Suddenly understanding, Karlene shook her head. "Not for fourteen or fifteen years, and not even then unless she wants to."

Relief came off them in waves. "So she doesn't *have* to be a bard?"

"No. She doesn't have to be anything she doesn't want to be." There was no need to mention that the odds of any person who could attract such attention from the kigh as an infant deciding *not* to be a bard were so small as to be essentially nonexistent. They'd dealt with enough for one day.

One day . . .

"By the Center of the Circle, Third Quarter Festival starts tonight!"

Frowning, Evicka began to count on her fingers. "That's in . . . Oh, my heart, you're right."

"It doesn't matter," Krisus sighed. "Not this year."

"It matters this year more than any," Karlene told them gently. "Grieving is a needful thing and it's enclosed by the Circle, but it can't be allowed to stop the Circle from turning."

"We don't have much to give thanks for."

"I realize you've lost a great deal." Her voice slid from sympathy into wonder. "But you have the strength that a loving family gave you and you have Ilka and you have each other and isn't that something to be grateful for?"

The young partners looked at each other over the baby's head.

"If I hadn't had you," Krisus murmured.

Evicka took his hand and together they turned to face the bard. "All thing beings enclosed, we think that we'd like to keep the festival."

Karlene smiled and taking each of them by an elbow, she pushed them toward the cottage. "Come on, we've got to get some kind of a harvest in, there's festival cakes to bake, and, if I'm going to Sing the Quarter around, I'm going to need some honey for my throat."

"Here, if you're going to be sitting around in my way, you can make yourself useful." When Kars stared at her in confusion, Ales closed his fist about the shaft of the wooden paddle. "Stir," she said, moving his arm around in a circle.

He looked down into the tub, smiled, and nodded. Using both hands he swirled the perforated paddle around and around in the batter. As grandmother had taken to her bed to rest up for the festival, his age entitled him to her place by the hearth. He'd spent the morning sitting and watching the bustle of festival preparations—trying to make sense out of the chaos. He didn't understand much of what was said, but he'd have time to learn the language later.

"What is?" he asked after a moment.

"Festival cake," Ales told him without looking up from the pot she was seasoning. "Enough for everyone in the settlement to have themselves a good healthy piece." Cuffing the shoulder of the boy chopping vegetables at one end of the heavy plank table, she sent him to the garden for a horseradish root. "Cake'll go in the Circle to be blessed at sunset, then cut and served and frankly, I think it needs more raisins. Keep stirring." Lifting a crock down off an upper shelf, she worked the stopper free and shook more dried fruit into the tub.

Kars frowned and worked his way through her somewhat disjointed speech. "Everyone eats?"

"That's right. Moment the service is over they descend on it like bears on berries. Nobody has to fake eating my festival cake, I'll tell you—I save spices all year for this. By the time this crew is done, there's never enough left over to bring in a mouse. Not that we need more mice after what they did to my bellflowers." She gave Kars a quick pat on the arm and a friendly smile. "Don't worry, there'll be enough for you. Jorin, hurry on out and see if those chickens have . . ." Turning, Ales remembered she'd already sent Jorin to the garden, and bustled out to check the chickens herself, throwing a not to be argued with "Keep stirring" back over one plump shoulder.

Everyone eats. Retrieving his pouch from its place under a bench, Kars worked the stopper out of the flask and poured the contents into the batter. When Jorin trotted back in, a plump root born triumphantly in grubby hands, he was stirring again as instructed.

"Mama?" Jorin asked, looking around.

Kars searched for the word. "Chickens!" he announced at last.

"All right!" Tossing his root on the table, he rubbed his hands against his shirtfront and extended a curved finger toward the batter.

"No . . ."

"It's okay." He grinned up at Kars. "I'm allowed to taste. Really."

"Jorin! You get your filthy hands away from that tub."

The boy whirled, saw his mother had both hands full of eggs, and, with a relieved grin, began briskly chopping vegetables once again.

"Kids," Ales snorted depositing the eggs safely in a bowl. "More trouble than they're worth." But she smiled fondly at her son. "Do you have family, Kars?"

"No more."

"I'm sorry."

"Have again."

She studied him skeptically, but in the end only shrugged and said, "Sure you will. Keep stirring." If he wanted to believe he was still capable of creating children, it was no skin off her teeth.

Outside the open door, Kiril took his son by the shoulder and the two moved with exaggerated silence toward the gate. "I see she's got our guest working," he said when he thought they were safely out of earshot.

"I don't like him, Papa."

"No? Why not?"

"He makes me feel funny."

Brows drawn in until they met over his nose, Kiril turned Edko around to face him, a hand on each shoulder. "Has he *done* anything to you, boy? Don't be afraid to tell me."

Edko sighed and shook his head. "It's nothing like that. It's just that when I'm near him . . ." He stretched out one bare arm. "It feels like there're ants climbing on my skin. He feels wrong."

Visibly relieved, Kiril ruffled the boy's hair. "It's probably just because we didn't think anyone older than Grandmother could exist."

"Well, yeah, but . . ."

"Cutters coming in!"

At the sound of the cry drifting up from the riverbank, Edko twisted out of his father's grip and raced for the gate, whooping with joy. Kiril took a step to follow and was nearly run down by Jorin charging after his cousin. The next few moments were chaotic as the family who remained in the stockade greeted those who were returning from cutting trees in the forest.

"Where's Enrik?" Edko demanded, clutching at the bronzed forearm of his older sister.

She laughed and shook herself free. "He spotted a hawk's nest halfway up a cliff and decided to go after one of the nestlings. We didn't want to wait, so he said he'd follow us down later."

"But the festival starts at sunset!"

"Listen, Sapling, I know the rest of us aren't worth much next to the glorious cousin Enrik, but you know what he's like. Once he gets an idea in his head, you couldn't shift it with an ax."

Edko sighed and turned away, searching the edge of the forest for any sign of his favorite cousin. His sister just didn't understand. Enrik was special. He was always willing to climb to release a deadfall, even when an uncle or aunt said it wasn't safe. He was the first into the river in First Quarter and the last out in Third. He could throw his ax up into the air and catch it behind his back. Sometimes maybe he took chances even Edko realized weren't too smart, but he cut the best willow whistles and he told the *best* stories.

Standing apart from the rest, released from his stirring duties by the pouring of the batter into greased and floured pans, Kars watched Edko watching the forest and slowly shook his head. The boy was demon-marked. He remembered other children lost to the demons. He remembered a boy not much older than this taken from his home. His throat tightened as he remembered the screaming that he'd tried for a very, very long time to forget.

Pushing one of the dogs aside, Karlene finished tracing a circle in the packed dirt of the square. Pulling the stake from the center, she coiled the four-strand measuring rope—each strand dyed to represent a quarter—and stepped over the line. A quick search of the communal buildings had found all the festival trappings recently gathered and made ready for use. Tears had flowed freely as they'd carried everything they needed over to the cottage.

Karlene laid the measure aside and squatted, a little dubiously, to lift the huge clay bowl of water. It was as heavy as it looked. Glazed the exact shade of green used in bardic robes, and etched inside and out with stylized water kigh, it had obviously been bought just for this purpose and transported carefully up into the mountains. It went over the hole where the stake had been and Karlene considered it a small miracle that none of the water spilled.

The four thick beeswax candles, set on each of the four compass points, were a lot easier on her back. Checking the position of the sun, she turned toward the cottage, but before she could call, Krisus hurried out with a basket.

"They're still really hot," he said, laying the steaming cakes in position. "Vicka's sure they're not cooked through."

"They smell great."

He smacked her hand away. "Oh, no, not until after the blessing."

Karlene sighed and began to pile vegetables. "I love festival cakes."

Krisus grinned at her. "Like my mother used to say, since you have to eat them, you might as well decide to like them." He half turned toward the communal kitchen. "Vicka! What about the . ."

"Cheese," she finished, appearing with a round in her arms. "You haven't left the baby alone?"

"She's asleep." But he set the last cake down and hurried into the cottage.

The last thing to be laid in the circle was the silver. From a dull nugget to a beautiful filigree representation of the four quarters, the individual pieces made a small circle of their own just outside the candles. Although it felt wrong when so many others had died, Karlene found herself thankful that the artisan who'd created the final piece of filigree had gone to Bicaz with the load of ore and lived to create again.

The sky had just begun to turn when they finished.

Krisus put the basket holding the sleeping baby in position, then moved to stand across the circle from Evicka. Behind each of them were a pair of lamps ready to be lit when it grew dark. The lamps were an addition to the service, the need for their light Kars' last legacy to Fortune.

Karlene draped her tricolored stole around her neck—a bard walking couldn't be expected to carry robes—and took a deep, calming breath. Gabris and the fledglings would be back in the Capital by now, Singing at the Empress' Center. Silently she wished them a happy festival and prepared to Sing.

Together, as the sky to the west became a glorious, streaked pinky-orange and the sky over the mountains to the east deepened into sapphire blue, the three adults sang the choral that gave thanks for the long, hot days of Second Quarter, and welcomed the cooler days and longer nights of the Third. Just as the sun set, Evicka and Krisus fell silent.

Fire kigh danced on the candles and in each of the lanterns, throwing more light than was possible for their size. Karlene Sang thanks for heat and light.

The Song changed, and the water in the bowl rippled although there was, as yet, no breeze to move it. Karlene Sang thanks for thirst quenched and cleanliness, for the power of the moving stream.

Ilka laughed and clapped her hands as the Song changed again and air kigh danced within the circle. Karlene Sang thanks for breath and the power given to the windmills.

The Song changed a third time.

Karlene turned in place, searching for the voice. There were chorals to be used if the bard Singing the service had less than four full quarters, and she'd just been about to begin one, expecting Krisus and Evicka to join in.

Somewhere, somewhere close, there was a bard Singing thanks to earth.

The dirt in the circle began to move and a kigh emerged. Karlene stared, her heart pounding so loudly she was sure its beat must throw off the rhythm of the Song. Without the ability to Sing earth, she'd never seen an earth kigh before but everyone knew that, where the other three quarters were essentially sexless, the earth kigh always appeared to be female.

This kigh did not.

Its shape seemed somehow familiar.

It was six, maybe eight inches high, broad-shouldered, short-legged, barrel-chested.

The earth Song ended, the last notes rumbling away into the gathering dusk, and the kigh began the Blessing. It was amazing that such a pure bass tone could come from such a tiny figure.

Instinct overcame shock and a half measure into the Blessing, Karlene added her voice. The harmony grew and rose until it touched the stars just appearing over the mountaintops. The sky seemed close enough to touch, the earth small enough to enclose in a protective embrace. For one glorious moment, the Singers became the Song and Karlene felt a presence she had thought never to feel again. Somehow, Jazep's kigh had not gone on when he'd died; it had, instead, gone to earth.

She Sang the gratitudes alone.

The earth kigh was the last to leave. It looked once around the circle, its calm gaze resting longest on the baby, then, arms spread in benediction, it sank out of sight.

*   *   *

Her own small festival service ended, Annice settled the
straps of her pack on her shoulders and set her feet on the
path the kigh created. She had too far still to go to allow
the night to stop her.

As she walked, she listened to a familiar voice Sing answers to her questions.

Gerek stood in an open window of Celestin's house and
listened to the sounds of Third Quarter Festival spilling out
of the Center. Marija only Sang fire and air, but the Bartek
Springs choir cheerfully filled in the other two quarters,
making up in volume what it lacked in bardic abilities. If
he listened closely, he could hear the rhythmic counterpoint
of Magda's footsteps sounding against the ceiling as she
paced back and forth across the room directly overhead.

Because Magda had emphatically refused to give her
word that she wouldn't attempt an escape during the service, bard and priest had decided she'd best stay right
where she was. Gerek had remained with her out of loyalty;
or possibly guilt, he wasn't entirely sure.

They'd be leaving in the morning.

Although he still wasn't exactly certain sure how they
were going to accomplish it, he and Bannon would be taking an unwilling Magda and Vree back to Elbasan. It wasn't
likely to be a pleasant trip.

Things were happening here that he didn't understand.

Digging his fingers into his beard, he scratched along the
edge of his jaw and wished there was someone around he
could talk to, someone who didn't already have their mind
made up. Scowling, he began to pace as well, falling into
the cadence still being drummed out up above. Apparently,
he was going to have to talk this over with himself.

"All right, Maggi's positive Vree and Gyhard can only
be healed by confronting Kars. Do I believe her? Do I
have any reason not to believe her?" If he accepted that
his little sister was a new and powerful kind of healer—
and considering that he'd been her first patient he'd be a
fool if he didn't—then he also had to accept that she knew
what she was talking about.

Next point.

"Do I want Vree to be healthy and whole? Of course I do." Perhaps he wasn't as much in love with the lovely, dangerous Southerner as he had been, but he still wanted only the best for her.

Gyhard was a thornier question. Gerek, as much as he hated to agree with Bannon, would've preferred Vree had let Gyhard float off into the great beyond back when they'd found themselves a body short. As she hadn't, and as Gyhard was now a very important part of Vree's life, Gerek supposed it would be best for Vree if Gyhard were healthy and whole as well.

"If a bard, say Karlene, gets to Kars first, then according to Maggi, Vree will never be whole." He didn't much like where this was heading.

Holding out his hands, palm up, Gerek lifted first one, then the other. "So I weigh Her Royal Highness' desire to have Vree and Magda returned to Elbasan against two lives." He sighed. "Three if Maggi thinks she's going to heal Kars as well."

While he stood there, staring at his makeshift scale, searching for an answer, a breeze from the open window brushed a chill across the back of his neck. Lifting a hand to rub at the gooseflesh, he wondered if it was from Annice. "Under the circumstances, she'd be more likely to send a full blown gale."

Find your sister. He chewed over her original message. It wasn't like Annice to be so unspecific.

"I've found her, Nees." His mouth twisted up into a wry grin. "Now what am I supposed to do?"

Believe in her.

The answer came from his heart.

Gerek nodded slowly, remembering. "All things being enclosed, that sounds like good advice," he said at last. Grinning broadly, he bounded up the stairs two steps at a time.

When he threw open the door to the priest's spare room, he found his sister tying the last knot in a rope made of torn bedsheets. "Good, you're ready to go," he said matter-of-factly. "Although this is very ingenious, we'll make better time if we take the stairs."

She glared at him, backing toward the tiny dormer

window. "What do you mean, we? Is this some kind of a trick? Because if you think I'm going to go quietly back to Elbasan with you, you're *wrong*."

"Trust me, Maggot, I don't think you'll go *quietly* anywhere. But as it happens . . ." He paused and spread his hands, the giddy feeling of relief that had come with making what he knew to be the right decision suddenly leaving him. "As it happens, Maggi, I think you're right. I think you and Vree and Gyhard need to get to Kars before the bards Sing him into or out of or all around the Circle. It's the only way to end this thing once and for all."

With a crow of joy, Magda scooped her bulging saddle-bag up off the floor, launched herself into his arms, squeezed him once, and ran for the door. "Come on! We've got to get Vree and get well away from here before the service ends."

"The kigh will still be able to find us," Gyhard reminded her as together they raced down the stairs.

"It doesn't matter if they know where we are," Magda told him, "as long as they don't catch us."

"You mean, catch you *again?*"

She punched him on the arm. "You looked just like Father when you said that. What have you done with Bannon?"

"Nothing at all. Bannon found someone willing to spend the festival giving thanks for getting laid."

"With a stranger?"

"He makes friends fast when he has to. Do you know what they've done with Vree's weapons?"

"All her stuff's in the kitchen."

"Good. I'll get *my* stuff and meet you there. See if you can find some journey food; if the bards stay here, there has to be some around."

A few moments later, saddlebags abandoned for a pack with shoulder straps, Gerek carrying Vree's weapons as well as his own, the two of them ran out the back door of the priest's house and toward the shed at the edge of town. Neither them looked back to see a shadow move away from the building and follow them.

. . . actually, Second Quarter Festival is the fertility festival because that's when things are blooming and, well, ready to be fertilized. First Quarter Festival celebrates new beginnings.

*Don't new beginnings usually come after *fertilizing*?*

She felt him smile—felt herself smile, knew it was him. *I'm just explaining how it is, Vree. I didn't make it up.*

So what are they singing about now?

He listened for a moment. *Right now, they're giving thanks for colley.*

For what?

It's a vegetable. I don't think you grow it in the Empire.

You're putting me on.

Afraid not.

They're giving thanks for a slaughtering vegetable?

Uh-huh.

People in this place have too much slaughtering time on their hands. Fingers laced behind her head, Vree lay on the pallet and stared up into the darkness. The priest had brought her food twice, the bard and Bannon standing by in case she tried something. All three of them had obviously wanted to talk but just as obviously couldn't with the others around. She had no idea what the priest wanted to talk about—who ever knew with priests? The bard wore an expression she'd grown used to during her time at the Hall and had there not been an audience would no doubt have blurted out the familiar, *"You really do have two kigh!"* Bannon had stared at her with an intensity that evoked unwelcome memories of the heat that used to burn between them.

He needs me, she'd said when they were gone.

So do I, Gyhard reminded her. *The question is, which of us do you need?*

I've made my choice, she'd snarled and stopped herself just in time from adding, *leave me alone.* Because that was the one thing she didn't want.

The distant singing changed and Vree wondered if they'd moved on to more important things, like maybe sausage and onions. *Gyhard, if you weren't locked up here, would you be there?*

You mean at the Center, for the festival? He hadn't been to a Quarter Festival since the brigand had murdered his first body and he'd murdered the brigand in turn. A long time. A very long time. *I don't know.*

Nothing to be thankful for?

It's not that. It's just the festivals are a part of a past I never expected to re . . .

Be quiet.

A sudden flash of insight and he understood what her question actually meant. *I didn't mean that I'm not thankful for you and—*

*Shut *up,* Gyhard! There's someone coming.* Rising to her feet in one swift motion, she faced the door, head cocked slightly to one side. *It's Magda and Gerek. They're coming to let us out!*

You can tell that from their footsteps?

No, I can hear Magda talking.

I can hear exactly what you hear and I don't hear . . . oh.

Relief at their approaching freedom making her feel a little light-headed, Vree grinned. *Given enough time, you may learn to listen.*

"Vree?" A familiar voice whispered her name through a crack between two logs. "Gerek came to his senses and decided to help. We'll have you out in a minute." The voice shifted direction. "What's taking so long?"

"It's dark, and I can't see well enough to undo the tie down."

Madga snorted, and Vree knew exactly what expression she'd be wearing. "So cut it! Honestly, Ger!"

Although there was only a crescent moon riding low in the sky, the almost total lack of light in the shed made the yard seem bright in comparison. With Gyhard's help, Vree managed to prevent a defensive response to Magda's enthusiastic hug.

"Where are my knives?" she asked urgently, putting the younger woman to one side.

She could see the flash of Gerek's teeth in his beard. "Don't I get thanked first?"

The slam of a throwing dagger sinking into the shed answered his question.

"You knew he was there." Gerek moved to stand in front of Vree and found himself shoved firmly out of the way.

Hands empty and held out from his sides, Bannon faced his sister across the yard.

Gerek reached for his sword. A slim brown hand clamped around his wrist like a vise, and the bit of blade he'd managed to draw was forced back into the scabbard.

"Not your fight," Vree told him in Imperial, so Bannon could understand. "This is just between the two of us."

"Don't you mean the *three* of us," Bannon sneered.

"Gyhard isn't involved in this."

"Oh, he slaughtering well is, but how much is my sister involved, that's the question!"

She stepped forward, away from the shed, away from Gerek and Magda. "Don't be an ass, Bannon. I'm in control, not Gyhard."

"Sure you are," Bannon scoffed. "That's why you walked away from everything you've ever known. Why you walked away from me."

"Things change."

"Not that much. Not all at once."

If he couldn't remember the choices he'd made while in her body, she couldn't forget. "It didn't happen all at once," she said softly. "What do you want, Bannon?"

"I told you. I'm taking you back to Elbasan with me."

Gerek shook off Magda's cautioning grip and, hands carefully away from his weapons, moved to stand by Vree's side. "Bannon, I think they're right. I've listened to what Magda has to say and I think they have to get to Kars before Karlene does."

"I don't give a rat's ass about Kars, or Karlene, or your sister, or you," Bannon told him with a pleasant and entirely false smile. "I want my sister back."

"Taking her to Elbasan won't change anything. In fact, it could make things worse. It could mean she'll *never* get rid of Gyhard."

Nice to be wanted.

He sounded so insulted, Vree fought a completely inappropriate urge to giggle—then scowled when she realized what she was doing.

"I thought Her Royal Highness ordered you to bring your sister back to Elbasan, Your Grace," Bannon reminded Gerek, although his eyes never left Vree's face. "Or does duty and honor mean nothing in this slaughtering country?"

"You let me worry about that," Gerek snarled. The hand

that had begun to drop to his sword hilt suddenly jerked up as Magda grabbed the back of his jacket and nearly yanked him right off his feet.

"Have you got a *death* wish?" she demanded, using her whole body to shove him up against the rough logs of the shed. "Or are you so stupid you actually think you could survive a fight with *either* of them?"

Gerek's mouth opened, then closed again as he took a good look. Neither Vree nor Bannon had drawn a weapon. There was no need. They were weapons. Although they stood perfectly still, mirror images of each other, something about them screamed of an incredible, deadly potential for movement. They were like bowstrings, pulled taut and waiting to be released.

The skies had cleared. Moon and stars gave light enough to throw Bannon's shadow almost to Vree's feet and to spill hers back into the deeper shadow of the shed. The songs of the festival seemed to be coming from a very long way away.

"What do you want, Bannon?"

You asked him that already.

I know. He didn't answer.

What are you talking about? He wants to take you back to Elbasan!

That's not the answer.

"What do I want?" he whispered mockingly. "I want you back."

With his face in shadow and his voice so low, he might have been Commander Neegan; he might have been their father. Whom she'd killed. "And what *I* want?"

"You can tell me what you want once that slaughtering parasite is out of your head." As he charged, Vree flung herself into the air. They hit the ground together with her legs wrapped around his neck, his eyes wide in disbelief. Half a dozen heartbeats later, she rose to one knee and checked to see that he was still breathing.

"That's it?" Gerek asked, peering from one to the other as though he were searching for an answer. "It's over?"

Breathing heavily, Vree stood and stared down at her brother, arms crossed tightly under her breasts. "The thing to remember when fighting an assassin," she told him bleakly, "is that you only get one chance. It's either over very quickly, or you've lost."

Gerek shook his head, still finding it hard to believe that anyone could move so quickly. "He never really thought you'd fight him."

"Yes, he did." Vree stepped back as Magda dropped to her knees by Bannon's body. "He just thought he'd win."

"You do realize that it's the next thing to *impossible* to shut off the blood to his brain without crushing his windpipe," Magda muttered, fingertips dancing over Bannon's throat.

"The *next* thing to impossible," Vree repeated changing the emphasis. "The first four people I tried it on died instantly, the next two choked to death slowly . . ."

Gerek, who'd been reaching out to comfort her, let his hand drop slowly back to his side.

". . . the seventh survived the first attempt but not the . . ."

Vree. That's enough.

I'm cold. She reached for him, and he came. *I don't know who I am anymore.*

Most of us never do.

How do you stand it?

By holding on tightly to anything you're sure of.

Don't leave me.

This time, Gyhard realized, she might have acknowledged the plea, but Magda stood and pressed two fingers against the back of Vree's wrist and they both fell silent.

"He won't stay unconscious for very long, you know. What do we do now?"

Gerek pushed past them and stuck his hands in Bannon's armpits. "We lock him in the shed," he grunted, dragging the smaller man backward into the building, "then we get out of here."

"He'll follow us."

"Not until someone lets him out." Gerek took one last look at Bannon's face, the pale oval just barely visible in the spill of light through the open door. He frowned, sighed, and pulled the door closed. Any questions would have to wait. "He has a plan for getting rid of Gyhard."

"What?"

What?

"Did he *tell* you that, Ger?"

"He told all of us. He said Vree could tell him what she wanted once that slaughtering parasite was out of her head."

Magda rolled her eyes. "That just means he wants Gyhard gone, not that he has a plan to get rid of him."

"No." Vree shook her head, the motion so minimal only Gyhard was sure of it. "Gerek's right. He was hiding something, and that's probably it."

"But in order to separate you and Gyhard, he'd need someone who can Sing the fifth kigh," Magda protested. "And *none* of the bards, even though they consider Gyhard an *abomination*, would risk it."

"None of the bards in Shkoder," Vree said slowly. "But now, there are bards in the Empire."

"No. Even Imperial bards wouldn't do that. You just don't understand bards."

Vree lightly caressed Bannon's throwing dagger still buried hilt deep in a log just to the right of the shed door. It was heavier than the one she'd lost; weighted for her brother's hand, not hers. "You don't understand the Empire," she said quietly.

Magda and Gerek stared at each other in silence for a long moment, a breeze stroking the hair back from their faces.

Finally, Vree turned, her expression unreadable. "Let's move. We still have to get to Kars before Karlene." Leaving Bannon's dagger where it was, she began buckling on her weapons.

"What about . . ." Gerek gestured at the shed.

"Maybe when he wakes up, he'll realize I've made my choice."

Maybe pigs'll fly, but I doubt it.

They're changing each other, Magda thought, watching Vree respond to Gyhard. She could feel the edges of their kigh, not so much overlapping as meshing, creating a new, shared area that was a part of them both. If this combining of kigh was a result of their feelings for one another—much the way echoes of her mother's kigh appeared in Stasya and Stasya's in her mother—then that was good. If, however, it was a result of their situation, then that wasn't good. But how could Vree talk about her feelings for Gyhard when he could hear every word? How could Gyhard speak of Vree? *I wish I could talk to them one at a time.*

"So how do we find Kars?" Gerek asked, shrugging the pack up onto his shoulders. "Where do we start?"

"We go east." Magda pointed along the bulk of the mountains, her finger indicating the heart of the star cluster Shkodens called the Sun's Herald. "I overheard Marija and Celestin talking. Jazep died . . ." She swallowed and tried again. "Jazep died in a mining settlement called Fortune that's due east of here."

Her night sight by far the best, Vree led the way across the graveyard, chance returning them to almost the exact place they'd been captured. At the edge of the trees, she threw aside a lifetime of training and looked back— although she had no idea of what she was looking for.

I think you do.

He's locked in a shed, Gyhard. If I couldn't get out of the slaughtering thing, neither can he.

So?

So he can't be following us yet. The festival service spilled out of the Center and filled the whole valley with song. *What are they giving thanks for now?*

He considered lying, decided against it. *Family.*

After the Blessing, the festival cakes were divided into generous portions and everyone ate. Some of them died quickly, cleanly. Some of them went into convulsions, soiling themselves as they thrashed and moaned. Ales screamed—a short shrill cry that forced Kars to clap his hands over his ears and hum to block the sound—then she ran at a wall over and over until she died in a bloody heap. Kiril had time to gather his dying daughter up into his arms. With her head lolling slack against his shoulder, he collapsed and died searching for his son.

The musty taste of decay coating the inside of his mouth, his back arched and his heels drumming the floor, Edko stared up into the dark gaze of a girl who seemed made of smoke. *If I knew who she was,* he thought, desperately trying to push death away, *I'd understand. If I knew who she was* . . . The darkness in the strange girl's eyes spread. It was too heavy. He couldn't breathe. When he understood, it was too late.

"Is he dead, Kait?"

Yes.

They were all dead. He could feel their kigh filling the hall; confused, crying, wanting to return. "Soon," he told them soothingly. "Soon."

Slowly, painfully, he stood and walked past the young and the old and the very young and the very old. There were too many dead. He would not have strength enough for everyone. As he had before, he must choose those who would be part of his new family. It would not be an easy choice but it was never an easy choice. He wanted to save them all.

All but one.

Kneeling by Edko's side, Kars straightened the boy's contorted limbs and lovingly kissed the pale cheeks. "The demons cannot get you now," he murmured. "I have done for you what no one would do for me." The memory of the rod rose and fell. He hunched thin shoulders and endured.

When it was over, he straightened and smiled. They would never have the boy.

Enrik heard the Singing as he approached the stockade and moved a little faster. "At least I haven't missed the entire festival," he told the half-fledged hawk wrapped securely in his shirt and carried close against his chest. He realized his coming down out of the forest after dark would be considered both dangerous and stupid by most of his extended family, but he personally figured it was only stupid if he didn't make it. Since he had, it wasn't. No one knew the forest better than he did. He'd just proven that.

Feeling more than a little pleased with himself, he picked up his pace, his feet sure on the path between the river and the stockade. "They better have saved me a piece of festival cake, or I'm going to stick my finger down someone's throat."

Then the dogs began to howl.

The fledgling stirred in his grip and he paused. Except for the dogs—and the Song he could still hear faintly behind their howling—the night seemed ominously still.

"Something's wrong." A sinuous black shape appeared suddenly out of the darkness. He cried out and leaped back as it brushed against his legs. A moment later, when his heart began beating again, he called himself several kinds of idiot as he realized it was just one of the cats.

Running *away* from the stockade?

Tucking shirt and bird both up into the broad crotch of an ancient willow, Edko ran toward the gate. The large cattle-gate was closed and barred, but when he lifted the latch on the narrow door cut into it, it opened under his hand. He stepped into the yard. The Song ended. Heavy bodies almost knocked him over as the family's dogs raced past him, flinging themselves through the open door and into the night.

He pursed his lips to whistle them back but made no sound, suddenly convinced it wouldn't be a good idea to announce his return.

In the spill of light from the hall, he could see the cattle crammed tightly against the near end of their pen. He'd seen the bull take on a mountain cat once, lowering its great shaggy head with its huge spread of horns and charging, bellowing in fury at the intruder. Until this moment, he'd thought nothing frightened them.

The Song began again. The hair lifted off the back of his neck, and although the night air was cool on his bare torso, he began to sweat. It wasn't a festival Song.

Every instinct screamed at him to run, to follow the dogs away.

Something had happened to his family.

He had to know what it was.

The Song had ended and begun again before he managed to force his protesting body across the yard. Through the slats in the shutters he could see Uncle Kiril standing with his back to the window, his daughter Anca by his side. Breathing heavily, his weight pressed against the outside wall, Enrik worked his way around to the door.

It took him four tries to grasp the latch and lift it.

RUN! RUN! RUN!

The urge was so great, he half-turned. The small door was still open. The night beckoned from beyond, promising safety.

He had to know what was wrong.

Teeth clenched, blood roaring in his ears, he stepped over the threshold and into the hall.

The toes of his boots pushed into something soft and yielding.

He looked down.

His mother stared sightlessly up at him, dried blood around her mouth from where she'd chewed through her lips. The dead were scattered all over the hall. Feeling as though he were dreaming, that none of this could possibly be real, he stepped over his mother's body and walked toward the place where his uncle and his cousin stood.

The Song grew louder.

An old man crouched over the body of his brother Ondro.

It was the old man who was Singing, Enrik realized suddenly—although how such an incredible Song could come from such a frail form he had no idea. *He's older even than Grandmother.* Except that Grandmother was dead, one arm smoldering in the hearth where she'd fallen.

Ondro twitched. His hand rose to clutch at the air.

Looking for an explanation, any kind of explanation, Enrik turned to Kiril.

Both his uncle and his cousin were dead.

They were standing.

They were looking at him.

They were trying to speak.

But they were dead.

The belief he was dreaming washed away in a horror so overwhelming it had to be truth. Enrik could smell the stink of flesh burning, of bowels voided, of vomit, of death. Everyone he loved was dead in this room. He began to shake as a scream built behind his ribs, pressing against the bone that confined it.

But worst of all, somehow, the old man's Song had made Kiril and Anca dead-not-dead.

Enrik charged forward screaming as Ondro, his dead brother Ondro, opened his eyes.

Kait, lost in the Song, reacted too slowly.

The old man looked up and saw death approaching. He pulled the living kigh from the charging body, held it within the Song until it stopped wailing and Sang it back in again.

Enrik's body dropped, knees slamming into the floor. It swayed back and forth and finally fell.

Kars crawled to its side and, with an effort, managed to turn it over. The chest rose and fell. The heart continued to beat. But a dead man looked up out of the hazel eyes.

Too far gone in madness to understand the unease he felt, Kars forced himself to pat Enrik's hand and murmur, "It'll be all right. You'll see."

The kigh rose up under Annice and dropped her forward onto her knees. Hands braced against the ground, gulping in desperate lungfuls of air, she fought to free herself from an overwhelming feeling of horror.

The basic tenet of her faith promised that all things were enclosed within the Circle.

But some things were not.

"Maggi! What is it? What's wrong?" Gerek grabbed his sister by the shoulders and shook her until she looked at him. Her eyes focused and high-pitched shrieks turned to frightened whimpering. He wrapped his arms around her and pulled her against his chest. "I have you. You're safe. Tell me what's wrong."

"Something horrible," she managed, then shook her head and started to cry.

Gerek looked over at Vree, who stood ready for a fight, a dagger in her hand. They'd stopped to catch a few hours of sleep before dawn brought pursuit, and although Gerek had insisted on standing watch, Magda's terror had woken them both. "She has nightmares sometimes," he explained. "Always has, ever since she was little."

"No." Magda pushed herself out of his embrace and wiped her nose on the back of her hand. "Not a nightmare. Something'd *happened*. Something so horribly wrong it woke me."

"What?"

"I don't know." She sank back on her heels, swallowing bile, suddenly very glad her stomach was empty. "But I can find it." A deep breath, intended to steady her voice, had no noticeable effect. "And when I do, we'll find Kars."

Eleven

Eyes wide, heart pounding so loudly it nearly drowned out the sound of steel-clad wheels rolling over dressed stone, Prince Otavas stared around him in horror at the high sides of the cart and the old man who held him prisoner.

"I have lost my heart," the old man said quietly. "I only want to find it again."

"I am *not* who you think I am!" Otavas cried as he had a hundred times before. "*They* know me!" He gestured toward the dead who sat silently watching, but they looked at him with no sign of recognition on decaying faces and, all at once, the prince knew that he'd never seen these people before.

Rising, he searched among the motionless men and women for a familiar face and found only strangers.

This is wrong, he thought. *There're too many.* There had only ever been two in the cart at a time and now he pushed past row after row of the dead/undead.

When he finally struggled through to the back of the cart, he found a tall, brown-haired man dressed in rough work clothes standing at the tailgate and gazing back the way they'd come. This man, too, was a stranger but, Otavas realized with a surge of joy, he was alive. His broad chest rose and fell in a steady rhythm and a vein pulsed in his throat at the edge of a day's stubble.

"I'm so glad I'm not alone," he sighed and took hold of the other man's arm. "Sometimes I think I'm the only living person left in the world."

Slowly, jerkily, as though he were not entirely comfortable in his body, the man turned.

"No . . ." Otavas tried to back up a step but was held in place by the unyielding press of bodies behind him.

"I live, but I am dead. I am dead, but I live. I live, but I am dead. I am dead, but . . ."

"NO!" Dripping with sweat, Otavas jerked up in the bed and fumbled with the lamp. He turned up the wick until the flame danced over the edge of the glass chimney and the shadows withdrew far enough to be endured.

Heart pounding, the prince lay back and stared at an unfamiliar ceiling. The dream had been so real, so terrifying and the worst he'd had for weeks. It left him feeling as though the life he'd lived since his rescue was the dream and his return to terror was the reality. He could see the old man's face, feel the rumble of the cart, see the countless pairs of endlessly staring gray and filmy eyes, hear a trapped and despairing voice say, *"I live, but I am dead."*

The words resonated, echoing forlornly over and over inside his head. Every time he closed his eyes, he saw, not the dead/undead but the living/undead, and that was infinitely more horrible still. It soon became apparent when the terror refused to recede, he'd be sleeping no more that night.

With trembling fingers, he pulled on a robe and picked up the lamp. He needed air; needed to stand under the stars and know he was no longer the captive of an insane—and an insanely lonely—old man. There was a terrace off one of the corridors in the royal wing that he thought he could find his way back to.

Ashamed of the control the past still seemed to hold over him, the prince moved silently by the door to his valet's tiny chamber. Of all his household, only Bannon understood. Had Bannon been guarding his sleep, there would have been a quiet voice and a strong hand to help chase the terror away. Without Bannon, he would have to exorcise the dark memory of the old man and the cart on his own.

The halls of the Palace were deserted. No guards stood outside the heavy wooden doors of individual suites, for only the most trusted of retainers came this far into the heart of the Citadel. Safe within his small circle of light, Otavas traced a path he struggled to remember, marble floors cold beneath bare feet.

To his astonishment, the terrace door was open and,

through it, he saw a slender figure bending over a pipe pointed at the sky. When the figure straightened and stepped back, Otavas recognized the profile silhouetted against the night.

"Please put out that lamp, whoever you are. I don't want my eyes to have to adjust all over again."

He understood just enough of the language to lick thumb and forefinger and quickly pinch off the end of the wick. The darkness jumped in at him and lest it show him memories he didn't want to see, he hurried out to stand by his cousin. "What are you doing out here in the middle of the night?"

Without any sign of the shyness she'd worn like armor during the three unending banquets they'd spent sitting side by side, Princess Jelena switched to Imperial and said, "Watching for falling stars. There're always a lot out toward the Broken Islands around Third Quarter Festival."

As his sight adjusted, he saw that she was bending over the eyepiece of a distance viewer—a much larger one than the sailors used and much, much larger than the collapsible leather cylinders used by the marshals of the Seven Armies. "Don't you have to be up before dawn for the sunrise part of the festival?" he wondered.

"Uh-huh."

He smiled at her preoccupied agreement. "Won't you be tired?"

"I'll stay up until after it's over. I've found it's easier that way." Apparently satisfied with what she saw, she straightened again and turned to face him. "What are *you* doing out here in the middle of the night?"

"I had . . . that is . . ." Something in the pale oval of her face, so nearly at a level with his own, made him think she'd understand. "I had a nightmare about . . . about what happened and I couldn't sleep."

"About the kidnapping?"

Otavas nodded and waited for her to tell him that he had to forget about it.

Her hand closed cool around his wrist—he could feel the sympathy in the touch—and after a moment, she tugged him forward. "Would you like to look through my starviewer?"

The sky held more stars than he'd ever suspected, and he backed away a little overwhelmed.

"I know." Jelena nodded. "It was like that for me at first, too."

"How did you get interested in . . ." Mere words didn't seem enough. Otavas waved a hand at the night.

She shrugged. "When I was younger . . ."

His grin flashed white. "Younger?"

"I'm fourteen, almost fifteen. And you needn't sound so superior, Your Imperial Highness who's barely three years older." But she smiled back at him before continuing. "When I was younger, I was afraid of the dark—I had to sleep with a lantern lit and everything. It was so bad that they even had me checked out by healers, and everyone started worrying that I'd never outgrow it."

"But you did."

"When I was ten, Jazep went to my grandfather and asked if he could try. His Majesty agreed and Jazep started teaching me about how the night is more than an absence of light. He taught me about the animals that live in it. About the flowers that bloom in it. And he showed me the stars. I haven't been afraid since."

"Jazep?"

She drew in a long breath and slowly let it out. "He was a bard."

Now Otavas knew why the name sounded so familiar. "The one who died?" When she nodded, he was surprised to feel a sense of loss, even though he'd never met the man. "He sounds like he was a really nice person."

"He was. He told me, well, he sang me a song, about falling stars being the lamps that light the way for babies being born." After a moment, she sighed and tossed her head, the dreamy tone—suitable for fables—gone from her voice. "There's a scroll in the Bardic Library from a stargazer in the south, the Sixth Province of your Empire, I think, and he says that the stars are suns like ours and that the world isn't flat, it's round."

"That's ridiculous."

"Maybe. I had the bards ask the kigh. Air and fire and water seemed to think it was a stupid question and wouldn't answer. Earth said, *The world is.*" Thumbs tucked behind

her belt, she rocked back on her heels and stared out
toward the harbor. "When I'm Queen, I'm going to send
ships out into the ocean as far west as they can go and see
if they end up in the east again."

Otavas tended to agree with the kigh. It was the stupidest
thing he'd ever heard—but somehow, it didn't seem so stupid
when Jelena said it. "When you are Queen," he murmured,
wondering where his tongue-tied little cousin had gone.

A wind, smelling of the sea, whipped around the edge of
the terrace and he shivered.

"Well, no wonder you're cold," Jelena declared, tugging
at the billowing sleeve of his robe. "Look at all you're
wearing. You'd better go in before you freeze."

That, he wholeheartedly agreed with.

"Tavas."

He paused, one hand on the terrace door, and turned.

"If the night gets too dark, and the dreams come back,
remember the stars."

The Emperor had been wrong. Lying back on the pallet,
mapping the graduations of dark on dark within the confines of a prison he couldn't escape, Bannon turned that
truth over and over in his mind. The Emperor had been
wrong; Gyhard was not controlling Vree. He'd fought beside Vree for too many years not to know when he was
fighting against her.

He swallowed and winced, his throat painfully bruised.
He'd tried to believe in her. He'd given her the benefit of
every doubt. All he wanted was for her to be a part of his
life again. Was that so terrible?

"It isn't you who left me, it's him."

"I chose."

This was the second time she'd chosen Gyhard.

The Emperor wanted Gyhard back in the Empire to pay
for his treason. The Emperor had bards who could rip the
parasite right out of Vree's head.

Then *she'd* know what it was like to be alone.

*Make the most of the night, Vree. When they let me out,
I* will *be after you and the next time, you'll get no warning.*

"Magda? Are you awake?" When there was no answer,
Celestin sighed deeply and unbolted the spare room door.

The child had sulked her way through both festival services and that, as far as the priest was concerned, was quite enough of that. Dark and disturbing dreams had interrupted what little sleep she'd had, and she was in no mood to continue excusing teenage extremes. "Magda, we have to talk. I brought you some festival ca . . . Oh, my."

She stared from the crude rope braided out of torn bedsheets to the dormer window she could've sworn was too small for even someone Magda's size to climb out. *Except,* she realized, *if she went out the window, there wouldn't still be a pile of ruined sheets lying in the middle of the room.*

"Oh, my." She said it again because there didn't seem to be much else to say.

Vree's weapons were missing from their place in the kitchen.

A pack and journey food had been taken from the storeroom.

Gerek had not slept on the pallet she'd had made up for him. His kit was gone, but Bannon's was still in the stable where he'd left it.

All four horses were still in the corral.

"I don't believe this is happening," she muttered as a black gelding lipped at her hair.

"Then don't stand so close to the fence," Marija advised, coming around the corner of the building, a half-eaten apple in one hand, her instrument case in the other.

Celestin stared at the bard in complete confusion. "What are you talking about?"

"The horse eating your hair. Why, what were you talking about?"

All things being enclosed, Celestin figured there was one more thing she had to know before she jumped to any conclusions. "I think you should send a kigh to find out who's locked in that shed."

A few moments later, an urgent message sped toward Elbasan.

The kigh found Liene resting on a bench set into the curved stone wall of the Center. She hadn't slept well. Dragging old bones out of bed for the sunrise service had left her feeling her age, and all she wanted to do for the next few moments was sit and listen to the cheerful babble of voices as those of the Bardic Hall, the Healers' Hall, and the palace who'd remained in the Citadel for the Third Quarter Festival milled about in the courtyard, chatting happily.

His Majesty stood joking with his treasurer about how the realm would soon have to strike new gold coins whether he dropped dead or not. "After twenty-seven years," he laughed, "the old ones are wearing out." It was obvious that both Her Majesty on his right and Healer Jonakus on his left, thought the humor in bad taste. Liene frowned and tried to remember the treasurer's name. She could remember his mother—Denyse i'Janina a'Albinek; a great body, a brilliant grasp of economics, and a tendency to giggle in bed—but the son, even though he was standing right in front of her, she couldn't recall.

I hate getting old, she grumbled to herself, tucking her hands into the wide sleeves of her quartered robe.

Her Highness, Princess Jelena, and her cousin, His Imperial Highness Prince Otavas were having what appeared to be a spirited argument off to one side of the semicircular yard. Watching with a critical eye, Liene wondered how the boy had gotten past Jelena's shyness. She seemed unusually animated. *Well, he's a good-looking lad. I suppose there's always the obvious reason.*

Its pointed features twisted in pique, the kigh stuck a long finger in Liene's ear to get her attention.

"Not my problem . . ." she grumbled when she finally worked out just what it was trying to tell her. Weight on her cane, she rose and Sang a gratitude before calling for Kovar.

"To be honest, I'm not surprised that His Grace went over to the other side, as it were. Magda's always been able to wrap her brother around her little finger, and he's infatuated with Vree."

Liene watched Kovar pace the length of the office and back again before she said mildly. "*Why* Gerek suddenly decided to join forces with Magda and Vree isn't the immediate problem. Marija needs to know what to do with Bannon. Should she keep him in Bartek Springs? Should she stop him from following?"

"Could she stop him from following?" Then he answered

his own question. "Of course she could, he's only got one kigh." Still pacing, he dragged at the ends of his mustache, realized what he was doing, and held out waxy fingers to Liene. "You're enjoying this, aren't you?"

"You bet. You became Bardic Captain at midnight and this is your problem. I'm retired."

"So you're not going to get involved?"

The old bard grinned at him. "Don't be ridiculous." The grin faded when she saw Kovar's expression suddenly change. "Look, you're conducting, I just thought I'd . . ."

He raised a hand and cut her off. "What if Gerek didn't decide to join forces with Magda and Vree? What if Gyhard jumped to Gerek's body?"

"No. Vree would have had to push him."

"We only have Gyhard's word for that." His lip curled. "We only have Gyhard's word for a lot of things."

"True," Liene acknowledged, "but then you're forgetting Magda. She'd never allow it!"

"Could she stop it? Would she even know it was happening before it was over?" Kovar sat on the edge of the desk, brows drawn in as he worked out possibilities. "Or maybe that's why they're going to meet up with Kars. We've been assuming Magda can Sing Gyhard into another body—how much do you want to bet Kars can? And he won't have her scruples."

"Now, you're forgetting Vree."

"Vree is afraid of Gyhard." Kovar remembered that first evening in the Bardic Hall—the rage that had belonged to a second intelligence flashing for a heartbeat in Vree's eyes, the fear he'd felt rolling off her like smoke. "I've seen it."

"I haven't," Liene snapped, then her face fell as she remembered her trouble with the treasurer's name. "I suppose I might not have noticed. No." She reconsidered. "You're wrong about that. She's not afraid of him although I'll grant you she may be afraid of what she feels *for* him."

"We don't have enough information."

"We could believe the story Magda told Marija; that Gyhard needs to put his past to rest before he can build a future."

Kovar snorted. "Magda is a romantic child."

"Magda is a healer of the fifth kigh."

"That doesn't matter. None of this matters." The new

Bardic Captain began pacing again. "We have to allow Bannon to go after them. People are dying out there at the hands of a crazed Cemandian bard and it's our responsibility . . ." He thumped both fists against his chest. ". . . to put a stop to it. Vree and Gyhard can't be allowed to interfere with Karlene stopping this maniac."

"And if Magda's right?"

"If Magda's right," Kovar repeated sharply, then he stopped and sighed. "It doesn't matter if Magda's right. As much as I dislike Gyhard, I like Vree, and I wish we could give her a happy ending. However, a happy ending for one person cannot outweigh the deaths of countless others. In the final chorus, we can't trust Gyhard. By his own admission, he is responsible for what Kars has become. We can't allow them to get together again. As long as Gyhard remains in Vree's body, Bannon is still the only chance we have of stopping her."

"You don't trust Bannon either," Liene reminded him. Both hands folded over the top of her cane, she leaned forward. "So your answer to Marija?"

"My answer to Marija . . ." The new Bardic Captain stood in the open window and watched a pair of kigh chase each other around a snapping pennant on the gatehouse tower. He frowned. "We're just whistling into the wind, you know. Kars is a bardic problem; stretching a point, Vree and Gyhard may be a bardic problem as well, but the other three are not. We have no right to stop Bannon from following anyone he chooses. He's broken no laws. We're not at war with the Empire."

"Her Royal Highness did make it clear that she wanted Magda back in Elbasan and she didn't want an unstable assassin roaming about the country."

Chin up and eyes flashing, Kovar spun around to face Liene. "The bards have not become the royal police force!" When he saw her expression, his brows drew in. "That was where you wanted me to arrive, wasn't it? Why didn't you just come right out and say so?"

The old Bardic Captain smiled up at the new. "Because now, you'll remember it."

"You're an obnoxious old woman; you know that?"

Her smile broadened. "I revel in it."

*   *   *

Watching Bannon quickly and efficiently stow supplies into a borrowed pack, Celestin debated with herself about offering to help. Not with his packing, he'd obviously done that countless times before, but with the other burden he carried. She didn't need to be able to read his kigh in order to feel the anger coming off him in waves, anger that went back beyond a night spent locked in a shed. This was a young man used to getting his own way and, in spite of evidence to the contrary, he seemed determined to continue.

Well aware that the young were often both angry and self-indulgent, the priest was equally aware that time was the only sure solution. Sooner or later, most discovered that they weren't the center of the Circle. On the other hand, most young people weren't angry, self-indulgent assassins.

On yet another hand, she'd seen his face when Marija—apologizing for the delay as profusely as possible with her limited Imperial vocabulary—had let him out of the shed. She could have sworn that, just for an instant, he'd hoped to see someone else and when he hadn't, he'd first looked hurt and then derisive and then there had only been a superficially charming young man, apparently more than willing to forgive.

Finally, she could stand it no longer. "Bannon?"

He turned and smiled. In a foreign land where he barely spoke the language, pleasantry was a crucial tool.

Now that she had his attention, she wasn't sure of how to begin. "Where do you go from here?"

A little surprised by a question with such an obvious answer, Bannon shrugged. "I get my sister."

"Why?"

His expression hardened. "Told to."

Celestin shook her head and laid a hand gently on his chest. "Why in here?"

Bannon met her gaze and was totally astonished to see that she seemed to really care. All at once, he was reminded of how Vree had held his face in both hands after his first target and asked him if he was all right. About to crow that the target had never touched him, he'd realized that she didn't want to know if his body had been wounded, she wanted to know how he felt. He'd turned in time to see them drag the body from the practice yard and discovered he felt nothing at all. When he'd told her, she'd nodded, like it was the answer he was supposed to give, but he'd thought, just for a moment, he saw sadness behind the patina of her training. He'd been twelve; Vree was thirteen.

But that Vree, his Vree, was gone.

For an instant, Celestin was reminded of how Dymek had looked when they'd told him Filip was dead. Confused and lost and unable to believe how such a horrible thing could have happened.

Then the instant passed. Bannon picked up a small sack of dried apples and stared down at it, as though searching it for answers. Finally, he looked up. He wasn't sure why it was important he make this woman understand; maybe because he thought she *could* understand. "Without Vree, like lost arm or leg."

"Without her you feel crippled?" When he nodded, Celestin spread her arms, her posture as nonthreatening as thirty years in the priesthood could make it. "But is it like losing an arm or leg or like losing a crutch?"

"Crutch?"

She mimed walking with a crutch then straightened as the assassin jerked toward her.

"It isn't like that!" Both hands curled into fists, Bannon shouted his protest in Imperial, using volume to replace the Shkoden words he didn't have. "She doesn't hold me up! She never held me up! We were partners, a team! The best slaughtering blades Jiir ever had! All I wanted was my body back and she betrayed me! First she saved the life of the man who tried to kill me and then she walked away. I'd leave her to rot in this slaughtering country if the Emperor didn't want her! I don't want her! He does! I don't care!" As the last word slapped against the walls of the small room, Bannon was horrified to find his eyes were wet. No one had ever looked at him with such sympathy before. He swallowed three or four times in quick succession and used the pain to find himself again.

Although she hadn't understood the words, the priest recognized the reaction. "It's frightening being alone, isn't it?"

"Alone?" The bark of laughter tore at the bruising on his throat. "His Imperial Highness Prince Otavas *need* me!"

"Good. I'm glad."

Her smile offered comfort. Terrified he might take it, Bannon grabbed up the pack and ran out the door.

"Ger, I'm fine. Honest." Pushing her hair back off her face with one hand, Magda shoved her brother away with the other. "I'm a healer, *remember?* If there was anything wrong with me, I'd know."

"You're shaking."

"I'm cold."

"It's a beautiful day."

She narrowed her eyes. "I didn't say it wasn't. If you want to do something *useful,* give me your sweater and stop fussing."

Gerek recognized her expression; she'd borrowed it from her mother and years of experience had taught him not to bother arguing. Yanking the sweater up over his head, he silently handed it to her.

"Thank you." Pulling it on, she spent a moment rolling up the cuffs, then sighed deeply and stood. Her calves ached from all the climbing, she had scratches all over both hands from pushing through prickly ash, and a low-hanging branch had left a painful welt across one cheek. "All right, let's get going."

Because he knew what Magda would say, Gerek looked to Vree.

Vree shook her head. "Karlene was closer than we were when she started, and Bannon won't have rested."

"Maggi . . ."

"Is a healer. She knows when she's ready to go on."

"She's leaving," Magda called as she reached the edge of the clearing. "And she wants to know if you two are coming?"

Gerek glared at Vree and jerked his head in the direction of his sister.

Vree moved to take up position just behind the younger woman's left shoulder. She didn't much like being between Magda and her brother, but as a marching order it made sense. Gerek could see over and around her; with their positions reversed, he was just too slaughtering big.

I don't think he loves you anymore.

Don't be an ass, Gyhard, he never did. He's a romantic. Probably falls in love every time he wants to get laid.

How exhausting for him.

Rolling her eyes, Vree reached ahead and lifted a low-hanging branch out of Magda's way. "Can you still feel the way we have to go?" she asked rubbing at the sticky sap smeared over the scar on the back of her hand.

Magda turned enough to show Vree a melancholy smile. "I think I'll always be able to feel it. It's like when someone's sick—not injured, but sick—and a healer can *feel* the wrongness. I can feel the wrongness in the world." She stumbled and would have fallen if Vree hadn't grabbed her elbow. "Sorry. I guess I have to pay more attention to where I put my feet."

"That's it, Maggi." Gerek's tone suggested he not be argued with. "Back to the clearing. You need a longer rest."

The two women exchanged a speaking glance.

"Don't get your bowstring in a knot, Ger," Magda advised, starting up the tumbled end of a rocky ridge. "I *need* to find this wrong and heal it. I *don't* need to rest."

Bannon dropped to one knee and studied the pattern in the clearing. He'd found where they'd slept and now he'd found where they'd rested. Shaking his head, he straightened and moved cautiously after them. *This pace must be driving Vree crazy.*

He caught up on the top of the ridge and froze as Vree motioned for her companions to be quiet. They weren't very good at it, he noted smugly; neither of them seemed to have any idea of how to stand absolutely still. While Vree might have heard something—he hadn't been moving as noiselessly as he could because he hadn't realized he was so slaughtering close—he'd make sure that she wouldn't hear anything else.

Predator patient, he waited. Once, his sister might have been able to outwait him, but that was no longer her decision to make.

"It was probably just a pinecone falling. Let's get moving."

His Grace was not a patient man. Bannon appreciated that. He let them gain some distance, then followed, watching for his chance. In the Empire, an assassin on target could kill anyone who got in the way. Two things kept him from sending a dagger into Vree's companions. The first; he was not, at present, in the Empire. The second; a good assassin seldom admitted that anyone was *in* the way. A good assassin took out the target regardless and Bannon had been the best.

One of the best, he corrected. The third reason, was that he had no intention of warning Vree he was coming. She'd beaten him once; he wouldn't let that happen again. They were going to pay for their treason—Gyhard for his against the Empire, Vree for hers against him.

"This is it," Magda declared, nodding at the river that cut through the bottom of the defile. "The river will take us right to Kars."

Gerek stepped forward, shrugging out of the pack as he moved. "Are you sure?"

Magda turned to face upstream and shivered. She could almost see the wrongness lying like a dark blot on the mountains. "I'm sure."

"Well, if we're going to follow the river, we'll have to find another place to climb down." Arm braced against his thighs, he leaned forward. "This is too loose and too steep." When he shifted his weight, a clump of dirt broke off the edge and bounced down toward the water, picking up other clumps and rocks as it went. "Maggi, step back. This whole thing's just looking for an excuse to give way."

With her eyes still locked on the evil in the distance, Gerek's voice seemed to come from very far away. Clutching her elbows, taking comfort in the familiar wool under her palms, she pivoted on her left foot until she faced him. "What did you sa . . ."

The last word became a scream.

Gerek grabbed for her, missed, and threw himself after her.

Feeling the ground roll out from under her feet, Vree leaped back.

What are you doing? Gyhard demanded.

He's going to bring the rest of that slaughtering face down on top of her. I follow, I bury them both!

We can't just stand here!

Oh, yes we can. Someone has to be standing when this is over to dig them out!

*   *   *

Bannon heard the scream, slid out of his pack and raced ahead. He arrived just in time to see Gerek disappear over the edge. Without slowing, he flicked a dagger down into his right hand.

Tumbling end over end, pushed along by the fall of earth and rock, Magda scrunched her eyes shut, closing out the terrifying kaleidoscope of images. Things were happening too fast for conscious thought. Her head bounced off the ground, a rock bounced off her shoulder, her arms and legs flailed about, sometimes moving with her, sometimes moving with the hill, and sometimes it seemed they were moving completely on their own.

She could hear Gerek shouting, but the roar of blood in her ears mixed with the grinding roar of the earth and drowned everything else out.

Then it was over.

Her arms slapped down on a gravel beach, her face smacked into her arms, a few final rocks slammed into her back. Half the hillside seemed to have landed on her lower body, pinning her left leg at a painful angle.

Blinking stupidly, she lifted her head and stared at the pattern a breeze was lifting the river into right under her nose. "Mama?"

Riding the crest of the fall, arms windmilling, weight back on his heels, Gerek fought to stay upright. Then an eddy sucked his right foot under. He started to fall forward. "NO!"

He twisted, rolled, and somehow ended up on his back, head pointing downhill, one leg buried, one leg kicking futilely at the air. He felt his sword rip free, one boot tear off, and got one arm up at the last possible instant to deflect a rock big enough to do serious damage away from his head.

His first indication that he'd reached the river came when his shoulders slid into something cold and wet, his neck whipped back, and the water covered his face. Coughing and choking he jerked forward, only to have the weight of the fallen hill push him back.

*   *   *

The kigh were beginning to grow nervous. Karlene picked a careful path to the river's edge and glanced upstream. Although they'd still answer her Songs, this was as far upriver as they'd go. It seemed, therefore, that upriver was the direction she had to travel.

As it wasn't specifically Kars that frightened them but the trapping of the fifth kigh to create the dead/undead, he must have found more of the living to destroy. There were small two- and three-family settlements all through these mountains; sometimes they grew into villages, sometimes the resource that created them played out and they were abandoned. The last recall Karlene had heard on this area was three years old, but she seemed to remember a timber-holding, a valley, and a river.

"There's no way around it," she sighed, disgusted with her inability to remember more detail. "I'm going to have to drop into trance."

Slipping her arms out of her pack straps, she leaned backward, letting it drop a handbreadth onto a waist-high, flat-topped boulder, then she squatted, flexing the stiffness out of her shoulders, and dipped a cupped hand into the water for a drink. Even one day into Third Quarter, the river held the memory of ice that had been and the promise of ice to come. A half-formed plan for a quick bath fled shivering. She sucked the cold water off her palm and bent to scoop out another handful.

A water kigh wrapped itself around her wrist. When she tried to free herself, it refused to let go. Behind it, two others spun about so frantically they created a half-dozen tiny whirlpools. At first, she thought they were warning her about Kars—the air kigh had been trying to get her to turn all day—but then she realized that Kars had nothing to do with their message: *Two children in the water. Hurry! Hurry!*

Karlene Sang understanding and wasted a moment or two convincing the three kigh to go back downstream and push the children out of the water if they could. Racing along the bank, splashing through the shallows, she wondered where a pair of children had come from and why the kigh had made that specific distinction. Usually, they referred to all non-kigh as flesh. Stumbling over a half-submerged branch, she decided it didn't matter. Had she not been available to take care of things, the water kigh would probably have avoided the area until the current swept the bodies away and then complained bitterly about it to the next bard who could Sing their quarter. It seldom occurred to them to attempt a rescue by themselves.

Scrambling across the neck of a rocky outcrop, hoping she wouldn't break an ankle, Karlene got her first glimpse of the raw gash on the side of the defile through a break in the heavy cedar. All at once, it became obvious how the children—whoever they were—had ended up in the water. She could hear them struggling, which made her hope they weren't badly hurt.

It was strange they weren't crying.

And then she saw the body at the water's edge. With no breath to spare for questions, Karlene covered the remaining distance faster then should have been possible.

A dark-haired man lay on his back, torso buried in such a way that his head and shoulders were pressed down into the river. A roll of water beneath him indicated that the kigh were attempting to do what she asked, but as he kept fighting them, struggling wildly to get free, they were doing little more than merely raising the water level.

Singing them away, Karlene waded out into the river.

Center it, there're two of them! The girl had been hidden behind the mound of earth and rock that had nearly buried her companion, but, as only her legs were buried and she'd landed short of the water, she could wait.

Ducking under a flailing arm, Karlene grabbed the young man's head, anchoring one hand in a short curly beard, and locked her eyes on his. **"Be still!"** she Commanded.

He went limp so quickly, she almost lost her grip. Without terror contorting his face, she discovered that he wasn't very old. A quick look showed that the girl was younger still.

Well, I suppose they're someone's children, she allowed silently.

Shuffling around behind him, she gritted her teeth against the cold, dropped to her knees, and let his upper body rest against hers. With the immediate possibility of his drowning averted, she took a deep breath and reviewed the situation.

Had she been able to Sing earth, it would've been a simple matter to free them; to free them both. As she didn't, and as she didn't really have a lot of time to waste before she lost all feeling in her legs, the solution would have to be more creative. Keeping her voice low and calming, she murmured, "I'm going to have the river wash enough of the dirt off you so that I can pull you out. Please, don't be afraid, and don't move."

"My sister's . . . downstream."

"She'll be all right."

His lack of reaction seemed to indicate that he'd dealt with bards before. Or that he was in shock. In this part of the country, the latter seemed more likely.

Her breathing deepening as she found her focus, Karlene shifted about just enough to see upstream, opened her mouth, and Sang. Gabris had often told her that she Sang the strongest water he'd ever seen. Time to prove it.

The water began to pull away from the far shore until a wave, three feet wide and four high, rolled toward them. Just before it reached her, it lifted and slammed, not into the young man's body but an inch higher, lifting the earth off him. Brown and muddy, it followed the Song back into the riverbed to avoid the girl.

When the wave ran clear, Karlene Sang a gratitude. The last kigh arced even higher into the air, twisted through itself, and sprayed them both. An instant after that, the river flowed as it always had.

The young man brushed at the remaining inch of earth on his torso with shaking hands. "Okay," he said. "I'm impressed."

A little shaky herself, Karlene shoved her hands into his armpits and pulled. "Frankly, so am I."

Protected by a thick sheath of muscle, he'd taken no real damage from his fall and it only took the two of them a few moments of silent struggle to free his legs, both of them realizing the girl had probably not been so lucky, neither wanting to be the one to say it.

The moment he could move, he scrambled over the remaining scree to the girl's side.

"Maggi? Magda? Are you okay? Are you hurt?"

Half out of the water, her teeth chattering and her toes numb, Karlene paused. Magda? The young man *had* looked vaguely familiar. "Your Grace?"

Gerek didn't bother turning. "Help me with her!"

Karlene had an uneasy suspicion she knew the only possible reason for Annice's daughter to be traveling so far from home. If Magda actually Healed the fifth kigh as the Imperial fledglings insisted, then she could only be out here looking for Kars.

When your mother finds out about this, she thought dropping to her knees and helping the heir of Ohrid scoop away dirt and gravel, *she's not going to be happy.*

Then she called herself several kinds of idiot. Annice had to know where Magda was—there could be no other explanation for the kigh telling her that *the children* were in the water.

"Ger, my knee hurts."

"I'm not surprised." He ran his hands gently over the joint before straightening it. "Is that better?"

"Little."

"Can you turn over and sit up if I bring your legs around?"

"I guess." She sniffed, wiped her nose on the back of her hand and tried to do as he asked. The world shifted and she clutched his arm. "Ger!"

"It's okay, Maggi, I've got you."

Leaning against his shoulder, she turned to where she thought Vree should be and the lines of pain were replaced by confusion. "Who are you?"

"Karlene." The bard sat back on her heels. "I was having a drink upstream. The kigh told me there was someone in the water." It didn't seem politic to mention to a grown man, and a nearly grown woman, that their mother was looking out for them—even if in this instance it had saved their lives.

Magda frowned and looked up at her brother. "Where's Vree?"

"Vree?" Karlene repeated, not entirely surprised. *I guess I was right about what they're doing here. Annice is really not going to be happy about this.*

Gerek forced his thoughts back before the water, before the fall. "She was right behind me."

As one, all three turned and looked up the slope. Gerek's boot-top protruded from the dirt about halfway up, but there was no sign of Vree.

Magda squirmed free of Gerek's grasp. "Vree! Vree!" She threw herself forward and collapsed in a slide of loose gravel.

"Maggie, stop it! Karlene's a bard! There's an easier way!" He pulled her back into his arms and turned to face the other woman. "You do Sing more than just water, don't you?"

"I Sing three quarters, but I don't Sing earth."

"So we can't find her!" Magda wailed.

"We can find out if she's under there at least." The air kigh were skittish and not inclined to help, but after a moment, Karlene managed to send one to the top of the cliff with Vree's description. It was gone longer than she expected and she could see by the growing fear on Magda's and Gerek's faces that they believed Vree had been lost in the collapse of the bank.

When the kigh returned a moment later, she had to Sing a question at it twice before she believed the news it brought.

"Vree's alive," she said at last, after Singing the indignant kigh a gratitude. "But Bannon has her."

The last time Vree had found herself bound, she'd opened her eyes to see Bannon studying her—or rather, Gyhard in Bannon's body. This time, she couldn't open her eyes as they were bound as securely as her hands and feet. This time, the rope tied wrists to knees to ankles and she was sitting in leaf litter, leaning against the trunk of a tree. This time, Gyhard and Bannon's positions were reversed.

Vree? Are you all right?

His voice drove multiple spikes of pain up through the crown of her head. *Why ask me? You're in here, too.*

I don't think he broke anything, Gyhard allowed after a moment.

Of course not. He's a professional.

He's a professional killer, Vree. That doesn't give me much faith in his ability to take us alive.

Imperial assassins try to kill only the target. It makes the Empire look bad if you leave a trail of bodies getting in and getting out.

So, where is he?

About six inches away from my right knee.

For the sake of their head, he toned down his exclamation of surprise. *How can you tell *that!**

The air patterns tell me something's there, and my nose tells me who.

All I can smell are trees.

We bathe more often in the Empire than they do here.

"I know you're awake, Vree. You can stop pretending." He sounded nervous and triumphant both, as though he'd beaten her at a game but wasn't entirely positive the game was over.

She turned her head to stare directly at him, although he'd know she couldn't see anything through the cloth tied around her eyes. "Why the blindfold?"

"A precaution in case the carrion eater decides he wants to be back in my body again."

I'd make better use of it, Gyhard snarled.

Vree tested the strength of the rope, felt the knots tighten, and forced herself to relax. "He can't jump unless I push him."

"And I'm supposed to believe you won't?" Bannon snorted. "I had the same training you did, Vree. Survive at all costs."

"No." She fought her way through the memory of Commander Neegan dying on her blade. "Not at all costs."

"He's changed you."

"I've changed."

She heard him stand, felt his shadow cross her body. "It's the same thing!"

His tone suggested there was no point in arguing. It was a tone Vree had heard frequently in the past. "Now what happens?"

"Now . . ." A branch snapped, silencing the background birdsong. "Now, we go back to the Empire."

By twisting her right wrist as much as possible, the upper buckle on her wrist sheath rubbed against the rope.

Given ten or fifteen days, you could probably cut us free.

Do you have a better idea? Vree snapped, struggling to remain outwardly serene, to give Bannon no weakness to exploit. "I thought you were taking us back to Elbasan?"

Another branch snapped. "Only on the way to the Empire. And Elbasan's a little out of the way when you consider how close we are to the border."

"You're going to take me across the border like this?" She could think of a number of alternatives, none of which she liked.

"No." He bent down and his breath lapped warm against her cheek. "I'm going to take my poor sick sister home on a travois." One hand lightly cupped her chin and turned her face toward him. "There's some pretty toxic fungus around here; I think they'll believe it."

She relaxed into his grip, softening her posture, drawing in a deep breath through a slightly opened mouth.

Bannon exhaled sharply and then backed away. "Forget it. You had your chance."

Vree! Gyhard jerked her chin up. *What are you doing!*

Trying to get him close enough to smack him in the face with my forehead.

Oh. She felt him release control. *Would that have worked?*

Probably not.

You're awfully calm!

I used to be an Imperial assassin.

Most Imperial assassins don't survive very long!

Muscles tensing and untensing, she worked the knots. *But they always believe they will.*

Vree . . .

Would you shut up! You're not helping! It was only a small crack and she hastily patched it over. Imperial assassins never left the Seven Armies. It was hard not to believe she'd have to answer for that. "What happens when we get back to the Empire, Bannon?"

"The carrion eater pays for his treason."

Imperial bards were still bards, but as she'd pointed out to Gerek and Magda, the Empire wasn't Shkoder. "And what happens to me?"

"The Emperor's willing to blame it all on Gyhard. You made your *choice*, Vree." Thrown back at her, the words hit her like a blow. Finally forced to acknowledge that choice, he was clearly going to make her pay. "You'll have to live with it."

Without Gyhard. Alone.

"I can't believe you told His Imperial Majesty about Gyhard."

He hesitated for an instant before answering and when he finally spoke, his tone was as much petulant as it was sarcastic. "Funny, I couldn't believe you saved the carrion eater's life."

"What about your treason, Bannon? What about your willingness to give Gyhard the prince in order to get your body back."

"Only you and I know about that. And I'm certainly not going to tell."

The implication was clear. "You think I won't?"

He leaned close again. His voice, although he'd obviously intended it to sound gloating, sounded a little sad. "I know you won't."

He's right, isn't he?

It wouldn't save you.

And if it would?

That's a really shitty question!

Gyhard fought to stay close as her anger tried to slam him away. *I'm sorry.*

You slaughtering well should be!

Bannon slipped his hands under her arms and quickly flipped her over twice, face down then face up, the motion too fast for her to take advantage of. The crosspieces of the travois pressed into her back. He was really going to do it. "Why, Bannon?" she asked.

At first she thought he wasn't going to answer.

"There was a hole in my life where you used to be. I wanted you back to fill it."

"Why didn't you fill it with something else?"

"Like you did?" he snarled. "Sorry, there weren't enough parasitic carrion eaters to go around."

"And when you woke up in the shed and you knew it wouldn't happen?"

"Oh, then I thought of something to fill the hole. An Imperial command. Remember duty, Vree? And honor? Oh, no. I forgot. You gave that up for the carrion eater, too."

She spat in his face. When the return blow came, she rolled with it, curled around the ropes and kicked him in the back of the thigh with both heels. He pitched forward and she threw her body up to meet his.

The back of her head slammed into his cheek and it was over a moment later.

"You're going to pay for that," he growled. "You're going to ... to ..."

Her own head ringing, it wasn't at all hard to believe she'd hit him hard enough to scramble his thoughts.

No. Listen.

All I hear are trees and leaves. She heard Bannon stand, heard him shuffle around making no effort to hide the noise his boots made in the carpet of dried leaves. A sound stroked the edge of her hearing, too indistinct to identify.

Incredibly, she heard Bannon walk away, his footsteps hesitant as though he went reluctantly.

Then the sound of his footsteps stopped and a familiar voice said, **"Albannon Magaly, do not move until I release you."**

Twelve

"Does anyone else think that dragging him along with us is a really stupid idea, or is it just me?"

Sitting by the fire with a wet tunic of Karlene's wrapped around her knee to keep the swelling down, Magda scooped up a pebble and threw it at her brother. It had been a long day—healers were unable to Heal themselves—and she didn't need him making it a long night. "What do you *suggest* we do, Ger? Leave him tied to a tree and come back for him when we've settled things with Kars? Or should I say come back to what's left of him. There are wolves around here, you know. And bears."

Gerek glared at her, past Bannon's blindfolded, bound, and hobbled figure. "At least being eaten by bears would have some dignity!" He turned on Karlene. "Look, if holding him captive is as temporary a solution as you say it is, why can't you keep him under Command?"

"Because it isn't good for him."

"And this is?"

"He could still kill you, Your Grace." The bard waved a hand at Bannon's semi-prone body—only the slow rise and fall of his chest, barely visible in the light from the leaping flames, indicated he was alive. "Even like that."

"Yeah, except he doesn't want to kill me. As far as I can tell, he doesn't want to kill anyone." Gerek pulled his sword, swung around, and viciously beheaded a small evergreen. Vree and Bannon both turned their heads to follow the swing of the blade although Bannon couldn't actually see it. "Kidnapping, yes. Murder, no."

When the weapon remained unsheathed, Karlene moved prudently to the other side of the firepit. "You're forgetting, Your Grace, that Bannon is an Imperial assassin."

"No, he isn't." The point of the sword rose until it was

on a level with Bannon's heart. "He's the personal body-guard of His Imperial Highness, Prince Otavas. He's no more an assassin than Vree is!"

The only sounds were the crackle of the flames, the lapping of the river against the shore, and a breeze pushing through the tops of the trees.

Finally, Magda shook her head. "Bullshit," she said succinctly.

"Maggi!"

At Gerek's outraged tone, Vree found herself looking toward Bannon to share the joke—except he couldn't see her.

"We may all be what the past has made us," Magda declared, ignoring her brother, "but we are just as much what we've made of the past. Vree made a choice, a conscious decision to break with her training. Bannon hasn't. By taking over his body, Gyhard forced him away from the army. By saving Gyhard, Vree forced him away from her, by giving him an order, the Emperor forced him into this confrontation. I'll bet he never chose to tell the Emperor that Gyhard was alive, it just spilled out one day."

"Maggi . . ."

This time, she jabbed a finger toward him, the light in her eyes not entirely a reflection of the fire. "And stop saying *Maggi* in that obnoxious tone, like you're trying to sound like Father. I hate it when you do that. I've spent the last two years learning to Heal, Gerek, and I know what I'm talking about. This isn't going to end until Bannon *actually* makes a choice!"

"I think you're both forgetting that Bannon isn't *actually* the problem," Karlene said softly, poking at the fire with a stick. "Kars is. And since I can't get rid of you . . ." She swept a resigned gaze around the circle of light. ". . . any of you, and since we're probably all going to have to cope with a great deal of very unpleasant death tomorrow, I suggest we get some sleep. So that we don't inadvertently cut off Bannon's circulation, I'm going to lullaby him and untie him for the night." A raised hand cut of Gerek's protest. "First of all, Singing him to sleep is nothing like keeping him under Command and secondly, if you don't trust me, Your Grace, stick your fingers in your ears."

He sheathed his sword, sank cross-legged to the ground, and did exactly that.

Karlene continued the Song for a few minutes after Bannon sagged against his bonds and then let it trail off. "He'll sleep until I wake him," she said easing him into a more comfortable position and loosening the ropes. Her gaze met Vree's and held it while Magda and Gerek settled down for the night. She wanted to say something, but had no idea of what. Finally, she shook her head, went back to the spot she'd chosen, and rolled herself up in a blanket. *So near and yet so far.* She sighed. *Cliché, but appropriate.*

Wearing every piece of clothing she'd brought, Vree moved closer to the fire and lay down, pillowing her head on one arm.

You know that either Gerek or Karlene would be willing to keep you warm.

Her brows drew in. *Don't start.* It had been an interesting evening; Gerek leaping to Bannon's defense, Magda standing up to him, Karlene suddenly acting like a corporal or a squad leader. *You know what I'm wondering?*

She felt him shift, as though he were settling in, getting comfortable for the night. *What?*

How much Shkoden does Bannon actually understand?

He didn't react to anything.

Vree closed her eyes and listened to the comforting sounds of people sleeping all around her. *Neither did I.*

From the far end of the valley, the timber-holding appeared peaceful enough.

"Is the gate closed?"

"I can't see from this angle, but there are some big, orange hairy things outside the stockade."

Karlene squinted but could only see gradations of brown on brown, broken by the occasional small evergreen and clumps of golden-leafed willows by the river. She hated being without the kigh; it made her feel as blind and bound as Bannon. "They're probably cows."

"Cows?" Vree shifted her grip on the branch and peered down at the bard. "Orange cows?"

"They're a mountain breed. They can live on just about anything and they don't mind the cold. Anything else?"

"Someone's . . ." About to say alive, she changed it to, ". . . awake. There's smoke. I don't see anyone moving around the piles of logs, though."

Kars could easily be the one who lit the fire.

Or not. If it were Kars, it would soon be over and Bannon would no longer be an inconvenience but a problem that had to be solved—one way or another. Trouble was, she couldn't think of another. "I don't see anything else. I'm coming down."

On the ground, Bannon frowned behind the masking blindfold. They used to spend hours, sometimes days, on reconnaissance; tucked into a safe vantage point they'd watch and weigh every inconsequential movement until they found the pattern. It drove him crazy, but Vree would insist. It was the way they'd survived for five long years when the life expectancy of an Imperial assassin seldom passed three. Today, in comparison, Vree had climbed up the tree, glanced around, and come straight back down again.

She'd changed in less than obvious ways.

"He's no more an assassin than Vree is!" Gerek's declaration chased itself around and around in his head.

What a load of slaughtering louse shit. He hadn't changed, not the way she had. A twig cracked as she came back down the tree, not making a lot of noise but not moving nearly as quietly as she could.

What's the slaughtering rush? he wondered. *If Kars is there, then hurrying saves no lives and might risk ours.* Bannon wasn't looking forward to running into the crazy old man with his hands tied behind his back and his ankles hobbled. While he wasn't completely defenseless, he certainly wasn't at his best. *At least His slaughtering Grace got them to drop the slaughtering blindfold while we're moving.* Once he would have trusted Vree to lead him blindfolded through an enemy camp. Not anymore.

Even sitting a careful distance away, Magda could feel the emotions rolling off Bannon like smoke. Besides the petty, self-absorbed jealousy, the "if I can't have my own way I'm going to eat worms" petulance, and the understandable anger at being captured, she could sense a deep hurt. Although she couldn't tell for certain without trance work, it seemed he honestly didn't understand how, after everything that had happened, Vree could've chosen to save Gyhard. *At least he's admitting she did choose.* Magda supposed that was progress.

When she sighed, Gerek turned. "Troubles, Maggi?" he asked, concerned.

She shrugged; Bannon's emotional state was none of his business.

"It's that wrongness, isn't it? Maybe you shouldn't go any closer."

Magda started. The wrongness was still there, like a great dark weight in the back of her mind, growing larger and heavier with every step they'd taken toward the valley, but she hadn't actually thought about it all morning. It frightened her how quickly she could get used to something like that. "I have to go." Her voice was a little too high, the words spilling out a little too fast. "I have to heal Kars."

Karlene went down on one knee beside the young healer. "There's only one way to heal Kars," she said softly. "And that's by returning him to the Circle."

"*. . . and when there is nothing left but pain, I will not deny my patients the embrace of the Circle.* It's part of the Healers' Oath." Magda sighed again and tucked a damp curl behind one ear. "Some pain only death can cure."

"And are you prepared for that?"

"I think so."

"Have you ever done it before?"

"No." Her chin lifted. "Have you?"

Killed someone. Taken a life. Even a life that should have ended years ago. It was the bard's turn to sigh. "No."

Magda shifted gaze and question to her brother.

He spread his hands; she already knew the answer.

When she looked at Vree, the ex-assassin shook her head and sighed. "I guess it's a good thing I came," she muttered dryly.

Bannon couldn't help it. He snickered.

Kars could feel lives approaching; five lives, moving slowly up the valley. One of them felt almost like the demon that had convinced his last family to leave him. There were differences, he would never mistake the two, but the similarities were terrifying.

Father?

"It's all right, Kait." She worried so. He was glad there were others now to keep her company. Such a young girl shouldn't have to spend all her time with . . . with . . . He reached for who he was, nearly touched it, and felt it slip away toward the five new lives.

They were moving closer. They were coming here. They would try to take this family away as they had taken the others.

"No." He shook his head, confused by names out of the recent past. Wheyra. Iban. Hestia. Faces half-formed in memory. Twisted fingers rose to stroke the necklace of bone that Anca and Kait had retrieved for him. He had no token from those three, from Wheyra, Iban, and Hestia, snatched from his side by the demon. Just as he had no tokens from the seven who'd been taken from him such a short time before. He hadn't even had time to learn all their names.

Gyhard.

His heart pounding, he turned toward the gate, but the approaching lives were still too far away to see. That name did not belong to one of his. Had never belonged to one of his. But it had left him, too.

They all left him.

"No. Not this time. This time I can protect you. Kiril, Ondro, close the gate."

As the two dead men shuffled forward to do as he commanded, he herded the other four together and got them moving toward the cool depths of the timber-holding's root cellar.

"If they cannot reach you," he told them happily, "they cannot hurt you." He waited by the door until Kiril and Ondro climbed down to join them, then smiled lovingly on all six, five of whom smiled involuntarily back at him, their lips already beginning to pull up off their teeth. "Wait here. When they are gone and you are safe again, I will come and get you."

He closed the door and sighed. He would miss them, but hopefully, they wouldn't have to stay there long.

Father, you need to eat.

"I do?"

Yes, Father.

Patting her cheek, completely undisturbed by his hand passing through the shadowy outlines of her face, he murmured, "You take such good care of me, Kait. What would I do without you?"

*   *   *

Enrik's tongue dragged across dried and cracking lips. While his kigh shrieked and fought within the confines of its prison, his body, driven by desperate need, shuffled forward until stopped by the rough wall of the cellar. Hands splayed out, he moved blindly to the right, face pressed up against a row of stone crocks. The earliest of all instincts opened his mouth and he sucked at the moisture dribbling down their sides.

"He's there." It suddenly became impossible to take another step forward. Not because she was physically exhausted, although she was. Not because the damage to her knee made walking painful, although it did. But because the dark wrongness had moved from the back of her mind to the front of her thoughts. If she squinted, Magda could almost see it, pulsing on the path they'd been following along the riverbank.

"You're sure?" Karlene asked, more for the sake of asking than because she doubted Magda's word.

The young healer nodded, swallowed once, swallowed twice, and began to shake so hard she lost her grip on the crutch Gerek had made her.

Without thinking, Gerek shoved the rope he'd been leading Bannon with into Vree's hands and raced to his sister's side. "It all right," he murmured into her hair as she flung herself into his arms. "I'm here. I've got you."

Vree stared down at the twisted hemp lying across her palm and slowly closed her fingers around it. Then she turned to look at Bannon who could have, should have, used that moment to escape. He was staring in turn at Gerek and Magda as though he'd never seen comfort offered before.

"*. . . if anyone talked about my sister the way you talk about Vree, I'd beat the living shit out of him.*"

Watching Gerek, Bannon felt as though he were forcing his way to understanding through an opposing army. He kept catching glimpses of it, but every time he thought he was getting close, another sword, another shield, another soldier, slammed into his way.

Because he was so totally unaware of her, Vree allowed her gaze to linger. In spite of the stubble, he looked younger than she remembered. *I wish . . .* Her mental voice trailed off.

What?

I wish that, just once, Bannon had held me while I cried.
Gyhard heard the thought so clearly he couldn't pretend he hadn't. *Did you ever give him the chance, Vree?*

Her chin rose and her mental voice maintained a bored nonchalance made completely unbelievable by the emotional turmoil surrounding it. *Don't be ridiculous. Assassins never cry; they allow the hurt to build up year after year after year until the only way they can find peace is to have their daughter kill them.*

Good thing you're not an assassin anymore. His tone matched hers, but he reached out with what comfort he could. He was no longer surprised when she accepted it.

Yeah. Good thing.

"I'm going to have to get closer."

Vree snapped her head around so quickly it seemed for a moment she was looking in two directions at once. *"You're* going to have to get closer?"

Karlene sighed. She didn't need this. "Look, Vree, I said I'd give you and Gyhard a chance with Kars but he isn't the only one behind that stockade. Before you do anything, I need to find out how many dead are walking in there."

"How?"

Both women turned to face Magda, who lifted a blotchy face from Gerek's chest. "There's *no* air kigh to send in, Karlene, and you'll *never* be able to Sing the fifth kigh from outside the stockade, not when they're total strangers. If you want to know what's going on in there, *I'll* have to do it."

"Maggi!"

She looked up at her brother. "You *know* I'm right, Ger."

He brushed at her cheeks with the palm of one hand then bent down picked up her crutch. "Okay," he growled. "It stinks, but you're right. Just be careful for a change."

"Okay. Fine." Karlene threw up her hands. "Let's all go. Let's make it a parade!"

Vree handed the rope back to Gerek and walked forward until she stood a hands span from the bard. "Do you really want to do this alone?"

Karlene's shoulders sagged and she shook her head.

"Then let's get this over with."

The three women walked single file up the path. Gerek and Bannon walked side by side.

"If anything happens to her," Gerek muttered, "I might as well kill myself because I'll never survive explaining it to Annice and Father. I'm going to be in deep enough shit if they ever find out why she's using that crutch."

"But is it like losing an arm or leg or like losing a crutch?" Bannon's memory translated the priest's words to Imperial.

Like losing a crutch.

They'd shared every important memory from the time he was six and Vree was seven. He knew that; he'd seen the memories in her head. But they weren't his memories.

When he had her tied, like a parcel to take to the Emperor, he'd been punishing her for what she'd done to him. Had he been punishing himself? No. That was ridiculous.

Two bodies, one will, she used to say when they were working. Two bodies, two people; undeniable after what they'd been through.

He stared past Magda and Karlene at the familiar line of Vree's back. She'd made her choice. And he hated it.

Hated her choice.

For the first time in his life, he stumbled and would have fallen had Gerek not instinctively thrown out a hand and caught him.

"Are you okay?"

Bannon looked from Gerek to Vree then back again. "I don't know," he admitted at last.

Gerek glanced ahead at his own sister. "That makes two of us," he muttered.

About halfway up the valley, they stopped to rest and drink from the river.

"It'll be late afternoon by the time we get there." Karlene passed around the last of the dried fruit. "Do we camp a safe distance away and get a fresh start in the morning or do we go right up to the walls, assuming we can finish before dark?"

Vree shrugged. "What difference does it make if we can't? The walking dead are no more dead at night than they are in the day."

"But the dark can hide so many other things . . ." The bard turned toward the stockade and her voice took on the rhythmic cadence of tales told.

"Worse things?" Vree asked pointedly.

They'd moved only a very little bit closer when Karlene had to pull out a set of multiple pipes and play them forward. Without her help, they kept veering off along water channels and animal trails, away from the river, away from the holding.

They found the half-eaten body of the young hawk at the point where the path left the riverbank. Magda gave a little moan as Vree dropped to one knee beside it. "What happened?"

"Probably a cat. Or two."

"Don't you *know?*"

"I know that no one crept up behind it and slit its throat, but more than that . . ." She straightened and glared at the young healer. ". . . I don't know."

"Vree . . ."

"Look, I was an assassin, not slaughtering Death herself! Just because it's dead, doesn't mean I know how it got that way!" She felt Bannon's gaze, met it, and saw he understood. Of course, he did. There were some things that only Bannon *could* understand.

And I can't?

It had begun to seem only natural that Gyhard could hear her thoughts. *No.*

Gerek's free hand curled into a fist and he took a step toward Vree. "I think you owe my sister an apology," he growled.

Eyes blazing, Magda turned on him. "I don't *need* you trying to protect me all the time, Ger. I am *perfectly* capable of taking care of myself!"

With his guard distracted, Bannon dove forward, hit Gerek in the lower back with his shoulders driving him to the ground. At the moment of impact, he got his feet under him, took a deep breath, and used his weight and momentum to rip the rope out of Gerek's slackened grip, taking the brunt of the pressure across the muscles on the back of his neck. After a day's walking, he knew the exact extent of his hobble and measured his steps accordingly as he ran.

"Albannon Magaly, stop!"

He stopped, but he tottered on the bank of the river. If

he could just force himself to fall forward, the current would soon sweep him out of range of Bardic Command and there were definitely no kigh in the water this close to the crazy old man. He swayed, began to fall; too late. A familiar arm dragged him back from the edge. Vree had realized exactly what he was going to do.

For a moment, they stood together side by side—the way they'd stood for most of their lives—then the moment passed. Vree shoved the rope into Gerek's hands and strode up the path toward the stockade.

"Vree!" Karlene ran to catch up, the others following. "It's not that easy!"

"Why not? Because the gate's closed?" Without slowing, she waved a derisive hand at the wall. "I could go over this in my sleep."

"Vree!"

When the bard grabbed her arm, she stopped so quickly Karlene stumbled forward another two paces. "Kars is behind that wall. Are we agreed?"

"Well, yes, but . . ."

"Then I am going either through it or over it and Gyhard is going to do whatever it is he has to do with Kars because I want something in my life settled. Do you understand?"

"Better than you think." Karlene sighed and, greatly daring, cupped the other woman's chin in her hand. "But dearling, I'm going to ask you the question you asked me this morning; do you really want to do this alone?"

The edges of Vree's laugh had unraveled just a little. "I'm *not* alone."

"I know." Karlene turned her head so that she could see Magda and Gerek and, because it was unavoidable, Bannon. "But Gyhard isn't the only person who cares about what happens to you."

Her breathing growing fast and shallow, Vree searched for a response and couldn't find one. The only thing that came to mind was a distinct desire to run—except that she didn't think she could control her legs.

"So what do we do next?" Gyhard asked through her mouth.

Tracing Vree's jaw with her thumb, Karlene let her hand fall away. "First, I Sing. Maybe we can get someone to open the gate."

Vree nodded and stepped back. She could feel Magda's gaze pushing against her and knew that although the bard hadn't noticed Gyhard's brief exposure, the healer had.

You seemed . . . *Terrified.* *. . . at a loss for words. I was just trying to help.*

I know.

You're not angry.

Why should I be? The Imperial Army put a great deal of effort into training me to act as part of a team. A little light-headed, she felt complete for the first time since Aralt's tower. While Bannon had been inside her head, he'd concentrated solely on getting out—he hadn't had a thought to spare for her and the barriers between them had been as thick as possible. Now, she ended where her abilities ended and Gyhard began where his started.

No barriers?

Do we need them?

He smiled. She never ceased to amaze him. *No.*

Magda frowned. She could no longer feel a definitive separation between the two kigh. That wasn't good. That couldn't be good. Could it? It was very hard to think so close to the stockade; the wrongness kept pulling at the abilities that made her a healer, leaving no room for coherent thought about anything else. She had to do something about Vree and Gyhard, but first she had to deal with Kars.

"Karlene, wait." Passing Vree, she hurried to the bard's side. "If I drop into a healing trance, I think I can tell how many damaged kigh there are. I might even be able to tell you who they are."

"Not if it puts you in any danger," Gerek protested. He pushed Bannon up against the only tree still standing in the immediate area and quickly secured him.

Shaking off the lingering effects of the Bardic Command, Bannon managed a strangled "No!" when Gerek reached for the blindfold.

The two men locked eyes for a long moment. Finally, Gerek nodded. He didn't have time to argue, not with Magda suggesting she open herself up to contact with the walking dead. Other reasons for giving in to Bannon's plea, muddier reasons, he ignored.

But when he reached his sister, it was too late for further protests to do any good. She sat on a section of log with her hands lying loose in her lap, her eyes half closed, and her breathing deep and regular. There were two vertical lines between her brows, and although he'd always thought healers healing were supposed to look serene, Magda looked distinctly unhappy.

"One living kigh," she murmured. "The dead, the dead are so hard to tell apart. I don't understand. They don't seem to care. How can they not . . . Oh."

That single syllable was the most heartsick sound Gerek had ever heard. "Maggi?"

"One of them cares. One of them cares very much." Tears spilled down both cheeks. "It's so *wrong*."

"How many are there?" Karlene prodded softly, not even noticing Gerek's scowl.

"More than three. Less than ten."

The bard glanced from the healer to the stockade. "There had to have been more than ten people in there."

"Kars is a very old man and these are the second set of companions he's Sung in a short time." Vree's gaze drifted down to rest on Karlene's face. "I doubt he could manage to bring back ten."

They were Gyhard's words, Karlene realized, and perhaps more than merely his words. All at once, she remembered what Gyhard had asked Vree every morning during their quest for the prince. *Are you still sane?* She wondered why she felt so much like asking it now.

"If you Sing now, Karlene . . ." Magda's voice, trembling but determined, cut off speculation. ". . . I can tell you if your Song has any effect."

Demons. Kars sat by the hearth and tried to control his fear for Kait's sake. The rod rose and fell once again in memory.

"Stop it! Stop it! Do you want the demons to come? Do you want them to destroy you?"

"I've been good. I've been good." He hadn't called the demons. Why were they here?

Father? Her eyes were wide and frightened, and her edges were beginning to spread.

"I'm sorry Kait. I'm so sorry." He wiped away tears and straightened as much as he was able. "Come here, child. You mustn't listen to the demons. They'll hurt you."

He wrapped his arms around her smoky image and Sang her Song to her over and over until she calmed.

No sound passed through the heavy earth insulating the root cellar.

"Karlene?"

Still Singing, the bards cocked an inquiring eyebrow at Magda.

"You might as well stop. Nothing's happening."

She Sang an ending, because the last thing they needed right now was more unfinished business, then said, "Nothing?"

"No." Magda sighed and swiped at the moisture on her cheeks. "Something started to happen, then it stopped. I think Kars was Singing, too."

Karlene snorted. "One old man is not going to be able to drown out my Song."

"Well, he has. And you needn't glare at me because I'm just telling you what was happening." She tucked a curl into the corner of her mouth and despondently examined the dusty toes of her boots. "We're going to have to deal with Kars first. Vree's going to have to go over the wall because she's the only one who can."

"But just open the gate," Karlene declared before Vree could move. She stepped in front of the ex-assassin and stared down into her face. "You are not to confront Kars until we're inside."

"You promised Gyhard could deal with him."

"And he can."

"But you want to be there."

"No." She wished she knew just what it was that felt so wrong. "I want Magda to be there."

Vree dragged the heavy sweater over her head and tossed it to one side. There'd be exercise soon enough to keep her warm and she didn't need the added weight.

"Vree!"

"I'll open the gate." She checked the release on her single throwing dagger, smiled, and flicked the bard's pale braid back behind her shoulder. "You worry too much."

Half a dozen running steps and she was her own height

up on the wall, clinging to a surface never meant to keep out human climbers. An instant later, she paused on the top, balanced easily between the points on two massive logs, fought the urge to look back at Bannon, and dropped out of sight.

Gerek laid an arm across Magda's shoulders as she sighed and wiped her eyes with the back of one hand. "You okay?" When she shrugged, he lightly kissed the top of her head. "If anyone can heal this mess," he told her softly, "you can."

A short distance away, Bannon fought the ropes that held him.

"Hush, child, hush. Tell me what's wrong." When the demons quieted, Kait had gone into the yard but almost immediately returned. Something had upset her, but Kars didn't understand what.

Two. Not one, two!

"Two what, child?" When he stood, she tried to push him back away from the door, but her hands passed right through him. "Just let me look, Kait. It isn't the demon. I'd know if it was the demon."

Leaning heavily on a staff he'd found, he pulled open the door and stepped outside, eyes squinting nearly shut in the sunlight.

Kars.

I know. Vree dropped the last few feet and moved away from the wall, eyes locked on the old man. She hadn't expected this; Kars, alone, no walking dead to protect him. *What do we do now?*

Gyhard felt as though his past had him in a vise and it was closing tight around him. *Lend me your body. Let me finish this.*

She hesitated, remembering how Bannon had shoved her aside, usurped control, and refused to give it back without a fight that had nearly destroyed them both.

I'm not Bannon, Vree.

Kars raised a twisted hand to shade his eyes. "Who's there?"

*   *   *

Vree?

One heartbeat. Two.

*Vree, the bards consider this to be a bardic problem. If we let Karlene in, *she'll* have to do something!*

Two heartbeats. Three.

Vree!

Yes.

She felt Gyhard surge forward. One moment she was Vree. The next, Vree and Gyhard combined, a joining so intense she almost lost herself in it. For that moment, she knew everything there was to know about him—his strengths, his weaknesses, his fears—and he knew the same about her. It was terrifyingly intimate and, because of that intimacy, the most incredibly sensual experience she'd ever had. Her whole body throbbed in reaction. As they slowly began to separate again, she couldn't help but think of sweat-slicked skin, welded together by heat and passion, pulling apart, inch by sticky inch.

Vree?

Pushed back into a corner of her own mind, Vree struggled to gain enough control to form a conscious thought. She could still feel her body but from a distance, almost as though she were feeling an outer layer of clothing. *I'm here.*

That was . . .

Yes. Looking through her eyes was like looking through a window that flickered every few moments. Kars had taken a step back toward the building. He seemed older, more tired than he had.

"Go away! We don't want you here!" So desperate to protect his family from the demons, Kars had forgotten how the world could attack with other weapons. He should have kept one of them with him to keep the living away. Kait did her best, but they didn't even seem to notice her as she swirled about their . . .

He shook his head and peered around the yard. He could see only one person, but he could feel two. And one of them felt achingly familiar.

Distracted for a moment by the graceful play of muscle over bone, a grace he now controlled, Gyhard stepped forward, hands held out from his sides. "Kars?"

"I know who I am." He hadn't for a long time, but the

knowledge had been given back to him. Stepping over the threshold, he struggled to close the door.

Don't let him get inside!

Gyhard raced across the yard and pushed against the planking. "Do you know who I am?"

The voice was wrong, but the kigh, he knew the kigh. "Gyhard?" Kars scowled through the wedge-shaped opening, barely visible in the deep shadows of the hall. "You went away. You came back, then you went away."

Swallowing around what felt like a dagger stuck crosswise in Vree's throat, Gyhard nodded. "I didn't have a choice." He could reach in, grab the front of what was obviously a borrowed robe, and yank the old man outside. Vree's hands were smaller than Bannon's but strong enough for what had to be done. He *should* reach in—but he couldn't.

"They always go away." The old man sighed, fingers stroking the necklace of bone. "I thought they wouldn't, you know, but they do."

"I know." In memory, Kars, young and beautiful and so dreadfully damaged, held out a cup of poisoned wine because he believed that the dead would never leave him.

"What is going on in there?" Gerek demanded, pacing back and forth on the hard packed earth in front of the gate. "Why hasn't she let us in?"

"She isn't . . ." Magda dragged a wet curl from the corner of her mouth and tried again. Closing her eyes, she reached out with all her strength. "She isn't in control anymore. Gyhard is."

Bannon shrieked in wordless fury and flung himself against the ropes.

Gyhard stepped back and held out Vree's hand. "Kars, please come outside. I've come to stop the pain."

Unable to do anything herself, Kait sped toward the root cellar. She couldn't open the heavy door, but neither could it keep her out.

Five of the others stood where they'd been left. The sixth sat crumpled in a corner. It wasn't like the others. It wasn't like her. She stopped in front of it.

Get up!

It ignored her. She could feel it frantically struggling against the tormented flesh that held it.

Five would have to be enough.

Kars looked at the hand stretched out toward him. "I can't leave now."

"It's time."

Just for a moment, it seemed that the insanity left his eyes and he was only a very old and very tired man "Long past time," he said softly. "But I've promised Kait I'd stay."

Gerek grabbed Karlene's shoulder, fingers sinking deep into the heavy sweater, and spun her around to face him. "Do something!"

"Like what?"

"How should I know? You're the bard!" He waved his sword at the stockade. "Sing something!"

"There are *no* kigh!" she reminded him through clenched teeth.

He pushed his face toward hers, and spat each word at her with separate emphasis. "Yes. There. Are."

"She's too far away!"

"Try!"

Jerking free of his grip, Karlene faced the stockade and pitched her voice to carry. **"Vireyda Magaly!"**

Gyhard barely held on as Vree surged forward. They meshed for a heartbeat, then separated again. *What the . . .?*

Karlene's using my name, like she used it at the way station when Bannon took control.

How could she know which kigh is dominant from outside the holding?

How the slaughter should I know? I've been here with you.

She's going to ruin everything!

"Vireyda Magaly!"

The second call was harder to fight.

Head cocked to catch the sound of the distant voice, Kars slid back into insanity, his eyes growing wider with every passing second.

"Vireyda Magaly, answer me!"

"Demons! A trick! A trap!" Gibbering in terror, Kars leaped backward, slamming the door.

"Shit!" Impossible to tell which one of them spoke, which one of them was in control.

The cabbage hit them just above the left elbow, numbing the arm and knocking them sideways. They turned and saw the dead approaching, their joined kigh too strong to accept the false comfort of denial.

Gyhard, give way. You can't fight them.

Neither can you! But he released her body, drawing quickly back within his original boundaries as she surged forward. The brief moment of unity brought a flare of heat that lasted long enough to be a dangerous distraction. *We've got to open the gate!*

Unfortunately, in order to confront Kars, they'd come too far in the yard. An ax balanced across her palms, one of the dead moved to stand between them and reinforcements.

Vree dove forward to avoid being brained with a stone crock of honey, rolled awkwardly because of the numb arm, and felt fingers close around her ankle, the touch so cold she could feel the chill through the leather of her boots. Writhing in the dead man's grip, she kicked up with her free leg, catching him on the point of his chin.

Teeth shattered as Ondro's head whipped back, but he didn't let go. Kait had told them the father was in danger. The father must be protected. He could dimly remember a man he'd called Father being set gently into a hole in the ground, but that memory had been stripped of power by the Song that held him. If Kait said the father was in danger, then Ondro would protect the father.

"Shit, shit, shit!" Narrowly avoiding a grab by the dead man's other hand, Vree curled up and drove the point of her long dagger into his waist, sawing it from side to side, severing tendons, separating the small bones. Suddenly, she could feel the air above her being pushed aside. At the perimeter of her vision, she could still see the woman guarding the gate—obviously, someone else had stopped to pick up a weapon. There was no longer time to waste on freedom. Flinging herself to the right, she dragged the dead man over with her and left a fold of her sleeve lying severed in the dirt of the yard.

* * *

"Now what's happening?"

"They're fighting."

"Who?"

Magda blinked and looked up at her brother. "The dead."

Gerek glared at the stockade then, snarling wordlessly, ran down the path to the tree where Bannon was tied. Barely pausing, he raised his sword. As it descended, Bannon twisted to present as small a target as possible.

"GEREK!" Magda rushed forward, hands outstretched, unable to believe what she was seeing.

Two more quick cuts and the ropes binding wrists and ankles were in pieces. Another and Bannon's knives spilled out of a split pack and onto the ground.

"Gerek, what are you doing!"

He grabbed his sister as she flung herself by him, but he directed his answer up the path at the bard. "Bannon's the only one who can get over the wall. Don't you dare call him back!"

Karlene's pale eyes blazed. "Are you threatening me, Your Grace?"

The steel point lifted. "If I have to."

Bannon ignored them. Scooping up the two throwing daggers and the long belt knife out of the pile, he sprinted for the wall, swarming up the same imperfections Vree had used, pausing as she had at the top. A quick glance down into the enclosed area showed him five to one odds. When his gaze tried to slide away as his kigh refused to deal with the dead/undead kigh below, he forced his focus back onto the fight. Vree was down there. And she needed him.

He saw her sever a hand to free herself and grimaced, remembering the fight with the dead soldiers at the ford. The dead didn't feel pain. Unless the bard could get inside the stockade and do whatever it was she did, this lot would have to be chopped to pieces before they'd give up. Five to one odds were no longer survivable.

With his feet braced against the inside of the logs, Bannon scuttled hand over hand along the top of the wall, his weight hanging from the rough points hacked into the upper ends of the logs. His right arm throbbed just above his wrist where it had been broken while Gyhard controlled his body. Swearing under his breath, he moved a little faster. He dangled for a heartbeat over the gate, then dropped, landing behind the dead woman with the ax.

Straightening, he grabbed the bar, began to lift, and flung himself to one side as an ax head thudded into the wood where his right shoulder had been. *Almost like someone told her I was there . . .*

Twisting the blade out of the wood with practiced ease, Anca swung again. She would protect the father.

The edges split the air an inch from Bannon's back as he dove under the swing and slammed his shoulder into her stomach. They hit the ground together, but with no air to be knocked from her lungs, she continued to flail about and managed to smack him in the side of the head with the ax handle.

Grunting in pain, he rolled clear and staggered for the gate. *Could use that pig-sticker of His Grace's in here right about now.*

On the other side of the yard, the severed hand still clutching her ankle, Vree dragged herself under a split rail fence and into the cow byre. At this moment, crawling through shit was a small price to pay. As a heavyset middle-aged man with arms like small trees chopped through the rails, she lurched toward the stable. From the stable roof she could get to the wall. Once on the wall, she could get out.

Slipping in the muck, she twisted to keep from falling, and saw Bannon lifting the bar on the gate. Her left arm snapped forward.

The throwing dagger embedded itself hilt-deep in Anca's armpit, grinding in the joint. The ax missed flesh and it bit deeply into wood. One arm dangling uselessly, she fought to free it.

Cut off from the stable, Vree picked up a splintered rail and smashed it into the face of the charging dead man. It slowed him down a little. With all her strength, she drove her heel into his knee. That shook off the clinging hand and slowed him down a little more. It didn't stop him.

Bannon kicked back, catching Anca in the ribs, hurling her away from both ax and gate. The sudden appearance of the dagger told him that Vree was back in control of her own body. Whatever had happened between her and

Gyhard before the dead attacked was no longer happening. *Kars kept calling Gyhard "my heart"; maybe he Sang his lost heart right back into his chest.* The thought of Gyhard trapped in an ancient ruin of a body with a crazy old man made him smile as he shoved open the gate.

Gerek's sword whistled down through the slowly widening space, deflecting the ax blow aimed at Bannon's head.

"Chop off her slaughtering arm!" he yelled scrabbling out of the way.

Momentum carried Gerek into the yard, but when it ran out, he stood frozen in horror, surrounded by the walking dead. His sword arm began to shake and the point fell until the tip dimpled the packed earth.

"Gerek!" Seeing only her brother's danger, Magda rushed forward.

NO! NO! NO!

Hands clutching her head, she screamed and fell writhing to the ground.

"Maggi!" The edge of his sword chopped through flesh and into bone. Jerking away from clutching hands, he fought to free the blade from a dead thigh.

Karlene Sang as she ran into the holding and that was all that kept her from falling as Magda had.

NO! NO! NO!

The voice shrieked denial in her head, trying to drown out the Song.

NO! NO! NO!

The pain was so intense she could hardly see, Karlene forced her voice to run up and down an eight-note scale. It was the best shield she could manage, and it wasn't nearly enough. Grabbing Magda's foot, she dragged the girl back out through the gate.

The shrieking stopped.

Wiping at a dribble of blood from a lip she didn't remember biting through, Karlene dropped to her knees and gently lifted Magda's head onto her lap. When the girl's eyes fluttered open, her heart started beating again. "Are you all right?" It was probably a stupid question, Karlene realized, considering how *she* felt, but it was the only question that came to mind.

Magda blinked and tried to focus on the bard's face. "Her name is Kait."

"Whose name?"

"The girl who kept saying no." Tears spilled over and ran down Magda's cheeks. "She's just barely hanging on to who she is."

"I'm not surprised." Setting Magda gently on the ground, Karlene got shakily to her feet. Considering the condition Kait's body had been in when she'd found it on the other side of the pass, and how long before that Kars had Sung the girl's kigh back into a parody of life, she was amazed Kait had any sense of self remaining at all. But since she did . . .

Leaning on the gate, careful not to cross over into the yard, Karlene Sang. Although she Sang everything she'd found out about the girl after returning with Prince Otavas to the Capital, Kait's kigh stayed just out of reach of her Song.

"She's protecting her father," Magda said, waving a shaky hand at the fighting. "They all are."

"Her father?"

"Kars. I think if Kars wasn't there, they'd stop fighting." She winced as Gerek parried blows from a maul. "I think."

A living fighter recoils from pain, leaving openings to be exploited; the dead do not. Unable to disengage long enough to run for it, Vree found herself pushed back against one of the buildings, an ax blade cutting patterns in the air inches in front of her face. Instinct flipped her right arm forward, but the dagger that should have dropped into her hand lay somewhere off the coast of the Broken Islands.

"Shit!" She ducked as the ax smashed through the narrow shutter behind her and swore louder as a splinter of wood embedded itself in her cheek.

"Vree! To the right!"

She flung herself sideways as the dead man catapulted toward her. Dropping to one knee under the flailing arms, she caught a glimpse of Bannon running something into his back.

Pinned to the wall by the steel point on the log gaff, Kiril struggled to free himself. He must protect the father. Pressing his palms against the wood, he pushed and, inch by inch moved backward, passing the shaft through his body. When his arms no longer reached the wall, he dug his heels in and kept moving.

Bannon grabbed Vree's arm and shoved her toward the broken shutter. "Karlene says Gyhard has to deal with Kars. Kait won't let her into the holding, and it's the only thing that'll stop this lot."

"What?"

"I'll explain later. Just deal with Kars." He ripped off the remains of the shutter and boosted her into the narrow opening. "Hurry up, before Gerek gets his legs chopped off. His Grace doesn't like hurting people."

"But they're dead!"

He flashed her a brilliant and achingly familiar smile. "Tell him."

NO! NO! NO!

Reeling backward, Karlene threw everything she had into Kait's Song. It was barely enough to chase the tortured kigh out of her head. Panting, most of her weight on Magda's shoulder, the bard shook her head. "All that seems to do is remind her we're out here."

Squatting by the hearth, a hand resting on the partially burned body of the old woman, Kars rocked back and forth Singing softly to himself, trying to drown out the Song of the demon. It wasn't working. One after another, the demon Songs that had been beaten out of him in his childhood welled up out of memory and built piteous harmonies in his head.

Lips caught between his teeth, his Song faded to a moan. He rocked farther back, beating his head against the fieldstone wall. Beating. Beating. He could still hear the demons.

"Kars, stop it." Breathing shallowly through Vree's mouth, thankful for her nightsight, Gyhard stepped carefully over and around the corpses and broken furniture scattered down the length of the dim room. "Hurting yourself won't drive away the kigh."

"The demons." The protest came out of the old man's mouth in a young man's voice.

"They're not demons, Kars. They're just the kigh."

"I don't want them. Make them go away, Gyhard. Make them go away!"

You've had this conversation before.

A long time ago. He stepped up onto the hearth and wrapped Vree's arm around the old man's shoulders, forcing his bleeding head away from the wall.

Kars buried his face against Vree's chest. "Hold me until they go away."

Her skin crawling, even though she wasn't exactly in it, Vree stared down at the tangled mat of gray hair. *Do what you have to.*

She could feel Gyhard's grief and his guilt as he took her hand and lifted the old man's chin until their eyes met. "Kars . . ."

He frowned. "Were you always a girl?"

Gyhard blinked. "What?"

"A girl. You're a girl. You weren't always a girl."

"No, but . . ."

His smile was everything it had ever been, "I didn't think so." Then the smile disappeared. "Why do you keep leaving me?"

"I never meant . . ."

"Yes, you did." The rheumy eyes narrowed. "You got on that horse and you rode away."

Gyhard. Do it!

Her hands closed around his neck. "I'm sorry."

Ignoring the hold intended to kill him, Kars shook his head. "Sorry isn't enough for what you did." Remembering another life he'd made his own, he filled his lungs with air and shrieked out a Song.

GYHARD! She could feel his kigh being dragged from her body. Forcing her consciousness past him into her hands, she changed her grip and twisted the old man's head around in one swift motion, snapping the ancient, brittle neck.

Gyhard!

I'm here.

She threw herself into him, not sure of what parts of her body were under her control and what were under his and not caring. He needed comfort, so she gave it, finding ways to hold him.

"Gyhard."

It was a name whispered with air pushed out of dead lungs. Meshed as tightly together as was possible and still maintaining separate kigh, they looked down at the body.

"Help me."

When Vree disappeared into the building, the dead tried to follow, throwing themselves futilely against the door Kars had bolted from the inside.

Forcing herself to think past the moment, Anca slowly backed away. She couldn't remember the kitchen. She couldn't remember exactly what it was for, but she remembered a door from the kitchen to the hall. The father was in the hall.

They had to protect the father. She began moving as quickly as possible toward the back of the building.

"Something tells me there's another way in!" Bannon yanked his borrowed log gaffe out of the wood, ignoring the rancid fluids smeared along its length, and ran after her. Slashing at her ankles, he brought her down. Planting the point in the center of her back, he leaped up into the air and drove it through her into the ground. It hadn't worked the last time, but it was all he could think of to do.

Jumping off the body, already rising moistly onto her hands and knees, he looked around for another target and saw Gerek leaning on his sword being noisily sick. Behind him, sunlight glinted on an ax as it descended. Even as Bannon raced forward, he knew he was going to be too late.

"Gerek!" Magda's scream echoed off the stockade walls.

Gerek straightened . . .

. . . started to turn . . .

Inches away from his shoulder, the ax fell from nerveless fingers and the blow that should have chopped through living flesh from neck to groin, skidded through the heavy muscle across the top of his shoulder on its fall to the ground.

Gerek cried out, clamped his left hand over the wound and swayed where he stood, blood pouring over his chest and arm. He would have fallen had Bannon not grabbed him around the waist and used his own momentum to get him moving toward the gate.

"Lucky we brought a healer with us, Your Grace." He dumped him into Magda's arms and turned once again to the yard. He had to stop the dead from getting to Vree.

Except that the dead had stopped.

They stood, or knelt, perfectly still, their faces blank.

Staggering back under her brother's weight, one hand clamped over the wound, Magda would have fallen had Karlene not lowered them both to the ground.

"Can you Heal him?"

Brows knit together, Magda took a quick look at the bloody gash, then clamped her hand down again, her relief so great it took her a moment to find her voice. "He doesn't need Healing," she sniffed, trying to sound unconcerned for Gerek's sake, "he needs to be sewn up and bound in clean linen packed with comfrey, but since I don't have a kit with me . . ." She sent a watery smile in the bard's direction. "I Healed Gerek while still in the womb. There isn't anything about his body I don't know. Which, I might add, is a *disgusting* amount to know about your brother, in spite of what the girls in the village think." Lower lip trembling, she drew in a deep breath and let it out slowly. Her eyes unfocused as she laid both shaking hands over the wound.

Gerek screamed and nearly threw himself out from under her touch.

An instant later, Magda sagged forward over an indented line of pale pink skin.

Her own heart beating uncomfortably fast, Karlene stroked damp hair back off Magda's face. "Are you all right?"

"I *hate* hurting people," she whimpered.

"It's only one quick pain against months of pain. I think Gerek understands."

"He passed out."

"I hear that often happens."

"I think I'm going to faint."

"Not now," Bannon called softly, in his thickly accented Shkoden. "Trouble comes."

With Kars' limp body cradled in her arms—he was nothing but skin and bones, the bulky robe weighed as much as he did—Vree crossed the yard toward the gate. The dead faces turned toward her as she passed, but that was the only movement they made. Vaguely aware of a confused wailing that seemed to come from the air around her, she laid the body down and turned to Karlene.

"He's dead." That was obvious to them all. The heads of the living never rested at quite that angle. "But he's still in there."

Thirteen

"It's been too long," Karlene said, sagging down onto her knees by Kars' body and pushing damp hair back off her forehead. "With the others, I used the Song to show them where they should go, but for Kars . . ." She sighed and spread her hands. "It's just not enough."

"We have to do something," Gyhard murmured through Vree's mouth.

"I know." Kars had been responsible for dark and terrible things, but he had suffered as much torment as he'd caused and had been trapped in the darkness far longer than any of his companions. Pity had proven stronger than revulsion and anger both. "Someone has to show him the way."

"You mean that someone has to die?"

Head bowed, exhaustion dragging her shoulders forward, Karlene nodded.

Vree, I . . .

No. Her body jerked with the force of her denial. *Not you.*

I have lived as much past my time as he has. He lifted a hand to stroke her cheek.

She lowered it again. *I don't care.*

Vree . . .

Don't leave me.

He looked down at Kars, at the tortured and undying creature his love had inadvertently created, then he looked into Vree's heart and wondered how many people were given such a second chance.

Leaning on the open gate, arms folded over his chest, Bannon nodded toward the neat line of dead bodies laid out along one side of the yard. "Should've thought before sending them off then," he snorted.

Karlene glared up at him. "They were suffering, and I had no way of knowing!" He shrugged and she barely resisted the urge to smack him. Besides, considering that he poisoned their entire family, I doubt any of them would be willing to do him a favor."

"Point," Bannon admitted after a moment's consideration.

"Thank you."

"No one dies," Magda declared from her place by Gerek's side.

Dropping her gaze to the young healer, Karlene gentled her voice. "It's the only way," she insisted softly.

Eyes narrowed into obstinate slits over purple shadows, Magda raised a hand from the rise and fall of Gerek's chest and pulled a curl of hair from the corner of her mouth. "Find another."

A heavy, uncomfortable silence settled over the living. Almost certain she could hear individual heartbeats, Vree asked, "What about Kait?"

Bard and healer both instinctively clapped their hands over their ears as the background wailing only they could hear grew in volume. It rose to a painful crescendo of grief and loss, slicing back and forth through their consciousness like hot, serrated knives.

"Hush . . . Kait."

The wailing stopped so suddenly its absence echoed.

Breathing heavily, Karlene nodded down at Kars' body, her gaze moving quickly enough to avoid eye contact. "Thank you." Looking up, she swayed and pushed a hand against the ground to brace herself. "Kait's as lost as Kars is," she explained when the world stopped moving.

"No one dies," Magda repeated, wiping her nose on the back of her hand. "Too many people have died already. Here, in Fortune . . ."

In Fortune. Karlene started. She could hear the music—if she could only identify the Song. Her fingers closed around a handful of earth. In Fortune, where all four quarters had been Sung the night of Third Quarter Festival. "Jazep!"

"Jazep's dead!" The protest brought a sudden renewal of grief. There were so many dead . . .

To Magda's astonished indignation, the bard laughed and

held out a fistful of dirt. "He's dead, yes, but he's not gone. His kigh went into the earth. He Sang Third Quarter Festival with me!"

Although Magda and Gerek stared at her in bewilderment, the absolute certainty in her voice kept them from arguing.

Rocking back onto her heels, Karlene surged up onto her feet, exhaustion pushed aside, words tumbling over each other in her eagerness to be heard. "Kait has no effect on the others because they can't Sing the kigh, but she kept attacking Magda and me because we can. Suppose, after Jazep Sang the dead away in Fortune, she attacked him? Suppose she's what killed him? He knows what she needs! What Kars needs!" She brandished the fistful of dirt. "That's why he stayed. To show them the way!"

"Even if that's true . . . ." Even with a limited understanding of how things worked, Vree had her doubts anyone, even a bard, would stick around to help the one who'd killed them. ". . . the dirt he went into is back in Fortune."

"Essentially, true; he went into the earth in Fortune *but* all kigh are part of a greater whole. There's only one earth kigh—just as there's only one air or fire or water." Exalted, Karlene threw open her arms. "Jazep's here, back in Fortune, checking out the gardens in Vidor—he's everywhere!"

"But I thought there were no kigh *here*." Vree jerked her head toward Kars without really looking at him. "Because of him."

"Jazep's a bard. Kars isn't going to be able to stop him."

"Even if you're right, Karlene . . . ." The young healer's subdued tone suggested she thought the possibility remote. ". . . we'd *still* have to Call his kigh."

"It's a fifth kigh," Karlene began, but Magda cut her off. "I don't *feel* it. I don't feel anyone but Kars and Kait. I can barely feel *myself*." She sighed deeply, looked up and held the bard's gaze with hers. "And *you* don't Sing earth."

"I do."

One moment Magda was sitting cross-legged on the ground beside her brother, the next she was wrapped in the embrace of a not very tall woman wearing travel-stained clothes and boots marked by a long, hard journey.

"Mama! Oh, Mama." Face buried against her mother's neck, Magda couldn't stop herself from bursting into tears.

Eyes closed, Annice murmured comfort with such fierce intensity that even Kars sighed and allowed his head to sag forward on the ruin of his spine.

Vree tried not to stare. *You have to believe her when she says everything's going to be all right.*

Gyhard smiled. *It wouldn't dare not to be.*

Swallowing sobs, Magda pushed herself out to arm's length, her face blotchy and her lashes in triangular clumps. All children believe that in times of trouble their mothers will miraculously come to the rescue, but Magda not only considered herself too old for that particular bardic tale, she'd never heard of it actually happening. "Mother, what are you *doing* here?" Then she scowled, the effect somewhat ruined by the grip she maintained on Annice's hands. "You've been using the kigh to watch me, haven't you?"

"You and your brother," Annice admitted easily, throwing a quick, grateful smile at Karlene. "But, as it happens, that's not why I'm here." She sighed and suddenly looked very, very tired. "I felt the dead walking, Maggi, and when Kovar told me you'd left Elbasan, I knew what you were going to do—what you had to do. Under the circumstances, I thought you might need some help."

"Magda shook her head. "Mother, if you were in Ohrid . . . I mean, we were *riding*—there's no way you could have got here . . ."

"Jazep made sure I'd arrive in time."

"Jazep?"

"Karlene's right. When I Sang earth at Third Quarter Festival, Jazep Sang with me as well. He led me here."

"Then you *know* what's going on."

Annice swept her gaze over the others, noting the blood on Gerek's shirt and his newly healed wound, noting two kigh in one body, noting the piled bodies of the dead, and finally noting the dead man watching her with what could only be called hope. "No, dear," she said, almost smiling in spite of accumulated horrors, "I haven't the faintest idea."

The sun was setting by the time explanations were over, and the valley looked as though it had been gilded with fire.

"Lost," Annice murmured, one hand holding tightly to

Magda, the other to Gerek as though keeping them from being lost as well. When Gerek had opened his eyes to see her bending over him, he'd smiled and said with very little surprise, "Hullo, Nees. Have you come to make it all better?"

"Yes." She'd kissed him on the cheek, helped him to sit up, and only then allowed Karlene to recount everything she'd missed since she came close enough to lose the kigh.

"Lost," she said again. She could feel Kars watching her from where he lay, wrapped in the gathering shadows. If he was lost, it was long past time for him to be found. She stood, and pulled both Gerek and Magda to their feet. "Well, then, let's get to it before we lose the light. Gerek, go sit over there with Vree and Bannon. All three of you, try to stay out of the way."

Brother and sister exchanged wary glances.

"Out of the way of what?" Gerek asked.

"The Song." She took Magda by the shoulders and walked her around to stand at Kars' head. Beckoning Karlene closer, she joined her left hand with Magda's right, then moved herself so that the healer stood between the two bards.

Karlene looked a question at Magda who shrugged, equally confused. As everyone's position received a last assessment, the younger bard murmured, "Annice, just what exactly are we going to *do*?"

"What has to be done. It'll all be over soon," she promised, squeezing her daughter's hand. Breathing deeply, she moistened her lips and began to Sing.

To her listeners it seemed as if the Song grew roots that reached down into the center of the earth. It thrummed through the ground and vibrated up through the soles of their boots. The Song was earth the way bards had Sung since the very first Song, but then Annice reached deeper, added the four notes of Jazep's name, and it became something more.

The kigh formed at Kars' feet. First head, then shoulders, then the barrellike torso, then finally the legs that weren't quite long enough to put the whole thing in proportion.

Magda blinked away tears and found a smile to answer the smile her name-father Sang at her.

For a moment, Jazep Sang with Annice, then the harmonies began to subtly change as he began directing the Song. They were Singing the fifth kigh, Karlene realized, but it wasn't the Song she Sang—it was more like a part of a larger Song, one she knew, although she had no idea when she'd learned it. Squeezing Magda's fingers in hers, she added her voice.

All at once, Kars' body was only that. A body. No longer a prison.

Jazep looked at Magda and nodded.

It took her a moment to understand and then she reached out with the part of her that healed. *It's time, Kait. They're waiting for you.*

In the last of the light, three translucent figures stood hand in hand. The young man, who, had he been born in another place would have been one of the greatest bards the four quarters had ever known, looked down at the ruin of his body and then at Magda. *Would you tell Gyhard I loved him, even when I forgot what that meant.*

I will.

And would you tell Vree that trust . . . His smile was sweet and a little tentative as he broke off and shook his head. *Never mind. I think it's something she has to learn for herself.*

The girl looked up at him with a puzzled frown. *You're not my father.*

No. He took her free hand with his, completing the circle. *I'm Kars.*

Jazep smiled on them both and although Magda was sure she heard him speak, she could still hear his voice in the Song. *Come, children. It's time to go home.*

As the earth kigh lost its shape, the Song rose until it filled the valley and for a moment, the moment between one heartbeat and the next, Magda heard another voice join in. Not Kars. A silent voice. A gentle voice. A strong voice. And one she knew.

All kigh were part of a greater whole. Earth kigh. Air kigh. Water kigh. Fire kigh. The kigh they called the fifth kigh because the bards had Sung four before it. *All* kigh were part of a greater whole.

Annice and Karlene Sang the gratitude alone. As the last notes rose up into a sapphire sky, they were nearly blown over by the rush of air kigh demanding their attention.

They barely noticed when Magda pulled her hands free and walked over to join the others by the stockade wall.

"You okay, Maggi?" Gerek asked, draping an arm over her shoulders and pulling her close to his side.

She nodded, then, as the euphoria began to fade, she frowned. Something still wasn't right.

Vree and Gyhard found him in the root cellar, pressed up against the earth wall. He'd obviously relieved himself where he sat, and he stank. At first they thought he'd hidden there from Kars but when they led him—not so much unresisting as uncaring—out into the yard, Magda took one look at him and began to shake.

"I think," she said through clenched teeth, "that I'm going to be sick."

"Smells bad," Bannon agreed, moving upwind.

"It's not that. He's dead. His body is alive, but he's dead."

Holding the lantern up by his face, Vree looked into his eyes and quickly looked away again. "She's right."

Gerek shook his head. "That's impossible," he began but fell silent when Vree turned toward him.

"I've seen enough of the dead to know when I'm seeing another," she snapped. "I don't give a shit if this one's breathing, he's dead."

I think, Gyhard told her slowly, trying not to remember the feeling of being dragged out into nothingness and suspecting that he'd never forget, *this is what Kars tried to do to me, just before you killed him.*

"A dead kigh in a living body." Magda chewed over the words. It should have been horrible, it was horrible, but suddenly all she could see was the answer they'd been searching for all along. "A dead kigh in a living . . . Gyhard!"

"What?" The exchange happened almost effortlessly now.

"This is *your* body!"

"What!"

"He can't *want* to stay, he's dead." Breathing shallowly through her mouth she stepped forward and took the unresponsive hand. "You *don't* want to stay, do you?"

When the body dies, I am free.

The word "free" reverberated off the inside of her skull. "Except *we* don't want the body to die. What's your name?"

Enrik.

"Okay." She released him and couldn't stop herself from scrubbing her hand against her thigh. Feeling as though she'd been stretched out by the events of the day, she gritted her teeth, determined to hold together until the end—she only hoped it would be soon. "Enrik here wants to leave. So Karlene..." She grabbed Karlene's arm as the two bards joined them and pulled her forward. "... Sings him out of his body and away."

"Maggi, this is a dead man in a living body!" Annice exclaimed just as Karlene demanded to know what she was talking about.

Magda sighed, explained, and finished with, "Once he's *out* of the body, Vree gives a little push and Gyhard moves in. Simple."

"Simple?" Gerek muttered. Bannon indicated complete agreement with the raising of both brows.

Gyhard studied Enrik in the lamplight. He was probably in his mid-twenties, brown hair bleached out by a working day spent in the sun, skin bronzed by the same. His nose had been broken at least once. His hands were rough, the nails ridged. It was hard to determine anything else under all the dirt. "The funny thing is," he said so quietly only Vree heard him, "my family owned a timber-holding. If I hadn't met up with those brigands, this might have been me."

You're going to do it?

He thought of all that it would mean. *If it can be arranged as simply as Magda thinks, yes.*

What about me? She could feel the emptiness surrounding her. Waiting. *What about us?*

Vree . . . Confused, he paused. He could feel her distress, but he didn't understand the source. *You'll still be you,* he hazarded at last. *And we'll still be us. The body's young and strong and . . .*

"No." Vree's head snapped back and her eyes narrowed. "NO!" You're not going to leave me, too!" She flung the lamp to the ground and in the sudden darkness raced for the gate.

Vree! What are you doing? Her fear pushed him into a tiny corner of her mind, blocking him from any kind of control, any kind of communication, but not from the desolate weight of her pain.

He'd asked her if she was still sane nearly every morning since Bannon had shared her body. Pummeled by the force of her emotional storm, he realized he'd hadn't asked it once since he'd taken Bannon's place. Perhaps he should have.

She'd almost reached the gate when something hit her from the right and took her to the ground.

This fight, Bannon won. He thrust his arms under hers and locked his hands behind her neck in a supposedly unbreakable hold just as Magda threw herself down beside them.

"Vree, listen to me. You haven't got time for this! Enrik says his body is dying, and he's not going to wait!"

"I don't care!" she spat. Bannon twisted so that her heel hit him only a glancing blow, got her to her knees and sat on the lower part of her legs. "I don't want it!"

"Why not? What are you afraid of? Vree, if you and Gyhard don't separate soon, you might not be able to. Your kigh are becoming so interlinked, even now you might not be able to find all of the bits of you and all the bits of him. You'll lose yourself in him and he'll lose himself in you."

"Yes."

Startled by the longing in that single syllable, Magda drew back. "But he *has* to have a body of his own!"

Vree shook her head. "He has me."

"He can't have all of you," Bannon growled.

"Not now, Bannon!" Magda snapped, "We've got to . . ."

"Maggi. Come here."

She turned to frown at her mother. "But . . ."

"No. Come here." Annice's voice took on not-to-be-argued-with tones.

Still frowning, Magda stood and slowly backed away until Vree and Bannon became a strangely shaped shadow in the night.

Annice stepped forward and put both hands on her daughter's shoulders, the grip equal parts comfort and caution. "Sometimes," she said, the past weighting her words, "people need to heal themselves."

"Let me go!"

"No." Bannon adjusted his hold. "Not this time. I let you go before, but I'm not doing it again."

Vree tried to smash his nose in with the back of her head but only hit a cheekbone.

"Vree, listen to me," he pleaded. "I understand what you're afraid of." Jerking back to avoid another blow, Bannon breathed in the warm familiar scent that all his life had meant he wasn't alone. "You're trying to do the same thing to Gyhard that I wanted to do to you."

"What are you talking about?" She'd intended it to be a snarl, but it emerged as more of a wail.

He knew what he meant, but he wasn't sure how to explain. Vree had changed, but so, he'd come to realize, had he. "You're not my arm or my leg, you're a separate person, with a separate life, and I have no right to try to make you into what I want. Being your brother doesn't give me that right. Loving you doesn't give me that right. The whole slaughtering Imperial Army doesn't give me that right. And you haven't the right to do it to Gyhard either."

She went limp in his arms and started to shake. It could have been a trick, but he didn't think so. As he gathered her close, she pressed her face against his shoulder in blind need. He tried to remember if she'd ever turned to him before and wasn't very surprised when memory told him their position had always been reversed. "I will always love you," he murmured into her hair. "Just because you've chosen to share your life with a carrion-eating *abomination* . . ." He stumbled a little over the Shkoden word. ". . . well, you won't get rid of me that easily. I guess that you can love him, too."

Too. Vree fought to find her way through the maelstrom roaring around inside her head. Assassins had no family but the army. But she'd had Bannon. Had loved Bannon with a desperate intensity because he was all she had. Because she'd been allowed to love Bannon, she was able to love Gyhard. It had never occurred to her that she could love more than one person at a time.

Suddenly released, Gyhard cautiously extended his control. *Vree?*

Her answer wasn't so much in words as a tentative opening of final barriers neither of them had realized still existed.

Becoming concerned by the lengthening silence, Bannon pulled back until he could look down into Vree's eyes. He'd looked into them too many times in the darkness to need light now. "Sod off, Gyhard. This is my time, not yours."

Gyhard stopped her as she started to stiffen. *Bannon's right,* he murmured, and withdrew as far as possible.

Releasing a breath she couldn't remember holding, the air leaving her lungs in a long shuddering sigh, Vree touched the comfort of Gyhard's presence and rubbed her cheek against Bannon's shoulder. The last time she'd held her brother, only her brother, their relationship unwarped by the training that made them blades of Jiir, she'd been seven and he'd been six. "Be my brother again."

"Just a brother with a sister? I wouldn't know how." He pressed his lips against the soft cap of her hair. "And neither, sister-mine, would you."

Vree sniffed and glanced over his shoulder at the shadowy figures of Gerek and Magda, peering at them in concern from the circle of light around a second lantern. "It doesn't look that hard."

"Magda!"

Karlene's urgent summons spun her around. "Oh no!" Diving forward, she helped the bard lower Enrik to the ground. "What's wrong? What is it?"

The body is dying.

"We know that, but . . ." Suddenly grabbing his shoulders, she shook him, hard. "Stop it!"

"Magda!" Karlene grabbed her hands and broke her grip. "What are you doing?"

"He's trying to die!"

"What?!"

"When the body dies, he's free! Enrik, you've got to hang on! Just for another minute or two!"

No.

"Yes!"

NO!

"I said, Yes!"

Ears ringing, Karlene caught Magda's chin, forcing her head up. "Magda, calm down! You're Vree's only chance. You can't fall apart on her now."

Vaguely aware that her mother was Singing a circle of fire kigh to light the yard, Magda stared across Enrik at Karlene. "Vree's and *Gyhard's* only chance," she snapped.

Karlene's mouth twisted into an approximation of a smile. "Yeah. Him, too."

Jerking her head away from the bard's touch, Magda pressed her fingers against the inside of Enrik's muscular wrist. His pulse felt thready, distant from her touch. "I can't let him die."

I am dead. Let me leave!

Leave? She could've smacked herself. Of course. There was no reason for the dead kigh to remain. "We have a bard here who can Sing you out of your body."

The body dies.

"No, it won't." It should have seemed stranger than it did, reassuring a dead man, but it had been a strange day all around. "We have a kigh without a body of his own to replace you."

His eyes met hers, and she looked away. Some things could be borne; some things could not. *If I am free, the body is dead.*

"But . . ." Then she understood. It worked both ways. If Karlene Sang Enrik's kigh out of his body before Gyhard's kigh was in it, the body would die. Therefore, Gyhard had to share the body, however briefly, with the dead man.

"All right." Vree looked from Enrik to Magda. "Explain why that's dangerous."

"We don't have time . . ."

Vree's jaw set. "Then explain quickly."

"But . . ." Realizing she had no choice, Magda threw up her hands. "Okay. Quickly. You know that living kigh don't like to be around dead kigh, especially not dead kigh acting like living kigh. *We're* all a little numb, so Enrik by himself isn't enough to cause us a lot of trouble but *we're* not stuffed in the same body with him and Gyhard *will* be. He might fling himself out again."

"Then I'll grab him again."

Magda sighed, spitting out a wet curl. "He might be caught in Karlene's Song and end up Sung away."

"I'm not going anywhere," Gyhard declared.

"What I'm trying to say is, he might *die*."

As Bannon's arm tightened around her shoulders, Vree closed her eyes for a moment. "And the alternative?"

"Things stay as they are."

"No." That decision had already been made. "Do what you have to do."

"I don't have to do anything right away," Magda reminded her gently, "you do. You have to push Gyhard out of your body and into Enrik's."

"Like giving birth," Bannon offered when Vree hesitated.

She elbowed him hard, just below the ribs. "That's sick."

Doubled over, gasping for breath, he managed a shrug.

"Vree, hurry! I'm losing the pulse!"

Do I have to make eye contact?

Gyhard nodded. *I'm afraid so.*

Ignoring the lines of sweat dribbling down her sides, Vree dropped to her knees and shot a warning glance at Karlene. "Are you ready?" When the bard nodded, she looked into Enrik's eyes. Over the years as a blade of Jiir, she'd looked into the eyes of the dead countless times—this time, the dead looked back. All the dead. "I can't . . ."

Death as practice. Death as profession. Death as escape.

There were too many. She could feel them gathering her into their company.

Vree!

Gyhard's terror jerked her back. Still teetering on the edge, she gathered up all her remaining strength and shoved everything she thought to be him through the dead and into Enrik's body.

Bits of her went with him.

Bits of him were left behind.

He didn't throw himself from her as Bannon had, but he went nevertheless.

Surprisingly, the actual doing of it hurt less than the fear of it had.

When at Magda's nod, Karlene began to Sing, Vree watched the dead man's kigh flicker and disappear. One by one, the dead of memory followed. When they were gone, Enrik's eyes held only the lifeless reflection of the surrounding flames.

The body breathed once. Twice. No more.

"NO!" Screaming in rage, Vree flung herself forward. "Get back here, you slaughtering carrion eater!" With every word she slammed both fists down on the broad chest.

"DON'T! YOU! DARE! LEAVE! ME!"

Warm fingers closed around her wrists and pulled her hands to either side. She pitched forward, barely stopping herself from smashing face first into Enrik's body.

"Vree . . . please stop." She knew the voice although it had never sounded so weak. "That . . . hurts."

"Gyhard?"

A swollen tongue dragged across cracked lips. "Wish you'd stop . . . calling me . . . carrion eater."

Pulling easily free of his hold, she sat back on her heels, her hands laced together in her lap as though she were afraid to touch him. "Gyhard?"

"Yes." He tried to cough and didn't quite manage it.

"What's wrong with him." Vree grabbed Magda's arm. "He sounds so . . ."

"Dehydrated. His body needs water."

"That's all?"

She wrinkled her nose. "Well, he could also use a bath."

Staring up at Vree's face, trying to memorize every curve, every line, Gyhard attempted a wink. "Remember the bath . . . at Elbion's?"

Magda was almost positive Vree blushed although the firelight made it difficult to tell for certain.

"What about Enrik?" Gerek asked, leaning forward for a closer look.

One palm resting lightly on Gyhard's forehead, Karlene shook her head. "He's gone."

"Witnessed," Annice said softly. "But what about Gyhard? Did sharing the body with a dead kigh hurt him?"

Before Magda could answer, Vree stared fixedly at Gyhard's face, searching for pain that went beyond the physical. "*Did* it hurt you?"

"No." Gyhard closed his eyes and felt the lingering awareness of being dead and trapped in life. It felt surprisingly like the guilt he'd shared a hundred midnights with. "But I . . . remember."

Karlene rocked back on her heels and stood. "All things being enclosed, I'm glad that's over."

Bannon caught her as she stumbled. "Is it?"

"It is for Enrik." She yawned and nodded down to where Vree and Magda were ministering to the abused body Gyhard now wore. "And it looks like Gyhard survived." The events of the day would be recalled and discussed in the Bardic Halls for years, but at that moment, Karlene was too tired to care. "Now, we've just got you two to worry about."

"What two?"

"You and Gerek. You, Your Grace," she said pointing a finger at Gerek, "were supposed to bring Magda back to Elbasan from Bartek Springs. I don't imagine Her Royal Highness is going to be too happy about your disregarding her wishes. And you," the finger moved to point at Bannon, "were given a direct order to bring Vree and Gyhard back to the Emperor. He's not going to be happy with you."

"All things being enclosed," Gerek muttered, scratching at the new skin on his shoulder, "I think I can deal with whatever Her Highness throws at me."

Unexpectedly pale, Bannon shook his head. "To disobey an Imperial order is treason."

Annice, still anxiously watching her daughter, snorted. "You leave the Emperor to King Theron, and you leave His Majesty to me."

"We thought it best to bury Kars' body with the others at the timber-holding."

"You're sure he's dead, Annice?" Theron locked eyes with her across the table. "You're sure this is over?"

"I'm sure."

"Good." He scowled at the bowl of clear broth and pushed it to one side.

Annice pushed it back. "Although there are a few loose ends."

"Of course there are." Throwing a crested linen napkin over the bowl, he glared at her. "Annice, I am not eating this slop, so you can just have a server take it away. I want a good thick chowder and an ale."

"Neither of which, I've been told, you can have." Putting her elbows on the table, Annice levelly regarded her brother and her king. She suspected he'd agreed to a private lunch immediately upon their arrival in order to circumvent the dietary order of his healer. As Lilyana had taken her aside and given her quick but explicit instructions, it wasn't doing him any good.

"You've been told," he repeated, crumbling a dry biscuit in disgust. "That's never stopped you before. You were *told* to remain at Ohrid."

"Stasya was there to give early warning if necessary and the Ducs of Ohrid were holding the pass long before you put a Bardic Hall in the keep—Pjerin was quite definite about that. *My* abilities were needed elsewhere."

"Which does not change the fact that you disobeyed a direct order."

"I couldn't stay there, Theron. Not when I *knew* what Maggi was going to do."

"You could have sent word, told me. You're quick enough sending the kigh about for other reasons."

She spread her hands. "I didn't want to chance having to disobey yet another direct order."

"I don't see what difference that makes," he muttered grumpily. "You're a bard. Bards are supposed to keep me informed." After a moment he sighed and sat back in his chair. "Oh, all right. The lot of you destroyed a very real threat to my people; I suppose that's as much defense as you need." Unexpectedly, he smiled. "Considering the lives this Kars had already taken and the ones he could have taken, I am very grateful he was stopped. I'd order a public celebration," he added brushing crumbs off his lap, "but I don't want the public to know about the whole horrific incident until the bards have had a chance to present this undead kigh thing in such a way as to cause the least amount of panic. I don't suppose you or Karlene had a chance to come up with anything on the way back to Elbasan?"

"On the way back to Elbasan," Annice repeated dryly, "Karlene and I spent our time answering questions from other bards—Kars' laying to rest having reverberated across the entire kingdom. The only time we got a moment's peace was when we were inside an inn, on the second floor, with the shutters closed, and blankets over our heads; at which point we were so exhausted all we did was sleep."

"And the others?"

She stared down into the red-brown surface of her soup, remembering short tempers and long silences brought about by exhaustion and emotional overload. The only high point had been watching Vree and Bannon attempting to reclaim their past, using Gerek and Magda as their template for a sibling relationship. "I can give you a full recall," she offered, "but you wouldn't enjoy it much."

"Then you can wait until after lunch." Theron sighed, removed the napkin, and picked up a spoon fancifully carved from a piece of narwhale horn. "Not that I'm enjoying lunch much. Magda has straightened things out with the Healers' Hall?"

"If she hasn't, she soon will."

Theron snorted, amused. "She's got that whole place wrapped around her little finger. What about the two doomed lovers? Who, not surprisingly, have been the inspiration for some truly bad ballads."

Delaying her response with a mouthful of broth, Annice thought back on Vree and Gyhard. From the little she'd seen, it hadn't looked good—Vree had ridden as far from the cart holding Gyhard and Magda as she could. Could love endure being ripped apart as theirs had? Had his moment of sharing a body with a dead kigh changed Gyhard in Vree's eyes? Annice shook her head, both in answer to her own thoughts and Theron's question. "I don't know. But, if they want to stay in Shkoder, you should give them some show of appreciation in return for taking care of Kars."

"Show of appreciation?"

"Land, money; you know, the usual."

"The usual? Annice, this is not something that happens quarterly." He raised a hand to cut her off. "I'll see that they're suitably rewarded—perhaps I'll speak to the Duc of Bicaz about that empty timber-holding. What about young Otavas' bodyguard?"

"I expect he's back guarding the prince's body." She leaned forward slightly, Theron having finally directed the conversation where she wanted it. "The Emperor arranged

Otavas' visit, you know, in order that Bannon would have a reason to be in Shkoder."

"No, I didn't know," the king growled. "And how do you know?"

"Bards know everything." Then her teasing smile vanished. "His Imperial Majesty wanted the boy to kidnap his sister and take her back to the Empire."

"Why?"

"Because he only found out that Gyhard was alive after he—they—left the Empire and Gyhard was apparently involved in a number of treasonous acts against the Imperial Throne."

His eyes narrowed as the brother disappeared within the king. "I assume you're referring to the rebellion he instigated as Governor Aralt and his intention to murder an Imperial Prince in order to take over his body?"

"You know about that?"

"Kings may not know as much as bards," he told her grimly, "but we're kept fairly well informed. I had been assured, however, that His Imperial Majesty thought Gyhard had died."

"Bannon blamed Gyhard for the loss of Vree, and he . . ."

"Decided to get even?" When she nodded, Theron shook his head. "Wonderful. An immature assassin. That aside, I was also informed that if Gyhard paid for those crimes, it would destroy Vree."

Annice spread her hands. "Vree and Gyhard are now separate people. Bannon could now take Gyhard back to the Empire without *physically* destroying Vree."

"Physically," Theron grunted. The emphasis made the alternative obvious. "What do you want me to do, Annice?"

"Intervene with the Emperor on Bannon's behalf."

"Intervene with the Emperor on behalf of an Imperial assassin refusing a direct order to deal with an Imperial treason?" Grasping the edge of the table, he leaned toward her, just barely maintaining a grip on his temper. "I don't think so."

She reached across the luncheon dishes and laid a hand over one of his. "Then intervene on behalf of a brother who doesn't want to hurt a sister he dearly loves."

Theron looked down at their hands then up at her face. He struggled silently for a moment then sighed, knowing when he'd been flanked. "I'll speak with Karlene. She knows the particulars better than anyone; perhaps we can work something out."

"What I find most curious, Majesty, is that the Emperor went to so much trouble." Karlene frowned down at the plush carpet covering the floor of the king's office, seeking answers in the pattern that turned and looped around upon itself. "Why send Bannon secretly when he could have just sent a message to you to have the traitor returned?"

"Perhaps he assumed I would agree with the bards that the innocent body worn by the traitor would not be destroyed. Understandable, since it was a pair of Shkoden bards who assured him Gyhard had been destroyed."

Karlene looked up to find the king regarding her with something less than approval. "But, Majesty, you did agree with the bards or you'd have sent them back the moment you were given my recall."

"The moment I was *eventually* given your recall," Theron amended.

Standing quietly to one side, Kovar winced.

"But since I have been assured from the beginning that this is a bardic matter," the king continued, shooting an unreadable look at the new Bardic Captain, then turning his gaze back to Karlene, "I would like to hear a bardic solution. With your help, and the help of my niece, Vireyda and Albannon Magaly and Gyhard i'Stevana have done Shkoder a great service and I would prefer that none of them be sent back to the Empire to be executed for treason. I would also prefer not to have to explain to His Imperial Majesty that Bardic Oaths supercede oaths sworn to him when he demands that I have you and Gabris executed for harboring a known traitor."

Karlene slowly shook her head. "He won't demand it, Majesty."

"That fond of you, is he?"

"No, Majesty. But if he were going to do it, he would have already done it. The Emperor wanted Gyhard back in the capital, but he wanted it done quietly. He wanted something and he wanted as few people as possible to know about it. He has to want Gyhard for something more than merely treason."

Theron's brows rose. "Merely treason?"

Kovar stepped forward before Karlene could answer. "What does Gyhard have that's worth such convoluted planning?"

The office fell silent as the two bards and the king spent a moment in thought. When Theron's stomach growled, he remembered his consort in tears, his heir pitched suddenly onto the throne, long lists of instructions from his healer, and innumerable bowls of broth. "I know," he said, remembering the pain, and terror, and the cold weight of death pressing against his chest.

"Eternal life?" Magda looked around the room at the king and the pair of bards and pulled a wet curl from the corner of her mouth. "Well, I *suppose* His Imperial Majesty might think that Gyhard had the secret of eternal life. I mean, he has lived a *very* long time moving his kigh from body to body, but it's no secret how he did it."

"How, Magda?" Theron demanded, eyes gleaming. "How?"

Recognizing where his interest originated, she smiled a little sadly. "All it takes is a fear of death so complete that you'd do *anything* to escape."

"There must be more," Kovar protested. "Or we'd have kigh jumping out of the dying all the time."

The young healer sighed. "You don't understand. You have to be willing, if only at that moment, to do *anything*." She stepped toward the desk. "Majesty, when you thought you were dying, did you fear death so much that you would have given an innocent life to survive?"

Theron slowly shook his head, left hand rising to twist his collar button. "No."

She nodded, satisfied. "And I don't think His Imperial Majesty would either."

"But there are those who would," Kovar pointed out.

"Those sorts of people," Magda replied, wondering why it was so obvious to her and so apparently difficult for anyone else, "are not the sort with the strength to throw themselves into the heart of their fear over and over again."

"But if Gyhard is such a person . . ."

"He isn't." Frowning, she reconsidered. "Well, I guess he *was,* but he isn't anymore."

"Magda, true love conquering all is a bardic tale." When she started to bristle indignantly, Theron leaned forward and held out his hand. "Child, the known path to immortality would be too great for anyone to deny."

"He doesn't have to *deny* it. He can't *do* it. When he was willing to die rather than take over Prince Otavas' body it was because he'd found something he couldn't do—which, I would like to point out," she added, chin lifting, "had *less* to do with the prince than it did with his *love* for Vree . . ."

In spite of the seriousness of the situation, both bards hid a smile at her tone. The young healer had matured a great deal since Vree and Gyhard had come to Elbasan, but she was still only seventeen.

"... at which time he lost his all-encompassing fear of death."

"You don't know that, Magda . . ."

"I *do* know that. I just spent *days* helping him anchor his kigh in the body he now wears."

"So he'll grow old and die just like the rest of us." Theron sighed. "Does he know?"

"Does it matter?" Magda demanded. "Immortality now has a price he's unwilling to pay. Why diminish him by telling him he couldn't pay it if he wanted to?"

After a long moment, Theron nodded, and sat back in his chair, thumb tracing the design of the crowned ship carved into the broad arm. "Why indeed? Which brings us back to the problem of His Imperial Majesty."

"The Emperor is a realist, Sire. He realizes that, occasionally, the birds he flies will miss their strike."

The other three people in the room blinked at Karlene in confusion. She cleared her throat sheepishly. "Sorry. You get into the habit of hawking analogies around the Imperial Court. Why not tell him that Gyhard is now just a man, no longer immortal and, furthermore, a man wearing a Shkoden body which cannot be executed for a treason committed by the body of an Imperial citizen. If you will not allow Bannon to remove Gyhard—in his new body from Shkoder—then whether or not Bannon is disobeying an Imperial order becomes irrelevant."

Theron snorted. "He won't like that much."

"For what it's worth," Magda offered earnestly, "I really, *really* don't think we could have stopped Kars without Gyhard and Bannon."

Within the masking of his beard, the king's lips twitched. "So I've been told." Twisting the ivory button between his fingertips—they'd stopped pulling off when his tailor began sewing them on with sailmaker's thread—Theron examined Karlene's suggestion from all sides. "It does have the advantage of being the truth," he said at last. "And it does solve young Bannon's problem, as even an Imperial assassin can hardly be expected to start a war by taking the man out of the country if *I* won't allow them to leave. However . . ." He glanced over at the beautifully detailed map that covered one wall of his office. Shkoder was a small country, bordered on three sides by mountains and the fourth by the sea. It was smaller than three of the Havakeen Empire's seven provinces and the Empire was running out of room to expand. ". . . we'd best come up with a way to sweeten the pot."

In the long, paneled corridor outside the king's private office, Magda fell into step beside Karlene and sighed. "I'm worried."

Shortening her stride, Karlene glanced down at the top of the healer's head. "About what?"

"Vree and Gyhard. Vree never came near him all the way back to Elbasan."

"She also never took her eyes off of him."

"Are you sure?"

"I'm sure," Karlene told her with sardonic emphasis. "Trust me, I would've noticed if she'd looked away."

Magda glanced up at the taller woman. "You like her, don't you? I mean, not just like but . . ." She could feel the blood rise to her cheeks.

"I could be a little in love with her, yes."

"Gerek, too," Magda said as they walked through a set of double doors and out into the public areas of the palace. "He's with Her Royal Highness, so I guess I'd better wait for him in his suite."

"Do you think he's going to need a healer?"

"Not unless he's forgotten everything Tadeus ever taught

him about charm." She smiled up at the bard. "Thanks for reassuring me about Vree and Gyhard."

"No problem." Karlene stood and watched the young healer effortlessly move through the crowds and wished she felt as reassured. As much as she might have wanted to believe otherwise, His Majesty had been right—true love seldom conquered all outside of a bardic tale.

"I had thought you understood that I wanted your sister and the assassin returned directly from Bartek Springs?" The Heir of Shkoder leaned back and locked eyes with the Heir of Ohrid over steepled fingers. "I believe my exact words were, 'I neither want my cousin with her unique and irreplaceable talents endangering herself by confronting this bardic abomination nor do I want an assassin with two not entirely stable kigh wandering around Shkoder.' "

"Yes, Highness, but after speaking with my sister, I realized she was right."

"And I was wrong?"

Gerek dropped gracefully to one knee. "And that you had less than complete information, Highness."

Onele's smile held edges that flayed. "I assume it never even crossed your mind that as there was a bard readily available I would like to be informed of any new information you acquired?" Her fingertips beat out an irritated staccato beat on the arms of her chair.

"Yes, Highness, it did cross my mind, closely followed by the fear that, should you still want me to return Magda and Vree to Elbasan, I would have to disobey a direct order."

"You would *have* to disobey a direct order?"

He inclined his head. "Yes, Highness, and I in no way wanted to put either of us in that position as we both believed we were acting for the good of Shkoder."

Onele stared at him for a long moment. Someday, when she was Queen of Shkoder, he would be Duc of Ohrid and the relationship between them would determine the security of her borders. "Get up, Gerek," she said at last. "And the next time, if it is possible, I should like to be consulted before you decide my instructions are no longer relevant."

Gerek's teeth flashed within the dark frame of his beard. "I guarantee it won't happen again."

The Heir accepted his assurance with a laugh. "I'd rather hear a guarantee that the abomination is truly gone."

"The bards and my sister are quite certain that he is, Highness." Frowning, Gerek tried to recall his sister's somewhat confused explanation. "Magda says his kigh has gone back into the Circle."

Onele rolled her eyes, an expression that reminded Gerek very much of her aunt. Although Annice would have probably snorted as well. "The priests keep telling us all things are enclosed, but I doubt sharing the Circle with such a man is going to make them very happy."

Having heard a small fraction of Kars' story, Gerek was surprised to find himself feeling sympathy for the ancient Cemandian. "He was what circumstances made him, Highness."

"Aren't we all. What about the others? The assassins?"

"Bannon has returned to his position with Your Highness' cousin, Prince Otavas. Vree . . ." He paused. "Gyhard was under Magda's care most of the way back to Elbasan. Vree seemed to be avoiding him."

"How unfortunate after all they've been through." The Heir of Shkoder cocked a speculative brow. "But I wouldn't have thought an Imperial assassin avoided anything."

"Highness, I am sorry but I didn't know what else to do but throw myself on your mercy." Down on one knee, Bannon stared fixedly at the carpet between Prince Otavas' feet. His Highness had been with a cousin when the seven of them had gone their separate ways upon arriving back at the Palace, giving him time to bathe and change. By the time the prince returned, he'd decided to tell him everything, from the moment he'd met with the Emperor until the moment the prince had welcomed him back. When he finished, he lowered his head until his forehead rested on his bent knee. "Highness, His Imperial Majesty gave me an order that I cannot obey."

"Are you saying that your inability to cause your sister pain outweighs your oaths to the Empire?" Otavas asked softly.

Mouth dry, Bannon swallowed nothing and nodded.

"But this Gyhard i'Stevana is a traitor to the Imperial Throne."

"Highness, when Gyhard was Aralt, he was a traitor to the Imperial Throne, but *this* Gyhard's only a man that my sister loves."

"He is the same man."

"No, Highness. I'm not the same man I was before I went into Ghoti. You're not the same man you were before Kars. Gyhard's not the same man he was before . . ." Bannon's hands closed into fists but he managed to finish the sentence. ". . . he fell in love with Vree."

"And she loves him?"

Bannon sighed. "Yes, Highness."

"Look at me."

Bannon looked up.

The prince met his gaze and held it. "You are disobeying an Imperial order and yet you returned here to me, risking arrest, risking being sent back to the Empire and a traitor's death. Why didn't you run?"

Surprised, Bannon opened and closed his mouth but no sound emerged. "It never occurred to me, Highness," he said at last. "Who would guard your dreams if I was gone?"

"Who indeed." The prince's brilliant eyes grew more brilliant still. "So for love of your sister, you refused an Imperial order and you returned to Elbasan for love of me?"

Had Vree felt this way, Bannon wondered. As if she'd been fighting her way *out* of a walled town? "Yes, Highness."

Otavas smiled. "Then, in order to keep you in my service, I have to keep you from being executed for treason."

"Yes, Highness. You'll speak to his Imperial Majesty?"

"I doubt that just my speaking to father would be enough." Love. Otavas repeated the word to himself; first in Shkoden and then in Imperial. Assassins could fall in love. And if assassins could fall in love, then anyone could. His voice rose and his eyes shone. "I have an idea."

Princess Jelena stared at Otavas in astonishment. "You want us to what?"

"Be joined. But not right now," he added hurriedly at her expression. "Look, Jelena, we both know we're due for political joinings. Shkoder is a small country, the Empire isn't. It can only benefit Shkoder to have closer ties. If when you're Queen, your consort is an Imperial Prince, well, that'll secure your borders for at least another generation. You're not quite fifteen, so nothing's going to happen for three years anyway, but wouldn't it be nice to have the threat of being joined to a perfect stranger taken away?"

Her eyes narrowed. "And what about us?"

Otavas backed up a step and wondered why he'd ever thought she was shy. "Us?"

"You and me. Especially you." She poked him in the chest. "Give me a reason that isn't politically based or you can just go home and have His Imperial Majesty join you with some fat old man in the Third Province whose ancestral lands happen to have access to a natural harbor."

"How did you hear about him?"

"The bards told me!"

His brilliant eyes sparkled. "You were asking the bards about me?"

"Tavas!" Smacking her palm down on the sketches of strange machines that lettered her desk, she glared at him. "I want a better reason than politics!"

"All right." He captured her hand. "I like you. A lot. Someday, if we give it enough time, I'll probably love you."

"Probably?"

"And even if I don't, I can't think of any way I'd rather spend my life than beside you, staring at the stars." When he bent his head to kiss her hand, she changed her grip and nearly pulled him off his feet.

"Come on."

"Where are we going?"

"To tell Grandfather. It is customary when you suggest a joining with the second in line to the throne, to inform the King."

"But you haven't given me an answer."

"Don't be ridiculous, Tavas." Her smile held a promise of shared exploration into the unknown. "I'd decided we were going to be joined during Third Quarter Festival."

Head reeling, the Imperial Ambassador left the king's office and hurried back to his own, his speed making the sweep of his robes against the polished floor sound like excited whispering. He had a great deal of work to do and was very grateful that his carefully worded communique would be sent through the almost instantaneous services of the Imperial fledgling still at the Bardic Hall.

His Imperial Majesty had to approve the joining, but that, he was sure, would be a mere technicality.

When Gabris bowed and left the room, the Emperor stared reflectively at the scars on his wrist. "So," he murmured without turning, "I have lost my first hawk."

"And the chance of immortality, Majesty?" Marshal Usef asked from his place to the right of the throne.

"Flown as well."

"You believe them, Majesty?" Greatly daring, Usef shook his head. "King Theron may be sheltering the traitor in order to gain the secret for himself."

"No. The Shkoden bards with their circles, and their connected quarters would never allow so dangerous a skill to continue to exist once they became aware of it." The Emperor frowned, reflecting on all he'd just been told. "It seems unlikely that the exact circumstances that created such a skill will probably ever occur again."

Marshal Usef shifted his weight but remained silent.

"So tell me, Marshal, would you be willing to die over and over, in order to live forever?"

The marshal thought about it for a moment. He had been in battles on his way to the command of the First Army and he'd seen a great many soldiers die in a great many unpleasant ways. "No, Majesty," he said at last, "I would not."

"Nor would I." The Emperor sat back and grinned. "I have lost the potential for an unpleasant immortality, Usef, but gained a hold on the Shkoden crown. Not an entirely bad trade."

"So you will give your permission to the joining, Majesty."

"Give it?" The Emperor laughed. "I've already sent them a pair of assassins, hooded and jessed, as a betrothal gift."

"Vree?" He would have thought she hadn't heard him approach except he knew better. "Every healer in the Hall took a poke at me and it seems they agree with Magda. This body took no permanent damage from holding Enrik's dead kigh."

"Good."

Reaching out to touch her shoulder, Gyhard let his hand fall back to his side. "Are you avoiding me?"

Vree stared out the window of the Bardic Hall at the wall around the Citadel and shook her head. "If I was, you wouldn't have found me."

"You barely spoke to me on the way back to the city."

"Magda said you needed to get settled in the body."

"And?"

"I was afr . . . I thought if I came too close I might pull you back here, into me."

"And we don't want that."

"Yes." She swallowed and closed her eyes. "Yes, I do. I missed, miss you, so much."

"I'm still here." Greatly daring, he gripped her arms and turned her around. His heart pounded a little less violently when she didn't object. He had no desire to end up on the wrong end of her reflexes. When she looked away, he sighed. "Is it the body?"

"What?"

"The way it looks?"

Holding her elbows, she shook her head. "I like the way it looks."

"Is it because of Enrik? Have I changed since touching him? Since touching death?"

"No."

As she didn't appear to be wearing her daggers, he lifted her chin until her eyes met his. Her skin was as soft as he remembered and her eyes as dark. "Are you still afraid I'll leave you?"

"No."

Her breath lapped warm down over his hand and Gyhard didn't think he could bear it. He'd waited so long to hold her. "Then what? Are you afraid of me? Of what I was? Of what I've done? Of what I did to Kars?"

"Of you?" She broke from his touch and stomped across the room and back. "Of you!" she repeated. "Of all the arrogant . . ." Then she saw he was afraid of exactly that— of what he did to Kars and the possibility of him destroying her as well. The anger left her as quickly as it had arrived, leaving her shaking and confused. "I'm not afraid of *you!* Not you. You . . ."

Stepping forward, she grabbed his arm. "You, I'm sure of. How could I not be. We know more about each other than any two people ever have." Her fingers dimpled the smooth curve of muscle, warm and resilient under her hand, and she forced herself to meet his gaze. His eyes, his new eyes were an indeterminate shade under brows that slanted down at the corners and up over the center of a crooked nose. It was a stranger's face, familiar because she so intimately knew the life that animated it. "I'm afraid of me!"

"Vree, do you love me?"

"You know . . ."

"I need to hear you say it."

She closed her eyes and touched the bits of him that remained with her, then opened them and took a deep breath. "Yes. I love you. But . . ."

Gyhard rolled his eyes; he should've known that was coming.

". . . I'm not used to having feelings."

"That's a load of ratshit. You always had feelings. You were just trained not to notice them. Now they're all breaking training at once."

Her gaze tracked the edge of his jaw, slid down the corded muscles of his throat, and lingered where his pulse throbbed just under the skin. "I feel like the first time I ever walked a roof. Like the next move is going to topple me off and when I hit the ground I'll break into a million pieces. Or like the first time I ever held a throwing dagger and I almost cut my own fingers off because it was so incredibly sharp and I didn't know how to use it."

"Do you know what I'm afraid of?" Gyhard asked softly. "That now I'm out of your head, you won't want me."

She took a step closer and breathed in the scent of soap and sweat and clean clothes. Of him. "I want you. I just don't want to fall off the roof."

"If you fall, I'll catch you."

She snorted. "You're up here, too."

"Then I'll jump after you."

"And if I cut someone's fingers off?"

He closed his hand over hers. "Won't happen."

"What makes you so sure?"

"I won't let it."

"You can't stop it! I can't stop it! Don't you understand, it's completely out of our control!"

"Is that why you practically ignored me on the way back to the city?" he demanded incredulously. "You didn't want to lose control in front of an audience?"

Vree had a sudden image of what would have happened had she surrendered to need surrounded by two bards, Gerek, Magda, and her brother, and hurriedly shoved it aside. "You don't understand!" she protested, cheeks flushed. "I've spent most of my life learning control, it's not that easy to surrender it!"

"I do understand. Like you said, we know each other better than anyone ever has. But you're not an assassin anymore; if you lose control, what's the worst that can happen?"

She stared at the walls, at the ceiling, at the empty hearth, anywhere but at him.

"Uncertainty might kill assassins, Vree, but it's the state the rest of the world lives in." His free hand cupped the side of her head, the callused edge of his thumb tracing the full curve of her lower lip. "You'll get used to it. And you'll never need to be uncertain of me; we're a part of each other."

Leaning into his touch, her tongue followed the path he stroked. "It's not like it was."

Gyhard swallowed and looked at the moisture glistening just above his thumb. All at once, the room seemed a great deal hotter. "It's better," he assured her, adding hoarsely, "there's no audience now. Maybe we should lock the door and see how much better it's going to be."

"Maybe . . ." She could feel the tempo of his heart quicken, and her heart began to beat in time. "Maybe we should."

"Karlene told me once that there would be no happy ending," he murmured against her mouth.

Teeth closing around his lower lip, she pulled her fingers from his because she wanted to use both hands. "Karlene," she said, finding certainty in opposition, "was wrong."

THE
QUARTERED SEA

For Alex:
Not quite the sequel he wanted,
but I'm afraid it will have to do.

One

THE fishing boat rose to the surface of the bay like an abandoned vessel of the old gods. Such was the angle that the masthead, draped in pennants of torn and dripping sail, had barely emerged before the bow broke through, water sheeting over the gunnels back into the sea. A moment later the stern followed, cradled on the crest of an unnatural wave. Long ropes of weed trailed off the rudder as though the depths had attempted to hold their prize.

Ignoring waves and wind, the boat cut across the chop toward a nearly identical vessel carrying four oilskin-wrapped people. Three of the four watched the approach, openmouthed. The fourth, a young man standing alone in the bow, watched the water and Sang.

A few moments later, the salvaged boat drew parallel with the other and stopped, both boats keeping their position as though held by unseen hands.

"That's her, that's my *Second Chance*." Leaning over the gunnels for a closer look, one of the identical trio pushed her hood back off salt-and-pepper hair and squinted into the spray. "Well, I'll be hooked and fried, they even brung up both pairs of oars." Half-turned toward the bow, she lifted her voice over the combined noise of wind and sea and Song, "Hey bard! We're close enough to use the gaff. Should I hook her in and make her fast?"

Still Singing, Benedikt shook his head and shuffled around on his damp triangle of decking to face the shore. Shoulders hunched against the chill, he changed his Song, and both boats began to move toward the gravel beach at the head of the bay where the tiny figures of the villagers paced up and down.

When the keels scraped bottom, he changed the Song again.

Two roughly human translucent figures rose up out of the shallows on either side of the bow and brushed against the ends of Benedikt's outstretched fingers like liquid cats. Closing his eyes, he allowed the four notes of the gratitude to linger a moment or two after the kigh dissolved back into the sea.

"'Right, then!" The owner of the *Second Chance* took command of the silence with an authoritative bellow. "Let's have some help here before the tide turns!"

His part in the salvage completed, the bard stayed where he was until it became obvious that there was nothing left to do but disembark. Clambering awkwardly over the side, he winced as the frigid water seeped into borrowed boots. The uneven footing threw him off balance. He staggered forward, then back, then forward again.

A sudden grip on his elbow kept him from falling.

The figure beside him, indistinguishable from all the others in the ubiquitous oilskins, was considerably shorter than his own six feet. Under his hood, he felt his ears burn. Bards were not supposed to need rescue. Especially not from rescuers so much smaller than themselves.

The hand remained around his elbow until dry land was reached, then it released him and rose to push back the masking hood. Fortunately, he recognized the face. Bards were not supposed to fumble for names either.

"Lucija."

The woman who'd offered her boat for the trip out into the bay smiled up at him. "Benedikt."

Wobbly on the slippery piles of beach gravel, he had no idea of what he was supposed to say next.

As though she sensed his unease, Lucija's smile dimmed a little. "That was an impressive bit of Singing out there; what with Tesia swamping right over the cleft and all. I never knew bards could control the kigh so deep."

He could feel the tension start to leave his shoulders. It *had* been an impressive bit of Singing, and he was pleased that she'd noticed. "It was nothing."

"Nothing?" Drawn around by the sound of her name, Tesia stomped over and smacked the bard enthusiastically on the arm. "You've given me back the fish, boy. That's an unenclosed sight more than *nothing*. Now you head over to my place around dark, and I'll cook you a meal that'll make a start at payin' you back."

"You don't have to . . ."

"I know that. I want to." She grinned around him at the younger woman. "I can see what you're thinkin', Lucija. You may as well come, too."

The entire village ended up at Tesia's cottage. From where Benedikt sat, there seemed to be a man, woman, or child in every available space—occasionally, two deep. Lucija had a seat close by, and the heat in her pale eyes made him wish his place of honor wasn't quite so close to the fire.

When they called for a song, he dried his palms on his thighs and lifted his quintara like a shield. He wasn't good in large crowds; there were just too many people to please.

"It's all right, these things happen." Up on one elbow, Lucija stroked the soft triangle of golden hair in the center of Benedikt's chest. "Don't worry about it."

It took an effort, but he kept his voice light. "Easy for you to say."

"Maybe you just need a little encouragement."

As her hand moved lower, Benedikt closed his eyes. When Lucija had finally come right out and invited him to her bed, he hadn't been able to think of a believable way to say no. He'd *wanted* to be with her, but he'd been afraid that exactly what had happened would happen.

It wasn't his fault really, it was the pressure. After his performance in the afternoon, he'd known that she'd expect an equivalent performance in the dark. He'd been magnificent out on the bay. The need to be that magnificent again—and the fear that he wouldn't be—had made him so tense. . . .

It would've been easier to raise another fishing boat.

"Maybe you're just too tired."

There was sympathy in her voice, not blame, but he couldn't have her telling others that Singing the kigh had exhausted him. Grasping at straws, he began a silent Song, calling up the one thing that had never failed him. Sleek, fluid, the image of the water kigh was not entirely human-seeming.

Not that it mattered.

"Ah, there we are."

"A lot of us fatten a pig and pretty much everyone keeps some chickens," Lucija explained, forking the strips of bacon onto Benedikt's plate beside the two fried eggs. "There's a limit to how much seafood a body can eat."

"It does lose its appeal after a while," Benedikt agreed with a laugh. "When I first went to the Bardic Hall, I didn't eat fish for almost a year."

"You're from a fisher family, then?"

He nodded around a mouthful of breakfast. "My three older brothers fish out of Three Island Cove," he told her when he'd swallowed, adding proudly, "They all go out to the deep water."

"Brave boys."

"Yeah, they are. Absolutely fearless. But not reckless," he hastened to explain. "Just really good at what they do. And my father's the factor at Three Island Cove. There hasn't been a surplus in the last twenty years that he hasn't convinced the Duc of Sibiu to pay handsomely for." One dark-gold brow lifted. "Whether she started out wanting the fish or not."

"Your father'd be bored stiff here, then. We're so close to Elbasan that all of our surplus is contracted in advance, and all we have to do is hand it over to the regular traders." Grinning and shaking her head, she sopped up egg yolk with a bit of toasted bread. "But you're a bard. You already know that."

"You've heard the rumors that we know everything, then?"

Her laughter added a special savor to the food and he almost stopped worrying about the impression he was making. He'd only been Walking on his own for a year and, sometimes, being a *bard of Shkoder* was as much a burden as a blessing.

"So, where do you go from here?"

"Fort Kazpar for the Queen's visit."

"So she's actually going through with it this quarter?"

"I don't know." Sighing contentedly, Benedikt pushed his empty plate away and picked up the heavy clay mug of tea. "I won't know until I arrive."

Lucija mirrored his movement. "Seems a shame you have to go all that way if nothing's happening. Can't you send a kigh ahead to the fort?"

The silence stretched and lengthened until the distant screams of scavenging gulls moved into the cottage to fill the void.

"Benedikt?"

"I Sing only water." Hands flat on the table, chin lifted, he dared her to comment.

"Ah." Looking somewhat taken aback, Lucija took a long swallow of tea before saying, "We had a Headwoman back when I was real young who could Sing water, but she decided to stay fishing rather than become a bard. Not that I'm suggesting you should've gone fishing," she added hurriedly when she caught sight of Benedikt's expression.

He felt the muscles tighten across his shoulders, the tension moving right down both arms and curling his fingers into fists. "If I'd gone fishing," he reminded her, "Tesia's boat would still be at the bottom of the bay."

"Hey, calm down." Hands making soothing motions in the air, Lucija gave him as much distance as the chair would allow. "We were all impressed by the way you Sang the kigh yesterday. Obviously, you made the right decision becoming a bard."

Shoving his own chair back with a shriek of protest, wood on wood, Benedikt stood. He'd hoped this time would be different, but it always came to the same thing in the end. "My thanks for breakfast and for last night, but I don't need your pity."

Arms folded, Lucija stood by her cottage and watched Benedikt grow ever smaller as he climbed to the top of the cliff, resolved that if he turned and waved, she wouldn't wave back. When Tesia came up behind her, smelling of warm pitch, she grunted a greeting but kept her gaze locked on the path.

"So, he's leavin' is he?" Without waiting for an answer, the older woman spat and added, "I never met a bard so uncomfortable at bein' the center of attention."

Lucija snorted. "I never met a bard I so desperately wanted to smack."

* * *

"Can't you send a kigh ahead to the fort?"

It always came to that. No matter how well he Sang or how long he spent playing song after song after song, in the end, they always found him wanting.

"I Sing only water."

His parents had been thrilled when Karlene had Walked into the village and discovered his talent. It explained why skills his brothers performed as easily as breathing came so hard to him. His father had bragged about the discovery up and down the road to Sibiu and even the duc had sent her congratulations. His mother had made him a new suit of clothes, his alone instead of outgrown bits and pieces. To have a bard in the family was a thing to be proud of. So what that he only Sang water—he was untrained. *"After training,"* they'd told him as they proudly sent him off to the Bardic Hall in Elbasan, *"you'll surely improve."*

They hadn't understood. He'd been taught Command, and Charm, and tricks of memory that allowed him to recall months of travel down to the tiniest detail. He could Witness in cases of judgment and be an integral part of any service in any Center anywhere the honoring of the Circle had spread.

But he would only, ever, Sing water. Nothing he could do, nothing he could be taught could change that.

He couldn't tell if his family was embarrassed for him or by him. Visits home were a trial; everyone smiling too broadly, making excuses to the neighbors, telling him too heartily that it didn't matter.

And it wasn't just his family. Even the other bards told him it didn't matter. *"There're half a dozen bards Walking through Shkoder who Sing only air,"* they told him. *"And don't forget Jazep. Jazep Sang only earth."* Jazep had been a fledgling with Annice, the Princess-Bard. Jazep had been the best teacher the Bardic Hall had ever seen. Jazep had died saving the kingdom. Benedikt was sick to death of hearing about Jazep and, when asked to play "In the Arms of the Earth," Jazep's song, he'd begun to deny ever having learned it.

"Can't you send a kigh ahead to the fort?"

He'd hoped Lucija would be different.

Settling the straps of his pack more comfortably on his shoulders, Benedikt turned toward Fort Kazpar and settled into the rocking stride the bards used when they needed to cover distance quickly. Unable to learn if the queen would be attending the ceremony, he had no choice but to arrive before her.

"Everyone understood why you decided against visiting the forts in First Quarter, Majesty, why you sent His Highness in your stead, but you can't do it again."

Jelena, Queen in Shkoder for almost exactly four full quarters, raised an imperious brow and leaned slightly forward, her palms pressed flat against the crested papers scattered over her desk. "Can't?" she repeated.

"Shouldn't, Majesty." The Bardic Captain carefully kept his tone neutral.

After a moment of narrow-eyed consideration, Jelena accepted his correction and sat back. "Why can't Tavas go again? He's willing, and the visits are only ceremonial. They serve no real function."

"On the contrary, Majesty." This time, Kovar allowed his voice to rise. "Even ignoring the very real function ceremony itself serves, it is necessary that you dispel the lingering fear amongst your people that the road to Fort Kazpar is ill-omened."

"Ill-omened?" The young queen shuffled paper from one pile to another. "Kings and Queens of Shkoder have traveled that road hundreds of times."

"Yes, Majesty, they have. Until a queen died."

"And then he dared—dared!—to remind me about my mother's death." Unable to remain still, Jelena paced from one end of the terrace to the other, the soles of her half-boots slapping against the wet granite. "As though I've forgotten!"

"Lena, I don't think he meant. . ."

"He meant it all right. The smug, self-satisfied windbag!"

Tucked up tight against the palace wall in a futile attempt to find protection from the Fourth Quarter chill, His Imperial Highness Prince Otavas, youngest brother of the Havakeen Emperor and the consort of Shkoder's queen, frowned as he watched his beloved travel back and forth and then forth again.

"He as much as implied that if I didn't go on this ever-so-symbolically-important ceremonial visit, I was being a bad queen."

As she passed, Otavas snagged Jelena's arm and pulled her to his side. With the thumb of his free hand, he smoothed the wrinkles from her forehead. "You are not a bad queen," he murmured, "but the Bardic Captain is right."

She jerked her head away from his touch. "Right?"

"Right," he repeated. "You've put it off once; if you put it off again, how much easier will it be to put it off a third time or a fourth?"

"So after the Bardic Captain tells me I'm a bad queen, Tavas as much as tells me I have to get back onto the horse."

"And do you think you should?" Magda asked, tossing her saddlebags onto a chair and shrugging out of her damp jacket.

"Do I think I should what?"

"Get back onto the horse." She hung the jacket on an iron hook by the fire and turned in time to see Jelena's lips thin. "Problem?"

"I am *not* a bad queen."

"I never said you were."

"You never said I wasn't."

"Oh, I see." Dropping down into the closest chair, Magda began working off her boots. "You followed me up from the stables so that I could tell you that I think it's too soon, that you can put off the visit to the forts one more time."

"No . . ." When the healer raised both dark brows, the young queen sighed. "Yes."

Magda smoothed all expression from her face as she studied her royal patient. In spite of the best efforts of tailors and valets, her clothing seemed a size too large, the embroidered velvet filled out with quilted under-tunics to keep out the cold. But the weight loss worried the healer less than the shadows that continued to linger under the hazel eyes. "It's been almost four quarters since your mother died, Jelena. I think that, if on your way to Fort Kazpar, you visited the spot where it happened, it might help you heal."

"I doubt it."

Boots tossed to the hearth, Magda stood, trying to decide if the protest sounded petulant or obstinate. Not that it mattered; queens could ill afford the luxury of either. "Jelena, you have *got* to move past the moment of your mother's death."

"So you've said." Jelena's left hand jerked up into the space between them, the royal signet inches away from Magda's face. "But how can I when everything I am, I became when she died? Her death made me Queen. How can I get beyond something I have to live with the rest of my life?"

"That's a question only you can answer."

Jelena's hand fell back to her side. "You are no help at all," she muttered, spun on one heel, yanked open the door and stomped off down the hall, her two guards hurriedly falling into step behind.

"Of course I'm worried about her," Magda snapped, "but keep in mind it's been barely four quarters since her mother died. Her spirit, her kigh, was wounded. That takes time to heal."

Behind the barricade of his desk, the Bardic Captain raised both hands in symbolic surrender. Although he could, as much as any of the bards, Sing the fifth quarter, the kigh carried by every living being, Magda i'Annice a'Pjerin was the first and, so far, the only person in Shkoder who could Heal it. That she was half his age made no difference; in this, he and everyone else in Shkoder—except perhaps her mother—defered to her.

Sighing deeply, Otavas leaned forward in his chair, slender brown fingers clasping and unclasping between his knees. "I hate to see her so unhappy. It's like the Jelena she was and the queen she is are two separate people. I just don't understand how she can feel guilty about something she had nothing to do with."

"The death of her mother made her queen," Magda reminded them, "and in her grief she began to believe that all those times she'd said 'when I am queen, I'll do this, or when I am queen, I'll do that,' she was wishing her mother dead."

Otavas cut her off before she could continue an explanation

he'd heard a hundred times. "Maggi, I understand it up
here." He tapped his temples with his fingertips then
pressed both palms over his heart. "But not here. It wasn't
her fault."

"Jelena has the same problem, Tavas." Of an age with
the consort and second cousin to the queen, Magda had
been more friend than healer until this last, dark year. "She
knows in her head it's not her fault, but she can't convince
her heart."

"If only she had something to distract her," Kovar
mused, one finger stroking the graying length of his
mustache.

The consort leaped to his feet. "Don't you start," he
snarled at the astonished bard, "I have had it up to
here . . ." His hand chopped the air above his head.
". . . with everyone in this unenclosed country wondering
why we haven't had an heir! There's nothing wrong with
either of us!"

Kovar opened his mouth and, with no idea of how to
respond, closed it again.

"It's not often you see a bard at a loss for words," Magda
murmured. When both men turned toward her, she shot
them her most professional *calm down* expression. Kovar
was quite honestly confused by the response he'd evoked,
but Otavas' kigh was beginning to feel as fragmented as
Jelena's and that wasn't good. "Jelena doesn't need a distraction, she needs to find acceptance. And, given the sudden tragedy that put her on the throne, it's only natural
the people should worry about an heir—although I realize
the speculation hasn't made this year any easier on her."
When Otavas continued to glower, she added, smiling, "No
one's suggesting you're not doing your part."

"Magda!" Ears burning, Otavas sat down, wondering if
the healer had read that fear off his kigh or if it had been
out on his face for anyone to see. Honesty forced him to
acknowledge, at least in the privacy of his own mind, relief
that his manhood wasn't being questioned over every dinner table or mug of beer in Shkoder.

"Which brings us back," Kovar said after a moment's
silence, "to the matter at hand. Her Majesty must lay the
tragedy to rest. She must make the journey to the forts."

"She knows that," Magda told him.

"But will she act on the knowledge?"

Magda tucked her hands into the wide sleeves of her Healer's robe and shrugged. "We three are her closest counselors and she knows how we feel; since she can't deal with how she feels, that may have to do."

The sound of heavy footsteps approaching drew their attention around to the door. Kovar separated the sounds and, his voice pitched to carry only within the confines of the room, announced, "Her Majesty."

The door swung open. Guards flanking her at a respectful distance, Jelena's gaze swept over healer, bard, and consort. "Is this a private meeting, or can anyone join in?"

She sounded, Kovar realized with a start, remarkably like her grandfather, the late King Theron. He'd had a way of using the same dry, very nearly sarcastic delivery to remind those around him just who, exactly, was in charge. The resemblance was disturbing, coming, as it did, from a young woman only a year or two past twenty.

"Well?"

Magda read excuses rising in Otavas' eyes and quieted him with a look.

Standing, Kovar bowed. "Your Majesty is always welcome in my office."

"Thank you. How fortunate you're all here. It'll save me the bother of repeating my decision." When she folded her arms, the royal signet flashed through a ray of sunlight slanting in from the window. "I've decided to go to the forts." Before anyone could respond, she added, "And you'll all be going with me."

Stonemasons had built Fort Kazpar and, across the water, Fort Tunov, up out of the stones of the headlands so that they seemed an extension of the cliffs. From the sea, the seam between the rock carved by the elements and the rock carved by hand was nearly invisible. By land, a small village and the well-traveled Capital Road leading up to the gate helped define the perimeter.

As Benedikt identified himself to the guard at the gate, he wondered what he'd do if he was challenged. *Stop being such an idiot. Why wouldn't she believe you? No one in Shkoder ever lies about being a bard. And even if she did challenge you, it's not like you couldn't . . .*

"So's Terezka expecting you today?"

Jerked out of his reverie, Benedikt repeated the only word he'd actually heard. "Terezka?"

"The bard who's already here."

"Terezka's here?"

Amused by his confusion, the guard nodded. "I was just talking to her, and she didn't tell me to keep an eye out for you, is all. Don't you guys usually send kigh ahead of you, or is this some kind of a surprise?"

Feeling a familiar tightening in the pit of his stomach, Benedikt straightened. "You should be expecting me. I'm here to Sing the queen's boat safely across the strait."

"You're that bard? That's wonderful!"

Somewhat taken aback, Benedikt searched her face for mockery but found only a visible complement to the pleasure that had been evident in her voice. "Why wonderful?" he questioned.

"Well if you're here to Sing the queen across the strait, then the queen's gotta be coming. Right?"

"I guess."

"You guess?" Stepping aside, she waved him through, eyes sparkling under the padded edge of her helm. "Hey, you're a bard; you don't guess, you know."

Recognizing an exit line when he heard one, Benedikt returned her smile, shoved his thumbs under his pack straps, and strode out into the sunlight of the inner bailey. It seemed that now *he'd* arrived, Her Majesty had no choice but to follow. It was a pleasant conceit, and he enjoyed it for a full half-dozen steps.

"Benedikt! Up here!"

He squinted toward the source of the summons and could just barely make out Terezka waving an enthusiastic greeting from the top of the inner wall.

"Keep moving, darlin'," she shouted. "I'll be on the ground by the time you're inside."

His smile broadening, he hurried toward the second gate. The older bard had been one of his favorite teachers when he'd been a fledgling. She'd never offered the reassurances the others had and so had been the only one to truly convince him that she found nothing lacking in his ability to Sing only water. He envied her indiscriminate way of sweeping those around her up into her excess of personality and agreed with her assumption that she was his closest friend among the bards.

He barely managed to get his pack off in time to survive her hug.

"Let me look at you." Shoving him out to arm's length, she swept a critical eye from head to toe. "I like the beard. Perhaps a little sparse on the cheeks, but it makes you look like a Petrokian pirate. What made you decide to attempt it?"

"A dislike of shaving in cold water."

"Wimp."

"Hag." Leaning forward, he kissed the top of her head. "Don't worry, I'm getting rid of it before the queen arrives. *Will* the queen be arriving?" he asked as he straightened.

"That's what they tell me."

"Nice to know I haven't made the trip for nothing."

"Nothing?" Grabbing one side of his pack-frame, she led him toward a heavy wooden door built into the inner wall. "How can it possibly be nothing when there's me?"

That night, they sang themselves almost hoarse in front of an appreciative crowd of guards and villagers. Buttressed by Terezka, Benedikt managed to ignore the tightening noose of attention and create two new verses to the ale house favorite, "What Would I Do for Your Love." Just before dawn, he collapsed into bed pleasantly buzzed by the certain knowledge that he'd met all expectations.

"But why the Bardic Captain?" Benedikt asked, not for the first time, as he walked Terezka to the village limits. "He's never come before."

"Have you not been listening to me?" Terezka demanded, shifting her pack into a more comfortable position. "Her Majesty requested his presence. This has nothing to do with you." The older bard sighed and frowned at the plume of her breath. "You know, when you get to be my age, you're not so fond of walking in Fourth Quarter. I should've agreed to teach again."

"Terezka, you seem to be ignoring the fact that Kovar Sings all four quarters. Four," he repeated. "Including water."

"Lots of bards Sing water, darlin', but none of them Sing it like you do. I've seen you Sing up kigh in a raindrop, and I can't think of anyone I'd trust more to sing the queen across the strait."

"You're deliberately not understanding—with Kovar here, they don't *need* me."

"Need?" She snorted, blowing a cloud of heated breath into the air. "Need has nothing to do with it. All bards who Sing water take turns Singing the queen across the strait, and now it's your turn."

He shoved his hands into his pockets. "Well, it's nice to be useful for something."

"You bet your ass it is. Plenty of people never know the place they're supposed to fill, but us, we're lucky. We have the security of knowing that our talent defines us. And as for you . . ." She stopped walking and, when Benedikt turned to face her, poked him in the chest with a gloved and emphatic finger. "There's nothing that makes a good-looking man less attractive than watching him feel sorry for himself. You're a bard of Shkoder, Benedikt—one of the few, one of the proud—and I've never met a bard that didn't have an ego big enough to hold the entire Citadel with room left over for Dockside. You hear me?"

"I hear you."

"What did I say?"

The corners of his mouth curled up. "That you think I'm too good-looking to feel sorry for myself."

"Ah. I see you didn't actually need that reminder about bardic ego." She studied his face for a moment then reached up and patted his cheek. "Just remember you're as much a bard as Kovar is, and if I wasn't freezing my ass off standing here, I'd pass on a few choice tidbits about our exalted captain." Leaning forward, she dropped her voice and murmured, "He has a tendency to be, well, windy in the morning."

Benedikt rolled his eyes. "I'll remember that."

Stepping back, Terezka grinned. "You will, you know." A quick glance at the sky brought on a tightening of straps. "If I don't get going, I'll never reach Planter's Basin before dark, and these old bones have no intention of spending the night without a bed." She thrust out her fist. "Good music, Benedikt."

He touched his fist to the top of hers. "Good music, Terezka."

"So that's it, then. Give me a kiss and point me up the Coast Road."

Having done as she commanded, Benedikt stood where she'd left him until a curve in the road took her from view. A breeze ruffled his hair as he turned back toward the fort, and he couldn't help thinking that, with him around, at least the Bardic Captain wouldn't be taken away from more important duties during the voyage.

"What do you think they're saying?" Otavas wondered, nodding toward Jelena and her grandmother. The two women were standing together on the palace steps, well out of the way of the jostling crowd of horses and riders that nearly filled the Citadel's main courtyard.

Magda looked up, twisted around in the saddle, and grinned. "Her Majesty, Queen Lilyana, is telling her grand-daughter, Her Majesty, Queen Jelena, that she should be wearing a heavier coat. Jelena is protesting that it's almost First Quarter Festival. Queen Lilyana is reminding her that we could still get snow and at the very least would she please put on a scarf. Jelena is insisting she'll be fine, but if it makes her grandmother happy, she'll wear the scarf."

As Magda finished speaking, the queen accepted a length of crimson fabric from her grandmother and wrapped it around her throat.

Kovar, on Magda's other side, turned his attention from the groom adjusting his stirrups and looked down a disapproving nose at the healer. "It is impolite to eavesdrop."

"I wasn't. When I said good-bye to Her Majesty—that is, Queen Lilyana—earlier, she was carrying the scarf. It didn't take half a lifetime of studying the fifth kigh to work out the rest." Reaching across the distance between their mounts, she patted the Bardic Captain on the shoulder. "Don't worry, Kovar. Cloud Dancer here is the calmest horse in the Citadel stables. All you have to do is stay in the saddle. She'll do the rest."

"I suppose it would be a waste of time to tell you I'm not concerned about my horsemanship?"

"It would as long as you maintain that white-knuckled grip on the saddle horn."

On the palace steps, Jelena kissed her grandmother,

descended into the chaos of the courtyard, and rose above it almost instantly as she accepted a leg up into the saddle.

"Are you all right?" Otavas asked softly as her groom led her horse into position beside his.

Jelena pulled on a pair of riding gloves, using the time to find a neutral expression before she turned to face her consort's concern. "Grandmother wanted to come with us, at least to the city limits, but I convinced her that my sister and the idiot courting her would be sufficient escort that far."

"Not to mention Bannon and two full troops of the Queen's Guard."

"Not to mention." A glance across the courtyard showed that the ex-Imperial assassin had taken up position where he could defend all possible approaches to his royal charges. "If Bannon's coming, why do we need the guard?"

"Even soldiers like to feel wanted."

"I suppose." Leaning back, Jelena peered around Otavas at the young noblewoman murmuring the Circle only knew what into her sister's ear. "The lady Marineka reminds me of my father."

Otavas couldn't see a resemblance, but as he spent very little time with Lord Jurgis, the queen's father, he realized he could be missing subtleties. "Is that a good thing?"

"I haven't decided."

Lord Jurgis was a hearty and athletic man who'd never been comfortable at court and, once he'd helped ensure continuation of the royal line, had spent very little time there. Except for state occasions where it was necessary they present a united front and during specific family celebrations, Queen Onele and her consort had lived separate lives—growing up, Jelena and her sister had used their father's country estates as a refuge from the duties and responsibilities that fell to them from their mother's position. Although he'd honestly grieved at the death of his queen, he'd returned to the country the moment her body had been interred. Jelena still wasn't certain how she felt about that; as much as she'd wanted his support, as long as he remained unchanged, safe in the country, he was still a refuge.

"Majesty?"

She jerked out of her reverie, glad of the groom at her bridle as her horse responded to her shifting weight by moving forward.

"The company is assembled, Majesty."

"Very well, then." She glanced up at the sky. Midmorning. The last time it had been midmorning on the sixth day of the third moon of the Fourth Quarter, she'd been standing on the steps next to her grandmother, waving goodbye. *If we leave now, we'll reach the place where my mother died by late tomorrow afternoon.* "Open the gates, Troop-Captain, and let's get this over with."

As the company moved out through the gate and into the city, Lilyana folded her hands inside her muff, fingers laced tightly together to keep her from reaching out and grabbing hold of her granddaughter. She smiled as the young queen rode away, experience hiding the lie. Given a choice, she'd have kept Jelena from going to the forts, kept her safely in the Palace, kept her off the road where Onele had died. Where the crown had been passed on. Again. Loss of a husband. Loss of a daughter. Lilyana didn't think she could bear it if she outlived a third monarch of Shkoder.

"Captain, we seem to have left the cheering crowds behind—at least for a moment. Would it be possible to speed things up a little?"

The Troop-Captain glanced over at his queen, then ahead at the road. "Majesty, with the sun in our eyes and the road following so close along the cliff, it would perhaps be safest to proceed at a walk."

Drawing in a deep lungful of sea air, Onele kicked both feet free of the stirrups and stretched her legs. "I've been on this horse for a day and a half, I've smiled and I've waved, and I've accepted half a dozen bouquets from small children. The sooner we reach Fort Kazpar the happier I'll be. I think we can risk a trot." When the Troop-Captain hesitated, she sighed. "This is my eighth trip out to the forts, Captain. We're as safe on this road as we would be riding down Hill Street in Elbasan. We'll just keep Stoyan here in the center of the company so that we don't lose him."

"*Majesty, you cut me to the quick!*" The young bard placed one hand on his heart and tightened the other around the saddle horn. "*Has my horsemanship so disgraced you?*"

Onele grinned as the Troop-Captain muttered, "*Horsemanship?*"

"*I did not fall off,*" Stoyan protested with dramatic dignity. "*I was dismounting and taken by surprise when the ground was not where I expected it to be. Although, I must admit, I agree with Her Majesty . . .*" He shifted uncomfortably in the saddle. "*. . . the sooner we get to Fort Kazpar, the happier I'll be.*"

"*So we trot,*" the queen announced.

Six horses, six soldiers in the Queen's Guard riding two by two, had already passed the nest when the bird decided to rise. Shrieking in panic or defiance or both, her wings drumming against the air, she catapulted into the air right under the nose of the queen's horse.

Eyes rolling, white showing all around, the gelding flung himself four feet to the right. Taken by surprise, Onele lost her stirrups and made a desperate grab for the saddle horn. Mane whipping her face, she slammed forward into his neck as he reared and flipped back off over the cantle when he landed.

The Troop-Captain had insisted that the queen ride on the inside position, away from the edge of the cliff. At first, he thanked all the gods in the Circle he had.

And then he realized it hadn't mattered.

Stroking sightless eyes closed with trembling fingers, Stoyan howled a lament onto the wind and the kigh spread the news that the queen was dead.

"This is where it happened?"

"Yes, Majesty."

"And the rock?"

"Her guard threw it off the cliff. It was the only vengeance they could take."

Jelena turned to look at her own guard, standing by the horses a respectful distance away. Every one of them had been with her mother that day.

"*Let them come,*" Magda had advised her when the Troop-Captain made the request. "*They need this as much as you do.*"

"Who built the memorial?"

"Fyona i'Amalica, a stonemason from Fort Kazpar, and Stoyan, the bard who was with her when it happened."

The stone pillar stood exactly as tall as the late queen. The crowned ship of Shkoder had been carved into its seaward face. The other three sides had been polished silken smooth.

"If you would allow me, Majesty?" When Jelena nodded, the Bardic Captain Sang the four notes of Onele's name.

From the stone, or the air around the stone, came a song wild with grief and denial. It wasn't long, but it didn't need to be.

"Stoyan's lament."

"Yes, Majesty."

She couldn't remember moving into the comforting circle of Otavas' arms nor could she remember crying, but his arms were around her and her cheeks were wet. Her body felt awkward as she stepped slowly forward and pressed both palms against the stone. This place, this monument, the lament—all three had nothing to do with her. Together they lifted the dark weight of her mother's death, the weight she'd carried since the day the Bardic Captain had told her she was queen and could finally do all the things she'd planned.

She waited until the stone turned warm under her hands, then she turned and started walking back toward the horses. "We should go."

His own eyes damp, Otavas fell into step beside her. She leaned gratefully against his support.

"Are you all right, *carimei?*" He murmured the Imperial endearment against her hair.

"I don't know." Every movement she made seemed to take more conscious thought than it ever had. "I feel empty."

A half-dozen careful steps behind, Kovar turned to the healer and pitched his voice for her ears alone. "Empty? Is that good?"

Most of her attention still on the queen, Magda shrugged. "That depends on what moves in to fill the space."

"This is Benedikt, Your Majesty. He'll be Singing your boat across to Fort Tunov."

As he straightened out of his bow, Benedikt found himself being examined by a pair of shadowed eyes.

"I've heard you Sing at festivals."

"Majesty?" All fledglings Sang in the Citadel's Center as part of their training so she'd definitely heard him, he just couldn't believe she'd remember.

"You Sang water. My mother once told me that she thought you could Sing the kigh out of a tear. I can't think of anyone I'd rather have Sing me across the strait. *And,*" she continued as he searched for a response, any response, "I read your recall on the floods in Seven's Bay back in Third Quarter. Good work."

He stammered his thanks, managing not to disgrace his training too badly although he barely heard the Bardic Captain's request for a meeting so they could discuss the next day's ceremony. When the consort's Imperial bodyguard snapped his fingers under his nose, Benedikt was astonished to see that the royal party had moved into the inner bailey, "I'm sorry." Feeling as though he'd could walk on water if the queen required it, he smiled apologetically at the waiting ex-assassin. "Do you want me?"

While golden-haired young men with that pouty just-smacked-in-the-mouth vulnerability weren't exactly his type, Bannon flashed him a predator smile on principle. "Maybe later. Right now, I need you to show me tomorrow's pattern."

A thick Imperial accent added strange emphasis to the words. "Pattern?"

"Where Her Majesty will be, where His Highness will be, where everyone else will be." When Prince Otavas had contracted to join with the Heir of Shkoder, Bannon had added the Princess Jelena to his responsibilities. No one had asked him to, but since his prince had thought it an excellent idea, no one had been able to stop him either.

Benedikt frowned. Kovar had told him he'd be attending the ceremony at the forts before his last Walk, almost as he was on his way out the Citadel gates. He'd had no time to read the recall of his immediate predecessor, but some things were a given. "You accompanied His Highness here in Second Quarter."

"I did."

"It'll be the same ceremony."

"Not quite. Her Majesty wasn't here in Second Quarter." Gripping the bard's shoulder a little harder than was strictly necessary, he turned him in a slow circle. "Those barrels weren't here in Second Quarter; two of the flagstones by the gate are cracked, there's a new half door on the stable, and there's evidence of repair on the rim of the well."

Benedikt whistled softly in amazement and remembered some of the stories floating around the Citadel concerning the ex-assassin. Apparently, those involving his obsessive attention to detail were true. Remembering other stories, a chill spread out from under the pressure of the gripping fingers and lapped against the bard's spine. If some were true, then all could be, and many weren't particularly pleasant. Although some were. An unexpected heat followed the chill, and Benedikt had to swallow before he could ask, "Is there any danger?"

"Always. But if you're asking if Her Majesty is in any danger . . ." Bannon grinned ferally. "Not when I'm around."

Benedikt didn't doubt that for a moment.

And as he pointed out the places the queen and her consort would stand, as he waited while Bannon calculated lines of sight, he couldn't stop thinking of how *he* was now one of the details the ex-assassin noted.

"You're looking solemn," Kovar commented quietly as he and Magda picked their way down a spiral staircase to the floor below the royal suite. "Is there a problem?"

"Not exactly. A couple of the guards are still carrying a lot of guilt about the late queen's death but I feel that escorting Her Majesty here safely should help them work through it and move on."

"Since we're speaking of Her Majesty . . ." Conscious of the way the stone bounced sound all around them, Kovar dropped his voice until the words were little more than a soft buzz against the healer's ear. "Shouldn't you be with her?"

"No. Otavas can do more for her right now than I can."

"You believe that His Highness can fill the emptiness?"

"I believe love will fill the emptiness," Magda told him, her tone leaving little room for argument.

Kovar nodded thoughtfully. "Ah, yes, an heir would help."

"That wasn't what I meant." Stepping out into the corridor, she turned and favored him with a disapproving scowl. "And they don't need you repeating the opinion of every other old fusspot in the country."

"Every *other* old fusspot?"

His indignant protest banished the scowl and drew a laugh. "Kovar, you're a year older than my father."

"And that makes me incredibly decrepit, I'm sure." He sighed, wondering, not for the first time, when the children had taken over. "And as I am so decrepit, I'd best have the room closest to the garderobe." When Magda indicated he should go ahead, he pushed open the door and glanced into the small rectangle. "All the comforts of home."

"And exactly like this one," Magda added, looking into the next room along. "A bed, a chair, and a washstand. I can see why the members of the court aren't exactly falling over each other to accompany Her Majesty on this trip. Can you imagine the Duc of Vidor's reaction to this?" She peered curiously down the corridor at another half-dozen identical doors. "I wonder if they've ever managed to fill their guest quarters."

"I expect young Benedikt's in one of them."

"Ah."

About to enter his room, Kovar paused. "Was that a professional ah, or a personal ah?" When Magda hesitated, he took a step toward her. "I know you saw him a great deal when he was a fledgling, but I'd thought all that had been dealt with."

Both Magda's brows rose and she folded her arms, suddenly looking much older than her twenty-five years. "All that?"

"The boy's belief that he wasn't worth much because he only Sang water. He's a fine bard, you know, does an excellent recall."

"In spite of his handicap."

Kovar drew himself up to his full height and stared down at the healer, mustache quivering. "I *never* said that."

"You didn't have to, I can feel your pity."

"Pity?" Only years of voice control kept him from shouting. "Benedikt is a bard of Shkoder, and he Sings a stronger water than anyone I have ever known."

"I'm aware of that." She cocked her head to one side

and held Kovar in a steady gaze. "But it's very rare for a bard not to be able to Sing air, isn't it? In fact, when a bard sings only one quarter, it's *usually* air. I can't think of another bard alive right now that doesn't sing air, can you?"

"You know very well there isn't." He pushed the words out through stiff lips.

"So you don't feel just a little sorry for Benedikt because he can't do the one thing all the other bards can do?"

"Of course, I feel sorry for the boy . . ."

"He's not a boy, Kovar. His voice broke late, and he'll be twenty before Second Quarter Festival."

"Fine. He's not a boy. And sympathy is not the same as pity. Jazep, your name-father, Sang only earth, the most restricted of all the four quarters, and I never felt pity for him."

"Because he never invited it. Benedikt does. Thanks to the misplaced enthusiasms of his parents, who were rather like ducks raising a songbird, he doesn't see what he has, only what he lacks. Not all the time, of course, or I'd have kept him with me longer—but often enough that he's convinced the rest of you it's a lack as well. He is a bard, after all, and bards can be very convincing."

"Do you think," the Bardic Captain growled, "that I should keep Benedikt from Singing the queen's boat across the strait?"

Magda smiled. "Why, if he Sings a stronger water than anyone you've ever known?"

After a long moment during which he reminded himself that throttling the young healer wasn't an option, Kovar expelled a long breath through his nose and spread his hands. "Thank you for the lesson. In the future I will try to keep in mind those talents Benedikt has, not those he lacks. There is no reason to feel sorry for a bard of Shkoder."

"Hey." Magda spread her own hands in turn. "You don't have to convince me."

The next morning Her Majesty, Queen Jelena, inspected the troops gathered in the inner bailey, then walked the walls to ensure they remained in good repair. While Benedikt Witnessed and Kovar Sang the air kigh to ensure that everyone in the fort could hear, she stood on an artificial cliff facing the sea and swore that Shkoder would not fall as long as Fort Kazpar stood.

Just after noon, the Troop-Captain handed his queen down onto the small boat that would take her across the Bache ky Lamer—the Mouth of the Sea in the old Riverfolk tongue—to Fort Tunov. Another captain, another troop would meet her on the other side. "Thank you, Majesty," he said as he released her hand.

Jelena nodded, a gracious smile carefully hiding emotional turmoil. As much irritated that Madga had been right as she was pleased that wounds—hers and her guards—seemed to be healing, she allowed Otavas to lead her away from the side so that the crew could cast off lines. Unfortunately, the morning's ceremony had done little to fill the emptiness left behind after the dissipation of despair. The ritual had required only a surface involvement and, looking back on it, she could barely remember what she'd said or done. She'd discovered during her long year of grieving that when performing many of the queen's duties, show sufficed where substance was lacking.

"We're away from the dock." Bannon nodded toward the deckhands stowing the lines. "Aren't you supposed to be Singing?"

"Me?" Suddenly realizing how stupid that must sound, Benedikt hurriedly answered the actual question. "No. Not yet." The ex-assassin had been close by his side all day; charming because he wanted to be, threatening because he couldn't not. Benedikt wasn't sure how he felt about the unexpected companionship. Or how he was supposed to feel. "I don't know why you're even here," he protested.

Bannon shrugged, a minimal rise and fall of one shoulder, deliberately infuriating. "I go where my prince goes."

"Any danger out in the strait will come from the sea." The waves grew choppier as they moved from the shore. "How can you protect him from that?"

"I can't. I guess I'll just have to depend on you."

Sarcasm blended so smoothly with threat, a bard couldn't have done it better. Benedikt stiffened. He didn't have to put up with that kind of attitude from anyone. Not even from an Imperial assassin. His muscles had actually tensed to turn and walk away when Bannon caught and held his gaze, and he suddenly realized that turning his back on this man was quite possibly the stupidest thing he could do.

Suddenly aware that they were standing alone, a considerable distance from anyone else on the ship, Benedikt's mouth went dry. "I won't let anything happen to him. To them. To their Majesties."

"Good."

Benedikt could clearly hear the consequences of failure in that single word. Walk away? What good would that do? Anywhere he went, Bannon could follow him.

Where do assassins sleep?

Anywhere they want to.

Imperial humor leaned toward the obvious.

"Benedikt!"

Jerked out of his search for a response by Kovar's summons, Benedikt realized it was time. He glanced down at the smaller man, who gracefully indicated that he should move toward the bow. Heart pounding, unsure of what he'd just gotten free of, he hurried gratefully to his place.

Carefully keeping his concern from his face, Bannon watched the younger man walk away. In eight years in Shkoder, he'd never met a bard so precariously balanced. *If he was a blade, I'd have him reforged.*

A product of Imperial Army training that many intended assassins didn't survive, Bannon'd often thought that the Bardic Hall, in insisting that bards were born not made, stupidly depended on talent at the expense of discipline. How they could justify sending this particular bard out into the world so ill prepared to face it, he had no idea. He couldn't decide if he was intrigued or appalled.

I am definitely going to have to keep an eye on him.

Benedikt felt the weight of Bannon's regard all the way to the bow. *It doesn't matter what he thinks. . . .*

Except that it did.

The moment he opened his mouth, he would be responsible for the safety of the queen and her consort. He'd be taking on Bannon's responsibility, and Bannon clearly didn't believe it was good idea.

As he stared down into the gray-green water, Benedikt's

fingers tightened around the rail. He should never have agreed to do this. Should never have risked . . .

"Any time, Benedikt."

He half turned, intending to make some kind of excuse to the Bardic Captain, but saw only the queen. Saw her smile at him, and nod.

"I can't think of anyone I'd rather have Sing me across the strait."

Her Majesty believed in him.

He wouldn't let her down.

The rest of the world, Bannon included, could go suck a wet rope.

As Benedict's Song rose over the myriad sounds of a ship at sea, the waves fell away until the boat rested in the center of a spreading circle of calm. The surface of the water gleamed like polished silver, and when Kovar leaned over the side, the reflection staring back at him was truer than he'd ever seen in any glass. Before he had time to wonder if Benedikt had misunderstood what he was to do, the boat rose gently up on the crest of a massive wave. The wave might have been made of a thousand kigh, or it might have been only one—although he, too, Sang water, Kovar couldn't tell.

With the boat cradled safely in the water's hold, Benedikt reached out with his Song and told the kigh what he needed them to do.

The wave began to move toward the opposite shore. Had it not been for the wind of their passage and the rapid approach of Fort Tunov, it would have been hard to believe they were moving at all, so perfectly still did the boat itself remain.

Wide-eyed, the boat's captain, who had made this journey a dozen times with a dozen bards, turned to stare at Benedikt, tracing the sign of the Circle on her breast.

Others in her crew hurried to follow her lead.

"You're astounded, aren't you?"

Kovar turned his head just enough to catch Magda in the corner of one eye, keeping most of his attention on Benedikt. Yes, I am," he told her.

"You couldn't do this, could you?"

"No, I couldn't."

The healer looked thoughtful. "I wonder if Benedikt knows that."

Standing at the rail, Jelena barely noticed the boat, let alone the kigh it rode. She had given reassurance when it was needed and now, one hand tightly gripping the polished wood, she stared westward out toward the Broken Islands listening to the voice of memory plan for the future.

"When I'm Queen . . ."

And she was queen. Not grief nor guilt nor anger could change that.

". . . I'm going to send ships as far west as they can go and see if they end up in the east again."

TWO

"YOUR Majesty, Your Highness, this is Lajos i'Lajosne a'Ulrik, the sailor."

"Thank you, Ermi." As the page left her office, Jelena studied the old man straightening laboriously up from a deep bow. Wind and sun had etched a thousand fine lines into skin the color of tanned leather. He wore his thin, gray hair pulled back into a narrow braid with blue beads hanging from the tie and similar beads threaded onto the long ends of his mustache—a style she dimly remembered as popular back when she was very young. His clothes were worn but clean and, judging by the fit of the tunic, he'd probably borrowed someone else's best for this meeting.

When his head rose high enough that she could meet his eyes, she smiled and said, "Thank you for coming, Lajos."

He returned her smile, his few remaining teeth in surprisingly good condition. "Your wish, Majesty, is my command." Before he dipped too far forward into another bow, he thought better of it and nodded instead.

"Please, sit down." Jelena had no difficulty reading a startled, *"Sit in front of the queen?"* in the way he looked from her, to the chair, to Otavas, and back to her again. She masked her impatience with a smile. "It's all right; you may be here for some time."

"I may?" The beads on the ends of his mustache danced out away from his mouth as he exhaled, "Beggin' your pardon, Majesty, but why?"

"I . . . that is, we . . ." Turning slightly, she included Otavas in the request. ". . . want to hear the story of the dark sailor."

"The dark sailor? You don't say? I done gave that story to the bards when it happened." His forehead creased and he rubbed at the ridges with the side of a bent finger. "They even done a song about it. Not meanin' no disrespect, but you musta heard it."

"Yes, I've heard the song, and I've read the original report." Jelena's fingers closed around the edge of a leather-bound journal borrowed from the bardic library. "But you were there, and I want to hear the story from you."

Lajos snorted and lowered himself down onto the chair. "Well, them bards just mighta put a bit more in the song than was in the story I gave 'em, now I think on it. The dark sailor," he repeated again as he settled. "We musta picked him up twenty, twenty-one year ago. . . . Twenty, that's it, 'cause it were the year Hanicka i'Gitka—she were our second mate—got herself a baby, and little Gitka's twenty next quarter. She's sailin' on the *Two Sisters* now, but she stops by to see what's left of her ma's old crew when she's in port." He sighed, caught sight of the queen's expression and, grinning unselfconsciously, brought himself back on track. "But you wants to know about the old days on the *First Ashore,* back when we took up the dark sailor.

"Until we was half a day out from the Broken Islands, it were just another voyage. Then we got caught in a storm. I'm tellin' you, Majesty, I ain't never been in a storm so wild." Both hands rose to sketch the storm in the air between them. "The winds come down out of the northeast like demons, like demons howlin' around the edges of the Circle, tryin' ta get in. A normal wind don't come out of the northeast," he explained solemnly, looking first to the consort and then to the queen, making sure they understood this. "Prevailin' winds is out of the northwest and that'll take you to the south current, and if you don't wanna stop in the Empire, you can ride all the way to the Gates of Hamilkas—he were a pirate what sailed the Fienian Sea and since it were the Fienians what named the gates . . ." He shrugged and continued.

"This storm blew so bad the captain, she thought of headin' back to the Islands, but by that time it were too late. We run in front of those winds, sails ripped all to ratshit— beggin' Your Majesty's pardon—timbers creakin' and groanin' like they was gonna split and send us to the bottom for five full days. I still wakes up in the night, hearin' them sounds and that sure I'm about to be drowned." The beads swung from side to side as he shook off the effect of the memories, then the intensity of the queen's attention locked his gaze back onto her face. "When the sky finally cleared, we was surrounded by more water than I ever seen before or since. No sight of land. No cloud that might tell a body where land was lyin'. And when it got dark, the stars was twisted all outa shape. We knew we was south, 'cause we knew some of the stars and it'd gotten right warm, but we had no idea how far west we'd been driven." The memory layered the slow, rocking cadence of a ship becalmed onto his voice. "We sat there, a day and another, all of us patchin' together what we could for a sail 'cause we knew if we didn't get a sheet to the wind, we'd never see home again. Late on the second day, a breeze come up from the south and, with it, what was left of a ship like I never seen before. It looked like it'd been caught in the bad-tempered twin of the storm what'd done us, and I'm tellin' you, Majesty, that boat were only half our size to begin with. Why it weren't bashed to bits I had no idea then nor none now. There was three dead on board—died of thirst we figured. They'd been out there longer than we had, that were for sure, and the storm had busted their water casks to kindlin'—three dead and one alive."

"The dark sailor."

Lajos nodded solemnly. "The dark sailor. Dark skin like in the south of the Empire." Pausing, he glanced toward Otavas. "Lot's darker than yours, if you don't mind me sayin', Highness. Dark as a Fienian's I'd say, but redder. And though his hair were black as a pirate's heart, it were straight and a Fienian's is mostly curly. Fact, it were so black that when the sun hit it, it were almost blue. His eyes was so dark they looked like they was all pupil and he had black designs on his chest—which didn't have a hair on it even given he were no boy—designs what were written right into his skin."

"These?" Forcing herself to show a calm she didn't feel, Jelena opened the journal to a faded sketch and turned it toward Lajos. Caught up in the story, Otavas leaned over for a closer look.

"If them's what I told the bards they looked like, then I guess they did." The old sailor shrugged apologetically. "Truth is, I don't exactly remember now."

"I thought the designs might be a map."

"A map?" The lines around his eyes deepened as he squinted at the page. "If you say so, Majesty. But I can't say that I see a map. Or ever did. But it were a long time ago," he added hurriedly as Jelena's face fell.

"Never mind, Lajos. Please, continue."

"Well, the dark sailor were ravin' when we found him. We didn't have no bard, so we couldn't figure what he was sayin', but we soon found that unless he were lookin' to the southwest, he wouldn't stay where we put him, so we made him a bed on deck. Me, I figured he had one of them fore-warnings that he'd never see his home again. He lay there, gettin' weaker and weaker spite of everything our old Jon could do—we didn't have no healer," he explained, "so old Jon, the cook, he done mosta the healin'—while the captain had us strip every bit of usable sail off the wreck. Next mornin', the dark sailor died. We put him back onto his ship with his friends, torched it, and pushed away. I seen the captain throw a handful of earth outa her personal altar onto it, givin' it all four quarters 'cause they was sailors, too, and there but for what the Circle enclosed was us.

"While we was watching the fire burn, a wind come up headin' east. We rode it all the way back to shores we knew. I always figured it was the dark sailor, thankin' us for not leavin' him and his shipmates for crab food."

"I am familiar with the song, Majesty. Slane—the bard who wrote it—and I were fledglings together." Kovar paused a moment to consider the most diplomatic way to continue, frowning down at a worn spot on the old carpet the queen refused to replace. "I just don't think you should base such an important decision on such a flimsy melody. Two full quarters passed before Lajos i'Lajosne even told the story to a bard, and that wouldn't have happened had he and Tadeus not met down in Dockside and ended up . . . uh . . ."

"In bed?" Magda offered helpfully. When Kovar shot her a black look, she smiled. "That *is* where Tadeus has always heard his best stories."

"And it is *not* something that should be discussed in front of the queen."

"I don't care where Tadeus first heard it," Jelena interjected, making it quite clear she expected both her advisers to behave. "According to the recalls I read, he offered the story to Slane because he thought it should go to a bard who Sang water, and Slane checked with the other crew in port at the time. They backed up everything Lajos said."

The Bardic Captain shook his head. "But to conclude that there's a whole new land to the southwest based on such a tale . . ."

"And what would you conclude, based on such a tale?" Jelena asked him dryly.

"Majesty, that is not the point."

"I think that's exactly the point. Answer the question."

"Sailors are known to exaggerate, Majesty." He could see she remained unconvinced. "I have even heard stories of giant kigh that turn the water of the sea into a trap for ships and a graveyard for sailors." Spreading his hands, he asked. "Surely if these kigh existed, we bards would know of them?"

"Why *surely?* You didn't learn of the fifth kigh until recently."

Once again, if the obvious differences were ignored, it might have been King Theron, sitting behind the desk. Kovar, who'd spent eight years as Bardic Captain under the old king, had to fight an instinctive reaction. Theron, he reminded himself, had been the voice of experience. Jelena was not. "The legends refer to water kigh, Majesty, and that is a quarter we have always known. If these giant kigh existed, surely we would have heard."

"So you're saying that the dangers are legendary?"

"I am saying, Majesty, that even though *some* of the reported dangers may be legendary, it is my opinion that it would be foolhardy to send a ship out into the unknown with such an untenanted hope of success."

"I thank you for your opinion, Captain." Sitting back in her chair, Jelena studied the bard for a moment or two. When the weight of her steady regard began to dip his brows toward the bridge of his nose, she turned her attention to Magda. "What do *you* think?"

The healer took a moment to glance at the man beside her. The Bardic Captain was sulking, uncomfortable with the queen thinking for herself. From the feel of his kigh, Magda suspected that he preferred Jelena unsure in her role and willing to embrace the advice of someone who'd seen more of life. Willing to embrace his advice. Perhaps it was time that he, too, came to terms with the young queen's sudden ascent to the throne. "I think, Majesty, that songs often provide valid inspiration."

"That's a platitude, not an opinion," Kovar snorted. "Not to mention complete and utter nonsense. There can be no good reason to send a ship out into the unknown."

Both hands flat on her desk, Jelena stood. Color burned on both cheeks, but her voice remained level as she said quietly, "I disagree. After careful consideration, I have decided to outfit a vessel and call for volunteers to crew her."

The older man folded his arms over his quartered robe. "I cannot approve such a ridiculous scheme."

"You forget yourself, Bardic Captain. I am Queen in Shkoder, and I am not asking for your approval."

"Now *that's* what I call healing."

Having strode half a dozen angry paces down the hall outside the queen's office, Kovar stopped and turned to glare at Magda. "Surely you don't approve of this?"

"Surely I do. We wanted Jelena to move past her mother's unfortunate death and accept that she's queen. I think we've succeeded admirably." Walking past him, fully conscious of him pivoting to keep her locked in the beacon of his displeasure, she frowned thoughtfully. "Let's see, the Council won't be meeting again until after First Quarter Festival. I expect Her Majesty will wait and make her announcement then. After that, things should get interesting."

Five days into the new quarter, Benedikt woke to find his hand in a puddle and a pair of tiny water kigh playing tag around his fingers. Cupping his hand so that they swam lazy circles on his palm, he asked them how much rain had fallen in the night.

Too much.

There had been heavy snowfalls in the high country throughout Fourth Quarter, enough to guarantee a certain amount of flooding in the valleys below as the weather warmed. Unfortunately, it had rained every day since First Quarter Festival. If it kept up, the flooding would be severe.

Pushed by a sense of urgency, he quickly packed up his camp and ate a cold breakfast while he traveled. Much of the path was wet enough that kigh rose up around his boots with every step. As much as he appreciated their company, that wasn't good.

He reached the village of Janinton just before noon, although, with the sun hidden beneath a thick blanket of gray cloud, he had to tell the time by the state of his stomach. He was looking forward to a hot meal when, just as he spotted the first cluster of villagers sitting miserably in the damp circle of their possessions, he heard the Song.

It seemed there was a bard already in Janinton; a bard who Sang water and was, even now, Singing the river away from the village.

Other bards could plan their paths to cover the country most efficiently; he had to show up and discover he was of no more use than a bottomless boat. Then he heard the desperation in the Song. The river's kigh were not responding.

Stripping off the encumbrance of his pack, Benedikt raced for the river's edge. Those last few notes, more wailed than Sung, told him he had no time to waste. The villagers called out to him as he pounded past, but he ignored them. Leaping over a wet chicken, too miserable to move out of his way, he rounded the last building and rocked to a stop.

The original settlers of Janinton had built in a bend of the Silverglass River. Most years when the water was high, the Second Quarter melt poured around the upper half of the bend and then spread out over the banks into the marshlands to the north. This year, something had clearly happened upstream and a wave of icy water roared directly toward the village, the only barrier a slender figure Singing to kigh that weren't listening.

The leading crest would reach the unknown bard in a heartbeat. Rushing forward, Benedikt sucked in a damp lungful of air and threw his Song toward the surging water. Dark with mud and debris churned out of the mountains, the flood smashed into the bend and began to rise behind the twisting, translucent bodies of the kigh. The other bard jerked around, but Benedikt had no time to acknowledge him. Weaving a complicated melody in and around the notes that held the kigh in place, he layered them along the path of the river, in some places three feet above the banks. On the other side of the village, he allowed the water to spill out of its translucent chute and into the marsh.

Toward midafternoon, a hand lightly touched his arm and a quiet voice wove itself into the Song where he'd be certain to hear. "Benedikt, you've taken the pressure off. The levees should hold now."

Should hold? Benedikt waved the interruption away. He would Sing until the flood had passed.

It was dark when that same hand gripped his shoulder and told him it was over, he could stop Singing. Somehow, he managed the four notes of the gratitude, releasing the kigh. When he looked down, he could just barely make out the river lapping against the toes of his boots.

"The village?" he whispered.

"Safe." The hand on his shoulder turned him around, then folded his fingers about the warm curves of a clay mug. "Drink this, Benedikt. The village herbalist says it'll ease your throat."

Using both hands, he got the mug to his mouth and took a tentative sip. "Tastes like goat piss and honey."

"Doesn't it always?"

He studied the pale oval that seemed to float in front of him as he drank, trying to put the features together into some sort of recognizable face. "Pjazef? You're supposed to be in Somes. Singing earth."

"I'm on my way to Somes, but I had to run an errand for the healers first."

Pjazef had finished training just as he was beginning. They'd never known each other well—which was amazing in itself considering how well rumor insisted Pjazef knew most of the bards and half the country—but, as far as Benedikt could remember . . . "Didn't think you Sang water."

"After today, I don't think I do either," the other bard admitted, taking back the empty mug and slipping an arm around Benedikt's waist. "Come on, I've got a bed all ready for you; we can talk in the morning."

"I can walk."

"Good. 'Cause you're too unenclosed tall. I don't think I can carry you."

Beginning to tremble, Benedikt surrendered and sagged against Pjazef's warmth. Left on his own, he'd have fallen where he stood.

Next morning, Benedikt crouched by the water's edge, peering intently down at the kigh. Everything he'd done yesterday could be destroyed today if the conditions upstream hadn't changed. In spite of the remarkable healing powers of the herbalist's tea, he hadn't voice enough to compel so he had to convince. Time after time, the kigh flung themselves away from his quiet Song, wanting to play. Finally, he got enough of an answer, straightened and turned.

"There's still plenty of runoff coming," he announced, wishing that, like the bard beside him, he could use the air kigh for volume instead of his abraded throat. "But it shouldn't be any more than the river and the wetlands can handle."

Gathered between the two bards and the first of the half-timbered houses, the half circle of villagers cheered. Pjazef grinned up at Benedikt, pitching his voice over the sound. "I said it last night and I'll say it again now. You were absolutely amazing. If I hadn't seen you do it, I wouldn't have believed it could be done."

Two spots of color high on his cheeks, Benedikt grinned. "I did do a pretty good job, didn't I?"

"Pretty good? Center it, man, you did what no one else could have. I had to try because I was here, but I fully expected to be swept away. My only hope was that I could Sing a strong enough water to keep from drowning."

Having heard a little of Pjazef's Song, Benedikt had his doubts.

"I'm just glad I was here to Witness for you 'cause the way you were Singing, your recall's going to be full of kigh and not much else. This is Urmi i'Margit," he added on his next breath as a middle-aged woman stepped forward, "the village headwoman."

Too quickly for him to avoid, Urmi dragged Benedikt into a vigorous hug. "You saved our homes," she told him, cheeks wet. "Probably our very lives, there's no way we can thank you sufficiently for what you've done."

The men and women behind her murmured in agreement. Releasing him, she swiped at her face with the palms of her hands. "If there's ever anything you need that the people of Janinton can give you, anything at all . . ."

Benedikt watched, astounded, as her eyes slowly slid together in the center of her face. A heartbeat later, Pjazef caught him and heaved him back more or less vertical. "I'm all right," he insisted as the shorter bard slipped a shoulder under his left arm. "I can walk."

"I know." There was a definite wink implicit in the tone. "I just like hanging on to you. Why don't we head back to the herbalist's, and you can spend a little more time recovering from saving the world."

"I didn't save the world."

"Then you can recover from saving this part of it. Unless, you're up to a bit of gratitude." Eyes crinkling at the corners, he glanced up through a fringe of russet hair. "The head-woman might think there's no way to thank you, but a couple of the younger villagers have come up with some pretty inventive ideas."

His tone made the general, if not the specifics, of those ideas quite clear.

The last thing Benedikt wanted to do at the moment was Sing, but sex came a close second. "I think I'll just go with you."

"Wise choice."

The herbalist's small house was dry and warm, and that alone would've recommended it, but it also smelled wonderful—a mix of summer meadows and woodland clearings. The two bards had spent the night in the downstairs room she kept for the sick, and Benedikt assumed he'd be returning there. Pjazef, however, guided him to the couch beside the stove. "This way you won't be so cut off from what's happening."

It would've taken too much effort to insist that he didn't mind, so he lay back and closed his eyes.

He had no idea how long he'd been asleep when the voices woke him.

"Don't fuss so, Pjazef, it's no wonder he's exhausted. The body is full of water, you know; he was Singing a different

Song to bits of himself even while he was Singing the river.
Let him sleep."

Benedikt forced his eyes open. "I'm awake."

The herbalist, a spare woman in her mid-forties, shot him
one keen look and reached for a covered pot on the stove.
Benedikt would've liked to have asked her what she'd seen,
but he didn't get a chance as Pjazef suddenly filled his line
of sight.

"I was beginning to worry." He dropped down on the
side of the couch and laid one hand lightly on Benedikt's
chest. "How are you feeling?"

Benedikt blinked at him, trying to focus. "How do you
make that sound like an invitation?"

Looking a little startled, the other bard brushed a bit of
hair back off his face, and smiled. "Practice," he suggested.

Her opinion of his practices plain on her face, the herbalist reached past Pjazef's shoulder and handed Benedikt a
familiar mug. "This lot should taste like goat piss and rasp-
berries," she told him. "You get that down you, and you
should feel more like yourself. And you . . ."

Pjazef recoiled dramatically from her smack on the
shoulder.

". . . you let him rest."

"I was only going to tell him the news from the Bardic
Hall."

"That's what you say," she sniffed as she gathered up a
wooden bucket of scraps and headed out the back door.
"And I'm sure you're sincere while you say it."

"How long have you *been* here?" Benedikt wondered as
the door closed.

"Just a little longer than you. Why?"

"Your reputation seems to have preceded you."

Unrepentant, Pjazef grinned. "I'm kind of memorable,
being the only redheaded bard."

"What about Sergai?"

"You call that red?" He ran both hands back through
shoulder-length hair the color of frost-touched leaves.
"He's a strawberry blond at best."

They were alone in the kitchen. Very conscious of the
warm thigh pressed up against him, Benedikt reminded
himself that for Pjazef flirting came as naturally as breathing. He didn't mean anything by it. When the silence

stretched, empty and echoing, he swallowed the last truly vile mouthful of herbal tea and said, "You have news from the Hall?"

"The Hall?"

"The Bardic Hall?"

"Oh. Yeah." *Mixed messages,* Pjazef thought, forcing his attention up off the full curve of Benedikt's lower lip. *That's what's wrong with the world.* He masked his disappointment behind a superficial, almost arch tone. "I Sang the Hall a report about the flood, or rather the lack of a flood, this morning before you woke up and . . . What's the matter?"

Benedikt's own report would have to wait until he returned personally to the Bardic Hall and gave his recall. "Nothing."

"Then you shouldn't frown like that. You'll make lines." He took his thumb and smoothed out the skin between Benedikt's eyes—and got the same lack of response he had before. *Oh, well, can't blame a guy for trying.* "You'll be happy to know that I finally got an explanation for all the lost ship stuff we've been getting from the kigh."

"We've been getting?" Benedikt snorted, staring into the bottom of the empty mug. The warmth of Pjazef's thumb clung to his forehead. He fought against responding and embarrassing himself.

"Oops. Sorry. You wouldn't, would you, 'cause none of the water you've been Singing has come from Elbasan, so the water kigh wouldn't know. It seems that the queen has decided to send a ship southwest from the Broken Islands to find the land the dark sailor came from. She's calling for volunteers. And she wants a bard to go along, but Kovar's against it."

That pulled an incredulous gaze up onto Benedikt's face. "He's not allowing it?"

"You're frowning again. He can't not allow it, now can he? This is the queen we're talking about, not some fledgling who wants to make a quick pile of coin at the Ax and Anchor—which, I'd like to point out, is not half as bad a place as rumor makes it. Anyway, I heard from Evicka that he's really singing low notes and minor keys about it. Nothing but doom and gloom. And Imrich says that you can't really expect anything else when the kigh are referring to it as the lost ship already. But Tadeus said he thinks every-one's overreacting and that if we paid attention, we'd real-ize that the kigh name any ship lost if it sails out of sight of land, so they're obviously not foretelling the queen's voyage. He also says that asking the kigh their opinion about something is a waste of time since we have no frame of reference for what they believe."

"You heard all this, this morning?"

"Plus that Evicka got her hair cut and it looks a lot better than those long braids, that the bolt of dark blue wool I ordered at the beginning of last quarter finally arrived, and that everyone thinks what you did with the river was amaz-ing. So what do you think?"

Benedikt had no idea that bards who Sang air spent so much time gossiping. Although he had to admit that in Pjazef's case he wasn't really surprised. "What do I think about what?"

"About this trip Her Majesty's planning. Calling for vol-unteers to sail off into the unknown. I mean, it's one thing to leave Shkoder to so to Petroika or to the Havakeen Empire, but this is another thing entirely. Doesn't Her Maj-esty realize that we're all part of the pattern that keeps the country strong?"

"And removing, say, *you* from the pattern would result in what? Complete collapse of the whole?"

Although he laughed at the conceit, Pjazef held to his opinion. "What would happen to Shkoder if we all went off walking on water?"

Walking on water was a bardic term used to describe those rare occasions when one of them took ship for for-eign lands. It wasn't what Benedikt had meant when he'd silently declared himself willing to walk on water for the queen—at least it wasn't what he'd meant at the time. "I think I'm going to volunteer."

Pjazef's reaction was everything he could have hoped for.

"Because you're too old, Tadeus."

The blue silk scarf tied around his eyes did nothing to hide the pique on the blind bard's face. "Too old?"

"You're fifty. Don't deny it, your age is a matter of re-cord." Kovar leaned back in his chair and rubbed at his temples with the heels of both hands. "And more importantly, you don't Sing water, a talent Her Majesty has decided is necessary for this idiot adventure. In case they run into those giant water kigh, I assume. And yes . . ." As Tadeus opened his mouth, he raised a hand, aware as he moved that the gesture was superfluous. ". . . the queen knows my opinion. It merely makes no difference to her."

Brows, still sleek and black, rose up above the scarf, personal indignation pushed aside. "My, my, someone's not happy about the fledgling leaving the nest."

"Her Majesty is perfectly capable of making up her own mind."

"Without your help?"

Lips pressed into a thin line, Kovar glared across his desk at the other bard. After a moment, he trusted his voice enough to say, "Was there anything else, Tadeus?"

"I *was* wondering if any other bards have expressed an interest."

"No."

"No?" Tadeus traced the brilliant embroidery on his sleeve with the tip of one finger. "I wonder why."

As he wasn't asking, Kovar saw no reason to answer.

"I can see why those who Sing earth might not be interested. They have a strong attachment to this piece of land, and I suppose many of the older bards have families they'd be loath to leave or physical frailties they'd be loath to risk, but I can't understand why the younger bards aren't leaping at this chance to discover songs that no one in Shkoder has heard." He lifted his head, and Kovar had the uncanny feeling that behind the scarf the blind eyes were staring directly into his.

"What good are new songs if no one ever hears them sung?" the Bardic Captain demanded. "We have no proof that there is land to the south and west, and we bards are too important to Shkoder to throw our lives away."

"Are we?" Again the black brows rose above the blue silk.

"Stop being irritating just because you can be, Tadeus. You know full well that we bards are the strength of a small country."

"So I've heard you tell the fledglings. We're all part of the pattern that keeps the country strong."

"Exactly."

"*Part* of the pattern, Kovar."

Outside the office window, a small brass bell rang an imperious summons.

Grateful for the interruption—arguing with Tadeus often resembled arguing with one of the kigh—the Bardic Captain stood and flipped up the latch that held the multipaned window closed during inclement weather. As he pulled open the left panel, he kept a tight hold on the frame lest the kigh decide to slam it back against the wall just for the joy of hearing things break. The wind-sketched outline of an elongated body separated from the bell, dove into the office, looped once around him, and delivered its message.

Kovar Sang his answer as it raced up and out of sight, then stepped back and closed the window.

"He's needed where he is?" Tadeus repeated behind him.

"You're all needed where you are," Kovar said wearily, turning to find the other bard standing barely an arm's length away. "Over the last four quarters we've had five losses to age and one to accident. Six dead and only two fledglings found. We haven't bards enough to lose one on this fool's quest."

"Shouldn't that be an individual choice?" Tadeus asked seriously, all affectations gone.

"No. Our duty is to Shkoder."

Recognizing a dismissal, Tadeus shook his head and walked unerringly to the door. With one hand on the latch, he paused and faced the Bardic Captain again. "I remember my oaths, Kovar."

And the blind bard's voice was so exquisitely controlled, Kovar had no idea where his emphasis lay.

The small assembly room had not been changed in living memory. From the carved rosewood throne, to the stained glass in the narrow windows casting multihued reflections on the polished stone floor, to the seal of Shkoder carved into the great roundel in the center of the ceiling, the room had been designed to quietly impress. Those standing before the throne at the edge of the low dais were left in no doubt of the power they faced. While much of the actual business of the realm was conducted in Council Chambers and in the monarch's private office, the small assembly room was used for the exchange of information, for the meeting of ambassadors . . .

. . . and to make a point.

"It has come to my attention, Bardic Captain, that you are denying your permission to those bards who wish to volunteer for the voyage." No need to define what voyage. Jelena's fingers were white around the arms of the throne. "Would you care to explain yourself?"

"I have not had to deny my permission, Majesty," Kovar told her matter-of-factly. "The only bard who has shown an interest does not Sing water."

The young queen leaned slightly forward without releasing her grip on the carved wood. Her knuckles were white and her voice suggested she barely kept her temper in check. "What of Benedikt? Or were you not planning on telling me he had requested a position on my ship?"

How had she known? Kovar wondered, trying to think past the sound of blood roaring in his ears. The kigh had brought the news directly to him and then left with his answer. He'd been alone at the window and Tadeus . . . Tadeus, that had to be the answer. He'd forgotten how far into a building the kigh were willing to go for the blind bard.

"I remember my oaths, Kovar."

No doubt where the emphasis lay now.

"Captain?"

He started, pulling himself back into the assembly room. "If you have had an opportunity to read Pjazef's report of flood at Janinton, Majesty, I think the situation amply illustrates my belief that all the bards are needed where they are."

"Let me reassure you, Captain, that I read both the day's reports and any new recalls nightly—" Her lips curled up into a tight, warning smile. "—as did my mother and my grandfather before her, and I value the work the bards do in maintaining Shkoder. The *Starfarer* will not leave Elbasan until the third moon of this quarter so, you see, I don't pull Benedikt abruptly from your pattern but give you a chance to reweave it."

"Majesty, you may not realize that Benedikt Sings only water."

"Then removing him will disrupt your pattern even less."

Jelena sat back as though it were settled. Looking up at her set expression, Kovar realized that it was. "I would appreciate it if you tell him to return to Elbasan, Bardic Captain."

Bardic Captains conducted, they did not control. Kovar had nothing to say to Tadeus.

Or rather, he had a great deal to say but as it all came down to "How dare you go to the queen behind my back?" and he already knew what Tadeus would reply he saw no reason to waste his time.

"I remember my oaths, Kovar."

Bardic Oaths were sworn to the greater good, which unfortunately left room for differences of opinions.

No, Tadeus had done all the damage he could, and if Kovar wanted to stop this blatant disregard of what was best for Shkoder, he needed to put his energy elsewhere.

"Magda, you must speak with her. She won't listen to me."

Setting her fluted glass pen carefully back in the inkwell, Magda sighed and looked up from her notes. "What do you want me to say to her, Kovar?" The healer laced her fingers together as he began an impassioned tirade against the exploration. Some time later, when he'd started to wind down and no longer seemed in imminent danger of exploding, she said, "Her Majesty listens to you, Kovar, she just doesn't agree with you."

He took a deep breath and slowly released the bunched handful of robe he'd been gripping. "And you?"

"Do I agree that she's sending a shipload of fools to their deaths? No. Do I agree that we have too few bards to waste one on this nonsense? No. Do I agree that you're doing the right thing in discouraging the bards from volunteering . . ." Before she could add one final no, Kovar interrupted.

"I am not," he growled, drawing himself up to his full height and glaring down at her, "discouraging the bards from volunteering. They have brains enough of their own to see this *exploration* for the death trap it is."

"And yet, if you hadn't been making it quite so clear

that you see it as a death trap, I can't help but think that some of the younger bards might be a little more willing to take the risk."

"Some of the younger bards?" he repeated with a harsh laugh, as nonmusical a sound as Magda, who'd spent her entire life among bards, had ever heard. "Tell that to Tadeus. The old fool is the only bard who thinks himself immortal enough to try."

"And Benedikt?"

"He doesn't think enough of himself to see the danger."

That, Magda had to admit, was a distinct possibility, but Tadeus was no fool. He was nearly of an age with Kovar, and so it was only to be expected that the Bardic Captain would have less influence on him than on the younger bards. Was this indicative, she wondered, of a split in ideology by age? "Perhaps I should speak to Tadeus."

"You might as well," Kovar told her tightly. "Since it seems you've nothing of value to say to the queen." Quartered robes whipping around his ankles, he strode for the door and paused, one foot over the threshold. Pivoting around, he pointed an inkstained finger at the healer. "This voyage is nothing but a personal indulgence by a monarch who doesn't seem to realize we have everything we need right here."

Magda sat where she was, forehead creased, until the staccato beat of his angry footsteps faded, then she slowly pushed back her chair, stepped out into the wide hall, and flagged down the first apprentice she saw.

"Find Tadeus, tell him I need to speak with him as soon as possible."

"Here, Healer?"

"Here."

She'd start with Tadeus.

And she'd call in a few favors to make certain that when Benedikt arrived back at the Citadel, he'd come to her before he spoke with the Bardic Captain.

The applause when he finished playing flung Benedikt up onto his feet and spun him around, heart beating so hard against his ribs he thought it might break free. "Pjazef! How long have you been standing there?"

"Just for the last song." A little taken aback at the reaction, he pushed his way through the last bit of dog willow. "Are you okay?"

Benedikt shook his head and then protested he was fine when he saw the concern on the older bard's face. "You shouldn't sneak up on people like that!"

"I didn't want to interrupt. It's a great piece, Benedikt. Did you just write it?"

He bent and carefully laid his quintara in the instrument case. "Why?"

"Because it sounds like a brook dancing down the mountainside, and there isn't anyone else who can interpret water like you do."

"Oh." Pleased, he straightened and nodded. "I finished it last night."

"Could you teach it to me?"

It hadn't been his for very long, but there wasn't a graceful way to refuse such a normal bardic request. "Sure." He bent back toward the instrument case.

Pjazef stopped him with a touch on his arm. "Not now. I have news." Brushing a bit of forest flotsam from the sleeve of his jacket, he grinned at Benedikt's expression and continued. "I have a message from the queen. Well, actually, it's from Evicka since she Sang it, but . . ."

"Pjazef!" Benedikt was not in the mood for a lengthy monologue of bardic gossip. He had a message from the queen. The queen.

"Right. You're to cut your Walk short by swinging around this side of Ohrid's border and cutting back through Vidor to arrive in Elbasan no later than the dark of the second moon."

"First Quarter?"

"First Quarter."

That was, indeed, cutting his Walk short. "Why?"

Pjazef spread his hands. "It seems you're going on a voyage."

"Me?" The queen wanted him. Benedikt felt a rush of joy so great that he couldn't contain it. Giving a great shout of laughter, he grabbed Pjazef around the waist and hoisted him up into the air.

The older bard laughed as well. "So you're happy about this?"

"Happy? Are you kidding? Out of all the bards in Shkoder, the queen has chosen me!"

As Pjazef's feet hit the forest floor, russet brows dipped down momentarily. That hadn't quite been the gist of Evicka's message.

Three

"THERE she is, Majesty, the *Starfarer*."

Jelena stared up at the ship, gaze sweeping along the curved side, out the bow, and alighting momentarily on each of the three masts. "She looks so bare."

"She'll look less bare once we've got her yards and sheets up," the master of the Elbasan shipyards told her reassuringly. "We're concerned right now about making her watertight, and we can't know that for certain unless she's in the water."

"She's not very . . ." Otavas paused but was unable to think of a tactful finish. "She's not very big."

"No, Highness, she's not," the master shipwright agreed. "Including her castles, she's only seventy-three feet long. The castles are those bits that rise above the main deck," he added, when both queen and consort turned confused expressions toward him. "She's got a twenty-one-inch beam over all and an air draft of seventy-one feet including her topsail. But she'll carry 2,360 square feet of sail when she's fully rigged, and you won't find a better bark in these yards."

Head swimming with nautical terms he barely understood, Otavas glanced down at Jelena. Although he suspected she understood no more of the description than he did, she was staring at the *Starfarer* with shining eyes, one hand stretched out as though to close the distance between them. He quickly suppressed a disquieting hint of jealousy, reminding himself that this visit had been his idea.

"I think she's beautiful."

"Thank you, Majesty." The master shipwright beamed proudly up at the hull, one scarred hand holding blowing hair back off his face. "I think so, too."

*   *   *

"So you've decided on a captain?"

"Lija i' Ales a'Berngards."

Otavas rested a thigh on the corner of the queen's desk and leaned across it until he could read the papers spread in front of her. "The merchant captain?"

Jelena studied his profile, a little confused by the smile in his voice. "That's right."

"Lord Dumin will be disappointed." Otavas and Dumin i'Janina a'Vasil, Lord High Commander of the Shkoden Navy had disliked each other on sight. Fully aware that Dumin considered him not only feckless but dangerously foreign, the prince thought the Lord High Commander a self-righteous, pompous, old *harnivatayger*—which had no direct Shkoden translation although a number of the younger bards were cheerfully working on it. While he wouldn't go so far as to wish the older man an injury, he wasn't above enjoying his disappointment. "He wanted you to chose a navy captain."

It suddenly became clear why Otavas found her choice amusing. "Yes, well, I wanted a captain who actually wanted to go on this voyage; not one encouraged to volunteer by Lord Dumin." Leaning back in her chair, Jelena twisted the royal signet around her finger. It had been sized to fit her just after her mother's death, but she'd lost so much weight during those dark quarters that only her knuckle kept her from losing it with every movement of her hand. "I didn't expect hundreds of volunteers—successful captains are seldom reckless captains—but neither did I expect to have so few to choose from. Fewer still after subtracting Dumin's politically motivated suggestions. And do you know why?"

Although he did know—at least he knew what Jelena believed—Otavas obediently shook his head, realizing that she was going to say it again regardless.

"Kovar," she declared, eyes narrowing. "There've been no songs wondering what might be over the next wave, no songs extolling the adventure of discovery. There've been no songs about this voyage at all, and the people of Shkoder know very well what that means. Kovar is against the idea, and the bards take their cue from him."

"And you can't tell the bards what to sing . . ."

"Or I'll be spending the rest of my life wondering about every new piece of information—is it the truth or is it what the bards think I want to hear?" Shoving back her chair, she surged to her feet and brandished a sheaf of maps at her grinning consort. "I don't care what that narrow-minded old man thinks, the *Starfarer* will find the homeland of the dark sailor, and when she comes back with proof, I hope he'll enjoy eating his words. And if she doesn't find the dark sailor's homeland, then she'll just keep going west until she lands in the silklands in the east, giving the Fienian traders the surprise of their lives and proving once and for all that the world is round. And Kovar can eat that, too." Pausing for breath, she finally noticed Otavas' expression. "What are you smiling about?"

He swung himself over the desk and scooped her into his arms. "I'm just happy to see you like this. Alive. Questioning. It's exciting." Pushing the maps aside, he drew her close. "I'm thinking," he murmured against her ear, "that maybe we should go on our own voyage of discovery."

Her eyes widened, then slid nearly closed as he took her earlobe between his teeth. "And discover what?" she sighed.

"Why not the center of the Circle?"

"Tavas!" But her protest at his irreligious comment carried little force. She arched her back as he unfastened the bottom three buttons on her tunic and slid a hand in under the outer layer of wool. "Now?"

"Now."

"Here?"

"Why not?"

The maps fell unheeded to the floor.

A familiar knock froze them in place.

One hand fumbling with Otavas' belt, the other entwined in his hair, Jelena turned scarlet and forced her voice into something resembling normal tones. "I'm busy, Nikki."

"Begging Your Majesty's pardon," the page's voice came muffled but audible through the heavy door, "but you asked me to remind you about that meeting with Lord Brencis and Lady Hermina. They're waiting for you in the small audience chamber."

"Tavas . . ."

"I know." He released her and stepped back so she could fix her clothing. "But it's lucky for you," he added, with a leer, "that I was raised to recognize the responsibilities of royalty."

Smiling distractedly, Jelena tucked her shirt back into her waistband. "Lord Brencis and Lady Hermina were instrumental in convincing the Council to agree to fund the *Starfarer* and her crew."

"Were they?" he asked softly, reaching out to fasten the buttons he'd undone. "In my opinion, the Council was so happy you'd found yourself again, they'd have agreed to almost anything you asked."

"Perhaps." Her fingers closed over his for a moment then she hurried toward the door. "But Lord Brencis and Lady Hermina were *perceived* as being instrumental, and you know as well as I do that needs a perceived response."

Laughing at her sudden descent into politics, Otavas blew her a kiss and began to fasten various buttons and ties of his own. He'd always known she'd be a wonderful queen, and now that they'd gotten through those four horrible quarters of grief and guilt, he was relieved to see he'd been right all along.

He only hoped she could come to an understanding with the Bardic Hall. Eight years in his adopted country had taught him that, eventually, everything in Shkoder came back to the bards.

Benedikt was at the Bardic Hall in Vidor before he heard the details about his captain's disagreement with the queen.

"Well, I wouldn't go so far as to say it was a disagreement," murmured Edite, the new lieutenant, leading the way into her office and motioning for Benedikt to sit. "Of course Kovar disapproves of this voyage, but he'd never go so far as to disagree publicly with the queen."

Arms folded over his quintara case—held shieldlike on his lap—Benedikt frowned. "What do you mean, of course?"

"We're a small country," she told him sharply, "surrounded by larger countries. Our attention must remain focused on the situation here at home, not on chasing some wild melody out over the sea."

"What situation here at home?" This was just one of the

many reasons why he hated not being able to Sing air. Every bard in the country knew what he didn't. There certainly hadn't been a situation back when he'd left Pjazef. Unless Pjazef knew something he wasn't telling. There *had* been a guarded tone to the older bard's voice.

"Benedikt?"

Jerked out of memory, he focused on Edite's face only to see an expression of impatient disapproval.

"When you ask a question, you should, at least, attempt to pay attention to the answer."

"Sorry."

"Yes, well. I said, the situation in Shkoder is the same as it has always been." She leaned back, hands clasped under the prominent shelf of her breasts. "If we allow our strength to be bled away . . ."

"I hardly think one ship will bleed much of anything away," Benedikt protested.

"One ship is where it starts. Where does it end?" Her dark eyes narrowed. "One bard lost is one bard too many; we're all part of the pattern that keeps the country strong."

Pjazef had used that exact line and, his memory prodded by repetition, Benedikt now knew where it came from. As Bardic Captain, Kovar had taught every fledgling since Liene had passed over the title a dozen years ago. Although Benedikt now remembered the lesson, it seemed to have had less effect on him than on the others. He could think of only one reason, only one way he was different. "Do all the bards think like you do?"

"Well, I certainly can't say that I know what *all* the bards think, but those who've Walked out of Vidor since First Quarter Festival have no intention of supporting the queen's fancy."

"Isn't that treason?" Behind what he hoped was an expressionless mask, Benedikt worked at pulling all the bits and pieces into a recognizable tune. Edite had been appointed to her position by Kovar. Although his choice for the lieutenant's position in Vidor had been limited to those bards who Sang all four quarters, would he have chosen Edite if she hadn't supported his views?

"I hardly think it's treason to have a different opinion than the queen."

"What about acting opposite to the queen's desires?"

"We do not act opposite to the queen's desires. We merely keep our mouths shut."

Edite's tone suggested that the discussion was over and she backed it up by rising and nodding toward the door.

Too angry for caution, Benedikt paused, half over the threshold and without turning, threw one last protest back over his shoulder. "When bards keep their mouths shut, it *is* an action."

Later that evening, in the largest ale house in Vidor, Benedikt took his quintara out of her case, wiped damp palms against his thighs, tried not to think of how many eyes, how many ears, were on him, and sang "The Dark Sailor."

The queen had remembered him, had acknowledged his work, had put her trust, her life in his Song.

He would not join this conspiracy of silence against her.

By the time he sought his bed, he'd sung the haunting ballad in three more ale houses and to a group of Riverfolk down by the docks. Although he couldn't see the air kigh swooping around his head, the night had become distinctly breezy by the final chorus.

The next morning, fingers white around the handle of his instrument case, he managed to look Edite in the eye and calmly say, "Am I not as entitled to have a different opinion to the Bardic Captain as he is to have a different opinion to the queen?"

"You don't Sing air," Edite told him sharply. "You don't know what other bards are thinking."

It was the first time any of them had ever come right out and said it. He only Sang water. He wasn't as good as the rest of them. Well, bugger them, too.

"I don't Sing air," he snarled, "so I think for myself."

He carried the look on Edite's face with him from the room—eyes wide, mouth opening and closing, she looked like a fish out of water. And if he'd alienated the people he had to spend the rest of his life with, well, he didn't Sing air, did he, so how would he know?

The anger prodded him to sing "The Dark Sailor" in every inn along the River Road.

Tadeus ran into an old friend on his way to the River Maiden so, what with one thing and another—mostly

another—it was late evening by the time he arrived at the
inn. Stomach growling, guided as much by his nose as by
the kigh, he hurried across the landward yard toward the
closest entrance.

"Fried fish and potatoes. Fresh fiddleheads in butter.
And, if I'm lucky," he told the breeze by his cheek, "stewed
pears in custard."

One foot on the porch step, he stopped and cocked his
head, a pair of breezes dancing through the silvered curls
above his ears. There was a bard already inside and he
was about to sing. When the kigh told him which bard, he
whistled softly.

That changed things. The River Maiden had long been
one of Tadeus' favorite inns, and he'd long been a favorite
of the inn's regulars—his sudden appearance would pull
attention away from the younger bard. That kind of grand-
standing would be rude at the best of times. Tadeus wasn't
sure what it might be called in these particular times.

*"In spite of everything I tried during his training, Benedikt
has hung on tightly to his feelings of inadequacy."* Magda's
shrug had admitted a weary defeat. *"But Benedikt is the
queen's choice and I don't even want to consider what will
happen should Kovar convince him not to go on this
voyage."*

Padding noiselessly across the porch, he cracked open
one of the double doors and slipped into the broad hall
that ran the width of the building. Designed to keep Fourth
Quarter winds from blowing in on the paying customers, it
held a number of pegs for wet weather gear and a Bard's
Closet tucked under a locked flight of stairs.

The noise from the common room masked any sound he
may have made as he crossed the hall and quietly Sang the
notes to open the closet door. Sifting the din into its com-
ponent conversations, he smiled as he shrugged out of his
jacket and lifted his harp free of her case. Word had spread
that there was a bard at the River Maiden and the room
was full. Good. The night's performances would deserve a
full house.

As a quick run of notes from the strings of a quintara
commanded something approximating silence, he moved to
a shadow just outside the archway leading into the common

room—a position that should keep him hidden if the bard by the fire happened to glance his way.

"The Dark Sailor" was a ballad, tied to the rhythms of the sea. Tadeus had never heard it sung as a defiant anthem before, and he wasn't entirely certain it was suited to the role. Not that it mattered. When a bard sang the way young Benedikt was singing, lyric and melody both were only the framework of the greater Song.

Defiance.

I am as good as any of you.
You can't tell me what to sing.
I stand by the queen.
So there.

Sifting the room for reaction, Tadeus grinned. Benedikt was young and handsome with a fine, strong, and, more importantly, bardic baritone. He could've sung the menu and still gotten an appreciative response from most of this audience—a trick Tadeus himself had tried successfully a time or two in the past. But if Benedikt wanted to do more than merely air personal grievances—if, say, he wanted to influence public opinion, to drum up support for the queen's voyage—he was going to need a little help.

In the moment between the applause and the next song, Tadeus stepped out into the light.

"Tadeus!"

The weight of the crowd's attention moving from him was almost a physical sensation, and its sudden absence brought on relief so overwhelming Benedikt felt nauseated. Swallowing convulsively, he stopped fiddling with strings that were already perfectly tuned and looked, with everyone else, toward the back of the room.

In spite of everything, he couldn't prevent a smile. The old bard certainly knew how to make an entrance. Dressed in spotless black, silver hair above the scarf over his eyes, silver buttons down the front of a velvet vest, one huge silver ring on the first finger of his right hand, he was the epitome of elegance and wouldn't have looked out of place at Court. Glancing down at his own travel-stained clothing, Benedikt scraped at a bit of mud with his thumbnail and wondered how Tadeus managed to keep so clean on a First Quarter walk when he couldn't even see the puddles to avoid them.

As the welcome rose to a crescendo, Tadeus bowed and moved slowly toward the fire. Crossing a crowded room was something he enjoyed doing, and he saw no need to hurry—after all, a blind man saw through his fingertips.

Laughing, he turned down several offers of company, one or two gratifyingly explicit, and stopped an arm's reach from Benedikt, bestowing upon the younger man the full force of his smile.

"May I join you?"

Confused, Benedikt nodded, realized what he was doing and said, "You can't stop me from singing 'The Dark Sailor.' "

"Of course I can't." Reaching behind him, Tadeus pulled a chair to the fireside and sat, arranging his harp on his lap. "You just sang it."

With a worried glance at the nearest tables, Benedikt pitched his voice for Tadeus' ears alone. "Then why are you here?"

"I always stop at the River Maiden on my way to Vidor." Frowning at the tone of a string, he reached into his vest pocket for his harp key. "You're causing quite a stir, you know. Most of the other bards think you've got a chip on your shoulder the size of the Citadel. That you're deliberately causing trouble. Unfortunately, this is an opinion shared by bards who would otherwise support your position."

The younger man stiffened. "I don't care what most of the other bards think."

"I know. You haven't exactly gone out of your way to make friends. Now, personally, I think that a bard, any bard, should be able to sing anything that doesn't contravene our oaths and that each of us have as much right to an opinion as our illustrious Bardic Captain."

"That," Benedikt muttered, "is not what our illustrious Bardic Captain thinks."

"If we're entitled to our opinion, Kovar's equally entitled to his. No matter how irritating, shortsighted, unimaginative, commonplace, provoking, and tiresome it might be."

Which was more or less what he'd said to Edite back in Vidor. Minus a bit of description. Benedikt's heart began to pound so loudly he could barely hear himself speak. He hadn't realized how good it would feel to have an ally. "*We're* entitled?"

Satisfied with his tuning, Tadeus tucked the key away and lightly ran his thumbnail over the strings. "I assume you know 'Search Beyond Tomorrow'?"

"Well, sure, but it's . . ."

"One of those feel-good songs everyone in this room probably knows." He turned his head, and Benedikt had the strangest feeling that the blind eyes were looking right at him. "It's a song about being open to new possibilities. When you're trying to change someone's mind," he added with a sudden grin, "it's always best to begin on common ground."

"It was different under Liene," Tadeus murmured into the darkness of the loft.

Benedikt turned toward the other bard's voice. "Different how?"

"You've heard it said that Bardic Captains don't command, they conduct?"

"Of course."

"Liene encouraged our individual strengths and expected us to do what we thought was right. While she quite often felt she knew best, she never tried to impose her opinions on the whole. She conducted a complex melodic line during her years as Bardic Captain."

"Are you sure that's not just wishful thinking about the good old days?" Benedikt muttered, punching his pillow. "All the elders in my village insisted the fish had fewer bones when they were young." Then he realized how that might be interpreted and winced.

"Age," Tadeus said dryly, "gives perspective. Kovar sees us as a group and wants to forge a group identity."

"We're all part of the pattern."

"So he keeps saying. But I'm afraid he only sees the pattern, not the parts. He's always been the cautious type, and now he's trying to make us all as cautious as he is."

Benedikt rolled over onto his back and stared up at the night. "Not all of us."

"No. Not all of us." Dry became positively desiccated. "If I wasn't so old . . ." Tadeus laughed as Benedikt mumbled an apology and went on in a lighter tone. ". . . and if I Sang water, I'd be going with you. Excitement, adventure, new lands, new people . . ." He rolled the list off his tongue. ". . . new songs."

"I'm not going for a song." At the other end of the loft, someone began to snore and was quickly silenced by a thrown boot, the tone and timbre of the thud unmistakable to bardic ears. Beside him in the Bard's Corner, Benedikt could hear only the silken whisper of Tadeus' breathing, could feel him waiting patiently for the rest of the answer. Before Benedikt could stop it, the past, so long pressed into dark corners, began to spill from his mouth.

"I was nine years younger than my closest brother—there were three of them—Pavel, Dusan, Nikulas—then me. I spent my entire childhood trying to catch up and never being quite good enough. They could do so many things that I couldn't. They were natural sailors, all three of them, right from the time they could walk, Nikulas a little younger even than that, if the stories were true. And they weren't just great sailors, they had an amazing affinity for fish. Any boat my brothers crewed came back riding so low in the water a fly landing too heavily would swamp it. You can imagine how popular they were in a village totally at the mercy of the sea.

"By the time I was old enough to go out, Pavel and Dusan had their own boat and there was only Nikulas left to spread the bounty among the fleet. You see, until they'd saved enough to go out on their own, Mother kept them rotating between the boats so no one boat had the advantage. My father was the village factor, and my mother's planning provided a solid power base for him to work from.

"They all expected to gain as much from me as they had from my bothers, but the first time I crewed, the boat nearly sank beneath me." He could still remember the gray swells, growing, rising, the fishing boat thrown from crest to trough as though caught between the paws of a watery cat. More confused than afraid, unable to concentrate on the tasks at hand, he'd lost an oar overboard, tangled the anchor line almost beyond salvaging, and had driven a triple hook deep into the ball of his foot. "Subsequent trips were worse, if anything, and finally the entire village decided I was a jinx. After the second time an abnormally high tide wiped out the drying racks, I wasn't even allowed to work on the beach. My father would've taken me with him, but the others were afraid I'd jinx his trading."

A familiar hand reached out of memory to stroke his hair. *"Sorry, son. Do you understand why you can't go?"*

Of course he'd understood. Did understand. His father had sided with the village. Against him. Although they were *all* very sorry for him, of course, and they always found him work to do far away from the water.

"You do understand why the sea behaved the way it did?" Tadeus asked softly.

Blankets clutched in damp fists, Benedikt realized he didn't have to answer this new question—the compulsion forcing his disclosure had passed. But once again Tadeus was waiting and, somehow, that seemed to be reason enough. "Karlene explained about the kigh when she tested me, how my talent attracted them."

"I hope she explained that only a very powerful talent would cause the kigh to show such an interest before your voice changed."

"Don't worry, she explained it all and everyone was very impressed." He paused to enjoy the memory of his moment in the center of the Circle and laughed bitterly at how quickly it passed. "They were impressed until they found out that I could only Sing water."

"I see."

"See what?"

"You're sailing into the unknown in order to prove something to all those people who don't think you're good enough."

"I am not." Drawing in a deep breath, Benedikt cursed himself for picking the scabs off his past. "If you must know, I volunteered because Her Majesty believes in me."

"When no one else did?"

"No!" The silence reminded him that bards can hear a lie. But he'd heard it himself, he didn't actually need reminding. "If I Sang air . . ." And then he remembered. "If I Sang air," he repeated smugly, "I'd be just another one of Kovar's drones."

"What are you talking about?"

It was the first time he'd ever heard Tadeus sound unsure. He wondered if it was the first time anyone had ever

heard Tadeus sound unsure. "You said that Kovar's trying
to make us all as cautious as he is. He teaches caution to
the fledglings, and after they start Walking, he keeps at it
with the air kigh. I don't Sing air, so I didn't get the reinforcement. He hasn't conditioned me to sing the same song
as the rest of you."

Bedding whispered as Tadeus shifted on his pallet. "Do
you have proof of this?"

"You Sing air. How often does he tell you to be careful?
How many of the bards he trained have volunteered for
this voyage? Only me. Because I don't Sing air."

"I think that's a tad simplistic. . . ."

"You would. *You* Sing air."

"Do try to remember who your friends are."

The edge beneath Tadeus' gently chiding tone cut
through his confidence and Benedikt felt himself deflate.
"I'm sorry. I didn't mean . . ."

"Yes, you did, but I accept your apology. And I admit
you may have a point."

"Well, thank you very much," Benedikt muttered.

"Don't sulk, Benedikt. It's quite unattractive." After a
moment, he added, "Are you sure you're not going on this
voyage to prove to Kovar he can't push you around?"

"No. Maybe. I don't know." Benedikt sighed and laced
his fingers behind his head. "You're beginning to sound
like Magda."

"Which reminds me, she wants to see you as soon as you
get back to the Citadel. She wants to impress on you how
important your going on this expedition is to the queen,
and, given Her Majesty's recent state of mind, how important it is you don't allow Kovar to talk you out of going."

He'd been trying not to think of what would happen
when he got back to the Citadel. "The queen believes in
me. I won't let her down."

"It might be better if you believed more in yourself."

"It might be better if you two shut up!" growled a voice
from the other end of the loft.

Tadeus rose up on his elbows, head cocked to pinpoint
the speaker. "Loomic? You shouldn't be able to hear us."

"Yeah? Then you oughta pay more unenclosed attention
'cause I can hear about one word in ten. Buzz, buzz, buzz;

voyage. Murmur, murmur, murmur; prove. Mutter, mutter, mutter; might be better. It's driving me nuts!"

"I've always said you had a touch of bardic talent. . . ."

"I don't give a crap about bardic talent, Tadeus. Not now. It's the middle of the unenclosed night, and *I've* got to do a full day's work tomorrow, unlike some decorative bits of fluff."

"Perhaps we'd best call it a night," Tadeus admitted, dropping his voice directly into Benedikt's ear. "Good night, Benedikt. Good dreams."

"It might be better if you believed more in yourself." Did he want to continue the argument past that point? "Good dreams, Tadeus." A few minutes later, he frowned. "Tadeus? Did Magda send you all the way out here to find me?"

"She might have."

"Pushy."

"Tell me about it. She gets it from her mother."

The boot bounced twice on the floor between them.

"What part of shut up do you two not understand?"

Next morning, the two bards walked together to the road and paused. Tadeus was heading east to Vidor, Benedikt west to Elbasan.

"I doubt I'll see you again before *Starfarer* sails," Tadeus said, rain beading on the waxed leather mask tied over his eyes, "so I'm going to gift you with my advice. Keep singing 'The Dark Sailor' if you want to, but remember that when you do, you're invoking a desperate desire for home, not a sense of adventure. If you're trying to change people's opinions about this voyage, you'll have more luck if you engage their hearts, if you get them to wonder about what's over the horizon." He grinned suddenly. "If, however, you're just trying to overwind Kovar's strings, then carry on as you were."

Benedikt protected his eyes with a hand as Tadeus' hood billowed out against the direction of the wind and the rain began to fall every way but down. "He seems angry enough now."

"What, this?" A quick four notes and the air around them stilled. "That wasn't Kovar. I'm heading for Ohrid and Annice seems to think I'm part packhorse. At least once a day she comes up with new lists of things I should bring with me. I'd ignore her, but I have no real desire to have her change the weather patterns over half the country." As a light breeze touched Benedikt's worried frown, Tadeus sighed. "I'm kidding. And now, as we've both got a long, wet walk before us, I suggest we say good-bye and get started." Reaching out, he gripped the younger man by the shoulders. "One last bit of advice; you're a bard now, Benedikt, let the past go."

"Concentrate on what I can do, not on what I can't." Benedikt snorted and stepped back. "Easy to say when you can do what I can't."

One ebony brow rose above the mask. "I was under the impression that, at the moment, you were proud of not Singing air, proud to stand apart from Kovar's caution."

"Well, yeah, but . . ."

"No buts." He held out his fist. "Good journey, Benedikt. Bring me back something nice."

"Bring you back . . . ? Oh. Right. Sure. Good journey, Tadeus."

As he turned into the angle of the rain, he tried to decide how he felt about having Tadeus' company in his rebellion. He was defying Kovar to go on this voyage because the queen believed in him; Tadeus would have gone for a song. *It's easy for Tadeus, he Sings air. He doesn't know what it's like not to be able to do something every other bard takes for granted.*

Three days later, with the smoke from Elbasan's chimneys smudging the evening sky behind him, Benedikt stood in the shipyard and stared at the *Starfarer*. She'd been painted pale blue and cream, the castles trimmed in a darker blue, and it seemed as though half a hundred pennants flew from every line.

"Beauty, ain't she?" said an admiring voice.

Shifting his pack, Benedikt turned.

"She's the best we ever built, I'm tellin' ya." Hands on her hips, the woman beside him kept her gaze locked on *Starfarer*. "Rides them waves so pretty you'd almost think she were Singin' the kigh."

There *was* a certain music in the way the water lapped against the painted wood, in the shump, shump of the heavy rope bumpers rubbed between the ship and the pier, in the dance of the pennants in the evening breeze. For the first time since Vidor, he felt a touch of the joy that had come with the news he'd been chosen.

"Yer sailin' on her, ain't ya?"

Surprised, he took a closer look at his companion. The leather apron streaked with tar and the sawdust in her close-cropped hair supported her statement that she worked at the shipyard. As far as he could recall, he'd never seen her before. "How could you tell?"

She smiled broadly enough to show a missing molar. "I know the look. You know 'When the Work is Done,' bard?"

"Of course I do."

"Then we should get along just fine." A callused fist thrust toward him. "Emilka i'Dasa. Call me Mila. I've signed on as ship's carpenter. I helped build her, so I figured I'd best make sure she makes it home."

"Benedikt." He touched his fist to the top of hers. "What look?"

"Say again?"

"You said you knew I was going because you knew the look. What look?"

Mila laughed. "We get a lot down here lookin' at her. Some of 'em, they look all disapprovin', faces scrunched up like an old apple, like they think we're wastin' time and money even buildin' her. Some of 'em, usually them that's too old or too young, look kinda wistful, like they can see the adventure but they know it's not for them. And a very few folk, the ones that're goin', they smile and their eyebrows kinda dip down in the middle like they're thinkin' . . ." She paused, caught Benedikt's eye, and turned his gaze back toward the ship. "They're thinkin' about all that water out there and they're thinkin', *I thought she'd be bigger.*"

Benedikt slipped into the Citadel through the Bard's Door and rolled his eyes as the notes of his name activated the message Kovar had left for him. All bards saw the

Bardic Captain as soon as possible after returning from a Walk; did Kovar think that he'd rebelled so thoroughly he wouldn't bother?

With good weather sending every able-bodied bard out into the country, the Hall was nearly empty. Even the year's two fledglings were gone, no doubt taking a short Walk up coast with Petrolis who thoroughly enjoyed teaching starry-eyed teenagers the more mundane aspects of their new lives. In Benedikt's opinion, for a bard who didn't Sing earth, Petrolis was just a little fanatical about latrine pits.

He saw no one as he made his way up to the second floor although he could hear the faint sound of a flute from somewhere up above. When the same three or four bars were repeated with minor variations, he suspected the song was a work in progress. It was a catchy tune and he hummed it softly as he went into his room.

In an effort to fight off the cold and damp, servers lit fires in the unoccupied rooms at the new moon and the full. Unfortunately, neither the occasional fire nor the bowls of dried mint could keep a place from smelling musty when it had remained essentially empty for a full quarter. Nose wrinkled, moving carefully in the near dark, Benedikt crossed to the window and opened the inner shutters.

Somehow, the room looked as abandoned as it smelled even though it looked very little different from when he was actually living in it. Shrugging out of his pack, he unbuckled his instrument case and paused, about to lift it up onto the small table. There was a slate propped up on the shell he used as a catchall dish. Someone had come into his room while he was gone and left him a note.

In case Tadeus missed you, it read, *please see me before you speak to Kovar.* It was signed, Magda.

"Does a healer outrank a Bardic Captain?" Benedikt wondered, smudging the chalk lines with his thumb. As a fledgling, he'd had significantly more long talks with Magda than the others. The talks had been intended to convince him that his lack of air made him no less a bard than the rest, but the mere fact that they'd singled him out for reassurance had shown him what they really thought.

Magda could only want to talk to him now about the queen's voyage. He knew what Kovar was likely to say, and he had no real desire to test his resolve against the full orchestration of the captain's opinion; therefore, it only made sense to begin defending his decision at the Healers' Hall.

Besides, from what Tadeus had said, Magda was likely to be on his side.

A quick wash and a change of clothes later, he started across the Citadel's outer courtyard. It seemed unlikely that Kovar would have the kigh watching for him, but since something as simple as a glance out a window could still give him away, he moved quickly.

"Benedikt!"

Not quickly enough. He turned to see Kovar hurrying across the cobblestones, looking distinctly displeased. Unfortunately, in direct confrontation, a healer did not outrank a Bardic Captain. He waited, shifting his weight from foot to foot as Kovar closed the distance between them, quartered robes whipping around his ankles like angry, multicolored cats.

An arm's reach away, closer than Benedikt would have liked, he stopped. "Are you unwell?"

"Unwell?" Benedikt repeated, confused. Expecting some kind of accusation, the question took him by surprise. Then he realized—in another three strides he'd be climbing the steps to the Healers' Hall. "No, I'm fine."

"I see." Kovar's tone suggested this answer came as no surprise. "Did you not get my message?"

Benedikt stiffened. "Of course I did."

"I wasn't suggesting you wouldn't understand it, Benedikt, I *was* wondering why you chose to ignore it."

"I'm not ignoring it."

The silence wondered why, then, he was going to the Healers' Hall.

"Magda wanted to see me." He hated how defensive he sounded and struggled for the voice control that should be second nature to a bard.

"Your responsibilities to the Bardic Hall should have brought you immediately to me. If you aren't sick, Magda can wait."

"Are you accusing me of ignoring my responsibilities?"

"Not out here," Kovar said pointedly and Benedikt suddenly became aware of the half-dozen guards over by the stable and the multitude of windows overhead. "Whatever our differences, we will not end up brawling like a couple of riverboat pilots out in public."

If he became recognized as the bard going on the queen's voyage, any argument would begin to attract attention. One or two of the guards were already looking their way. The thought of attracting a crowd, of a face staring down at him from every one of those windows, from the Bardic Hall, from the Healers' Hall, from the Palace, made Benedikt's palms itch.

Stepping to one side, Kovar half turned back the way he'd come. "Shall we discuss this in my office?"

He could say no. Say no and walk right into the Healers' Hall. But as much as he despised himself for it, he didn't have the courage. To walk away from Kovar now would turn a difference of opinion into something much more significant.

He nodded and fell into step beside the Bardic Captain. It was likely to be an unpleasant interview and he couldn't blame himself for trying to postpone it. *If Magda's as concerned about the queen as Tadeus thinks, why isn't she out here supporting me?*

"Benedikt?"

The high-pitched voice turned both bards around.

The page slid to a stop and grinned up at Benedikt, panting slightly. "Her Majesty would like to see you."

"Tell Her Majesty he'll be up momentarily."

An indignant gaze lifted to Kovar's face and thin arms crossed over royal livery. "Her Majesty wants to see him *now.*"

"Her Majesty hasn't seen the Bardic Captain in ever so long," the page confided as they entered the Palace through one of the smaller, private doors. "She sees other bards and reads all the recalls and stuff, but she doesn't see him. She saw you cross the courtyard from upstairs and sent me to get you."

The queen herself had come to his rescue. Benedikt felt his mouth curve up into an idiotic smile he couldn't seem to stop.

"This way, follow me." Racing up the stairs, the page turned on the landing and stared mournfully down at

Benedikt. "I wish I was going on the *Starfarer* but they say I'm too young. I'm not."

"Of course you aren't."

Benedikt jumped, but the page merely turned as though Bannon appeared silently behind her all the time. Perhaps he did.

"Hi, Bannon. Where's His Highness?"

"You tell me."

Ignored for the moment, Benedikt realized that, in spite of an imposing presence, the Southerner wasn't significantly taller than the page he quizzed.

"Um, it's late afternoon, you're not with him . . ." Her face lit up. "He must still be meeting with Chancellor Cecilie."

"About?"

"The new Fienian ambassador."

"Correct." The minimal movement of his head was clearly a dismissal. "I'll take the bard from here."

"Her Majesty told me to get him." She folded her arms. "Did Her Majesty send *you?*"

Bannon smiled. "No."

After studying him for a moment—and Benedikt would've much to know if she saw threat or promise—she returned the ex-assassin's smile. "Okay, you can walk with him, and I'll go on ahead so I can announce you when you arrive, and if I get in trouble with the Page Master, you've got to get me out of it."

"Deal."

"Bard?"

It took a moment for Benedikt to realize what she wanted. "Oh. Witnessed."

As the page raced up the remaining stairs two at a time, Bannon motioned for Benedikt to join him on the landing. They took half a dozen steps in silence.

Benedikt could feel himself wanting to babble, to fill the stairwell with nonsense just to cover the drumming of his heart. He only wished he knew why. Perhaps it should have been fear, but it wasn't.

"This voyage is very important to Her Majesty."

Only a bardic ear could have detected the difference in Bannon's voice. To anyone else he would have sounded the same as when he'd been speaking with the page—friendly, unconcerned. Benedikt could hear the warning, but he couldn't think of a safe response.

"His Highness has said that the *Starfarer* has given Her Majesty back the self she lost in grief."

They climbed another three steps.

"Do you understand why I'm telling you this?"

"I think so." A step apart, they were eye to eye. Benedikt tried to look away and couldn't.

"Your captain has made his feelings on this clear—he disapproves of the trip but if the ship sails without his approval, he doesn't want a bard on board."

"I've already agreed to go."

"What happens if your captain gives you a direct order to stay?"

"It doesn't work like that."

"Then what if he tells you that your going will split the bards, make them less able to do their work, that you must respect his opinion, keep a united front for the sake of everything that makes a bard?"

"He wouldn't . . ." But looking into the gold-flecked eyes, Benedikt knew that Bannon was right. That was exactly what Kovar would do. Announcing a threat to the good of the many was his greatest power. "I don't know what I'd do."

Bannon cupped Benedikt's chin in his hand, fingers and thumb indenting the flesh along the jaw just on the edge of pain. "I do."

"You're not a bard." To disagree with Kovar was one thing. To place himself in opposition to what it meant to be a bard, that was something else entirely. "You don't know what it's like."

"And I don't care what it's like. If your captain shoves at you from one side, remember that I'm here, on the other."

His breathing a little ragged, Benedikt pulled away. "You can't threaten me."

Bannon's gaze followed him, expression unreadable. "Then call it support, you fool."

Bannon handed the bard back to the page outside the door to the queen's solar and continued on his way without a backward glance. Shoring up another's insecurities was a new experience for him but, with any luck, he'd managed to exert a force equal to that of the Bardic Captain, enough to keep Benedikt from collapsing under the weight of *being a bard*.

Bards. Everything in Shkoder came back to the bards. Right now, everything in Shkoder came back to Benedikt.

Absently rubbing the lingering warmth of Benedikt's skin on his fingertips, he sighed. All he could do was see to it that Her Majesty's choice got onto the boat. The rest of the slaughtering country would just have to work things out on its own.

"You've seen the *Starfarer?*"

"Yes, Majesty."

"What did you think?"

Remembering Mila, Benedikt smiled. *I thought she'd be bigger* was not the answer the queen was looking for, so he told her another truth. "I think she's beautiful, Majesty."

"Isn't she." Eyes gleaming, Jelena smiled down at her secretary. "Taska, have I got time to take the new Fienian ambassador down to see her tomorrow?"

"I'm sorry, Majesty, but no."

"Majesty, please . . ." Her tailor muttered his plea through a mouthful of pins. "If you keep moving, your hem . . ."

"My apologies." She stilled, and the tailor's assistant draped another piece of fabric over her shoulder. "What about after Council?"

"You're meeting with the Duc of Vidor, Majesty."

"Oh, well." Sighing philosophically, she turned her attention back to Benedikt. "You'll just have to sing him a song describing it."

"Yes, Majesty." But that wasn't the song he wanted to sing.

"This voyage has given her back the self she lost in grief."

The difference between this Jelena and the Jelena he'd Sung across the strait was like the difference between a running river and a stagnant pool. If he was all that stood between her and the loss of her joy, then Kovar could do his worst. He was insulted that everyone seemed to think he wouldn't be up to the responsibility.

"What is it, Benedikt? You're frowning."

"Am I? I beg your pardon, Majesty."

Risking another reprimand from her tailor, Jelena moved farther into the room. She liked the way he looked at her. He'd done it at Fort Kazpar and he was doing it again now. He made her feel worthy of the risk the *Starfarer*'s crew was about to take in her name. There were those on the Council who suggested it might be better if the *Starfarer* carried a bard able to Sing more than one quarter but, for the sake of that look, Jelena would not, could not, imagine any other bard in Benedikt's place. "His Highness and I will be going with you as far as the Broken Islands."

His Highness meant Bannon, and Bannon meant . . . Actually, Benedikt didn't know what Bannon meant; figuratively and literally most of the time. He resisted the urge to rub his jaw. "You honor us all, Majesty."

She laughed. "Carrying crowned ballast is hardly an honor." Her outstretched hand was a symbolic gesture, given tailors and secretaries and tailor's assistants there was no way to physically bridge the distance between them. "Thank you for volunteering, Benedikt. If I could have chosen any bard, I'd have chosen you."

Bards could hear the truth. At this moment, and he couldn't insist on any more than this moment, she meant what she said.

"Majesty, please . . ."

Murmuring apologies, Jelena allowed the tailor to place her back in the center of the low pedestal. "Could you sing me something, Benedikt? Something to keep me from moving and destroying Edgard's work."

He wanted to reassure her, to tell her that he wouldn't let her down, so he sang her "The Dark Sailor." Not the way he'd been singing it, as a protest, but as a gift. When he finished, she smiled down at him and said softly, "I don't want you to worry about anything Kovar says to you.

Later, in the Bardic Captain's office, during an interview that was just as unpleasant as he'd anticipated, where all the possibilities Bannon had suggested were thrown at him, Benedikt held on to the memory of the queen's smile, so almost everything Kovar said made no impression at all.

Almost.

"All right, Benedikt. If you won't consider the good of the bards, then consider the good of the *Starfarer*. You only

Sing water! Think man! What if a storm comes up or you need to send a kigh for help?"

"Then I'll Sing water. Or do you think they'll be worse off with me than with no bard at all?"

"That's not what I said."

"You didn't have to." Benedikt stood and stared down at the captain through narrowed eyes. "You want me to consider the bards? Well, how about this; by sending a bard on *Starfarer*, we support the queen and by sending me, we send the bard you can most afford to lose. As far as I can see, the bards win either way." Heart pounding, triumph making him feel like throwing up, he made it out of the office before Kovar could voice a protest.

Or agreement.

Four

MAGDA stood with two friends just off the end of the gangplank, their healer's sashes allowing them a prime position as well as protecting them from the rough jostling of the crowds. Behind them, the people of Elbasan packed the pier and the waterfront, personal opinions on the value of the voyage keeping no one from enjoying a warm, sunny day and a celebration paid for by the crown. In front of them, the gangplank length of empty pier away, the *Starfarer* bobbed gently on the light chop.

Supplies and trade goods had been loaded. The captain and crew were on board.

"What's taking so long?" Magda wondered, bouncing up and down. Not particularly tall, she couldn't see a thing when she turned except hundreds of other people, all waiting for the arrival of the queen and her consort.

"I can see the pennants!" Jerrad, one of the other healers, announced. "They've made it to Lower Dock Street."

A sudden rise in the volume of cheering toward the other end of the pier backed up his observation and the crowd began to rearrange itself into two crowds flanking a wide aisle. A curse and splash marked the spot where someone went off the edge and into the water. A moment later a man's voice yelled "He's okay!" and the healers relaxed.

"I can't believe you'd rather stand out here with us peasants than parade to the docks with the royal party," Jerrad shouted by Magda's ear.

She grinned and ducked as one end of a streamer escaped the hands holding it and flapped over her head. "What?" she yelled up at him, "And miss all this?"

Once it had been determined she wouldn't be going with them . . .

"Because no matter how it may have seemed over the last

four quarters, I'm not your personal healer. Johan is. He goes, Majesty; I stay and get some work done."

. . . personal good-byes had been said in the quiet of the royal apartments. As friend and cousin, she'd enthused with them over the possibilities unfolding and demanded that they bring her back a souvenir from the Broken Islands. As a healer, she'd kept her mouth shut. Jelena was healing; the idea of the voyage had brought her out of her grief, and Kovar's opposition to it had strengthened her hold on the crown. Grinning, Magda wondered if Kovar had any idea of how helpful he'd been.

"You look like a cat that's been into the cream," Jerrad told her. The streamer retrieved, they straightened.

"Are you surprised?" demanded their companion, one hand clutching her healer's sash as though afraid she might lose it. "She's surrounded by overstimulated kigh. Everyone who touches her is giving her a buzz. She'll be sizzling before this is over, you mark my words."

"Anzie!" Cheeks burning, Magda smacked Jerrad on the arm before he could add his quarter gull's worth. "That's not how it works!"

Anzeta's answer got lost in the roar of the crowd.

A pair of standard-bearers, each carrying the crowned ship of Shkoder over the symbols of the five principalities and the leaping dolphin of the Broken Islands, took up position at the bottom of the gangplank. They braced themselves as the silk banners, rising more than a bodylength over their heads, caught the offshore breeze and threatened to send them out to sea.

With everyone else craning for a first glimpse of the queen, Magda was the only one who saw their expressions of relief as the air around them, and only around them, suddenly stilled. As she'd seen no bards actually on the pier, she assumed Kovar was making himself useful from his place in the procession.

Four of the Queen's Ceremonial Guard, their long pikes topped with pennants similar to those flying from the *Starfarer*'s rigging, took up position just in from the standard bearers. Her view blocked by a broad shoulder clad in gleaming armor, Magda bumped her hip against Jerrad until he moved down far enough for her to see again. The guard, a young woman she knew by sight, was grinning.

Leaning forward, Magda aimed her voice at the edge of the ceremonial helmet. "Someone's going to get a strong laxative in her beer one of these nights." The grin vanished.

Her Majesty, Jelena, Queen of Shkoder, High Captain of the Broken Islands, Lord over the Mountain Principalities of Sibiu, Ohrid, Ajud, Bicaz, and Somes, looked terrific. Under her blue-and-cream travel clothes she remained a little thin, but her eyes sparkled and her cheeks were flushed with excitement. Magda felt as proud of the result as if she'd been personally responsible for it.

Two steps behind the queen, Otavas looked as incredible as he always did. He smiled and waved to the crowd as they called his name, but Magda could see that most of his attention was on Jelena and most of his joy was for hers.

Six or seven paces back, Bannon and Benedikt walked side by side.

His hands folded into white-knuckled fists by his thighs, Benedikt seemed to be doing his best to ignore the crowd. Magda could read his kigh from across the pier—she suspected she'd be able to read it from across the city. He loved the adulation. He was terrified of the possibility he might fail in front of so many.

Magda had to admit that, had it been her choice, she'd have chosen a more stable bard—by default, any other bard. On the other hand, it was quite clear that the queen's faith in him had done more for his self-esteem than she ever had.

Right at the moment, he was thinking that he should never have listened to her and should have boarded earlier with the crew; she could see it in his face.

Bannon's face, on the other hand, gave nothing away. As far as Magda knew, the possibility he might fail, at anything, had never entered Bannon's head. To her surprise, he suddenly looked directly at her and winked.

"Magda!" Anzeta followed the path of the wink and was astounded to see it answered. "You haven't! Have you?"

Magda put on her best healer-of-the-fifth-kigh expression. "What do you think?"

"I hate it when you do that."

Behind the ex-assassin and the bard, a careful distance back of the boarding party, walked four priests from the Center in the Citadel, the Marshal of Shkoder, most of the members of the Queen's Council, and the Bardic Captain. From the look of it, Kovar and Benedikt had never had as much in common as they did this morning—Kovar, too, was doing his best to ignore the crowds.

After that first disastrous interview, he hadn't spoken to the younger bard. *"Why should I, Magda? He doesn't listen to a word I say."*

Privately, Magda had very little sympathy for Kovar. Tadeus was right, he was attempting to make all the bards as cautious as he was himself, and it was frightening how well he'd succeeded. But he wasn't her patient, and it wasn't her business.

When the queen reached the top of the gangplank, the captain of the *Starfarer* stepped out to meet her, and the cheers of the crowds doubled in volume once more.

During their single meeting, Captain Lija i'Ales a'Berngards had gained Magda's full approval. She was a tall, thin, practical woman who dealt with difficult questions by first staring into the distance as though she could see the answers there. For all Magda knew, she could.

Magda had briefly met with all the members of the crew. Far from shore, sailing an unknown sea, was not the time to discover that one of the people confined on a tiny island of wood had a less than healthy kigh.

With queen, consort, and captain at the rail, Benedikt paused halfway between ship and pier, wet his lips, and raised his hands. By the time he spoke, there was silence enough for him to be heard.

"Shkoder's Throne," he said simply, and began to sing.

The sound of the anthem crashed over Magda like heavy surf, and she threw herself joyfully into it, adding her own voice to the din. She'd heard it sung better but never louder; the crowd on the left side of the pier seemed to be trying to drown out the crowd on the right.

On the *Starfarer,* the flag of Shkoder rose to the top of the mainmast, caught the breeze, and spread the crowned ship out against an azure sky. Jelena was smiling so broadly, Magda suspected her cheeks would hurt for the remainder of the voyage.

As the last line of the anthem deteriorated into screams of approval, Benedikt, looking a little battered by the volume, hurried the rest of the way up onto the main deck.

The crew on board drew the gangplank in while crews standing by on the pier released the lines. The priests, tokens of the four quarters divided amongst them, stepped forward and enclosed both vessel and voyage in the blessing of the Circle.

Since the noise level made it unlikely that a kigh would respond, a pilot boat took the *Starfarer* out to mid channel where she and the two ships accompanying her as far as the Broken Islands swept out of the harbor on the ebbing tide. A little larger, the *Starfarer*'s companions carried the rest of the queen's company and would provide a way for her to return home.

"Almost makes me wish I'd volunteered," Jerrad murmured as they waited for the crowds to thin.

Anzeta poked him in the ribs. "They wouldn't have let you go. Those of us with the talent are too precious to risk."

"They let a bard go."

"That's different. Bards need to keep finding new songs. The last thing we need to find are new injuries. And speaking of bards—" She jerked her chin, and Magda turned, knowing what she'd see—she could feel the many prickly bits of his kigh jabbing into her.

"Magda." Kovar nodded at her and then past her at the others. "Jerrad and Anzeta, isn't it?"

"That's right." Grabbing Jerrad's arm, Anzeta tugged him around. He began a protest but stopped as he saw who'd joined them. "If you'll excuse us, we were just going to get something to eat. The smell coming up off that sausage cart made me hungry."

Magda nodded. She could see no polite way of dumping the Bardic Captain and going with her friends—the downside of position in the Citadel. "I'll see you back at the Hall, then."

"If they're actually going to eat one of those sausages," Kovar murmured as he watched them make their way down the pier, "they'd both better be very good healers."

"That's an unfair stereotype," Magda protested. "Perpetrated by bards and that stupid sausage song: *I bit into a sausage and found half a fly . . .* That can't have made you lot very popular with the street vendors."

"Actually, they said it improved their business. Not our intent I assure you." Hands tucked into the cuffs of his quartered robe, he turned to stare out into the harbor. "I sent Evicka along on the *Sand Hawk*." He nodded toward the distant sails. "That's the *Hawk* there on the left. Her Majesty seems to have forgotten that the crown never travels without a bard, and as she's determined to throw away the one she has with her now, she needed another for the trip back."

Gulls crying challenges over bits of garbage filled the pause.

"Her Majesty saw me for a moment yesterday. Do I have you to thank for the meeting?"

Magda shrugged. "I may have said something."

Try to see it from his position, Jelena. You spent four full quarters leaning on his knowledge and experience, seeking his advice on everything from foreign policy to replacing an old tunic then, suddenly, you're not listening to him at all. He feels tossed aside, abandoned. Is it any wonder he overreacted?

"I tried one last time to convince her not to send these people to their deaths. She accused me of overreacting and said I want to keep her dependent."

Magda winced.

"She said that I've asked the bards to choose between their queen and me. As though refusing to have any part of this fool voyage has anything to do with loyalty to the crown. I never heard anything so ridiculous in my life."

"And you told her so?"

"Of course I did."

She's no longer my patient, and he never was, Magda reminded herself. *This is none of my business. Pity I can't just knock their heads together.* "What *do* you want, Kovar?"

"I want to keep Shkoder safe, and to do that I need every available bard."

Reaching out, Magda laid her hand lightly on Kovar's arm. "Safe from what?" she asked softly.

Slowly, deliberately, he turned his head and stared down at her for a moment or two, lips pressed so tightly together they disappeared under the fringe of his moustache. Then

he shook himself free of her touch. "You wouldn't understand," he said, pivoted on a heel, and strode away down
the pier.

Magda watched him go, noting how the stragglers, still
standing about in groups of two or three, called out to him
as he passed. There *had* been a bard on board the *Starfarer,*
and Kovar *had* come down to the docks to give his support
to the sailing. For most of Elbasan, most of Shkoder, that
would lay to rest the rumors of a split between Her Majesty
and the Bardic Captain. Laying the substance of their disagreement to rest wouldn't be so easy.

"Safe from what?" she'd asked.

And under her touch, Kovar's kigh had answered, *"Change."*

Having insured that his instrument case was stored safely
below in the corner he'd claimed as his, Benedikt leaned
on the rail amidships and watched the shore slip away. All
around him, members of the crew tied off lines, stowed
last-minute supplies, and took care of the hundred-and-one
tasks that began every voyage—albeit a little self-
consciously under the fascinated gaze of queen and consort.

Leaving the bowl of the inner harbor behind, they soon
passed the last of the smaller, private docks. Not long after,
the land began to climb up onto the cliffs that edged the
harbor's throat, north and south, until they ended at the
Forts and the Bache ky Lamer, the Mouth of the Sea. The
rock face had just cut off his view of the land beyond when
a kigh lifted out of the water and passed on a message
from Evicka.

Are you excited?

He turned, saw her on the forecastle of the *Sand Hawk,*
and waved. During his second year as a fledgling, the healers had been forced to amputate her legs, and she'd been
confined pretty much to the Citadel ever since. It had been
her flute he'd heard his first night back. Nagged by Tadeus'
criticism—"You haven't exactly gone out of your way to
make friends"—he'd sought her out, ostensibly to learn the
new piece she was working on, actually to prove Tadeus
wrong.

Although philosophical about her loss, she'd been so excited at a chance to Walk on water as far as the Broken
Islands that the air kigh had broken two windows in the

Hall and a cistern had overflowed into the cellars the night Kovar had told her she was to go. But was *he* excited?

Not yet.

With a breeze from the wrong direction lifting the hair back off his forehead, Benedikt watched the kigh rise almost even with the *Hawk*'s deck to deliver his answer. He thought he heard Evicka laugh as she sent it back to him again.

Then look behind you.

Behind? He turned.

Standing barely an arm's reach away, his balance unaffected by the motion of the ship, Bannon smiled. "Trade secrets?"

"No, we just . . ." Suddenly realizing what the older bard had meant, he felt his cheeks burn, the heat not at all cooled by the breeze now blowing lazy circles around his head. "Um, excuse me for a moment." When Bannon gracefully indicated he should do what he felt had to, Benedikt turned, Sang briefly to the kigh, reinforced the Song because he knew Evicka'd be expecting a response, and sent it back to the other ship. Where it drenched her.

The breeze vanished.

"Why did you do that?" Bannon asked, leaning on the rail beside him.

"I don't Sing air." He shrugged and tried to keep from sounding defensive. "It was the only way I could get rid of the kigh buzzing around u . . . me."

"You don't think that was an extreme reaction?"

"No. Why?"

"That bard has no legs."

"So? She has a towel."

Taken by surprise, Bannon laughed aloud.

Benedikt relaxed at the sound—it came without the overt manipulations of the ex-assassin's smile and had no expectations he'd fail to live up to.

Still smiling, Bannon rested his weight on his forearms and, while appearing to watch the scenery, studied Benedikt's reflection in the water. It seemed that under the nerves and patchwork armor, Her Majesty's pet bard had a sense of humor to go with his pouty good looks. *It's three days to Pitesti; I wonder what else he's hiding . . .*

Finding out might be an amusing way to kill some time.

*   *   *

Approaching the Bache ky Lamer, *Starfarer* cut her way
through a river of liquid gold toward the center of the strait
and the point where the sun would touch the sea. Pennants
marked with a crimson circle were hoisted on all three ships
and the crews fell silent as Evicka and Benedikt Sang the
sunset. Their voices rose to fill the space between the cliffs—
first air and water alone then together for the Gloria.

In the pause that followed, Benedikt moistened his lips
and waited for Evicka, as senior, to begin the choral that
would take the place of the two missing quarters.

Instead, from Fort Kazpar, squatting gray and impenetrable to the North, came the unmistakable sound of Terezka's
soprano Singing fire. Spiraling down from the heights, it
seemed, on the deck of the *Starfarer,* as though the sun
itself was singing. When she finished, all three bards lifted
the Gloria again and, as the last note faded, a male voice
began to Sing earth from Fort Tunic.

Pjazef, Benedikt realized. Much younger than Terezka,
he didn't have the projection to bridge the distance across
the strait, but Singing earth that didn't really matter. The
cliffs themselves resonated to his Song.

All four quarters rose to close the Circle as the ships
slipped from between the cliffs and into the sea.

"All right you lot, look to those lines! We need to make
the Arrow Head before dark!"

Jolted from the lingering aftereffects of the Song by the
mate's bellow, Benedikt gripped the rail as *Starfarer* hit
heavier chop. Behind him, Evicka, Terezka, and Pjazef
would be exchanging news—although given the other two,
he somehow doubted Terezka would be able to get a kigh
in edgewise. For the first time since Vidor, he felt his lack
of air; felt excluded and a little lonely.

"Benedikt?"

He turned, careful of his balance, and bowed. "Majesty."
When he straightened, he noticed that her eyelashes were
clumped together in damp triangles. "Is something wrong?"

"No. Everything's right." Her smile trembled at the corners as though the emotions creating it were too great to
contain. "I've heard the sunset Sung a thousand times but
never like that. I've never felt so enclosed in the Circle, as

though I was a part of everything and everything was a part of me. Thank you."

"Recent research based on Karlene's experience with the fifth high has indicated that when the four quarters are Sung correctly, the fifth is evoked." But Kovar's lesson, learned way back in his first year as a fledgling, would be a dry and pedantic response to the queen's joy.

"You're welcome, Majesty." Benedikt returned her smile. "I'll tell Evicka, and she can pass your thanks on to the others."

Stepping forward into the curve of the bow, Jelena pressed herself against the rail. Wondering what he should do—there being very little between the queen and the sea—Benedikt glanced around for Bannon. He found the ex-assassin amidships, talking with Prince Otavas. Clearly no one who mattered thought the queen was in any danger with only a one-quarter bard by her side.

All at once Benedikt's tongue felt too big for his mouth, and he doubted he could Sing if he had to.

"I don't believe in omens," Jelena said quietly, unaware of the turmoil her trust had provoked. "I don't believe in things that can't be measured or proven. The dark sailor existed, so therefore his homeland exists, and I'm sending the *Starfarer* to find it. But what happened in the strait, two bards with the right quarters there at the right time, that seemed like an omen to me. Kovar would say, *Coincidence, Majesty, is a bard's stock in trade,* but if all things are enclosed in the Circle, can't coincidence be those things falling into place?" Eyes locked on the horizon, she drew in a deep breath of the salty air. "I choose to believe that Song was an omen—a good omen, the best of omens—and that *Starfarer* will succeed beyond our wildest dreams."

"We'll do it for you, Majesty," Benedikt told her. But he said it so softly, only the wind heard him.

That night, the three ships anchored in the lee of the Arrow Head, the huge outcrop of rock that marked the most eastward point of the Broken Islands. Although many captains of deep-keeled vessels risked the passage between the islands on moonlit nights, that wasn't a risk the captain

of *Starfarer* was willing to take, not with queen and consort
tucked up in her cabin.

As a quiet voice announced the first half quarter of the
fifth watch, Lija i'Ales climbed into a hammock slung in
with the mate and settled to sleep. There'd be plenty of
risk ahead. No need to tempt the sea.

Jelena's great-grandfather, King Mikus, had been the last
ruling monarch to visit the Broken Islands. It had been
near the start of his reign, and he'd come with enough ships
and troops to leave bearing the title, High Captain. As the
relationship, political and economic, had turned out to be
to the benefit of all parties, the title had remained comfortably with the crown of Shkoder. Both Jelena's grandfather,
King Theron, and her mother had made multiple visits
while they were heir. Jelena had been planning her first
trip when her mother died.

By the time the three ships reached Pitesti, and the deepest harbor in the islands, they'd acquired an accompanying
flotilla of smaller craft. With Evicka Singing all flags and
banners to their best advantage and Benedikt parting the
waves before the *Starfarer*'s bow, Jelena, Queen of
Shkoder, made an entrance worthy of her ancestors.

Although a massive rock jetty had been begun, ship's
boats were still the only way to land in Pitesti Harbor. As
Starfarer's boat approached the shore, it became obvious
that the entire Council had come to the gravel beach to
meet the queen.

"As well as every man, woman, and child on the island,"
Otavas noted.

"And a number of other islands as well, Highness." Eyes
narrowed, Bannon stared disapprovingly at the crowds. "So
many strangers puts you both in danger. If I may suggest,
you should both stay in the boat until your people have
gained a little more control."

Jelena laughed. "These *are* my people, Bannon. They're
not strangers, and there's no danger."

"Majesty . . ."

"Don't worry, Bannon. I'll have Benedikt Witness both
your objection and my refusal to listen to you. If anything

happens, it won't be your fault." Smiling broadly, she twisted around on her seat. "Benedikt?"

"Witnessed, Majesty." But as they drew close enough to pick out individual expressions, Benedikt began to wonder if perhaps Bannon wasn't right. Although everyone seemed excited, no one looked terribly happy. He turned and noted that her Majesty's six Ceremonial Guards, coming in on the boats from the other two ships, were too far back to do much guarding.

When the sailors shipped their oars in the shallows and leaped out to drag the boat the last few feet up onto the beach, an old woman moved out of the crowd and walked slowly forward. The staff she carried, carved with an entwined pattern of kelp and topped with a leaping dolphin, clearly had a ceremonial function although, as she leaned her negligible weight against it, it also worked well as a support.

Jelena stepped out onto the shore.

In the silence that fell, Benedikt could hear Evicka, about half a dozen boat lengths behind him, Singing softly.

"Jelena, Queen of Shkoder, High Captain of the Broken Islands . . ." Carried by kigh, the old woman's voice rang out over the harbor. ". . . are we, the people of the Broken Islands, of Shkoder or are we not?"

A gesture from Prince Otavas held Bannon where he was as Jelena answered. "You are."

"Then why have we been slighted so?" The staff lowered to point at the *Starfarer*. "You send a ship to seek the land of the dark sailor, and yet you ignore the best the sea has to offer. Why have none from the islands been asked to sail for you?"

Jelena spread her hands. "Why would I ask such a thing through emissaries? No. Captain Lija i'Ales a'Berngards has chosen only eighteen of the twenty in her crew, the other two she hopes to find here." Without pausing, she raised her voice and lifted her arms to shoulder height. "Are there two among you with heart enough to sail in search of the unknown?"

The roar from the crowd needed no help from the kigh to make itself heard. As the old woman handed the staff to a nearly equally old man and clasped Jelena in her arms,

Benedikt noticed a bicolored robe—blue and green, air and water—in the first line of islanders. It had to be Tomas, the senior of the two bards in the islands.

No doubt warned of his attention by the kigh, Tomas looked up and mimed wiping his brow.

The celebration lasted two days and watches were arranged so everyone on board the three ships could take part. On the morning of the third day, Captain Lija chose the final two members of the crew and then began the serious business of loading extra water casks and as much food as possible.

"Shouldn't you be down there helping?"

Snapped out of his reverie by Tomas' question, Benedikt straightened and turned. He'd been standing with his forearms on the peeled cedar rails that edged the rooftop deck of the combined Healer/Bardic Hall—a position he'd come to enjoy on board ship—watching the activity down in the harbor. "You know how we're all taught as children never to allow a bard to do anything you can do yourself?"

Tomas smiled. "I've always thought it's how we bards acquired our reputations—we're only ever asked to do the impossible. Or at least, the unlikely."

"Well, I was told in no uncertain terms that they knew what they were doing and didn't I have something bardic to take care of." He shrugged. "Her Majesty wanted me to give you my recall of the trip this far, so I thought now would be a good time. If you're available."

"Of course I am. Did you want to work out here?"

"If we could." Benedikt waved an enthusiastic hand out over the rail. "If I don't look down, it's almost as if I'm back at sea—blue above and blue below.

"Yes, well, you can be thankful you're not here in Fourth Quarter," Tomas muttered, frowning out at a passing cloud, "Then it's gray above and unenclosed cold down below. I'll go get my writing materials, and we can set up over there in the corner out of the wind."

As recalls went, it didn't take long. They could still hear the *Starfarer*'s mate shouting instructions down on the beach when Tomas brought Benedikt up out of his light trance and handed him a glass of honeyed tea for his throat. "That's one, then." He frowned down at the topmost page.

"Legible but not pretty, I'm afraid. Liene was always appalled by my penmanship. Do we pass this straight over to Her Majesty's secretary or give it to Evicka to take back to the Hall?"

Benedikt cradled the heavy glass in both hands. "Actually, Her Majesty wants you to copy it—there should be plenty of time before she sails. You're to keep the original and give the copy to her secretary."

"But . . ." Uncertain of just how exactly he'd intended to word his protest, Tomas settled for running both hands up through his thinning hair. "Did her Majesty say why?" he asked at last.

Surprised by how miserable he felt thrust back between the queen and the Bardic Captain, as though the three days they'd already sailed counted for nothing at all, Benedikt nodded. "She doesn't trust Kovar to deal fairly with the recalls from *Starfarer*."

Tomas' jaw dropped. Up until that moment, he'd considered the expression merely a figure of speech but there was his jaw, hanging loose. He snapped it shut. "Has it gone that far?"

"Apparently."

"I'm not saying Kovar doesn't have a point," Tomas muttered, "there's few enough of us for Shkoder . . ."

"So you don't think I should be going?"

The challenge in his tone lifted Tomas' brows. "I think you're a Walking bard and fully capable of making your own decisions," he said sharply, "And I think Kovar's forgotten that we were never intended to be a political entity. We Sing the kigh, we bring the people to each other, and anything beyond that is an individual concern."

Somewhat abashed, Benedikt plucked a leaf off a potted herb and rolled it between his fingers. If the scent released was supposed to be soothing, it wasn't doing much good. "The only high note in this whole mess is that by tomorrow's tide, it won't have anything to do with me."

By the time Imperial assassins made their move, they knew more about their targets than their targets knew about themselves. Ever since Benedikt had made him laugh on the *Starfarer*, Bannon had been observing the bard. It had been unexpectedly hard to keep his distance, but he had no intention of starting something—even something brief and physical—with a man so insecure and was actually a little appalled to find himself wanting to.

Amongst other things, he'd discovered that there were only three people in Pitesti Benedikt felt comfortable with. Evicka, who had no legs, and Tomas, who Sang only two quarters in a four-quarter position, he saw as handicapped as himself and relaxed around them. Her Majesty, whom he adored, he saw as the one person who didn't expect him to fail. Concentrating on his noble effort for the queen, he hadn't yet given a thought to the people he'd be sailing with.

"It ought to be an interesting trip."

Benedikt jerked around, wondering how anyone, even an ex-assassin could get that close to a bard on a pebble beach without being heard.

Reading the thought off the other man's face—not difficult as it was a reaction he often, and deliberately, evoked just for fun—Bannon grinned. "No second thoughts?"

Confused by the absence of edges in Bannon's smile, Benedikt shook his head. "Don't worry. I won't let Her Majesty down."

"Would it surprise you to find out that I'm not worried about that?" Impatience sharpened Bannon's tone. He'd asked an innocent question and had it treated like an accusation. Why was he even bothering? "No one is slaughtering worried about it except you."

"You *were*."

"The only way you could've let Her Majesty down was by not showing up." Smiling tightly, Bannon spread his hands. "And here you are."

They stood in silence for a moment.

Surprised and irritated by how easily Benedikt had taken him from amusement to annoyance, Bannon breathed in through his nose and out through his mouth, attempting to regain his equilibrium. Up until this moment, he'd thought only his sister could have that effect on him.

Benedikt's gaze flickered over the beach, the sky, a wheeling gull, and finally settled back on Bannon. It seemed that every time he turned around of late, the southerner was there in the background. *I think of him, and there he is.*

Every time.

"Why are you here?" he asked at last.

Wondering that himself, Bannon chose to answer the general rather than the specific. He turned and indicated the queen and her consort standing talking to Evicka and the eldest of the Pitesti Council by one of *Starfarer*'s boats. "Her Majesty and His Highness are going back out to the ship to address the entire company before you sail. Where they go, I go. Looks like you're not quite rid of me."

Wondering why he felt slightly cheated by that answer, Benedikt shrugged. "I'm not trying to get rid of you."

Their small section of the beach seemed suddenly, impossibly, silent.

After a moment, Bannon nodded. "Good."

Standing on the aft deck, looking past the crew gathered amidships, past the forecastle, the bow, and out of the harbor, Jelena gave half a moment's thought to ordering the anchor raised and *Starfarer*'s nose pointed out to sea. Exploring the unknown was her dream, had been her dream since the first night she'd stared through a distance viewer at the stars; she wanted to be there to share the discovery. *If I weren't queen* . . . She sighed. If she weren't queen, there would be no *Starfarer*. Nor would there be a *Starfarer* if she hadn't decided to *be* queen. Kovar would never have allowed it.

"You can't go with them, Lena." Otavas' breath lapped at her ear "Let's let them go."

She turned her head enough to smile into her consort's incredible eyes, unsurprised he'd know what she was thinking. Taking a deep breath, she held up a gold coin between thumb and forefinger. The crew below fell silent, all eyes locked on her hand.

"I have one of these for each of you; a gold Jelena." A little embarrassed still by the coin that bore her name, she ducked her head. The twenty men and women on the main deck murmured their approval and, looking up again, she smiled. "It is, of course, too small a reward for what you dare, and when you return, there will be many more." A pause while that received the anticipated reaction. "I want you to have these coins now," she continued after a moment, "for a purely selfish reason. When you see them, when you hold them, you'll think of me. In this small way, I can be a part of your adventure." She spread her arms. "May the Circle enclose you and protect you and bring you all safely back home."

For a heartbeat there was no sound at all.

The cheers that followed the silence were so loud they echoed back from the buildings of Pitesti.

To Bannon's horror, Jelena walked down the ladder to the deck and personally handed out the coins. Everyone, from the ship's jack to the captain had a moment with the queen before she left, a word and a gentle touch that would carry her with them more surely than any coin.

Finally standing by the rope ladder that led down to the boat and back to shore, she reached out with both hands and drew Benedikt to her. "You are my eyes and my ears, Benedikt." Stretching up, she kissed him on both cheeks. "I can't wait to hear the Songs you'll bring me."

Benedikt could only bow, his chest too tight for words.

"Now we leave our hearth and home."

"Heave, hard o're, heave ho." The main yard began to rise, mainsail spilling off below.

Standing in the very spot on the aft deck where Queen Jelena had stood, Benedikt tossed the next piece of the chanty down to the crew. "We follow aught but dreams alone."

"Heave, hard o're, heave ho. Heave ho, on we go." The great square belled out, lines tightened. "Heave, hard o're, heave ho."

"Now we leave familiar shores," He could hear the lateen rising behind him.

"Heave, hard o're, heave ho."

"Seeking lands not seen before."

"Heave, hard o're, heave ho."

"Mains'il secured, Captain." With the ease of long practice, the mate's voice inserted itself into the rhythm of the chanty.

"Heave ho, on we go. Heave, hard o're, heave ho."

"I can't say I'm not glad to see them go," Otavas murmured, watching Jelena who was still watching the empty horizon. "Perhaps now, things will get back to normal."

"I hope so, Highness." Bannon forced himself to watch the crowds and not the same horizon as the queen. *I slaughtering hope so.*

"Actually, we'll be near familiar shores for a while." The captain leaned back so Benedikt could see her finger trace their route on the map. "We'll run south before the prevailing northerlies, keeping to the western trade routes as far south as the Astobilies. If this wind stays with us . . ." She traced the sign of the Circle on her breast. ". . . that should take no more than six, seven days. We'll refill our water casks, take on fresh stores, and start west from there. First-quarter winds by the Astobilies blow from the east and the ocean around them is as calm as a millpond. Northern waters are dark and cold and the winds cruel and fickle. There's no reason I know of suggesting we can't sail into the unknown in comfort."

She looked up at the bard and smiled, the skin at the corners of her eyes folding into deep creases. "Doesn't sound much like an adventure, does it?"

Benedikt sputtered, aghast at having his thoughts read so easily.

"There'll be adventure enough before we're finished, lad." The captain lightly tapped the paper where figures of giant kigh rose out of an empty sea. "I promise you, you'll come home with songs enough for a dozen bards, and you'll see and hear plenty to enthrall the queen." She paused, stared past Benedikt for a moment, then brought her attention back to the young bard, "I want your word that while you're on board this ship, you'll not Sing the kigh without my express permission."

"But . . ."

"No buts. No exceptions. When it comes to matters between this ship and the sea, I must be the final arbitrator. A ship must have only one Captain."

"I would never . . ." he began, recognized her expression for what it was and realized she would accept only one answer. "I give you my word."

"Well, bard, wadda ya think?"

Benedikt shuffled over to give Mila room at the rail. "It's nothing like a fishing boat," he admitted.

"I should think not," the carpenter snorted. "Fishin' boats stink of fish. Comparin' my grand lady here to one of them runts is like comparin', uh . . ."

"Artur's snoring to a song?"

She snickered approvingly. "Aye, you've got it."

Artur's snoring had kept most of the crew awake two nights running. It was the only flat note in *Starfarer*'s melody. The morning of the third day, three of the company had held him down while the cook forced him to snort a spoonful of brandy up each nostril. Benedikt had no idea if the cure worked or if Artur stayed awake lest it be tried again, but the snoring stopped.

He hadn't expected just how different *Starfarer* would be from a fishing boat. He'd known she'd be much larger than anything that had ever sailed out of his village but that was only the most obvious of the differences.

Fisherfolk, even those, like his brothers, who fished the deep water, navigated by dead reckoning. The *Starfarer* found her way by compass. An invention of the Fienians, it was set on a brass pillar on the aft deck and minded by the officer of the watch.

"I've no idea how the unenclosed thing works," the mate admitted scratching his beard. "But it does. This bit here that always points north, it's mounted on a gimbal so it swings with the motion of the ship. Those thirty-two points on that circular card it swings over; they tells us what way we're headed." After a moment, staring down into the binnacle, he shook his head. "I guess I do know how it works, but I'll be unenclosed if I could tell you why. It was Her Majesty's idea to install it; she's got a right mechanical turn of mind."

Too big to be steered by a single sweep, *Starfarer*'s rudder was controlled from a tiller in the aft castle. While this offered the helmsman welcome protection from the elements, he could see very little and had to be conned by the officer of the deck.

"Through this?" Standing by the helm, Benedikt peered up through the brass tube that led to the deck above.

"Oh, aye." Leaning on the heavy tiller, Janina watched the bard indulgently as he poked about. "You'd be amazed at how loud sound comes through. Mind you, once you know what's what, you can keep a steady course by the feel of the helm. Here." Adjusting her grip, she straight-ened, moving her body back away from the wood. "You have a go."

"I couldn't . . ."

"We're right straight now, best time." She waggled heavy brows suggestively. "You know you want to."

He did.

"Just tuck yer butt in here. Aye, that's it. Now wrap yer arm around like mine. Put yer weight back on yer heels like. If you have to turn her, you'll want to be using yer whole body." Releasing the tiller, Janina moved only far enough to allow him her old position—still close enough for body heat to warm the air between them. "You've a nice lot of muscles for a bard."

"We do a lot of walking," Benedikt told her absently, distracted by the song of the sea resonating in the tiller. He felt as though *Starfarer* was his instrument and he could play whole concerts on her with the slightest movement.

"Walking?" She leaned back and looked down. "Aye, that's nice, too, but I was talking of yer back and arms." The sleeve of his shirt compacted under her fingers. "If there was something else you might like to try out later like, I'm willing."

Her touch got through where her words might've been lost. "Uh, thanks, but . . ." He indicated she should take back the tiller. When she did, he stepped away and faced her. He'd studied the ship's roll back in Elbasan, Janina was two years older than he was, unjoined, no children. The entry hadn't mentioned the dusting of golden freckles across all exposed skin, eyes almost turquoise, and hair that seemed to ignite in the sun. Nor did it mention the breadth of her shoulders and hips and the deep round bells of her breasts. Suddenly afraid he was staring, he took another step away and spread his arms. "Where?" he asked hoping she'd recognize a request for information not an oblique acceptance.

Janina laughed. "I forgot this was yer first time out. Well, there's no real privacy that's for sure but there's places less public than others."

"Please don't take this the wrong way, but . . ." He shook away a disturbing vision of performing in front of the crew. ". . . I couldn't."

"Don't fret. I'm not insulted. It takes time before you get used to living in each other's breeches." She winked. Explicitly. "But when you are used to it, the offer stands."

It wasn't his last offer, but he couldn't shake the thought of watching eyes. He wasn't all that fond of *singing* in front of an audience—and that, at least, worked out well because sailors weren't all that fond of being sung to. They preferred, he discovered, to be sung with.

At dawn and dusk, Benedikt Sang the sunrise and sunset and led the crew in the chorals.

"Every day?" he asked the captain in astonishment.

She raised a brow. "Feeling overworked?"

Under normal circumstances, he reacted badly to sarcasm, but on board ship the captain held rank equivalent to one of the ancient gods. "It's not that. I thought only the Centers Sang sunrise and sunset every day. I didn't know sailors were so religious."

"Religious?" The captain looked thoughtful. "I wouldn't say that, but when we're out too deep to anchor, on nights with cloud or without a moon, we sail blind. Sunset, we ask the Circle to enclose us. Sunrise, we give thanks that it did. Not religious." A half smile curved a long line around one side of her mouth. "Practical."

During the day, the crew taught Benedikt the Songs of the sea, frequently adding increasingly salacious verses to those commonly known. He'd never be able to sing any of them to the queen. In return, he spent his evenings making the connections that kept Shkoder strong, telling tales of the land and her people to an audience who'd never been away from the sea.

Almost within sight of the Astobilies, *Starfarer* ran into a calm. The sails hung limp from their yards and the heat baked the moisture from wood, rope, and flesh. By the afternoon of the third day, the captain finally allowed Benedikt to Sing the kigh.

"This is no riverboat," she warned him. "We're deeper keeled than anything you've ever had the kigh move." Watching the last sail lowered, Lija shook her head and wrapped one hand around the quartered Circle medallion she wore. "It's bad luck to Sing the kigh into the sails; it causes the wind to turn against you."

"That's not really relevant," Benedikt reminded her peevishly.

"It is if I say it is." She turned a warning glare toward him. "If the water kigh don't want to help, don't force them, don't plead with them. The sea's capricious enough, I don't need her actively irritated."

Benedikt's song called a glistening tumble of bodies to gather about the ship and by evening they'd moved *Starfarer* far enough for a freshening breeze to cause the sails to be raised again.

The captain broached a cask of sweet rum and they toasted their bard far into the night.

Benedikt had never been so happy in his life.

In the Astobilies, they filled the water casks yet again and took on barrels of pickled beef. Benedikt was not permitted ashore and for safety's sake the crew were forbidden to mention there was a bard on board. The only other bard ever to sail as far as the Astobilies had barely managed to escape the interest of the prince.

"I can protect myself," he muttered, not really wanting to go ashore until it had been denied him.

"Can you protect all my crew? And this ship?" the captain demanded. "And remember, you'll be the one who tells Her Majesty why we went no further."

Instead of exploring a strange, exotic port, Benedikt stayed on board, working on his recall of the voyage so far. Captain Lija had promised, as there were no other Shkoden ships in the area, she'd pass the sealed scroll to an Imperial ship heading north. He knew he should have been grateful for the time to prepare the recall and for the opportunity to send it to his queen, but for the three days *Starfarer* remained at anchor, the tides were the highest the Astobilies had ever known.

For the next ten days, the eastern trade winds blew steadily, and Benedikt savored every morning. He Sang a new song daily to the beauty of a dawn that kindled the clouds and tinted the sails a delicate rose. The sea was smooth and the air so fresh, every breath promised new beginnings. He grew to love the smell of the dew drying on the wooden decks, and as that faded, he happily replaced it with the scent rising from a cup of sah.

"Named for the sound the first Astobo made as he picked the dried bean up out of the sun and breathed in that intoxicating bouquet." Pjedic, the cook, matched action to words, bean dwarfed between a meaty thumb and forefinger. "Saaaah," he sighed as he exhaled. "This, I truly believe, is the fragrance at the center of the Circle."

"Why," Benedikt wondered, almost as entranced as the big man, "has no ship ever brought barrels of these beans back to Shkoder?"

"A few make it back, a precious few and for nearly the price of a bottle of brandy, those of us who note what ships are in harbor and know the ports they've visited can enter the haven of a select ale house in Dockside and remember mornings like these."

This was the first Benedikt had ever heard of *select* ale houses in Dockside. There were a couple that Bard's Hall warned their people not to enter alone, but somehow he didn't think those were the places Pjedic meant.

"You see, my friend the bard," the cook continued, "these precious beans travel oh so very badly. Time and moisture are their mortal enemies."

"Fish shit," grunted Mila, leaning into the galley to refill her plate. "The stuff may smell good, but it tastes like boiled bilge water and sawdust."

"That, my dear, is because you have the palate of a barnacle."

"And I ain't given' it back neither." She flicked Benedikt's coin as she passed. The first day out she'd drilled a hole in the gold Jelena for him so that he could hang it about his neck. "We coulda just had Cookie talk at the sails and saved yer voice."

"I have a dream, friend bard," Pjedic began when they were alone again. "Someday, I'll find a way to keep the beans both fresh and dry and I'll open a small place just up from Dockside, where discriminating patrons can enjoy a cup of sah together with those of like mind."

"Witnessed," Benedikt told him and raised his cup.

As the days passed, he never tired of the constant play of light and color on the bellying square sails; silver in moonlight, black in starlight, cloth of gold at sunset, white as the clouds themselves at noon. Occasionally, a black squall came up from windward but passed harmlessly with only a brief lashing of rain—the crew stripping down to stand naked in the fresh water. For days the sheets and braces needed no attention except to alter the nip on the block so they wouldn't chafe through. One by one, the crew brought their stories to where Benedikt stood in the bow, leaning over the rail and watching the silver flash of kigh dancing in the bow wave.

"There's little enough adventure at sea, if'n yer lucky. No, it's once you make landfall, that's where the adventures start. I recalls once landin' in the Empire, Sixth Province, Harak it was. There was an army garrison there, and I met me a corporal, not real tall but oh, so pretty . . ."

"Me da was a sailor. Me ma never knew which sailor, but I guess it's in me blood . . ."

"Yer family's fisher folk? Well, fillet me sideways—mine, too. Let ya in on a secret, though. I can't stand fishin'. Love the sea, can't stand fishin . . ."

"Them birds up there? Look sorta like brown gulls? We call 'em sky rats. I shot one once. Cross bow. Slapped it right onta the deck. Tasted like fish shit . . ."

"My family wanted something better for me, but I can't think of anything better, can you? With a fair and steady wind singing in the rigging . . ."

Sometimes, Benedikt forgot why they were there, forgot the dark sailor, forgot the search for the unknown, forgot the young queen waiting patiently back in the Citadel surrounded by stone instead of sapphire white-capped sea. When the glint of gold against his chest jolted his memory, guilt swept away in the rush of great waters alongside. At night, he watched wide-eyed as familiar constellations twisted and new ones appeared.

After ten days, the captain had the bottom sounded, but they were deeper than the line.

That afternoon, Benedikt climbed to the stern rail and found the mate there before him, glowering back at their wake. "What's wrong?"

The mate shook his head without turning. "It's this unenclosed wind. It keeps up, we'll never beat back against it."

Back. It was first anyone had mentioned going back.

That night the wind changed. Tacking against it, *Starfarer* made less distance but the mate stopped glowering.

Five days later, Benedikt began to notice a growing unrest in the crew. They'd been out of sight of land much longer than any of them had been before, and he began to hear the words, "go back," muttered more and more often.

No. He wasn't going to fail at this as well. He would not return empty-handed to the queen. Using the familiar tunes and rhythms of the chanties, he began tease the crew with the possibilities lying ahead. Some were absurd, some were obscene, and some appealed to that most basic of emotions: greed.

"Do I understand correctly; you're telling my crew there's gold in the land of the dark sailor?"

The dawn choral had been sung, the sun was safely in the sky. Benedikt turned to the captain and shrugged. "I've also told them there'll be three-legged whores and rivers of beer."

"And you may continue to do so with my blessing." Her tone suggested she knew full well why he'd been singing such songs. "But I don't want them thinking of gold when we . . ."

"Land ho!"

The cry from the ship's top brought everyone out on deck, jostling, crowding at the rail, squinting into the distance.

Benedikt felt some of the tension leave the muscles of his back. Unfortunately, the land turned out to be no more than a cloud bank above the western horizon.

"It's an unenclosed shame," the mate told him as *Starfarer* returned to her original course and her crew returned to abandoned tasks, "but it's not unusual. You stare at the same unenclosed sea, day after day. You strain your eyes for a sign that the Circle hasn't shit you out to rot alone. You start to see what you want to see." His teeth flashed white in the shadow of his beard. "Me, I wouldn't mind seeing that unenclosed river of beer."

The air hung hot and heavy as Benedikt walked to his place on the bow rail. Like most of the others, he wore only a pair of thin cotton breeches and sweat clung to his exposed skin like a film of oil. Swinging aside the queen's coin, he scratched at the damp hair on his chest with one hand and let his weight drop forward onto the other arm. The clouds on the horizon had grown darker and closer and were unmistakably not land.

"If we turn around right now, we'll be home by Third Quarter."

He could only see her hands without turning but there was no mistaking the voice. Mila.

"I'm not sayin' he'll have found another bedmate by then, but the longer we're gone, the better the odds. You know what I mean?"

"If you're worried about keeping his affections, why did you leave?"

She sighed. "I never really had his *affections.* And I figured this might impress him, you know. Dangerous adventures, finding a new land."

"I thought you came to keep an eye on your ship?"

"That, too."

"When *Starfarer* sails back into Elbasan Harbor," Benedikt told her, dropping into a storytelling cadence, eyes locked on a kigh beckoning to him from just below the surface, "with all flags flying and a thousand strange and wonderful new things crowding the decks, it won't matter if he's taken another bedmate. He'll be so impressed that you've been to the other side of the world that he'll be impressed right out of the arms of that bedmate and back into yours."

"Yeah?"

"Yeah."

He could hear the smile in her voice. "Then I guess we'd better get somewhere so's I can bring him back somethin' pretty." She picked at a scab on the back of her left hand for a moment. "You leave someone behind, Benedikt?"

About to say no, he found himself thinking of Bannon.

"I'm not trying to get rid of you."

"Good."

At the time, he'd thought it a threat. He'd stood and watched Bannon walk away and wondered why the other man was so angry. All at once, he wasn't sure that the heat had come from anger. Had Evicka, with her teasing *Are you excited? Then look behind you.* sensed something?

He'd never been a great percussion player but, even so,

this had to be the worst timing ever. Here he was, sailing across uncharted seas toward an unknown shore and suddenly realizing . . . what?

Fear, anticipation, desire—he didn't know which—dragged a chill down his spine.

Mila pulled an answer out of his silence. "What, no one? A good-lookin' young guy like you?"

Her tone pulled his head around. She smiled knowingly at him. "It's okay. You don't got to tell me. You left without anything settled between you." The scab came free, and she rubbed at the pale, new skin beneath. "I guess we both got someone we think we got to impress."

Before Benedikt could protest, a sudden gust of wind flattened their breeches against their legs.

Frowning out at the cloud, Mila straightened. "I don't like the feel of that."

And that was almost all the warning they got.

Five

THE first violent squall came on them so suddenly, it split the main course and blew the furled forecourse and mizzen out of their gaskets, whipping them to ragged ribbons in a few moments. Stripped down to bare poles, *Starfarer* scudded before the wind, laboring heavily.

"Bard!"

Attempting to make his way aft without being decapitated by a line or flung overboard, Benedikt jerked toward the sound, lost his balance, and fell into the aft castle, slamming his shoulder against the wood. Strong fingers wrapped around his arm and dragged him into a more-or-less upright position.

"Now," Captain Lija declared, her mouth almost on his ear, "might be a good time to Sing."

Benedikt opened his mouth, but the wind whipped his answer away.

They staggered together, hip to hip, as the bow slid up another crest and raced down the far side.

The captain's grip tightened. "If you were waiting for my permission—"

A line torn loose smacked into the wall over Benedikt's head hard enough to dent the wood.

"—you have it. Sing!"

"The kigh will never hear me!" he yelled. "Not over this wind."

"They sure as fish shit won't hear you if we go to the bottom!"

A wave, crowned with foam and anchored in darkness, broke over the side, smacking the Starfarer down into the sea. The crew, fighting desperately to secure the whirling, striking snake's nest of ropes, hung on to what was at hand as the rushing water wrapped around their waists and tried to drag them into the depths.

Miraculously, *Starfarer* fought her way free, groaning and shaking but gaining the surface. As certain death poured back off the decks, the pin Mila held broke. She had no time to scream as the water closed triumphantly around her.

Shoving himself away from the captain, Benedikt Sang.

Almost absorbed back into the sea, the wave paused and reformed into a vaguely human shape, the struggling figure of the ship's carpenter clearly visible inside. A featureless face turned toward the bard.

He added a command to the Song.

The huge kigh hung motionless beside the ship for a moment, then it leaned forward and dropped Mila out onto the deck.

Benedikt saw her cough once, twice, and that was all the attention he could spare as the kigh turned toward him again. He added layers to the Song, and a second kigh rose to join the first, then a third, a fourth, and a fifth. For every kigh there was one less wave.

Finally, *Starfarer* bobbed gently, ringed by a barrier of translucent bodies that kept the waves at bay. Essentially, the kigh listened to the same Song that had held the flood from Janinton; essentially, in the way that *Starfarer* and a river-boat were sister ships.

Janinton had been exhausting only because of the time he'd spent Singing. This was different. Benedikt had never had to reach so far into himself to find a Song. Among those who believed all things were enclosed in the Circle, all kigh were said to be part of one greater kigh. A Song to any one kigh was believed to be a Song to them all. Benedikt had never doubted that.

These kigh had never been Sung to.

They listened, intrigued, but he could feel how precarious the balance was. His Song weighed against the violent passions of the storm. He had to do something, something more to hold their attention.

So he Sang seduction.

The captain backed away as a translucent hand reached out to lap its fingers against the bard's bare chest. She watched, concerned, as, eyes closed, Benedikt moved out onto the main deck and each of the kigh wrapped their touch around him in turn. If they were responding to him, the wet cotton breeches made it quite clear he was equally responding to them.

The ship began to rock gently back and forth to the rhythm of the Song.

The muscles and tendons stood out in hard relief on Benedikt's throat. Rivulets of sweat began to draw their own salty paths down damp skin.

With glowers and gestures, the mate sent the crew back to their unfinished tasks. As the captain approached, he leaned toward her, her words barely louder than her breath.

"How long do you think he can last?"

The storm screamed through the rigging, furious at being denied its rightful prey. It swept down, blew over the decks, caught up the queen's coin Benedikt wore, dragged it to the length of the leather cord, and slapped it back against his mouth. The ship jerked, once, twice then, eyes still closed, Benedikt licked the blood from his lower lip and forced his voice over the shrieking of the wind. The gentle rocking began again.

The mate snorted and turned his mouth to the captain's ear. "He's barely twenty. If he's lasted this long, he should be able to last all day."

Outside the ring of kigh, the sea raged. And waited.

With the sun behind a barricade of green-gray cloud, time passed unmarked. Wide-eyed and silent, the crew watched the storm throw itself against the constant fluid motion of the kigh and tried to hear past the winds for any faltering of the Song.

Benedikt had no idea how long he'd been Singing. He couldn't feel the deck beneath his feet or the pain in his lip or the wet cotton clasp of his breeches. He could feel the Song. And the kigh. They didn't so much Sing with him as within him. He ran up one series of notes and down the other, the kigh never allowing the Song to build to the point where he'd have to bring it to its only possible conclusion.

He could still hear the wind, the creaking and groaning of the tortured masts and spars, but he ignored it just as he ignored the roar of his own blood in his ears, the racing of his heart, and the taste of copper in his mouth. There was only the Song. And the kigh.

"They're gonna kill him."

The captain forced her gaze off the bard and down to the woman by her side.

Hair whipping about her face, Mila kept her own eyes locked on Benedikt. "They'll just keep takin' it till he's got nothin' more to give."

"He's a bard," Captain Lija reminded her quietly. "This is what they do."

That brought Mila's attention around. She snorted. "This is *not* what they do. At least not that I ever heard of. He's givin' them too . . ."

A sudden violent gust of wind won the battle it had been waging and ripped a line and pulley free of its mooring. Mila threw the captain hard back against the rails, grabbed for the wildly swinging rope and missed. They whirled around together and watched the weighted end swing wide across the deck, missing Benedikt by inches.

Other hands reached out, other hands missed. Rope and pulley began the return.

"Benedikt!"

He heard his name. He tried to ignore it. Couldn't.

The ship stopped rocking.

Benedikt opened his eyes.

At the bottom of its arc, the pulley struck him a glancing blow against the back of his head. Had it struck him full on, it would have silenced him forever. As it was, it stopped the Song.

He blinked once, twice, sustained for a moment by the kigh. It almost felt as though he went with them as they left, driven out of his own body by shock and pain.

It had happened too fast for reaction, too fast for anything but Mila's one desperate cry. The crew watched in stunned silence as Benedikt crumpled apparently boneless to the deck.

The kigh drew back, peaks folding over once again into foam-capped crests as the storm threw itself past any lingering form and against the Starfarer.

As though making up for lost time, cross seas created dangerous pyramidal waves that broke over the ship from stem to stern. Bruised and battered, the captain fought her way in from the aft rail and fingers white around the upper end of the brass tube, she shouted directions to the helm below. With half the stores gone, the Starfarer was under-ballasted. If they turned to, the waves would roll her over and take her straight to the bottom.

Smashed down onto the deck by Benedikt's side, Mila could do nothing more than keep his face above water as the sea threw them back and forth. The deck tipped. His head lolling against her shoulder, they began to slide.

Then something grabbed the waistband of her breeches. The wet fabric dug into her stomach, stretched, and held. They stopped sliding and actually began to move against the angle of the deck.

The angle changed.

Still cushioning Benedikt with her body, Mila slammed into Pjedic's unyielding bulk. The sea swirled around them unable to gain ground, the irresistible force hitting the immovable object.

"We'll take him to the galley!" he bellowed. "But I suggest we do it on our hands and knees."

Together they began dragging Benedikt toward the forecastle. They moved slowly, careful not only for his sake but for their own. When waves broke over them, Pjedic hunkered down and created a pocket of calm in the lee of his body. Against all evidence, Mila began to think they'd make it.

And then the sea drew back. For a moment, the decks were dry and the wind fell as silent as the bard.

The cook and the carpenter slowly turned.

Rising up off the bow was a wall of water.

Starfarer slowly began to turn.

"Helm! Maintain heading!" The captain's command bounced back and forth between the walls of the trough.

The wave no longer rose directly off the bow.

Starfarer continued to turn.

The wave rose up beside them.

It trembled.

It fell.

"I should have sent a bard who sang air as well as water." Jelena stepped away from the window without having seen either the sunlight or the new growth that painted the courtyard topiary in pale green. "I never thought it would be so hard not have news."

"You sent the bard who wanted to serve," Otavas reminded her.

"But not necessarily the best bard. It was an emotional choice, not a rational one. I chose Benedikt because I was angry at Kovar for assuming that *he* had the final decision. Perhaps if I'd waited . . ."

Otavas rose and drew the queen into the circle of his arms, "You wouldn't have found anyone more anxious to please you. That has to count for something."

Grabbing his shoulders, she locked her eyes on his. "Have I sent them to their deaths?"

"You haven't sent anyone, Lena." He cursed Kovar silently for not only putting the thought into his queen's head but for repeating it so often she almost believed it. "They all volunteered, and they all knew what they were getting into. Magda touched every single kigh on board that ship and they were all willing to dare the unknown. You made something possible that many of them had only dreamed about."

"I know." She dropped her head against his chest and sighed. "I'm being stupid. I just hate waiting."

"Speaking of waiting, the Fienian ambassador . . ."

Jelena laughed at his tone and pushed him away. "Is he still attempting to take Bannon from you?"

"He is." Otavas plucked his gloves off the mantle and slapped them down into his other palm. "We're going riding this afternoon; theoretically to exchange nonbinding opinions on the trade route and the taxes my brother, the Emperor, is proposing, but I expect Bannon will be discussed."

"In a nonbinding manner?"

"Count on it." He stroked her cheek with the back of his hand as he straightened from their kiss. "They're all watching, you know: Fienia, Petrolka, even my most Imperial brother. They're all waiting to see how this venture of yours turns out, and they're all cursing themselves that they didn't dare to send a ship out first."

"There's nothing stopping any of them from sending a ship out *second*," Jelena snorted.

"Perhaps, but Fienia, Petrolka, and the Empire are all

ruled at this time by men and men, my darling love, would rather not make an attempt at all if they know they'll come in second."

"*Starfarer* was certainly no secret. I'm surprised they didn't try to beat us out of the harbor."

"With Kovar opposed, they didn't think you'd go through with it."

She reached up and tugged gently at the point of his short beard. "More fools them."

To Otavas' surprise, Bannon was not waiting outside the royal apartment. When questioned, one of the duty pages pointed to the double doors at the end of the long hall and asked if His Highness would like him fetched.

"Thank you, no. I'll fetch him myself."

The balcony on the other side of the double doors was the balcony where he and Jelena had first really spoken without the rules of rank between them. She still used it to view the western stars.

Bannon turned from the railing as Otavas stepped outside, saw who it was, and dropped gracefully to one knee, "My apologies, Highness, I meant to stay only a moment, but I . . ." Explanation trailing off, he dropped his gaze to the toes of the consort's boots. He knew, they both knew, he had no business being anywhere in the royal wing but with his prince or outside his door.

"I assume you had a reason for wandering off?"

The ex-assassin looked up, saw that his prince was smiling, and sighed. "Do you remember, Highness," he asked in Imperial, "how it feels when there's a huge storm overhead? Not Shkoden storms but the storms back home when the sky seems low enough to touch and the hand of Cieri reaches down to flatten the land?"

A little surprised by the reference to the empire's god of storm, Otavas motioned for Bannon to rise. "I remember. Why?"

"That's how I feel now, Highness." He lifted the edge of a glance to the brilliant blue sky above and shrugged. "I don't know why."

Otavas glanced up as well. It would be hard to imagine weather less likely to evoke the misery of an Imperial storm. "Perhaps these feelings have nothing to do with weather," he said, continuing the thought aloud. "Could it have something to do with your sister?"

"No, it's not Vree. And it's not you nor Her Majesty." Bannon turned to face the west again, knowing his prince would forgive the slight. "I don't know how I know that, but I do."

"Then who?"

He shook his head, almost wishing it had been one of the few he cared for because then he could answer foreboding with action and drive it away.

As near as Otavas could tell, Bannon was at least as much annoyed by this unwelcome feeling as he was distressed. Both responses would have to be defused if they were to ride that afternoon. Personal sympathy aside, the company of a distressed assassin would be almost as dangerous as that of an annoyed one. There were very good reasons the Imperial army trained emotions out of their blades of Jiir. He moved to stand beside Bannon at the railing, their shoulders touching. "Perhaps it's the Fienian ambassador."

Which was so ridiculous Bannon forgot himself and said so.

Otavas grinned. "He's about to spend at least half of the afternoon courting your service. I know I'm feeling foreboding about that."

"I'd never leave you, Highness."

"I have no doubt of that. I'm just afraid you may think he's more trouble than he's worth and put a knife in him."

Gold flecks danced in Bannon's eyes. "Would you like me to, Highness?"

"Yes. But since diplomacy forbids the order, we'll both have to put up with him." Otavas laid his hand for a moment on the other man's arm. "Come. Let's hope your storm warning is nothing more than anticipation of an extremely tiring afternoon."

"As you say, Highness." But as he smiled and bowed and led his prince back into the royal apartments, he hadn't lost the feeling, the certainty, that something had gone very wrong.

The day *Starfarer* had sailed had been the first time in years Kovar had gone to the harbor. He was the Bardic

Captain. Every bard in Shkoder was his responsibility. He almost never left the Citadel.

Standing on the end of the wharf, staring down into the brackish water, he realized that this was his eleventh trip since then. One more, he thought, watching the shadow of a fish disappear under the wharf, and he'd have an even dozen. And there would be one more. And one more after that. And as many as it took until he knew that Benedikt was safe.

Missed Councils were unimportant since the queen had no use for his counsel.

Air kigh sent for news would not go out of sight of land. They'd never been asked before, and no one knew what Songs to Sing.

He had bards all along the coast, north and south, waiting for a message. Water kigh dispersed at the best of times and not even Benedikt could keep one on a straight course from so far.

There were no messages today just as there had been no messages on any of the ten previous trips.

He turned, walked in to shore, and began the long climb up the hill.

I should have stopped him somehow. I should never have let him leave the pattern. But all he'd done was fight with him, allowing the boy no room to back away from his foolishness. *If my pride has gotten him killed.*

His pride. And the queen.

"Look, look at this!" Jelena brandished the bardic scroll at Otavas as he entered their apartment. "It came this afternoon while you were out riding. It's from Benedikt! They made it safely as far as the Astobilies fifteen days ago. They're sailing west from there. The captain expects steady winds and smooth seas!" She tossed the grimy scroll into a chair and grabbed him by the collar. "Isn't this amazing!"

"Amazing!" he repeated, reflecting her smile.

"I wish I was with them!"

"I'm glad you're not."

"You'd be with me of course."

He widened his eyes. "So we'd be lost at sea together? I don't think so."

"Don't be an idiot." Releasing him with a kiss, she scooped up the scroll again. "Everything's fine."

"Hentee! Come and see!"

The boy put down the stick he'd been poking sand crabs with, sighed, and straightened. "If it's another dead sacfish, Mija . . ."

"It's not." At the other end of the small beach, his sister continued to dig, throwing sand behind her like a puppy. "It's made!"

"Made?" Hentee started to run. Children who returned stuff lost from the village fishing boats were often given shells from the deep water. His best friend Hootay had a big old shadow shell with only two broken spines. More than anything else, Hentee wanted a bigger shell than his friend.

By the time he reached his sister, she'd paused to study what she'd found. It was flat and round, bigger around than his head, and it gleamed a shiny gray against the black sand. Nudging her aside with his hip, Hentee bent and picked it up.

"Hey!"

He ignored her. The bit that had been in the sun was warm and the rest, the buried bit, was cold.

Mija pushed up against his elbow, digging her head against his shoulder. "What is it?" she demanded.

"I don't know." Palm flat against her scalp, he pushed her away. "Mamon needs to shave your head again." If the edge had been sharp, he might have thought it a weapon, but the strange stuff it was made of sort of rolled under itself all around.

"You know what I think it is? Do you? I think it's a plate."

"It's not like any plate I ever saw."

She hissed through the space where her front teeth used to be, her opinion of his greater experience obvious.

"It has a picture in the middle." He rubbed at the raised image with his thumb and both children leaned in for a closer look. "I think this is a boat."

Mija hissed again.

"No, look. This is the part that floats and this is the mast and this here in behind is the sail."

"Wrong shape."

"Different shape," Hentee corrected smugly. He knew he was right. Tentatively, he licked at the edge. All he could taste was salt. It rang against his teeth.

"What's that in front of the sail then?" One fat finger poked at the ship.

It was flat on the bottom and had points on the top. "A flower. This never came off one of our boats, Mija."

"Then from where?"

It was round and shiny gray. Hentee looked toward the horizon where a pale moon was just barely visible against the sky. "From Xaantalicta."

Mija followed his gaze and her eyes widened, "Do you think she dropped it?"

"I don't know. But I heard Papon say it's almost time for the change."

Loud voices approaching the far end of the beach jerked them both around.

"It's the big kids," Mija whispered. "They'll take it!"

"Not if they don't see us. Come on." He grabbed her arm and pulled her toward the jumble of rock that marked the end of the sand. "We'll hide in here until they go."

"But Sorquizic will be rising soon! Mamon says we're not to go into the rocks when Sorquizic is rising!"

"Don't be such a baby. Sorquizic won't be rising for ages yet." Half lifting, half dragging, he got her up onto the first rock. "This is ours, and they're not getting it."

The word *ours* worked like he knew it would. Twisting free of his grip, Mija began to climb. When she was safely out of sight, he tucked Xaantalicta's treasure under one arm and followed.

"If they look over that edge, they'll see us," she told him as he dropped down beside her.

He looked up the way she was pointing and realized she was right. "Then we'll wade out around this rock and hide on the other side. They'll never find us there."

"Never?"

"I promise."

Looking dubious, Mija slid into the water.

Since he was taller, Hentee moved to the outside and together they waded around and onto a tiny enclosed triangle of sand.

Waves lapping at the backs of their knees, both children stood and stared.

"Did Xaantalicta drop this, too?" Mija breathed at last.

Hentee shook himself as his sister's voice broke the spell. "Don't be silly. It's a man."

"But he's all yellow."

"It's a man," Hentee repeated but with less certainty. It looked like a man, that was true, but it was bigger, much bigger than even his Papon who was one of the biggest men in the village, and Mija was right, it was very yellow. The skin was almost brown, but there was yellow hair on its head and darker yellow hair on its face and around its pee-er and on its chest instead of a man's tattoos. Nestled in the hair on its chest . . .

"Is it dead?"

"No. Now shut up." Handing Mija Xaantalicta's treasure, Hentee waded ashore and squatted by the great yellow thing's side.

"What, Hentee? What?"

"I don't know." He reached out slowly and pinched the leather thong between thumb and finger, lifting the disk that hung from it up onto its side.

A narrow beam slanting out from the late afternoon sun found its way through a cleft in the rocks and touched the disk with glory.

Hentee swallowed hard. "Gold. Mija. It's gold." Under the band of sunlight, skin and hair gleamed golden as well. "Tulpayotee. He's sent a warrior to fight the change!"

Mija hugged their treasure tighter. "You shouldn't be touching him. I'm telling!"

"I'm not touching him!" Still holding the thong, Hentee turned to glare at his sister. "I'm just touching . . ."

A huge, damp hand closed around his.

Hentee screamed.

"You say a pair of children found him on the beach?"

"Yes, gracious one."

"They ran for their father who ran for the Ooman who ran for you?"

"Yes, gracious one."

"Good. I like to have these things straight in my mind.

If rumors of his existence come to me from other sources, I'll know who is to blame."

"Yes, gracious one."

"You may go."

"Thank you, gracious one. I am unworthy of your time."

The only sound for some moments was the shuffling of sandals growing increasingly distant.

"Take him to my personal physician. Tell her; if the golden man dies, so does she."

Six

AFTER death, so said the priests, the fifth kigh—the kigh of self—is gathered back into the Center of the Circle to rest and be cleansed until it is spun a physical form again. Benedikt was vaguely aware of being carried, of warm, wet cloth, bright light, and of liquid voices he thought belonged to the kigh who had saved him. For if all things were enclosed in the Circle, would his kigh not be there as well? As bits of memory floated by—the storm, the Song, the cowardly retreat from sudden pain—the thought of the kigh was the only thing that made bearable the knowledge of his failure.

He was swimming for the surface and for air, fighting against a great weight of water. Behind him, in the darkness, swam horror. Above him, in the light, was rebirth. His heart pounded. Surely his lungs would burst. One arm broke through. And then the other.

He opened his eyes.

The light was dim, the silence that of a large, almost empty space. He wore the body he'd spent twenty years growing into although he wore it with unaccustomed awareness. *These are my feet. These my legs. I move my fingers so . . .* His tongue reported oil on his lips but couldn't identify the flavor.

The soft shuff, shuff of approaching footsteps froze him in place, eyes half closed, hardly daring to breathe.

He felt a touch against his foot, saw a small, dark hand. The touch moved lightly up his leg, he saw arm and shoulder . . .

A girl. No, a woman, full breasts and hips pressed against her cream-colored shift, but she was so small he could easily tuck her under one arm. Her skin held the deep, rich tones of old copper and both of her upper arms were marked by an intricate design of interlocking black patterns. When he dared open his eyes a fraction more, he saw a profile dominated by an imposing angle of nose. Etched with silver, her dark hair had been gathered at the nape of her neck and fell down her back in a single braid.

One hand resting just above his knee, she turned. Her eyes widened and she started, fingers tightening on his skin. Then she frowned, said something he understood to be an admonishment—she clearly considered it his fault she was startled—and quickly left the room.

Benedikt had barely begun sorting out this new information when she returned accompanied by another woman, no taller, perhaps ten years older, and clearly of higher status. What he could see of this second woman's shift had been bleached white, and over it she wore some kind of loose multicolored coat. She had a black pattern drawn on one cheek and her multiple braids had been decorated with small white feathers.

She stood at the foot of the bed, and at her command the first woman slipped an arm behind his shoulders and tucked pillows behind him until his upper body reclined at an angle. Her breasts were soft and heated against his shoulder and he could feel her nipples through the thin fabric of her shift. His ears began to burn as he realized he was responding.

A sarcastic comment from the woman at the foot of the bed took care of that.

Smiling, the woman who'd lifted him placed a cup to his mouth.

He hadn't realized how thirsty he was until the cool water splashed against his lips. Eyes half closed, he gratefully drained the cup and sank back into his pillows exhausted by the effort of so much swallowing. An imperious thumb pried one eye open again. He had barely time to recognize the woman from the end of the bed before he found his head pushed forward and the back of his skull undergoing a close examination. When her touch sent shards of pain bouncing around behind his eyes, he found strength enough to wrap his fingers about her wrist.

She effortless broke his grip and said something to her companion, the musical tones of the strange language making it no less clearly a command.

The other woman knelt and touched his chest, drawing his gaze to her face. "Ochoa," she declared, fingertips denting the fabric between her breasts. Then she touched his chest again, lifting both brows in an obvious question as she did.

It took him a moment to remember how to work his mouth. "B . . . Bene . . . dikt." His eyes widened at the sound of his voice and all at once he realized what it meant. "I'm not . . . dead."

Ochoa patted his chest encouragingly.

If he wasn't dead, perhaps there were others! Ignoring the pain, he jerked his head from side to side. The silence hadn't lied. The room was large and empty of all but his bed. No other beds. No other . . .

A firm grip on his chin stopped his movement, and a sharp admonishment held him in place.

Ochoa, still kneeling by his side, made it quite clear that he was to remain still.

Benedikt caught her gaze and held it, hoping to make her understand by intensity alone what he needed to know. "Am I . . . the only one?" When she frowned, clearly confused, he repeated the question. He hadn't realized he was crying until, shaking her head, she reached out and traced the path of a tear down his cheek.

There were no other beds.

As the other woman released his head and stepped back, he groped for the comfort of the queen's coin.

Gone.

Gone!

His nails dug frantically into his chest.

"Bene Dikt!"

Something cold was shoved under his fingers. Cold and flat and round. Gulping air, he blinked away tears enough to see. On one side, the queen's profile. On the other, the crowned ship. With the coin safe within the cage of his fingers, Benedikt sagged back against the pillows and deep water claimed him again.

"I begin to think he might live."

"The gracious one will be pleased," Ochoa muttered dryly.

Her companion snorted. "I admit to some joy myself, given Tul Altun's command."

"You don't really believe he'd have tied your life to the stranger's?" Ochoa asked, stepping back so that the other woman would cross the threshold first. "To Bene Dikt's?"

"If it was the gracious one's will . . ."

"Imixara!"

"However," the Tul's personal physician continued, moving through her outer room to the herbarium, "I believe in this instance he was merely making certain I understood how important the stranger is to him."

"And do you?"

"I understand the gracious one wants the stranger to live."

Accepting the reproof in the physician's voice, Ochoa bowed her head and murmured an apology, "Do you believe he's one of Tulpayotee's warriors, come to challenge the change?"

Imixara, who, arms crossed, had been scanning the contents of the woven shelves, turned to face her favorite assistant. "No, I do not. Would one of Tulpayotee's warriors have taken an injury that made his eyes so sensitive to light."

"If he is to work against Xaantalicta in the darkness . . ."

"The stranger is a *man* and not a very old one at that, given his little display earlier."

"Not exactly a little display," Ochoa observed, beginning to grin.

The two women locked eyes, and neither could repress a snicker.

"Yes, well, at least our young giant is proportional." Crushing a dried leaf between thumb and forefinger, Imixara shook her head and moved onto the next rack of shelves where she began dropping leaves and the occasional flower into a small basket. "You're not pronouncing his name correctly. It's Benedikt, one word. He paused only to catch his breath."

"Are you sure?"

"I *have* heard the effects of injury before."

Ochoa murmured another apology. "When will you tell the gracious one that the stranger, Bene . . ." Caught in the pause, she rushed to finish before Imixara thought she was being deliberately defiant. ". . . dikt, is awake."

"Not until he can stay awake for the duration of the tul's interest. Meanwhile, make an infusion." The basket of herbs changed hands. "Have him drink a cup cold every time he awakes. If he indicates hunger, he may have clear broth. Under no circumstances is he to rise to relieve himself. Continue using the gourds." A bell rang in the distance. "If the tul doesn't need me after I've checked his fluids, I'll drop in to look at Benedikt this evening." She paused and leaned back out of the alcove that separated her rooms from the hall. "And for glory's sake, shave him. He's a man, not an animal."

"Shave how much of him?" Ochoa asked with some concern. The young stranger was quite definitely the hairiest man she'd ever seen.

Imixara stopped in mid step. "Good question. Shave his face. The tul can decide himself if he wants the hair removed from other places."

"He cannot speak to me?"

"No, gracious one."

"Does he understand what I say?"

"He seems to understand a great deal from tone and context, gracious one."

"Does he? Good." Gathering up the folds of his robe in one hand, Tul Altun crossed to the bed and stared down at the young man lying in it. "You are certain he is nothing more than he seems?"

"I am certain he is a young man, gracious one." Imixara shrugged, both hands lifting to cup the air. "More than that he will have to tell you himself."

"Fine. See to it that he can."

"Yes, gracious one."

The tul smiled down at the golden-haired, golden-skinned, pale-eyed stranger. "It *is* possible that Tulpayotee gave one of his warriors a man's form to better assess the strength of his followers."

"It is possible, gracious one." Twenty-four years of practice kept Imixara's voice respectfully neutral.

"Benedikt." Tul Altun lingered over the unusual name

and smiled when the pale eyes widened. "We'll have much to speak of, you and I. Learn quickly."

Suddenly chilled in spite of the damp heat lying across him like a blanket, Benedikt watched Tul Altun leave the room and listened, frozen in place, until the sound of his footsteps faded away. Ochoa had named his visitor before he arrived—although whether it was title, name or a combination, Benedikt wasn't sure—and had made it unmistakably clear that he was her lord and the lord of a great deal more besides. Whether she was warning him to beware or only behave, she needn't have bothered. Benedikt had seen the kind of easy arrogance Tul Altun exhibited in only one other person. Bannon. An ex-Imperial assassin who knew, bone deep, that he could bring an unpreventable death to everyone around him.

I have plans for you.

Those might not have been Tul Altun's exact words, but Benedikt would have had to have been deaf not to have heard the meaning. Even a non-bard would have understood.

Physical and cultural differences made it difficult for Benedikt to judge the other man's exact age by appearance alone, but unless he'd had voice training, tone and timbre put him between twenty and thirty. He wasn't much taller than the women. While he seemed to be carrying no excess flesh, neither was there much muscle apparent through the opening of the loose, multicolored coat, similar to the healer's but finer and cut long enough to drag behind him on the floor.

Ochoa wore a single braid, the Healer between ten and twenty, their lord many, many more. It had probably taken Tul Altun's barber hours to weave the tiny, perfect plaits and fix a green feather in each. The braids, Benedikt concluded had to be a status symbol—only the very rich and powerful could afford to waste that kind of time. It made sense; back in Shkoder the wealthy wore clothing they couldn't get into without the help of servers. Here, wherever here turned out to be, where it was far too hot to be laced into anything, hair clearly served the same function.

Reminded of the heat, he realized how thirsty he was

and reached for the mug of water beside his bed, thankful
that for the last couple of days Ochoa had let him out of
bed to use a pot. When he could walk to a privy, he'd be
more thankful still. When he could walk on out of here . . .

And go where?

Perhaps he could convince Tul Altun to give him a ship.
I have plans for you.

Perhaps fish would sing. Benedikt couldn't decide if Tul
Altun's expression had been speculative or predatory. Not
that it much mattered.

He sagged back against the pillow and wondered. *What
next? What do I do?"*

What would Bannon do?

Benedikt stared up into the shadows that clung to the
ceiling surprised by the comfort he found in such a simple question.

What would Bannon do?

He'd survive.

"No, you're too valuable to me to be wasted as Benedikt's tutor." Imixara pulled a braid forward and stroked the
dove's feather laced into it. "We must find someone born
to the house—the tul won't want him to pick up a common
accent. We need someone young so that he can believe he
has a friend—that belief may be useful to the tul later. It
had better be someone male just in case they get very
friendly—the tul won't want any golden bastards toddling
about." The tul's personal physician glanced up as Ochoa
made an indeterminate noise and smiled. "Were you planning to comfort him yourself? Try to remember what herbs
to use and when to use them."

"I'm not saying I want to comfort him," Ochoa protested. "I'm not saying I haven't thought about it," she
quickly added to cut off the other woman's incredulous
response, "but he's young enough to be my son."

"Your son still works with Bon Kytee?"

"He does."

Imixara glanced up at the circular calender. "Xaantalicta
will hide her face in two days. The Bons have to be back
to the house for the service. Find out if Bon Kytee has
returned and, if he has, inform him that I speak with the
tul's voice and I have another position for your son."

"You'd do that for my son?"

"No, foolish one, I would do that for you. I have no children of my own to bring to the tul's attention, why should I not advance your son's position in the house?"

Ochoa leaned forward and gently kissed the other woman's cheek above her physician's tattoo. "And it will irritate the glory out of Bon Kytee."

"That *had* occurred to me."

Language lessons began with Benedikt reclining against his pillows and Xhojee, Ochoa's son, kneeling beside the low platform of the bed. His teacher was a year younger— determined by the simple process of banging chests and holding up fingers—and had answered, just by entering the room, the question of where the kigh had brought him ashore.

He wore only high sandals and a short unbleached skirt, belted with multicolor netting threaded with shells. There were netting bands on both wrists as well. Like his mother and the healer and the lord, he had thick, dark hair, drawn back and then split into two short braids. He had no hair on his legs or his arms or his chest. What he *did* have in the center of his chest was a dark drawing, somehow set right into the skin.

The dark sailor had worn "patterns drawn in darkness etched above his heart."

Benedikt clutched the queen's coin and tried not to weep. He had reached the land of the dark sailor, but there would be no answers, no wonders returning back across the sea to delight Her Majesty.

Xhojee had not inherited his mother's hawklike profile nor her bedside manner, but Benedikt ignored the undercurrent of discontent and concentrated on mastering words enough to ask what Tul Altun had planned. Although his new teacher seemed not to care how fast or even if he learned, language was a bardic skill that had nothing to do with the number of quarters Sung.

A few days later, Imixara pronounced her patient fit to be moved, and the lessons continued in what Benedikt was made to understand were his rooms.

"All mine?" he asked, clutching close his sleeveless robe. Imixara looked impressed. "All yours," she told him, then turned to Xhojee. "He seems to understand a great deal. I will see that the tul knows of your success."

"I cannot take the credit, Physician." Xhojee bowed, a momentary expression of pleasure replaced by resignation. "If I were not here to teach him, Benedikt would learn from the birdsong. He takes in meaning like a sponge."

"Then perhaps the tul should hear of your honesty." She nodded toward the wall of shutters, "He may go out onto the terrace if it rains or at night. I do not want him in Tulpayotee's sight until I am certain it will not blind him."

"Does Tulpayotee punish his warrior for becoming a man?"

The sarcasm in Xhojee's voice drew Benedikt out of the adjoining bathing room.

"Don't ever take that tone with me, young man." The physician tapped him on the chest with a polished fingernail. "I will ignore your sulks for your mother's sake—don't think for a moment I haven't noticed—but if you ever speak to me like that again, I will have your head shaved and return you to the children's compound. I don't care what attitude Bon Kytee put up with from you, do you understand?"

"Yes, Physician."

"Good. Let me know the instant you believe him capable of conversing with the tul."

Benedikt bowed as she nodded toward him, then waited until her footsteps died in the distance before crossing to Xhojee. When the other man turned toward him, he poked his finger toward his chest, rolled his eyes, and mimed an overreaction.

The tall golden man did a wicked imitation of the short dark woman. Xhojee couldn't help it, he started to laugh.

So Benedikt expanded on the performance.

A few moments later, they sagged against the wall, exhausted. Xhojee couldn't remember the last time he'd laughed so hard. Then Benedikt jabbed his finger at the air and it set them off again.

Gasping in, gasping out lungful after lungful of air, Xhojee thought he was going to be sick, his stomach hurt so. He managed to bring the last of the giggles under control and realized that the gnawing resentment at being dragged away from his position with Bon Kytee was gone. The laughter had released his grip on it. He felt cleansed.

Breathing finally back to normal he turned to Benedikt, still gasping for breath beside him, a little worried that his student hadn't seemed to have recovered.

Benedikt wasn't certain when the laughter had turned to tears, he'd moved so effortlessly between them. It was as if in allowing the one, he'd somehow left himself open to the other. Drawing in great gulping breaths, he closed his left fist around the queen's coin and punched his right into the wall, over and over. The steel bands around his chest were gone, and all the grief and all the fear came pouring out. He was making some kind of horrible noise, he could hear it but he couldn't stop it.

Captain Lija was dead.

Pjedic was dead.

Mila was dead.

The *Starfarer* would never return to Shkoder.

. . . to the queen.

. . . to Bannon.

He had failed again.

Xhojee barely managed to catch the bigger man when his knees buckled. All he could do was guide the collapse to the floor and use his own body to cushion the impact. Bracing his back again the wall, he tucked the golden head into his shoulder and searched his heart for words of comfort. When he couldn't find any Benedikt would have understood, he tightened his grip and quietly sang a cradle song. To his surprise, although the weeping continued, it lost the wild sound that had frightened him so. When he finished, he sang another and another until Benedikt finally slept, exhausted.

Settling them both a little more comfortably, Xhojee brushed his lips against the golden hair and sighed. All of a sudden, in spite of his lost position with the bon, his life didn't seem so bad.

"No, you're karjet if you have more than one braid so to the karjen, the one braids, pretty much anyone is karjet. If you have six braids, then anyone with seven braids or more is karjet."

Benedikt frowned. "Then what is person with six braids called?"

"That depends. He's a karjet to anyone with five braids or less but just a person with six braids to anyone with more braids." Xhojee scrubbed his face with his palms. "It's like an oven in here. Let's take a break. Is there any juice left?"

"No, there are . . ."

"Is."

". . . is no juice left. Will I have more juice?"

"Will you get more juice? Sure."

Scooping up the pitcher, Benedikt walked to the alcove that led out to the hall. The louvered shutters separating the terrace from his suite were the closest things to doors he'd seen. Privacy seemed to be maintained by closetlike entries—with the outer door in the side wall at one end and the inner door in the opposite wall at the other end—and a hanging string of bells placed so that they were impossible to avoid.

He wasn't permitted to go out into the hall—not that he was sure he wanted to while wearing only a knee-length skirt—but if he put the empty pitcher outside the alcove and retreated back into the room, in a few moments the bells would ring, and he could retrieve it refilled. It was a spooky system. When he'd asked about it, Xhojee'd explained that the tul had given orders he was not to be seen.

"I don't see them?"

"No. They don't see you."

It didn't seem to make much sense, but by now he knew better than to question the orders given by Tul Altun. Tul was his title, Altun, his name. Actually, his full name was Kohunlich-tul Tulpay Altun. Tul Altun for short. Kohunlich was the house he was head of—Benedikt knew that house meant more than dwelling but didn't quite understand how much more. He was twenty-four years old and had been tul since he was sixteen. Tul meant he was the male head of the house. His sister was the female head, which made no sense to Benedikt at all, but Xhojee had promised it would in time. Tulpay was a name to honor Tulpayotee, the sun. Because he was tul, he didn't have a name to honor Xaantalicta, the moon, although everyone else did. Everyone except Tul Altun's sister, Xaan Mijandra, who didn't have a name to honor Tulpayotee. Xhojee's full name was Kohunlich Payo Alans Xhojee. The whole thing made Benedikt's head ache. He'd explained in turn that he only had one name and left it at that.

And the tul had a use for him, although Xhojee didn't know what it was.

The bells rang. The pitcher was full.

"Is too hot," he agreed as he filled Xhojee's glass and passed it over. "Open shutters all the way?" The louvers were open, but the shutters themselves were closed. "Maybe find breeze?"

"If it was cloudy out there, sure, but not with Tulpayotee glaring down on us. Your eyes are still too sensitive."

"Not."

"Hey, I'd be perfectly happy to let you go blind in order to get a breeze in here, but Imixara would skin me."

"I explain with Imixara."

"*To* Imixara. Wouldn't matter, she'd still skin me."

Benedikt gave up, stretched his legs out on the floor, and leaned against the triangular stone back rest. He hadn't expected it to be as comfortable as it was, but in the heat it was a lot cooler than the pile of cushions they used after dark. Xhojee had snickered derisively at his explanation of chairs. Since there were no drafts and cool floors were to be welcomed not avoided, Benedikt supposed he understood the lack. He took a swallow of an unidentifiable fruit juice and stared down into the amber liquid. "You sing good."

"I sing . . . ? Oh. I wasn't sure you'd even heard me."

They hadn't spoken of that afternoon and although nightmares of bloated, crab-eaten faces threw him out of sleep every night, Benedikt had managed to keep his grieving private. Sometimes, lying awake in the dark, he softly sang what he remembered of the first lullaby, and it helped.

"I heard. Good voice. True."

"Thank you." Too far reclined to bow, Xhojee tapped his tattoo. "What about you?"

He could see his reflection in the juice. "What about me, what?"

"Do you sing?"

The kigh had smashed the *Starfarer,* taken her and all on board her to the bottom of the sea.

Benedikt shook his head. "Not very good."

                              *   *   *

Unable to sleep, Benedikt stared up at the ceiling.
Shadow hid the complex tile pattern, flowed down the
walls, and pooled around the furniture. Head aching,
Benedikt couldn't decide wether he was the source of the
shadow or its destination—whether it poured out of, or
into, his heart. The dim light seeping through the open
louvers managed to push the shadow back, and all at once,
Benedikt wanted to be on the other side of that fragile
barricade.

He slid out of bed and into a loose robe, its weight lost
amid the dark weight of memory he carried on his shoulders.
Feet bare, he padded quietly to the first shutter, unlatched it,
and pushed it open just far enough to slide through.

Barely on the terrace, not really outside, he paused and
listened to the silence. Xhojee slept in a small room just
off his, an attendant's room—he'd laughed when Benedikt
had asked him if he'd minded—and slept lightly enough to
have heard the soft sigh of the folding hinges. It wasn't that
Xhojee would insist he stay inside; he'd been on the terrace
after dark and in the rain a number of times, but, following
orders, Xhojee would insist he come along.

Benedikt wanted to be alone.

His rooms were on the second floor. The broad terrace
overlooked a large enclosed courtyard filled with fruit trees
and a garden so lush its growth masked the first-floor
rooms. There were other terraces—on his side of the square
as well as on the other three—and all but his had been
screened by huge pots of plants.

About fifteen feet from the building, a low sculpted stone
wall provided more of a decorative than a functional barricade at the edge of the drop. Benedikt walked to it slowly,
welcoming the feel of the cool tiles beneath his feet—the
stored heat of the day having long since been given up to
the night.

Then a shadow moved. Heart in his throat, Benedikt
froze in place, hardly daring to breathe.

A gray cat, larger and more angular than the cats at
home, launched itself off the stonework and into the
branches of a flowering tree. From there, it seemed to flow
to the ground like smoke, disappearing into shifting patterns of gray and black. Once his heart started beating

again, Benedikt was glad to see it. They had cats at home, in Shkoder, and just for a moment home didn't seem so terribly, horribly far away.

The stars, barely holding their own against a lightening sky, were not the stars of home. They might have been the stars that had kept watch the last few nights on board the *Starfarer*, but Benedikt wasn't sure. It was as if the storm had driven all the extra details of the trip out of his head, leaving him only with the painful certainty that he was responsible for the sea's victory.

The upper edge of the low stone wall pressing into his thighs, he hugged himself and listened to the quiet. As the sky grew paler and paler and the gardens below more and more distinct, greens and golds replacing black and gray, it felt as though the world were waiting for something.

Then a bird began to sing. The very uppermost tiles on the roof across the courtyard were touched with gold. A hundred birds joined the first.

Dawn.

Without stopping to think, Benedikt drew in a deep lungful of air and began the sunrise song. He started softly, for he hadn't sung a note since he'd lost the Song that held the kigh, carefully working around the highs and lows as he warmed up. He'd sung the sun into the sky every morning on board *Starfarer*. His voice knew what to do with no conscious direction.

The last of the stars disappeared, the line of gold moved down the tiles. Eyes blurred with unshed tears, Benedikt drew in a deep breath of warm, damp, scented, unfamiliar air and surrendered to the Song. It filled the courtyard and terraces perfectly and then lifted up to touch the rising sun.

As the last note faded, Benedikt heard rustling down below and abruptly remembered where he was. *I've probably terrified that cat.* He blinked, rubbing his cheeks with sweaty palms, and glanced down. Half a dozen wide-eyed faces stared up at him. Then half a dozen more. A breathy murmur drew his attention up to the terraces where karjet and karjen alike clutched robes and stared.

"Benedikt . . ."

He turned. Xhojee stood barely an arm's reach away, his eyes open so wide the whites showed all the way around, his focus on the far side of the courtyard.

Benedikt turned again. He could see a slight figure, a sheet clutched about his waist, dark hair loose on his shoulders. Even after a single meeting, there could be no mistaking that stance.

Tul Altun had heard him Sing.

"Benedikt, what have you done?"

"I assure you, gracious one, I was in the temple. This stranger's song touched Tulpayotee. I felt him stir. The rumors must be true."

"What rumors?"

"That you give shelter to a warrior of Tulpayotee. There can be no other explanation."

Tul Altun frowned and turned to pluck a date from the platter of fruit by his elbow, his pair of barbers following the motion smoothly and continuing to braid. "You're sure it was the stranger's singing that invoked the god?"

"Yes, gracious one. Why has he been here so long without being brought to me . . ." As high priest of the house temple, Ooman Xhai took risks others of House Kohunlich wouldn't dare—it was his right to argue religion with the tul—but there were still lines even he didn't cross. Suddenly aware he'd come perilously close to one such line, he folded his hands over his yellow robe and hurriedly continued. ". . . so that I may help him find his feet in this world?"

"He'll have your help in time."

Uncertain of where the tul's sarcasm was aimed, Ooman Xhai settled for the safest response. "Thank you, gracious one."

"Think nothing of it." The tul sat back and motioned that his barbers should hurry.

After a moment, Ooman Xhai cleared his throat. "May I stay and speak to the stranger, gracious one?"

Remembering how he'd been dragged from sleep by visions of the sun, Tul Altun nodded. "Yes, I think that might be a good idea."

"Follow my lead. When I kneel, you kneel. When I rise, you rise. Unless the tul tells you to rise, then you do what he says and don't worry about what I'm doing."

"I feel better if I have my *breeches*."

The Shkoden word pulled Xhojee around. "What are you talking about?"

"My *breeches*." Benedikt waved his hands around the thin skirt he wore. He couldn't have felt more self-conscious if he'd been naked. "For my legs."

"I don't know what you're talking about." Xhojee grabbed the other man's arm and jerked him back into motion. "Don't stop walking. When the tul commands an audience, you don't dick around in the halls discussing your legs."

"Not legs. Clothes."

"You look fine." He swept a quick glance over his charge, head to toe. The new sawrap clung low to slim hips and fortunately Benedikt had a well-shaped foot because all he had so far were open house sandals. The only problem Xhojee could see was all the hair. Arms and legs were thick with the stuff, there were gold curls in the center of the broad chest, and the line of hair that ran down from the navel to disappear behind the sawrap met up with more hair than Xhojee really wanted to think about.

"I dangle!" Benedikt protested, ears red.

"Yeah, well, don't worry about it. Once we reach the tul, everything'll crawl back up inside."

The wide halls were deserted, but as they hurried toward a distant flight of stairs, Benedikt thought he heard movement from every alcove, eddies of air that stroked quiet whispers from the hanging bells. Once, an awed voice murmured "Tulpayotee" and then fell silent.

Tulpayotee was the god of the sun, or in the sun, or maybe just represented by the sun; Benedikt wasn't sure, Xhojee's explanation seemed to have involved all three possibilities.

"Xhojee, when I Sang, have I broken religious . . . uh . . ." He didn't know the word.

"Have you broken religious?" Xhojee's laugh held no humor. "You woke the tul. Isn't that enough? Somehow, I doubt you woke the god. And even if you did, we'd probably be in less trouble. All right. We're almost at the stairs. From now on, be quiet. Do you understand?"

"Don't talk."

"Don't talk. Don't sing." Xhojee smiled nervously and

clapped the other man on the arm. "Especially, don't sing. And by the way, if that's not singing very good, I'd like to hear what you consider very good to be."

"It's just . . ."

"Don't talk. Remember, you call him gracious one if you have to speak to him. You keep your eyes locked on his feet if you don't. Unless he tells you differently. And don't volunteer anything."

"What is volunteer?"

"Don't offer him more than he asks for. Now, be quiet."

The stairs were broad and awkward to descend. They led down into a large square room with no outside walls. A line of guards, alternating men and women, stood facing out into the courtyard and another, identical line, faced out into what had to be the world beyond the house. Set into the wall directly opposite the stairs, was a huge set of stone doors carved with a bas relief of nightmare imagery.

They were the first doors Benedikt had seen, and they were a full two stories high.

Xhojee hurried across the room and pulled one open.

"Counterbalanced," Benedikt muttered trying to see where they'd hidden the weights. A glare from Xhojee pressed his lips together. Surely they couldn't be in *that* much trouble just because he'd woken the tul?

The stairs on the other side of the door were more awkward to climb than the first set had been to descend. Benedikt knew that some keeps were built with uneven stairs in case an enemy got through the outer defenses. He was pretty sure the older parts of the keep in Ohrid, the parts where Annice maintained her Bardic Hall, had been built using that design. These, however, seemed to be more for humiliation than defense, to keep those approaching the tul off-balance. By the time the upper hall was finally gained, it was impossible not to feel clumsy, tired, and frustrated.

Benedikt had believed the tile work adorning the walls and ceiling in his room was elaborate. In comparison to the tile work in the long hall leading to the tul's chambers, it was virtually nonexistent. Instead of plain geometric repetitions, tiny tiles, no bigger than a thumbnail, had been used to create pictures on the walls. The colors were brilliant and the pictures exquisite—in spite of the dim morning light and the speed Xhojee insisted he maintain.

The tul had no door at his chamber, but the alcove was so narrow they were forced to walk in single file and it turned twice, becoming almost a hall in its own right. A single string of golden bells chimed musically for each of them.

Benedikt barely had time to note that Tul Altun wasn't alone before Xhojee dropped to one knee. Right arm between his legs in the hope he could keep his skirt down, Benedikt followed.

Sandaled feet walked across the room and stopped in front of Xhojee. The metal on the sandals had been gilded and the toenails trimmed square and polished. As the other man had been wearing a floor-length yellow robe, they had to be the tul's feet.

"Does he still understand more than he speaks?"

No mistaking the tul's voice. Or the effect of the tul's voice. Although the question had been directed at his companion, sweat beaded Benedikt's bareback.

"Yes, gracious one."

"Can he speak for himself?"

"He sometimes gets words wrong, gracious one, but he can make himself understood."

"Good. Wait in the hall, I will speak with you later."

"Yes, gracious one."

Benedikt listened to the sounds of Xhojee leaving and tried not to feel abandoned by his only friend. Xhojee had no more choice about leaving than he did about staying. The sandals moved more fully into his line of sight.

"Just what were you doing this morning, Benedikt?" The tul's pronunciation made the final tee almost a syllable on its own.

"I were Singing the sunrising, gracious one." Remembering Xhojee's warning not to volunteer, he closed his teeth on an explanation he didn't think he had the words for anyway. In either language.

The other person in the room gasped, and a yellow hem swayed into Benedikt's view. "Gracious one, out of his own mouth, he was evoking Tulpayotee!"

"He said no such thing, Ooman. Benedikt, look at me."

Benedikt swallowed and lifted his head. He was enough taller than the tul that even kneeling their faces weren't that far apart. Given differences in decoration, they were dressed identically.

"Do you know who Tulpayotee is, Benedikt?"

"Yes." The tul's expression indicated he should continue. "He is God of Sun. Or is Sun. Or the sun is his . . ." He didn't know the word for symbol, so he came as close as he could. ". . . sign."

Tul Altun nodded. "The Ooman thinks you were singing to Tulpayotee this morning. Were you?"

Remembering how his Song had risen to touch the sun, Benedikt nodded, hoping he hadn't broken any religious taboos. "Could have, gracious one."

"Really?" Tul Altun walked around behind the kneeling man and lifted a strand of the golden hair. It was long enough to braid, but he'd given orders it be left loose. Watching the colors change as it spilled through his fingers, he actually spent a moment wondering if the god had truly blessed him before reminding himself of his physician's certainty that this was just a man. A man with an appearance he could exploit and apparently a few other talents as well. "Can you sing the same song tomorrow morning, Benedikt?"

"Yes, gracious one."

"Good. You'll sing it tomorrow in the temple, and we'll both see if the Ooman tells the truth."

With the tul still behind him, Benedikt's gaze flicked over to the other man. His head had been shaven and covered in black patterns that extended out onto his cheeks.

"Although I've done what I could to keep your existence secret, there are those in this house who believe you've come from Tulpayotee, that you're one of his warriors here to prevent the change. It turns out that Ooman Xhai listens to rumors and, after this morning, he believes them. What do you think now that you've seen him, Ooman?"

"The invocation, his appearance . . ." The priest shook his head. "Can he be anything else?"

"A good question. Why don't you go out onto the terrace and think about it?"

"Yes, gracious one."

Although he'd never seen the shaved man before and

had no idea if he were friend or foe, Benedikt found it difficult to breathe as he watched him leave. There was something very disturbing about having the full attention of the tul.

"Who are you really, Benedikt? Where do you come from?"

Startled, Benedikt looked up and met a penetrating stare looking down. It was clear that whatever the priest might believe, the tul did not. "I come from over the sea, gracious one." They had a long, complicated name for the sea but Benedikt couldn't remember it. "From a land called Shkoder. It are very far away. We were on a ship, there were a storm." He swallowed and spread his hands to give himself time to regain control of his voice. "Now I am here."

"Do you know where here is? Do you know where you are?"

"I am in Petayn, gracious one, in the House Kohunlich."

"At the feet of the tul."

"Yes, gracious one." His tongue felt thick as he answered. Or maybe he was reading way too much into a simple statement; he couldn't tell.

Smiling, appreciative of the discomfort he'd caused, Tul Altun slowly circled the kneeling man. "How did you do what you did this morning?"

"I have told you, gracious one. I Sang the sunrising."

"And Tulpayotee just happened to respond?"

"I don't know, gracious one." He shrugged a little. "Not to me."

"Nor to me." Except there had been those dreams of the sun . . . "But if the god responds to priests, why not to a poor shipwrecked sailor? Will the god respond tomorrow?"

"I can only Sing, gracious one."

"I suppose that will have to do." The stranger wasn't as golden as he'd been when he first arrived, but his eyes were still the color of an evening sky. Perhaps the god looked down and was himself confused. It was a pity about all the hair, but it would help to set him apart. "Stand," he commanded, stepping back. A moment later he shook his head. "No, you'd best kneel again. It isn't good for anyone to be so much taller than his tul."

"I am sorry, gracious one."

The tul caught his arm as he began to sink back toward the floor. "It was a joke, Benedikt."

The tul hadn't actually been joking. No matter what he'd said, the emotion in his voice made his feeling on the matter quite clear. It *wasn't* good for anyone to be so much taller than the tul, but as there was nothing Benedikt could do to be shorter, he straightened.

"Your body is damp." Tul Altun spread one hand on the warm air rising from Benedikt's chest and leaned slightly forward. "And there is a musky scent . . . not entirely unpleasant. Why is that?"

Ears burning, Benedikt hung onto his skirt with both hands. The tul smelled faintly of cinnamon, and the sharp, exotic scent only made his reaction worse. There wasn't a Petayn word for it so he used Shkoden. "I *sweat,* gracious one." Born and raised in the heat, the Petayans didn't seem to sweat, and his sweating had fascinated Xhojee as much as it now did the tul—although his reaction to Xhojee's fascination had not been so extreme.

"You are uncomfortable in these clothes."

It wasn't actually a question, but it seemed safest to agree. "Yes, gracious one."

"Have clothing made as you would wear in your own land. Tell your attendant that you speak with the voice of the tul; he'll see to the details."

It took Benedikt a moment to realize that his attendant could only be Xhojee. Attendant to a warrior of Tulpayotee—he could just hear Xhojee's reaction to that.

"So what did you do in Shkoder over the sea?" A sudden thought locked the nil's gaze back on Benedikt's face. "Were you a priest?"

"No, gracious one." About to declare himself a bard of Shkoder, Benedikt paused. There was no word for *bard* in Petayn, perhaps that was a sign. Time after time, he'd proved himself not particularly adept at carrying the responsibilities that came with the position, perhaps it was time to put them down. Besides, he was a bard in Shkoder because in Shkoder people recognized what a bard was. Here . . . "I Sang, gracious one."

"You sang?"

"No, gracious one, I Sang." About to explain about the

kigh, a dark glare from the tul closed his teeth on the difference.

"I understand. You sing. I heard you this morning. An entertainer," he added eagerly, almost to himself, "will be an asset. You've been trained to perform?"

Benedikt nodded. "Yes, gracious one."

"Good." Circling around him once again, he tapped the taller man in the center of his chest. "Do you know what I want from you, Benedikt?"

"You want I should pretend to be a warrior of Tulpayotee?"

"Gracious one."

A deaf man could have heard the warning.

"Gracious one."

"Very good. Yes, I want you should pretend to be a warrior of Tulpayotee." The tul's eyes narrowed. "This morning's happy accident has convinced Ooman Xhai you are who rumors—my rumors—say you are. I had my doubts that your looks alone could do it so perhaps Tulpayotee is smiling on my attempt."

Attempt to do what? Benedikt wondered.

"If you can evoke the god on demand, however, it occurs . . ." His voice trailed off, and Benedikt had the impression the tul was staring into a future he couldn't wait creating. Considering the predatory edges in his smile, it wasn't likely to be a very pleasant future for everyone involved. "As for this morning," he said, suddenly re turning to the present, "you're pardoned for waking me. Don't do it again."

Benedikt watched the tul walk over to a low dais, step up onto it, and sink gracefully onto a pile of cushions. *What if I don't want to pretend to be a warrior of Tulpayotee?* He had a feeing that his choices were limited, that the tul, who had made it quite clear from the beginning that he'd had a use for him, would not take a refusal well. Did it matter? *What would I pretend to be instead?* His gaze locked on the smooth planes of the tul's face, he discovered he didn't want answer.

"I won't finalize my plans until I know how useful you can be. After tomorrow morning . . ."

Maybe I should warn him that he's counting on the wrong bard . . . man.

The tul paused and focused on Benedikt once again. "What is it?"

His attention felt like the calm before the storm that had driven the *Starfarer* to the bottom of the sea. He'd had no control over that storm either. "Were there others found like me, gracious one?"

"Like you? You mean the others on your ship? No." Tul Altun shook his head, slender braids tipped in scarlet feathers sweeping across his shoulders. "I sent my people out to scour the beaches, but you were the only one found."

"The only one . . ."

"Yes, the only one." The tul's expression spoke concern, his tone triumph.

"The tul want to see you now."

Now left no time for anything but a quick squeeze of Benedikt's arm as Xhojee hurried into the chamber wondering why his mother had thought it such a good thing he be brought to the attention of the tul.

Benedikt stood where he was for a moment, until he heard the bells at the other end of the entrance chime, and then he started back to his rooms. He'd been told not to wait. He hoped that meant the tul assumed he could find his own way, not that there'd be no point in waiting as he wouldn't be seeing Xhojee again.

Through the stone doors, standing in the open hall, Benedikt looked out at what little of the world he could see past the shoulders of the guards. Would they stop him if he tried to leave? And would they stop him with words or with the barbed points of their spears?

And where would I go?

"We're lucky, we have the security of knowing that our talent defines us."

Redefines us, Benedikt corrected the Terezka of memory as he started up the second flight of stairs. *He wants me to be a warrior of Tulpayotee.*

And what does that involve?

I'm sure he'll let me know.

The halls were empty again. He wondered how they, the other inhabitants of this huge building, knew when he'd be returning. Surely the tul hadn't insisted they stay hidden from the moment he left his rooms until he was safely tucked away again?

All at once, he had the sudden fear that there weren't any others. He hadn't seen the healer or Xhojee's mother for days. Perhaps he, and Xhojee, and the priest, and the tul were the only four people left in the world. And Xhojee had been taken away from him.

All 'right, so he hadn't gone out of his way to make friends among the bards, but wasn't it enough that he'd never see those few again?

The faint sounds of his footsteps, the only sound he could hear, seemed to grow louder, to echo, to slam against his head until he had to stop and put his hands over his ears.

"I sent out my people to scour the beaches, but you were the only one found."

He hadn't realized how much he'd held onto the hope, deep in his heart, that there'd been other survivors. That he hadn't failed them all.

That hope was gone.

Empty heart, empty halls; hands still clutching his head, he stumbled back to his rooms, bounced back and forth from wall to wall in the entrance, and finally ended up in the bathing room where he teetered on the edge of the deep tile tub.

The water was tepid and scented with one of the flowers from the garden. He stripped off skirt and sandals in seconds and slid into the bath. The tub was large enough that he could lie down with his head under the water.

So he did.

The tul would just have to consider him ungrateful.

A familiar touch lifted him back into the air again.

Blinking water from his eyes, Benedikt stared at the ripples where the kigh had been. This was the first kigh he'd seen in Petayn, but then this was the first time he'd tried to drown himself. Pushing wet hair back off his face, he got his feet beneath him and began to rise. The water clung to his body, pulling him back.

He allowed the water to win although he could have broken its hold. When he softly Sang the four notes to call the kigh, it reformed so quickly it had to have been waiting for the call.

Had probably been waiting every time he'd bathed. If all kigh were part of a greater kigh, changing the water was of no significance.

Reaching out a nearly human hand, it touched his check.

"I am the only one who survived." He spoke in Shkoden. "Why?" The fluid body reformed behind the blow from his fist. "Why did you save me and not the others?"

The kigh didn't answer. Benedikt hadn't expected it to, its presence was answer enough. He was a bard of Shkoder.

Had been a bard of Shkoder.

Tears, three, four, a half a dozen fell into the water and the kigh drew them into itself. For a moment, Benedikt thought he could see them, separate saltwater droplets, as little a part of the whole as he was a part of the life he now found himself living.

When the kigh leaned forward, he leaned back and, weeping quietly, accepted the comfort it offered.

Seven

A very young priest, his head only partially tattooed, came for Benedikt while it was still dark. He woke to see the boy bending over him, fingers on his lips, and he slid out of bed without waking Xhojee.

He'd still been in the bath when the other man had returned, and he'd thanked all the gods in the Circle that he'd made it very clear from the beginning he preferred to bathe privately. He'd managed some kind of reply to Xhojee's worried call and then, a few moments later, managed to Sing a gratitude and dismiss the kigh.

"I have told the tul everything I know about you," Xhojee had said with a smile when he emerged. *"I'm to continue giving you instruction."* Some time between the tul and the suite, his hair had been divided into six braids. The smile had disappeared as he got a closer look at his charge. *"Are you all right? Should I send for the physician?"*

Benedikt had shaken his head and sunk down onto the bed. He didn't need the physician, he needed not to be alone. So Xhojee stayed.

It was cool so early in the morning, and Benedikt gratefully put the loose robe offered by the young priest on over his skirt . . . his sawrap. When he slid his feet into his sandals, the boy hurriedly put his hooded lamp on the floor and knelt to lace them. Embarrassed, Benedikt tried to pull his foot away, but a stern glance told him quite clearly to stop.

Apparently, warriors of Tulpayotee didn't lace their own shoes.

The temple was not in the main building. Benedikt followed his guide down to the open hall—lit now by lamplight, the two lines of guards still on duty—and around to the eastern part of the square where an open archway led to a wide tiled path. Although it was still too dark to see clearly, the lush growth of the courtyard garden seemed to be missing here. In both directions, he could see grass, cropped sheep-pasture short, blending into the darkness.

At the end of the path, a flight of stairs covered the entire side of the building—all four sides of the building Benedikt realized when he reached the top. He snuck a glance back over his shoulder and was amazed to see that he was even with the top of the house. Essentially, the temple of Tulpayotee stood on a huge platform, three stories high.

The actual temple appeared to be made primarily of columns, roofed but open on all sides to the weather. As Benedikt stood staring, the young priest offered him a leather flask and indicated he should drink. The water was warm from being held next to the boy's body and tasted faintly of honey and herbs. The sudden thought that they were trying to drug him disappeared as he realized he'd never have been able to sing with his throat dried by sleep and the climb. He smiled his thanks.

The boy's only response was to take back his empty flask, point toward the center of the temple, and then start back down the stairs.

Tul Altun and Ooman Xhai were waiting by a large, square block Benedikt took to be the altar. The light changed as he moved toward it and, glancing up, he saw that the roof ended where the altar began. Considering the violent storm he'd witnessed from the safety of his rooms, he figured some services had to be distinctly unpleasant. Although perhaps Tulpayotee, being a god of the sun, wasn't worshiped in the rain.

The tul, the loose hair rippling over his shoulders making him look younger, softer, pointed an inarguable finger. "Stand there." The command proved the implied softness to be illusion. "Sing as the sun rises."

The position put the altar between Benedikt and the sunrise.

No one seemed inclined to talk much after that, so Benedikt shifted his weight from foot to foot and wished that the whole thing was over. What if it didn't happen? What if he sang the sunrise and nothing manifested?

This is crazy. This isn't my god. I shouldn't be here.

Then he remembered that the tul had planned to use him right from the beginning, probably from the moment he'd been carried unconscious off the beach, long before he'd Sung the sunrise, and a failure this morning wouldn't change that. He was, by his own admission, merely waiting to finalize his plans.

That didn't actually make Benedikt feel much better.

The sounds of the night began to fade and, one by one, the stars were extinguished by the coming day.

Benedikt took a step away from the altar and felt, rather than saw, the tul turn toward him. He forced his lips apart. Bards do not hit wrong notes, the talent that makes them bards makes that impossible—Benedikt had been told that time after time while in training, but the opening notes he managed to squeeze out of his throat were as close as any bard had ever come.

"I doubt that would call pigs," the tul muttered.

Anger replacing the first flush of embarrassment, Benedikt locked his eyes on the distant flush of gold and filled his lungs. Sliding into the vocals—*"Oh, light of day we greet you . . ."*—he held nothing back, playing his voice like an instrument. His ribs expanded painfully far, his highs had never been so high, his lows so low, or his tones so ringingly clear.

On the edges of his vision, he saw Tul Altun and the priest turn to face the altar. Ooman Xhai looked beatific— in spite of his shaven head and tattoos; the tul looked predatory. They were both doomed to disappointment. Technically brilliant, the song was emotionally flat. The sun would rise, regardless, but Benedikt knew that the only thing he was evoking this morning was a sore throat.

And then, as the first low rays of light touched the altar, he felt something stir; not a god but the prayers and promises, the fears and joys of all the people who had come to this temple, who had stood where he stood and believed in something larger than themselves. Opening his arms to the light, he stopped showing off, gentled his voice, and added his Song to theirs.

A soft exclamation from the priest dropped his gaze to the altar. There, in the center, lay the golden translucent form of a newborn baby boy. A heartbeat later the infant opened his eyes and became a thousand tiny suns that spun off into the sky.

Benedikt let the last note fade, then, breathing heavily, he stumbled forward and lightly touched the altar's edge. The stone was warm.

When a hand closed around his arm, he jerked back, afraid he'd broken a temple taboo, but instead of censure he saw only awe on the face of Ooman Xhai. This close and in this light, the priest was older than Benedikt had first assumed, the tattoos had distracted from the deep lines around his eyes and at the corners of his mouth. There were tears running down both his cheeks.

"Yesterday, the god could barely be seen, but now, when you sing in his house, he favors you greatly."

"That was the god? A baby?"

Ooman Xhai smiled. "Every morning Tulpayotee is born. Every evening he dies." He stepped away from the altar, pulling Benedikt with him and indicated that the bard should look down. The ages of the god marched around the sides of the stone in gilded bas relief; an infant at sunrise, a man in his prime at noon, an ancient at dusk. "There are small services for the priests at the beginning and end of each life, but the people come at noon when he is strong enough to carry their need. If there are enough people and a strong priest, or merely enough priests, we can evoke the god as a young man and he is able to intercede in the lives of his worshippers."

"Do you sing?"

"Not as you sing; we wrap our voices around the heartbeat of Tulpayotee and lay out the measure of the god. If *you* would sing at noon . . ."

"I'm sorry." To his surprise he was. In the light of what had just occurred, there could be no question of the priest's sincerity. "I only know songs for sunrise and sunset."

"It doesn't matter." The tul's voice cut them apart. "I don't need you to be a priest." As the Ooman bowed over the altar and began to pray, he pulled Benedikt aside. "The god seems to like whatever it is you're doing. Can you repeat this?"

"At sunrise, in a temple . . ." He could still faintly feel the touch of those other kigh. ". . . yes, gracious one."

"Good. Is there anything else you can do that I should know about? Any other hidden talents?" *It's not wise to keep things hidden from your tul.* The meaning was so clear, he might as well have said the words aloud.

"I Sing . . ."

"So you keep saying. So I heard. Or do you have songs to evoke other powers?"

"Water, gracious one."

"Water?" The tul rolled his eyes. "What can you make water do?"

Benedikt shrugged. "What do you want it to do, gracious one?"

"Nothing. Water is of no use to me." He turned to face the altar and smiled. "But this, this is. Return to your room, Benedikt. The change is coming, and the Ooman and I have much to discuss. Oh, one more thing—this." His gesture included altar, temple, and sunrise. "No more singing to gods unless it's by my command."

Benedikt had already decided on his own that there'd be no more Singing the sunrise. Evoking a god, even an infant one, was just a little more than he felt capable of dealing with. He bowed and turned to go, but Ooman Xhai stopped him. Reaching up, he slipped a cool hand behind the taller man's neck and drew his head down until he could murmur, "Thank you," against Benedikt's forehead and seal the words softly with a gentle touch of his lips.

"Enough of that."

Doubting very much that the priest's blessing could stand against the tul's disapproval, Benedikt hurried away.

"And what was that in aid of?" Tul Altun demanded as the sound of Benedikt's footsteps descended the stairs. When the priest turned toward him, he noted that the old man seemed calmer, more sure of himself.

"I merely thank him, gracious one, for showing me the birthface of my god."

"This isn't about you and it isn't about Tulpayotee. It's about me." Pushing his loose hair impatiently back off his face, the tul walked out to the edge of the temple and stared out toward the coast where Benedikt had been found. "*I* have a chance to strengthen *my* position before the change."

"How, gracious one?"

"Think about it, Ooman; what would be the result if I took my warrior of Tulpayotee to court and had him invoke the god in the Great Temple?"

"You would attract the attention of the Tulparax, gracious one," the priest answered promptly. "The Sun in Splender would consider you blessed by Tulpayotee."

"So he would." One so blessed would gain the favor of the court, and those in favor of the court were those given powerful contracts and commissions. Until Benedikt, his future had been bleak at best, but now he could feel the possibilities stretching out before him. "Which is why we're going to court and you're presenting Benedikt in the Great Temple."

That got the priest's full attention. "I am, gracious one? Now?"

"No, not now. I have a few plans to put in motion before we leave—but soon. The Tulparax won't live much longer and if I don't strengthen my position before the change, my loving sister will quite happily destroy me."

"Gods are for the gullible."

Nodding thoughtfully, Benedikt reached across the low table and plucked a piece of steaming fish out of its leaf wrapping and popped it into his mouth. The tul seemed to think that, given his performance in the garden, there was no longer any need for him to remain hidden. Two giggling karjen had taken a long look at him when they brought in the food. Both were nicely rounded under their shifts and he'd taken a long look at them in return. One of them was missing the smallest finger on her left hand. "Then how do you tell me of the golden baby?" he asked mildly when he'd finished chewing.

Xhojee scowled, well aware he was being patronized. "How do I *explain* the golden baby? A trick of the light." He snorted. "A trick of the priests."

"The priest was as surprised as Tul Altun. He thanked me."

"The tul?"

"The priest."

"For glory's sake, Benedikt, do *you* think you evoked Tulpayotee?"

"If I understand evoked, no. I give form to what was there."

Xhojee snorted again. "*That* is what it means to evoke."

Benedikt shrugged. Some day, he'd take Xhojee to the temple and show him, but he saw no need to waste his morning on an explanation that could only suffer through lack of common vocabulary. "The tul wants people to believe I am a warrior of Tulpayotee."

That drew Xhojee's attention off the fruit paste he was spreading. "He does? What people?"

"All people as far as I can tell."

Squirming backward far enough to miss the low table, Xhojee banged his forehead into the floor. "All hail great warrior! Tulpayotee blesses me with your presence."

"Stop it."

"I believe what my tul tells me to believe." Catching the grapes Benedikt threw, he moved back to the table and continued eating. "Did he say why?"

"The tul did not explain to me but he said, yesterday, '*There are those in this house who believe you have come from the court of Tulpayotee, that you are one of his warriors sent to prevent the change.*' "

The next few moments involved a great deal of back pounding as Xhojee attempted to cough up the mouthful of flat bread he'd inhaled. "You sounded . . . just like him," he gasped when he could speak. "Don't do that!"

"Sorry."

"I hope so." Wiping streaming eyes with one palm, he took a slow, careful mouthful of chilled mint tea.

Benedikt waited until he swallowed. "Xhojee, what is the change?"

The younger man sighed and stared into the depths of his tea. "The Tulparax is dying."

"Who?"

"The Tulparax. The Sun in Splendor."

"The high priest of Tulpayotee," Benedikt guessed.

"That, too. The Tulparax rules all of Petayn."

"The Tulparax is a man?"

Xhojee looked insulted. "Of course."

"And his death is the change?"

"No. His death causes the change. When the Tulparax

dies, his heir, the Xaantalax, the Rising Moon, takes the throne.''

A lifted hand paused the explanation for a moment. Benedikt felt a need to regroup. "The Xaantalax is a woman? *And* high priestess of Xaantalicta, the moon?" When Xhojee nodded, he nodded, too. Petayn titles were so derivative they made certain associations unmistakable. "When the Xaantalax is on the throne, Xaantalicta is stronger than Tulpayotee?"

"If you believe in that sort of superstitious crap," Xhojee snorted. "What it really means is that Xaantalicta's priests become more powerful and that *they* collect the daily offerings while Tulpayotee has only the four monthly festivals to pay the bills.''

"I forget you was apprenticed to a tax collector." Benedikt ducked a thrown grape. "So that is the change? The sun for the moon?"

"Not all of it. When the Xaantalax takes the throne, the Xaans will command the great houses. Xaan Mijandra, the tul's older sister will rule House Kohunlich.''

"And what happens to the tul? He gets tossed out on his ear?"

"She won't hit him." Xhojee looked appalled. "She probably won't even see him; he keeps his personal holdings and the bons make sure that the tax rolls of the house are given over to her. Imixara hates the bons, because they'll be taking the power away from the tul whom she's taken care of all his life. She *really* hates Bon Kytee, but I think that's personal.''

"So around here . . ." Benedikt waved his arm to take in the immediate area. ". . . nothing changes?"

Xhojee stared down at a cold and congealing piece of fish. "I don't know," he said at last. "The Tulparax was on the throne for thirty-seven years. I've never known a change. My mother was a child when the last change happened.''

Benedikt thought about the predatory young man who was currently Kohunlich-tul. If he willingly stepped down into second place, it would be only so that he could attack his opponent from behind. "What if the tuls don't want to give up power?"

"But it's the xaan's turn, they have to. The tax rolls will

have passed and no one will deal with the tuls because they no longer speak for the house. All they can do is wait for the next change."

Wait? Somehow, Benedikt didn't think so. "Tul Altun said some people thought I was a warrior of Tulpayotee sent to prevent the change."

"That's because they've only known Tulpayotee. They thinks he's real, and they think he's going to stop it, but they're wrong. He isn't, he won't, and you aren't, so it doesn't matter what they think."

"I've decided you're to have religious instruction. A warrior of Tulpayotee should know something of the rituals of his god." The tul paced a circle around Benedikt and stopped too close to his left shoulder. "Xhojee assures me you have the vocabulary."

It wasn't a question, but his pause suggested a response was called for. "Yes, gracious one."

"Good. One of the junior priests will be joining us shortly. Ooman Xhai feels it should be his responsibility, but I don't want the shine wearing off this morning's performance. Do you understand what I'm saying?"

Benedikt jumped as the tul began playing with his hair. "You do not want him to realize I am only a man, gracious one."

"Exactly."

"The symbol of House Kohunlich."

"Good." Xhojee touched another pattern on his chest. "And this?"

"The symbol of your apprenticeship to the bons."

"Good. And this?"

"A brand new symbol of Tulpayotee." After two days instruction with an intense young priest who wore the symbol inked into the skin between his eyes, it was the one symbol Benedikt never got wrong. And if he was to be a warrior of Tulpayotee, that was probably for the best.

"Benedikt. Good. I have people here who want to meet you."

As Benedikt moved farther into one of the terraced rooms on the first floor, he noted that some of the tile work appeared to have been recently repaired and the exposed walls had been given a fresh coat of paint. He also noticed that the room held the most people he'd seen in one place since he'd arrived at the house of the Kohunlich-tul.

Ooman Xhai stood just off the dais, at the tul's left shoulder, tattooed head bowed, hands thrust into the sleeves of his yellow robe. He looked up as Benedikt entered and quickly down again. He might have been frowning, but the tattoos made it impossible to be sure.

Two guards, male and female, flanked each side of the door and two more the low dais. A young karjen—or at least a boy Benedikt assumed would be karjen when he had hair enough to braid—stood by a tray table of food and drink, ready should the tul decide to refresh himself. Two slightly older karjen stood by the open terrace doors, each holding a large woven fan.

He noticed that both sets of guards, bracketing his path, were taking full advantage of their position to stare at him without appearing to. The karjen, caught between their curiosity and their tul, did the best they could.

The two people who wanted to meet him were both men, one about the same age as the tul, one considerably older. Both wore their hair in multiple braids, the braids then braided and decorated with feathers. Neither style seemed as elaborate as that of Tul Altun although given the dark-on-dark shadows in their hair, Benedikt found it difficult to be sure. Tul Altun, he noted, wore three long and iridescent green feathers, the whole arrangement falling so elegantly onto one shoulder he made the other two seem coarsely overdone. Although they also sat on the dais, their heads were much lower than the tul's.

Looks like he had a riser added before company came. An unnecessary addition in Benedikt's opinion. Tul Alton's eyes blazed and drew attention the way a moth was drawn to a flame. Benedikt wasted a moment wishing he Sang fire.

Both men stared at the bard. The older man opened a fan of red feathers and waved it slowly back and forth in front of his face.

Tul Altun smiled. "Benedikt, these are the Becan-tul and the Campeche-tul. They wanted to see you for themselves."

Dropping onto one knee, Benedikt noted how everything—position, tone, the tul's smile—indicated that the Becan-tul and the Campeche-tul were by no means equal to the Kohunlich-tul. House Kohunlich was one of the six upper houses. Benedikt was willing to wager that House Becan and House Campeche were not.

"Stand, Benedikt."

He straightened, resisting the urge to tug at his sawrap. At least the heavy leather girdle gave it some weight against his hips.

"He is everything you said he was," the Becan-tul murmured, eyes wide.

"He is not as golden as you said he was," the Campeche-tul amended, his expression vaguely petulant behind the fan.

"No, he isn't." Tul Alton's words were honeyed but the honey dripped from the edge of a very sharp blade. The continuous movement of the Campeche-tul's fan paused, and Benedikt hid a smile. Clearly, he wasn't the only one who'd heard the steel. "Why is that, Benedikt?"

"I need to be more in the sun, gracious one."

The tul's silent approval allowed him to release a breath he hadn't remembered holding.

"Then I suggest you spend more time out of doors."

"Yes, gracious one."

"Take your . . ." Only a bard could have heard the pause as the tul decided on the most effective way to refer to Xhojee. ". . . guide with you when you go."

"Yes, gracious one." He added a flourish to his bow, the merest hint of Tadeus, and was rewarded by a flash of honest amusement crossing Tul Altun's face. A small thing, but his heart pounded as he left the room.

"Oh, my," the Becan-tul sighed after a moment. "He is magnificent. Tulpayotee in the flesh. Such shoulders. Such hair. And his eyes, have you ever seen such eyes? And his voice—it stroked feathers up and down my spine."

The Campeche-tul snorted. "You don't honestly believe this stranger has anything to do with Tulpayotee, do you?"

"He wears Tulpayotee's symbol around his neck. And his looks . . ."

"Yes, yes. We know what you think of his looks." He slapped the folded fan down into his other palm. "But do you believe he comes from Tulpayotee?"

"I, well . . ." Catching up a cushion, the Becan-tul looked

beyond his companions to the priest. "Ooman, what do you think?"

Ooman Xhai sighed, the sound as different from the Becan-tul's earlier exhalation as was possible. "I have seen him invoke the god at sunrise."

"So do priests," the Campeche-tul snorted. "That proves nothing."

"But combined with his looks . . ."

"Exactly," Tul Altun broke in. "What do you think the result would be if I took him to court?"

"And gave him to the Tulparax?"

"Shut up, Gonzile. You're more of an idiot than your father was." The Campeche-tul glared the younger man's protest into irritated and unintelligible muttering then continued. "The most religious members of the high houses remain at court to be near the Tulparax and have, as a result, been there to receive power from the throne. Should you arrive with this golden stranger, you will appear to have been blessed by the gods."

"And one so blessed by the gods would be also blessed by the state."

"He'd be tested by the priests."

Tul Altun inclined his head toward his priest. "Ooman?"

"He will pass the tests."

"But will he cooperate?" The Campeche-tul raised his fan to forestall any response. "I ask only because men of power are not always predictable, and the gods never are."

"The gods," Tul Altun told him dryly, "are infinitely predictable. The sun rises, the sun sets. The moon waxes, the moon wanes. Have no fear, this warrior of Tulpayotee will cooperate. He's a stranger here, and he is *mine*."

"Yours?" When Tul Altun nodded, he fanned himself thoughtfully for a moment. "Then I also am yours," he said at last. "In the understanding that one so blessed by the gods and then by the state will bless others in turn."

"To what extent?"

"Blessing enough so that I may have the Uxmal-xaan assassinated before the change. My niece cannot stand against her, and I will not see my house absorbed."

"Her heir?"

"A child. Seven, perhaps eight years old. Interhouse rivalry over regenting will keep them busy until my niece finds her strength."

"Agreed."

"Wait." The Becan-tul held up both hands. "I don't understand. Are we saying that this stranger is really and actually a warrior of Tulpayotee?"

"I'm saying that you should judge for yourself."

"If he *isn't* from Tulpayotee, who is he?"

Tul Altun smiled and stroked one finger down the length of an iridescent green feather. "Exactly."

"There have been no headaches?"

"No."

"No spots before your eyes? No pain in the light?"

"No."

"Physician, the tul said Benedikt must go out in the sun." Xhojee threw up both hands, walked across the room and back again. "Good weather doesn't last forever in this season; what more do you want?"

"I want him to survive the experience," Imixara told him tightly, turning Benedikt toward the light and peering into his eyes. "You're lucky I was here when he returned for you. And if you call me *physician* in that tone of voice again, I'll put so much laxative in your soup, you'll be shitting out your brains. Close your eyes."

Grinning broadly, Benedikt obeyed.

"Now open. Are you sure there's no pain?"

"I'm sure."

"All right, then." She patted him on the shoulder. "You may wander about during the youth and the age of the day, but you are not, do you hear me, not to be out as Tulpayotee gains his manhood."

"I hear you." Early morning and late afternoon, Benedikt translated. Not at midday. They weren't hard terms to agree to as even the tiny lizards that hunted bugs on his terrace sought out shade at noon.

"He is now officially out of my care," Imixara told Xhojee as she passed. "Which makes him your responsibility." Pausing in the doorway, she threw a grin back at him. "I've brought you to the attention of the tul with a vengeance, haven't I? Your mother is pleased."

"My mamon will never have more than karjen because of that old woman," Xhojee muttered when the sound of the physician's footsteps had faded. "She says she stays with her out of love. Can you believe it?"

Benedikt shrugged, trying and almost succeeding in not thinking of anything, or anyone, at all. "Love is confused."

"I think you mean confusing." He jerked his head toward the door. "Let's go before the tul finds out you've been stuck in here instead of out obeying his expressed desire."

They went to temple. An acolyte burnished the images of the god on the altar, but otherwise they had the place to themselves.

"You can see a lot from up here," Xhojee panted as they climbed the last few steps.

In the full light of day, the house was resplendent with both colored tiles and paint. One hand shading his eyes, Benedikt doubted he faced so much as a handspan of undecorated wall. Down at the far end of the huge building, three tiny figures worked on what had to be perpetual upkeep.

"There should be a team responsible for each side," Xhojee said, following the direction of Benedikt's gaze. "I was almost apprenticed to one of the plasterers. Good thing I turned out to be quick with numbers."

"What do you mean, should be a team?"

"I mean there isn't. And don't ask why," he added hurriedly, "because I don't know."

Benedikt watched the work for a moment. "Is the tul in trouble?"

"The bons bring him the taxes . . ."

"That's not what I meant."

Xhojee shrugged. "You're the warrior of Tulpayotee, you tell me."

The acolyte's wide-eyed gaze followed them as they crossed from the inner to the outer edge and Benedikt remembered a question he'd been meaning to ask.

"Why do the priests shave their heads? I thought shave was what you did to children?"

"We are all children in the house of the gods." Xhojee snorted. "Or at least that's what they say. If I went in under the pillars, I'd have to unbraid my hair. I *should* unbraid it even out here—that's probably why we're being stared at."

Benedikt smiled at the acolyte who tossed his cleaning rag out of sight behind the altar and bowed.

"Or maybe it's because you've been sent from the god."

"I haven't."

"You have if the tul says you have." Dropping his voice. Xhojee punched the other man lightly on the arm. "Besides, what else have you got to do?"

Fortunately, since Benedikt had no answer, the view from the outer edge of the temple drove the question right out of his mind. "The sea."

"Sorquizic. Not worshiped but respected. Giver of bounty. Dangerously unpredictable—not that I need to tell you. Do you want to go closer?"

He wrapped his fingers around the queen's coin. "Yes."

Colored gravel had been used to create a broad path from the temple to the shore.

"Stay on it," Xhojee warned. "If you go into this longer stuff, you won't be able to see the snakes."

Set back from the tiny crescent of black sand beach, a dozen wooden posts supported a roof over what looked like the pieces of a boat.

"The tul's, before he was tul," Xhojee explained. "They say he used to come down here a lot, but now the boat master's left pretty much on his own. He lives over there behind . . . Benedikt?"

But Benedikt wasn't listening. Stumbling a little on the loose sand, he walked until he stood just beyond the touch of the surf. This sea did not look as if anyone had ever been shipwrecked in it. It stretched out toward the horizon, turquoise, then blue, sunlight kissing the upper curves of lazy waves.

It was hard to believe that under the beauty, under the seduction, lay the broken remains of the *Starfarer* and the bodies of her crew.

He could see the kigh beginning to gather, not the huge kigh of the outer sea but smaller, familiar kigh that he knew from the shores of home. He wanted to Sing, Sing his grief, Sing his loneliness, Sing his sorrow, but he held his lips tightly closed. Not even Xhojee knew about the kigh. He had begun to tell the tul about them twice, and now he found himself glad that they weren't a part of what the tul wanted from him. The kigh were still his alone.

"Is this where I was found?"

"No. That way." A gentle touch turned him to the south. "The village is in the next cove; two children found you a bit beyond that."

"Can we go there?"

"It isn't far, but I don't know if the tul wants you seen in the village."

"Did not they already see me?"

Xhojee thought about that a moment. "Good point," he admitted at last. Squinting up at the sky, he looked dubious. "I'm not sure we can get there before you have to go back inside, but . . ."

His next observation was cut off by the sound of sandals against gravel. A very young man, his hair a short brush over his scalp and the skin around the first of his tattoos still red from the needle and dye, pounded down the path, onto the beach, and fell to his knees as his feet sank into the sand. "The tul," he gasped, "wants to see the warrior of Tulpayotee."

"So you were out in the sun, were you?"

"Yes, gracious one." Only the tul remained in the room.

"Some of your skin is touched with red." Gathering up the folds of his robe in one hand, Tul Altun rose, walked over to the kneeling man and laid the fingers of his free hand on Benedikt's shoulder. "It's heated. You haven't injured yourself, have you?"

"No, gracious one. The heat will fade." Tul Altun's touch was as cold as his tone had been, and it sent an involuntary shiver skittering across the muscles of Benedikt's back. A line of sweat ran down his spine. His skin felt tight, too small for his body in a way that had nothing to do with a minor sunburn.

The touch became a caress that lifted strands of hair, and rested for a moment on the other shoulder. "It doesn't seem to be fading. Never mind, I brought you here for other reasons. Why do you think I wanted Becan and Campeche to see you?"

He had a sudden vision of a dancing bear Petrolkian traders had brought to his village when he was boy. It wore a coat and a hat, and it shuffled about on its hind legs pretending to be a man.

"Benedikt?"

"Because if one assumed to be from the god is in your house, you will be in a strong enough place to find . . ." He didn't know the word for allies. ". . . to find friends."

"And why do I want to find . . . friends?"

"To be stronger at the change."

"Who told you of the change?"

There was something in his voice, a dark edge, that made Benedikt suddenly afraid for Xhojee's safety. "You did, gracious one. You spoke of it to the priest."

"Did I? And then you had the boy explain?"

"Yes, gracious one."

"Ah." Pivoting on the ball of one foot, the tul sank gracefully back onto the cushioned dais amid the billowing, multicolored folds of his robe. "You're right about your presence in this house; the rumors alone have brought me some small benefits, and today I've secured the support of Becan and Campeche—lesser houses, but they'll help strengthen my position. You see, Benedikt . . ." He leaned forward, eyes glittering, "I'm taking you to court."

"To court, gracious one?"

"Oh, yes. Do you know what the Campeche-tul asked me, Benedikt?"

"No, gracious one."

"He asked if you'd cooperate. Perhaps he truly believed you were a warrior of Tulpayotee and that, therefore, you had a choice. You understand that you don't, don't you, Benedikt? You owe me your life, so I choose what to do with it."

He would have died on the shore if not for the tul. Perhaps he should have died, but he hadn't. He wondered, briefly, what kind of life that Petrolkian bear had lived before it began its impersonation. What had brought it to the coat and the hat and the shuffling walk. "You can't make worse choices than I have," he sighed.

"Good. Come . . ." A gesture indicated the cushions on the lower dais where the Becan-tul had sat. ". . . and I'll go over more of what you'll need to know to survive."

Survive. There was that word again.

What would Bannon do?

Survive.

"Gracious one, if they find out I am not from the god but survived from a shipwreck, what will happen?"

"You'll die. So if you have any idea of throwing yourself
on the mercy of another house when we arrive in Atixlan,
it wouldn't be wise."

"I have no idea of doing that, gracious one." He sank
awkwardly down into the cushions.

"Very nice." The tul waited as, ears crimson, Benedikt
shoved his sawrap down between his legs. "But what happened to the *breeches* you were to have made?"

"They are not ready, gracious one."

"Why not?"

Benedikt spread his hands apologetically, "I never paid
attention to how they were sewn. Without a pattern . . ."

"I want you in *breeches* for court. Am I to wait on the
pleasure of this karjan tailor?" He threw the braided skein
of hair and feathers behind his shoulder. "Would the loss
of a foot encourage him to sew a little faster?"

To his horror, Benedikt realized this was not a rhetorical
question. Spinning around, he locked eyes with the tul.
"That's insane! You can't take a man's foot just to make
him sew faster!"

Tul Altun stared at him for a long moment, nostrils flared
and lip curled. Then he leaned back, lifted a handbell from
between the cushions, and gave it one violent swing.

A guard appeared while the summons still echoed off the
walls. She had to have been waiting in the hall—although
the hall had been empty when Benedikt had arrived moments before. Guards and karjen appeared and disappeared
so quickly, he'd begun to suspect the walls were hollow.
The guard approached the dais, rapped her spear butt twice
on the floor, then waited for orders.

Benedikt knew the tul was about to prove he could do
exactly what he said he could. He was no longer punishing
the tailor, he was teaching Benedikt to think before he
spoke.

"Please forgive me, gracious one." Charm, like Command, was a bardic skill Benedikt had never had the self-
confidence to fully master but it was a bardic skill and he
used what he could of it now. Sliding off the dais, he rose
up on one knee, head bowed. "I should have said, **please
don't.**"

"You should have said nothing at all," the tul snarled.
"This does not concern you." He drew in an audible breath

and said, a little more calmly, "Why do you care about this tailor?"

"Where I come from, gracious one, the punishments are not so severe."

"But you are not *there* now, are you?"

"No, gracious one." In the dark on dark of the tul's gaze, Benedikt saw a mutilated tailor and truly realized for the first time that he was not in a world he knew. He had one card left to play. "Will you not grant the mercy of Tulpayotee?" he asked, using just enough Voice to touch the words with power.

Behind him, the guard gasped and Benedikt risked a glance at Tul Altun's face. The finely arched brows were knit together, but after a moment he slowly smiled.

If cats could smile, Benedikt thought.

"The mercy of Tulpayotee is not to be ignored," the tul allowed graciously. A raised hand dismissed the guard. "Very convincing," he declared when they were alone again. "If you can be that convincing at court, we should have nothing to worry about."

We? Benedikt wondered. But the tul continued speaking before he could ask.

"Ooman Xhai will arrange your visit to the Great Temple as soon as possible after we arrive. You'll sing, just like you did in the temple here. That, and your appearance, should be enough to convince most of the court you're from the god. I'll do what I can to keep you from having to deal with awkward questions, but the Tulparax will want to speak with you and that I can't control."

He motioned for Benedikt to rejoin him on the cushions and waited until he settled before asking, "What will you say when he asks you if you come from Tulpayotee? Remember, to do me any good, you have to make him believe the lie."

"Then I won't lie, gracious one." Benedikt risked a small smile. "I'll ask him, in turn, if the sun is not the giver of all life."

An ebony brow rose. "Are you sure you're not a priest?"

Tul Altun studied and discarded a piece of melon. Examined and rejected a bunch of grapes. It was the waiting that was the hard part, the preparing.

It would have been easier to have had Benedikt killed and his golden body found in such a way that the blame was laid on one of the other houses. On the Kohunlich-xaan if he could have gotten close enough.

"My sister has killed a warrior of Tulpayotee!" He took a bite from a piece of fresh sugar cane and threw the rest aside. Unfortunately, although the rumors would have weakened her, they wouldn't have strengthened him.

"And why waste a perfectly good warrior of Tulpayotee?"

Sometimes he caught himself believing that Benedikt came from the god. Sometimes he caught himself wondering if there might not be other uses for him.

The tul needed him.

The tul's plan would not succeed without him.

He was the only person in Petayn who could do what the tul needed.

Tul Altun needed him in a way his parents and his village hadn't with three older brothers who so excelled at what they did. Needed him in a way the Bardic Hall hadn't with so many others who could do so much more.

Benedikt sagged back into the kigh's liquid embrace, his head against the side of the bath, one hand closed around the queen's coin.

Needed him in a way Her Majesty hadn't. She'd only needed a bard who Sang water, she hadn't needed him.

"You are my eyes and my ears, Benedikt." Stretching up, she kissed him on both cheeks. *"I can't wait to hear the Songs you'll bring me."*

Benedikt banished the memory. "There are dozens of bardic names she could have substituted for mine," he told the kigh, his voice rough.

"You are my eyes and my ears, Karlene." Stretching up, she kissed her on both cheeks. *"I can't wait to hear the Songs you'll bring me."*

"You are my eyes and my ears, Ziven." Stretching up, she kissed him on both cheeks. *"I can't wait to hear the Songs you'll bring me."*

"You are my eyes and my ears, Aurel." Stretching up, she kissed her on both cheeks. *"I can't wait to hear the Songs you'll bring me."*

"STOP IT!" Shrinking back from the echos, he stared

down at his right hand, blood welling up in two half moons where the edges of the coin had cut into his palm. Breathing heavily, he dropped it against his chest and offered his hand to the kigh. For a heartbeat, the translucent features were tinted pink.

"You see," he told it hoarsely, "I've let go of the past."

By some blind turning of the Circle, he was the only one who could help the Kohunlich-tul strengthen his position before the change.

No responsibilities. He makes all the decisions.

So?

He's using you.

But he was used to that. He'd been a bard of Shkoder, and Shkoder used the bards.

What of the tailor?

Benedikt couldn't ignore his own abilities enough to deny that the tul had been entirely serious. But if that sort of casual cruelty went on as often as the matter-of-fact suggestion seemed to indicate, the house should be overrun with missing limbs. And it wasn't.

Benedikt closed his eyes, trying not think of a predator's smile as the kigh wrapped around him and began to move. A small, dry noise in the back of his throat was almost a laugh.

He couldn't decide if the smile belonged to Bannon or the tul.

He didn't Sing fire, and he was going to get burned.

"My sister knows he's here. My eyes and ears tell me she's moving to confront me at court."

"Why at court, gracious one?"

"If she discredits me at court, power shifts in her favor. And, if this golden stranger turns out to actually be what I say he is, she's there to try and take advantage of any benefits that may fall to House Kohunlich."

"Is Benedikt in danger, gracious one?"

The tul smacked his barber's hand away from a green feather and pointed to a white. "Does Tulpayotee not protect him?"

Ooman Xhai gestured toward the window. "Tulpayotee hides his face today. He will not see if Benedikt is in danger."

"Then I'll have to protect him, won't I?"

"But your sister has eyes and ears as well, gracious one."

"And the heads of two are being used in the ball court—although I may remove the larger, he rolls distinctly to the left." Ebony brows drew in as though a thought had just occurred. "Are you suggesting that I *can't* protect him?"

"No, gracious one."

"Good. Stop wasting time worrying about my sister. She may be a very successful gambler, but she's not fool enough to try anything until we're on the road."

"We'll have some distance to travel before we reach Atixlan, gracious one."

"Which is why we'll be traveling with Becan and Campeche. If that isn't security enough for you . . ." He shot an irritated look out the window at the pounding rain. ". . . perhaps you'd better pray Tulpayotee reappears before we leave so that he can keep an eye on the warrior he sent us."

After the two giggling karjen—and always the same two giggling karjen, Benedikt noted—had cleared away the remains of breakfast, the string of bells chimed softly.

"Your rooms," Xhojee mouthed.

Benedikt grinned and, in his best multibraid voice, commanded the visitor to enter.

A thin man, short even for a Petayn, poked his head timidly around the corner. "Pardon," he murmured. "But I think I have finished."

"Would the loss of a foot encourage him to sew a little faster?"

Benedikt jerked at the memory, waved off Xhojee's question, and told the tailor to come in.

Frowning slightly, Xhojee got to his feet and glanced between the two men. "If you'll be busy for a while," he said. "I've got some things to do."

Distracted by thought of mutilations, Benedikt waved a hand in Xhojee's general direction. "Yeah. Sure." When Xhojee snorted, he actually focused on the other man. "What? You'll be back, right?"

Rolling his eyes, Xhojee bowed. "Of course I'll be back, oh, warrior of Tulpayotee."

The tailor made a small sound in the back of his throat.

"Stop it, you idiot." Benedikt stepped forward and froze

when it looked as if the frightened man might drop to his knees. "You're not the idiot," he clarified, gesturing at Xhojee. "He is." In a strange language it was harder to pitch his voice so that there'd be no question of belief, but he did the best he could. "You have nothing to be afraid of."

"The warrior of Tulpayotee is in a gracious mood today," Xhojee added solemnly.

Benedikt whirled to face him, trying unsuccessfully not to laugh. "Would you get out of here!"

"As you command, great one." Bowing with every step, Xhojee backed from the room, disentangled himself from the string of bells, and disappeared.

The tailor looked as though he might follow at any moment.

"The *breeches*," Benedikt prodded gently.

"Ah. Yes. The *breeches*, great one."

"Not great one. Benedikt." The tailor seemed so shocked Benedikt sighed. "Just not, great one; all right?"

"Yes, gr . . ." Flustered, he shook out the garment he'd been clutching to his tattoos. "I think I have solved the problem of the fabric between the legs. If you would try them . . ."

They fit the way Benedikt remembered breeches fitting. He settled himself to the left, buckled the waistband that crossed over much like the top of a sawrap, and stared down at his fabric-enclosed legs. It felt weirdly confining in places and very loose in others.

"The legs must be wide," the tailor explained when Benedikt mentioned it. Twitching a seam straight, he searched for an explanation that wouldn't sound insulting. "When it is hot, you are damp," he said at last. "The fabric is very fine. It will stick."

This made sense—the only time he wasn't covered in a fine patina of sweat, and sometimes not so fine a patina, was while he was in the bath.

Benedikt glanced down at the blue chalk line angling out from his crotch. "Can I guess I don't get to keep these?"

"Keep? No. These are my pattern. With these I can make you many *breeches*."

"Just one pair I can keep would be fine," Benedikt muttered, stripping and reaching reluctantly for his sawrap;

modesty in this case merely wasted time. Not only was there nothing the tailor hadn't seen, there was very little he hadn't measured.

When the small man left, still adjusting chalk lines, Benedikt wiped the sweat from his chest with the palm of one hand. The rain that had been pounding down since before dawn had made it no cooler. Only wetter.

Smiling suddenly, he walked out onto the terrace.

He staggered a little as a gust of wind slammed a sheet of rain into him, then he found his balance, threw back his head, and opened his arms to the sky. Another man might have had trouble breathing but around Benedikt's nose and mouth the driving rain became a gentle mist.

A second gust brought a wave of jasmine up from the garden below.

A third brought the cold, dark, almost oily scent of wet stone.

A fourth brought the warm, salt smell of the sea.

He was standing on the deck of the *Starfarer,* the storm crashing all around him. He opened his mouth to Sing, but there was no Song powerful enough to stop this particular storm.

Saltwater joined the fresh on his face as he made his way indoors and leaned, water pouring off him, against the wall.

He had to Sing the *Starfarer* to rest.

Xhojee was probably with Tul Altun. Benedikt suspected he reported to the tul every morning. If he wanted to Sing the *Starfarer* to rest, he had to go now.

Singing softly under his breath, he stepped out into the hall. He passed one karjen who frowned at the water dribbling off his sawrap and sandals, but the Song was enough to keep her from looking directly at him.

Still Singing, Benedikt made his way to the temple exit. He moved unnoticed out of the house, up the broad stairs, across the deserted temple, and down, toward the sea.

He stayed on the path more by feel than sight—*Although any self-respecting snake is probably inside . . .*—and he found the beach by falling onto his knees in the sand.

The wind was stronger here. It blew great holes of visibility into the rain. As Benedikt got to his feet, the boatshed appeared suddenly to his left. Behind the hull of the tul's boat, an old man stared at him from under lowered brows.

The wind shifted and boatshed, boat, and boat master, if that's who he was, were gone again.

Standing ankle-deep in the sea, Benedikt turned in the direction Xhojee'd said he'd been found and began a new Song, weaving his voice into the sounds of the storm. It opened a path before him, and he moved quickly along the shore. He wasn't certain how far his voice would carry, but he hoped the weather would keep everyone safely in doors. Whether for their safety or his, he wasn't sure.

Passing the village, he paused a moment and directed the Song just long enough to see a large grouping of huts. Less than what could be survived in back in Shkoder but here, with nothing but the unrelenting heat, lattice-work walls made the only kind of sense. When a curious dog stuck its head out a doorway, he redirected the Song and moved on.

The kigh showed him where to go.

When he'd crossed another beach and reached a rock outcropping, they rose out of the sea and let him know he must go over or around.

They wanted him to go around, to walk out into their embrace.

He went over.

Sheltered from the storm, the small crescent of sand was an island of calm. Head bowed, Benedikt stood silently for a moment catching his breath. When he looked up, it seemed that the sea and the sky had become one, the rain so heavy even the kigh blurred between the boundaries.

As a wave washed over his feet, he wet his lips, and Sang.

He Sang his pain at his failure. His guilt because he'd been expected to save them and hadn't been strong enough.

He Sang for the loss of life, for the loss of dreams.

He Sang, asking for a forgiveness the kigh couldn't give. All but one of those who could were dead, and that one was far, far away.

He had failed *her* most of all, for she had entrusted those lives to him. He held one low note and then another a little higher. If he could only let her know it hadn't been her fault but his . . .

She would wait and wonder and finally, when hope was gone, she would blame herself. He would willingly give his life to take that pain from her, to place the blame where it belonged.

And only water lay between them.

It might as well have been an ocean of sand or fire. If he couldn't save the *Starfarer,* how could he hope to convince the kigh to carry a message across the unknown width of an angry sea?

The Song became a wail, then a sob.

The kigh moved up the beach and tugged at his ankles, at his knees, at his thighs.

Come, lose yourself in us.

Almost.

He took a step forward.

He remembered.

There was someone who needed. Someone to give his life purpose. One more person he must not fail.

One more chance.

He clutched at it and managed to Sing a gratitude.

Eyes wet with more than rain, Benedikt staggered backward until his back pressed hard against the surrounding rock. The sudden pain of sharp edges scraping over bare skin brought him a little distance and he realized that even a gratitude would not keep the kigh away for long. He had to move away from the sea before he gave in and became a part of it.

He turned.

A cloth pressed down over his mouth and nose.

A smell like rotting orchids.

Blackness.

Eight

"KOHUNLICH Quilax, the old boat master, saw the Benedikt by the sea, gracious one." Eyes focused on the wall over the tul's head, the guard gripped her pike with white knuckles. When the tul was this angry, it made very little difference who was to blame. "He said the warrior of Tulpayotee headed south, along the shore."

"He saw? He said?" Eyes narrowed, the tul paced slowly around behind her. His hands were empty, but the skin between her shoulder blades itched regardless. "He saw the warrior of Tulpayotee heading south, and he did nothing?"

"Yes, gracious one."

"Your Five went after him?" He stood beside her now, leaning close enough that she could feel his breath hot on her shoulder and smell the cinnamon he'd had rubbed into his hair.

"Yes, gracious one." As the Five's Second, it had been her responsibility to report back to the tul. *You work your way up from nothing, and then you're in the wrong place at the wrong time.* Starving on the house periphery with her siblings had never looked so good.

"Rejoin them." The pause held her in place; he clearly wasn't finished. "On your way, kill the boat master."

"Yes, gracious one." Relief made her almost light-headed as she spun about and hurried from the room. Death would walk House Kohunlich until the warrior of Tulpayotee was found, and every step it walked with someone else meant there was one less chance that it would walk with her.

Tul Altun remained motionless for a moment, standing facing the place where the guard had been.

"Shall I send one of the temple workers to retrieve the boat master's body?" Ooman Xhai asked softly.

Jerked from his reverie, the tul slowly turned toward the priest. "No. His body will be left to the gulls."

"Gracious one, the boat master has served you, and your father before you, faithfully all his life." The priest spread his hands imploringly. "To die for failing you is one thing, but to be denied the final rites . . ." His voice trailed off at the expression on the tul's face.

A weighted silence settled.

And lengthened.

"Your position allows you a great deal of license, Ooman." The tul's voice pinned the priest's title to the silence. "It would be safest if you did not presume more influence than you have."

Even the oldest, most faded tattoos stood out in bold relief against the sudden paling of Ooman Xhai's skin. He opened his mouth, closed it again, and said finally, "Your pardon, gracious one."

"And now you." Tul Altun ignored the apology and moved slowly across to the kneeling figure before the dais. "What do I do about you?"

A line of blood still dribbling from one corner of his mouth where the tul's ring had split his lip, Xhojee stared mutely at the floor.

"You were with me when Benedikt left." The backs of two fingers stroked a bruised cheek. "You returned to me immediately after you found him gone." The hand slipped under the younger man's chin and lifted his head. "It's very difficult to find fault with you, but Benedikt is still missing and fault, after all, must . . . be . . . found." With each of the last three words, the tul's grip tightened until his fingertips drove into the soft flesh of Xhojee's throat.

Found . . .

Xhojee clawed at the tul's wrist and gasped out his suspicions. Released, he sagged forward, desperately sucking in air. He could barely hear the tul snapping out orders through the roar of blood in his ears, and surely it was the pounding of his heart he felt not the vibrations of a hundred feet running for the tiny cove where Benedikt had washed ashore.

When the silence settled again, he became aware of a single gilded sandal thrust into his line of sight.

"Why didn't you mention this earlier?" The tul's fingers tightened in his hair.

"I didn't know he—Benedikt—had gone to the shore, gracious one."

The fingers tightened and released, tightened and released.

"Granted."

The sandal moved away and Xhojee fought to calm his breathing. If they found Benedikt in the cove, the worst was over. If not . . .

"Someone besides the boatmaster must have seen him." Moving out onto the terrace, the tul savagely ripped a feather from his hair and began methodically stripping it to the shaft. "He didn't fly from his room to the shore. There may be more shadows than people in this house, but the halls are never entirely empty unless I order it so. And I didn't." He flung the shaft aside, spun on his heel and reentered the room, glaring over Xhojee's back at the priest. "I want to know who was in the halls with him."

"It is a large house, gracious one," Ooman Xhai protested. "The house master may not know *exactly* where anyone is."

"She'll find out, then, or she'll be joining the boat master on the shore."

"Gracious one . . ."

Tul Altun ignored him. Robe billowing out behind, he strode to the dais and threw himself down into the cushions. "If I lose Benedikt, I lose Becan and Campeche and my best opportunity to gain power before the change. Remember, Ooman, your position wanes with mine. Have we had any luck in poisoning my sister's brat?"

"No, gracious one. But a son of your own . . ."

"And has a woman of high enough house announced her willingness to carry that son? No. What woman would align herself with the Kohunlich-tul right before the change when he controls so little and the Kohunlich-xaan has a son of her own she'd like to ensure inherits? Without Benedikt, I won't live to see the first festival after the change."

Eyes wide, Xhojee shook his head.

The motion caught the tul's attention. He gave a harsh bark of laughter. "You didn't know it was so bad?"

"No, gracious one."

"No. Why would you." His lip curled. "My sister gained control of our father when I was too young to prevent it. He adored her and never realized that she'd added up the years the Tulparax had ruled and had decided she'd better start preparing for the change. She poisoned him slowly, protecting him from my attempts to end his life before all the power of the tul was lost. When I finally managed to have him killed, the bons came to me, but that was all. I could do little more than keep myself alive. Benedikt gave me hope." He stared at nothing for a moment, then brought his gaze down to meet Xhojee's. "It is far worse to lose hope than to have never had it."

Xhojee had no memory of the last tul. He'd still been in the children's compound when the Kohunlich-xaan had taken her father away. His hair had barely begun to grow when the bons returned and his apprenticeship had begun. The distant image of Tul Altun had represented power and splendor for all of his life that mattered. To be brought, as he had been, to the attention of the tul, was the dream of every karjen in the house.

To discover that the power of life and death over every man, woman, and child in the compound and the surrounding lands was no power at all left Xhojee's thoughts reeling. "Perhaps," he began, faltered under the lack of interest in the tul's dark eyes, and forced himself to start again. "Perhaps Benedikt will be found at the cove, gracious one."

"Perhaps he has returned to Tulpayotee," Ooman Xhai offered gloomily.

"But he's . . ." Xhojee's voice trailed off as he realized that the priest truly believed Benedikt had been what the tul declared him. He glanced over at the tul and found himself coloring under the heat of a bitter smile.

He wasn't at the cove.

"He was there, gracious one. We found the marks of his sandals; but he wasn't alone. There were other sandal marks, normal sized, sunk deep into the sand behind his."

"Sunk deep?"

"Yes, gracious one. As though the man was heavier."

The tul stared at his hands, not really seeing them. He couldn't return to the life he had before. Not because he'd breached his own security in going to Becan and Campeche; they were lesser houses, even he could handle them. *No, I've begun to move forward. I can't go back.*

Decision made, he surged to his feet and was viciously amused to see discipline hold as the guard who'd brought him the news jerked but remained in place.

"Empty the temple," he snarled as he swept from the room, "I want everything with a godmark in that cove. Tulpayotee has returned in strength after the storm, and I want answers."

The black sand all but steamed under the heat of the noon sun. Sorquizic had withdrawn from the land, and there was room enough for the five senior priests and the twelve junior priests to crowd together in front of the flat rock designated as the altar. The temple workers, each bearing a single god-mark on their shaved heads, perched around on the rocks and stood knee-deep in the sea. Tul Altun, his many braids clubbed back and secured with a length of golden wire, watched impatiently from the highest of the surrounding ledges.

As the priests chanted cleansing prayers, Ooman Xhai laid out the symbols of Tulpayotee—the rayed disk of gold, the triangular dagger, and the bowl of dried corn. Beside them, he set what they had of Benedikt—a few hairs from his bedding and an unwashed sawrap. Here, in the place where Benedikt had been found and then lost again, it would probably be enough.

The cleansing prayer ended.

Ooman Xhai raised his hands. Each of the junior priests began beating out the measure of the god on the small drums hung around their necks. The senior priests chanted the evocation.

Sunlight poured down onto the altar. Shaped by the high priest, it took on the form of a young man in his prime. The voices of the priests low and urgent, they created a background rhythm that would hold the image of their god in place.

Scooping up the dagger in his right hand, the high priest

extended his left over the bowl of corn and pierced the fleshy mound of his thumb. The image of Tulpayotee watched as one large drop of blood fell into the bowl.

Ask, it commanded, outlines shimmering.

Ooman Xhai raised his head so that he could stare directly into the sun. "Where is your warrior called Benedikt?"

In a caravan.

"Where is the caravan?" he asked, outstretched hand beginning to tremble, breathing beginning to quicken. He could see nothing but golden fire.

On the causeway to Atixlan. The shimmer grew more pronounced.

Eyes burning, his entire body shaking, lips pulled back off his teeth, he managed to suck in enough air for one last question. "Who commands the caravan?"

The Kohunlich-xaan.

As Ooman Xhai collapsed onto the sand, the image of Tulpayotee shattered into a thousand points of light that spun up and away until they were lost against the sky.

On the altar, nothing remained of Benedikt's hair except a fine line of ash. The inside waist of the sawrap had been badly scorched.

"Send him to me the moment he recovers," the tul commanded with a nod toward the fallen priest. "Tell him we're leaving for Atixlan and the court of the Tulparax as soon as possible."

The first thing he remembered was throwing up. It was also the second and third thing he remembered. As his stomach twisted and his throat convulsed, he had the vague idea that there should be more to life than a fight to breathe through the taste of bile.

"What's the matter with him?"

A woman's voice, only academically interested. She didn't care one way or the other.

"He's reacting badly to the orchid distillate, peerless one."

"Will he live?"

He found himself almost hoping that he would not.

"I expect so, peerless one. He's already much better than he was."

"Then accept payment for the body, and my people will see that you get the rest when and if I can speak with him."

"There is one thing more, peerless one. He was singing the entire time I followed him along the shore, and when he reached the small cove, it seemed the sea was answering."

"Answering how?"

He could feel damp ground under his cheek. He wanted to shout, "Don't tell her!" but he couldn't find his voice, and he didn't understand why, or even what, she wasn't to be told.

"Waves rose up, peerless one, and moved to his singing."

"The waves obeyed him?"

"Yes, peerless one."

"Really?"

"I would never lie to you, peerless one."

"True enough."

He heard something whisper close to his head but he couldn't make out the words.

"Tell my caravan master that you speak with the mouth of the xaan. You're to have one quan more than we agreed."

"The information pleases you, peerless one?"

"All information pleases me."

It was clearly a dismissal.

He heard the whispering again, closer, and the small part of his mind that wasn't concentrating on breathing said, *silk*.

"Have that idiot killed. He can obviously go in and out unimpeded through my brother's perimeter, and I don't want him going back in and selling the location of our guest."

"Yes, peerless one."

"Where do you really come from?"

She was talking to him now, her voice holding no more or less expression than when she'd ordered the death of—of whoever it was she'd ordered the death of.

"Did my foolish little brother actually believe he could pass you off as a warrior of Tulpayotee?" Something—a foot, a shoe—prodded him. "Clean him up and bring him to me when he can speak."

"Yes, peerless one."

Benedikt. He was Benedikt. The door to memory had

barely opened when another stomach spasm slammed it closed again.

For a moment Benedikt thought he was lying on the deck of his brother's fishing boat, watching the sail luff as they came about—except that his brother's sails had never been dyed so many incredible colors. And then he remembered.

He was in Petayn and had slipped out of the house of the Kohunlich-tul in a storm to Sing peace to the crew of the *Starfarer*. He had gone to the small cove where he'd been found and had just Sung a gratitude when someone pushed a cloth soaked in a foul-smelling liquid in his face.

His stomach churned at the memory, but it had been too thoroughly emptied to do anything more.

He was lying, curled up on his side on short grass and the canvass he could see moving in the wind was the wall of a tent.

"Did my foolish little brother actually believe he could pass you off as a warrior of Tulpayotee?"

Which seemed to indicate that the tent belonged to the Kohunlich-xaan. Tul Altun's sister.

This cannot be good. Moving slowly, his head balanced on his neck like an egg balanced on a stick, he got one hand flat against the ground and pushed until he flopped over onto his back.

"He's awake!"

A tiny, pointed face framed in a soft fringe of hair popped into his line of sight.

"Can you talk?"

His throat felt like he'd been swallowing sea urchins whole. "I think . . ."

"Good." The face withdrew. A small hand fumbled at his waist and the next thing he knew his sawrap had been unwrapped and pulled from beneath him. "Do him now."

The water had obviously been sitting in the sun, and Benedikt drank as much of the warm liquid as came into his mouth, not really caring how clean it might be.

"If you can get him on his feet, I could do a better job."

The face reappeared. "Can you stand?"

Drawing in what felt like his first full breath in years, Benedikt blinked the water from his eyes. "Yes. I can stand." He wasn't actually positive that he could, but showing weakness right now seemed like a really bad idea. In the end, both the girl attached to the face and the boy who'd been throwing the water, had to help.

When he reached for the queen's coin, Benedikt's hand closed around his wrist. "Leave it be."

The boy shrugged and returned to his leather bucket. "I guess I can see how he might come from Tulpayotee—now that he's not covered in his own puke. He is kind of big and golden."

"Big anyway," the girl grunted as she ducked under his arm and tried to keep him on his feet, "But awfully hairy."

By the third bucket of water, Benedikt could stand on his own. When the girl approached him with a drying cloth—*towel*, he reminded himself—he pulled it from her hands. "Thanks, but I'll dry myself."

"Up to you." The girl told him. "But do it fast 'cause the peerless one won't wait forever, and you really don't want to face her with no clothes on."

Nodding agreement, the boy held out a clean sawrap. "It's still gonna be short, but it was the longest in the caravan."

"Caravan?" Benedikt didn't recognize the word. "What is a caravan?"

"This is." Her gesture seemed to take in more than just the partial bit of tent they stood in.

"The Kohunlich-xaan is traveling?" Handing back the towel, he reached for the sawrap.

Expressive eyes rolled. "Well, yeah. The peerless one is traveling in her caravan." Her tone suggested that he had asked quite possibly the stupidest question she'd ever been forced to answer.

The sawrap *was* too short. As he secured the waistband as low on his hips as he dared, Benedikt thought longingly of the growing stack of breeches back at Tul Altun's compound.

"There's no way anyone had sandals that'd fit you so you're gonna have to do without." After a critical sniff, she splashed him with lime and handed him a wide-toothed wooden comb. "Put this through your hair, and I'll tell the guards you're ready."

"Guards?"

"The peerless one never takes chances even though I heard you're not dangerous."

Mildly piqued, he frowned down at her. "You heard I'm not dangerous? From who?"

She shrugged. "People talk in the bath. I hear you're from a long way away and your boat sank and you washed ashore. The Kohunlich-tul was gonna pretend you were from the god 'cause of how you look. He was gonna say that you were here to prevent the change, but that's just stupid 'cause no one can stop Xaantalicta from rising."

It seemed Tul Altun hadn't been exaggerating when he'd said his sister had spies everywhere.

When the girl ducked around the edge of a canvas flap, Benedikt saw that one foot turned in and she walked with a limp. Not that it seemed to slow her down any.

Turning toward the boy, he asked, "Why did the xaan have me . . ." Not surprisingly, Xhojee had never taught him the word for kidnapped. ". . . taken?"

The boy snorted. "The peerless one's not gonna let you help the tul to more of Kohunlich's power, now is she?"

It was the first time Benedikt had ever seen a tent with a corridor. When a pair of guards escorted him from the bathing room, he found himself standing astounded at one end of a narrow hall. Straight ahead, maybe twenty feet away, was an exit from the tent. On his right, three more doors like the one he'd just used. On his left, a seemingly unbroken expanse of brilliantly colored canvas. Underfoot, equally brilliant carpeting. At least he assumed it was equally brilliant, the dim light filtering through the canvas ceiling didn't quite reach the floor

He could hear a low murmur of voices. One, male, baritone if Benedikt had to guess, rose up out of the mix for a word or two but not long enough for him to make out what they were saying.

He could smell burning lamp oil and lime and, remembering, scratched at the dried lime juice on his chest.

The guards, who wore ornately decorated breechcloths instead of sawraps, were both men and both significantly shorter than Benedikt—although they carried themselves in such a way he wouldn't have dared to mention it. The overlapping pieces of their broad metal collars clanging quietly with each step, they marched him a dozen paces forward and turned him to the left. The wall was not, as it turned out, unbroken.

A string of tiny silver bells chimed as one guard pushed the canvas aside and brusquely motioned that Benedikt should enter.

The first thing Benedikt noticed, as he was intended to, was the tiny woman sitting amidst the piles of cushions on the dais. Everything in the room pointed toward her; all the people, all the things, the patterns painted on the canvas, even the light from the lamps. It wasn't overt, but any stranger walking into the room would have his attention captured and diverted.

The second thing he noticed were the huge palm frond fans turning slowly under triangular openings in the ceiling. Although they managed to keep warm air made warmer by the press of bodies from being completely unbearable, Benedikt had already begun to sweat. The moisture running down his sides made him feel self-conscious in a way that the sawrap couldn't—after all, he wasn't wearing significantly less than any other man in the room.

The tiny woman on the cushions glanced up from the piece of paper she held and beckoned him closer.

When he got a better look, his eyes widened in surprise. This was the Kohunlich-xaan? This tiny, plain woman was the powerful sister who'd stripped Tul Altun of power?

Then she met his gaze, and just for an instant he saw a woman who could inflame a bardic imagination into the worst kind of excess. She knew exactly who she was and what she was capable of. No doubts. No self-delusions. It wasn't arrogance, although the arrogance was there; it was knowledge, a truth incontestable.

Then it was gone.

No, he decided, not gone, contained. And, once seen, unforgettable.

Power had burned off her brother in a violent aurora. If the Kohunlich-tul was fire, the Kohunlich-xaan was ice.

If asked, he had no doubt she'd describe herself as a practical person and that it would be a completely accurate description.

She wasn't smiling, but neither was there any overt

displeasure in her expression, and Benedikt began to hope—although what exactly he was hoping for, he couldn't have said. The odds were not good that she'd return him to the tul.

As he walked forward, bare feet making no noise against the carpets, heads began to turn and conversations died. There were a number of karjen on the edges of the crowd, but most of the twenty or so men and women standing about wore multiple braids and some wore the kind of complicated hairstyle Benedikt had previously only seen on the three tuls. He saw no shaven heads covered in tattoos and would have been willing to bet that a small cluster of hooded white robes represented the priests of Xaantalicta. Dropping to one knee before the xaan, he found himself comparing the crowded tent to the tul's empty room and wishing he were back in the latter.

"So . . ." The cool, almost liquid tones confirmed that it had been the xaan's voice he'd heard while lying semiconscious, "*Are* you a warrior of Tulpayotee come to prevent the change?"

There didn't seem to be much point in keeping up the pretense when even the xaan's bath attendants didn't believe in it. "No, peerless one."

"Then who *are* you, Benedikt?"

He wondered what he should tell her. Given what the bath girl knew, he suspected his time with the tul had been thoroughly analyzed by the everyone in this room.

Who was he if he wasn't a warrior of Tulpayotee?

He was a bard of Shkoder.

No. He had been a bard of Shkoder. . . .

Now, he was a man without a country, or a position, or even the dubious comfort of an uncomfortable situation he'd begun to understand.

He'd heard someone shifting around beside him, but the open-handed blow took him completely by surprise. His head snapped back, and he tasted blood.

"Answer the peerless one, dog!"

A high-pitched yapping drew laughter from the crowd.

"Gently, cousin. My Shecquai thinks you insult him."

Pushing his hair back off his face, Benedikt turned to glare up at the man who'd hit him but instead found his attention caught by the smallest dog he'd ever seen. Mostly white with black marking around eyes and ears, it had a rounded head, bulbous dark eyes, a sharp little muzzle, and legs no longer and much thinner than his fingers. Standing on the edge of the dais, front paws braced, it continued to yap at him until the xàan called it back to her lap. When it turned, Benedikt saw that it was very obviously male and seemed to be making up in some areas what it lacked in overall size.

As the dog settled, the xaan glanced back down at the papers she still held, then fixed him with an impatient frown. "My time is valuable, Benedikt."

It was an almost gentle reminder, completely at odds with the sudden violence that had preceded it.

Who was he?

Who had he been or who was he now?

The man she'd called cousin shifted his weight impatiently.

"I'm a man, peerless one, from far across the sea." Benedikt forced his voice into a storytelling cadence, using it to distance himself from what had happened. "We had traveled many days from land with nothing but the sea and sky for company when a great storm swept down upon us. The ship was destroyed, and everyone on it drowned except for me. I washed ashore in Petayn. The people of the Kohunlich-tul found me, lying on the sand where the waves had thrown me, and they took me to his compound."

"You speak the language well, considering your short time among us. Better even than some of my own." She smiled toward her cousin.

"I serve my xaan in other ways." Benedikt could hear an answering smile in the cousin's reply and, from the corner of an eye, Benedikt saw him bow. Although of average height, he was so heavily muscled, so broad through the chest and arms, that he seemed short.

"Why do you speak our language so well, Benedikt?"

"I have a gift for languages, peerless one."

"Really? What other *gifts* do you have?"

A woman's voice made a quiet observation, and Benedikt felt his face burn.

"Clearly you have excellent hearing," the xaan declared dryly, then added, "when I want your opinion, Hilieja, I'll ask for it." She swept a serene gaze over the room. "The next person who deliberately embarrasses my young guest loses their tongue." The gaze returned to Benedikt. "I apologize for my cousin's lack of manners. You were about to say?"

Confused by the realization that both statements had been equally true—the Kohunlich-xaan had sincerely apologized and just as sincerely threatened to remove the tongue of a relative—Benedikt stammered, "I Sing, gracious one." He realized what he'd done a heartbeat too late as another backhand, less casual than the first, flung him to the carpets.

"I suppose we should have expected as much," the xaan murmured as he dragged himself back onto one knee. "I'll excuse your error; this time. Don't make it again. Now then, the singing. You sang at sunrise in my brother's house."

"Yes, peerless one." Wiping blood from the corner of his mouth, he wondered how much she'd heard. About the first song? Definitely. The courtyard had been full when he'd finished, there was no chance her spy—spies—could have missed it. Had she heard about the second song, when the god had manifested?

"And in his temple."

"Yes, peerless one." But had she heard that he'd invoked the god?

"Interesting that you've found a god to worship so soon after arriving in our land."

"Worship?" Even to his own ears that protest sounded a little shrill. "I don't worship Tulpayotee, peerless one."

"No, of course not. Or you wouldn't have been willing to pretend to be one of his warriors. That's sacrilege, you know."

"Sacrilege?"

"Don't worry, I'm sure it was my brother's idea. You were merely making the best of the situation at hand."

"Yes, peerless one."

"I shall have to ensure that you receive some proper religious instruction, then."

Benedikt could hear people moving about, but with his back to the greater part of the room, he couldn't see who. The sound might have been coming from the corner where he'd seen the clump of white robes.

"Not now, Yayan," the xaan sighed. "I'll let you know."

She couldn't have found out about the invocation, Benedikt decided, relief making him feel nauseous again, or she'd have surely said.

"I hear also that the waves obey you."

He had to clench his teeth and swallow bile. Fortunately, his stomach had been empty. She was watching him with nothing more than mild curiosity, but he couldn't shake the feeling she knew exactly how he'd reacted. "Yes, peerless one."

"Obviously not very well, considering what happened to your ship."

As his head jerked up, a large hand came down on his shoulder and closed in a painful warning. *She's right,* Benedikt reminded himself, memory banishing the anger. He watched the xaan watch him, ignoring the response to her jest. When the laughter died, he said, "Obviously not, peerless one."

She nodded once, satisfied, but with what, he had no idea. Under more-or-less-similar circumstances, Tul Altun had said that water was of no use to him. With no knowledge of the kigh, how would the xaan interpret . . .

"Sing for me, Benedikt."

Jerked out of the whirlpool his thoughts were forming, Benedikt stared. "Sing, peerless one?"

"Yes."

The last thing he wanted to do was to sing, here and now, in front of these people and this woman. "I know only simple songs in your language, peerless one."

"Then sing in your own language."

"This position . . ."

"Stand."

The single word cut short further discussion. He would sing, or he would . . . She hadn't actually left him another option.

Running his tongue around the inside of his mouth to gather moisture, Benedikt swallowed and stood. His throat burned from the vomiting, his head ached, and the second blow had left his right cheek swollen and hot. If the xaan wanted him to sing, he'd give her the only song that seemed to fit the circumstances. Fortunately, he'd sung it so many times as he'd traveled toward Elbasan, he could sing it in his sleep.

Breathing deeply, he closed his eyes and remembered what Tadeus had told him.

"Keep singing 'The Dark Sailor' if you want to, but remember that when you do you're invoking a desperate desire for home, not a sense of adventure."

A desperate desire for home sounded about right to him.

When he finished, the silence was so complete he could hear the soft whisper of the fans moving through the air. He could feel the connection he'd made with the kigh all around him, could feel tears on his own cheeks that he didn't remember crying.

He opened his eyes to see the xaan staring up at him. The song had touched her, too, but not in the way he'd intended. Power recognized power.

Then, to Benedikt's surprise, she dropped her gaze and absently stroked the small dog on her lap. "You were a performer back in your distant home?"

"Yes, peerless one." He felt calmer than he had in a long time. "Although performing was only part of what we did."

"You can tell me the rest later." This time, when the xaan glanced up at him, Benedikt saw only honest amusement. "I'm not at all surprised my brother planned on using you to better his position. Only a complete idiot would have ignored the opportunity. Who knows, it might have worked. You would have spent the rest of your life living a lie—but he cares little for that.

"Personally, I have no need to better my position, but I could use someone who can occasionally make me forget there are several dozen problems constantly requiring my attention." Her smile suggested weariness although nothing else agreed with the smile. "Will you become a member of my household, Benedikt? Unlike my brother, I can't offer you a large role to play, but I would like it if you sang for me now and then."

Briefly, Benedikt wondered what would happen if he declined the invitation. But only briefly. He wasn't fooling himself that the xaan offered any more choices than the tul did. The only difference he could see, was that the tul had assumed compliance and the xaan had asked for it.

Does that count when the question only has one answer?

Feeling as though he'd been pulled from a rushing tide

only to be sucked down by the undertow, Benedikt bowed as gracefully as he was able to in the short sawrap.

"I would be honored, peerless one."

And if it sounded more as if he'd said, *Why fight the inevitable,* no one commented.

"Good. I'll see to it that you're taught some new songs."

"You'll have to ride covered, Benedikt, I'd rather not have every peasant we pass screaming Tulpayotee and rushing the caravan. You'll have more freedom after the change, of course."

"I understand, peerless one." His hair, divided into six feather entwined braids felt strange and tight, but it was the best indication that he was a part of Xaan Mijandra's household rather than a curiosity to be confined and exhibited. *Xhojee had six braids when he got back from that first meeting with the tul.* He found it difficult to maintain a fatalistic attitude against the xaan's acceptance of him.

Whether he liked it or not, he was starting over.

"Yayan Quanez doesn't approve of how I've dressed you."

The hooded robe he wore was white and identical to that worn by the priests of Xaantalicta only much, much larger. The xaan's tailors had made it while the xaan's barber had been braiding his hair.

The high priest snorted, her breath pushing out the gauze that filled the opening of her hood and masked her face—gauze left off Benedikt's robe. "While I understand the necessity, peerless one, he is not a priest. He violates the symbolism."

The fourth passenger on the platform, the muscle-bound cousin of the xaan, echoed the snort. "How could he be a priest? He's a man."

Benedikt hid a smile. Even the shadowy outlines of Yayan Quanez's face were enough to interpret her expression.

"I know he's a man," she snapped. "That is not the point. When people look at me, they see a representative of Xaantalicta. When they look at him, they see a lie."

"But his face isn't covered."

"That's not the point, Hueru." The crescent moon tattoos on the backs of her hands stretched as she clutched a double handful of white fabric and thrust it toward him. "People see what the robe symbolizes and not what it covers."

"Which is why he wears the robe, Yayan. The symbolism will survive. Yayan Quanez is my mother's sister," the xaan explained, turning to Benedikt. "She's been anticipating the change her whole life, waiting for her god to take ultimate power—it makes her . . . cranky."

Xaan Mijandra had a very different relationship with her priests than the tul had, Benedikt realized as the high priest muttered behind her gauze. But then the oomans were about all the companionship the tul had.

The xaan ignored the muttering. "What do you think of Petayn, Benedikt—now that you're getting a chance to see it."

"It's very beautiful, peerless one."

"What's beautiful about the laborers of a lesser house working in fields?" Hueru muttered.

"This lesser house is one of our allies," the xaan reminded him.

"They're still fields of laborers, peerless one." Arms behind his head, so that the tattooed muscles of his chest and the taut ripples of his abdomen showed to their best advantage, he lay back against his woven support and closed his eyes. "Wake me when there's something interesting to see."

The xaan raised a thin eyebrow but said nothing, so Benedikt returned to watching the scenery, determined to find it fascinating because Hueru found it dull. He hadn't forgotten either blow—his cheek would bear the mark of the second for some time—nor had he forgiven. Thrust into yet another situation where his choices were made for him, he clung to his anger, using it like an anchor. It was the first uncomplicated emotion he'd had for some time.

Panels of the same gauze that masked the features of the priests hung down around the platform but did little to obscure the view. Up above, a brilliantly patterned square of silk provided welcome shade. The platform itself rode on top of a storage compartment almost a man's height deep that held both the xaan's personal tent, the household tent, and most of their furnishings.

Although large, long-necked, vaguely sheeplike animals

called coloas carried packs and pulled small carts, the actual forward movement of the caravan was provided by the single and double braids who served the xaan. Two long poles with many smaller crosspieces extended out from the front of each of the three large wagons. Two shorter poles trailed behind.

At his first sight of men and women taking their places by the poles, Benedikt had been appalled, but Hueru had made it quite clear that he was to climb the ladder, sit down, and shut up. He found himself searching for the girl from the bath, wondering if her limp excused her or made an expected service painful and difficult. He didn't see her at the xaan's poles, but there were two other wagons.

Getting under way was as bad as he'd imagined it could be—backs straining, heavy, ridged sandals digging into the causeway, angry voices demanding a greater effort. Once the wagons were moving, it didn't seem so bad.

The causeway had been built up with hard-packed gravel and kept as smooth and as level as possible. The wagon wheels were so large and narrow that very little of them came in contact with ground at any one time. The pace never moved above a fast walk. The xaan's staff could catch up, climb the ladder, conduct their business, and climb back down again all without interrupting the steady forward movement of the caravan.

Friends pulled or pushed side by side, talking or singing. Even the four junior priests walked at a crosspiece, robed and gauzed.

"They'd be walking anyway," the xaan had pointed out, amused by his reaction. "I don't use whips or chains, and those who call the cadence walk with the rest. There are brakemen for the hills, and I don't travel during the heat of the day. If you weren't so noticeable, you could try it yourself and see that I'm not forcing my people to endure untold hardships."

Benedikt, who had walked from one end of Shkoder to the other, carrying almost everything he owned on his back, found it difficult to argue. Later, he found himself watching the fields pass by and not even thinking of how.

"Xaan Mijandra cannot sleep and wants you to sing to her."

Having just gotten rid of the senior groom, who seemed to determine to teach him the chorus of a dozen songs he didn't actually know the verses to, Benedikt opened one eye and peered wearily up at the old woman looming over him. Before the groom, he'd endured an incredibly long dinner in the big audience chamber surrounded by strangers who also had six braids and nothing else in common with him—although the caravan master had attempted to include him in a conversation about causeway repairs. All he wanted to do was spent a quiet moment trying to absorb the day. "She wants me now?" he sighed.

Backlit by the small lantern hanging from the central crosspiece of his small tent, the xaan's senior attendant gave Benedikt much the same look she'd have given a bug found in the bedding. "No. She wants you to sing to her tomorrow so that she can sleep tonight. Get up, fix your hair, and follow me."

The server had two braids, Benedikt had six. *It seems the number's less important than the head the braids are hanging from,* he reflected, reluctantly doing as he was told.

The xaan's personal tent was only slightly smaller than the household tent. Two guards stood under the awning that protected the entrance from the weather but, to Benedikt's surprise, they were the only two guards he saw.

He followed the attendant across a sitting room, through a belled flap in the inner wall, and into the xaan's bedchamber. The bed, a thin mattress over the ubiquitous dais, looked large enough for six or seven people, but it held only the xaan and her dog.

As they entered, the dog's head rose, his ears went up like triangular flags, and he began to bark, bouncing stiff-legged forward and back on the embroidered coverlet.

"Hush, Shecquai!" Smiling fondly down at him, the xaan reached out and scooped him back to her side where he continued to glare at Benedikt even as he thoroughly licked her fingers. "Leave us, Zulich."

The attendant bowed and backed out through the canvas wall.

Uncertain of protocol, Benedikt decided to err on the side of caution and dropped down onto one knee.

"Ah, Benedikt. Does your tent suit you?"

Benedikt's small tent had been raised close to the xaan's at the point of maximum privacy and minimum time needed to get to her side should she send for him. To his astonishment, the senior tent raiser had a number of such positions drawn on a map of the camp with the lines of sight drawn in and the time needed to reach the xaan marked precisely in each.

The tents of dependents with more than five braids and no blood tie consisted of two long, supple poles, crossed and pegged at the middle with their ends shoved into the earth. A square of thin waxed convas was arranged over the frame as the occupant required—illusion of privacy balanced against necessary air flow.

"The tent suits me fine, peerless one."

"Good."

Benedikt stared down at his bare feet and wondered, as the silence stretched and lengthened, if he was supposed to speak next. He'd been brought here to sing; should he just start?

It was very quiet. The multiple layers of fabric between the xaan and the camp made the silence seem weirdly muffled.

And then he realized where here was.

They were *alone* in her bedchamber. Him. And the xaan. And that barking rat. Trust? Or a test? Or . . . He'd been alone with the tul more than once but never in his bedchamber. He felt his ears begin to burn.

"You aren't very old, are you, Benedikt?"

Startled, he raised his head to find her watching him speculatively.

"Don't worry, I'm not belittling your manhood. I was wondering if your relative youth makes it easier or harder to be so far from your home."

He spread his hands, attempting to appear unaffected by her interest in his feelings. "Having never been any older than I am, I cannot say, peerless one."

"Well put," she acknowledged, her mouth curving momentarily up into a smile. "But still, it must be difficult to be so different from everyone around you. Every face you see emphasizes how alone you are."

Her casual sympathy almost undid him. Not even Xhojee, intent on following the tul's commands, had realized how

alone he'd felt. Tears pricked at the inside of his lids and
it took him a moment to find his voice. "Not *your* face,
peerless one."

It was the kind of charming, throwaway compliment that
Tadeus might have used, but Benedikt meant it. For the
first time since he'd opened eyes in the tul's compound,
someone had seen him. He felt as though he were suddenly
doing more than merely surviving; that he'd started to actually live again. *I'm not wearing the bear suit anymore. . . .*
He could never thank the xaan enough for that.

She leaned back against her cushions, the dog curled up
in an indignant, wide-eyed ball by her side. "Pinch off that
lamp to your right and come closer."

A few moments later, he stood by her bed, shifting his
weight from foot to foot, wondering what came next.

The xaan looked up at him and shook her head. "You're
far too tall. No, don't kneel. Sit. Can you sing when you
sit?"

"Not as loudly, peerless one."

"Volume won't be necessary tonight."

The bed came up to Benedikt's mid-calf—an awkward
height at the best of times and more so under these particular circumstances. He sat as gracefully as he could and as
near to the edge as possible.

The dog lifted its tiny head and growled.

"I don't think he likes me, peerless one."

"Shecquai doesn't like most people, but he'll get used to
you in time." Half lidded, her eyes glittered in the remaining lamp light. "What are you wearing about your
neck? It is *not* a sign of Tulpayotee, or I would have had
it removed."

Removed. Lost. Like all the rest. Benedikt's hand closed
around the coin. "It's a token from my *queen*, peerless
one."

"Queen?"

He didn't know an equivalent word so he'd used the
Shkoden. "My Xaantalax. She rules my land."

"Ah. Should I be jealous?"

Anyone else might have thought she was flirting, but
even as off balance as he was, Benedikt was still a bard.
Xaan Mijandra had meant the question as asked. "No,

peerless one." And reluctantly he added, "She's a part of my past."

"You still wear her token."

Slowly, his hands rose to the thong and lifted it over his head. He felt as though he were watching himself do it—too shocked to stop himself. Dropping the coin into his right palm, he closed his fingers tightly around it.

The xaan made no further reference to his queen or the coin, but he could feel her approval and that helped. A little.

"I often have trouble sleeping when I travel," she told him, stroking the dog. "Can a song brush away the day's distractions and help me rest?"

"Shall I try, peerless one?" When she nodded, he sang one of the songs Xhojee had sung to comfort him the day he'd fallen so desperately apart; a children's song about an old woman who tucked the animals into bed, but because there were so many animals, it was daylight before some, like the bats and the anteaters, were asleep. Although the small dog stared at him throughout, occasionally quivering with indignation, the xaan visibly relaxed. He could have ensured that she slept but remembering how she'd reacted to "The Dark Sailor" he was afraid she'd be aware of the manipulation.

When he finished, she sighed sleepily. "A stranger sings the songs of my childhood better than my own people. I'll have to make certain you learn others." One hand waved a minimalist dismissal. "Many of the great houses keep personal entertainers, but I never have. Perhaps I was waiting for you."

Standing, he bowed. "I'll try to be worth the wait, peerless one."

I am the personal entertainer of the Kohunlich-xaan, he thought as he left the tent. He grinned at one of the guards and was pleased to see the flicker of a reaction in spite of discipline.

It felt great to know who he was again.

Hueru pushed aside the canvas at the end of Xaan Mijandra's bed and thrust himself forward into the room. "I don't like him being alone with you, peerless one."

She yawned. "I don't care."

"I know what he meant when he said he'd try to be worth the wait. He was being familiar."

"He was trying to impress me."

"Impress you?" Hueru scoffed. "You aren't impressed so easily."

"No, I'm not."

"Do you believe the waves obey him?"

"He does."

"The waves obey *him*? Does he think we're fools, peerless one?"

"No. He doesn't, which is why I'm inclined believe him."

"I don't believe it," Hueru muttered, shaking his head. "I still say the Kohunlich-tul intended you to take him so that he could turn on you from within your defenses."

"Don't be an idiot. Benedikt is of more use to my brother with my brother." The xaan sat straighter, rippled hair falling forward to bracket the swell of her breasts. The movement distracted Hueru as she'd known it would. It was a game she played with herself, seeing how little flesh would make him hers all over again.

As for Benedikt, she could recognize threat as she recognized power, and he was no threat. He wanted a place to belong. She could give him that—and he would give her everything he had.

Hueru forced his gaze back to the xaan's face. "You shouldn't let him so close to you."

Her brows rose, "Don't presume to tell me what I should or should not do," she suggested softly.

Reacting to her tone, Shecquai opened one eye and growled.

"Your pardon, peerless one." Curling his lip at the dog, Hueru stepped closer to the bed, his shins pressing against the edge of the platform. "Do you want him, peerless one?"

"Do I what?" Her laughter brought a sleepy yap from the dog. "Don't be ridiculous. He's too young, he has no understanding of what's happening around him, and he's far too hairy." Stretching out an arm, she slid a hand up under Hueru's sawrap. In her experience, once a person began to think with their crotch, it became increasingly hard for them to dissemble. "Do *you* want him?"

"Peerless . . . one."

"You do. Why? Because he's so much larger than you? Never mind. You can't have him. No one has him; willing, unwilling."

"Why not?"

Up under the sawrap, her fingers closed and Hueru gasped. "Because I said so." Benedikt was hers, and when the time came, she'd let him know exactly what that meant.

The waves were behaving strangely.

Bards who Sang water had no fear of the sea, but Karlene paused knee-deep and checked the beach to see that her clothes remained high and dry. She had others in her pack, but they'd been well worn during the Walk she was just finishing and she'd as soon not put them on again before she reached the Bardic Hall in Elbasan and the whole lot of them had been boiled.

"The older I get," she muttered to the wind, "the more I consider a good laundry the ultimate sign of civilization."

The sea moved like cool silk against her skin as she waded deeper until she finally threw herself forward into the waves' embrace. To her surprise, they set her back on her feet again.

Skimming the water off her face with both hands, she rolled her eyes and Sang the four notes to call the kigh.

There were more kigh in the cove than she'd ever seen in one place before. No wonder the waves had been behaving strangely.

It took her the rest of the afternoon to work out what they were trying to tell her. Each of them held a piece of the message—a single note, a half a tone, a tear.

Sorrow diffused over a very long distance.

Nine

KARLENE hadn't slept for almost two days. All she wanted was a chance to fall into her bed and stay there for an equivalent time. Later, when body and mind were functioning again, she'd grieve properly for the loss of Benedikt and all the bright dreams that had died with him. The old wood-and-leather chair creaked as she shifted her weight, impatient for the Bardic Captain to finish his deliberations.

"I think," Kovar said softly, pulling one end of his mustache hard enough to distort his lip, "I think this is the sort of message that should be delivered personally to the queen by the bard who received it."

"What are you talking about?" Rebalancing her head on her neck, Karlene glared across the desk at him. "I sent you word by air when I left the cove."

"*The sea tells me the* Starfarer *is lost*—not exactly something I could take to the queen."

"You haven't told her?" Too tired for dramatics, Karlene covered her face with both hands. "I don't believe this."

"I thought it was important she hear such news directly from you."

"From me?"

"I doubt she'd want to hear it from me."

"But you're the Bardic Captain!" When Kovar made no reply, Karlene dropped her hands and found him looking obstinate. "Center it! Don't tell me you haven't made up."

"Her Majesty is not interested in my opinions." He purposefully shuffled papers from one pile to another. "I do my job, and we maintain as little contact as possible."

"Contact is part of your job," Karlene snarled. She'd never have spoken to her captain in such a way had she not been so exhausted but, having started, she decided to get the entire judgment off her chest. "This *situation* is not good for us, it's not good for Her Majesty, and it's sure as slaughter not good for Shkoder!"

Kovar's brows drew in over his nose. "I find your use of Imperial Army oaths distasteful."

"Imperial Army oaths?" The younger bard stared at him, openmouthed. "That's all you have to say?"

"I needn't defend myself to you or to anyone else." His tone made it quite clear the discussion was over. "Do you really think Her Majesty would want to hear about the *Starfarer* from me?" he continued, voice too reasonable. "All things considered?"

Her burst of indignant energy spent, Karlene could only numbly shake her head.

"Good. You should find her in the small audience chamber. If not, Marija is on duty at the Palace and will be able to tell you where the queen has gone."

Dragging herself up onto her feet, Karlene paused, one hand on the back of her chair. "Was I the only bard the kigh found?"

"There were other bards by the sea," Kovar acknowledged reluctantly, "but none who Sing so strong a water."

The only bard who Sang a stronger water than Karlene was Benedikt. The knowledge hung in the air between them.

"The others don't know, do they? You haven't even told the bards that one of our own is dead."

Kovar's chin rose, his eyes narrowing defensively. "The queen must be the first informed."

The sea tells me Starfarer *is lost. . . .*

There really wasn't much else to say. The *Starfarer* was lost and Benedikt was dead.

The queen could have been told, should have been told the moment Kovar got her message and the bards told directly after that. It wasn't right that a bard had died and no one mourned him. Granted, Benedikt had more than his fair share of the arrogance and insecurities of the young and was, at best, prickly company, but that still didn't make it right. He was one of theirs. He was a bard of Shkoder.

Dashing a tear away with an angry hand, Karlene entered the Palace through the Dawn Doors and beckoned to the first page she saw.

"Go to the Healers' Hall and find Magda i'Annice a'Pjerin," she told him. "Tell her it's extremely important that she meet Karlene immediately outside the small audience chamber."

"What if she can't come?" he wanted to know, bouncing on the balls of his feet.

"She **has** to come." The bardic emphasis probably hadn't been necessary, Karlene realized as the page raced away—at his age, every message he carried was of equal and vital importance—but she needed to be sure Magda would be there. The queen had invested so much of herself in *Starfarer*'s voyage, only the Circle knew how its loss would affect her.

There were three people already waiting in the hall outside the small audience chamber. Seated in various anticipatory postures on benches along one wall, they were attempting to look serene about the wait under the steely gaze of the queen's secretary. Karlene recognized the harbor master and the new head of the Glassmakers' Guild, but the third man she didn't know. Pitching her voice for the secretary alone, she leaned over the desk and said, "I have to see Her Majesty."

"You're a bard." During the moment she studied her face, Karlene bit back half a dozen scathing replies to that bland observation. "Karlene, isn't it?"

"That's right.'

He glanced down at his appointment book. "And why do you need to see Her Majesty?"

"I'm a bard, remember. I have information." She sagged forward so that her elbows were on the desk and they were eye to eye. "It's what we do; we gather information and make it available to the crown so that well-informed decisions can be made for the good of us all."

To her surprise he smiled, showing deep dimples in both cheeks. "When was the last time you got any sleep, Karlene?"

"Almost two days ago. Why?"

"Just wondering. There's a representative from the Furriers' Guild in with her now but she shouldn't be much longer."

"Thank you." Strongly suspecting that if she sat down she wouldn't be able to get up again, Karlene crossed the hall to a bit of smooth paneling and set about propping it up. She could feel the eyes of the other three, feel them wondering what business she had that was more important than theirs. *They'll know soon enough.* . . . Tears pricked against the inside of her lids, and when she closed her eyes they rolled slowly down her cheeks, and into the corners of her mouth.

Magda arrived before the Furriers' Guild finished their business. Her impatient expression disappeared as soon as she came close enough to read Karlene's kigh. "What's wrong?" she asked quietly, closing a hand around the other woman's arm.

Karlene told her.

"And you want me with you when you tell the queen?"

"Unless you think you should tell her."

"No. As much as I hate to admit it, Kovar's right. This has to come from you."

"And here I thought I was due for a tedious meeting with the harbor master," Jelena laughed, beckoning bard and healer closer. "What's happened that you've upset Johan's . . ." As Karlene stepped out of the shadows and into the late afternoon sunlight streaming into the chamber through a high window, the queen's smile vanished. "Tell me," she said quietly.

Karlene wet her lips and swallowed. This would be the third time she'd told the story since arriving back at the Citadel. It should have gotten easier. It hadn't. Hoping for the distance she'd need to finish, she fell into a storytelling cadence. "I was two days out of Elbasan, Majesty, and I stopped to bathe in a small cove just north of Gull's Head Point . . ." She left nothing out, not her amazement at the number of kigh nor her feelings as each gave up a piece of the message. ". . . and the only thing I can conclude, Majesty, is that the kigh have brought us news of Benedikt's death and the loss of the *Starfarer*."

In the silence that followed, someone laughed outside in

the courtyard, and all three women glanced toward the window.

"The message was shattered, spread over a great many kigh." Jelena locked her gaze on Karlene's face as though she could gain the answer she wanted by force of will alone. "The *Starfarer* may be lost, but there must be survivors. If Benedikt died, who Sang the news to the kigh?"

"No one, Majesty. When a bard dies, the kigh carry the emotional imprint of the last moments of life and surrender it only when they reach another bard."

"But with so many kigh carrying so many pieces, you can't be absolutely positive," the queen insisted.

"Unfortunately, Majesty, there're only a few ways those pieces go together. They were nothing *but* emotional imprint and they all agree that the *Starfarer* was lost," Karlene had to swallow hard before she could continue. "He, Benedikt, was thinking of you when he died."

"Of me?"

"Yes, Majesty. He was asking for your forgiveness."

"Forgiveness?"

"For failing you."

A tear trembled on Jelena's lower lashes and fell to splash unheeded against her breast. "How could he have failed me? He dared so much. How can forgiveness be all he asks of me?"

Karlene took a small step closer to the queen. "As I understand it, Majesty, he also asked you to believe in him, and I think he wants to be forgiven for that as much as for falling before the storm. He doesn't want you to blame yourself."

"Foolish, foolish Benedikt," she murmured as much to herself as to the women listening. "And I would tell him so if he weren't dead." Her fingers opened and closed on the arms of her chair, and she stared at them as though they belonged to someone else. Then she drew in a deep breath and lifted her head. "Thank you for bringing me this news, Karlene. As dreadful as it is, it would be more dreadful still not to know. Will there be a service Sung for Benedikt in the center tonight?"

"I don't know. It's Second Quarter, there are almost no bards in Elbasan. . . ."

Jelena's chin lifted. "There are others who cared for him.

Tell the Bardic Captain that there will be a service Sung and that His Highness and I will be there."

Close to tears again, Karlene bowed. "Thank you, Majesty."

"Magda will stay with me, but you'd best go and get some sleep."

Karlene shook her head. There was nothing she wanted more, but . . . "I need to tell the others."

"One last Song, then let the air kigh carry the burden for a while. You need some rest." Trembling lips formed themselves into what was very nearly a smile. "And if anyone tries to keep you up, you tell them you've been commanded to rest by your queen."

"Thank you, Majesty."

"Karlene?"

She paused, one hand on the door.

"Why were there so many kigh?"

"It happened a long way away, Majesty. Ripples spread."

Karlene didn't wait for Kovar's approval. She stepped outside the Palace, called the kigh, and Sang Benedikt's passing into the air. When she finished, the kigh circled her once, ethereal hands outstretched as though in comfort, and then it flew straight up where it either met or became a half a dozen other kigh.

The residents of the Citadel were so used to bardic Singing, none of them paid her any attention as she crossed the courtyard toward the main doors of the Bardic Hall.

"Karlene?" Evicka opened one of the floor-to-ceiling ground-floor windows and beckoned her over. "Is it true? No. Sorry. Of course it's true." She rolled her chair back out of the way so Karlene could enter the lounge and grabbed the other woman's sleeve. "What do you know?"

"Little more than I Sang." She regretted her abrupt answer when Evicka flushed and tried to make up for it by telling her the entire story and asking if she'd reply to any Songs that came in.

"Of course. You go get some sleep." Releasing Karlene's sleeve, Evicka spun her chair to face out the window again. "I was the last bard to see him alive, you know."

"I know."

"He could be an irritating little shit at times, so ready to

take offense, but he was awfully cute and I kept thinking
that once he'd been a bard for a few more years he'd figure
out how it worked and . . ."

"You could jump him?"

"Well, fall over on him anyway." She folded her hands
on her stumps and drew in a breath that quivered around
the edges. "Will we Sing for him tonight? There aren't
many of us in the city."

"We'll Sing. Her Majesty informed me that Benedikt had
other friends and that she and His Highness will be
attending."

Evicka snorted. "Well, that ought to be put a set of pipes
up Kovar's butt."

Once the world stops rocking back and forth so violently,
Karlene promised herself heading out into the hall and up
the stairs, *I'll ask her why she's so happy about that.* Things
had clearly gotten a lot worse around the Bardic Hall than
anyone had been willing to Sing.

Perhaps it was just because they were listening for it,
but Karlene's Song seemed unusually loud inside the small
audience chamber.

"The windows do open onto the main courtyard," Magda
murmured as the last note faded. "And I suspect she Sang
the moment she stepped outside."

"Did you understand any of it?" Jelena asked, her fingers
white around the arms of her chair.

"Only the grief. I can hear the emotions when bards
Sing the kigh, but if they don't use words, not the actual
communication."

"Only the grief," Jelena repeated. She shook her head.
"I suspect this time that was the actual communication."

Magda stepped forward and laid one hand on the queen's
arm both for comfort and to get a clearer reading of her
kigh. Under the thin linen, muscles were rigid, and under
an outward composure lay pain and guilt.

Well aware of what the healer sensed, Jelena sagged back
into her chair. "If I hadn't sent them out searching for a
land across the sea, they'd all still be alive. This is my
fault."

"And who did you coerce?"

"No one. They were all volunteers."

"And do you control the storms?"

"No. Not here in Shkoder nor so far out to sea." A gesture stopped the next question unvoiced. "I understand in my head that this loss, these deaths, are not my fault, but here . . ." Her free hand touched her breast. ". . . here I will always feel it. I had to say it once, myself, just to hear how it sounds because you know as well as I do that everyone will be saying it soon."

Magda tightened her grip, just a little. "Not everyone," she said, surprised her voice sounded so steady. She'd been afraid that the loss of *Starfarer* would throw Jelena back into despair, but her kigh held none of the twisted, self-loathing that had blighted that first long year after the death of Queen Onele.

The *Starfarer* had made Jelena actually *be* the queen in a way that the death of her mother had not. To realize her dream, she'd had to take up both the power and the responsibilities of the throne. She'd held both long enough to be able to put neither down. That was good to know but was it worth the loss of twenty lives?

There'd be many in Shkoder willing to answer that, but, answering only for herself, Magda didn't know.

One of the twenty had been a bard.

"Will you see Kovar?"

Jelena jerked around and stared wide-eyed at the healer. "See the Bardic Captain? Now? No. I'll see him tonight at the Center. That'll be soon enough!" She paused and laughed shakily, a little embarrassed by her own vehemence. "I couldn't bear to see him now, not when the news is still so raw and painful. He'll be all *I told you so.* . . ."

"It was not exactly unexpected news."

And not exactly *I told you so,* but close enough. Palms flat on the Bardic Captain's desk, Magda leaned forward. If she hadn't been able to feel the grief in his kigh, she'd have been unable to stop herself from slapping him. "Her Majesty will need your support through this."

"My support?"

"Everyone's support."

Kovar matched the healer glare for glare. "The support

of the families of *Starfarer*'s crew? The support of the bards when one of their own, of the few, has died? If she'd listened to me . . ."

"If she'd listened to you, she'd still be trapped in the guilt of her mother's death." Realizing that if she stayed within arm's reach she really would hit him, Magda stepped away. Both her parents had tempers, and she'd never felt so much their child.

"If she'd listened to me, Benedikt would still be alive."

"You don't know that!" She whirled around, took three steps from the desk and three steps back. "A rock could have fallen on his head. A bandit could have jumped him from behind. A cut could have gotten infected when he was Walking far from help." He sat there, expressionless, and she couldn't believe the arrogance of the man, "How can you possibly believe that your directions are all that keep the bards alive!"

"I have to believe it. They are my responsibility."

Change leaves us unprepared, undefended.

If we keep the pattern strong, the edges can't unravel.

When we Walk too far, we weaken the pattern.

When we Walk on paths unknown, we weaken the pattern.

Reeling under the onslaught of Kovar's kigh, Magda barely managed to stand her ground.

When one of them dies, a piece of me dies.

Magda thought she had a pretty good idea of what pieces of Kovar had already died. Had she been concentrating so intently on the queen she hadn't seen how badly the Bardic Captain needed healing?

A Healer can't be everywhere at once.

It was one of the first things she'd learned.

Sometimes it helped.

Moistening her lips, she managed a close approximation of her usual professional tones. "Kovar, I need to see you."

"You will see me tonight, at the Center."

He'd known what she'd meant and had deliberately shut her out. All she could think of was the stupid joke the apprentices at the Healers' Hall found so funny. *How long does it take Magda to change her clothes? That depends; her clothing has to want to change.*

"I will see Her Majesty at the center tonight as well," Kovar continued. "And I think she owes me an apology."

*   *   *

"Karlene, if you would Sing water, Evicka air, and Marija fire . . ."

"If no one minds, I'd like to Sing fire."

"Tadeus!"

He hugged Karlene, bent and kissed Evicka, then gathered the other half-dozen bards into his smile, before turning to unerringly face Kovar. "I was just east of Riverton when the kigh told me. I'd have sent word, but I wasn't sure I could make it in time."

Kovar nodded. "If Marija doesn't mind."

"Please, Tadeus, Sing fire." Marija blew her nose into a large handkerchief and fixed him with a damp gaze. "I hate Singing memorials. I'm just no good at holding back tears, and that always puts the fire out."

The others smiled at the joke, weak though it was. Tadeus, his own eyes wet, put his arm around her shoulders and pulled her close. "Who Sings earth?" he asked. "None of us here . . ." And then he realized, his voice trailing off.

Kovar sighed. "I was not happy with Benedikt for going against my wishes and going off on this voyage, but that doesn't mean I am unwilling to Sing for him." He paused and stared at nothing for a moment before softly adding, "Or that I will not mourn him." Then he shook himself and brought his attention back to the moment. "One more thing before we go to our places. Those of us at the service tonight will tomorrow personally go to those families of The *Starfarer*'s crew who live close at hand. We are not the only ones to suffer loss, and it's best the truth reaches them before rumor."

When it was Karlene's turn to Sing, she Sang the song the sea had given her.

"Bardic Captain."

"Majesty."

Kovar had left the gallery as the last choral ended and had placed himself by the Second Quarter doors, the doors that led from the Center to the Palace. The queen couldn't help but see him. She would apologize for not trusting his judgment. He would graciously suggest that they never speak of it again, and then they could get on with the monumental task of keeping Shkoder safe. There had been any number of things she could have used his advice on over the last quarter, but with the exception of the *Starfarer,* there'd been no real damage done.

He would be so happy when things were back to normal. No matter what rumor suggested, he had not enjoyed their estrangement nor prolonged it in an attempt to gain personal concessions from the queen.

Who seemed to be waiting for him to speak.

Very well. He would give her the opening she needed.

"A great loss, Majesty."

"Yes, it was." She seemed older than he remembered, and she had her grandfather's way of locking her gaze on the eyes of those she spoke to. Her eyelashes were clumped together, as though she'd been weeping. "I will be sending the bonus I promised the *Starfarer*'s crew to their families. Would the Bardic Hall like to pass on Benedikt's to his parents, or will I send it directly from my hand?"

"As Your Majesty wishes."

"Then I will send it directly from my hand. From what I know of Benedikt's family," Jelena added bitterly, "it will ease their grief to know he was owed a great deal by the queen."

Confused, Kovar shook his head. "I don't believe you owe him a great deal, Majesty."

"You're wrong, Bardic Captain. I owe everyone on that ship a great deal." Her gaze released him and she turned away. "Benedikt most of all."

He couldn't bring himself to say, *So you admit I was right.* It had to come from her, from the queen, freely and unprovoked. He watched her walk away, her arm tucked in the consort's and her head near Otavas' shoulder, and he silently cursed her for a foolish, stubborn child.

"I didn't know you knew Benedikt so well," Evicka murmured as she bumped down the steps toward the Bard's Door.

Following close behind her, Tadeus sighed. "He'd been wounded, but he was healing. In time . . ."

"Yeah." While Karlene steadied her chair, she flung herself into it off the third step. "Me, too."

Dark brows rose from behind a strip of scarlet silk. "As flattered as I am at your opinion of my stamina, I'm old enough to have been his grandfather. In that respect, my appreciation was purely aesthetic."

When Evicka looked up, Karlene spread her hands. "Hey, mine, too."

"You're both so limited," she told them reproachfully, maneuvering her chair over the threshold and through the narrow door. "Did I ever tell you what Benedikt did to me on the way to the Broken Islands. We'd just left the harbor . . ."

As the other two headed back to Bardic Hall, reminiscing, Karlene leaned back against the cool stone of the Center and looked up at the stars. After having Sung a surprisingly poignant earth, Kovar had left the building ahead of the other three quarters. Now, with Tadeus and Evicka gone, she was alone.

The four stars the bards called Night's Quarters were rising over the Palace. Karlene wondered if Benedikt had been able to see them that last night before the storm. Although she'd been the one to discover his talent and bring him to the Bardic Hall where he belonged, she hadn't known him well. It seemed no one had, and that upset her almost as much as his loss.

"Karlene? Can I talk to you?"

"You're asking?" She didn't have to see Bannon standing in the shadows, or even recognize his voice. He was, after all, the only person in Shkoder who could sneak up on a bard. Then she frowned. They weren't exactly friends, but she knew the ex-assassin better than most, and he'd sounded honestly in need. Regretting her flippancy, she stepped over to a bench and sat. "Here?"

"Here's fine."

He dropped down onto the other end of the bench and sat silently staring into the darkness. There wasn't light enough to see his expression, but Karlene would've sworn his silhouette looked awkward. Ex-Imperial assassins were never awkward. "Is there something wrong with Vree?"

"What?" Bannon jerked then shook his head. "No. She's fine. Seems to be getting the hang of that whole motherhood thing." He drew in a deep breath and let it out slowly. "His Highness told me you were the one who found out about Benedikt." Another breath. "I need to know exactly what was said."

"Why?" When he turned to look at her, her eyes had adjusted enough to see one emotion after another cross his face, and the pain they revealed made her speak without thinking. "Bannon, were you in love with Benedikt?"

She thought he'd look away, but he didn't.

"I don't know. He was an irritating, arrogant, insecure little pissant. And too pretty. Way too pretty. I'm really not fond of that soft pouty look. And he was young."

"Too young."

That brought back a bit of the Bannon she knew. "The same age difference as between you and Vree," he growled.

Karlene acknowledged the point.

"I never even touched him, but I can't stop thinking about him. And it was irritating the slaughtering shit out of me. And now he's dead." He leaned toward her, eyes locked on hers. "I don't believe he's dead. Shouldn't I feel differently if he's dead?"

"How do you feel?"

"Like I want to grab him and shake him until his nose bleeds for putting me through this crap!"

Greatly daring, she reached out and laid her hand over his. "I'm no expert, but it sounds like love to me."

To her astonishment, he let her hand lie for a full three heartbeats before tossing it off. "Tell me what the kigh told you."

So she did.

When she finished, he exhaled loudly, as though he'd been holding his breath the entire time and said hoarsely in Imperial, "Slaughtering, stupid, gods-abandoned idiot. You don't slaughtering Sing to a storm, you batten down and ride it out. You know what the worst of it is?" he added, switching back to Shkoden. "He's dead, and I'm never going to slaughtering know."

"How he feels?"

Bannon laughed. "How I feel. Or what I feel. Or even if I feel anything at all."

"And yet you can't stop thinking about him."

He rose fluidly to his feet; all awkwardness gone, all predator again. "If any of this makes it into a song, I will kill you."

Imperial assassins didn't bother making elaborate threats. Karlene watched him stalk off into the shadows and sighed. The others would be wondering what had happened to her. They'd spend the night singing and sharing memories, a steady stream of kigh coming and going from the bards out Walking. The night would become their touchstone, their mutual recall of one of their number, of Benedikt.

Hopefully there'd be enough of them that they could piece together a true song in spite of how little each of them seemed to know. They'd be like the kigh who'd brought the news of his death across the sea, she realized.

Sorrow diffused.

Ten

IT had been raining for five days, a constant gray deluge so pervasive that it turned the air to water and made it hard to remember a time when the world had been dry. After spending the first day in camp, the Kohunlich-xaan had ordered her caravan back onto the causeway.

"If I'm going to be damp and miserable," she declared tightly, pulling her shift away from her body between two tinted fingernails, "I'm going to be damp, miserable, and moving closer to Atixlan."

At the xaan's order, four karjen had fought the downpour and replaced the roof on the wagontop shelter. The stretched canvas wasn't exactly waterproof but neither had the tents been, Xaan Mijandra sat under a second sheet of canvas draped down from the center of the first, Shecquai curled up on her lap looking distinctly put out, the two of them as far from the sides as it was possible to be. The high priest, Hueru, and Benedikt shifted around to avoid the leaks and endured an occasional gust of rain in through the gauze sides. There *were* canvas sides, but the weather remained so hot no one would have survived their use.

The running of House Kohunlich continued. As far as Benedikt could tell, the only difference the rain made was in the disposition of those who climbed up onto the wagon with information for the xaan.

Those who pulled and those who pushed no longer talked or laughed or sang. Although the ground drained quickly and the hard-packed causeway remained essentially firm underfoot, they had to fight the rain for every breath. It pounded heads down. It rolled shoulders forward. It added not discomfort but misery. The junior priests who would not remove their robes of office and strip down to shifts suffered the most. After the caravan had stopped for a second time rather than run over a priest pulled down by the wet weight of her robes, the xaan ordered all four to the last position on the rear poles.

"If I can't order the priesthood into sensible clothing, I can at least see to it that they won't inconvenience the rest of us when they fall."

"There are two other wagons, peerless one," the high priest reminded her as they waited out the adjustment.

"Your point?"

"If they fall behind this wagon, they could still be in danger from the one following."

"Then tell them to take off their robes."

"I can't do that, peerless one. As priests of Xaantalicta, even junior priests, they have the obligation to be identifiable."

"Then stop complaining."

The wagons were some distance apart, but the small two-wheeled carts and members of the xaan's household with braids enough to avoid a place at the shafts filled the space. Fallen priests, Benedikt realized, would have to be nimble to regain their feet before something or someone ran them over. "Perhaps we should wait until the rain stops, peerless one."

"I don't wish to wait." She fed a bit of meat to the dog who gulped it down and began digging through her robe in search of more.

"But . . ."

"Nor do I intend to justify my actions to you."

Behind her, Hueru's expression suggested any further argument would be met with violence.

Benedikt touched his tongue to his lip and the not-quite-healed reminder of the back of Hueru's hand. No doubt, one or two of those walking would help the fallen. They were priests, after all. They were in no real danger.

The wagon lurched forward.

"Sing for me, Benedikt." Lifting Shecquai to rub the top of his head against her cheek, the xaan sighed. "Give me something to think about besides this unending rain."

"It rained in the dark of Xaantalicta," Yayan Quanez murmured behind her gauze. "With such a sign, we should have expected it to rain until she smiles on us again."

"Is your name Benedikt?" the xaan snapped, glaring at

the high priest. "When I want your opinion, as meaningless as it is, I'll ask for it."

"Your pardon, peerless one."

This weather is enough to make even a kigh unhappy, Benedikt reminded himself, a little taken aback by the venom in Xaan Mijandra's tone. Quickly examining and discarding over half of the Petayan songs he knew, he finally settled on the improbable journey of a farmer trying to get his *kuskis* to market.

The final disastrous verse—involving the *kuskis,* two members of the city guard, three pitchforks, and a goose—evoked an actual smile from the xaan.

Basking in her approval, Benedikt took a long drink of lukewarm water, then, at the xaan's command, started in on the rest of the songs he'd been learning from the members of her household.

It seemed that every waking moment he hadn't actually been with Xaan Mijandra, someone had been singing at him. Although no one with more than three braids had been involved, he'd had no privacy and very little sleep since joining the caravan. Every evening, he thanked all the gods in the Circle that he ate in the same tent as the xaan, albeit some distance away. On his own, he'd have missed every meal. Even taking a piss had gained him an anthem, another lullaby, and a rhyming explanation of why a banana was better than a man that he decided his current audience probably wouldn't appreciate. He only wished he'd had time to actually talk to some of these people; they came to him, they sang, they left. He knew no one's name that he hadn't overheard, nor anything about them.

He missed Xhojee, missed having someone he could just talk to without guarding every word he said, and, probably because of the amount of music he was suddenly exposed to, he missed having other bards around more than he had at any time while he was with the tul. It wasn't even specific bards he missed—although Evicka would have enjoyed the song about the banana once he'd explained the dimensions of the unknown fruit—he missed just knowing they were there. *I guess I miss being part of Kovar's stupid pattern.*

Fortunately, two dozen new songs in a short time left him too busy to be very lonely. Although none of the songs were lyrically complex, he had to completely rework a number of the tunes as more than one of his teachers sang in impossible keys.

The xaan didn't seem to mind the new melodies. Benedikt suspected she didn't even notice.

Singing from the top of the wagon, he tried to fit what songs he could to the cadence of the walkers. The chance that he might be easing their drudgery helped to lessen a vague, undefined guilt.

Late afternoon, on the fifth day of rain, the caravan came to a sudden halt at the point where the causeway moved from cultivated land and onto the heart of the broad river delta that held at its center the Atixlan, the capital city.

"Our way is under water, peerless one." The caravan master balanced on one of the huge wheels and peered apologetically into the shelter. "I sent a man across the flood and the causeway appears to have held but, unless the xaan commands, I will not risk any of the wagons. What may be solid under one man . . ." An eloquent gesture finished the thought.

"I have as little desire to lose a wagon as you do." Lips pressed into a thin line, she locked her gaze on his face. "So, caravan master, what do you suggest?"

"We must return to the last freehold and make camp, peerless one. Once the rains stop, the causeway will quickly reappear."

The xaan exhaled sharply, drawing an interrogative bark from the dog. "Whose stupid idea was it to build a causeway in such a place?" she demanded, looking as though she'd like to bark herself.

"It is only a problem for the wagons, peerless one. And it is unusual that one of the great houses would be traveling at this time of year."

"Not one," the xaan told him shortly. "All. I'll let the Tulparax know you disapprove of the season he chose to die."

Up at the front of the shelter, Benedikt stared out past the poles and the exhausted men and women who crouched beside them. It was still raining but lightly. On its own, it would be a miserable day. Compared to the four just passed, it wasn't all that bad.

Up in front of the poles, in front of the double line of guards, a hundred-foot dip in the landscape had filled with water. What looked like swamp on both sides of the causeway had risen, met in the middle, and kept on rising. Given the lay of the land, Benedikt could only assume culverts under the causeway handled the more normal amounts of rain.

A huge drop of water came through the canvas and landed hard enough to soak immediately through the shoulder of his robe.

The xaan knew he Sang water even if she didn't know exactly what it meant. She hadn't mentioned it since that first interview, but then, neither had he. He waited, listening, but only heard her issuing terse instructions to the caravan master, none of which involved him.

Had she forgotten?

From what he'd observed over the last few days, he doubted she ever forgot anything.

"I hear also that the waves obey you."

"Yes, peerless one."

"Obviously not very well . . ."

Benedikt had thought at the time she'd been mocking him, but he'd gone back to the memory again and again, and now he was certain she hadn't been. She'd been asking for confirmation. She'd been making an observation based on what she knew.

And she didn't think much of it.

Benedikt could almost understand why his abilities had been trivialized in Shkoder. Unable to Sing air he was crippled around other bards. But no one Sang air here. Or fire. Or earth. Or anything except water.

Another drop of rain collected in the canvas and fell, striking him in the same place.

Clearing the water from the road, ensuring that the caravan could move forward without delay, would do nothing to mitigate his failure with the *Starfarer,* but it should impress the xaan. Or at least convince her that he was more than he appeared.

This is your life now. The more you have to offer, the more she'll respect you, the better your chances.

Turning to face her, he bowed in the Shkoden way, and said, "Peerless one, I can clear the water from the causeway."

Hueru's bark of laughter was cut short by the xaan's

quiet, "Do it, then." She waved the caravan master off the wheel, then looked up at Benedikt. "Can you follow him?"

"Yes, peerless one." It would feel good to move, to use his body after sitting for so long. "The robe . . ."

"Remains on. And the hood stays up. For your own safety," she reminded him pointedly as he opened his mouth to protest.

"As you wish, peerless one." Sliding under the gauze wall, he lowered his body over the edge of the wagon and groped for the wheel's hub. A rough hand gripped his calf and directed his step. Balanced precariously, he threw a quick smile down at the caravan master, suddenly thankful for the voluminous folds of fabric around his legs. When he'd asked to get rid of the robe, he hadn't really thought about climbing down the wheel in nothing but a sawrap and sandals. *Although, with all that unbleached cotton plastered against their skin, everyone looks vaguely naked anyway.*

Suddenly, now that he'd brought the observation to the front of his thoughts, all he could see were breasts and buttocks and soft pouches of flesh swinging forward against wet fabric. Water wrapped up around his feet as he walked, clinging more than water should.

"That boy couldn't move water in a bucket," Hueru growled, absently rubbing at his tattoo with the palm of one hand. "The waves obey him, my ass. Do you see any waves out there?"

Standing beside him, the xaan ran a fingernail down the cleft of his spine. "So, if he fails I'll punish him and make you happy. Shall I punish you for doubting my judgment if he succeeds?"

"If he succeeds in moving the water out of our way, peerless one?" Hueru laughed, good humor restored by the ridiculous thought. "If he succeeds," he declared, thumbs behind the waist of his sawrap, chest thrust out, "you may punish me as you see fit."

"Out there in the middle, it's as deep as your shoulders—well, my shoulders anyway," the caravan master amended with a sideways glance up at Benedikt's height. "Current's slow, though. Easy enough to move against. If you're planning on diverting the flow, I don't know where you're gonna move it to. You've got *bajos* on both sides . . ."

"*Bajos?*"

"You know, water over mud and rotting plants—you should smell this place as it starts to dry up."

Swamp, Benedikt translated.

"Oh, sure there's a few *chowcis.*" He waved toward a clump of moss-draped trees up to their lowest branches in water. "And that there's an old *atix*—we'll start passing plenty more of them as we get closer to Atixlon—but right here there's no solid ground. Nothing to build a levee out of, nowhere to anchor it if there was, and no way the Kohunlich-xaan would give you the time to build it." He looked up at Benedikt again, "How many warm bodies you gonna need to help you do this thing you're going to do?"

"None."

"None? A word of advice, boy, from someone who's had six braids longer than you've been alive; if you can't do what you told her you can, your best bet would be to walk out there and drown yourself. It'd be quicker and a lot less painful."

"He's just standing there."

"I'm not blind, Hueru. If you have nothing useful to say, I suggest you say nothing."

Benedikt could see the kigh waiting for him out in the deep water, waiting for him to come to them. He gave the caravan master's suggestion a moment or two of careful consideration. The beckoning bodies of the kigh made it almost tempting, "As soon as the causeway clears, begin moving the caravan forward. I can hold the water for as long as necessary, but I'd rather not Sing myself hoarse."

"Sing?" The caravan master sighed deeply and clasped Benedikt's arm for a moment before moving away. He'd been at that first interview where the xaan had taunted the boy about waves and ships and the like. Assuming that it concerned the boy's time with the tul, he hadn't been paying much attention. Clearly, Benedikt was a great deal more deluded than he'd thought. Just as clearly, the xaan had called his bluff.

It was a pity. The boy really did have a nice voice and

the caravan master had enjoyed every opportunity to hear him sing—or more exactly, overhear him sing for the xaan. *Oh, well, if he's going to sing now, at least I'll hear him once more before he dies. . . .*

Wishing he could ditch the robe and feel the rain actually on his skin, Benedikt moistened his lips—*Funny they should be dry when everything else is so wet*—and began. The four notes to call the kigh were really just for tradition's sake. He never had to call them anymore.

In the shallower water on the far side of the flood, half a dozen bright pink birds lifted broad-billed heads on rope-like necks, and stared.

"He's singing," Hueru scoffed, arms folded. "Does he expect the flood to just move out of his way if he asks it nicely?"

Watching the pattern of ripples on the water's surface, the xaan's mouth curved up in a triumphant smile. "Yes," she said. "He does."

When the kigh finished pushing the flood back, the small flock of pink birds had returned to their interrupted meal—the clear implication that whatever was happening was none of their business.

Benedikt added a sequence of eight notes to dry the gravel, then walked to the lowest point of the causeway. Still Singing, he stood with his back against one translucent wall of water and faced the other. According to the kigh, the stone culverts beneath the gravel had neither collapsed nor washed out; they were merely full. Half turning, the movement dropping his hood down onto his shoulders, he paused to enjoy the expressions on the faces he could see. Then he beckoned the caravan forward.

At that instant, and just for that instant, the sun found a break in the clouds.

"Tulpayotee . . ."

The murmured name could have come from one throat or a dozen. Heard through the filter of Benedikt's Song, there was no way for the two women up on the front of the wagon to tell for certain.

Beside the xaan, Yayan Quanez hissed through her teeth. "They know he isn't! He told you so himself."

"People believe what they see," Xaan Mijandra remarked thoughtfully, with no understanding at all in her voice, "It *is* a remarkable resemblance. Just think of how he would have looked with his hair loose and out of that robe."

"He defiles the robe," the high priest snarled.

The xaan took a moment to let the astounded caravan master know he should get things moving, then favored Yayan Quanez with a speculative gaze. "Is that all you have to say?"

"I have said it from the beginning, peerless one."

"Fascinating that you fixate on an article of clothing and miss the point entirely. Hueru," she turned to her cousin who watched wide-eyed and silent as the first of the guards stepped between the walls of water, "do you recognize the significance of what Benedikt has done?"

His breath coming in short, sharp, gasps as though he'd just run a great distance. Hueru shook his head. "He moved the water from our way, peerless one."

"There, you see, even Hueru understands."

He faced her then. "Did you know he could do this, peerless one?"

"He *told* me he could do this. In fact, he told us all. It's hardly his fault if you didn't believe him."

"Then our agreement . . ."

"Don't worry, cousin. I remember our agreement. But I have no intention of holding you to it . . ." Her pause was exactly long enough to give him hope. ". . . here and now."

Shecquai began to bark as the wagon started to roll.

"Hush, little one. Even the *hartilcos* are paying no attention, and you're certainly braver than a bird."

Frowning, Hueru stepped forward and clutched at Xaan Mijandra's arm. "You can't intend the caravan to pass through there, peerless one!"

"I *can't?*"

He snatched his fingers back.

The xaan stared at him for a moment, her expression of disbelief becoming annoyance. "Here and now suddenly seems like a good idea." Calling to the caravan master, she had the wagon stopped. "Get down and pull, Hueru."

His mouth opened and closed, but no sound came out. "Now."

Benedikt had no idea why Hueru had suddenly been put to one of the poles at the front of the xaan's wagon. He didn't go willingly, that much was certain. *I bet his mother never warned him about his face freezing like that. Serves him right, the arrogant shit.*

At first, he thought the delay in moving forward again had to do with Hueru—who was definitely enjoying his new position much less than the men and women around him were—but then he saw an older man shaking his head and singlehandedly trying to back the entire wagon away from the divided flood. His eyes were so wide they showed white all the way around, and his cry of inarticulate terror rose up in counterpoint to the Song. Too far away for Benedikt to try figuring out the complex pattern of his tattoo, the single braid and sawrap gave no clue to the old man's occupation in camp.

No one had ever been afraid of what he did before. The realization that someone feared him, created an interesting and not entirely unpleasant sensation.

The old man's fear had begun to affect those around him by the time the caravan master got to his side. With most of his attention on holding the water, Benedikt couldn't quite make out the shouted exchange of words. Finally, the caravan master pried the old man's fingers from his crosspiece and dragged him bodily away from the wagons.

"Give him to Javez and Intega," the xaan called down from the wagon top. "Tell my cousins you speak with the mouth of the xaan. They're not to hurt him, but they're to see that he continues traveling with us. I'll deal with him later."

When the wagon finally got moving again, Benedikt glanced up at the xaan and found her not quite as awestruck as he might have hoped.

"Our young singer is wiser than he looks," Xaan Mijandra acknowledged, stroking the dog nestled into the curve of her arm. "See how he stands halfway across the parted flood? If he'd sent us on ahead, I'd have suspected a trap. If he'd gone through before us, reaching the other side before we began to move, again, I'd have suspected a trap. By standing there, in the middle, he knows that I know he can't release the flood without drowning himself and, if I can't trust him not to kill me, I can at least trust him not to kill himself." She nodded slowly. "Easily manipulated doesn't always mean stupid."

The priest glanced nervously from side to side and finally focused on the backs of her hands and her crescent-moon tattoos. "Hueru is Benedikt's enemy now, peerless one."

"So?"

The guards passed him, eyes front—the only indication of their emotional state the white-knuckled grips around the shafts of their spears. As they drew even with him, both lines swerved a half step away. Fear or caution, Benedikt didn't know, but he liked the feeling of power it gave him.

As though aware of his scrutiny and the thought that went with it, the closest guard turned his head a fraction of an inch toward him, lip curled. *I don't like this,* his expression said, *but I'm not afraid of you.*

All but two of those pulling the xaan's wagon kept their gazes locked on their footing. All but two . . .

The first stood at the second crosspiece on the near side. As he passed, he looked up and Benedikt clearly saw him mouth the name of the sun god, Tulpayotee. Suddenly realizing his hood lay on his shoulders, Benedikt grabbed it with both hands and yanked it back up over his hair.

Not everyone had seen him. With any luck, he hadn't completely alienated the high priest—who fortunately had considerably less influence on Xaan Mijandra than Ooman Xhai had on Tul Altun.

The second gaze he encountered belonged to Hueru. *What's he so mad at me for? It's not my fault he's pulling the wagon.*

As the xaan passed, he thought of asking the kigh to rise and acknowledge her presence but, without knowing how long it would take for the entire caravan to reach the other side of the flood, decided not to risk it. The odds were good he'd be Singing for some time, and loss of control would impress no one.

"I can't make out any words, but it's a pretty song," the xaan noted thoughtfully as the wagon creaked into the lowest point of the crossing and began to climb the low hill on the other side. "I wonder if the power's in the song or the one who sings it?"

Her hands scrubbing around and around so that the fingers of one continually stroked over the tattoo on the other, Yayan Quanez kept her gaze locked on the narrow wooden planks beneath her. "Does it matter, peerless one?" The question quavered slightly.

"Of course it matters, Yayan. If the power is in the song, he can teach it to others. If the power is in the singer and that singer is mine . . ." Her voice trailed off, touching four or five possibilities as it went.

The coloas seemed intrigued by Benedikt's Song. Everyone of them swiveled a ludicrously small head toward him and gave him a supercilious look of approval as they passed. Most of the people accompanying them kept their eyes locked on the back of the xaan's wagon although two of her cooks continued plucking chickens as they walked, oblivious to *where* they walked.

The second and third wagons had no choice but to follow the xaan down between the walls of water, terror of the known far outweighing that of the unknown.

"It seems I underestimated you, Benedikt." She saw that the admission pleased him. Good. It was supposed to. "The waves do indeed obey you. Although saying that water obeys you would be more accurate, wouldn't it?"

"Yes, peerless one."

There had been a freehold not far past the flood and the xaan had decided to camp one more night rather than arrive at Atixlan after dark with her people still openmouthed at the impossible. By morning, they'd know what she wanted them to think.

When Benedikt had rejoined her on the wagon, she'd said only, "Thank you. We'll talk later," before closing her eyes and leaning back against her cushions. She'd almost been able to hear him wondering why they weren't talking now and had known the moment she'd reopened her eyes at the freehold that he'd convinced himself she'd been too overwhelmed to find the words for an immediate reaction.

"I hear also that the waves obey you."

"Yes, peerless one."

She'd known at the time he'd been telling the truth but had no intention of admitting, in front of everyone, that she didn't know what that truth implied. He was a stranger; who knew what strangers could do?

She did.

Now.

She'd kept him by her side as the tents went up, and led him immediately into a private audience.

"You saved me a great deal of inconvenience this afternoon, Benedikt. The rain could have kept us out of Atixlan for days."

"I'm glad I could help, peerless one."

He was, too. He reminded her a little of Shecquai as a puppy. "Tell your barber tomorrow that you speak with the mouth of the xaan. You're to have eight braids."

"Thank you, peerless one."

"Was what you did this afternoon the extent of your power?"

"No, peerless one."

A brow rose. Clearly the thought that she believed removing the water from the causeway had taxed his abilities upset him. "Are you telling me that parting the flood was easy for you?"

"Shallow, slow-moving water is always the most responsive."

"Is it?"

"Yes, peerless one."

He had his chest thrust out in a hairier imitation of Hueru's favorite posture. On her cousin, she found it amusing—he had nothing beyond his conceits, after all—but as much as Benedikt's assurance had pleased her, she wasn't going to put up with that posture from him.

"Would the water obey anyone who knew that song?"

"Not song, peerless one. Song. The emphasis is slightly different."

"Is it? Answer my question."

Deflated by her tone, Benedikt stared at the xaan for a moment, confused. It had never occurred to him that anyone would assume the Song could have an effect without the bard. The Song couldn't exist without the bard. "The power is mine, peerless one. I have a . . ." How to explain something so intrinsically inexplicable? ". . . connection with water."

"Through the song?"

"The Song expresses the connection, peerless one."

"And have you connections with anything else?"

Her tone suggested she already knew the answer, and he'd better be careful that he matched it. But he didn't have connections with anything else, Benedikt reflected bitterly. What could she have heard? He'd done almost nothing but learn Petayn songs and sing them to her since joining her caravan. And before that . . .

Could she have heard about him evoking the god? She clearly knew what Tul Altun had planned for him. "If you mean the sunrise song, peerless one—that wasn't connecting with Tulpayotee but with the people who worship him."

Her eyes narrowed. "You connect with people?"

"Not always, peerless one, but sometimes a Song touches . . ." He couldn't give her the kigh. He'd intended to, he'd intended to give her everything, but when he opened his mouth to say the word, the sense of betrayal almost choked him. ". . . something inside."

He didn't think she noticed the pause.

If you were going to mention the kigh, why didn't you mention them before? You told her the water obeyed you. Not the water kigh.

Water kigh would have meant a long explanation that would have given the xaan not only water, but air, and earth, and fire as well. With one quarter explained, any reasonably intelligent person would arrive at the rest. *And I don't want to live this new life as the person who Sings only water.*

It sounded good. If memories of being drawn into a liquid embrace hadn't been taking up so much space in his head, he might even have believed it.

"Yes, I'm sure most songs touch something inside." The xaan clearly disapproved of such blatant sentimentality. "Can you make people obey you as well as water?"

About to deny the ability—he'd been absolutely pitiful at Command and only moderately better at Charm—Benedikt suddenly realized that the xaan *expected* him to say no. She didn't believe he could do it.

He remembered the feeling he'd had during that moment of power over the frightened old man and when the guards had taken that half step away—it was a heady, addictive feeling. It was probably what the xaan felt all the time.

If you could feel like that, her tone said, *you would. You don't, so you can't. I ask only because I don't like to leave these things unsaid.*

He thought about explaining bardic oaths—*I will not use the kigh for gain*—then remembered he wasn't exactly a bard anymore and that here, in this new land, he was making it up as he went along.

"I can Command, peerless one."

This time she heard the inflection. "Then why haven't you?"

"And what would I Command, peerless one?" Benedikt spread his hands for emphasis. "Take me home? There's no point in asking for the impossible. Give me a place in your household? You've already done so."

"Yes, I have. And now I discover you're so much more than you appear." The xaan lifted a small string of bells and gave it three short sharp jerks.

One of her guards slipped silently into the room.

"Command him," she told Benedikt, flicking a polished fingernail toward the guard. "I need to see what you can do. Have him bend down and touch his toes."

Trying not to panic, Benedikt rose up off his knee. *You can do this,* he told himself. *Guards are used to being commanded.* Breathing a little faster than he had been, he turned and moved two steps closer to the guard.

Who looked up and sneered.

Benedikt recognized the sneer. The same guard had given him much the same look as he passed during the flood Song. After a moment, Benedikt caught the older man's gaze and managed to hold it. **"Bend over,"** he said, **"and touch your toes."**

The guard blinked once, shook his head as though he were dislodging flies, and peered over Benedikt's shoulder. "Is it your wish, peerless one?"

"No. It is not. Again, Benedikt."

Ears red, Benedikt shifted position until he regained the guard's gaze. **"Bend over and touch your toes!"** He heard embarrassment force his voice up on the last word and fought unsuccessfully to keep it down.

The guard's answering snort held all he would have said had his xaan not been able to hear.

The failure, although bad enough, was not the worst, Benedikt reflected as the guard slipped back through the canvas. The worst was that the xaan had expected him to fail.

"There are those born to command and those who take command." The xaan stood, rising gracefully out of her cushions. "You are neither. I am both. I am obeyed because my people recognize the benefits of doing what I ask far outweigh the consequences of refusing."

The top of her head barely reached the middle of Benedikt's chest. When she moved, her breasts swayed under a thin covering of brilliantly died silk. He thanked all the gods in the Circle that she hadn't told him to kneel again because that would have put his eyes and her breasts at roughly the same level. "I understand, peerless one."

"Do you? I hope so. I enjoy your singing and don't want to lose it."

Compliment or threat? Benedikt was discovering truth could have many interpretations.

"Does water obey everyone in this land you come from across the sea?"

"No, peerless one. Only a few are born with the ability." Fewer still without the ability to Sing air, but she didn't need to hear that.

Unfortunately, she heard something. "What are you hiding from me, Benedikt?"

What—if not the other kigh . . .

"We, that is, I, have a very good memory." In this, at least, he knew he could make up for his inability to Command the guard. "I can recall every word you have ever said to me, peerless one."

She listened to him repeat their first conversation and nodded. "That might be useful, but remember what I have said to you is not as important as what I am saying to you."

Do not forget that your position is only as secure as I say it is at this moment.

Her actual meaning was so obvious it hardly qualified as subtext. She had moved very close to him. Close enough that he could feel the air warming between them. She smelled wonderful, like sun-warmed limes. His mouth began to water.

"Tell me how your abilities can be of use to House Kohunlich."

It wasn't what he expected her to say. Although he didn't know exactly what he had expected. She was so close he found it hard to think. "You, uh, you sleep better when I sing to you, peerless one," he stammered.

"Not of use to me personally, Benedikt. Of use to House Kohunlich."

"At home, I mean back in Shkoder, we Witness . . ."

"You're not in Shkoder, Benedikt."

"I . . . I know, peerless one." He had to move away. Or he had to touch her. It didn't really matter which. His body argued for the latter, his mind for the former. Caught between them, he could only stay where he was, hoping she didn't look down.

"Benedikt?"

"Peerless one?"

"I want you . . ."

She wanted him? His erection vanished so quickly it might never have existed.

". . . to go to your tent and think of a way water can be of use to House Kohunlich."

Relief mixed with embarrassment rushed the blood to his face so quickly it made him lightheaded. He couldn't bow, there wasn't enough room, so he backed up, one hand groping behind him for the opening in the wall. His fingers had just closed on the edge, when the xaan stopped him.

"One more thing, Benedikt. Did my brother know about this?"

This? It took him a moment to bring his mind back to what *this* meant. "I told him I could Sing water, peerless one. He said water was of no use to him."

She nodded thoughtfully, a fringe of blue-and-black-banded feathers brushing against her cheeks. "My brother is an idiot."

As he doubted she wanted agreement, Benedikt bowed then and backed out under the overlap. He didn't, couldn't, draw in a full breath until he was safely in the next room where the air still carried her scent but not as strongly. He was useful to her. It was a start.

"How about *you* bendin' down and touchin' your toes, singer?"

The softly growled question lifted all the hair on the back of Benedikt's neck. Distracted by his reaction to the xaan, he hadn't noticed the guards standing with their backs to either side of the slit in the canvas wall. The guard he'd failed to command was now inches behind his left shoulder.

"I got a song I wanna make you sing . . ."

Pulling himself back together, Benedikt turned and, using his height to its best advantage, dragged a disinterested stare over the guard's body. "I doubt it," he snorted as the man glowered. "You can't sing along with a *zados.*"

The zados was a very small horn that children hummed into, creating a noise that resembled a swarm of angry wasps. A young karjen had shown him one.

The other guard snickered. "He's got your number, Cazzes."

"Shut up."

"You don't think a *zados* might be a bit generous?"

"I said, shut up."

Benedikt left the tent, moving quickly to avoid his saw-rap settling in any one place. After that interview with the xaan, he'd have accepted an honest invitation from just about anyone. *I wonder if she knows she has that effect on people?*

"Has he relieved himself?"

"Yes, peerless one."

"Good." The xaan took her dog from the hands of his senior attendant and indicated that the guard should fold open the door to her large assembly room.

Benedikt, she had needed to see in private. This next bit of business required an audience.

"Your name is Kohunlich Porez. You are my senior lamplighter."

The old man raised hopeful eyes to the xaan's face while all around, her attendants, her priests, and those karjen who could leave their tasks without inconveniencing her looked impressed. She knew they were wondering how she managed to remember not only the name but the position of such a lowly member of the household, and—given that she knew such a thing—they also wondered what else she might know. Which was exactly what was intended.

She noted those who looked particularly nervous before turning her attention back to the senior lamplighter. "You're here because this afternoon you refused a direct order from your xaan."

Porez shuffled forward on his knees, hands uplifted in supplication. "I was afraid, peerless one."

A number of those listening reacted to the old man's declaration with surprise—he hadn't been expected to offer a defense.

"Your fear is no concern of mine," Xaan Mijandra reminded him wearily. "You can be afraid of whatever you want. You can be afraid or in love or just generally pissed off—that's your life and it does not involve me. But, you are of House Kohunlich and I am the Kohunlich-xaan. I gave the order to move forward, and you did not move."

"Peerless one, the water, the stranger, the flood . . ."

"I gave the order to advance *my* wagon through that flood. By refusing, you showed the world you doubted my decision."

"Peerless one . . ." His whole body shaking, he collapsed facedown on the carpet.

The xaan stared at him for a moment, her left hand rhythmically stroking the dog. "Since he didn't want to walk, take his legs."

Wailing inarticulately, Porez scrabbled toward her on his belly, clawing at the carpet with fingers and toes.

"And his tongue, too if he can't learn when to be silent."

The wailing became a low, continuous moan as two guards hauled the old man to his feet, dragging him from the audience chamber and out the back of the tent. His legs dangled, unused, as though they were already no longer a part of him.

The xaan sighed and glanced around at the silent faces of her household. "I'm sure I don't have to tell any of you that Benedikt's solution to our flooding problem is not to be discussed." She smiled at the low murmur of agreement, agreement reinforced by the fate of the old man. "Now then, you'll all want to get cleaned up before the evening meal. Not you, Otypez," she added as they began to disperse. An inarguable gesture indicated that the eldest of her physicians should approach the dais.

When they were alone, except for the servants raising the outer walls and setting out low tables for food at the other end of the room, she murmured. "You've been drinking."

Otypez bowed, a bit unsteadily, the movement causing the fine silk of his robe to whisper secrets to itself. "From the moment the lamplighter refused to move forward, peerless one."

"Don't let it interfere with your work."

"It never does, peerless one." He blinked bloodshot eyes at her and added bitterly, "It never has."

"Good. A legless lamplighter is of no use to me. See that he doesn't survive."

Rubbing at the physician's tattoo on his cheek with one shaking hand, Otypez nodded, brilliant green feathers flashing in amongst the gray of his many braids. "It will be as you command, peerless one."

"I know." She watched him leave, noted how he took a serpentine path to the exit, and shook her head. He had been her father's physician, so she granted him a great deal of license. There were, however, limits.

Still, as long as he's useful . . . Pleased with the way the day had turned out, the xaan set Shecquai on the ground and made her way to the exit, the dog dancing at her heels.

Porez had no children back in the children's compound, he had no life partner, and both of his parents were dead. The trick in applying an object lesson was not to create a martyr. It was the first lesson her aunt, the last Kohunlich-xaan, had taught her.

Just wet enough to be miserable by the time he crossed from the xaan's tent to his own, Benedikt dropped cross-legged onto the dead center of his pallet and the last, small island of dry, any and all physical urges discouraged by the clammy slap of damp cotton sawrap against skin. Rubbing at the moisture trickling down his face, he glared out at the rain. While the canvas above was essentially waterproof, the rug on the ground was not, and the whole camp smelled of damp wool and mold. Fortunately, there was water enough for frequent washing—Benedikt had been trying very hard to not overhear what people were growing in personal crevices.

"There's got to be some way water can be of use to House Kohunlich," he muttered, scraping mud off his sandals with the edge of his thumb nail. "Because there's certainly enough of it around. I've never seen so much unenclosed ra—"

A muffled wail cut across his complaint and brought him to his feet. He could hear no words, only an inarticulate terror so strangely familiar that it lifted every hair on his body.

He took a step out into the rain, back toward the xaan's household tent, and stopped as the sound did. It wasn't repeated. Whatever had happened was over.

In Shkoder, he'd have investigated and not been satisfied until he knew who had cried out and why. In Shkoder he'd been a bard with all the rights and responsibilities that entailed, but here he was still trying to make a place for himself, and that place didn't yet include the right to go charging into a situation he knew nothing about.

The rain began to soak through the shoulders of his robe.

The camp was strangely empty, Benedikt could hear karjen working over in the kitchen area, could smell the evening meal cooking but could only see the guards standing outside both of the xaan's tents. There should be more people moving about, talking, laughing, snarling about the weather, making plans for later in the evening should the xaan not need them. There should be *someone* trying to teach him the inane words to a tuneless song. This was the longest he'd been totally alone and awake since joining the caravan.

So what do I do?

A quiet murmur of voices, like the sudden sound of distant waves answered his question. The voices grew louder as the flaps of the household tent were folded back and Benedikt watched in amazement as everyone in the caravan seemed to come boiling out. First the members of the xaan's family in varying degrees of silks and feathers, then a white clump of priests, then the caravan master talking to

someone Benedikt thought was one of the junior barbers—
where junior clearly referred to rank, not age. The number
of braids per head grew less until only a steady stream of
single braids were exiting the tent.

The karjen seemed subdued, Benedikt noticed although
they hurried off to their evening tasks too quickly for him
to get more than a vague impression of mood.

Only Hueru noticed him, standing motionless in the rain.

When Benedikt had chosen to sail on the *Starfarer,* he
had believed Kovar hated him for it. If that had been hate,
it was a weak, lukewarm response compared to the emotion
that burned in Hueru's eyes.

Benedikt stopped himself from taking an involuntary step
back and his hands formed fists within the masking folds
of his robe. If it came to a fight, he'd bring Hueru down
in the biggest puddle he could find. He doubted he'd even
have to Sing anything.

Hueru's lip curled, and already impressive muscles
seemed to swell. Then Javez, one of the other cousins—a
term the xaan applied to most of the relatives traveling
with her regardless of actual connection—draped an arm
over his shoulders and tugged him away, talking urgently
in the big man's ear the whole time.

One breath. Two. Benedikt's heart began to slow. Was
this how Bannon felt when a challenger thought better of
it and backed away? Somehow Benedikt doubted Bannon
felt vaguely nauseous, but the memory of the ex-assassin—
even a memory brought on by the threat of violence—was
surprisingly comforting. *I know you didn't think much of
me,* he told it. *But considering how I washed up on shore,
naked and alone, I haven't done so bad.* If anyone could
appreciate survival, it would be Bannon.

The last of the karjen left the tent, and the camp came
to life around him.

Why had Xaan Mijandra deliberately excluded him from
whatever it was the rest of the caravan had been involved
in? As a punishment? In spite of his failure with the guard,
she'd seemed pleased with him when she'd sent him to
his tent.

They had to have been talking about him.

He smiled as he realized there could be only one

explanation for Hueru's reaction. Xaan Mijandra had told
them about his rise in status. The xaan's attention was moving elsewhere, and Hueru was jealous.

A line of karjen carrying low tables and dishes went into
the household tent while another group began rolling up
the outer canvas walls exposing the gauze inner walls.
Barely managing to keep the rolled canvas from slipping,
they scrambled out of the way as an elderly man emerged.
A fast recall identified him as Otypez, the best dressed and
most highly braided of the xaan's physicians.

As he cleared the awning, he staggered slightly and
stared in surprise up at the rain. Before Benedikt could
move forward to help, he drew a bottle wrapped in woven
straw from under his robe and took a long swallow. Not
sick, the younger man realized, drunk.

Otypez had barely moved out of Benedikt's line of sight
before the xaan came out of the tent. Two guards moved
into position before her, two fell into place behind, and a
pair of karjen, their hair still too short to braid, flanked her
holding a piece of waxed canvas stretched between painted
poles. Protected from both the elements and more mundane dangers, the xaan made her way to her personal tent.

Queen Jelena, Benedikt remembered suddenly, had arrived at Fort Kazpar on horseback. Accompanied by
guards, yes, but if it rained, she got wet. Her Majesty traveled considerably lighter than the xaan, not only in personal
effects but in sense of importance as well.

Somehow, Benedikt couldn't see Xaan Mijandra allowing
the Bardic Captain to maintain a public disagreement.
She'd use his guts to tie her braids.

His movement hidden by her guards, Benedikt backed
up until his heels hit the rug. While he had no intention of
going inside his tent, like a small boy sent away while the
adults talked, neither did he intended to jeopardize what
status he might have gained by appearing to blatantly disregard the xaan's wishes.

At the exact point on her path where the guards had
moved far enough forward but the karjen holding the canvas weren't yet between them, she glanced over and smiled
approvingly at him.

Heart pounding, Benedikt felt as if he'd just won some

rare and wonderful prize. Next time he got the chance, he definitely would have the kigh rise and acknowledge her.

"What happened to the woman who usually lights my lamp?" Benedikt asked, watching a harried young man touch his lit taper to the wick.

"She's senior lamplighter now, and I got the whole shittn' camp to light on my own." His eyes widened as he turned and realized who he was talking to. "I shouldn't have said that. You took me by surprise, askin. No one with more'n two braids ever asked me nothing before. Please, I'm sorry."

"Hey, it's okay." Stepping forward, Benedikt used enough Voice to sooth. "This is a big camp, you've got a right to complain."

The lamplighter flashed him a grateful smile, admitted he didn't know no songs, dropped the burned end of the taper into his bucket of hot coals, and ran off.

"I guess I'll have to wait to find out what happened to the old senior lamplighter," Benedikt remarked philosophically to the night. The xaan would send for him shortly, but until then he wanted nothing more than a chance to lie down and digest an indigestible meal. If he lived in Petayn another hundred years, he'd never get used to baked grubs, four inches long, as part of the main course. It wasn't that he disliked the taste, it was more that they were, well, baked grubs.

Arms folded behind his head, he stretched out and stared up at the lamp, watching the shadows flicker as the night air danced around the flame. For some reason the patterns they made reminded him of the terrified cry he'd heard earlier in the evening.

The strangely familiar cry.

Eleven

BENEDIKT woke early the next morning after a restless night, his sleep plagued by a kaleidoscope of images. Most, he couldn't remember, but two, repeated over and over, he carried with him into the day. In the first, his mother held him by the shoulders, screaming at him that his brothers had drowned. *"You knew they were dead, you just weren't paying attention! You never pay attention to anything but yourself!"* In the second, Bannon stood beside him as the waters over the causeway parted and asked, more seriously than he had on the beach at the Broken Islands, *"No second thoughts?"*

Lying in a puddle of his own sweat, he stared up at the lamp. His mother and Bannon. "I'd love to know what Magda would make of that combination," he muttered. Magda had believed that dreams could be the kigh's way of talking to the conscious mind. Benedikt had believed that was a load of fish shit and had told her so. This morning, he'd have given almost anything to have heard her say it again.

"Great, a dream of my mother calling me selfish makes me homesick. My childhood must've been more pathetic than I thought." Sighing, he sat up and reached for his sawrap, his mother's accusation chasing Bannon's question around and around in his head. He'd dreamed of Bannon a lot right after leaving the Broken Islands, but this was the first one in a while, and he had to admit that the other dreams had been considerably more enjoyable.

As his body reacted to the memory, he reminded himself that he'd be in Atixlan by noon and in a bath as soon as possible after that.

It had stopped raining during the night. A pale yellow sun sat on the horizon, and the camp gleamed in the near luminescent light of early morning. Standing outside his tent, Benedikt had the strangest feeling that he was seeing clearly for the first time since he'd come to Petayn, Everything he looked at—the tents, the wagons, the coloas in their corral, even the guards—all seemed defined by the shadows stretching out behind them. The largest, darkest shadow stretched out behind the xaan's tent, and he stared at it for a long moment, holding his breath so as not to disturb the perfect quiet.

Then a bird shrieked in the surrounding bajos, half a dozen more answered it, two servers walked over toward the cooking area carrying strings of fish, and something took a chunk out of the side of Benedikt's neck.

"Center it!" His fingers came away bloody, the body of a small insect crushed in the gore. Flicking his hood up, Benedikt hurried toward the bathing rooms. Six braids entitled him to a gentler version of the wash he'd had his first day in camp.

Eight braids didn't seem to change the service any.

Sluiced down and dripping wet, he scooped out a handful of the soft soap and, after banishing his two bath attendants to the side of the tent, lathered. He'd come to the point where he could cope with them being there, but he still drew the line at having them help.

As the girl limped over to the reservoir with her bucket, he realized it was the same pair who'd cleaned him up for his interview with the xaan. Usually embarrassment added to the pressure of others waiting moved him in and out as quickly as possible, but this morning, with dreams lingering, he found he wanted to talk.

"So where have you two been for the last six days?"

The boy looked startled. "We didn't go anywhere, karjet."

It wasn't the first time he'd been called karjet, but having awakened already susceptible to emotional overreaction, he missed Xhojee so badly he ached with it.

"You don't go out of your way to make friends."

And now he'd lost another one.

Stop it. He's with the tul, you're with the xaan, and they're not exactly a close family.

"You don't have to call me that," he said, pushing Xhojee out of his mind. "I'm no different than I was." He added enough Voice to the protest to set them at ease. It didn't take much. He was so different from everyone else they obviously had trouble thinking he could then be different from himself. "I just wondered why I hadn't seen you . . ." A self-conscious wave took in the small canvas room. ". . . here."

"It's 'cause you've never been up this early," the girl told him, setting her filled bucket on the grass. "We're most junior, so we're here first—and that's why we washed the puke off you. Most days, by the time you're up, we're off gettin' more water, and the older ones are in here. We seen you, though. And we hear you sing. I was gonna sing you the three monkeys song, but . . ." Her shrug eloquently told how another had beaten her to it. "You're still awfully hairy."

"You're never gonna get two braids," the boy hissed, handing over the first bucket of rinse water. "You don't learn to shut up, you might not even get one."

Although she gave a defiant sniff as she switched her full bucket for his empty one, Benedikt thought she looked a little worried.

"It's okay," he said. "I don't mind."

"Others do," the boy muttered darkly.

"His hair's growing faster, so he'll get his braid first," the girl told Benedikt as he poured one last bucket of water down his back. "So he thinks he's the boss of me. But I'm not gonna be a junior bath attendant forever. When I get to Atixlan, I'm gonna learn about pipes and cisterns and stuff, and I'm gonna get my second braid makin' sure he's got enough water to clean up with."

"You like water?" Benedikt asked her, wrapping a towel around his waist and sitting on the low leather stool to be shaved.

"I like pipes."

He'd have preferred to shave himself as he had with the tul, but he had no blade of his own and those provided were slightly curved. The one time he'd tried to use the unfamiliar shape, he'd made such a mess that the xaan had laughed and told him to not do it again.

"I don't want people thinking you've been ineptly tortured."

Lifting his chin, he wondered a little nervously just how

much experience these two children had had. Out of the corner of his eye, he saw the boy smile for the first time.

"S'okay," he said, moving around so that his lean stomach pressed against the back of Benedikt's head. "They wouldn't let us do this to a karjet if we didn't know how."

"Did you have bath attendants with the tul?" the girl asked from over by the reservoir.

"He didn't even have braids with the tul."

"Oh, yeah."

"I had a bath, though," Benedikt protested. "I had a whole bathing room."

"But no attendants?"

"Well, someone cleaned it, but there was no one like you two."

"See?"

The blade finished a final sweep of his throat and Benedikt turned his head. "See what?"

"We heard that the tul's got almost no karjen in his household. That it's just him and his ooman and the bons."

"Where did you hear that?"

"People talk in the bath." Smiling broadly, she limped out into the tent. By the time Benedikt finished drying off she'd returned with clean clothes. "The senior leather worker finished these for you last night," she said holding out a pair of sandals.

Although they looked ludicrously large dangling from her small hand, they fit perfectly. The clean sawrap was still too short, but under the robe it didn't much matter.

"You're lucky you got it," she told him as he sniffed it distastefully, then put it on. "It's not rainin', so there's gonna be about six different kinds of blood bugs swarmin' around until we're outa the bojos."

Benedikt rubbed at the itchy welt on his neck. "And when will that be?"

She rolled her eyes. "When we start cross the river just before we get to Atixlan."

"You've been to Atixlan before?"

As the boy snorted, she grinned. "No, but like I told you, people talk in the bath."

He paused at the exit and, as there was no one waiting, glanced back. "What are your names?"

"I'm Herexi." She jerked her head toward the boy, who

sighed the sigh of the elder and wiser. "This is Domez. Are you gonna sing 'The River Dances' today?"

"Maybe."

"Please."

"I'm not sure I remember it."

"You sang it yesterday!"

"I did?"

Hands on her hips she scowled at him. "Yes!"

Grinning, Benedikt held up his free hand in surrender. "I'll sing it if the xaan allows. Okay?"

"Well, yeah." Clearly that went without saying.

As the First—the xaan's Troop-Captain as near as he could translate the position—pushed past him and into the bathing room, Benedikt waved and dropped the flap. It felt good to be appreciated instead of merely useful.

On his way to the barber, he realized that had been the longest conversation he'd had with anyone but the xaan since leaving Xhojee.

That morning, they broke camp even later than usual. The wagon boxes, once reassembled, had to be hung with silvered ropes caught up behind huge silver disks embossed with the spread hands and crescent moon symbol of the Kohunlich-xaan. Blue pennants with silver tassels flew from poles on the wagon tops, and the plain gauze curtains that usually hung around the xaan and her companions had been replaced by gauze embroidered in blue and silver along both the top and bottom.

As the sun rose higher, great clouds of biting insects swarmed out of the bojos.

The xaan stood it as long as she could but finally called a sudden halt to the refurbishing, ordering the caravan out onto the causeway.

"You can finish before we reach Atixlan," she told the caravan master, a drop of blood running down her cheek. "We're not staying here another moment. And I'm *telling* the Tulparax what I think about the time of year he chose to begin dying," she added, grinding the words out through her teeth. Handing Shecquai, wrapped in a protective bit of gauze, up to Hueru, she climbed up to join him on the wagon top. "Benedikt, get up here. We're leaving."

The entire caravan agreed with the wisdom of presenting

a moving target. Had it not been for the double row of guards setting the pace out in front, Benedikt suspected that the cadence caller would have had the xaan's wagon moving at a trot.

Just out of sight of the capital, a fresh breeze cooling the bloody welts on exposed skin and lifting small waves on increasingly less muddy water, the caravan master called a halt.

The guards replaced leather greaves and vambraces with silvered metal and added white plumes tipped with blue to round helms—the size and number of plumes rising with rank. Finally, they draped the pelts of great spotted cats down their backs, tying them over their metal collars by the front legs. They looked both barbaric and beautiful and Benedikt found himself searching for a song for the first time since the kigh had taken the *Starfarer* down.

Behind a hastily erected canvas barrier, the priests exchanged robes no longer white for robes so brilliantly clean they were difficult to look at in the sunlight. Yayan Quanez wore silver embroidery almost as high as her knees, the senior priests a little less, and a gleaming thread wove around the hem of the juniors. Although the high priest remained with the xaan, the rest left former positions and fell in, massing behind the guards.

Girdles of silver-and-blue net were handed out to those at the wagon crosspieces and the coloas' harnesses were quickly fitted out with silver tassels.

Faster than Benedikt thought possible, the whole glittering caravan began moving again.

"Keep your hood forward," the xaan told him, "or you'll have to wear the gauze. Fortunately, you're not too dirty. Remember to ignore the people."

You've gone to a lot of trouble to impress people you're about to ignore, Benedikt thought.

Atixlan was a lot larger than Benedikt had expected and, unlike Elbasan which had grown undirected between the harbor and the Citadel and spread from there, it had obviously been planned. Even from the far side of the river he could see that the streets had been laid out in a grid around a central square of huge buildings.

As the causeway put down stone arches and crossed the

river, Benedikt found his place on the wagon harder and harder to bear. Bards walked.

"What is it, Benedikt?"

He spread his hands apologetically. "I feel isolated from the people, peerless one."

The xaan stared at him for a moment, nonplussed, one eyebrow raised. "Good," she said at last, and that was all Benedikt dared say about that.

The caravan came to a halt between a pair of temples bracketing the Atixlan end of the bridge. The temple to the left had been built in the familiar square shape of Tulpayotee and even before the caravan had stopped, three priests and half a dozen temple attendants had emerged and arranged themselves on the broad steps. The attendants were swinging spiked orbs at the end of lengths of chain, and not even a coat of gleaming yellow enamel was symbolism enough to hide their function.

The temple to the left rose up on the same platform of steps but the pillars at the top were arranged in a circular pattern. A single priest, almost indistinguishable against the white marble, waited halfway down the stairs.

Benedikt watched in surprise as the caravan master approached the priests of Tulpayotee and handed over a purse. He must have made some noise, for the xaan gave a quiet snort and said, "Until the change, Tulpayotee collects the toll."

Yayan Quanez muttered something behind her gauze, words lost but bitterness clearly audible.

"Soon," the xaan told her. "Soon."

The wagon began moving again. Xaan Mijandra turned and nodded toward Xantalicta's temple. The lone priest acknowledged her gesture with a graceful bow.

"I see the Xantalax took my advice and replaced Yayan Laruta with someone younger. I only hope they'll have temple attendants ready and waiting."

"Do you expect trouble, peerless one?"

The xaan glanced over at Benedikt, her face expressionless. Hueru, who'd been silent all morning, stirred, anticipating punishment to be meted out. Xaan Mijandra raised a hand and stilled him.

"I expect the change," she said.

*   *   *

The outer edges of the city weren't much like the cities Benedikt had left behind. Not only were the buildings on both sides of the causeway made of thick adobe, painted in a visually painful kaleidoscope of colors and patterns, they were farther apart than anything in either Elbasan or Vidor. *No need to huddle together for warmth,* he decided, sweat running down his sides under the robe.

The caravan moved farther up and farther in through heated air thick with the smells of civilization. They were unimpeded by traffic, and Benedikt wondered if the xaan had sent news ahead to clear the road or if the people of Atixlan got themselves out of the way when they saw her coming. He suspected no one in their right mind would challenge her to the right of way. Small crowds had gathered at each of the cross streets, although he wasn't sure if they were waiting to cross or merely enjoying the spectacle. A few of those watching wore the familiar unbleached shifts, sawraps, and house tattoos, but most wore multicolored cloth that clashed with the walls around them.

Close to the causeway, the noise seemed muted although Benedikt could hear the normal sounds of life and commerce rising up from unseen streets.

The buildings began to get bigger, walls surrounding them, flags flying from the rooftops—building materials aside, very much like the houses of the wealthy and wellborn in Elbasan. The causeway, which had been climbing slightly, leveled out again, and Benedikt could see a large open area directly ahead.

A strip of trees and gardens appeared on either side of the wagons. Already overstimulated after so many days of nothing but rain-drenched fields or bajos, Benedikt blinked in amazement at the rainbow stripes that had been painted around the trunks of some of the trees. A thick stone wall topped with steel spikes ran behind the gardens and behind that, a three-story building that seemed to go on, unbroken for a very long time. Gardens, wall, and building all ended in the largest paved square Benedikt had ever seen. Six huge buildings filled three sides and on the fourth . . .

This time, he knew he made a sound; he just wasn't able to prevent it.

"The Great Temple," the xaan told him quietly. "Soon it will be ours again."

It was a temple of Tulpayotee on an almost unfathomable scale. There was a large double entrance at ground level and then six or maybe seven stories of stairs rising up to the pillared platform. It was the temple where he was to have Sung the dawn as a warrior of Tulpayotee.

"It looks like my brother has arrived before us."

Arrived where, Benedikt wondered, and then he realized that the caravan was pulling up in front of one of the six huge buildings and that a blue-and-gold flag was flying from the southwest corner. Two things hit him at once. The first, was that he was no longer traveling toward his new life, he'd arrived. The second, was that the xaan's brother had arrived before them.

The tul had arrived before them.

Tul Altun was in Atixlan.

"The Kohunlich-tul can't be here," Hueru growled, getting to his feet as the wagon stopped. "We left days before he did."

"I doubt he took the causeway. He won't be here long, so he wouldn't have had much to transport."

Benedikt watched understanding dawn on the big man's face, followed closely by an unpleasant smile.

"He must be desperate, peerless one. The change . . ."

"Will happen soon enough." She passed Shecquai over to his junior attendant, waiting on the ladder with a basket. "And I'd like to be unpacked before it does."

The front of House Kohunlich, the building, had been divided into thirds. Each of the exterior pieces had an identical entrance—double latticework doors within a pillared colonnade. The central portion had been exquisitely tiled in more shades of blue than Benedikt had realized existed, with gold accents to the left and silver to the right.

In spite of an eerily empty square and no sign of life from any of the other buildings, Benedikt couldn't shake the feeling he was being watched. Glancing up, he thought he saw a familiar face at a third floor window. *Xhojee?* Then the window was empty.

Don't be an idiot, he told himself. *Why would the tul bring Xhojee to Atixlan? You're only seeing him because you want to see him.*

As the xaan walked toward the door on the right, it opened, and a middle-aged woman wearing multiple braids took three steps forward and dropped to one knee. "Your return to Atixlan is greeted with joy, peerless one."

Xaan Mijandra indicated that the older woman should rise, then looked down at her barking dog and smiled. "It seems Shecquai remembers you, Serasti. He is . . ."

The other door opened; Benedikt felt his chest tighten as a smoldering voice said, "He is out of Shecquaz, our father's dog, is he not? There is a resemblance."

The xaan raised a cautioning hand as her guard moved forward and turned to face her brother. "You have a good eye, Altun. I doubt you saw our father's dog more than twice."

"I have a good memory."

Benedikt wondered if anyone besides himself heard the double meaning.

A pair of guards followed the tul out the door but stayed next to the building as he walked closer to his sister.

He's daring her to do something. Even from a distance Benedikt could see the glitter in the tul's eyes. The feeling of being watched grew stronger, and he wished he could put the bulk of a wagon between himself and the other five great houses.

"Your son was well when you left him?" The tul's emphasis on the last four words leaned an innocent question toward provocation.

Her expression unchanging, the xaan turned to the woman beside her. "Serasti?"

"A bird arrived this morning, peerless one. Your son was fine when it left the compound."

The tul spread his hands, the concerned movement in complete contrast to his tone of voice. "So many terrible things could have happened while that bird was in flight."

Hueru jerked forward one step, two, before the xaan stopped him with a raised brow. "Thank you for your concern, Altun, but I have complete faith in my son's security. I wouldn't have left him otherwise. It's a pity you haven't children of your own to worry about."

"I have plenty of time."

She smiled at him then, an older sister's smile to a younger brother who wasn't very bright. "Of course you do."

Benedikt could almost feel the heat of the hatred that flared behind Tul Altun's dark eyes.

"If you'll excuse me," the xaan continued, "it's been a long morning, and I'd like to change."

The word *change,* even thrown away as it had been, hung over the group.

"The Tulparax is still alive," the tul told her, smoldering tones now in flame.

"Good. Then I'm in time to pay my last respects." She stepped forward, and Benedikt wasn't surprised to see the tul back instinctively out of her way although there'd been no overt menace in her movement—much the way there was no overt menace in the movement of the ice fields that swept down over the north lands.

He watched her as she passed him, smiled mockingly at Hueru, then looked Benedikt full in the face, aware of what he'd seen within the masking hood. "I didn't know that Xaantalicta admitted men to her priesthood," he purred.

Benedikt had to remind himself to inhale before he could speak. The tul burned even brighter than he remembered. "She doesn't, gracious one."

"It's a disguise, then?"

"Yes, gracious one."

"So you've decided to switch sides?"

He saw the xaan pause, waiting for his answer. "The Kohunlich-xaan has given me a place in her household, gracious one."

"You were *mine* first."

Although his face flushed and his heart began to beat uncomfortably hard, Benedikt shook his head, courage bolstered by the place he was making for himself. No more a performing bear . . . "I am my own, gracious one."

The tul stared at him for a moment, then threw back his head and laughed with what looked very much to be sincere enjoyment. "Your own?" he said. "Sun above, that's priceless. Thank you, Benedikt, for that bit of entertainment."

Sudden anger caused his cheeks to burn hotter still even as it touched his voice with frost. "You're welcome, gracious one." A man who needed a lie to gain even a part of his own power had no right to laugh at him. Benedikt bowed and followed the xaan into the building, catching up with her just inside the doors.

"You handled yourself well with my brother, Benedikt."

"Thank you, peerless one." He pushed back his hood, hoping the shadows in the hall would hide the color of his face.

"Serasti, take Benedikt to a room suitable to his braids and send the tailor to him immediately. He needs clothing that fits him."

Eyes locked on impossible coloring and size, a hundred questions chasing themselves across her expression, Serasti said only, "Yes, peerless one."

"He's a shipwrecked sailor, Serasti, and he sings beautifully."

"Ah." Curiosity satisfied for the moment, the house master gathered up her robes and started up the flight of stairs that curved down into the hall.

Benedikt bowed to the xaan, and followed.

"You liked the way he handled the tul, peerless one?"

"Yes, Hueru, I did."

Climbing as quietly as possible, Benedikt strained to hear the conversation wafting up from below.

"*I* would have killed him, had you given me a sign."

"I know. I thought about sacrificing you, but you're still more use to me alive."

Hueru laughed at the xaan's jest.

She wasn't joking, Benedikt thought.

The room suitable to eight braids was just that, a room, large and pleasant with access to the small balcony that ran along the courtyard side of the second floor but in no way comparable to the suite he'd occupied in the tul's compound. *But this I've earned,* he reminded himself. *The room and everything in it is rightfully mine.*

"You'll want to wash before the tailor arrives," Serasti told him. "This room shares the bath directly across the hall. It has no attendants while the xaan is in the country, so you'll have to wait until a pair are released from the wagons."

"I don't need the attendants." When her brows went up and the corners of her mouth tucked down, it took him a moment to realize what he'd forgotten. "Karjet."

Serasti sniffed, only slightly appeased. "You know how to operate the cisterns? The boilers? The showers?"

"I can operate the showers," he protested indignantly.

"Fine. Do so." Nostrils flaring, she looked as though she smelled something unpleasant. "I expect you'll be using the shower frequently." Turning on her heel, she left the room.

"It's the *robe!*" She made no response although she had to have heard and Benedikt sighed. He'd already bathed once today. In fact, he'd probably bathed more since he'd arrived in Petayn than he had all the rest of his life. "It's not my fault it's always so hot here." He used the robe to wipe sweat from his sides as he crossed the hall.

The shared bath had an alcove entry hung with bells instead of a door. A huge wooden tub and its boiler filled one corner. It was a soaking tub and built for more than one occupant at a time. Benedikt had never seen one before, but he'd read about them in recalls bards had sent from the Havakeen Empire. Although it was deep enough for the kigh, with no door, attendants, and bathing companions, Benedikt doubted he'd be calling them any time soon.

"I'm going to have to see what I can do to get more braids," he muttered, pushing aside a beaded curtain and stepping into one of the half-dozen shower alcoves. It was no different from his shower at the tul's compound. Opening the lever, he let the lukewarm water from the cistern pour over him, then, turning it off, he scooped soap up on a cloth and began to wash.

The xaan wanted him to think of a way water could be of use to House Kohunlich but, at the moment, all he could think of was how water could be of use to him.

The division of the front of the house continued its entire length. One outside third belonged to the xaan, the other to the tul, and the center held a divided courtyard. The wall between the halves had a guarded door in the middle of it, but Benedikt doubted that it had been opened in recent memory.

Finally wearing a sawrap that fit, Benedikt walked in the gardens, waiting for the xaan to have time for him. In the two days they'd been in Atixlan, he hadn't been called to sing her to sleep nor had she joined her household for any meals. Feeling forgotten, Benedikt made himself feel even worse by spending all his time thinking about Xhojee and the tul on the other side of the wall. He *had* seen Xhojee at the front of the house; while standing out on the balcony, he'd seen him again in a third-floor window staring at the xaan's part of the house. Once he'd seen Benedikt, he'd disappeared.

Benedikt could think of only one reason why Tul Altun would have brought Xhojee to Atixlan. The tul wanted him back.

But the xaan knew he wasn't a warrior of Tulpayotee. And the xaan's people knew. As far as Benedikt could see, the tul would gain nothing but his sister's enmity by repossessing him although, given the nil's performance the day they'd arrived, that might be all he was after.

At least living with the tul I had someone to talk to. It was incredibly frustrating knowing his one friend in Petayn was on the other side of that wall and might as well be in Shkoder for all the time they'd be able to spend together. He wouldn't have given the wall a thought had it not been separating him from Xhojee, but as it was, it made him feel like a prisoner. Pacing along its length, he listened for sounds from the other side and heard nothing.

The call of falling water drew him at last to a small fountain screened on two sides by flowering vines. Water poured from a pair of clasped hands, cascaded down three white ceramic basins, and finally spilled into a round pond where tiny silver fish swam over a blue ceramic bottom. Given that Petayn taste tended toward overdoing both color and design, it was the prettiest thing he'd seen.

Smiling, he settled onto the intricately carved stone bench that curved around the edge of the pond. A few moments later, the kigh were dancing to his Song, the tiny fish flashing silver within them. Their joyful response eased his need for Xhojee even as it increased his desire to throw himself into their embrace—it was probably fortunate that the water was so shallow.

An approaching conversation, only partially blocked by the vines hiding him from the speakers, seemed to indicate that his Song had been overheard. *It doesn't matter,* he reminded himself. *They know what you can do.* So with part of his attention on his imminent audience, he continued doing it.

There were three of them, two women and a man, and although they'd fallen silent by the time they were standing behind him, he could feel their interest. Changing his Song slightly, he had a kigh leap up from the pond to the first basin and back again, still carrying the fish.

"Oh, look what he's making the water do!"

Intega's breathy tones were unmistakable and made it very likely that the man in the trio was Javez, her twin.

"Oh, can you make it go all the way to the top?"

Aware he was showing off but unable to help himself, Benedikt Sang two kigh up to the pair of hands, had them form a single vaguely human shape at the top and bow, then split apart and chase each other back to the pond. Intega's requests and increasing delight kept him busy for the next few moments. Then feeling his voice begin to burr, he Sang the kigh a gratitude and finally turned around.

Their reaction was everything Benedikt could have hoped for. Even Javez was impressed and told him so.

"It's like something out of one of the old tales," he said, clapping Benedikt on the shoulder. "The man who talked to water." He rolled the words off his tongue, then grinned. "It could be a companion tale to the old woman who lived in the sea."

"The old woman needs an old man," Intega protested, pressing up against his side. "Benedikt is young, he needs a young woman. Don't you, Benedikt?"

"Look how red his ears are turning." Yexli, the second woman—girl really, Benedikt doubted she was even as old as he was—was the youngest of the xaan's "cousins" who'd accompanied her into Atixlan. Her braids, although heavily interwoven with feathers, were still quite short. "You're making him uncomfortable, Intega."

"Am I, Benedikt?" Reaching out, she stroked the golden triangle of hair in the center of his chest. "It's soft. I've been wondering."

"Wondering?" he repeated, wishing he could think of something a little more original to say. "Really?"

"Don't get your hopes up," Javez laughed, smacking his sister's finger away. "Xaan Mijandra's told everyone not to touch." He laughed again at Benedikt's reaction. "You didn't know that, did you? Since you're too big to need her protection, I'd say she's got you marked for herself."

"No . . ."

"Can you think of another reason?"

Actually, he couldn't.

"I don't think that's fair," Intega protested, still a warm weight against Benedikt's side.

"The xaan doesn't have to be fair," her twin reminded her. "She's the xaan. You ought to get all that hair shaved off and get yourself a house tattoo, Benedikt." He tapped his own chest in the thickest part of the design. "You couldn't have one like this, of course, but the needle master would know what you're entitled to."

"Maybe he's afraid it'll hurt," Yexli snorted. The skin above her elbow was still red and puffy around the interlocking blue-and-black design that circled her arm above the elbow. "It doesn't."

"Your pardon." The house master managed to make the interuption sound neutral, but in no way did her tone defer to the cousin's superior rank. "The peerless one wishes to see Benedikt now."

Intega sighed and peeled herself from Benedikt's hip.

"Here, fix your feathers," Javez muttered, reaching out and doing it for him. "Can't go to the xaan with your feathers all cocked up."

Yexli looked rebellious, although at what Benedikt wasn't certain, and moved out of his way.

"Adjust your sawrap," Serasti sniffed as she spun on one heel and led him back toward the house.

When the sound of their sandals against the gravel paths had faded sufficiently, Intega dropped down onto the bench and scrubbed both hands in the pond. "He was damp."

"That's what you get for plastering yourself all over him," her brother sniffed. "I don't know why he keeps all that hair. He's like an animal."

"So he's damp and hairy—tell me again why we were being nice to him?" Yexli asked, kicking the gravel up into ridges.

"We were being nice to him, infant, because he's in the xaan's favor." Javez sat beside his twin and flicked water up at the younger girl. "She obviously plans to use him to benefit the House and, if he succeeds, that'll give him influence with her. Influence he'll be able to use for his friends."

Yexli wiped the droplets off her face and scowled. "He doesn't have any friends."

"Nonsense. He has us."

Sarasti stopped so quickly just outside Xaan Mijandra's private terrace that Benedikt almost stepped on the edge of her robe. Leaning toward him, she shot him an irritated glare when she realized that his ear was a considerable distance above her mouth.

Trying not to smile, Benedikt bent over.

"The xaan is not alone," the house master told him, grabbing a braid and pulling him so close her breath lapped against the side of his face. "Be respectful, and do not embarrass the House." She released him with a final tug for emphasis and pushed past him onto the terrace.

"I have brought Benedikt, peerless one."

"Thank you, Serasti."

The house master turned, flashed Benedikt a silent warning, and left him standing alone on the edge of the multicolored tiles. Remembering her admonishment to be respectful, he dropped to one knee.

"Get up, Benedikt, and come closer."

Studying the xaan's companions from under his lashes, he did as he was told. Seating arrangements suggested that the two women were of equal, or very nearly equal, rank as the Kohunlich-xaan. Although they both wore an uncountable number of tiny braids Benedikt suspected the woman to Xaan Mijandra's left wore some kind of a wig. Her hair couldn't possibly have grown that long in the few years she'd been out of the children's compound.

She tossed her head, as though somehow aware of his scrutiny. "My mother always makes *her* house master kneel."

"Your mother never leaves her house, Omliaz," Xaan Mijandra reminded her, amazing Benedikt with the patience she showed such a petulant comment. "Both my house masters are alone for a portion of the year. I need to show I trust them."

"What does that have to do with kneeling?" the younger woman demanded.

"By not insisting she kneel, it means I respect what she does for me. Besides, she's a cousin."

"My mother makes the whole family kneel." Omliaz looked down into her glass and frowned. "This is empty. My mother's karjen would never allow a guest's glass to be empty," she added as a karjen Benedikt didn't recognize hurried forward to fill it.

"Your mother never has guests," the woman to Xaan Mijandra's right slurred. Benedikt suspected she, at least, was not drinking fruit juice. "No one goes near her since that thing with the Shanshich-xaan."

"That was an accident!" Omliaz protested hotly.

"Sure it was. And it was a coincidence that your mother's brother had fathered the next Shanshich-xaan."

"Well, that didn't matter, did it? Because she died, too."

"Because no one wanted so close a tie between House Shanshich and House Calakroul."

Omliaz leaned forward, eyes narrow. "When I am xaan . . ."

"When that happens," Xaan Mijandra interjected, "and given your mother's health it will happen soon, you must begin with a clean slate and not bring your mother's mistakes into *your* rule of the house."

"My mother made no mistakes."

"Really? Your Aunt Leyza believes differently and seems willing to work with the other great houses."

From the expression on Omliaz's face, Benedikt assumed that Aunt Leyza was another claimant for the soon-to-be available position of Calakroul-xaan.

"I'm willing to work with the other great houses," she muttered.

"Good." Xaan Mijandra fed Shecquai a small piece of melon, then looked up at Benedikt. "Sing for us now, Benedikt."

Glad he hadn't been forgotten about—there being few things less comfortable than hovering on the edge of a conversation unable to join in and equally unable to leave—he bowed. "What song would the peerless one like to hear?"

She turned to the older woman. "Rayalmi?"

Benedikt found himself being scrutinized by a pair of small dark eyes nearly hidden in folds of fat. "Do you know this? *'I came down from the mountains for battle/down to the still hot air of the plain./My blade it ran red with the blood of the dead./I'll not see my home in the mountains again.'*"

"Oh, that's cheerful," Omliaz muttered into her glass.

The heavy-set woman had a good voice, the slurring less

evident when she sang than when she spoke. Benedikt
knew the song. One of the guards had sung it to him while
they were on the road. Breathing deeply, he set himself
into a light recall trance and began.

When he finished, it was so quiet in the courtyard that
the sounds from the aviary on the roof seemed to be coming from just beyond the terrace. Rayalmi wiped damp eyes
on the wide sleeve of her robe and motioned for a karjen
to refill her glass. Omliaz stared at him openmouthed until
she realized he'd noticed, then she brought her teeth together with a snap.

"Well, what do you think of my shipwrecked sailor?"
Xaan Mijandra asked.

"He's too tall and too hairy . . ."

I'm getting really tired of hearing that, Benedikt decided.

". . . and I don't think he looks anything like a warrior
of Tulpayotee." Omliaz threw herself back into her cushions and bit into a piece of fried spice bread. Voice, movement, and expression all adding an emphatic, *so there.*

"Who cares what he looks like," Rayalmi sighed. "That
voice."

"I think he should sing for the Tulparax before he dies."

"You're going to kill him?"

"Before the Tulparax dies, Omliaz."

The sudden sensation of drowning faded and Benedikt
drew in a long, grateful breath.

"My brother is in Atixlan, and I want the Tulparax to
meet the true Benedikt in case something goes wrong before the change and he's presented with the lie."

"A reasonable precaution," Rayalmi admitted, gesturing
for another drink. "But it won't be easy for the Kohunlich-
xaan to gain the ear of the Tulparax—even this close to
the change."

"True." One hand stroked Shecquai, but that was the
only movement Benedikt could see.

"Why aren't you having him sing for the Xaantalax?"
Omliaz demanded.

"Because she'll want to keep him. The tuls won't allow
the Tulparax to take anything from a xaan."

"My nephew has just been made an attendant of the
bedchamber. He's fond of me—the change being so close
there was no reason for him not to be. I'll invite him over

for the evening and see what I can do. I assume you'll want to be with Benedikt all the time?"

Xaan Mijandra smiled. "It seems a reasonable precaution."

"Doesn't it." Amused about something—the lack of trust between the great houses if Benedikt had to hazard a guess—Rayalmi shifted her bulk and gazed curiously up at him. "Do you play any instruments, Bene . . . dikt." She stumbled a little over the unfamiliar name.

"Yes . . ." He suddenly realized he had no idea of how to address her and shot a panicked plea toward Xaan Mijandra. Somehow, given the convoluted Petayn social structure, he doubted a simple karjet would do.

"Yes, *peerless one,*" she told him. "This is the Palenque-xaan."

He bowed his thanks. "Yes, peerless one." The words seemed wrong applied to another, but he covered his unease and continued. "I play pipes and the *quintara.*"

"These were lost when your ship sank?"

"Yes, peerless one."

"I don't know that second thing—the quitata, was it?— but we've certainly pipes about. My senior attendant plays for me. Very pleasant to have around." She emptied her glass and held it out to the side for a refill, confident that a karjen would appear when needed. "You might consider sending for an instrument maker and getting this boy re-outfitted, Mijandra. If he plays half as well as he sings . . ." Glass refilled, the end of the thought got lost in its depths.

"Why does he have eight braids?" Omliaz asked suddenly.

"Because that's what he's worth to me," Xaan Mijandra said levelly. "Rewards are as important a motivation as punishments."

The younger woman tossed her head again and, closer now, Benedikt realized that the braided hair was all her own.

Moving with exaggerated care, Xaan Rayalmi set her empty glass on a small table and yawned. "Sing me something cheerful, Ben . . . edikt. Give me a tune to hum as I haul myself back across the square."

Xaan Mijandra nodded her permission, and Benedikt sang "The Coloas Chorus," hiding as he did a moment's regret he hadn't been rescued by House Palenque. He couldn't help think that Xaan Rayalmi would know what to do with a bard.

Called to the xaan's bedchamber for the first time since arriving in Atixlan, Benedikt paused to smooth his hair before he reached the string of silver bells. Still tightly braided and feathered, it didn't really need smoothing, but he needed that extra moment to compose himself. He couldn't stop thinking of what Javez had said that afternoon.

"Since you're too big to need her protection, I'd say she's got you marked for herself."

For herself. His mouth was dry, and he'd had to wear one of his new blue-on-blue robes over the nonexistent camouflage of his sawrap.

She probably just wants you to sing, he told himself sternly. *The same thing you did for her on the road.*

He found the thought of the xaan . . . and him . . . together . . . equally arousing and terrifying. Would she ask, he wondered, or assume? The tul would assume. Why am I thinking of him now?

"What are you doing?"

Benedikt leaped backward. "Nothing," he coughed, choking on spit.

The xaan's senior attendant narrowed already narrow eyes. "Then get in here. The peerless one is waiting."

Shecquai lifted his head off the bed and growled as Benedikt came into the room. He seemed fuzzier, looking less like a starved rat than usual.

"He's just had his bath," the xaan announced, following Benedikt's line of sight and smiling fondly down at the tiny dog. Returning her attention to the attendant on his knees, rubbing oil into her feet, she lifted his chin on two fingers, caught his eyes with hers, and asked, "Are you done?"

It wasn't really a question, and the attendant realized it as much as Benedikt.

"Yes, peerless one." Picking up the glass flask of oil, he stood, bowed, and hurried from the room.

"Good. We're alone."

Would she come to him, or should he go to her?

The dog gave him a "one step closer to her and I'll rip your ankle off" kind of a look.

"What did you think of the Palenque-xaan?"

Benedikt blinked. "Peerless one?"

"The Palenque-xaan." Two vertical lines appeared between plucked brows, "I want your impression of her."

Feeling as though he was coming about into the teeth of a gale, Benedikt banished hopes and fears and attempted to consider the question. "Xaan Rayalmi is a powerful ally of House Kohunlich, peerless one."

"She wouldn't have been here if she wasn't an ally." Rising, Mijandra walked to the bed and sat down, gathering Shecquai into her lap. "Why powerful?"

"You treated her as an equal, peerless one."

"And Omliaz?"

"You were instructing her, peerless one. You and the Palenque-xaan."

"And why would we be doing that?"

"Because her mother spoiled her and you can't have an . . ." . . . *untuned quintara in the band.* Shkoden metaphors wouldn't be understood and he didn't know any Petayn ones. "You can't have a xaan of a great house who doesn't know the rules."

"What makes you think her mother spoiled her?"

"Her hair, peerless one. She never had her head shaved in the children's compound, so she was probably raised to consider herself as xaan."

"What's wrong with that? It's very likely, she *will* be xaan."

"Overindulged children seldom make good leaders, peerless one."

"Then why would I support Omliaz over her aunt?" Her tone suggested he think carefully about his answer.

Benedikt shrugged. "I can think of two reasons, peerless one. The aunt is older, less easy for you to mold, or House Calakroul has something you need and you can get it more easily from the girl."

"House Calakroul controls the land nearest Atixlan. The Calakroul-tul is a religious idiot and no problem, but House Kohunlich had no guarantee of safe passage after the change. Thus I bring Omliaz under my influence. You see the things that are in front of you. That's a rare skill, Benedikt. I'm impressed." Lips stained a deep red curved up into a smile.

Flustered by her praise, Benedikt bowed in the Shkoden way. "I was trained to observe, peerless one."

"Can you train others?" she asked as he straightened.

"I can try, peerless one." Fortunately, it hadn't been that long since he'd left the Bardic Hall.

"Good. There's something I need you to do for me first, but after that, we'll see how good a teacher you are." As Benedikt wondered if teaching entitled him to more braids, the xaan settled back against her cushions. "I've been at the palace much of the last three days. Tell me everything that's been happening here."

Wanting to show her that his earlier observations were no accident, he reported much the way he would have reported to his Bardic Captain, mixing observed detail with overheard bits of conversation. When he saw he had the xaan's full and complete attention, he lightly embellished a story one of her "cousins" had repeated about the tul.

"Where did he hear that story, I wonder?"

"I think it's common gossip, peerless one."

"Of course." She raised a hand when he would have continued. "Sing to me now, Benedikt."

Interesting evening, he thought three songs later as he made his way back to his room. *Not at all what I expected.*

His ears burned as he remembered his earlier expectations. He didn't know why Xaan Mijandra had told the others to stay away from him, but she, herself, was clearly more interested in his mind than his body. Head up, gaze locked on the not too distant future, he could see a day when he became her primary councillor. Indispensable. Doing the job a Bardic Captain should be doing were he not an opinionated old fool.

"Stick that in your four quarters and bang it, Kovar. Watch me learn what not to do from your example."

He had a future.

The xaan's cousins were trying to make friends. Xaan Mijandra, herself, was impressed by him.

For the first time in what seemed like forever, he felt secure. *And if the bath is empty, maybe I can even get laid.*

*   *   *

"Hueru, what do you think of the Palenque-xaan?"

He snorted. "Fat old coloas who drinks too much. Don't know why you put up with her."

"And Omliaz?"

He looked down at the xaan suspiciously. "Why, peerless one?"

"Because I asked you."

"She's got a great body."

"What does her body have to do with House Kohunlich?"

"It doesn't, peerless one." Hueru swallowed nervously. "You did ask."

"True. I did." She sighed and moved Shecquai off her lap. *There are times,* she thought as Hueru sat beside her and nuzzled his face into the rippled mass of her hair, *that I regret not being able to trust the more intelligent members of my family.* Which reminded her. "When you leave here, see that Hilieja has her tongue notched for repeating gossip."

Twelve

WONDERING if the barber had braided his wet hair extra tightly, Benedikt scratched his head and walked out onto his tiny balcony to get a look at the new day. "Maybe I shouldn't have laughed when he told me he had a good voice," he muttered, trying to ease the tension on his scalp.

Although thick cloud combined with the surrounding walls to keep him from seeing the sun, the distant chanting and drumming from the Great Temple told him it couldn't be long after dawn. He'd been amazed to discover that the square and the great houses surrounding it had been constructed in such a way as to carry the sound of the prayers to as many of the faithful as possible—no one but Benedikt seemed concerned about sleeping after the change when the priests of the moon would be in charge. *Maybe you get used to it after a while. . . .*

Scratching his head again, he took a moment to congratulate himself on what he'd already gotten used to. Had anyone ever told him he'd not only eat fried honeybee larva but like the combination of sweet and spicy, he'd have assumed they were out of their mind. And although he hadn't gotten used to the heat, he had gotten used to the lack of clothing the high temperatures demanded. He'd more or less gotten used to the braids.

Benedikt leaned his forearms on the balcony railing and stared down into the courtyard. He'd thought he was used to living on the edge of things—of no help to his village on the boats, without the ability of every other bard to Sing air—but his old life put him in the center of the Circle compared to how he lived now. He hadn't realized how used to a bard's welcome he'd become until he ended up where no one knew what a bard was.

"Oh, stop feeling so unenclosed sorry for yourself," he

muttered as he straightened. "Considering that the kigh dumped you here, naked and alone after having failed to save any of the lives entrusted to you, you've done better than you deserve. You have a position of some importance with a very powerful person which will only improve as she realizes what you can do. You *could* be faking a god connection for the tul, remember."

From where he was standing, he could just barely see the edge of upper bowl of the fountain through the greenery. It wasn't really that he didn't go out of his way to make friends, he just wasn't very good at it. Anticipating the moment they'd discover he was less than they thought always left him guarded and uneasy. He knew that some of the other bards had thought he was full of himself, but they didn't understand. *They* could Sing air.

He grinned as he tugged at a particularly annoying braid. Singing air was no longer an issue. "Here in Petayn, they'll only discover what I can do and that'll make that whole friendship thing a lot easier. Which is a good thing," he added in Shkoden as a tiny, ruby-throated, iridescent green bird caught his attention. "Because unless I'm talking to you, I'm spending far too much time talking to myself."

Ignoring him completely, the bird backed out of a huge red blossom and flew up and over the dividing wall, taking Benedikt's gaze with it. Squinting a little to keep it in sight, he realized there was a figure in one of the tul's third-floor windows. *Why not?* He waved.

As the figure moved forward, out of the shadows and into an identity, he waved again, more vigorously. Xhojee looked startled but waved back.

Distance made communication difficult. Shouting would draw the attention of both halves of House Kohunlich and as far as mouthing the words, Benedikt doubted he'd be able to recognize the shapes of a language he'd only just learned the sounds of.

"I'm . . ."

He brought one hand in and thumped himself on the chest.

". . . happy . . ."

Forefingers drew a broad smile in the air in front of his mouth.

". . . to see . . ."

Two fingers then a line drawn out from both eyes.

". . . you."

An exaggerated point across the courtyard.

Xhojee smiled and, using the same system, signaled back, "Me, too." Then suddenly he grew serious, scanned the xaan's side of the building, leaned forward, and beckoned.

"You want me to come over there?" Grasping the balcony railing with both hands, Benedikt tried to work out a gesture that meant, *I can't.*

"What are you doing?"

Had he not been holding the railing, Benedikt was fairly sure he would've gone over it. Heart pounding, he whirled around and glared at Serasti. Had he not been certain he was doing something he shouldn't be, it would have been a more convincing glare.

"I asked you a question, Benedikt." Blue-on-blue robe whipping around her bare legs, the house master strode toward him, one hand outstretched as if to pluck him bodily from the railing.

Trusting Xhojee to have faded back, Benedikt stepped out of her direct path and drew himself up to his full height. "I was looking at a bird," he told her, using enough Voice that she had to believe it, telling himself that he wasn't using his training to support a lie. He *had* been looking at a bird.

Serasti peered out into the courtyard, inspecting the tul's side of the building through narrowed eyes. "A bird," she repeated. "I see." When she turned toward him, Benedikt had the strangest feeling that, in spite of the way he towered over her, she was looking down her nose at him. "The Kohunlich-xaan wants to see you. Now."

Knowing that he'd think of a hundred clever responses later, when it would be far too late for them to be of use, Benedikt sighed and fell into step, following one pace behind the house master's heels.

Benedikt leaned back in the small cart and stared at the stubby tail of the coloas flicking flies off its rump. He knew he should be happy about being out of the house, even hidden by the enveloping priest's robe, but something nagged at him. "Why does the house master dislike me so much, peerless one?"

"It's not dislike, it's distrust. You came to me from my brother." Xaan Mijandra paused while the coloas' groom shifted her grip on the cheek strap and clucked to get the animal moving. "Serasti expects you to betray me," she added when guards, coloas, cart, and following pair of guards, were moving toward the street directly opposite the Great Temple.

Startled, Benedikt squirmed around and stared at her, his nose pressing against the gauze. "How?"

"You could strangle me while you sing, arrange the body so I appeared asleep, then be gone, back to my brother, before my death is discovered."

The xaan sounded so matter-of-fact about her own murder that Benedikt found himself at a loss for words. Gaze locked on House Carakoul's outer wall, not really seeing the green-and-gold tile work, he tried to work out the result of such an action. When he spoke, he matched her tone. "If I returned to your brother after strangling you, peerless one, the other great houses would know he had something to do with your death."

"He'd insist you went crazy, remove your tongue lest you implicate him, and hand you over to the authorities. Appearances would be satisfied and, after a great deal of pain, you'd be as dead as I was."

"And the house master thinks I'd be stupid enough to do that?" he demanded, adding a quick, "peerless one?" and a muttered, "I'm not stupid!" before she could answer.

"You wouldn't sacrifice yourself if my brother asked you?"

"No, peerless one."

She studied him measuringly over the edge of her fan. "What if I asked you?"

Once again, Benedikt realized that the xaan did not ask rhetorical questions. Would he sacrifice himself for her? He'd have sacrificed himself for the *Starfarer*. He'd have sacrificed himself for Queen Jelena. He supposed he'd have even sacrificed himself to save Janinton from the flood—it was what bards did, after all. Squirming under the weight of the xaan's regard, he considered his options. A "yes" would be a lie. A "no" would not only be a lie but, he suspected, a really bad idea. So . . . should he lie to himself or to her? Survival suggested the former, integrity the later.

"I don't know, peerless one," he said at last, hoping ambiguity would cover both options.

The fan waved slowly, back and forth. "Anyone else in my household would have said yes without hesitation."

"But would they have meant it?" He bit his tongue, but it was too late. The words had slipped out before he could stop them. It was an instinctive, bardic question. *A self-righteous, suicidal question,* Benedikt corrected. *We aren't a bard anymore.*

Out of the corner of one eye, he saw the fan stop moving.

"What difference would that make?"

And she meant that question just like she meant every other. Thankful for the masking gauze, Benedikt opened and closed his mouth and finally fell back on, "I don't know, peerless one."

"Exactly." As the fan began moving again, she patted him lightly on the thigh with the other hand.

Benedikt would have been a lot happier about that had he not just seen the coloas' groom pat a woolly shoulder in much the same way.

". . . I'd say she's got you marked for herself."

Maybe. But he was beginning to get the feeling sex had nothing to do with it.

The road they were on went straight from the square to the docks. While not as wide as the causeway, it was clearly one of Atixlan's major streets.

As they moved by the lesser houses, Benedikt's attention was caught by the rumbling of a heavily laden cart. A quick look while they passed the mouth of an alley set between garden walls showed him the back end of the cart piled high with garbage. It hit a bump while he watched, and a cloud of flies lifted off the surface of the pile.

"Peerless one, there was a body . . ."

"You seem shocked." The xaan, herself, seemed mildly amused by his reaction. "Don't people die in Shkoder?"

"Yes, but we don't throw them out with the trash." They were past the alley now. "I saw a foot sticking out of a garbage cart."

"Just a foot." Now she looked bored. "Then you don't know it was a whole body, do you?"

"No, but . . ."

"You're supposed to be a priest of Xaantalicta, stop squirming."

He sat still as the xaan commanded, but he also stared down every side street and alley they passed, afraid of what he'd find amidst the debris yet unable to stop examining it.

Leaving the houses of both greater and lesser families behind, they entered a commercial area where the occupants of those houses found amusements and necessities of the quality they demanded. The farther they moved from the square, the less discriminating the shops until, finally, they moved between the large, grayish-yellow bulk of warehouses.

Benedikt straightened and drew in a deep breath. Even overlaid with a hundred other smells, there was no mistaking the salt tang of the sea. He hadn't realized how much he'd missed it.

"Been feeling confined lately?"

"A bit, peerless one." He should have known she'd notice. She noticed everything.

The road ended with the warehouses. The groom led the coloas out onto a broad paved thoroughfare that followed the curve of a deep, bowl-shaped harbor. Five huge stone piers jutted out like teeth around the bottom curve of the bowl, with smaller docks clustered closer to the open sea on either side. A sudden breeze from the right brought a familiar stink and Benedikt figured he had a pretty good idea of where the fishmarket had to be.

Used to the constant bustle of the harbor at Elbasan, he was amazed to see almost no activity on either ships or shore. *Maybe it's the heat.* The air was so heavy and still, his breath barely made it out through the gauze. A quick glance up at a gray-green sky, amended the theory. *Or maybe it's because we're about to get very wet.* In his admittedly limited experience, Petayn didn't have such a thing as a light shower.

He wasn't the only one to check the sky.

Prodded by bellowing in a language he didn't understand, sailors suddenly swarmed over a low, sleek ship, tying down lines and dragging canvas over the cargo piled into the open hold.

They were heading, the coloas moving more quickly than it had been, toward the same pier.

"All the way to the *Kraken*," the xaan commanded as they passed a pillar marked with the hands of House Kohunlich.

The dressed stone of the thoroughfare extended out onto the pier. As the metal reinforcement in the guards' sandals rang against it, the man doing the bellowing turned to check out the noise.

Must have bardic ears, Benedikt thought, amazed he'd been able to hear anything over the combined sounds of his yelling and his crew's compliance.

"Peerless one!" The volume remained constant although the language changed. Shouting what could only be instructions to keep working over his shoulder, he bounded up the ladder to the pier and fell into step beside the xaan's cart, apparently unconcerned when it didn't stop.

Coarse dark hair had been cut short around the front half of his head but hung loose over his shoulders—the first unbraided hair Benedikt had seen outside Tulpayotee's temple—and the puckered line of an old scar was all that marred the gleaming copper skin of a muscular chest. Dark eyes gleamed under heavy brows, and the smile that split the broad face showed a front tooth inset with jade. "My heart sings at the sight of your beauty, peerless one."

"I'm surprised to see you here, Ah Chak. Not many ships continue trade at this time of year."

"All the more profit for those of us who do, peerless one." He dropped his voice to a near conspiratorial whisper. "Word is, Petayn's sun is setting."

"If you mean the Tulparax is dying; yes, he is."

"I will rejoice when you are paid the fee for docking and not your brother. Has the news of the Aliphat's most recent attempt to take Balankanche reached your ears? Three ships were lost and with them most of their crews. The Aliphat swore on the sacred rock that she'd return again when the rains are done. The yards of Becan hum with the building of many small, deep-keeled ships."

"Many small, deep-keeled ships," Xaan Mijandra repeated thoughtfully. She turned to face Ah Chak fully for the first time as the cart stopped in front of a two-masted ship flying the colors of House Kohunlich, a great wooden squid tucked up under the bowsprit. "After the change, I will personally deal with your docking fees."

His smile broadened. "The peerless one is generous as well as beautiful."

"Only when she's dry."

Arms spread, palms facing out, Ah Chak bowed and backed away.

Benedikt hurriedly followed the xaan out of the cart and up the gangplank, the guards visibly straining to maintain her dignified pace. Every line on the ship stood out in stark relief against a glowering sky that seemed close enough to reach out and grab. Hoisting up his robe for faster movement, he began to count under his breath.

On four, he reached the deck and the first drops of rain slammed dark circles into the sun bleached wood. On six he stood on the threshold of the cabin, waiting for the ship's master to finish greeting the xaan. He stepped into the dim shelter just as the clouds grew tired of restraint. The last thing he saw before nearly solid sheets of water blocked his view, was the philosophical expression on the face of the coloas. He couldn't see the groom, but he suspected she was looking a little less accepting.

When the rain stopped a short time later, the very wet crew of a waiting pilot boat rowed the xaan's ship out to the mouth of the harbor.

Out of his robe, Benedikt stood on the deck and tried not to think of how much water there was all around and of how loudly it called to him. The xaan hadn't told him they were going on a voyage. She'd told him she wanted his company but not for what. Chased on board by the rain, he hadn't had time to think about what he was doing. Now, unfortunately, he had nothing but time.

Once the sails went up and only the open sea lay ahead, he paced up and down the center line of the deck, as far from both railings as he could get.

"The xaan wants you inside."

By the time Benedikt turned, the guard had already started back to the cabin leaving him no choice but to follow. He ducked under the low lintel and paused to let his eyes grow accustomed to the gloom. Xaan Mijandra sat cross-legged at the rear of a small dais, a large map spread out in front of her.

"Frightened, Benedikt?"

"No, peerless one." When he saw her expression, he spread his hands, and sighed. "Yes. Maybe. I don't know."

"Sorquizic beat you once. I'm going to give you a chance to even the score."

"Peerless one?" He had no idea what she was talking about.

"Come here."

He came.

"Look at this."

He sat on the edge of the dais and looked at the map. There was no sign of Shkoder or the empire or even the Antibolies. *Idiot. Why would there be?*

"This is Petayn." One hand swept down from the mountains to the sea. "Atixlan is here. We control the coast as far north as here." A tinted fingernail tapped the map a considerable distance from the capital. "And south to Becan, here. This is Balankanche." The fingernail traced the outline of a large island.

The island had been drawn an equal distance from both Petayn and Becan. "Who controls Balankanche, peerless one?"

"No one. In the time of the last Xaantalax, the islanders traded with both Petayn and Becan." Xaan Mijandra settled back against a wicker rest, habit stretching out a hand to scoop an absent Shecquai into her lap. Recovering smoothly, she laced her fingers together and continued. "Balankanche had . . . has . . . huge deposits of gold. The Xaantalax decided to add those deposits to the riches of Petayn. After ensuring that no Balankanche trader would be able to return and give warning, she sent a fleet to take the island. They met the Becan fleet just before they arrived at Balankanche. That unexpected conflict gave warning enough."

"The islanders were ready for them when they landed?"

"They never landed. Although mostly abandoned on the mainland, the worship of Sorquizic was strong on Balankanche. The priests went out in small boats and prayed to their god who took every one of them to the bottom— unfortunately, along with most of the remaining Petayn ships. No one has been able to get a ship of any kind near any part of that island since." She paused and looked

Benedikt right in the eye. "The sea rises up and prevents it."

Watching the rippling shadows thrown across the map by the swinging lantern, he had a horrible feeling he knew where this was going.

The xaan's smile had all the warmth of a curved blade. "Water listens to you."

"If we're going to take Balankanche, we have to do it now, before the Aliphat tries again." They were leaning on the bow, the xaan braced comfortably against the railings, Benedikt standing uncomfortably behind her. "The xaan who captures the island will capture most, if not all of Petayn as well. The Xaantalax has survived the years of the Tulparax's dying, in spite of having several living female relatives, because I threw my strength behind her as did the houses that follow my lead. I made sure she came to depend on my strength rather than develop her own. After the change, I would have been the second most powerful person in Petayn."

Would have been? Benedikt wondered. He realized this quiet explanation was probably as close to bragging as the xaan ever came, but he didn't feel at all relieved to discover that even the mighty needed to be reassured occasionally about how clever they were.

"Then you came into my hands. At first I discounted your so-called powers—who wouldn't, you couldn't even save your own ship, after all—but you dealt with the flood and I began to ask myself, why second? Why not first? It isn't unheard of for houses to rise and for other houses to fall."

The matter-of-fact way she announced what amounted to a palace coup, lifted the hair on the back of Benedikt's neck. It made the tul's desire for power look like childish pique at being denied what he considered his fair share. "Peerless one, isn't the Xaantalax the earthly representative of Xaantalicta?"

She cocked an eyebrow back over her shoulder at him. "Your point?"

"Doesn't that make her almost divine?"

Xaan Mijandra grinned and scooped a handful of blowing

braids back off her face. "Trust me, Benedikt, if I capture Balankanche, I'll be divine enough."

"Island, ho!"

"There, peerless one." Benedikt pointed past her at a blue-gray smear against the horizon.

"I see it. Now, let's see how close we can get before we're stopped."

They came close enough to see interior mountains and the blurry, undefined outline of a good-sized town, then the waves began to move almost at right angles to the wind. The *Kraken*'s master brought her around and, with minimum sail up, maintained a course more or less parallel to the disturbance.

"Any closer, and Sorquizic will stop us."

"You want me to Sing you through Sorquizic's barricade, peerless one?"

"No. If you can't remove it entirely, I want you to Sing my *fleet* through Sorquizic's barricade."

"Your fleet," Benedikt repeated as he walked to the part of the railing closest to the unusual wave pattern. When he leaned over the side and stared into the water, he saw what he expected to see—the giant kigh of the depths. One of them rolled to the surface, became part of crest and trough, and beckoned him in. He thought of Xhojee beckoning to him that morning and wondered if he'd known what the xaan had planned. *Don't be a fool. How could he?*

"Can you do it?"

"This isn't . . ." He dried suddenly damp palms on the front of his sawrap. "This isn't like the flood, peerless one."

"More difficult."

It wasn't a question, but he answered it anyway. "Much."

He heard her sigh and walk forward until she stood very close behind him. The billowing folds of her robe wrapped around his bare legs. "I can't say that I'm not disappointed." Her hand was cool where it gripped his arm. "But I understand. You're not a priest of Sorquizic, how can you undo what they set in motion."

He stiffened. "It's not that, peerless one."

"You lost your confidence when you lost your ship?"

"No . . ."

Her grip tightened, then released. "It's all right."

It was *not* all right. She'd brought him out here expecting him to fail, and he was not going to fulfill that expectation. Benedikt moistened his lips, worked up enough saliva to swallow, and Sang the four notes to call the kigh. It was enough to get their attention but not enough to pull them out of their pattern.

You come to us, they replied.

He felt himself responding, reaction to the kigh mixed up with reaction to the warm presence of the xaan, and he threw himself into the Song, away from the distraction of his body.

Caught up, thrown about, he was a pebble in a current, his rough edges worn smooth by the unceasing movement of the water all around him. He wasn't Singing the pattern the priests had set in motion with their sacrifice so many years before, it was Singing him and, had the kigh not helped him learn the Song of Sorquizic, he would have drowned standing dry on the *Kraken*'s deck.

When he finally Sang the gratitude and came back to his body, he found himself pressed painfully tight against the railing. At some point, although he couldn't remember when, one of the kigh had come to him. He was dripping wet and the deck around him was soaked. Not all the moisture on his sawrap had come from the sea.

A hand touched his shoulder and he half-turned, clutching the rail for support.

The xaan's mouth moved, but he could hear nothing over a Song almost too large to be contained within one bard's head. She frowned, and spoke again. "The barricade is still there, Benedikt."

Nodding, he managed to gain control of his voice and wasn't surprised to find it little more than a rough whisper. "But now I know how it was built, peerless one, I can create a Song to remove it."

"Now?"

"No. It'll take time."

"How much time?"

He rubbed saltwater from his eyes and considered the complexities of a pattern twenty-three priests had died for. "I don't know, peerless one."

"That's three times today. I'm beginning to dislike that answer."

When she moved toward him, he tried to step back, but

his hips were already pressed against the side of the ship. There was nowhere to go but into the sea.

Trapped.

Barely back in control of his own thoughts, really not up to marshaling a defense, he asked himself what Bannon would do and didn't much like the answer. He hadn't known the ex-assassin well, but he had a feeling that if approached by a beautiful threatening woman, Bannon wouldn't have backed up.

Standing so close Benedikt's sawrap dampened her robes, the xaan stared up at him. "I must have Balankanche before the end of the rainy season. You have a limited time to create your Song."

"Peerless one. I must turn the *Kraken* now if we're to reach the harbor before sunset."

At the ship master's interruption the xaan closed her eyes and shook her head. "Of course," she murmured. Opening her eyes, she sighed. "Do it. A limited time," she repeated to Benedikt as the minimal crew raced for the lines. "Get yourself something to drink. You look like you could use it."

Completely confused, Benedikt blinked stupidly down at her. Had she just been threatening him?

Wrapped in a coloas wool blanket and sipping a carved wooden mug of honeyed wine, Benedikt followed the xaan to the stern, and together they watched Balankanche disappear from sight.

"Amazing how much power that miserable little blot on the horizon represents."

Benedikt watched the xaan watch Balankanche. He'd never seen her look so animated. Her eyes were shining, there were spots of color on her cheeks not entirely the result of the wind, and her voice had dropped to a throaty purr.

"You are as little aware of your fate as the Xaantalax."

It took him a moment before he realized that "you" referred to the island.

"Power should go to those best able to wield it." Whirling around, she stared up at him, dark eyes burning, "Don't you agree, Benedikt?"

Very glad he had no wine in his mouth to choke on,

Benedikt managed a strangled, "Yes, peerless one." For the first time, she showed the kind of raw power that blazed so continually off her brother. For the first time he realized he was in just as much danger now of being burned as he ever had been with the tul.

And I still don't Sing fire.

How could he have ever thought she was cold?

He felt—no, he knew—he was about to do something very, very stupid. Maybe it was the wine, but he didn't think so.

Dropping the blanket, he took a step toward her.

Out in the water, the crest of a wave rose higher still as the kigh responded.

She reached up and laid heated fingers against his chest. "The survivors will go to the mines. Perhaps I'll put Hueru in charge of the operation. He'd like that."

Survivors? When Shkoder had conquered the Broken Islands, it hadn't been entirely bloodless but neither could the losers have been referred to as survivors.

Survivors implied slaughter.

When she turned to face the island again, he didn't stop her. Wrapping himself in the blanket, he stepped away to think.

In spite of another downpour, the *Kraken* reached the harbor before full dark to find the pilot boat—her crew even more wet and miserable than they had been—waiting to take them back to the pier.

Wearing his priest's robe, thankful for the masking gauze, Benedikt followed the xaan and her guards down the gangplank and into the cart. Whether it was the same cart or a different one, he had no idea—he couldn't tell the coloas apart and he hadn't looked very closely at the groom.

He felt as if hadn't looked very closely at anyone during his time in Petayn.

Survive.

Survivors.

He was a survivor. It wasn't so bad.

Careful not to move his head and give away his interest, he stared at the xaan. All traces of the passion that had so nearly sucked him under were gone. She hadn't asked him if he would Sing an invasion fleet to the island. She'd assumed that if he could, he would.

The xaan said nothing on the return journey through Atixlan, leaving Benedikt free to chase half-formed thoughts around the inside of his own head. Perhaps she assumed he was already working on the Song.

The city streets were packed as the cooler evening air brought out buyers and sellers, lovers and the lost, and those who just wanted to be seen. Any other time, Benedikt would have stared in fascination at the parades of people, shifts and sawraps in incredible color combinations, heads wearing anything from one braid to a dozen, but this time he barely saw them. Sounds and images pounded against him like another cloudburst with as little lasting effect.

They reached the square just after the ending of the sunset service. Small clumps of people were heading back to the greater or lesser houses or to the heart of the city beyond. Trying to seem as though he were paying no attention, Benedikt searched the clumps for Xhojee or the tul but was unable to find either.

"Say nothing of your journey today."

Drawn from his search, Benedikt followed Xaan Mijandra from the cart and into the house.

"If anyone asks," she added just before Serasti met them, "say your mouth has been closed by the hand of the xaan."

"Yes, peerless one." From the look Serasti shot him, he realized the house master had not only heard but didn't much like the idea of him having secrets with the xaan. So she didn't trust him. So what.

The xaan had his evening meal sent to him in his room along with a stack of paper, a ceramic jar of ink, and a metal pen. Ignoring the food, Benedikt picked up the pen and turned it between his fingers. Dipped, the ink ran down a spiral path to a smoothly rounded point, similar to the glass pens of the Fienians the Bardic Hail used for writing recalls. A quill needed to be cut several times during a recall, but a glass Fienian pen lasted forever—as long as no one dropped it.

When Benedikt deliberately dropped the metal pen, it rang against the tile.

This was something he could have brought home. Something useful. Something wondrous. The paper was better too. White, smoother, and more flexible at a similar thickness. The librarians would have loved it.

He hadn't thought about going home for a while.

The xaan wanted a Song that would help her destroy a people.

Xaan Mijandra explained the supplies when she sent for him that night. "You mentioned once, at a meal, that you could read and write."

So he wasn't the only one who recalled the conversations she might have missed. "Only in my own language, peerless one."

"I don't care what language it's in. Have you begun?"

"It isn't the sort of Song you write down, peerless one."

"That's not what I asked you."

He knew that but he'd been hoping he could, if not change the subject, move it sideways. Wishing he could risk using Voice, he spread his hands and said as calmly as he was able, "Peerless one, I swore an oath not to use my abilities to harm others."

"You didn't swear that oath to me."

"No, peerless one."

"I see."

Startled, he looked up and met her gaze. It had sounded as though she actually understood.

"Fortunately," she continued, "you won't be harming others. You'll just be moving a bit of water out of the way." Her mouth curved up into something that roughly resembled a smile. "Where's the harm in that?"

"It's the intent, peerless one."

Her expression no longer resembled a smile in any way. "My intentions are none of your concern. Your job is to provide me with access to Balankanche before the end of the rainy season."

And if he didn't do what she wanted, what happened then? Did he lose everything? If, when he moved the flood from the causeway, someone had shoved an enemy into the wall of water and drowned them, was that his responsibility? If all he did was move a bit of water out of the way . . .

"It would help if I had an instrument, peerless one."

"I'll send an instrument maker to you tomorrow."

* * *

Xhojee didn't come to the window at sunrise although Benedikt waited on his balcony until he was almost late for the morning meal.

Talk around his table centered on one of the junior priests who'd gone into convulsions the night before after eating from a bowl of deep-fried duck intestines.

"You know how the gauze kind of dangles while they eat?" one of the guard Seconds asked as she passed Benedikt a bowl of steamed egg and beans. "She ripped it right off her face."

"Wonder what they used for a marinade," the senior record keeper snickered.

"We're not entirely sure," the junior physician answered seriously. "Physician Otypez is still running tests."

"Why would someone want to poison a junior priest?" Benedikt wondered, appalled.

The others at the table turned as one, and stared.

The Second recovered first. "They weren't trying to poison the priest, you hairy moron, they were trying to poison the xaan."

"The dish was intended for the xaan's table, but she decided she didn't want it," the record keeper explained. "So she sent it to the priests."

"The strange thing is," the physician said, leaning forward slightly, "the karjen who tastes the xaan's food had no reaction."

"Didn't taste *that*," snorted the Second.

"Did," the physician corrected. "And the xaan made him finish the whole bowl. Nothing. Otypez thinks it was a poison targeted specifically to the xaan, and the priest just happened to be sensitive to the same thing."

The Second looked as though she didn't believe a word of it. "Question is, how'd it get into the food? The peerless one should've had more than one of the kitchen staff punished."

"Punished?" Benedikt repeated.

"Yeah." The record keeper sighed. "And with the change so close and both halves of all the great houses full, do you have any idea how hard it's going to be to replace that man with someone reliable?"

"Bet the priest'll be replacing the taster," the guard offered.

The junior physician looked doubtful. "*If* she regains consciousness."

"But she's a priest," Benedikt protested.

Everyone seemed to think that was very funny and he realized that although these were the people in the household he knew the best—there weren't many six to eight braids, it was too many for servants and too few for family, and they not only shared a table but a bath—he didn't know them at all. He felt a little like the priest must have, choking on something everyone else could eat with pleasure.

Glancing the length of the room, he saw the xaan nod as she sipped her tea, a minimal, businesslike gesture in response to whatever Hueru was telling her.

She'd put the survivors of Balankanche in the mines and Hueru in charge of the survivors. He'd enjoy that.

"I spent the day in the herbarium," the physician noted, spreading honey thickly on a small, round biscuit. "Who do they think is responsible for the poisoning?"

The Second shrugged, reaching across the table for the last piece of baked banana. "It was probably the tul, but there's only one way for most us to know for certain." The others waited while she chewed and swallowed. "Just keep an eye on the other houses until someone dies."

"*That* could just as easily be a family quarrel as retaliation," the record keeper stopped eating long enough to point out. "I wonder if it was Hilieja. She is the Xaan's heir, and she just had her tongue notched."

"So what *were* you doing in the herbarium?" The senior record keeper leaned over and pointedly poked the junior physician in the shoulder. "Looking for a *seasoning* the tul's people couldn't trace?"

Everyone thought that was pretty funny, too.

Benedikt thought that no one in the household of the Kohunlich-xaan would have any trouble with any part of the invasion of Balankanche.

Was he or was he not a member of the household? And if he wasn't, what was he?

*   *   *

The instrument maker had a set of multi-reed pipes essentially identical to the set Benedikt had lōst with the sinking of the *Starfarer* and, after a spirited discussion over the many possible types of stringed instruments, seemed determined to attempt a quintara.

"It's only a bigger *okalie,* yes?"

Benedikt had picked up one of the tiny, three-stringed toys, laughed and agreed, and felt better than he had in days.

Unfortunately, it didn't last long.

"You have your instrument, Benedikt." The xaan cast a dubious look at the pipes. "Now get to work, I expect a return on my investment."

With a Song of Sorquizic caroling in his head, Benedikt went back to the fountain. He needed a friend. He needed someone to tell him what they thought he should do.

What would Bannon do? he asked, watching the kigh dance down from the uppermost basin.

Survive.

But the survivors would go to the mines.

He turned the pipes over in his hands, passing them back and forth, learning their weight and feel so that he could better find their song. For the first time since he'd washed ashore, he missed his old pipes, but the differences between the old and new were barely noticeable—more in decoration than construction. Each reed had been stained a different color and even the leather bindings were dyed.

Finally raising the pipes to his mouth, he blew a tentative scale. They had a good sound. A bit breathy, but he was willing to allow that might be a weakness in technique. It had *been* a while.

He let the music wander where it would, noting, out of habit, some bit of melody he might make use of later, but mostly just playing what he felt. It wasn't a very happy tune.

Even the fountain seemed to have slowed in response.

When he looked up a short time later, he realized he had an audience. Showing off a little, he added a chorus of "Three Dancing Pigs," then lowering the pipes, smiled. "Hello, Herexi."

"Did you make that up?" she demanded. "Not the pig stuff but the stuff before?"

When he nodded, she limped over to his side and looked at him with concern. "Why're you so sad? You got eight braids."

Benedikt shrugged and dropped the pipes on his lap. "Braids aren't everything."

"That's 'cause the peerless one gave you eight of them," Herexi snorted. "I'm not sayin' it wasn't pretty, though. Just sad. Those yours?" She jerked a pointed chin toward his lap.

He grinned, remembering their last conversation.

"Yeah, these are *my* pipes. Have you found yours?"

The girl drew herself up to her full height. This put them pretty much eye to eye, although Benedikt had remained sitting. "I," she said proudly, "am a training pipe attendant. When I get my braid, I'll be a junior pipe attendant."

"Congratulations."

"The pipes in this place are so great," she confided. "I thought the country house had pipes but not like here. Pipes all over. Like for this fountain, they go right down under the garden. There's these old tunnels under the house where you go to fix them. Tunnels even older than the house—from the olden days. One of the junior pipe attendants, he told me that they go out under the square and to all the great houses 'cause there used to be a temple to Peta where the square is now and the olden days people used to use the tunnels to get there. I get to go in them a lot 'cause some of them are small and I'm smallest."

"Olden-days tunnels must be dark and scary."

She glanced around, as if making sure Benedikt would be the only one to hear such a confession. "A little." Then she shrugged and the grin returned. "But it's part of doin' the pipes. So, if you don't mind . . ."

When Benedikt indicated she should go ahead, Herexi balanced one-legged on the lowest basin, her bad foot dangling down as a counterweight, and jabbed her fingers into the fountain's source between the two stone hands. Her brow furrowed, and she jabbed again.

The water began falling faster and Benedikt realized the slowing had been a mechanical problem—a pipe problem—and nothing to do with his song.

"Well done."

"You just wait till they let me at the cisterns," Herexi told him gleefully.

"Did you want me to play you something?" Benedikt asked hurriedly as the girl turned to leave.

She paused and looked back at him. His ears started to burn as he realized she was looking back in sympathy. He didn't need her sympathy, the xaan had given him eight braids.

"Maybe another time," she said softly. "I gotta go back to work now."

"Sure."

The fountain seemed to be laughing at him as she limped away.

That wasn't the kind of friends he needed. He needed someone who could give him advice, not a half-grown ex-bath attendant with a plumbing fixation.

The xaan went to the palace that afternoon, so Benedikt ate his evening meal in his room, then blew out his lamp and went to sit on the tiny balcony, staring at the tul's half of the house. As his eyes became accustomed to the darkness, he could make out the dark gray-on-gray rectangle of Xhojee's window—not that it did him any good, the two halves of House Kohunlich were no closer in the dark than in the daylight.

"I don't want to do it," he admitted and could almost hear Xhojee answer, *So? What you want has nothing to do with what the xaan commands. Wouldn't you obey the commands of your, what was that word, queen?*

"No. Not a command like that, not one that would result in the slaughter of a whole people. The bards of Shkoder take oaths."

First, you're not in Shkoder. Second, you're not a bard, you're the xaan's—well, I don't know what she calls you, but you're hers. The xaan's reaction is likely to be a whole lot different than your queen's.

Benedikt sighed and sagged back against the cool stone of the wall. "You're a lot of help."

His choices were simple. He could do what the xaan wanted, help her conquer another people, and secure his place high in House Kohunlich. Or he could refuse.

He could hear singing, very faintly, from the kitchens— probably the cook who'd found the time to give him three songs while they were on the road. For all his size, he sang a pure, light tenor that reminded Benedikt of Tadeus. Back in Shkoder, he'd have taken his pipes down to the kitchens and the two of them would have made music long into the night. In Petayn, karjet didn't socialize with karjen.

"I don't like it here very much," he admitted to Xhojee's window. The new life he'd made for himself had turned out to be one he didn't want to live. Problem was, he didn't think he could stop living that life and keep living.

Living the tul's lie would have been easier.

He dreamed that night about the day he'd left home for the Bardic Hall—except in the dream he wasn't fourteen and he was wearing a sawrap and braids. Karlene didn't seem to notice, but Benedikt cringed every time she looked at him, expecting her to laugh.

"The training's going to be pretty intensive for the first couple of years," she said as she settled her pack on her shoulders. "You'll learn to control your voice, listen to the kigh, recall, witness, command, charm, and probably pick up a second instrument. It's funny," she turned to him and smiled, "but every new bard that comes in already plays something."

"Why is that funny?" he asked, pulling at his sawrap and hoping they wouldn't meet anyone on the road. With every step he took it got shorter. *If this keeps up, I'll be wearing nothing more than a belt and sandals long before we get to Elbasan.*

"It's funny because the xaan only brought in the instrument maker this morning."

Even to the dream Benedikt that didn't sound right, but Karlene continued before he could protest.

"Mostly you'll learn how to be the string that holds the shells of Shkoder together."

"What shells?"

She slipped off a necklace of polished shells that one of the village women had given her just before they left. "Hold out your hands." When he did, she draped the necklace over his palms. "Think of this as our way of life here in Shkoder. The shells are all the bits and pieces that way of life is made of and the bards are the string, holding everything together."

"I'm going to learn to be string?" Suddenly realizing his hands were wet, he looked down at what he held and saw that the shells were turning to water that dripped through his fingers and sank into the packed gravel of the causeway.

The causeway was in Petayn and Karlene had never been in Petayn.

It didn't seem to matter because Karlene was turning to water, too. He tried to scoop her up, contain her somehow, but the ground absorbed her too quickly, and he was left holding nothing but another piece of damp string while the xaan's wagon came crashing toward him.

Heart in his throat, he woke up drenched in his own sweat, still hearing the thunder of the runaway wagon. Then he realized, it was thunder indeed and, although his room was so hot and so damp it was like trying to breathe underwater, he managed to draw in a calming breath.

"Other guys my age dream about sex," he sighed, getting out of bed and padding naked to the balcony.

Lightning flashed, close enough to illuminate the courtyard in stark black and white. Thunder crashed, and the sky opened. Benedikt spread his arms and welcomed the deluge. A hundred kigh flowed over him, into and around each other, continually replaced, continual sensation. He thought of Karlene turning to water and slipping away and wished that he could join her. Then it almost seemed like he had; as his knees buckled, he grabbed the railing to keep from falling.

The hundreds of kigh continued, and arousal began to build again.

And again.

Finally, he realized that if he wanted to survive the night, he had to get out of the rain. He fought his way back to the safety of his room, sinking down cross-legged to the floor as his legs gave way beneath him on the other side of the raised threshold. After a while, when his breathing returned to normal, he grinned and murmured, "Nothing left but another piece of damp string. I hope it was as good for Karlene."

He felt better than he had in a long time. He was tired, but the kigh seemed to have washed away mental clutter along with physical tensions. For the first time in ages he was thinking in one language instead of bits and pieces of two, even the dream had been in Petayn.

If he was looking for the symbolism behind the dissolving shells, he didn't have to look far since it seemed that Shkoder had, indeed, disappeared.

The string remained.

Bardic oaths weren't made to Shkoder, they were just made.

"I'm going to learn to be string?"

Benedikt swallowed a lump in his throat and stared down at his wet hands. Without Shkoder, he was no less a bard. He'd been asking the wrong question all along.

"Not what would Bannon do," he told the rain. "What would Benedikt do?"

Without a visible moon or stars he had no idea of how much time he had until dawn. All he could do was hurry and hope he had enough.

At least it doesn't take long to dress . . . In sawrap and sandals, he scooped the queen's coin off its hook and dropped it over his head. With the coin's cool weight scything a familiar pattern against his chest, he shrugged into the priest's robe and slipped silently out past the string of bells into the corridor. He felt bad about leaving the pipes behind, but when it came right down to it, they weren't his, they were the xaan's.

The house was completely quiet and absolutely dark. One hand against the wall and the other holding the robe away from his legs, Benedikt moved as fast as he could through the blackness. One door, two doors, three doors, and nothing. Given room enough to spread, the darkness seemed to gray over the stairs to the first floor.

The doors would be guarded. Two by the front portico, two by the kitchens, two by the stables. It would have to be through the front, then.

Giving thanks that the Petayns went for cluttered color not furniture, Benedikt made it safely though the public rooms to the front of the house. Standing on the half flight of stairs that led down to the ground floor, he could see the dark of armed figures through the open stonework to either side of the door.

He wished now he'd paid more attention to either of the

guard Seconds when they'd complained about night watches. He had no idea when or how often the watches changed.

Although, as I've no idea what unenclosed time it is now, it wouldn't help if I did know.

The sound of the rain covering any noise he made, Benedikt moved as close as he could get to the door without actually touching it, and began to Sing.

After a few moments, the guard on the right shifted in place and muttered, "Xaantalicta save me, I can barely keep my eyes open."

"Your eyes close, and the xaan'll sew them shut," the other hissed. "You don't sleep until your watch is done."

Had it not been raining so hard, Benedikt doubted that his lullaby would have worked, even adapted to the situation. But the kigh seemed to lend him strength and finally, his pectoral chiming softly, the guard on the left sagged down out of sight, murmuring, "Glad that's over." The guard on the right, already on the ground, only snored in reply.

Still Singing, Benedikt opened the door, stepped over an outflung arm, and hurried toward the edge of the portico. Masked by rain and hood and gauze he changed his Song slightly and, in spite of the danger, waited until he was sure both guards had roused before moving on.

"What's that?"

Heart pounding so loudly he could hardly hear, Benedikt kept walking.

"Just a Priest of Xaantalicta. Closer it gets to the change, the more of them are out walking around in the night."

The guard's voice dropped to an irritated mumble. "Hate those faceless robes. Makes them look like . . ."

Benedikt strained to catch the last word, but it disappeared under the weight of the falling rain. Now he was safely away from the xaan, there was only one place he could go where she wouldn't be able to get her hands on him again.

Balankanche.

The rain stopped as suddenly as it had started while Benedikt was still in amongst the expensive shops. He hadn't gone much farther when the sky cleared, and he saw, to his horror, that the east had begun to gray.

Eyes locked on the dawn, he picked up his robes and ran. He didn't see the other priest until he was almost on top of her.

She whirled around as he skidded to a stop, arms windmilling.

"Is that you, Aralich? I thought you weren't going to . . ." And then she noticed his feet, and his hands, and his height. "You're not . . ."

Desperate, Benedikt flung back his gauze with one hand and hers with the other. He got a momentary glimpse of a middle-aged face twisted with anger, then he caught her gaze in his and said, **"You see only a priest of Xaantalicta— one of many. No differences."**

He'd never been good at Command, but need lent him strength.

"Watch where you're going," the priest snapped, her gauze falling back into place as she pushed past him. "Honestly, if you young priests were where you were supposed to be on time, you wouldn't have to run all over Atixlan every night. Things weren't like this when I was young, I'm telling you. If this is what the change is going to bring . . ."

At which point her voice merged with the distance and the sound of Benedikt's sandals against the street.

As shutters were thrown open and the day began, he had to slow to a walk. His Song could distract from his size and his sex but not at a dead run—he simply didn't have breath enough for both.

It was farther to the docks than Benedikt remembered, and the sunrise services of Tulpayotee were well underway before he reached the relative safety of the warehouses. With trade slowed by the rainy season, there shouldn't be many people about, but he kept Singing anyway. It would only take one person saying, "Strange looking priest," to draw a crowd and end his one chance to save himself and Balankanche.

As he emerged out onto the docks, a group of karjen, hurrying along the harbor's edge, barely glanced at him. A carpenter, passed him by muttering about the hour and swinging her hammer so that it Sang counterpoint for a

measure or two. Two cats, intent on a pile of fishguts, ignored him completely.

The docks of the great houses held no ship smaller than
the *Kraken*. Size didn't matter—the kigh would take anything that floated anywhere he asked. The problem was,
ships like the *Kraken* had crews on board at all times. Probably no more than two or three people if they weren't
expecting to sail that day, but that was two or three people
more than Benedikt wanted to handle. Once on the open
sea, he would need all his strength and then some to control
the kigh.

One of the smaller fishing boats would have been perfect,
but with the fleet already out, he had to fall back on his
second choice, the pilot boat. Unfortunately, at low tide
without a mast, it was too small to be seen above the edge
of the piers. Logic said it should be tied up near shore, but
to be certain he didn't miss it, he'd have to go all the way
out to the very end of each pier and look down.

Unless . . .

If each of the great houses had their own . . .

No. Or if they did, House Tayasal, the holder of the first
pier, berthed theirs somewhere else.

Keep calm, Benedikt told himself, fighting the urge to
run. *There's nothing unusual about a priest walking around
the docks.*

At least he hoped there wasn't.

The pilot boat that had taken the *Kraken* in and out of
the harbor hadn't been left tied at House Kohunlich's pier.

As he passed the *Kraken,* the hair on the back of Benedikt's neck lifted and when he turned, pulled by the feeling
that something was very wrong, he saw the ship's master
standing at the rail. Although he held a steaming cup of
something in one hand, he wasn't drinking. He was staring
directly at Benedikt. Because he'd seen a too tall, too male
priest of Xaantalicta only days before, the Song had to
work harder to convince him he wasn't seeing it again.

Feeling a little light-headed—he'd never realized it was
possible to both Sing and hold his breath—Benedikt
gripped the queen's coin through his robe and Sang a little
louder, loud enough to cover the sudden increased pounding of his heart.

*   *   *

"Gone?"

"Yes, peerless one."

"I see." Shecquai tucked into the crook of her elbow, the xaan stood, shook out her robe, and strode toward the door. Without breaking stride, she beckoned Serasti up beside her. "Send half the guards not on duty to the docks now. Remind them that Benedikt will be wearing the robes of a priest of Xaantalicta. They're to hold every priest they find. The rest of the guard will be with me."

The house master shook her head. "But your brother, peerless one."

"What about him?"

"Surely Benedikt has gone to him. I have *seen* him staring at the tul's windows."

"And I've seen him staring at the sky. That doesn't mean he's sprouted wings and flown away."

The tone was clearly a dismissal, and Serasti hurried off, still shaking her head.

Hueru watched the house master leave, then followed the xaan into her dressing room.

"You have eyes and ears in your brother's townhouse?" he asked as one of the junior attendants replaced the xaan's house sandals with streetwear.

"Of course, I do."

"And he isn't there?"

"My brother?"

"Benedikt."

"No." She handed Hueru the dog and allowed the attendant to replace her robe as well.

"Do you have eyes and ears at the docks, peerless one?"

"Don't be ridiculous."

"Then how do you know that's where he is?"

"Benedikt is young and easily manipulated, but he's no fool. He knows there's only one place he can go where I can't reach him." With Shecquai back in the crook of her arm, the xaan brushed past her cousin. "He's either already at the docks or he's on his way there, and I will not lose him."

"You're sure they're searching for him?" Tul Altun crossed the room to stand by the open stonework that overlooked the Great Square. Four Fives of his sister's guards had just formed up and marched off, leaving . . .

He rested his forehead against the polished stone.

. . . leaving too many guards still in the house for him to make a move that had any hope of success. Hope of success had been in very short supply lately.

"You're sure?" he asked again.

"Yes, gracious one. The Kohunlich-xaan's house master checked to be certain he wasn't here."

"Good." When the tul turned, his smile had regained a certain feral cast. "Tell my First you speak with the mouth of the tul. He's to put as many guards as I can spare in house sawraps—I don't want news of this getting back to the tulpayotee. Tell him they're to find Benedikt first."

"I could search as well, gracious one."

The tul studied Xhojee for a moment, as though weighing where the younger man's loyalties lay. "Go."

Benedikt had begun to doubt the pilot boat's existence. He'd searched the piers of all the great houses and found nothing. A ship from House Calakroul had come in, sails furled and oars out, without using a pilot boat at all. From what he overheard, they'd spent the night before anchored just up the coast and waited for daylight before making the attempt. Which did him no good at all.

Caught between the crowd that disembarked and the crowd that boiled out from the warehouse and the crowd that gathered from nowhere just because something was happening, Benedikt began to lose control of his Song. He found himself trying to influence individuals instead of the group as a whole. He began to receive a few curious glances.

And then a few more.

Clutching the coin, trying not to hurry, he started toward the smaller piers along the left arm of the harbor. No one tried to stop him, no one even shouted after him, but he couldn't help feeling as though they were all watching him walk away. He'd reached the point where he'd have gone to sea in a coracle if he could have only found one.

He heard the guards before he saw them. Only guards, in this land of minimal clothing, rattled as they walked. Heart in his throat, he dove flat behind a pile of wicker baskets. When no one raised a hue and cry, he squirmed carefully around and peered out.

They were the xaan's guards, no mistaking the uniform. As he watched them spread out, Benedikt realized this wasn't a random search—they'd come straight to the docks and expected to find him.

Curious about where and why the guards of House Kohunlich were going in such a hurry so early in the morning, about a dozen people had followed them out from between the warehouses. There were now a number of small crowds milling about on the docks, but among them, no priests of Xaantalicta. It didn't matter what he Sang, the guards would be looking for the robe. Glad to be rid of the gauze at least, he slipped it off and stuffed it between two baskets. Which was when he saw the boat.

Not much bigger than a coracle, it lay on its side between the baskets and one of the buildings. There were no oars, but that didn't matter if he could get it into the water. He could only hope it was watertight because it was the only chance he had.

The guards were searching the piers of the great houses first. All he had to do was get the boat up and onto his right shoulder where it would mask his head and most of his body. He could only hope that one pair of legs under a boat would look pretty much like any other.

First, he had to get *to* the boat.

Drying damp palms on his sawrap, he got to his feet and glanced over the top of the baskets. As long as the guards continued searching the piers for just a few more minutes . . .

He reached the boat and swung it up onto his shoulder in one easy motion then, hissing in pain, he jerked his head to free his hair, trapped between shoulder and crossbrace.

Oh, that's got things off to a good start.

Eyes locked on the water, he hurried toward the harbor edge, wanting to run, and knowing he couldn't.

Cazzes had no idea why the xaan's singer had run away, and he didn't want to know. If he found him, he'd get some of his own back for the *zados* crack and that was good enough for him. Besides, guards never asked questions. He had a good life, and he wasn't about to mess it up by wondering what could have happened to make a man throw away eight braids.

He was still thinking about braids when he glanced up and saw the small boat being carried toward the water. Still thinking about braids, he was looking at the spot where the boat covered the head of the man carrying it. A strand of golden hair flickered for an instant over the upper gunnel.

Shouting for his Second, he started to run.

Once the shouting began, Benedikt shifted his grip on the boat and raced toward the water. He could hear the guards closing fast, but the water was barely a dozen strides away. He was going to make it.

He had to make it.

He didn't see the cat although he heard it shriek as he tripped. Twisting as he fell, he threw the boat as hard as he could and, moments after he smashed knees and elbows into stone, heard it hit the water. The retaining walls were lower here, no more than four or five feet high. All he had to do was throw himself off them after the boat. The kigh would do the rest.

Scrabbling to his feet, he took one step, two, and launched himself forward.

Arms closed around his legs and dragged him down.

His hips hit the edge of the harbor wall, and he barely managed to protect his face as momentum slapped him down toward the vertical stone. He could see the boat, so close below, as he fought to drag himself over into the water.

Then other hands grabbed hold and pulled him roughly back onto the shore.

When they rolled him over, he found himself staring up into a circle of almost familiar faces.

"Gag him," commanded a voice beyond the circle. "If he can sing a flood . . ."

On his knees, straddling Benedikt's body, Cazzes took the strip of cloth someone offered and leaned forward. "This'll teach you to call mine a *zados*," he murmured as he tied it tightly underneath the golden hair. Straightening, he pushed a finger in under the corner of the singer's mouth, now stretched and disfigured, and checked that the gag wouldn't shift. Then he grinned down in triumph at his captive.

He expected to see anger or fear, wouldn't have been surprised to see him begging silently behind the gag, but the strange blue eyes looked up into his with such raw desperation that it caught his breath in his throat.

What could have happened to make a man throw away eight braids?

He didn't want to know.

Rising, he stepped aside but, when one of the others prepared to deliver a vicious kick to the stranger's side, he stepped back and blocked it.

"Well done, Cazzes." The Second clapped him on the shoulder, then glared around at the rest of the guards. "The xaan only wants us to hold him, she'll give him what he deserves herself. Tie his hands, then move him away from the water. And find something to cover him with before someone screams Tulpayotee and the xaan has *our* balls for breakfast."

"Your balls," muttered one of the women as the Second moved the crowd away in the name of the Kohunlich-xaan.

Cazzes watched while the singer's hands were tied, while a futile escape attempt was almost absently dealt with, then he bent down and yanked him to his feet.

When the gag went on, Benedikt stopped fighting. It was almost funny that they bothered. He'd been hiding behind a Song since before sunrise and he didn't have strength enough to control even one of the guards, let alone the half dozen who held him. Almost funny, but not quite. He couldn't fight his way free, and voiceless, all hope was gone.

He knew they were talking about him, but all he heard was a dull roar of sound. Two guards forced his arms together behind his back while a third tied his wrists. Hoping they'd be distracted while they worked, he tried to throw himself backward into the harbor. They stopped him without really trying.

Then strong fingers wrapped around his upper arm and heaved. Benedikt stood, staggered, and a surprisingly gentle touch steadied him.

The touch, an unexpected kindness, cut through the insulating despair and right into his heart. It brought the world back into focus. Out over the water, a gull shrieked and he wished he could echo the cry.

The despair in the blue eyes changed, focused, but didn't lessen. Cazzes cursed himself for a fool. *Don't look in his eyes!* He tightened his grip again.

By the time the xaan reached the harbor front, the guards had Benedikt on his knees by the pillar that marked the House Kohunlich pier, his discovered robe pooling on the ground around him. Guards, groom, and coloas emerged from between the warehouses at full speed and clattered to a stop. The coloas looked vaguely surprised by how fast it had been moving. Stepping out of the cart, Xaan Mijandra might have been arriving to inspect a warehouse ledger but Hueru's expression was one of dark anticipation.

His house tattoo covered by the bib of a leather apron and his hair back in a single braid, Xhojee pushed as close to the edge of the crowd as he dared. A few dozen men and women lingered just beyond the area of the harbor claimed by House Kohunlich, wondering what was going on and more interested in it, whatever it turned out to be, than in going back to work. When the Kohunlich-xaan arrived, the interest level peaked. Three or four karjen wearing house tattoos scurried off and the rest settled down to enjoy a bit of street theater.

Telling himself that his tul would want to hear of how the xaan dealt with Benedikt's capture, Xhojee stayed.

"I don't have time for this, Benedikt. You are going to Sing for me, one way or the other. Willing, unwilling, I don't really care." She slipped two fingers under his chin and lifted his head so she could stare down into his face. Her thumb came around to stroke the gag. "You're willing to die so that doesn't happen, aren't you? Too bad. Dead, you're no use to me."

She stepped back, looking thoughtful, and Benedikt felt sweat roll down his sides. If she wasn't going to kill him, she'd try to force him to agree to Sing. He glanced beyond her to Hueru. It wasn't difficult to see where the force would come from. He'd never been beaten, never even been badly hurt. He'd never been so frightened in his life, but he was a bard—he hadn't been for a while but he was again—and a bard would never agree to destroy a people.

No matter what.

Although no one in the crowd had a very good line of sight—the surrounding guards saw to that—everyone knew what was coming. Remembering days and nights his peace of mind would have just as soon he'd forgotten, Xhojee clenched his fists, and yelled, "That's a priest of Xaantalicta! The houses can't punish a priest!"

"I can have that fool taken care of," Hueru muttered.

"No. I don't want the rumor that I'm punishing a priest to get back to the xaantalax. It must be killed now."

"Take the robe off him."

As annoyed by her cousin as by the interruption, Xaan Mijandra shook her head. "And start a new rumor that he's a warrior of Tulpayotee; I don't think so."

"Don't take the whole robe off him, then." One hand clutching hood and hair, Hueru hauled Benedikt to his feet and flipped the bottom half of the robe up over his head.

Face covered by the fabric, Benedikt struggled but the guards behind him maintained their hold.

"Peerless one, if you would move the guards aside."

A gesture opened a line of sight to the crowd.

"Take a good look at your priest!" Hueru roared.

The crowd roared back. As the guards closed ranks again, Xhojee knew he'd spent the one chance Benedikt had and bought nothing more than a short delay in the inevitable.

As Benedikt was thrown to his knees again, Xaan Mijandra patted her cousin approvingly on the arm. "Well done." Reaching out, she dragged the bottom half of the robe down into place and held Benedikt's wildly staring eyes with hers. "Your defiance has created quite a spectacle for the people of Atixlan, and I don't appreciate it." Still staring into his face, she beckoned to Hueru. "Since he wants to run away, take his legs."

This was more than just a beating. Benedikt jerked back, unable to help, himself then fought for calm. *Evicka has no legs. And is no less a bard.*

Sword half drawn, Hueru stepped forward only to be stopped by the xaan's hand on his chest.

"You can live with that, can't you, Benedikt? Interesting." Her fingernails tapped thoughtfully against Hueru's tattoo. "If he can't see, he can't run," she said slowly, allowing her arm to fall back by her side. "Take his eyes instead."

Breathing heavily, Benedikt found his gaze locked on Hueru's hands. The big man flexed them as he advanced, jabbing the thumbs into the air the way he'd jab them . . .

Stop thinking about it! Tadeus is blind, and he's certainly no less a bard.

But Tadeus has eyes! The second thought was a silent wail, inside his head.

I said, stop thinking about it!

"Wait."

Hueru snarled down at Benedikt then turned. "Yes, peerless one?"

"It bothers him, but not enough."

Relief made Benedikt dizzy, and he swayed where he knelt.

Motioning for Hueru to move aside, the xaan stepped forward again. She stroked one finger up the column of Benedikt's throat then ran it along his lower lip. "You really would rather die, wouldn't you? And because you'd rather, you won't. But . . ." The finger tapped against the gag. ". . . if I can't use you, neither will anyone else."

Her eyes were very black. Unable to look away, Benedikt felt as though she had his kigh squirming on the ends of two dark daggers.

"Hueru."

When she released him, Benedikt sagged, only to be yanked back upright by a guard.

"Yes, peerless one?"

"Cut out his tongue."

He saw the dagger from the corner of one eye.

Without a tongue, he'd be voiceless forever.

Voiceless.

The dagger caught the light as Hueru turned the edge toward him.

Forever.

If the gag had removed hope, this shattered it into a

million pieces that shredded Benedikt's resolve. He threw himself at the xaan's feet, screaming, crying, begging.

Rough hands grabbed him and hauled him back to his knees. Terror took over, and he fought them with everything he had left, shrieking his surrender through the gag.

The blade touched his cheek.

A moment's pressure, and the gag was gone.

"Peerless one! Please . . ."

Hueru's fingers dug into his jaw.

The xaan turned slowly. "Let him speak, cousin."

When Benedikt looked up into her face, he knew he'd lost. He swallowed and forced the words through chattering teeth. "I'll sing for you. Just, please, don't . . ."

She studied him for a long moment.

He felt sick. He hated himself so much he wanted to puke. But he couldn't take the words back.

"You'll sing for me?"

He couldn't say it again so he nodded and hoped that would be enough.

"Good. Hueru, take an eye anyway. I want him to remember this later."

He didn't actually believe it was going to happen until Hueru grabbed his hair in one hand and pressed his thumb against the bottom of his right eye.

He started to scream as the pressure built.

And he kept screaming.

Those not of the xaan's household who were still on the docks, pretended they didn't hear.

Out in the harbor, a wave formed.

The xaan watched it grow, and when it reached the height of a tall man, Benedikt's height perhaps, she tapped her cousin on the shoulder. "Get him into the warehouse. Now."

Benedikt stopped screaming as Hueru threw him over his shoulder, one bloody hand bright red against the white robe. He moaned once as his head flopped down against the shorter man's hip. Again as blood dripped onto the stone. One final time as Hueru dropped him on the warehouse floor and turned to help the guards with the door.

They got it shut just as the wave hit.

"Is he doing that?" Hueru demanded.

"He was." Xaan Mijandra looked down at Benedikt and

prodded him gently with one toe. "He isn't doing anything now. I expect the waters will retreat."

"You *expect,* peerless one?"

When they opened the door, the stones of the harbor front were steaming in the morning sun, washed clean of Benedikt's blood.

Dagger in one hand, Bannon crouched by the side of his bed. Not even such a dream could make him break years of training and cry out, but it had been close. Breathing heavily, he stood and slipped the dagger back into its sheath with trembling hands.

Karlene had been wrong. Benedikt was still alive. He'd bet his life on it.

Assassins' hands never trembled.

Thirteen

OTYPEZ straightened and, wiping his hands on the damp cloth his assistant held out to him, turned to face the xaan. "I assume you want him to live, peerless one."

"I do."

"Then it would have been better had you waited to discipline him until you had a physician immediately available."

"I expect you to keep him alive, regardless."

The physician sighed. "As you wish, peerless one."

"Keep his throat lubricated . . ."

"Lubricated, peerless one?"

Her expression hardened at the interruption although her tone remained reasonable. "Lubricated. You're the physician, you figure it out. If he loses his voice, you lose yours. I need him functional as soon as possible."

"Begging your pardon, peerless one . . ." Otypez glanced back at the motionless figure on the bed and continued without sounding remotely apologetic, ". . . but how do you define functional."

"Able to function—walking, talking, standing, singing, thinking." Gathering the trailing edges of her robe up over one arm, she paused on her way to the door. "You've done this before, Otypez. Just do it again."

"She's never wanted them thinking before," Otypez told his assistant dryly as the bells noted the xaan's departure.

Without the senior physician's protective history, his assistant pretended not to hear.

Five days later, Benedikt stared at the xaan's feet without really seeing them. The world had taken on a flatness, a permanent reminder of his weakness and his betrayal of his oaths. Because it was easier than thinking for himself, he'd done everything the physician had asked of him and his eye was healing well. His kigh still bled, would bleed, he knew, for the rest of his life.

"I want the solution to the Song of Sorquizic by Xaantalicta's next rebirth. Twelve days, Benedikt. That's all."

He wanted to say he'd forgotten the song, that the terror and the pain had driven it right out of his head, but he didn't have courage enough to lie to her. "Yes, peerless one."

Second Quarter had been kind to the Broken Islands with lots of warm sunny days and very few of the devastating storms that blew in so suddenly from the Western Sea. Leaning over the railing on the third-floor deck of the combined Bardic/Healer Hall, Adamec squinted against the reflected sunlight and watched a small boat sail into Pitesti Harbor.

"Lisbet's in early. If she's full, she must've run into an early school."

Tomas grunted distractedly as he wondered just how much of young Aniji's last recall he needed to put into the quarter's report. "The trouble with remembering everything," he sighed, "is that nothing becomes trivial enough to leave out."

"Tomas, are you listening to me?"

"You said it's too early for Lisbet to go to school. I don't think Elbasan needs to know what the Captain of Shatterway fed her for dinner, do you?"

Adamec sighed. About to turn and offer his assistance, he took a closer look as the crew leaped out of the fishing boat and began dragging it high onto the pebble beach. "I think something's wrong."

"And I'm tellin' you, Tomas, it's *not* a storm. Sky's as clear as it is over your head, but there's somethin' right wrong about those waves." Lisbet rubbed a scarred hand through close-cropped hair, shaking her head. "I've been sailing out of this harbor 'most every day since I was sixteen, and I've never seen waves act like that before. It was like the regular waves were bein' overtook by these other waves."

"I'm sorry." The bard spread his hands apologetically. "I don't understand."

"Okay." She took a deep breath. "Waves got rules. I don't need to tell you that, you Sing water, you probably know it better'en me. These waves were not followin' the rules. It was sorta like a big, big ripple catchin' up and ridin' right over the waves that were already there."

"Were they big waves, the ones not following the rules?"

"No. Not yet."

"Not yet?"

"That's what I've been tryin' to tell you—I took a look through my glass, and behind them little waves there's something big comin'."

"But not a storm."

"If it is, it's like no storm I've ever seen."

"Due west?"

"And headin' this way fast."

Frowning, Tomas waded out into the harbor, his bicolor robe floating around his calves. He Sang the four notes to call the kigh and then, after a moment, he Sang the same four notes again. The kigh were there, in the water, but they weren't responding. He got the impression that they had already been called and were simply too busy to bother with him.

"This isn't good."

Back on shore, Lisbet rolled her eyes.

Fortunately, the air kigh were willing to listen and Tomas Sang them out to warn the rest of the fishing fleet. When the kigh rang the storm bell hanging on each boat, the fleet would make all speed to a safe harbor.

"We're still gonna lose some," Lisbet told him grimly as he came ashore. "It's comin' that fast."

Tomas shoved his feet back into his sandals and yanked the laces tight. "All right, then, I'm going to the western arm to meet it. Maybe I can do something from there. I'll let Aniji know what's coming, and she can Sing warning to the west coast settlements."

"Bard?"

He paused, half out of his robe, glad he hadn't take the time to remove his short breeches when he'd thrown it on. He'd never heard Lisbet use that tone before, and it lifted the hair on the back of his neck.

"What's happening?"

"I don't know."

Tomas was no longer a young man, and since Aniji had come to the Broken Islands, doubling the number of bards, he hadn't done as much walking as he once had, but fear put wings on his feet. He couldn't have run faster had all the demons of the Circle been behind him—instead of in front of him as he feared.

By the time he reached the seaward side of the harbor's western arm, he was breathing so heavily, he could barely stand. The first few waves that smacked up against the rocks could have been square for all he noticed. When he finally got his breath back and managed to focus, he stared in astonishment at the sea.

It looked like a storm approaching except that there was no storm. Up above, the sky arced a clear and pale blue all the way to the horizon, but down below, huge gray-green waves crashed and roiled, crests rising ten, even fifteen feet above the troughs. Whatever it was, it stretched as far north and south as Tomas could see.

When he Sang to call the kigh, he very nearly choked on the last note. The waves were full of kigh. Or perhaps they *were* kigh, he couldn't tell for certain. He did know they were the biggest kigh he'd ever seen, somehow drawn up from deep water and speeding straight toward him.

Tomas Sang a strong water, but these kigh wouldn't listen to anything he Sang, and the pain they Sang back at him nearly drove him to his knees. He didn't understand what could have happened to have hurt them so, nor would they give him any kind of an answer beyond the pain. He hadn't known the kigh could feel pain.

High on the rocks, he should have been safe enough.

Then the first wave hit.

Eyes widening, he watched it rise, stared into a wall of greenish-black, and barely had presence of mind enough to jam himself in behind a boulder before it crested. For a heartbeat, he was completely engulfed, saltwater in his eyes, his nose, his lungs, the pain the kigh carried cutting through to his heart.

Then the water was gone, running back through cracks and crevices to the sea, and only the memory of the pain remained.

Coughing and sputtering, Tomas dragged himself up far enough to look over his shelter.

The waves were parting, going around the island.

By the time he found his voice, the giant kigh were gone, and they'd added the kigh from the shallows to their bulk.

They were taking the pain home.

And if home wasn't the Broken Islands . . .

The kigh dove through the open window of the small audience chamber and into Karlene so hard it very nearly knocked her over. Hair flying in all directions, she Sang it calm enough to deliver its message.

Jelena watched the bard pale. "What is it?" she asked before the older woman could speak.

"It's Tomas, from the Broken Islands, Majesty." One hand holding her hair in place, Karlene Sang the kigh a gratitude and sent it on its way. "He commands all bards who Sing water to the coast immediately."

"Commands? Does he say why?"

"The kigh seem confused, Majesty." *Pain is coming? That makes no sense.* "But I got the impression that something dangerous is on its way."

"A storm?"

"The air kigh say no, but . . . ." She watched as a kigh came back into the room and circled her head. "Excuse me, Majesty, I *have* to get to the harbor."

"Of course."

Karlene had taken two steps toward the door when the senior member of the Imperial Trade Delegation moved into her way, "Begging Your Majesty's pardon," he said, turning toward the queen, "but without a bard to Witness our negotiations . . ."

"The negotiations can wait," Karlene snapped, wishing her oaths allowed her to Command the pompous little man out of her way and into a midden.

The Imperial delegate ignored her. "Begging Your Majesty's pardon, but the Emperor is most insistent we conclude as soon as possible. He fears this disagreement has already gone on too long."

"Karlene, go." Settling back in the rosewood throne, Jelena stared down at the delegate as the bard raced from the room. "The Emperor does not rule here."

Out in the hall, Karlene dodged around a pair of pages, and nearly ran straight into Tadeus. "You heard?"

He nodded. "They came to all of us, not only the bards who Sing water. I thought Her Majesty might need someone else to Witness."

"You're a wonder. What about him?" A jerk of her head indicated Bannon hovering impatiently behind Tadeus' right shoulder.

"His Highness wanted to accompany you to the harbor." Bannon explained. "Tadeus said it might be dangerous, so I was the compromise. If this summons is so urgent, shouldn't you be moving?"

"You're right." Spinning around, Karlene grabbed one of the pages. "Find Magda. Tell her to meet me at the harbor—at the royal wharf—**right away.**"

"Why Magda?" Bannon demanded as they left Tadeus by the assembly room and raced through the Palace, scattering courtiers and servants alike.

"The kigh said something about pain, and a kigh in pain can only mean Magda."

They burst out through one of the smaller doors and ran across the courtyard, Bannon easily matching Karlene's longer stride. The bard on the gate—*Air and earth,* Karlene noted absently as they passed—waved them on with one hand while sketching explanations for a pair of puzzled guards with the other.

As they crossed the wide road that circled the Citadel and started down Hill Street, they could see the harbor sparkling in the distance. Given the angle of the street and the amount of traffic it wasn't going to be a pleasant run, but when Karlene hesitated, three kigh dove toward her, urging her to hurry.

"At least it's downhill," she muttered and uttered a silent prayer to whatever gods were listening that she didn't break an ankle before they reached level ground.

Hill Street took them all the way to Lower Dock Street, and crossing Lower Dock Street put them in Dockside, close enough to the harbor to change the smell and the feel of the air.

"I don't like this," Karlene declared, stumbling to a walk.

"That's because you're out of shape," the ex-assassin told her scornfully.

She ignored him. Turning to the posse of children they'd acquired on their mad dash through the center of Elbasan,

Karlene used just enough Voice to send the lot of them home.

"What if some of them didn't want to go home?" Bannon asked as they covered the last bit of ground side by side.

"Better than . . . what they'll face here."

In spite of her heavy breathing, there was something in Karlene's voice that reminded Bannon of why he had come, of the danger Tadeus had said was too great for the prince. "What is it?"

"I wish I knew." She'd have given a great deal to have been able to define the foreboding. Unfortunately the only definition that seemed to fit was the one the air kigh had provided.

Pain.

To her surprise, Kovar was on the royal wharf before them.

"I was trying to spend a quiet afternoon with my cousin," he explained. "She has a shop in White's Lane." He waved a hand out over the harbor. "I don't see a storm."

Karlene shook her head, trying to listen to the waves and hearing nothing she could make sense of. "That's not what's coming."

"Well, if it isn't a storm, what is it, that's what I want to know?" Mustache fairly bristling with indignation, Kovar stepped around a pile of rope. "Why wasn't Tomas more precise?"

"I don't think he could . . ."

Both bards were nearly blown over by the force of the sudden wind, and even Bannon was rocked back on his heels. He watched and listened as they Sang, voices wrapping around each other and around the wind. Then the air was still.

"What . . ."

Karlene waved him quiet and began a new Song as Kovar faced the water.

"All vessels get to shore immediately. It doesn't matter where, just get off the water. All crews pierside, secure your vessels, then get to shore. Now."

Carried by Karlene's Song, Kovar's voice boomed out over the harbor. As half a dozen small boats and two larger ones came about, and the wharfs began to look like an anthill stirred with a stick, he sagged down onto a crate. "Do you think they'll have time?" he asked numbly.

Eyes locked on the west, toward the long arm where the harbor spilled into the sea, Karlene shook her head. "Not if it's already through the Bache."

"If what's already through the Bache?" Bannon demanded.

"Kigh," Karlene told him shortly, then began to Sing air into sails.

"What kind of kigh?" demanded a new voice.

Only Bannon turned toward Magda.

"Kigh from the deep sea," Kovar said, his attention on the breezes darting about his head. "They're slamming into the coast from one end of Shkoder to another. Ziven's at Fort Kazpar, he says it's almost as if they're looking for something. Petrolis is at Eel Cove. They've lost two boats, maybe four people. There're bards all up and down the coast trying to calm the sea, but nothing we Sing is working."

"And now it's coming here?"

The Bardic Captain nodded. "Look at the angle on those waves."

"But why did Karlene want me?"

"The kigh that came to her said something about pain," Bannon explained when Kovar shook his head.

"These kigh are in pain?"

With all sails full and the boats making the best time they could for shore, Karlene stopped Singing and finally turned toward the healer. "No," she said softly. "I think these kigh *are* pain."

"That doesn't make any sense," Kovar sputtered.

"Maybe not," Karlene admitted. She pointed past Magda's shoulder. "But we're about to find out for sure."

The waves that came rushing from the narrows were green and dark and larger than anything that had ever been seen in the sheltered harbor, even during the worst of the Third Quarter storms. Karlene and Kovar Sang in unison and in harmony, and nothing made any difference. Bannon barely had time to grab Magda and scream at her to hang onto something when the first wave hit.

Then they were under water.

Since fighting would do no good, Karlene relaxed and let

the wave take her. As her feet left the pier, she half expected to be slammed into the side of the nearest ship but there was nothing but water all around her. She tumbled, unable to tell up from down, her whole world the kigh and what they were trying to say. The pain made it hard to concentrate on anything *but* the pain.

And then, just as her chest began to tighten and her body cry for air, she understood.

With the last of her air, she Sang four notes.

A heartbeat later, she lay coughing on the pier, Magda, Bannon, and Kovar beside her. Dragging herself up onto her knees, she realized the harbor had gone completely calm.

"Blood."

Wiping at the saltwater running out of her nose, she turned and found Bannon kneeling beside a deep red puddle. "Yours?"

He shook his head.

"The kigh left it," Kovar said quietly. He looked up at the younger bard. "I heard you, under the water, but I couldn't make out the actual notes. What did you Sing?"

Karlene licked salt off her lips. "The four notes of Benedikt's name."

"The kigh couldn't bring Benedikt home," Magda said, her voice unsteady, "so they brought his pain."

The Bardic Captain shook his head. "But Benedikt's dead."

The cry that burst from Bannon's throat drew all eyes to him. He lifted both hands from the pier, palms stained red. "Dead men don't bleed," he said.

"But the kigh said that the *Starfarer* was lost. That it sank in a storm and everyone died." Jelena gripped Otavas' hand, her fingers white around his. "If everyone died, how could Benedikt still be alive?"

A murmur, echoing the queen's confusion, ran around the room. Every ranking Palace official, most of the nobility in residence, almost half the Council and one or two officials from the city had crowded into the large assembly room for an explanation. Rather than have a thousand rumors started, the queen had commanded the bards, the healer, and the ex-assassin—the four who'd experienced the disaster from the inside—into the large assembly room the moment they returned to the Palace. So far, the explanation hadn't clarified much.

Karlene glanced over her shoulder toward the Bardic Captain. When it became clear he wasn't about to answer, she stepped forward. "Benedikt Sings the strongest water the Bardic Hall has ever seen, and he seems to have a more . . . personal relationship with the kigh than any of the rest of us. It's not impossible that the kigh would save Benedikt even while they destroyed the *Starfarer* and her crew."

"Then why didn't Benedikt Sing the *Starfarer* safe?"

"I'm sure he tried, Majesty. I suspect that the kigh saved him after the ship had gone down. This . . ." She waved a hand, unable to think of what exactly to call the brutal pounding the coast of Shkoder had undergone. ". . . visit today wasn't Benedikt's idea. He didn't tell the kigh to bring his pain home, they just did it."

"They just did it," Jelena repeated.

"Are you sure that's what was going on out there?" Otavas asked quietly. He raised his free hand before anyone could protest the question. "I'm sorry, Karlene, but first you told us Benedikt was dead with all the others and now you tell us Benedikt is alive. You had to have been wrong at least once—is it possible you're wrong today?"

"No, Highness." Heads turned as Magda answered for the bard. "The first message had diffused into hundreds, maybe thousands, of kigh. This one didn't. I felt the pain." She had to swallow before she could go on. "The pain of the wounds Benedikt had taken and the pain of being so far from home—of being so completely and utterly alone."

Some of that pain made itself heard in Magda's voice, the rest of it, resonating in her kigh, made itself felt throughout the room, touching each kigh in turn.

After a moment, Iancu i'Nadina, the Queen's Chancellor, coughed into his fist, drawing all eyes. "If Benedikt is alive, Majesty, what do the kigh expect us to do?"

Bannon made a sound low in his throat.

Magda, who'd stayed close by the ex-assassin's side ever since he'd bathed his hands in Benedikt's blood, reached over and lightly laid two fingers on his wrist. He started at the touch of her kigh and jerked away, but the sound stopped. "We're expected to do the right thing, Chancellor. No more but certainly no less."

"Which is?" the chancellor insisted.

"We will send a ship to bring him home." Jelena's words rang in the room like a trumpet call. Releasing Otavas' hand, she stood and swept an uncompromising gaze over the faces staring up at her. "I will not abandon one of my own."

"Majesty." The Chancellor's voice was apologetic but firm. "The Council will never agree. We have already lost a ship and twenty lives. Will we risk twenty more to save one?"

Jelena's brows drew in at the sounds of agreement coming from the crowd.

"We lost more lives today, Majesty." The Chancellor spread his hands. "There isn't a fishing village up coast or down not mourning their losses. Isn't that enough?"

Otavas saw Jelena's shoulders stiffen, and he moved up to stand behind her. No matter what decision she came to, he knew she'd added the day's deaths to the deaths she already carried, and he wanted her to realize that she didn't have to carry them alone.

She drew in a deep breath and her chin rose. "Abandoning Benedikt will not bring those people back."

"And those you send out to rescue him," the Chancellor prodded gently. "What of them?"

The sounds of agreement and disagreement grew momentarily louder, then shut off as Jelena raised her hands. Before she could speak, Kovar stepped forward.

The Bardic Captain had said very little on the way back from the harbor and nothing at all during the explanation of why the sea had thrown itself with such fury against the Shkoden coast. His shoulders were bowed under his quartered robe and his face was not only pale but almost gray. Those of the court, who'd barely seen him since the *Starfarer* had sailed, thought he was growing old.

The bards and Magda realized he'd aged that afternoon.

As he approached the dais, the nearer edge of the crowd drew back so that he stood alone. He drew in a deep breath, gathering strength much as Jelena had, and slowly lifted his head.

"Majesty, when you send a ship for Benedikt, bards

strong in both air and water will sail on it. I will send strength enough to fill the sails and calm the sea. No more than you do we abandon one of our own.''

"That isn't how you felt when the *Starfarer* sailed," the queen reminded him coldly.

Kovar closed his eyes for an instant, then met her gaze. "I was wrong, and I most humbly beg Your Majesty's pardon." Gathering his robe up out of the way, he dropped to one knee. "The bards are Your Majesty's to command. *I* am Your Majesty's to command."

The room had gone so quiet, Jelena's surprise could almost be heard.

Karlene stepped forward and knelt behind Kovar's right shoulder. Hardly had her knee touched the marble when Tadeus dropped gracefully down by her side.

Feeling a hysterical giggle rising in the back of her throat and viciously suppressing it, Magda knelt where she stood. Under normal circumstances, Shkoden monarchs would be knelt to en masse only once in their reign—during the final moments of their coronation, in a final acknowledgment of their sovereignty. As she heard Bannon kneel beside her and the rustle of clothing as more and more of those in the room were caught up in the moment, Magda felt kinder toward Kovar than she had since First Quarter. *Trust a bard to find the symbolic gesture. . . .*

Brows drawn in, the Queen's Chancellor stared out over the kneeling crowd in disbelief. Then he shook his head and smiled. Lowering himself carefully to one knee, he turned the movement into a truncated bow. "Majesty, it appears we are *all* yours to command."

"So, Benedikt, how is my Song coming? Will you be finished on time?"

"Yes, peerless one." She asked him that question, or a variation on it, every night. Benedikt didn't know why as he no longer had the courage to answer any other way. It was always Song, never song, she never missed the emphasis, and somehow, that bothered him more than the rest. He braced his fingertips against the floor as she walked around him, her palm brushing the soft stubble on his head. He'd lost much of his sense of balance when he lost his eye and it didn't help that the xaan's touch sent deep shudders through his body that he could neither prevent nor show.

Her robe trailed a silken caress across the bare skin of his back. He swallowed hard as his body reacted. Barely breathing, he watched her as she came around his blind side and settled before him on her bed. Brushing a rippling fall of dark hair behind one shoulder, she tucked her feet up under her robe and nestled Shecquai against her hip.

The dog licked a front paw, ignoring Benedikt completely as if no longer considering him a threat.

"Sing *'The Mountain Maiden'*, Benedikt. It has a gentle melody that always relaxes me."

"Yes, peerless one." He spent his day in his room—the same room as before the loss of his eye, only guarded now—but every evening he was brought to the xaan to sing. Perhaps she liked to see how well she'd molded him to obedience, perhaps she'd just grown used to her nightly lullaby. He didn't know, he couldn't care. He did as he was told and he sang.

When the guard returned him to his room, Benedikt sank down on the floor and leaned against the stone backrest. Singing for the xaan, the constant struggle to show nothing of what he felt, left him too numb to work on the Song of Sorquizic during what remained of the evening. Perhaps— if even once—he'd succeeded in hiding his emotions from her, it might have been different. Perhaps, but he didn't think so.

It wasn't the fear that gave him the most difficulty.

He stroked his palm over his head, much as she had, and trembled at the memory of her touch. Her gentle caresses were far more dangerous than Hueru's brutality. He was so afraid of her; he needed to know she was no longer angry with him, and every time she fulfilled that need, he felt himself tottering on the edge of a dark precipice.

He found himself wanting to please her.

He had broken that afternoon on the wharf. He remembered every word he'd screamed, every promise he'd sobbed, every plea for mercy. He'd agreed to break his oaths and use the kigh as a weapon.

Had the xaan been able to use him immediately, the pieces he'd broken into would have been forever scattered.

But she couldn't. And every day, while he worked on find-ing an answer to the Song of Sorquizic, he remembered he was a bard of Shkoder. And every night, he managed to step back from the precipice and work on putting the bro-ken pieces of himself back together, one at a time.

Trouble was, there probably wouldn't be enough time for him to finish, and his courage seemed to be broken into the smallest pieces of all. If he truly wanted to keep his oaths, all he had to do was fling himself, head first, off his balcony. Twenty-three priests had already died to keep Balankanche safe. What was one foreign bard?

All he had to do . . .

But he couldn't.

If he wanted to save both Balankanche and himself, he had to come up with another way.

His hand rose to the edge of the linen bandage over his eye but didn't actually touch it. He knew he couldn't get to the island before the xaan caught him.

Who was strong enough to protect him from the xaan?

Not the tul. Benedikt had a feeling that the tul was only alive because his sister hadn't bothered to kill him.

"After all," he sighed, stretching out his legs and staring out through the open balcony doors at the falling rain, "why risk upsetting the Tulparax so close to the change?"

He began to frown and stopped as the movement pushed painfully at his healing eye. If he was right, and the tul was only alive because the xaan didn't want to upset the Tulp-arax, then all he had to do was find a way to put himself under that same protection.

Perhaps as a warrior of Tulpayotee.

All things considered, he could live such a lie.

But to get to the Tulparax, he had to first get to the tul.

Benedikt sat up and peered out to the space where the tul's half of the building was unseen, black on black in the rain. Serasti had told him, with a significant degree of satisfaction, that if he was seen even glancing across the courtyard, he'd lose the other eye. He hadn't been out on the balcony since and now, heart in his throat, he dropped his gaze to the flickering flame dancing in the small lamp beside him on the floor.

The clipped wings of his courage couldn't carry him across the courtyard, so how?

The guards on his door wore cotton plugs in their ears and even if he could get by them, he didn't think he could just walk out the front door, not anymore. They'd all be watching for him, and they'd taken his priest's robe away.

Out of favor, he had no friends to call on for aid.

So, not over. Not through. Under?

If he could get into the tunnels Herexi mentioned . . .

If he could find his way to the tul . . .

If he wasn't captured again . . .

If he wasn't . . .

Benedikt dried damp palms on his sawrap and fought to breath through the fear in his throat. If.

Too may ifs.

If broke him back into pieces again.

"She's essentially the same ship as the *Starfarer*." The master of the Elbasan shipyard tucked his thumbs behind his wide leather belt and rocked back on his heels, watching the activity down on the pier through satisfied eyes. "She's not as new or as pretty, but the *Silver Vixen* is as good a ship as ever came out of these yards."

Jelena swept a worried gaze from bow to stern, noting four different crews of carpenters and twice that many assorted trades she couldn't identify. "Will she be ready in time?"

"Count on it, Majesty. The upper harbor took the brunt of the assault—kigh hardly touched us. By the time you get a crew on her, she'll be ready to sail."

"Good."

The master shipwright peered sideways, past the queen and her consort at the front of the royal party to—surprise, surprise—the Bardic Captain. Although the latter wasn't looking too good, he still hoped Her Majesty had kicked the sanctimonious old coot right in his tunemaking ass before accepting him back into her good graces. "I hear there're more bards going this time," he said.

"Three. Karlene, Evicka, and Jurgis," Kovar answered without taking his eyes off the ship. Everyone in Shkoder knew what bards were going and how well they Sang; the yardmaster was deliberately digging at him, making him pay for his earlier stubborn stupidity. He wasn't the first, and he wouldn't be the last. Kovar accepted such mild censure, half wishing for stronger accusations to help allay his feelings of guilt. "Karlene Sings a strong air and fire and a stronger water. Evicka and Jurgis both Sing a strong air and water. They'll be picking up Jurgis at Fort Kazpar; he's got to come down the coast."

All three bards had been trained under Liene. The bards he'd trained, the younger bards, would have gone if he'd asked, but none of them had volunteered. He had a lot more than Benedikt to pay for.

"Isn't Evicka the bard with no legs?"

That pulled Kovar's attention off his failings. "The loss of her legs hasn't affected her voice," he said coldly.

"Never suggested it had." The yard master rocked back on his heels again. "Was thinking she was a wise choice, actually. *Vixen*'ll be a bit crammed for space, and she'll take up less room."

Kovar narrowed his eyes suspiciously, but there was nothing in the other man's face to suggest he'd intended anything more than he'd said. Still . . .

"What's happening down at the pier?" Jelena's question cut short Kovar's annoyance.

"Where, Majesty?"

"There." She pointed. "Where the mate is taking names for the crew."

The Bardic Captain Sang a quick series of notes—not even quite a tune, to the kigh—who sped down and back. "It appears we have three volunteers who won't take no for an answer."

"And not the first time," the yardmaster muttered. "We could hardly fill the *Starfarer*, but it seems like everybody wants to go rescue young Benedikt."

Nobody mentioned, although everyone thought, of how the difference could only be a result of bardic support.

The first day, the line of potential sailors had stretched from the pier, along the shore, past the lumberyard, and almost to the gate. Fortunately for Hanicka i'Dasa, the *Vixen*'s beleaguered mate, nine out of ten volunteers were completely unsuitable.

The numbers had dropped off as positions were filled, but as the royal party approached the disturbance, it became clear suitability was still an issue.

It was just as clear that the two men and the woman at

the front of the line were not going to take their rejection without a fight.

"But if you'd just listen . . ."

"To you and to everyone else?" The mate sighed and shook her head. "Look, I appreciate that you want to help, but you know nothing of . . ." Her eyes widened. "Majesty!" The table rocked as she surged to her feet and made a wild grab for her inkwell.

Bannon caught it before it spilled and handed it to her with a small, mocking bow.

Gaze locked on the queen, Hanicka ignored him. "Captain Juzef is in Riverton, Majesty. I'll send someone for him."

"There's no need," Jelena told her with a smile. "I just wondered what was going on."

"Majesty?" The younger of the two men stepped forward. "We're from Janinton, Majesty, and we want to help rescue Benedikt."

"Janinton?" The queen stared at nothing for a moment then refocused on the anxious face before her. "That's in Bicaz, isn't it?"

The young man looked relieved. "Yes, Majesty, it is."

"But that's days from the sea."

"Yes, Majesty, it is." The mate's tone suggested everything could be explained by that statement. "None of them ever even saw the sea before they got to Elbasan. They've no experience at all."

"We were chosen because we're the best archers in our village, Majesty." The young woman stepped forward as well, her chin high and the line of her jaw determined. "You'll need those who can fight once the sea's been crossed. And we're not stupid. We can learn what we need to so we're pulling our own weight on the ship."

"Archers." Jelena's brows drew in unhappily. "How did you hear there'd be fighting?"

"Stasya, Majesty. She'd Walked from Ohrid to check on the village 'cause of the First Quarter floods.

"And Stasya says there'll be fighting?"

"She said that's what the kigh said, Majesty."

Jelena glanced at Kovar who shook his head. "They didn't say it to me, Majesty, but that doesn't mean they didn't say it."

"Majesty?" The final member of the trio joined his companions in front of the queen. "Benedikt saved Janinton, he saved our village. He put himself between us and a flood out of the mountains, between us and a rushing wall of ice-cold water filled with crushing debris. He risked his life to save our homes, our land, our lives. He stood there all day and Sang himself hoarse, and not one drop of water got past him. We owe him, we all owe him, everything we are. Please, Majesty, let us help."

Jelena felt Otavas' hand rest lightly on her shoulder. She looked from face to face, then turned toward the mate. "Find a place for them," she said.

"But, Majesty . . ."

"I said no, Magda, and I meant it." Jelena dropped into a chair and rubbed her eyes. "I've asked the Healers' Hall to provide two volunteers for the voyage, but you're still the only healer in Shkoder who heals the fifth kigh and you're simply too precious a resource to risk. You can't go, and that's final."

"I felt Benedikt's pain in the kigh, Jelena. He needs me."

"And he can have you as soon as they bring him back, but you're not going." Most of her face still hidden behind her hands, she sighed. "What would I do if I lost you, too?"

"No, Tadeus."

"It's because I'm blind, isn't it?"

Kovar sighed and set both palms flat on his desk. "Tadeus, not only do you not Sing water but you've never been to sea, and," he continued quickly before the other bard could comment, "although you still Sing a strong air, you don't have the range you once did."

Even the scarf over Tadeus' eyes looked indignant. "So it's because I'm old."

"Yes." Kovar spun his chair around to look out the window, to the west, to the sea, to Benedikt. "But I know how you feel."

"Oh?"

"I can't go either."

Otavas stepped through the double doors, indicated Bannon should stay where he was, and crossed the balcony to his side. Of late, when the ex-assassin couldn't be found, this was where he was, staring toward the west. *Although, couldn't be found isn't entirely accurate,* Otavas mused, settling against the railing, *since I always know exactly where he is.*

"I'm sorry, Highness. I thought you were with the Council until late this afternoon."

The prince waved a hand toward the sun, a bare hands' span above the horizon. "It is late this afternoon, Bannon."

"Highness, I'm . . ."

"Sorry. Yes, I know." Leaning on his left elbow, he reached out with his right hand and turned Bannon toward him—knowing his touch was one of two, or maybe three, that wouldn't provoke old instincts. "Why haven't you asked me?"

Bannon closed his eyes for an instant and when he opened them again, the misery on his face hit the prince like a physical blow. "How could I?" he whispered. "The risk is so great—if you let me go and something happens, who will guard your back? If I go to him, I leave you unprotected."

Another man might have mentioned that Shkoder was not at war and the only dangers the consort might encounter could easily be taken care of by someone less specialized but Otavas knew Bannon's protection was only another word for Bannon's love, so he smiled and tightened his grip. "You went to him the moment you knew he was alive. There's only one way I'm going to get you back. I've already told Captain Juzef of the *Vixen* that you'll be sailing with him."

"Highness, I . . ." Bannon's mouth worked, but no sound emerged. Spinning back toward the west, he slammed his fists, one after the other and then both at once, into the railing.

"Are you all right?"

Sucking air through his teeth, Bannon managed a shaky smile. "I'm a slaughtering idiot, Highness. Thank you."

"You're welcome."

And neither man mentioned that although Otavas wouldn't need Bannon's specialized skills, Benedikt might.

Fourteen

PERCHED on a bale of rope, Evicka waved at the distant figures of Broken Islanders gathered on the western arm, then dropped to the deck and palm-walked forward to the bow. "So here we are," she declared, heaving herself up onto a barrel so that she could see over the rail. "Sailing due west into unknown seas."

"Southwest," Karlene pointed out. She waved a hand toward the distant horizon off the starboard side of the ship. "That's west."

"Bardic license. Sailing vaguely southwest just doesn't start the chorus off right."

"It's the unknown seas part that concerns me," Jurgis admitted, not turning from his place by the rail. "The world seems to be bigger than we thought it was, and Benedikt could be anywhere."

"The kigh know where he is." Karlene knew she sounded more definite than she felt. Both the other bards knew it, too, but she hoped they'd been able to fool the crew. They'd all sent air kigh out to find Benedikt and all received identical answers—he was too far away. Only the water kigh could get them close enough to find him, but none of them knew if the water kigh would cooperate. So far they'd been less than helpful.

"What happens if we can't get an answer out in deep water?" Jurgis asked, finally turning and tucking a strand of pale blond hair behind his ear.

Karlene shrugged. "We keep sailing southwest until we get an answer."

"But we don't know how far south or west is far enough. We could sail right by him."

"Pessimist," Evicka grinned. Her companions both had that north-coast, sun-kissed look she preferred in a bedmate and she had every intention of taking the opportunities offered by long nights at sea. Yes, it was a terrible thing that the *Starfarer* was lost. Yes, it was a terrible thing that Benedikt had been so badly hurt. But she had no intention of dwelling on either. Bad things happened—who knew that better than she did?—-but life went on.

Spreading her arms, she tucked one stump under a strap on the barrel top to help her keep her balance on the pitching ship and dramatically declaimed, "We are bards of Shkoder, and we do not abandon one of our . . ."

Jurgis and Karlene exchanged a questioning glance.

"One of our what?" Karlene asked.

Serious now, Evicka pointed. "There. Do you see it?"

They turned together.

"I see a wave . . ."

Karlene frowned as Jurgis' voice trailed off. "It's not a wave. It's a kigh."

"If it's a kigh, it's the biggest unenclosed kigh I ever saw," Evicka muttered.

"It's a kigh," the older woman repeated. She swallowed to moisten her throat, then Sang the four notes to call their distant companion closer.

It didn't respond.

Each of the bards tried. Then in pairs. Then all together. Harmony. Unison. Nothing worked. They could hear sailors gathering behind them, beginning to mutter, as aware as the bards that they needed the kigh if they hoped to find Benedikt.

"It's just like when they hit the coast." Jurgis pushed hair back off his face with both hands. "Nothing we Sang made any difference."

"I'm an idiot."

The other two bards glanced over at Karlene.

"That's a little harsh," Evicka offered. "We're not having much luck either."

Gripping the railing so tightly her knuckles whitened, Karlene Sang the four notes of Benedikt's name.

The kigh rose up, higher, higher, until even those on board with no bardic ability at all realized this was more than just a wave. It lingered for a moment, water behaving the way water didn't—couldn't—behave then it dove toward the southwest, surfaced, and dove again. The ship surged forward along the same path. As one, all three bards looked over the side.

"Do you think we ought to tell the captain that we're not doing this?" Jurgis wondered. "That the kigh have decided to take us to Benedikt on their own?"

"If that's where they're taking us," Evicka said thoughtfully.

Lifting her gaze from the giant forms within the water, Karlene sighed. "I think I'd better go tell the captain not to fight the current."

"What should we do?"

"Sing your memories of Benedikt at it, at them, see if you can get them to respond. But be careful," she cautioned as she turned to go, "don't make them jealous."

"Jealous?"

Evicka grinned. "Karlene thinks Benedikt has a more, *personal* relationship with the kigh than the rest of us."

"More personal?" Jurgis took another look over the side and whistled softly. "Okay. I'm impressed."

Captain Juzef wasn't happy about giving over control of his ship to the kigh, but since he'd known from the beginning it was likely to happen, he acquiesced with at least an outward show of good grace.

Karlene left him discussing the situation with the mate—as she didn't even know what a mizzen *was,* she saw no need to stay—and made her way amidships to the slender figure standing motionless by the rail. "Are you all right?"

It was a good thing she hadn't expected an answer because she didn't get one. Behind them, the crew fought to get the sails down, the canvas sheets having become more hindrance than help. "The kigh will take us right to him, Bannon. We'll be there in time."

"Don't be more of a slaughtering idiot than you have to be," Bannon snarled in Imperial. "You have no way of knowing that."

"I was trying to be comforting."

"Comforting?" He turned toward her, eyes narrowed. "If you hadn't got that first message wrong, we'd have saved him before . . . before . . ." Unable to voice what they'd both felt in the wave, he turned away again.

"We don't know that for sure. I'm not making excuses,"

she added hurriedly as he tensed. "Since that day on the wharf I've gone over and over the pieces a thousand times—in recall and out—and given what we knew about the kigh then . . ." One hand gestured toward the too large, too regular waves around the ship, ". . . not what we know now, I came to the only possible conclusion." Karlene closed her eyes and allowed the wind to brush a tear from the end of her lashes "But I **am** sorry."

"For what?"

She could hear the curl in his lip even if she couldn't see it. "For your pain. For his. For Her Majesty's. For mine."

They stood together, remembering, as the giant kigh carried the *Vixen* farther and farther from shore.

"You . . ." Bannon cleared his throat and tried again. "You mourned him, too."

It was forgiveness of a sort. Karlene leaned on the rail beside him, staring out at nothing, inside the circle of pain his kigh projected. Magda would have known what to say; all Karlene could do was be there, just in case.

"If he dies . . ." The ex-assassin's voice was so soft, only a bard could have picked it out from the sounds of another twenty lives on a small ship. "If they kill him before I get there, I will destroy them. I will destroy anyone with his blood on their hands."

Remembering Benedict's pain, Karlene wanted to say she'd help. She didn't because she knew Bannon had spent too much time around bards to believe her and lying to an ex-assassin, even in kindness, was less than a good idea. But remembering Benedikt's pain, the muscles along her jaw tightened and she said instead, "Witnessed, and we won't try to stop you."

Bannon's hand covered hers for an instant, long enough for her to know he'd found at least a little of the only kind of comfort he'd take.

Xaantalicta would be reborn in two nights. Benedikt turned his pipes over and over in his hands, comforted by the familiar feel of the bound reeds. He was running out of time.

He knew how to defeat the Song of Sorquizic and unraveling such a complicated, intricate, powerful Song had taught him more about Singing the kigh than all his time in the Bardic College. Although nothing could be certain until he actually Sang, he was fairly sure he could Sing open a passage to allow the xaan's fleet through and then close the barrier again lest other ships follow. If not, he knew he could dismiss the barrier completely.

He hadn't yet told the xaan.

When she asked him, as she did nightly, if he'd be finished by the rebirth, he truthfully answered yes. Truth or lie, it didn't matter as that was the answer she wanted to hear. She'd discover which in three days.

Two nights. Three days. All the time he had left.

He had a plan; he only needed the courage to use it.

Three days. He didn't have to do it now.

Sighing deeply, Benedikt stopped turning the pipes and stared out at the curtain of rain. The rain was a necessary part of his plan. The rain had filled the cisterns to overflowing and, if chance left watchers in the garden, the rain would keep them from looking up. If he waited, and the sky cleared . . .

It's the rainy season. I could safely wait until tomorrow.

Behind the bandages, the empty socket throbbed.

Or even the day after.

He lifted the pipes to his face, laid his mouth against the familiar shapes, and set them aside again without even exhaling over the holes.

If I'm caught . . .

All the xaan needed was his voice. She could, and would, destroy the rest of him to ensure his service. It was easier to be defiant before the failure of defiance had been paid in blood.

I am a bard of Shkoder.

But was he? He'd given it up once. Could it be taken up again so easily? Had he managed to cobble together enough pieces to call himself a bard of anything? And if he had, would the shape hold against the sorts of pressures the xaan could bring to bear.

There was only one way to be sure.

Benedikt brought the pipes to his mouth again and closed his eye. He could feel the kigh confined in the cisterns, waiting for his attention, and as he blew the first four notes, he felt them respond. The guards had grown used to him playing bits of tunes over and over. With any luck, they'd think that was all he was doing now.

Of course, his luck hadn't been especially good of late.

His Song drove the kigh against the walls of their prisons, searching for weak points and, once found, slamming into those weaknesses again and again. Water cut riverbeds into mountainsides and wore those same mountains smooth. The floor quivered and a heartbeat later, the roar of blown masonry and rushing water combined to drown him out. He stopped playing, listened to the guards shouting in the hall, and waited.

"You! What are you doing?"

Benedikt turned toward the door and opened his eye. "Working on the Song for the xaan." He let his fear spill into his voice to help the lie. "What happened?"

"Never mind," the guard snarled. "Keep working, *karjo*."

Karjo. Roughly, no braid. It didn't apply to either children or priests of Tulpayotee and was, as near as Benedikt could determine, one of the most potent insults in the Petayn vocabulary. The xaan had ordered his head shaved, not to disturb him, a foreigner, but to evoke a reaction in those around him. Even guards who'd given him songs now treated him with heated disdain.

Bowing his head as the guard left, Benedikt waited until he heard the bells over the sound of the chaos beyond, then scrambled to his feet. Earlier, he'd gathered rainwater into a deep metal basin, pushing it into the far corner of the room, and now he stood over it, watching the kigh and praying to all the gods in the Circle that this would work.

Bards who Sang air strongly enough could echo Songs off distant objects so that the effects were felt long after the bard had left the area. It was mostly a party trick, amusing but not very useful. Benedikt planned on using a version of the trick to help him escape.

He piped the four notes to call the kigh, added a short sequence he'd been playing over and over for days, then asked the kigh for their help. In the basin, the water started to spin. The metal basin began to hum. Faster. Louder. Finally, the kigh recreated the short sequence of notes.

Benedikt started to breathe again. It wouldn't fool anyone up close, but from the chaos in the hall—those cisterns had held a lot of water—it should sound as if he continued to practice, too frightened to use a god-given opportunity.

Which was very nearly the truth.

Xaan Mijandra calculates everything to her benefit, he reminded himself as he hesitated. *She* won't *take my voice.* He raised his hand to the place on his chest where the queen's medallion had rested. The xaan wore it now, reforged into a pair of earrings. *I won't let her take my honor.*

Singing softly to the rain, he paused on the raised threshold between room and balcony. When he was sure the kigh knew what he needed, he stepped outside, pulled himself up onto the railing, and swung around the dividing wall to the next balcony. The rain pressed him hard against the stone. The kigh couldn't hold him, but they could keep him from falling. Had he been able to see more than a hand's distance in front of his face, his lack of depth perception would have probably caused a misstep and sent him to his death on the multicolored paving stones of the courtyard below. As it was, he had to depend on his sense of touch, and that hadn't changed.

Hurrying across the next balcony, Benedikt heard his name spoken and froze in place, his heart nearly deafening him with its terrified pounding. Then he realized it came, not from the room itself, but from the hallway beyond. Someone, caught in the cascade of water from the cistern, was wondering why he couldn't sing this flood back as well.

If they went to get him, and he wasn't in his room . . .

"Ain't gonna happen. Xaan said he's to stay in that room, and that's where he's stayin'."

"But the water . . ."

"Take it up with the xaan."

Some members of the xaan's household might risk initiative, but not the Guard. The Guard followed orders. Although he hadn't appreciated it at the time, Benedikt thanked all the gods in the Circle that the xaan had seen fit to waste a guard on his door.

Wanting nothing more than to crawl into a corner and be sick, he forced himself to keep moving along the eight balconies to the wall over the kitchens. As he rested, sucking air through the rain, he could hear screams of outrage as the artiste who prepared the xaan's meals raged against the sudden flood in his domain. Although he couldn't maintain it, Benedikt found himself smiling briefly. The kitchen cisterns were as large as the bathing cisterns and had been just as full.

From the outside lip of the last balcony, he gripped the railing and managed to find toehold enough on the kitchen wall that all his weight didn't slam suddenly onto his outstretched arms. Dangling put him less than three feet from the ground. He was significantly taller than the people the house had been built to contain.

He dropped.

The rain came down thicker around him.

There had been a guard in the courtyard under his balcony, but that balcony was now some distance away. Between all the shouting from inside and the sound of the downpour smashing into the building, he should be safe.

Should be.

For the moment.

Now he had to get past the kitchen, into the cellars below, and then into the passageways below that. From overheard conversations, he knew there were at least two levels of cellar under the kitchen; he could only hope that they held an access to the old tunnels.

Getting past the kitchen turned out to be surprisingly easy. Between the initial destruction when the cistern blew and the continuing destruction caused by the xaan's cook, no one noticed either a bent figure racing for the stairs or the way those stairs got suddenly darker.

In the first cellar, Benedikt carefully set the lamp he'd taken from its bracket onto the floor and took a moment to still a rising panic. His empty socket throbbed in time to his heartbeat, the pain a constant reminder of what he'd face if he were caught.

If they found me in the house, I could say I just wanted to help with the flood. But if they find me down here . . .

He turned back toward the stairs, then turned himself around again. The cellar was quiet, the only sound the dripping of water from the floors above.

If you're a bard of Shkoder—be one. Pick up the lamp and find those tunnels.

*　　*　　*

"What is going on here?"

The karjen dropped to one knee with a splash. "The cisterns, peerless one. It, they . . ." He really didn't have an explanation for what the cisterns had done. "Your rooms are flooded, peerless one."

"She can see that, you fool," Hueru growled from behind the xaan's left shoulder. "Tell her something she doesn't know."

Visibly tensing, the karjen stammered, "There's water everywhere, peerless one."

A light touch on his tattoo stopped Hueru's forward movement. "Leave it."

"Peerless one, you've returned early!" Serasti bustled out of the xaan's bedchamber wearing only her shift, her arms filled with billowing folds of multicolored cloth. "The Tulparax . . .?"

"He lives, although there was an assassin dismembered in his private garden last night."

"Whose?"

"The remains were mostly eaten, impossible to tell." A brief flash of what might have been satisfaction was quickly replaced by the sardonic lift of a brow. "Have I returned at a bad time?"

As Hueru snorted, Serasti glanced down at the damp fabric in her arms and flushed. "The cistern wall collapsed into your bathing chamber, peerless one. Flying masonry has destroyed most of the tile work, the boilers were smashed, and the water had barely slowed by the time it reached your wardrobe. We're saving what we can, but the damage . . ."

A lifted hand cut off the flow of explanation. "Yes," Xaan Mijandra acknowledged softly, "water can be more dangerous than we suspect." She nodded toward the kneeling karjen. "He said cisterns."

"Yes, peerless one. All three."

"All three?" Her tone suggested she found it more interesting than upsetting. "Where is Benedikt?"

Serasti's fists clenched, bunching her burden into disapproving rosettes. "In his room, peerless one. The guard checked on him immediately, and he has been heard since."

Hueru's lip curled. "Singing?"

The house master nudged the kneeling karjen with her foot.

"N-no, karjet," he stammered. "Playing the pipes."

Xaan Mijandra lifted the trailing edge of feathered robe she'd worn to court as a rivulet of water reached the mosaic at her feet, spread into the spaces between the tiles, and divided into a thousand tiny streams. "I think I'll go and have a word with him."

"It will be difficult, peerless one. The cistern wall is blocking the upper hallway."

"I go where I please in my own house."

It was almost a warning.

"Yes, peerless one."

"It's still raining." The xaan glanced toward the ceiling, "Have you closed the cistern intake on the roof?"

"Yes, peerless one. It was the first thing I ordered when I was told what had happened."

"Good." She turned, Hueru following like a shadow. "You see, cousin, I told you Serasti excels at her job. You shouldn't repeat such unfounded rumors."

Enjoying the sudden flash of fear on the house master's face, Hueru grinned. "I won't do so again, peerless one." It didn't matter that he never had.

The entrance to the old tunnels had to be fairly obvious if the pipe attendants used them for maintenance. Unfortunately, the cellars were large and Benedikt's one small lamp threw more shadows than illumination. Time after time, he started toward a certain opening in the wall, only to have it disappear when he came closer.

He began to fear the tunnels were hiding on his blindside. His search lost all system as again and again he staggered into the darkness on his left.

He began lighting other lamps as he found them.

It didn't help.

"Benedikt is not in his room, peerless one!"

"And the pipe music?" the xaan asked, continuing to feed Shecquai bits of melon.

"It came from a bowl," Hueru snarled. "I smashed it."

"Of course you did."

Stopped in mid-stomp by her matter-of-fact tone, Hueru's brows drew in. "You aren't surprised he's gone, peerless one? I could have sworn that he broke when I took his eye."

"He did," she told him, wiping juice from her hands with a scented cloth. "Apparently, he put part of himself back together again; enough to force the water through the cisterns to cover his escape."

"Force the *water,* peerless one?"

The xaan ignored her cousin's confusion and continued, speaking more to herself than to him. "The flood has gained Benedikt the freedom of the house, but it won't have distracted the guards on the exits." Pausing, she frowned slightly. "They'd better not have been distracted. Where's the First?"

Hueru jerked away from the platter of sliced fruit. "Making sure the failure of the cisterns wasn't meant to cover an attempt on your life, peerless one."

"It wasn't. Find him. Have him make certain Benedikt is still in the house, then have the house searched." Scooping up the small dog, she settled back on her cushions. "There are a limited number of places a one-eyed karjo that size can hide. When he's found, he'll pay for the damage he's done."

Benedikt found the entrance to the tunnels in a small room in the lowest level of the cellars. It was the second room he'd looked into. Sweating in spite of the cooler air, he'd peered into the first, expecting to see the desiccated body of a forgotten prisoner, and had seen only a double stack of small stone crocks.

Dungeons aren't the xaan's way. If she has a use for you, she puts you back into a parody of your life, reminding you constantly not only of what you've lost but of what you can have again if you only behave. If she has no use for you . . . .

He remembered the body he thought he'd seen on the waste wagon and the xaan's reply.

"People die, Benedikt."

Dying would have been so much easier.

The tunnel was a great deal older than House Kohunlich, an arched passageway carved from the rock for a people still shorter than those who'd replaced them.

Hunched over his lamp, following the signs of use, Benedikt didn't look too closely at either the crumbling walls or the piecemeal attempts at repair. He ducked under angled, worm-eaten beams, stepped over piles of loose rubble, and tried not to think of the weight of stone above him.

Herexi had said she used the tunnels to get to the pipes under the fountain. The fountain was very close to the wall separating the xaan's half of the house from the tul's. If he could only get to the fountain, surely he could find a way across to safety.

Cazzes approached the house Second cautiously. His actions on the pier had made him a Second of Five and he was now discovering the downside to the promotion. Even such a small addition to his tattoo meant he was no longer hidden safely in the ranks. "Second?"

"What?" she growled, lifting her sandal as a sudden stream of water washed a pile of cut vegetables past her foot.

"We found lamps lit in the cellars."

"So?"

"The kitchen karjen say they didn't light them."

The Second smiled grimly. She'd shared food with the missing karjo before he'd lost his braids, and she couldn't help but feel that had tainted her slightly. Others who'd been in her position assured her it didn't, but she'd be happier if she were the one to return the fugitive to the xaan. "You, go find the First and tell him. The rest of you . . ." Her voice filled the kitchen, pulling the guards from their search. ". . . come with me."

He found the fountain by listening for the song of the water in the pipes, although an ancient rockfall closed the side tunnel to anyone even half his size, preventing him from actually reaching it. Standing with one hand on the damp rock and the other clutched tightly around the handle of his lamp, he tried to orient himself to the world above.

If the fountain was to his left, then the tul was to his right.

Unfortunately, the main tunnel continued parallel to the wall, heading out toward the Great Square.

Herexi had said that the tunnels connected the great

houses to the site of an old temple under the Great Square. Perhaps he had to find that temple before he could make his way back in to another building.

Perhaps Herexi was wrong and the tunnels had collapsed everywhere but under the house of the Kohunlich Xaan.

Pushing his free hand against the edge of his empty socket, trying to press away the pain of a heated spike being driven back into his skull, Benedikt lifted his lamp and moved carefully through the rubble toward the Great Square.

It was simple really; he could go forward, or he could go back, and going back wasn't an option.

"Into the old tunnels?" To Cazzes' surprise, the First looked pleased. "Good. Rejoin your Five and tell the Second to follow him in. I'll have another group try and cut him off at this end."

Sketching a quick salute, Cazzes hurried less than enthusiastically back to the cellars with the message. He hadn't even known the tunnels existed until they'd followed the lamps into the lowest cellar and a quick search had turned up the ancient stonework. Clearly, the First not only knew they were there but knew of other accesses and planned to use them.

"Yeah, but I'll bet he won't be going down into the dark, dangerous things," he muttered. "Don't find house Firsts and Seconds marching into the realm of the dead with the rest of us."

Chasing the xaan's runaway out in the city was one thing, chasing him down into the bowels of the earth was another thing entirely.

A sudden draft indicated another passage to his right. Another passage leading back to the house. The wrong direction. Benedikt took his hand from the wall to protect the tiny flame in his lamp and froze.

Voices.

Guards.

He should have known there was more than one way into the tunnels. Should have known the xaan knew they were there and had worked out a way to use them to her advantage.

He should blow out his lamp, find a dark corner, and hide.

Glancing toward the house, he saw the glow of lanterns in the distance. They were bringing enough light to fill the corners. There was nowhere to hide. He had to keep moving.

He turned his lamp down as far as it would go, put his left hand back on the wall lest he miss the passageway he needed and began a desperate, bowlegged run.

There were lights in the tunnel behind him when his left hand finally fell away into nothing. Relief making him almost sick, he turned toward the tul and safety.

Relief lasted three steps. The side tunnel had been filled in with loose stone.

As far as he could tell, none of the pieces were larger than his head. Given time, he could clear the passage. But time was the one thing he didn't have. The guards would find him here, trap him here, take him to the xaan. . . .

Benedikt bit off an involuntary moan and hurried back to the main tunnel. The lights were closer.

Breathing heavily, he started running, tripped, and slammed one knee painfully into the debris covering the floor. Lifting his lamp, he saw that a section of the arch had fallen, leaving a jagged, unbraced hole behind. Either the maintenance had ended or this was a recent collapse—either way, it seemed he was now in as much danger from the rock itself as from the guards.

"I see his lamp!"

The tunnels presented him with the triumphant cry, wrapped in echoes and joined by the slap of sandals against stone.

They were farther away than they seemed.

He still had a chance.

Careening off rough walls, bare skin scraped and bruised, Benedikt threw himself forward, no longer caring where he ran to as long as he got away. His back screamed protests, but he couldn't straighten. Every movement jangled half-healed nerves in his empty socket, filling it with fire, but he couldn't stop.

He scrambled up and over rockfalls. He threw himself down and under another section of collapsed roof propped to knee height on two slabs of stone. He squeezed past jagged edges, opening new lines of pain on back and chest.

If there were side tunnels, he didn't notice.

He had to get away. He couldn't let them take him back.

But the lights were still behind him when he reached the dead end. Another rockfall.

The tiny part of his mind still clinging to rational thought kept him on his feet and spun him about, frantically searching for another way.

The flame in his lamp flickered and he froze. Without even such a pitiful light, he couldn't run, and if he couldn't run . . .

Run where?

Despair brought with it false calm. Benedikt sagged against the stone that trapped him and drew in a long shuddering breath. He could see the lanterns, hear the guards coming closer. He could wait or he could go to meet them and get it over with a little quicker.

"Maybe," he whispered, amazed at being able to speak at all, "if I charge them, they'll kill me."

His sawrap slapped against his legs as he stepped forward, spraying water down his calves.

Water?

Stumbling around to face the rockfall again, he found the glistening line that ran from ceiling to floor and back along the wall until it disappeared into shadow.

Frowning, he bent lower and followed.

The shadow hid a crevice.

His lamp, thrust in as far as his arm could easily go, suggested an opening beyond—another tunnel, a natural cave, Benedikt neither knew nor cared.

The crevice was wide enough to allow a small man turned sideways to pass.

Benedikt was not a small man.

Still . . . He swallowed and forced his right shoulder into the crack after the lamp. . . . *there's less of me than there was.*

Stone pressed against his throat as he angled his head into the only possible place that would pass his skull. Head unshaven, he would never have made it. His hair would have caught on the rough rock and trapped him.

Why would anyone give up eight braids?

Here's a reason.

He could feel hysteria rising and bit it back.

Chest. Hip. Right leg bent almost into a squat.

Ribs creaked but slick with sweat and blood, his chest moved through.

Left hip. Left leg. Left shoulder.

Everything except his right hand was in the crevice.

Fighting panic, Benedikt struggled toward the lamplight a hair's width at a time.

His right foot pushed into freedom.

The gouge of rock into his groin, forced forward by the unnatural bend in his legs, was just one more pain amidst the many. He'd have ignored it except that the sawrap caught, and with movement so minimal it had strength enough to hold him fast.

All he could hear was the pounding of his heart, but he knew the guards were closer. Soon, they'd find him. Yank him out. Drag him back . . .

He had nowhere to put the lamp; he had to hang onto it or be plunged into darkness. His left hand fought to find purchase on the rock, to push against the friction of the wet fabric.

A moment's panic added a little more blood, but it wasn't enough to slide him through.

What would Bannon do?

He couldn't help it, he started to laugh. Bannon was half his size. Bannon wouldn't have gotten stuck.

Cazzes frowned. "Did you hear that?"

The guard beside him nodded and held the lantern higher. "It's the dead. The dead live underground."

"The dead don't live, asshole. And they sure as shit don't laugh."

"Shut up, both of you," growled the house Second from the back of the pack. "We let this karjo get away, and the dead will be the least of your concerns."

Trite, Cazzes allowed, but true.

The two clumps of guards had come together, then separated once again, half to check the tunnels behind to make sure their quarry hadn't hidden himself until they passed and half moving on toward the Great Square. As the tunnels moved out from under House Kohunlich, they'd spotted their quarry's light and given chase.

Once or twice they'd lost the light and the Second—with them still to Cazzes' surprise—had sent reluctant guards into every nook and cranny they'd passed.

At the moment, they'd lost the light again; Cazzes wasn't looking forward to taking his turn alone in the next nook and or cranny they found.

With his weight held by the stone, Benedikt hooked his right heel on the crevice's edge and used the muscles of his legs to drag himself free of the rock's embrace. Teeth clenched, eye shut, explosions of light filling his skull, he began to move. Amid a hundred other bits of pain, he couldn't feel the sawrap dig into his waist. Nor could he feel the ties begin to part.

"Rockfall up ahead, Second."

"So I see."

"Whole tunnel's blocked, and there's no sign of the karjo."

"Then find out where he's gone."

When the sawrap finally gave way, Benedikt came out of the crevice like he was being birthed a second time. Naked, covered in blood, he slammed down onto a sandy floor and lost his hold on the lamp. He lay there for a moment, breathing shallowly, beyond both panic and despair, and then opened his eye.

A small flame flickered in the darkness. The lamp, cradled in a pile of fine black sand, had not gone out. The last few precious drops of oil hadn't spilled. The darkness hadn't won.

Taking strength from that simple gift, Benedikt crawled forward, lifted the lamp and looked around.

He was in a small round cave, with walls that had once curved down to become colonnaded entrances to a myriad of tunnels. Time had blocked many of the tunnels, but some, he thought, were open still.

In the center of the cave was a seated statue of a woman.

There was only one possible place the karjo could have gone.

"Give Cazzes a lantern," the Second commanded.

"If there's only one place the karjo could have gone," Cazzes argued, "why don't we all go?"

The Second glanced over at the shadowed crevice and hid a shudder. She'd heard the same stories in the children's compound as the others.

The dead lived underground.

"First," she told him, "you make sure."

As Benedikt moved around to the front of the statue, he wondered why the head seemed so out of proportion. The body had been carved along generous lines, broad hips and rounded shoulders cradling generous swooping curves of breast and belly, but the head seemed small and almost delicate.

Then he saw that the head had not actually been carved.

". . . *there used to be a temple to Peta where the square is now, and the olden days people used to use the tunnels to get there.*"

The remains of a skull, sat on the pedestal of a stone neck, the jawbone wired into place. It had been a very long time since this ancient goddess had chosen a new avatar.

A muffled curse pulled Benedikt around and he realized he could see a line of light near where he'd entered the cave.

No, not near.

The guards were in the crevice.

There was blood on a bit of jagged stone by Cazzes' cheek. It glistened in the lamplight and told him they were very, very close.

Shuffling sideways, attempting without much success to keep the new and tender part of his tattoo from touching the rock, he choked off a curse as his foot came down on something soft that wrapped a damp fold up over bare toes.

Hanging the lantern on a projecting rock, he managed to hook his finger around it and bring it up to where he could see.

A sawrap.

The karjo was naked and injured, and, Cazzes reminded himself, just barely recovered from the loss of an eye.

He hadn't been able to look away when the xaan's cousin

had taken the eye. It had been no more brutal than many a punishment he'd seen and certainly no less than the runaway deserved, but somehow it had meant more. He hadn't been able to stop thinking of the despair he'd seen in those strange blue eyes.

He couldn't stop thinking of it now as he closed his fingers tightly around the crumpled sawrap.

The karjo, Benedikt, was harmless. He had a smart mouth, sure, and maybe he could push water around, but Cazzes had seen him embarrass himself in front of the xaan.

If he backed out of the crevice, if he said it ended barely a body length in and the karjo could not have gone that way, would the Second believe him?

Benedikt didn't know why the first of the guards hadn't already come through into the cave, but he was willing to believe the goddess had something to do with it.

"Peta, please," he whispered, his free hand staining her thigh with blood as he dropped to his knees. "Help me."

Staring up at the empty sockets of the ancient skull he touched the cloth wrapped over the place where his left eye had been. Tears ran down his cheek.

The goddess cried with him.

Heart racing, Benedikt lifted the lamp higher.

No. Water dripped from the ceiling above, ran down the rounded curves of ancient bone, and dripped dark promises onto the stone breasts.

The rock all around the cave was saturated with water.

"Cazzes! What's taking you so long?"

The harder he tried to think of something else, anything else, the more the despair in those eyes filled his thoughts.

What harm would it do to let the kid go?

He felt the movement of the rock before he heard the Song that caused it.

Heard the Second yell a moment later.

"Get him out of there now!"

Felt hands grab his wrist and yank him back into the tunnel as the world collapsed around him.

Fifteen

"YOU'RE certain you can't clear the rockfall?"

"Yes, peerless one. When we moved one rock, another two fell. If we'd kept going, we would have collapsed the tunnels right back into your cellars. Perhaps miners . . ."

"No." The xaan cut off the nervous flow of words before they provoked her into a more definitive response. Two steps took her from the house Second to the filthy, bleeding guard kneeling beside her. "You had your hands on him when the rocks began to fall?"

"I'm sorry, peerless one." Right hand cradled against his chest, Cazzes held up the sawrap in his left. He'd been clutching it when the rest of his Five had pulled him from the crevice, and he hadn't argued with the Second's assumption. He knew he should have been terrified by how close he'd come to betraying his xaan, but somehow it just didn't matter. The certain death of the karjo, of Benedikt, bothered him more. He didn't know why.

"You caught him on the pier as well?"

Her question took him by surprise. He hadn't realized she'd been told. "Yes, peerless one."

"And you were the guard he failed to command."

"Yes, peerless one." He was amazed she'd remembered. *Too* much attention from the xaan always ended badly. The terror smashed through whatever had been holding it back and he swayed where he knelt.

"Is he injured?"

"Not badly, peerless one," the Second began.

Xaan Mijandra cut her off. "Take him to a physician. He has served me well."

The last was almost a ritual statement of praise. Cazzes struggled to feel the joy he should have with little success.

The xaan waited until the Second helped Cazzes from

the room, then she turned to her First. "I thought the tunnels were closed off."

"The pipe attendants use them, peerless one, to . . ." He paused and finished a little sheepishly. ". . . attend to their pipes."

"Then find out which of the pipe attendants has been speaking to Benedikt. He didn't stumble into those tunnels by accident."

"And when I find out, peerless one?"

"Deal with it."

"Yes, peerless one."

"He'll likely die in the tunnels," Hueru offered when the First had left them alone.

"Best case scenario," the xaan agreed, stripping an iridescent green feather to its shaft with tiny vicious movements of her fingers. "If he doesn't, he's going to wish he had."

Benedikt's lamp had gone out just after he left Peta's cavern; the last of the oil burned, the darkness enveloping him like deep water. He should have been terrified, but he wasn't. Whether the ancient goddess continued to aid him or he was just emotionally numb, he neither knew nor cared. He set the useless lamp aside and moved on.

The xaan couldn't find him in the darkness.

Eye closed, humming the Song of Sorquizic softly to himself, he crawled on, one hand in the tiny stream of water that guided him. Water would save him. Water had always saved him. Although he clambered painfully over rockfalls and inched forward flat on his belly through a horizontal crack in the rock, there were never obstacles so great he lost track of the water.

Until it disappeared under the lip of a worn stone.

Kneeling carefully, Benedikt opened his eye.

The darkness no longer pressed so heavily against him. There was distance, depth, shades of darkness where for so long there had been nothing at all. Reaching out, he stroked an opening a little higher than his head, a little narrower than his shoulders. Breathing heavily, he inched forward.

The distance grew a little more distinct.

His shoulder brushed against an object more yielding than stone. Warmer. Rougher. It took him a moment to remember what it was called. Wood. Curved. Fitted. Round. A barrel.

The water had disappeared beneath an ancient lintel.

He was in a cellar.

His nose led him to the kitchen.

Benedikt wasn't sure he could make it up the final flight of stairs, but he pulled himself up into the light along the smell of roasting pork. Gripping the wall for support, he levered himself up to his knees and stared around. The xaan's kitchen had barely been large enough to contain her staff; with food and equipment added it bulged at the seams. This room was as large but almost empty except for the half-dozen karjen at the far end of the room . . .

"Assassin!"

. . . and the one behind him.

He went down without a fight and lay quietly under the weight of his young attacker, too tired to care what was going to happen. *Far* too tired to do anything about it.

Whatever it was, it seemed to involve a lot of shouting.

He kept his eye closed and tried to remember that this was happening to him, but it wasn't easy. His body seemed unattached, not really a part of him, no longer his concern.

"If this is some kind of a joke . . ."

"No joke. We caught a karjo assassin."

"Why tell me?"

Benedikt stirred and moved his head away from the small hand pushing at the bandage over his eye. Something familiar . . .

"So you can tell the tul."

The tul? There were eleven tuls. One for each of the great houses and one for each of the lesser houses. *You see, I was paying attention.*

"He's at the palace."

Very familiar.

"You can tell him when he gets back, karjet."

"The karjo assassin's only got one eye."

That came from the skinny boy sitting on his chest. Eye open. Benedikt tried to focus on his face, couldn't, and focused instead on the red edges around a brand new tattoo centered on a thin chest. Boy indeed. Had just gotten his house tattoo. That should have meant more, but he couldn't seem to make it.

"And he's naked."

Shadows darkened as everyone drew in for a closer look. Benedikt waited for the inevitable.

"And he's hairy."

"Hairy?" The familiar voice became a familiar touch and a familiar face. "Benedikt?"

"You know the karjo assassin, karjet?"

Xhojee sat back on his heels, staring at the filthy, bleeding body before him. "This isn't an assassin, this is a warrior of Tulpayotee."

"This?"

Benedikt couldn't help smiling at the disbelief· in the boy's voice—for all it wasn't funny.

"This. Get off him and go get the physician. The rest of you can get back to work."

"We should help you guard him."

"He's not going anywhere." When the two of them were finally alone—although the karjen had only gone to the other end of the kitchen, Xhojee reached out and gently stroked an abraded shoulder. "What happened to you?"

Benedikt dragged his tongue over his lips. Back in the tul's country house, Xhojee had told him a story about how, unwilling to wait for a change, the moon fought to cover the sun until only a circle of light was left. Those who stared at the battle went blind. Somehow, the story seemed apt.

"I got eclipsed," he said.

"Benedikt is with the tul, peerless one."

"My brother?" Surprise pushed the xaan's usual, calm tones to a higher pitch. "Are you sure?"

Serasti bowed. "Positive, peerless one. The karjen you placed in your brother's house spoke to her brother this morning at the trash heap. Benedikt staggered into the kitchens last night and was taken away by the physician. The girl said he did not appear to be badly injured."

"Good."

"Shall I send for the First, peerless one?"

"The First? Why?"

"So that before you go to the palace, you may make plans to get Benedikt back."

"No, I don't think so." Carefully keeping her left hand

and its wet nails away from her robe, Xaan Mijandra moved to gaze out through the stone latticework that overlooked the Great Square. A party from House Calakroul was heading toward the palace.

Confused, the house master shuffled closer. "The guards seem to think at least one of the tunnels between your house and your brother's could be cleared. A Five could . . ."

". . . find itself picked off one by one as it crawled through the opening. My brother is not always a fool, Serasti. He knows how to defend himself."

"But, peerless one, Benedikt . . ."

"I don't think I'll bother getting Benedikt back right away." While she'd been busy covertly arranging a fleet and weapons, Omliaz, she who would be the Calakroulxaan, had become very close to the xaantalax. Sooner or later—probably sooner—the silly chit would mention that the Kohunlich-xaan had an exceptional singer in residence. The xaantalax would want to hear him sing and, if she liked him well enough, would want to add him to her own household. House Kohunlich was powerful but not powerful enough to refuse a direct request from the xaantalax. Yet.

How much simpler, Xaan Mijandra mused as she watched the Calakroul banners disappear behind the Great Temple, *to tell the xaantalax that Benedikt has run to my brother. After the change, the xaantalax can order Altun to give him up and thus avoid a lot of potential unpleasantness during these unstable times.*

How unfortunate for the xaantalax that after the change will be too late.

"Peerless one?"

"I know my brother, Serasti. Benedikt has only one thing to offer him now. When he tries to use it, I'll be there to take it away." Smiling serenely, she waved her unpainted nails at the housemaster. "Send my adorner back in, would you. I don't want to be late arriving at the palace."

"You didn't exactly take care of yourself while you were gone, did you?" Imixara held Benedikt's jaw firmly and turned his head from side to side. "It seems Sorquizic was kinder to you."

His reaction pulled his face from her grip. For a moment the Song of Sorquizic drowned out conscious thought. "Why do you say that?" he managed at last.

"I say it because the sea didn't take any body parts." Rising, the physician held out her hand for a scented cloth. "And having saved your sight, I'd have preferred you hadn't lost part of it to the xaan."

Benedikt fought to keep his voice steady. "I tried to get away."

"We know." Xhojee knelt by the other side of the bed. "I was the one in the crowd who yelled that the xaan couldn't punish a priest."

"That was you?" He remembered the voice and the moment of hope it had given him.

"The tul sent us out looking for you when he heard you'd run." A braid tipped with a red-and-black feather fell forward as Xhojee ducked his head. "I'm sorry."

"For what?"

"For not finding you before the xaan's guard." He looked up, needing Benedikt to believe that he'd tried. "I wasn't even sure it was you at first, because of the robe, then I covered my tattoo and got as close as I could. Xaan Mijandra was smart using the robe. It covered just enough to hide your strangeness and what it didn't cover, well, no one ever looks too closely at prisoners of the great houses. I stayed until they took you into the warehouse."

Tears filled Benedikt's eye and spilled down behind his ear and onto the bed. Just to know that he hadn't been alone . . . "Thank you."

Xhojee flushed as Imixara cleared her throat, glad she'd drawn the other man's attention. Everyone in the room but Benedikt knew he'd stayed only because the tul would have wanted him to.

"The eye is healing as it should. Now that you're clean, I see that most of the new damage looked worse than it is." The physician stepped back and motioned Ochoa forward. "A few days of this salve on your knees and across the stitches I put in your hand and there should be no scarring." *Physical scarring,* she added silently, watching the way he reacted to Ochoa's touch.

Hearing voices outside the room, she moved the string of bells aside and stepped out into the hall.

"Well?"

"If you'd let Ochoa finish tending him, gracious one, then you can speak without interruption."

Tul Altun dismissed her response with an impatient wave of one hand. "Did my sister leave me enough to use?"

"Your sister only removed his eye, gracious one. The injuries he received in the tunnels will heal."

"What about his voice?" Ooman Xhai leaned past his tul and clutched at the physician's robe. "Can he still sing?"

"He hasn't done any singing since he arrived last night so I couldn't say, although his speaking voice seems much as I remember it."

The priest clasped his hands together and sighed. "Tul-payotee is merciful to his warrior."

"Not that *I've* noticed," Imixara observed with thinly veiled contempt.

"Has she broken his spirit?" The tul demanded, his question cutting through the ill will between priest and physician.

"Kohunlich-xaan is a dangerous person, gracious one."

"Just answer the question."

Imixara's lips thinned and she spent a moment deliberately provoking the tul with her silence. She hadn't approved of the way he'd exposed himself by coming to Atixlan and she used every opportunity to remind him of that. Finally she said, "Bent, gracious one, but not broken, or he would have never made it back to you. Go carefully if you want to make use of him."

"Thank you for your advice, physician." The tul's voice was cold.

Imixara bowed and, as Ochoa came out of the room, took her assistant's arm and included her in the dismissal.

"What did you say to him?" Ochoa whispered when they were safely away.

"I merely told him to go carefully with Benedikt."

"Merely?" the other woman snorted. "Why didn't you just tell him to poke your eye out, too?"

"No one told me she shaved his head."

Looking anxious, Xhojee rose to face the tul. "It seemed unimportant beside the rest, gracious one."

"The rest?" An edged gesture moving Xhojee aside, Tul

Altun walked to the head of the bed and frowned at Benedikt. "The rest I could work around, but not this! This ruins everything." Drawing in a deep breath, the tul closed his eyes for a moment and visibly forced himself calm. "You owe me, Benedikt. I, the Kohunlich-tul, had to go to the tuls of two lesser houses and convince them to keep quiet about a plan *I* had approached them to support. Fortunately, they had no wish to come to the attention of the Kohunlich-xaan." He glanced up, toward the window and his sister's half of the house, then back down at the karjo she'd sent him. "What am I supposed to do with you?"

"Gracious one . . ."

"Quiet. The physician said I was to be careful." Almost to himself, he added, "I wonder what *she* thought I was going to do." Reaching down, he stroked his palm lightly over the golden stubble.

Staring up at the ceiling, Benedikt tried not to tremble. He had no defenses left against gentleness, not even gentleness intended to provoke.

Fingers cradling the soft, round curve of the other man's skull, Tul Altun turned Benedikt to face him, catching his gaze and holding it. "You can't be my warrior of Tulpayotee, you're just not golden anymore. The tulparax would never believe in you."

"But he can call up the god, gracious one!" Ooman Xhai shifted his weight from foot to foot on the other side of the bed. "He can sing in the temple and call up the god."

Ignoring his high priest, the tul continued speaking quietly to Benedikt. "Even if you could sing Tulpayotee right into the bed of the tulparax, you wouldn't get the chance because, more importantly, the people around the tulparax wouldn't believe in you. And looking like you do now, if we smuggled you into the temple, you wouldn't sing out two notes before you were brutally silenced."

"Your priests could protect him, gracious one."

This time, the tul looked up. "The four I brought to Atixlan against the priests of the Great Temple? Do you have some *connection* with Grand Ooman Cuauhtemoc you haven't mentioned?"

Glancing from Benedikt to his tul, Ooman Xhai shook his head. "No, gracious one . . ."

"I thought not. Go away, Ooman, I'm tired of your interruptions."

"But, gracious one . . ."

"Now."

Recognizing that it had become dangerous to stay, the priest bowed and left the room.

Maintaining his grip on Benedikt's head, Tul Altun waited until he heard the bell before continuing. "In spite of what Ooman Xhai seems to think, you're of no use to me. My sister, however, clearly wants you." There was a hint of desperation in the tul's dark gaze. "What would she give me to get you back?"

Benedikt swallowed and didn't answer.

"Wouldn't it be worth keeping him just to annoy her, gracious one?"

"Would it?" Smiling tightly at Xhojee, Tul Altun straightened and flicked the sleeve of his robe back into place. They all knew that if the xaan decided to move against him, the tul wouldn't have the resources to stop her. "If she wants him badly enough, she might be grateful."

"He brought you the tunnels, gracious one."

"Yes, the tunnels. How interesting that no one in my household seemed to know they were there. Now they're found, do I fill them in, so preventing my sister from using them against me, or do I clear them out, so I can use them against her. Your return . . ." Sarcasm weighted the words. ". . . as welcome as it may be to Xhojee and Ooman Xhai, is not without problems, Benedikt."

As the dark gaze settled on his face, Benedikt had the strangest impression he was looking into a pool of still water and seeing a reflection of a familiar despair, of a man very near the end of his resources. With the death of the tulparax, the Kohunlich-xaan would move quickly to replace her brother with her son, and in Tul Altun's eyes was the certain knowledge there was nothing he could do to stop it.

Benedikt felt as though he'd been struggling in high seas and had unexpectedly discovered he could touch bottom. "If you return me to your sister, she'll see it as a sign of weakness," he said softly.

"Suppose I return you in pieces? She clearly wants you alive."

"So do you."

"Do I?"

He wondered if the tul even noticed they were speaking as equals. "I can give you the power you need to survive the change."

The tul stiffened. "Xhojee, out." When they were alone, he turned the full force of his attention on Benedikt. "You can give me my sister?"

"No, gracious one." No longer weighted by intimidation, Benedikt pulled himself up to a sitting position and drew in a deep breath, tasting the cinnamon scent that had come into the room with the tul. "I can give you Balankanche."

"You told me you sang water." The tul stared down at the bowl where only moments before the contents had divided themselves into four equal parts. His mouth thinned as he transferred his gaze to Benedikt's face. "You should have told me what it meant."

"You stopped me from doing so, gracious one."

"So?"

Even given their new relationship, there really wasn't a safe answer to that. "It didn't mean anything until I learned the Song of Sorquizic."

"But you would have learned it for *me,* had I known."

The protest had an edge Benedikt hastened to dull.

"You wanted a warrior of Tulpayotee, gracious one, not a bard of Shkoder."

"I did, didn't I." The tul's lip curled. "I should have let the Ooman stay, he'd have named you a warrior of Sorquizic instead." Without looking down, he pushed at the bowl with his foot. "You can do this to the barrier?"

"Yes."

"It makes no difference," he snarled as the water spilled and spread over the tile floor. "Unlike my sister, I have no fleet."

"You don't *need* a fleet, gracious one." Benedikt wondered if assuming conquest was a family trait or a national one. "I'll take us through the barrier on the single ship. You'll negotiate a treaty with the islanders and then return to the Tulparax with a way for him to get his hands on the gold of Balankanche."

"But not all of it," Tul Altun protested.

"More than he has now."

The tul nodded reluctantly, alternately crushing a feather and fluffing it out again. "True enough. But what makes you think the islanders won't kill me on sight?"

"Gracious one, they're as locked on that island as you are locked away from it. I guarantee there will be those open to trade. The rich and powerful are always open to more wealth and power, and you'll be the way they'll get it. You'll be the way the Tulparax gets it. And you'll get a good bit yourself."

Brows drawn in, the tul studied Benedikt for a long moment. "And what's in it for you?"

"When you return to Atixlan, you'll leave me on the island."

"Do I look like a fool!" Throwing the feather aside, Tul Altun got to his feet in a billowing cloud of multicolored silk and glared down at the younger man. "I leave you on that island, and I'll never get through the barrier again."

"I think the islanders would have something to say about that, gracious one, after having promised them the riches of trade."

"No, I want you with me. You're too valuable to let out of my sight."

"I'm too valuable to risk losing." He had to stop his hand from rising to touch the new bandage over his eye. "Balankanche is the one place where your sister can't get to me."

And they both knew she'd try.

"Suppose she gets to me?"

For all the careless way the tul tossed off the question, Benedikt realized he actually needed an answer. "You need to get to the island and back before the tulparax dies. The balance of power will shift in your favor."

"The Tulparax could die any time. What if it doesn't shift quickly enough?"

"Then ask yourself what would the Xaantalax rather have, the goodwill of the Kohunlich-xaan or the gold you'll bring into her treasury? I'll open the barrier for you alone." When the tul hesitated, Benedikt added, "You might also point out to her how very powerful the Kohunlich-xaan has gotten and how it isn't unheard of *for houses to rise and for other houses to fall.*"

Tul Altun's eyes widened. "That could have been my sister's voice."

"That was your sister's voice."

"She said as much to you?"

"She didn't expect me to leave."

For the first time since he'd entered the room, the tul smiled. "No. She didn't. But how to make the xaantalax believe . . ."

"It shouldn't take much." Benedikt found himself returning the smile just because it had been so long since someone had smiled at him. His cheeks felt stiff. "You people are always trying to kill each other; that's got to make her just a little paranoid. The prospect of all that gold should get you an audience at least."

"It should," the tul agreed. Then his smile slipped into something more speculative. "You've changed."

Benedikt shrugged and tried to keep any real emotion from showing in his voice. "I had to rebuild what I thought of as myself after your sister took my eye. If I wanted to hold together, I didn't have time to use anything but the strongest pieces."

"And now you offer this new, more definitive, you to me. Why?"

The question burned. Tul Altun was both intrigued and flattered, and Benedikt felt the muscles across his back relax. "You're the only chance I have," he said simply. "Just as I'm the only chance you have."

"I'd kill or maim you just as easily as she would if it suited me."

"But not as coldly."

After a long moment the tul nodded and wrapped warm fingers around Benedikt's wrist. "No. Not coldly." It was an acknowledgment, if only a momentary one, to an equal. "We have to move quickly before my sister does. She knows you're here."

"She has a *spy* . . ." Unable to think of the Petayn word, he used the Shkoden. ". . . one of her people in your house."

"I know. So much easier to keep the old eyes and ears than remove him and have to go looking for his replacement." He shot Benedikt a disdainful glance as he moved away from the bed. "Try and remember that I have survived this long without you."

"I beg your pardon, gracious one."

"Good. And while you remember it, remember also that what isn't spoken can't be overheard." A toss of his head lifted the feathers braided into his hair. "Now I'm about to let my sister know how your trip through the tunnels left you a blithering idiot and how nothing you say makes sense. What kind of idiot would believe that a song would open the barrier of Sorquizic?"

"And she'll believe that?"

"She would never believe that we'd work together . . ." The tul paused just inside the door and threw an edged look back at the man in the bed, gratitude and resentment equally mixed. ". . . karjo."

"Gracious one, his hair will grow, and you can put him in the sun again." Frowning deeply enough to pull the tattoos on his scalp out of shape, Ooman Xhai clutched at the tul's robe. "To return him to your sister might give you immediate gain, but it would lose you the future." He snatched his hand back as the tul's gaze flicked down to his fingers then up to his face. "Gracious one, please. The eye does not matter. He is still a warrior of Tulpayotee."

"After what my sister has done to him, I doubt it." Tossing a skein of feathered braids back over his shoulder, the tul motioned Xhojee back into the room, "Go, talk to him. Perhaps you can make more sense of his raving."

Confused, the younger man slipped back inside.

"I should speak with him, too," the priest began, but Tul Altun cut him off.

"No. My sister has him convinced he's a warrior of Sorquizic."

"Sorquizic?" Surprise stopped him in his tracks and he had to hurry to catch up. "There haven't even been priests of Sorquizic for generations."

"There's one now."

"But why, gracious one?"

"How should I know?" the tul growled. "But you can rest easy, I'm not giving him back. At least I'll die knowing I took something of hers."

"You're not going to die, gracious one."

"Do you know that for a fact?"

"Gracious one?"

"I thought not." Robe whispering against the floor, he swept toward his private apartments. "If I'm to wait on the Tulparax today, I'd best get ready."

"But, gracious one; Benedikt?"

"Leave him alone. He's of no use to me until he comes to his senses."

Crossing the room, Xhojee wondered if Benedikt had lapsed back into unconsciousness. His head lolled against the wall, and something about him suggested he just wasn't there. "Benedikt?" To his relief, the startlingly blue eye— not less startling for being on its own—opened and fixed on him. "The tul says you were raving."

Sliding back down in the bed, Benedikt managed half a shrug. The strength he'd used to convince the tul had been almost all the strength he had, physically and emotionally. "Maybe I was." He expected the younger man to ask what he'd been raving about, but Xhojee only sat down and watched him carefully. Finally, he had to fill the silence himself. "You've gotten close to him since I left."

"Left? I thought you were taken."

"I wouldn't have been if I'd stayed inside." And if he'd stayed inside that day, how would things have been different? He used the pain from his missing eye to chase the thought away. "Well?"

"He hasn't many people he trusts."

Compared to his sister, Tul Altun didn't have many people, period. Still, when he came right down to it, he was no more alone than the xaan. Benedikt wondered if all the great houses were like that, or if fate and the kigh had played a cruel joke with their choice. "And he trusts you?"

"As much as anyone."

"You blushing?"

Xhojee's cheeks flushed a little darker. "No." He rubbed at the edge of his tattoo where a new addition to the pattern still itched and watched exhaustion paint shadows over the hope on Benedikt's face. Although it had vanished almost instantly, that same unexpected hope had marked the tul as he'd come out into the hall.

There could be only one reason for hope.

Xhojee had seen exactly what Benedikt had gone

through to get away from the xaan, and he saw daily what the tul went through as the certainty of the change moved closer.

A common enemy. A common solution.

He had no illusions that the tul's household wouldn't meet the same fate as the tul.

A common solution indeed.

His hope was that the other two knew what they were doing because, based on what he'd seen before the bathing and the bandaging, he strongly suspected that if Benedikt came face-to-face with the xaan, he'd fall apart.

"Benedikt, what's the xaan like? I'm sorry," he added as the shadows darkened. "I just wondered if she was like the tul."

"Sort of. On the surface. They're both . . . what's the Petayn word for animals that eat other animals?"

"Predators?"

"Yeah. The tul is like a leopard." Benedikt, who'd grown up surrounded by cats, had been fascinated by the size of the pelts the xaan's guard wore over their ceremonial armor. "He's dangerous. Unpredictable. Personal. Stretching the metaphor, he likes to play with his food."

When Xhojee winced but didn't disagree, he went on. "The xaan is quicksand. Not exactly a predator but the same idea. She gives no warnings, plays no games. A traveler sees a leopard, steps off the path to avoid it, and disappears. It's not that she waits for her prey to come to her, she just *always* happens to be where it is."

He watched Xhojee thinking about the wet sand closing over his head, the terror rising in his eyes, and wished he'd kept his mouth shut. It was just such a great image that it had gained him a little distance from the reality. He looked for a way to give that distance to Xhojee. "I know it's supposed to be a disgrace, but there's an upside to having had my hair shaved. My head's cooler."

Jerked out of his reverie, Xhojee stared at Benedikt's pale scalp. "Then they ought to shave the rest of you," he said.

"Your brother doesn't believe that the karjo, Benedikt, can do what he says he can, peerless one."

"Good." The xaan held Shacquai on his back in the crook of her arm and absently scratched his chest. "Did my ears and eyes mention what my brother doesn't believe?"

Serasti nodded. "Yes, peerless one. Your brother says that the karjo has come out of the tunnels raving that he is a warrior of Sorquizic."

"Interesting. Do we know what Benedikt actually said to my brother?"

"No, peerless one. The boy couldn't get close enough. The tul has allowed no karjen into the karjo's room. Today, while he was at the palace, there was a guard posted."

"So we know what my brother wants us to know."

Confused, the house master looked past the xaan to Hueru, who shrugged.

The xaan set the dog onto his feet and watched indulgently as he began digging in a cushion. "Altun hasn't searched for my eyes and ears since just after he came to Atixlan. He knows I have someone in his household. What comes from his mouth to me is what he wants me to hear."

"So he *does* believe what the karjo says?" Hueru asked, frowning.

"That's impossible to tell."

"But, peerless one . . ."

"Don't strain yourself, cousin. Tell the First you speak with the mouth of the xaan; I want to know immediately if anyone in my brother's house takes more than one step toward the harbor."

What he knew of Benedikt marched visibly, point by point, across Hueru's broad features—the flood on the road, the wave on the pier. . . . "Is he a warrior of Sorquizic, peerless one?"

The xaan lifted ebony brows into a sardonic arch. "Does it matter?"

"She's watching the house and everyone in it." Wearing only his sawrap, Tul Altun turned from the window and held out his arm so that Xhojee could began removing the designs painted from fingertip to elbow. "I, however, am only watching her and she's still at the palace."

"She doesn't . . ." Benedikt waved a hand at the disappearing body paint.

"She wouldn't. It's a style from the Tulparax's youth. He's fond of it, so those in attendance on him wear it."

"Does it help?"

Xhojee looked shocked at the implication of pandering, but the tul smiled. "Not that I noticed." When his arms were clean, he crossed to the bed. "Imixara said you slept most of the day. Have you regained your strength?"

"Does it matter, gracious one?"

"No. Tomorrow night is the rebirth of Xaantalicta. She'll come for you then, so she can use you as soon as she has you. Having lost you once, she won't move before she has to and risk losing you again. We have to be out of here and away before then."

"But she's watching the house."

"So? If in the cool of tomorrow morning, while the streets of Atixlan are full of people, I leave here with banners flying, with you and all my guard, what can she do? Start a pitched battle in the street? No. She can kill me in the privacy of my own home, that's a family matter, but a great house taking its quarrel to the street would bring the guards of the tulparax and immediate execution, House Kohunlich and all its assets claimed by the palace. It's a very old law that keeps up appearances for the common people and ensures a certain amount of political stability. All she can do is send her guard after us and all we have to do is get to the harbor before her. If she cuts us off, we'd have to retreat back to the house."

Where it's legal for her to kill you, Benedikt added silently. It was a strange system, and he found it hard to believe it worked as well as it seemed to. "Do you have a boat?"

The tul examined the sheen on his fingernails. "We'll take the *Kraken.*"

"Her boat?"

"No." His upper lip curled. "The *Kraken* belongs to house Kohunlich and I am the Kohunlich-tul." Eyes glittering in the lamp light, he smiled. "Until the change, I am the head of the house and the ship master will obey me."

One dry summer, Benedikt had seen lightning start a forest fire. Something in the tul's smile reminded Benedikt of that now. The ship master would either obey or die—a dead master would no doubt bring the mate around. It wasn't a scenario Benedikt cared much for, but he couldn't see that they had a choice; he had no more chance of controlling the tul than he'd had of controlling that fire. "If you can get us onto the *Kraken,* I'll make sure she can't be caught."

"You're sure he's sent no one to the harbor?"
"Positive, peerless one."
"And that he's not spoken in private to . . ." She ran over which of the great houses had deep-water ships in Atixlan. "The Shanshich-tul or the Palenque-tul?"
"We had him watched all day at the palace, peerless one. The Shanshich-tul was not present, and he never approached the Palenque-tul."
"Interesting."
The First bowed. "What do we do now, peerless one?"
"Now we prepare to get Benedikt back."

The lookout had spotted land at midday, and the kigh had brought the *Vixen* into shore cloaked in a heavy fog. During the course of the day, the captain had chewed three pipe stems to splinters. The bards had taken turns reassuring him with only partial success.

"It feels like we've sailed off the edge of the world." Jurgis murmured, tucking a strand of hair back behind his ear.

"You're not helping," Karlene told him shortly. During the day, it had been just barely possible to make out the shadowy outlines of the bow from the sterncastle but since they'd lost even the filtered sunlight, visibility had dropped to an arm's length. Lanterns remained unlit but ready, and bows had been given out to all crew members who could shoot. Karlene had instructed the kigh to keep them away from other ships and made objects like piers, but she wasn't certain of either how much they'd understood or were willing to cooperate.

Sitting on the bench built into the rail, her stumps allowing her to face the sea, Evicka leaned over the side and trailed her fingers through the fog. "I don't know whether to Sing air or water to this . . ." Frowning, she straightened. "We've stopped."

"Are we here, then?"

All three bards turned to face the captain.

"And if we are, where might here be?" he continued.

Karlene cocked her head. "I can hear breakers, we're close to shore."

"I don't know how you can hear anything in this unenclosed fog," the captain muttered. Leaning over the amidship rail, he whistled softly to catch the mate's attention. "Hanicka, send down a line." Turning back to the bards, he added, "A person shouldn't have to whisper orders on their own ship. I'll be unenclosed glad when we've picked up Benedikt and are well away."

They waited silently while the depth was taken and Hanicka climbed up to the sterncastle with the measurement.

"How much?"

She repeated it.

"There's nothing under us!"

"There are kigh under us," Karlene reminded him. "I promise you, the kigh won't let us run aground."

"Well, if we've arrived, what do the kigh want us to do?" the captain asked tightly.

"Yes, what?" Seemingly out of nowhere, Bannon appeared by the captain's side. For the first time since they'd left Shkoder, he was wearing both belt knife and wrist sheaths. "Ask the kigh where I can find Benedikt."

"You?" Evicka shook her head. "You can't go ashore, you don't even know the language."

"I'm not planning on talking to anyone."

"Forget it, you're . . ."

Eyes locked on Bannon's face, Karlene cut the other bard off. "You're wasting breath, Evicka. He'll go anyway, so we might as well send him to the right place." Walking over to the rail, she Sang the four notes to call the kigh and then the four notes of Benedikt's name.

The *Silver Vixen* rocked slightly as the kigh replied.

Unfortunately, they didn't know where Benedikt was, only where he'd been.

"If he was on that ship," Bannon growled as the two-man dinghy was lowered as quietly as possible over the side, "someone there knows where he is now. At the very least, I'll get some idea of the situation before you three march in with a rousing chorus of wind and water."

"You still don't speak the language," Evicka reminded him.

"If I can't make myself understood . . ." His tone suggested that wasn't likely to happen. ". . . I'll bring the slaughtering someone back here for *you* to talk to."

She reached out and patted him on the thigh. "Good enough."

"Bannon?"

Eyes narrowed, he paused, half over the rail.

Karlene suddenly found she couldn't say everything that needed to be said, so she settled for, "Be careful."

"Assassins don't survive if they're careless," he told her, and disappeared.

When she heard the kigh moving the dinghy away, she sighed. "And assassins aren't at their best when they're in love."

The fog had broken into patches like low-lying clouds by the time Bannon entered the harbor and had disappeared entirely as his boat drifted almost directly under the high, curved prow of a ship and bumped silently against a massive pier.

There was no moon, but the unfamiliar stars were bright enough for Bannon to note the carved squid wrapped around the bow. According to the kigh, Benedikt had sailed on this ship, had Sung to them from it, had been hurt on the pier beside it.

Hurt. Apparently the kigh, as translated by Karlene had no gradations of pain.

Bannon did.

Benedikt had been tortured on the pier next to this ship.

When I find out who did it, Bannon promised as he tied off his boat and climbed through shadow, *I'll make that person wish they'd never been born.* A good assassin killed instantly. This time, he'd make an exception.

The sailor on watch stiffened as Bannon passed, sensing a threat he couldn't see. He spat a question into the darkness, but by the time he turned toward the right set of shadows, Bannon was gone.

While part of the ex-assassin reveled in the chance to put fatally acquired skills to work once again, the rest noted low voices coming from inside the sterncastle. Voices but no lights. It didn't sound like the sort of dialogue that went with sex, but he couldn't think of another reason for the lack of lights nor could he think of a better time to get some information. People interrupted in the midst of sex were usually too rattled to put up any kind of a defense.

His soft boots making no noise on the deck, he sped aft. Up close, it began to sound more like an actual conversation.

Then why are they sitting in the slaughtering dark. To his surprise, the walls weren't solid planking but make of louvered shutters like many of the walls back home in the Empire's Sixth Province. Bannon supposed that made sense, the temperature seemed about the same. But, if the crew had come on deck to get out of the heat below, why were the shutters closed? Unless they weren't supposed to be in there. On the *Vixen,* the roughly equivalent space was the captain's cabin.

Barely breathing, he listened to the rise and fall of conversations, trying to determine just how many of the crew were in there. None of the words sounded familiar and even the cadences were strange. He identified two speakers, then three, then a fourth said something that could have only been Benedikt, and the others laughed.

Bannon's lips drew back off his teeth, and his belt knife was in his hand.

The fourth voice continued, exaggerating fear with high-pitched babbling, then he ended with a shriek, a pause, and a word that sounded very much like, "Oops." The others thought he was hysterically funny.

Kicking in the shutter, Bannon threw himself on the fourth voice, dagger aimed up under the ribs, going for the safer body kill in the dark.

But the dagger met unexpected resistance.

And there were a lot more than four people in the room.

"The sun's up." Karlene scowled at the sky. "Or as up as it seems willing to get. Bannon won't be back now until tonight."

Evicka heaved herself up onto her barrel and peered out into the fog. "If he comes back."

"He's just got caught by daylight and is holed up somewhere safe."

"You sure?"

"He's an Imperial assassin. He sneaks into cities, villages, camps, whatever, and kills people. This time, he's trying to save someone, it's probably got him a bit confused."

"And if he doesn't come back tonight?"

The ship rocked slightly, and a sudden gust of wind shifted everything not nailed down.

"We go in after him. Them."

As Karlene strode off amidships, Jurgis came out of the forecastle shirtless and yawning and walked over to Evicka. "What got the kigh all worked up?"

Evicka jerked her chin toward Karlene's rapidly disappearing figure. "She did."

Jurgis sniffed the breeze then leaned back against the rail. "I guess we got lucky, then."

Dragging her fingers through disheveled hair, Evicka snorted. "Lucky? How do you figure that."

"She forgot she also Sings fire."

"Gracious one, I must protest this sacrilege."

"What sacrilege?" Arms folded, the tul turned to Ooman Xhai while Xhojee continued to paint black patterns on Benedikt's head. "If he is, as you believe, a warrior of Tulpayotee, why would the god mind him pretending to be a priest?"

"A warrior perhaps, but *not* a priest."

Tul Altun waved the protest aside. "I'm sure he can cope with the demotion."

"I'm finished, gracious one." Xhojee stepped back and studied his handiwork. "But I think your adorner could've done a better job."

"Probably. Had I wanted my adorner to know." The tul examined Benedikt critically and smiled. "If I get the chance, I'll have to thank my sister for both giving me the idea and for shaving your head. Stand up."

Thinking that the tul's smile had become increasingly reckless as the morning progressed, Benedikt shook out the folds of his yellow robe and stood.

"You're still too tall."

"My apologies, gracious one."

"Never mind. Nothing we can do about it now." He glanced down at the measure of fabric Xhojee had inexpertly sewn to the bottom of the robe, and his lip curled. "Fortunately, you'll be in the cart, so your height will be less easy to see."

"In the cart, gracious one?" A sudden realization drew Ooman Xhai's attention from the fake tattoos on Benedikt's head. "But if he's in the cart . . ."

"Then you're walking. Or staying here. I don't care either way."

The Kohunlich-tul, Xhojee, Benedikt, a disgruntled Ooman Xhai, and every guard the Kohunlich-tul had in Atixlan save those actually on the doors, waited in the vestibule for a karjen from the stable to bring the cart around. They left the building in their order of march and by the time the last three guards were in line, the first three were moving.

"A fast walk," Tul Altun instructed the karjen holding the coloas' bridle. "But don't run. A run through the streets of the capital," he added for Benedikt's benefit, "would attract the attention of the other houses."

"Your sister and her guard ran through the city." Remembering how quickly the xaan had been traveling when she arrived at the harbor after he'd been caught, Benedikt had to suppress a shudder. "The other houses didn't seem to notice."

"They noticed, and they stayed out of her way. When the powerless run, however, it means something entirely different. It draws the scavengers to feed." The tul's eyes glittered, their dark centers reflecting back the sunlight like polished stone and Benedikt could feel an almost feverish heat rising off him.

"Are you all right?"

"Why wouldn't I be?" His laugh held the faint cadences of hysteria. "I was just thinking of how Balankanche's gold would buy me power enough to ensure a Kohunlich-xaan that's easier to live with. I'm sure Mijandra's trained the cousins to be properly subservient."

"But your sister . . ."

"When the gold gets me the ear of the Xaantalax, my sister will suffer the fate of all those whose reach exceeds their grasp."

They were neither of them very pleasant people, Benedikt

reflected as their small procession began to pass the more expensive shops and their shoppers. The only real difference was the that tul's position forced him to cooperate rather than compel. Still, if it came to a choice between death by leopard and death by quicksand, Benedikt preferred the former.

"I'd kill or maim you just as easily as she would if it suited me."

"But not as coldly."

Had the tul ordered his eye removed, there would've been emotion involved, not a dry taking-care-of-business. *At least I could've gotten a song out of it,* he thought, slumping lower in the seat. *It wouldn't have been a total loss.*

But nothing else would've changed, he reminded himself. *But if I at least had a song, I'd be ahead.*

"Stop sweating, Benedikt. The designs on your head are smearing."

"Your pardon, gracious one." Tul Altun was clearly not the only one affected by the day's activities. *At least I'd have a song? I'm losing my mind.*

"Gracious one!" Breathing heavily, a karjen with the tul's tattoos on her arms fell into step beside the cart. "Two Fives of the xaan's guards have left the Great Square at a quick march."

"Good work." The tul's voice had picked up a manic edge. "Tell the house First you speak with the mouth of the tul and that we need to move a little faster."

For the first time, Benedikt appreciated a social system that arbitrarily cleared the way for the great houses. In spite of crowds in the lower town, their pace never faltered, and as far as Benedikt could tell, no one was hurt. Reaching the harbor safely, they clattered across the stones, and right out onto the House Kohunlich pier.

"Run." Gathering up his robe, Tul Altun leaped from the cart before it had quite stilled. Benedikt followed less gracefully. "Now I deal with the ship master," he announced, grinning wildly as they approached the gangway, "and then we're gone."

"Not quite."

The calm declaration stopped both men in their tracks. Benedikt didn't know how the tul felt, but he was glad he'd eaten so little back at the house. He'd never wanted to vomit quite so badly as he did on hearing that voice.

Two guards stood on either side of the upper end of the gangway, crossbows trained on the tul. Her hair braided with hundreds of tiny white-and-blue feathers, the xaan appeared between them and started down toward the pier followed by Hueru and a double row of guards.

The tul backed up a step and then another, Benedikt following. Neither man had to turn to know that the sudden slap of cleated leather on stone behind them was the rest of the xaan's guards, blocking escape.

"Don't worry," the xaan told them as she stepped off onto the pier and her guards took up position. "I won't start a fight that will destroy our house. My people won't prevent your retreat."

"If you were already here, why even bother to have us followed from the square" the tul asked scornfully. The contempt in his voice suggested he couldn't care less about her answer. Only the many small movements of his hands, arms, and head betrayed him.

"If I hadn't had you followed, you might have realized where I was and gone somewhere else. Right at the moment, the guards behind you are only preventing the curious from interrupting our conversation. I can't have that."

"Can't you?" Tul Altun's gaze swept his guards, then hers. As it swept over Benedikt, he had a terrible fear he knew what the fire in the tul's expression meant, "If I'm going to die anyway, it might be worth dying now to ensure that you're executed, too."

"Melodramatic nonsense. I'm not interested in killing you."

Hueru looked startled but the tul's laughter cut off his protest unspoken.

"Since when?"

"Since Benedikt. I have bigger plans now."

"And what if I, too, have bigger plans and don't want to give Benedikt up?"

"You don't have to. He'll come back to me freely. If you allow that, you can live a long and prosperous life."

"And if I stop him from going back to you?"

"I'll take him later, and you'll die."

"If I kill him rather than let you have him?"

"You'll die a heartbeat after the Tulparax. Slowly, since you'll have annoyed me." No one could have looked more reasonable than the Kohunlich-xaan. "You have one logical choice."

The tul tossed his head, gold and black striped feathers lifting in his braids. "How do I know you'll let me *live a long and prosperous life?*"

"It doesn't matter," Benedikt broke in.

The tul turned on him. "It matters to me!"

Eye locked on the xaan, Benedikt shook his head. "I won't return to her freely and if I'm forced, I won't Sing."

"Yes, you will," she said softly. Behind her, Hueru grinned.

"Or I'll die?"

"No." Holding her braids back out of the way with one hand, she turned just enough to direct their attention back to the ship. "He will."

Between the two guards at the top of the gangway were two more, holding a bound, but still struggling, man. All three were bleeding from multiple wounds.

"Did he try and escape *again?*"

"Yes, peerless one. But we've got him tied tightly enough this time."

"That's what you said the last time."

"Sorry, peerless one, he's just . . ."

"Never mind." The xaan sounded more weary than annoyed as she cut off the explanation. "Lift him so that Benedikt can see his face."

Benedikt didn't need to see his face. He'd known who it was by the shape, by the movement, by the blood. He didn't know how, or why, but he knew who.

"Bannon."

The night had been a long one. Bannon considered his physical injuries minor compared to the shame of being caught. Imperial assassins might die—often died—while taking out a target, but they were never captured. This was all Benedikt's fault. Bards, nothing but trouble.

Then he'd heard Benedikt arrive and had realized he had only one last chance to be of any help at all.

He failed and took very little comfort in knowing how close he'd come.

When the very dangerous woman in charge had commanded he be displayed, he lifted his head before the guard could pull it up by the hair. His eyes widened. The pretty, golden boy he'd stupidly expected to see was gone, replaced by a gaunt, one-eyed man with black paint making a mess of his shaven head. Only the full mouth and its pouting lower lip hadn't changed. When it formed his name, Bannon went limp in the guard's hold.

Assassins depended only on themselves.

Assassins weren't supposed to fall in love.

I slaughtering surrender, all right?

Briefly, he wondered if it had been this bad for his sister, but since Vree had never spent the night tied and wrapped in a stinking net in a rat-infested bilge, with four less than friendly guards, he doubted it.

He'd almost rescued himself when you arrived. I have to let him finish it.

Eyes locked on Benedikt's face, he nodded and working mouth and throat behind the gag, said, "It's up to you."

Only a bard could have heard him.

Benedikt stiffened. He felt as though he were drowning. And then he realized. He only sang one quarter, but that quarter was water and by all the gods in the circle, after what he'd been through, he wasn't going to drown now. He straightened, no longer hiding his height but using it.

The xaan's eyes widened. "You have hidden strengths after all. Good. Too late, but good. Your friend crept on board my ship last night. The only word he understood was your name, so I kept him for you. He wasn't easy to keep either; he killed three of my guards, one of them after they took his blades away. So if you go with my brother, your friend dies slowly. If you come back to me, he gets to live as long as you cooperate. And if you so much as sing a single note, my guards will kill you both."

In the silence that followed, the sounds of the harbor, the sounds of men and women who pulled a living from the sea, rose momentarily to the foreground as the fishing fleet returned. Beyond the barricade of guards, Benedikt realized with some surprise, life went on. This little drama only mattered to those involved.

Except that . . .

If I go to the xaan, I'll be responsible for the destruction of an entire people. If I don't . . .

Rescue came from an unexpected source. Throwing off Xhojee's cautioning arm, Ooman Xhai stepped forward to stand by Benedikt's side. "This man is a warrior of Tulpayotee," he said, the complete and utter absence of doubt in his voice forcing belief. "He is nothing to do with you."

"A warrior disguised as a priest?" Hueru snorted. "He was more believable wearing the woman's robes of a priest of Xaantalicta."

"My . . ." The xaan paused and nodded at her brother, ". . . our cousin has a point."

The Ooman stiffened. "Your ignorance does not change what he is."

"True. Then let him prove it. If he is a priest of Tulpayotee, let him call to his god and have his god answer."

To her surprise, the ooman stepped back and said. "Very well. Benedikt, call the god."

"This is ridiculous."

"You offered him a chance to prove it."

"Oh, very well." She folded her arms and glanced impatiently up at a clouded sky. "When he fails, it will put *that* lot of rumors to rest at least.

Benedikt moistened dry lips, "I have to Sing . . ."

"No."

"If you don't allow him to prove it, you may trust my ooman's word," Tul Altun murmured, smiling.

The tul's guard had seen Benedikt in full golden glory. Xaan Mijandra remembered the beam of sunlight just after he split the flood and realized, so had hers. Glancing around the surrounding circle of guards, hers and her brother's, she realized that if she didn't allow Benedikt to fail now that the words had been spoken, there would be trouble later.

"Fine. Sing. But one wave, one ripple out in that harbor and both you and your friend here die."

He'd called the god in a temple, with a song he'd sung a hundred times. But here? And even if he could call the god, that wouldn't save Bannon.

There was no rain. Nothing he could use.

"You're wasting my time, Benedikt."

And then he remembered the herbalist in Janinton. He'd been lying in her kitchen, not quite awake, listening to her explain to Pjazef why he was so tired.

"The body is full of water, you know; he was Singing a different Song to bits of himself even while he was Singing the river."

What would Bannon do . . .

. . . for him?

He Sang the four notes to call the kigh.

He'd taken an oath not to use the kigh against others, but the xaan stood condemned out of her own mouth.

"You'll just be moving a bit of water out of the way. Where's the harm in that?"

He looked into the xaan's eyes and, using what he'd learned from the Song of Sorquizic, he Sang to her.

"What the . . ." Jurgis grabbed for the rail as the *Silver Vixen* suddenly jerked forward. The volume and variety of cursing suggested he wasn't the only one taken by surprise. Bracing himself, he leaned over the bow and Sang a question to the kigh.

"Well?"

He straightened and slowly turned to face the other two bards and the captain. "Benedikt's Singing."

"To them?"

"No."

"Then why . . .?"

Jurgis shrugged. "As near as I can tell, they think he needs them."

Kariene blinked. "They *think?*"

Jurgis shrugged again. "So it seems."

The ship flung itself out of the fog and into hazy sunlight. Riding the crest of a massive wave, the *Vixen* crossed the broad mouth of a swollen river and raced toward a low point of land capped with a brilliantly patterned tower.

The captain whirled around, scanned the faces staring up at him and pointed. "You, Janinton, grab your friends and bows and get up in the lookout. This is what you came for. The rest of you, prepare for . . ." He shot an irritated look at the bards behind him. ". . . anything."

They swept around the point without slowing, so close

they could see the reactions of the people out working in small, square fields. Ahead, at the base of a deep harbor, they saw a red-roofed city rising up onto a plateau.

Kariene Sang Benedikt's name to an air kigh and was almost blown off her feet.

Xaan Mijandra's mouth opened. And closed. Covered in a sheen of moisture, she fell to the pier. Her knees snapped up to her chin with an audible crack of bone on bone and her face collapsed in on itself. All those watching had seen death often enough to know it again.

Benedikt Sang a gratitude and fell silent.

Stepping forward. Ooman Xhai lifted one of the xaan's arms. Flesh that had moments before been plump and round was now dried and desiccated as though it had spent months roasting under a burning sun. "The judgment of Tulpayotee," he said. Releasing the xaan, he held both palms up to the sun and began to pray.

Ignoring the priest's drone and the uneasy murmuring all around, Benedikt met Bannon's astounded gaze and held tightly to the thought that he'd just saved hundreds of lives. That he'd just saved *this* life, and that was all that really mattered.

He'd just moved a bit of water out of the way.

The xaan's guards shuffled in place, unsure of what to do. The xaan was dead, and they knew the means if not the method of her death. Should they not avenge her?

The tul's guards shuffled in response. Their god had spoken, and the enemy of the tul was dead.

Up on the *Kraken,* Cazzes felt the world tottering and came to a decision. Maybe the xaan's death was a judgment of Tulpayotee, maybe it wasn't. He didn't really care. From his vantage point it had seemed that Benedikt's one remaining blue eye had been slightly mad while he sang and Cazzes knew whom to blame for that madness.

"The peerless one asked for proof," he said into the rising tension. "The god did no more than give her what she asked for." As all eyes turned toward him, he took the quarrel from his crossbow and laid the bow down.

The xaan's First stared up at him for a long moment, then he glanced down at the body. Even the xaan's hair had gone dry and brittle and, while he watched, a breeze in off the harbor pulled half a dozen feathers out of the braids and danced them down the pier. "Stand away," he commanded.

Almost everyone stepped back a pace.

Ooman Xhai continued his prayers and beside him, Hueru stared at the wizened remains of his xaan, of his lover. He looked up at Benedikt, and one hand rose to touch the edge of his left eye. There had been one judgment of Tulpayotee, the gesture said. Why not another?

"Your protection, gracious one!" Diving forward, he threw himself to his knees at Tul Altun's feet. "I only did what she told me to!"

The tul stepped back in disgust. "Don't ever touch me," he said, drawing his robe out of the other man's grip. "You are no cousin of mine."

"Gracious one . . ."

"Your next word will be your last. Second?"

"Gracious one?"

"See that this karjo stays where he is and doesn't crawl off." Pushing past the kneeling man, he glanced up at the *Kraken* as he walked to Benedikt's side. "And you two, release the friend of the warrior of Tulpayotee. No," he said quietly as Benedikt began to move forward. "Stay here. They'll bring him to you."

They brought him so quickly Benedikt had no time for further protest.

"I can stand on my own," Bannon growled, shaking free of restraining hands.

. . . and barely time to catch him before he hit the pier. "You're hurt."

"A little," Bannon admitted, turning his head and spitting a mouthful of blood out onto the stone. "Mostly I'm stiff from being tied." He raised a hand and stroked the back of his fingers over Benedikt's cheek. "What about you."

"I'm okay . . ."

"Are you?"

Benedikt blinked, confused. Wasn't he? "Oh, you mean the eye." He felt his ears redden. "I've nearly healed."

"So I see."

There was a speculative, almost amused tone in the ex-assassin's voice Benedikt didn't understand. Nor, he found, did he want it explained.

"So these are *breeches?*"

"Yes, gracious one."

The tul stroked a gaze over Bannon's body. "They look hot. So it seems you weren't the only survivor, after all."

"Survivor?"

"Of the wreck."

Benedikt stiffened and stared down at the man in his arms. It was an understandable assumption except that Bannon hadn't been on the *Starfarer.* "H-how?" he stammered.

"Did I get here?" Bannon grinned, winced as it pulled his torn lip, and stood, Benedikt reluctantly rising with him. "The kigh came to Shkoder and told us you were in trouble, so we came to rescue you."

"We?"

"Did you think I came on my own? Well, I would've, but three bards, two healers, and a whole shipload of people came along to help bring you back."

"Bring me back?" Benedikt shook his head in disbelief. This wasn't making any sense. "That's . . ."

"Not possible? Don't take my word for it, then." Placing both hands on the taller man's shoulders, Bannon turned him around to face the harbor. "Here comes our ride."

The crowned ship of Shkoder flying from bare masts, the *Vixen* made an impossible curve around three fishing boats and, at the last second, turned sideways to the House Ko-hunlich pier and came to a full stop.

"Assassins are trained to notice things," Bannon murmured at Benedikt's back.

Benedikt's knees felt as if they were going to buckle, and he couldn't catch his breath. The best he'd dared hope for was a protected life on Balankanche. He'd never dared to hope that one day he'd get to go home. *Fool. How else could Bannon have gotten here?*

The fingers of one hand dug into the wood of the railing and the other keeping Jurgis from leaping ashore, Karlene stared down from the forecastle at the incredible figure the kigh told them was a bard of Shkoder. "Are you two all right?"

Since Benedikt seemed no more capable of speech than anyone else on the pier, Bannon answered for them both. "More or less."

Jerked from his prayers by this new arrival, Ooman Xhai stared up at the ship and the golden-haired, golden-skinned bodies at the rail. "The ship of Tulpayotee!" he cried.

Tul Altun rolled his eyes. "I can't let you go," he said quietly, leaning toward Benedikt.

"You can't keep me," Benedikt told him, drinking in the sight of the familiar faces.

"Because you're a warrior of Tulpayotee?"

"No. Because I'm a bard of Shkoder."

"Are you? Really? After everything that's happened to you?"

Turning, Benedikt stared down into the heat of the tul's gaze. He still couldn't Sing fire, but now it didn't matter. It had taken him this long to remember that water could put fire out. "Yes, I am. Really. *Because* of everything that's happened. Besides, you don't need me. You have all of House Kohunlich now."

The tul glanced back at Hueru, still on his knees, and nodded slowly. "True."

"And this much attention from your god should advance your cause with the Tulparax."

"Also true."

He was smiling so broadly his cheeks hurt. "And there're three archers in the lookout who'll kill anyone who tries to stop us getting on that ship."

"I had noticed that, yes."

Eyes on the tul, recognizing the only other predator on the pier now that the woman was dead, Bannon pushed forward. "Come on, Benedikt. We're leaving."

"Leaving?"

"As in going. Now."

Benedikt took a deep breath and let Petayn drop away. As he turned, he met Xhojee's gaze and raised a hand in farewell. "Thank you for being my friend."

The younger man grinned. "It wasn't so hard most of the time. I'm glad your old friends came for you."

"Benedikt!"

Breezes that were more than breezes pulled at his robe. "Coming."

*   *   *

The *Silver Vixen* sped out of the harbor as fast as she'd sped in, and no one followed—a sudden torrential downpour probably as much to blame as anything for the lack of pursuit. Propelled by the kigh instead of sail, the *Vixen* raced through the nearly solid sheets of rain like a fish.

Everyone but the helm and the lookouts crowded belowdecks while Benedikt was thoroughly examined by the two healers—although he kept sending one of them to Bannon who kept sending her back.

It took the rest of the afternoon and into the night to tell the bare bones of his story to an enthralled audience, and by the time he got to the death of the xaan, he was too tired to make excuses.

"When you saw Bannon, you must have known . . ."

"What?"

Karlene ran both hands back through her hair, searching for the words, but Benedikt didn't give her the chance.

"I must have known that the kigh had taken my pain all the way to Shkoder? That my *pain* would be enough to change Kovar's mind about sending a ship across the sea when nothing else of mine—except the unfortunate fact that I only Sang one quarter—had ever made the slightest impression? That Her Majesty would think one bard worth the risk of so many other lives? Especially when that bard had failed her so badly?"

"Her Majesty doesn't believe that, Benedikt; or do I need to give you her message again?"

"No." Bardic recall had insured that none of the queen's words had been forgotten and bardic mimicry had provided the tone and timbre of the queen's voice, but he wouldn't really believe until he could kneel at her feet and she forgave him. He stiffened, ready for an argument.

To his surprise, Karlene only shrugged. "We all screw up sometimes—as Bannon keeps reminding me—then we make what amends we can. We learn from our mistakes, and . . ."

". . . and eventually, we set on with our lives. But what about the families of the dead?" He stared searchingly into her face. "Is it enough to say that if I'd been given a choice I would have died to save them?"

"You're a bard, Benedikt, they already know that."

Some of the tension left his shoulders. "Yeah, I guess they do." Ducking his head, he stared at his new reflection in the waves below. "When I saw Bannon, all I could think of was . . . I mean, I couldn't . . . I didn't . . ." He sighed and surrendered. "You know."

"I know." Karlene copied his position on the rail. It was cute that this new, self-assured, *bardic* Benedikt couldn't put his feelings into words any better than an ex-assassin, but it didn't solve their problem. "You used the kigh to kill that xaan woman."

"I know. I called it something else, but I knew I was doing it. At the time, it seemed worth it."

"And now."

She was standing on his blind side, so he had to turn most of his upper body to actually look her in the eye. "If you're asking if I'd do it again under the same circumstances, then yes. If you're asking if I regret doing it . . ." He paused and examined what he felt. "I had two choices: Bannon's death or hers."

"What about yours?"

"No." To Karlene's surprise, he smiled. "I didn't want to die, but I would have if had been the only way to protect the island."

"Because there're just some things that bards of Shkoder aren't willing to do?"

It was Benedikt's turn to look startled. "Yeah, something like that."

"Do you know what the kigh say about what you did?"

What he did would only ever refer to one thing. "No, what?"

"That you just moved a bit of water." And the opinion of the kigh would weigh heavily when it came time for Benedikt to face judgment. "There isn't another bard in Shkoder who could have done what you did."

"Would have?"

"Been able to. Your relationship with water is going to become the stuff of songs."

A sudden wave curved high against the ship and extended an almost hand to brush Benedikt lightly on one cheek.

He watched the kigh retreat, then turned back to Karlene.

"You didn't expect to rescue an oath breaker. I've complicated things, haven't I?"

"Yes."

"Sorry you came and got me?"

She leaned forward and kissed him lightly where the kigh had caressed. "No."

"The way I saw it, you'd pretty much rescued yourself by the time we got there."

"I'd created a sort of life for myself out of compromise."

"All lives are compromises, Benedikt. Don't let the bards tell you different. Look at me, I had to stop killing people."

Benedikt looked at him. After a moment, he smiled. "Yeah. Me, too."

"I've never heard Bannon laugh like that before," Jurgis murmured. "Maybe this thing with Benedikt will work out."

Sprawled in a coil of rope, Evicka twisted around until she could see the two men by the rail. "Hope he realizes it's going to be a damp threesome.

When Bannon had stopped laughing and other questions had been answered without words, he looked back toward the vanished shore and said, "Do you think we'll ever see them again?"

Thinking he looked more like a Petrokian pirate now than he ever had, Benedikt glanced up from his reflection and asked, "What do you mean?"

"Well, they have ships and they know we're out here, somewhere. What if they come looking?"

"They won't find us, I learned a new song while I was away."

Unsure of the connection, Bannon frowned. "Just one?"

Benedikt waited until the Song of Sorquizic faded back into memory. "Just one that counts."